The Exciting Rediscovery of E. R. Eddison
and his Masterwork of Fantasy

THE WORM OUROBOROS

"A new climate of the imagination. Its effect is not evanescent, for the whole life and strength of a singularly massive and consistent personality lies behind it. . . . Every episode, every speech, helps to incarnate what the author is imagining. You could spare none of them. It takes the whole story to build up that strange blend of renaissance luxury and northern hardness."

—C. S. Lewis, in *On Stories*

"Authentic dream, fantastic far beyond invention and natural beyond all possibility of unbelief."

—Arthur Ransome, author of
Swallows and Amazons

"In [Eddison's] towering fantasy, the sweep of his invention and the grandeur of his style, I find something more than high talent— a vein of genius, setting him apart as one of the most remarkable writers of our age."

—Sir George Rostrevor Hamilton

"A ROMANCE OF A WORLD THAT NEVER WAS. . . . ITS LANDSCAPES ARE MAGNIFICENT. ONE LIVES IN IT."

—Hilaire Belloc

"A LITERARY EVENT OF THE FIRST IMPORTANCE."
—Orville Prescott

"A REMARKABLE PERFORMANCE."

—H. Rider Haggard, author of
King Solomon's Mines

QUANTITY SALES

T·H·E
WORM
OUROBOROS

BY E. R. EDDISON

Introduced and Annotated by
PAUL EDMUND THOMAS

With a Foreword by
DOUGLAS E. WINTER

With Illustrations by
KEITH HENDERSON

A DELL TRADE PAPERBACK

A DELL TRADE PAPERBACK

Published by
Dell Publishing
a division of
Bantam Doubleday Dell Publishing Group, Inc.
666 Fifth Avenue
New York, New York 10103

ISBN: 0-440-50299-3

Printed in the United States of America

Published simultaneously in Canada

July 1991

10 9 8 7 6 5 4 3 2 1

BVG

ACKNOWLEDGMENTS

THE Parents Association of Breck School in Minneapolis has helped pay for my three journeys to England, and without its help I would not have been able to delve so deeply for so long into E. R. Eddison's notes, letters, books, and manuscripts. The staff of the Duke Humphrey Library in the Bodleian Library of Oxford University greeted me with smiles and nods every day as they helped me sort through their Eddison collection. Mrs. Anne Hamerton and the staff of the Taylor Institution Library of Oxford not only brought the books of Eddison's Trinity College bequest out of storage for me, but they gave me a comfortable place for consulting them. The Public Library of Marlborough also gave me easy access to Eddison's bequest of books. Mrs. A. Heap and the staff of the Local History Library in the Central Library of Leeds cheerfully hefted the weighty boxes containing Eddison's manuscripts, and they made special scheduling sacrifices to facilitate my research. I heartily thank all the people of these institutions.

I am grateful to the Bodleian Library of Oxford University and the Leeds City Libraries for giving me permission to quote unpublished material housed in their collections.

I thank the Cambridge University Press for giving me permission to quote from E. R. Eddison's translation of *Egil's Saga*. I thank the University of Chicago Press for giving me permission to quote from Richmond Lattimore's translation of *The Iliad of Homer*. And, I thank the Oxford University Press for giving me permission to use the first and second editions of *The Oxford English Dictionary* in the writing of many of my explanatory notes.

Especially, I thank Jeanne Cavelos of Dell for her constant enthusiasm for this project and for my part in it. And most of all, I thank E. R. Eddison's daughter, Mrs. Jean Gudrun Rucker Latham, and his granddaughter, Mrs. Anne Al-Shahi, for the encouragement and friendship which they have given me for seven years and out of which this new edition sprang.

P. E. THOMAS

CONTENTS

FOREWORD

TO

The Worm Ouroboros

BY DOUGLAS E. WINTER

The Worm Ouroboros, that eateth its own tail . . .

I FIRST read these words more than twenty years ago. They seemed magical, an invocation of something locked deep inside me— something dark and dangerous, and yet desperately alive. They intrigue me, uplift me, haunt me, even today; and I introduce them to you with the anxious delight of a child who wishes to share a special secret. You hold in your hands the best single novel of fantasy ever written in the English language.

Eric Rucker Eddison (1882–1945) was a civil servant at the British Board of Trade, sometime Icelandic scholar, devotee of Homer and Sappho, and mountaineer. Although by all accounts a bowler-hatted and proper English gentleman, Eddison was an un- mitigated dreamer who, in occasional spare hours over some thirty years, put his dreams to paper. In 1922, just before his fortieth birthday, a small collector's edition of *The Worm Ouroboros* was published; larger printings soon followed in both England and America, and a legend of sorts was born. The book was a dark and bloodred jewel of wonder, equal parts spectacle and fantasia, laby- rinthine in its intrigue, outlandish in its violence. It was also Mr. Eddison's first novel.

After writing an adventure set in the Viking Age, *Styrbiorn the Strong* (1926), and a translation of *Egil's Saga* (1930), Eddison de- voted the remainder of his life to the *fantastique* in a series of novels set, for the most part, in Zimiamvia, the fabled paradise of *The Worm Ouroboros*. The Zimiamvian books were, in Eddison's words, "written backwards,"[1] and thus published in reverse chronological order of events: *Mistress of Mistresses* (1935), *A Fish Dinner in Memison* (1941), and *The Mezentian Gate* (1958). (The final book was incomplete when Eddison died, but his notes were so thorough that his brother, Colin Eddison, and his friend George R. Hamilton were able to assemble the book for publication.) Although the books are known today as a trilogy, Eddison wrote them as an open-ended series; they may be read and enjoyed alone or in any sequence. Each is a metaphysical adventure, an intricate Chinese puzzle box whose twists and turns reveal ever-encircling vistas of delight and dread.

Eddison's four great fantasies are linked by the enigmatic character of Edward Lessingham—country gentleman, soldier, statesman, artist, writer, and lover, among other talents—and his Munchausen-like adventures in space and time. Although he disappears after the early pages of *The Worm Ouroboros*, Lessingham is central to the books that follow. "God knows," he tells us, "I have dreamed and waked and dreamed till I know not well which is dream and which is true."[2] One of the pleasures of reading Eddison is that we, too, are never certain. Perhaps Lessingham is a man of our world; perhaps he is a god; perhaps he is only a dream . . . or a dream within a dream. And perhaps, just perhaps, he is all of these things, and more.

Eddison was exceptional in his embrace of the *fantastique;* in his fiction there are no logical imperatives, no concessions to cause and effect, only the elegant truths of the higher calling of myth. Characters traverse distances and decades in the blink of an eye; worlds take shape, spawn life, evolve through billions of years, and are destroyed, all during a dinner of fish. These are dreams made flesh by a dreamer *extraordinaire.*

"There was a man named Lessingham dwelt in an old low house in Wasdale . . ." (p. 1) Thus *The Worm Ouroboros* introduces Lessingham and his lady, Mary, the first glimpse of the tragic romance that will haunt the Zimiamvian novels. Lessingham retires, alone, to the mysterious Lotus Room, a place of contemplation and opiate calm—there to sleep, perchance to dream. "Time is" (p. 3), speaks a little black bird, and a shining chariot, drawn by a hippogriff, arrives to fetch Lessingham to Mercury. His destination is not the first planet from the sun, but a medieval Norseman's nightmare of our own Earth, "all gray and cold, the warm colours

1. E. R. Eddison, *The Mezentian Gate* (New York: Ballantine, 1969), p. xi.
2. E. R. Eddison, *Mistress of Mistresses* (New York: Ballantine, 1967), p. 356.

burnt to ashes," (p. 174), save one: the crimson of blood. It is a grim world, peopled by Demons and Witches, Imps and Pixies, Goblins and Ghouls—all of them human, and all of them at war. Swordplay and sorcery and Machiavellian intrigue are the order of the day; vengeance and feuds, betrayal and bloodletting, as common as the dawn.

The heroes of this majestic Romance are the Demons, ruled and captained by the three brothers—Lords Juss and Spitfire and Goldry Bluszco—and their cousin Brandoch Daha. Valiant in war, courtly in speech and stance, these are heroes in the classical sense, superhuman, violent, passionately alive, with the ferocious good looks and fate of fallen angels; if there is a single certainty, it is that those who befriend them will die. The Demonlords are demigods who struggle for a kind of savage nobility, forever pursuing a sentimental, romantic code that places word before deed, death before dishonor. Their trials are many, and painted brightly with blood.

Arrayed against the Demonlords are the Witches of Carcë, purveyors of a blackness "which no bright morning light might lighten" (p. 362). Their king is the crafty warlock Gorice XII, an egromancer "full of guiles and wiles" (p. 39). Skilled in grammarie, he lurks forever in his citadel, which stands "like some drowsy dragon of the elder slime, squat, sinister, and monstrous" (p. 354). At his side are his warlords: brave Corund, the bearish Corsus, the insolent Corinius, and "the landskip of iniquity" (p. 366), the renegade Goblin Gro—philosopher, schemer, and traitor by nature. No blacker and more dastardly crew of scoundrels could be found; yet Eddison's passion for them is obvious and intense.

The struggle between the Demons and Witches is nothing less than epic; the battles of this modern *Iliad* rage on land, sea, and air, taking us from the ocean depths to the lofty pinnacles of heaven. Among its finer episodes are the "wrastling for Demonland," which pits Goldry Bluzco against the King of the Witches and sets an entire world aflame; the fog-clouded siege at Eshgrar Ogo; the harrowing ascent of Kosthra Pivrarcha and the struggle there with the beast mantichora; the bloody battle at Krothering Side; the flight of the hippogriff to the gaunt peak of Zora Rach; and the playing of the final trumps at the dark citadel of Carcë.

Eddison's prose is archaic and often difficult, an intentionally affected throwback to Elizabethan and Jacobean drama. His characters are thus eloquent but long winded; they speak not of killing a man, but of "sending him from the shade into the house of darkness" (p. 229). In his finest moments Eddison ascends to a sustained poetic beauty; listen, for example, to the haunting premonition of the Goblin Gro: ". . . in my sleep about the darkest hour, a dream of the night came to my bed and beheld me with a glance so fell that the hairs of my head stood up and pale terror gat hold upon me. And methought the dream smote up the roof above my bed, and the roof yawned to the naked air of the midnight that laboured with fiery signs, and a bearded star travelling in the houseless dark. And I beheld the roof and the walls one gore of blood. And the dream screeched like the screech-owl, crying, *Witchland from thy hand, O King!*" (p. 24–25).

At other times the reader is virtually overwhelmed with words. Palaces and armory were Eddison's particular vices; he describes them with such ornate grandeur that page after page is lavished with their decoration. The reader should not be deterred by the density of such passages; like a vintage wine a taste for Eddison's prose is expensively acquired, demanding the reader's patience and perseverance—and it is worthy of its price. These are books to be savored, best read in the long dark hours of night, when the wind is against the windows and the shadows begin to walk—books not meant for the moment, but for forever.

The Worm Ouroboros inevitably has been compared with J.R.R. Tolkien's later and more popular *Lord of the Rings* trilogy; apart from their narrative ambition and epic sweep, the books share little in common. (Eddison, like Tolkien, disclaimed the notion that he was writing something beyond mere story: "It is neither allegory nor fable but a Story to be read for its own sake" (p. *xliii*). But, as the reader will no doubt observe, he proves much less convincing.)

If comparisons are in order, then I suggest Eddison's obvious influences—Homer and the Icelandic sagas—and that most controversial of Jacobean dramatists, John Webster, whose blood-spattered tales of violence and chaos (from which Eddison's characters quote freely) saw him chastised for subverting orthodox society and religion. The shadow of Eddison may be seen, in turn, not only in the modern fiction of heroic fantasy, but also in the writings of his truest descendants, such dreamers of the dark *fantastique* as Stephen King (whose own epics, *The Stand* and *The Dark Tower*, read like paeans to Eddison) and Clive Barker (whose *The Great and Secret Show* called its chaotic forces the *Iad Ouroboros*).

Eddison would have found this line of succession, like the cyclical popularity of his books, the most natural order of events:

the circle, ever turning—like the worm ouroboros, that eateth its own tail—the symbol of eternity, where "the end is ever at the beginning and the beginning at the end for ever more" (p. 178).

You hold in your hands a masterpiece.

DOUGLAS E. WINTER
Alexandria, Virginia
September 1990

INTRODUCTION

WHEN 1922 opened in England, it seemed an unpropitious year for romantic fiction about other worlds. The great Pre-Raphaelite romancer William Morris had been dead for twenty-five years. The science fiction novels of H. G. Wells and the faerie tales of Andrew Lang belonged to the generation past. C. S. Lewis was writing mythic narrative verse, but the luscious floating islands of *Perelandra* lay, undreamed of, fifteen years in his imagination's future. J.R.R. Tolkien was inventing mythology and writing poetic prose relating his history of the Valar and the Elves, but it would be ten years before he would read *The Hobbit* to C. S. Lewis and fifteen before his imagination would forge the Rings of Power. Mervyn Peake was only eleven years old. H. Rider Haggard was still writing, but his bright star was fading, and death lay three years in his future. Only the Irishmen Lord Dunsany and James Stephens and the American James Branch Cabell held popular English attention with the kind of romantic fiction that has, in the last two generations, been ambiguously labeled as fantasy literature.

In 1922 the modern writers held the literary field. Gertrude Stein's salon flourished in Paris, and on occasion Ernest Hemingway and Ezra Pound chatted in her sitting room. James Joyce found in Paris a press for his already serialized *Ulysses*. D. H. Lawrence was traveling in Australia and writing *Kangaroo*. Virginia Woolf finished *Jacob's Room*. And, T. S. Eliot cut and laid a cornerstone of the modern age when he composed *The Waste Land*.

Nearly every generation has writers who look backward, who do not join their contemporaries in seeking new literary forms but rather take inspiration from older writers. E. R. Eddison is one of these. Eddison's literary work, though in some ways as modern as Eliot's and Pound's, belongs to the nineteenth century, to the aesthetics of the Pre-Raphaelites, of Swinburne, William Morris, Andrew Lang, and Walter Pater. Eddison wrote his first and longest novel in his late thirties. It is a book full of four decades of living, reading, studying, and imagining. It contains a strangely archaic and romantic story of heroic adventure on the planet Mercury. It has little in common with the modernist literature that dominated the decade, but an intrepid young publisher named Jonathan Cape saw genius in it, and published it in 1922. This novel is *The Worm Ouroboros*.

1. The worm ouroboros: "all is one"

Ouroboros (ουροβοροσ) is the name given to an ancient Greek symbol of a dragon or serpent pictured devouring its own tail. No one knows the symbol's exact age, but its first appearances occur in treatises on alchemy composed in Alexandria during the third and fourth centuries A.D.[1] An obsolete science, alchemy was based upon theories nearly opposite to the principles of modern chemistry. Chemists have shown that matter exists in more than one hundred elemental forms. Alchemists theorized that matter had one perfect form consisting of four components united in perfect proportion: Fire, Air, Earth, and Water. The Alexandrian alchemists explored methods for altering the proportions of the four components within substances; they wanted to transmute disproportionate matter to proportionate or golden matter.[2] The ancient alchemists often wrote using allegory and symbolism to describe technical processes. In their treatises the ouroboros symbol usually occurs with the inscription "All is One" (εν το ηαν),[3] and serves to symbolize several important doctrines that the alchemists attempted to prove: the ultimate unity of matter; the potential perfectability of imperfect matter; matter's circular pattern of birth, growth, decay, death, and rebirth; and the circular returning of an impure substance to its pure source through the alchemic process.[4]

"I cannot but remember such things were That were most precious to me"

It would be hard to find a more apt symbol for the working of E. R. Eddison's imagination than the ouroboros. While composing, Eddison's imagination worked upon memories of influences and experiences entering his active thinking consciously or unconsciously. Memories of stories conceived in childhood, of hills and meadows walked in Lakeland and the Pennines, of orchestral music heard in London's concert halls and works of art seen in London's galleries, and, most important, of books and books enjoyed and studied through thirty years: at any moment Eddison's composing imagination could hold memories of many things. So, the ouroboros can symbolize the continuous returning of old thoughts to Eddison's new imagining. This thinking pattern has the circular shape of the ouroboros since it departs from present time, moves into the past, and returns with memories to the present. Like the dragon biting its tail, the circle has no breaks: Eddison's current thinking unites the separate memories that enter his imagination. And, like the dragon that destroys itself and yet remains alive, this circular process of remembering and imagining resurrects and revivifies the dead and digested time of past thought and experience.

The alchemic process itself provides a metaphor for Eddison's composing method. The memories of reading and other experiences held in Eddison's conscious thinking were, like "base" metals, alloyed and rendered malleable by Eddison's imagination to fit his prose. Because he combined several literary influences in new, unattempted ways, he essentially reproportioned these influences and made new matter from them. And when Eddison's alchemic imagination works perfectly, it produces not just pure matter, but gold.

Some of Eddison's greatest strength as a writer lies in this alchemic composing method of combining eclectic literary materials. If you know Eddison's sources, your mind's eye will see shadows and your mind's ear will hear echoes of these influences as you read, but you will smile when you realize that in sensing these things you are perceiving only the parts of a whole which, in its wholeness, is not imitation but creation. For example, one of Eddison's characters may have the disposition and attitudes of Achilleus, he may speak like Macbeth, he may write like William Caxton, he may wear clothes like those of Henry of Navarre, and he may carry weapons like those of Lancelot, and yet he will be not merely a combination of these figures but a new character. Because *The Worm Ouroboros* makes use of so many different kinds of sources, it eludes genre labels. This novel is part epic, part romance, part adventure story, part myth, part faerie tale, and part fantasy.

The best way of describing the nature of this eclectic novel is to compare it to the main literary sources which inspired it. Much of this book, of course, originated solely from Eddison's imagination, and it grew and developed over thirty years. But much came from other sources, as Eddison asserted to Keith Henderson, his brother-in-law and the first illustrator of his books: "The *Worm* . . . is influenced at every turn, consciously or unconsciously, by every writer whose work I have loved."[5] Of course, not every influence over four decades can be discussed here, so while I have documented many of the minor influences in the notes at the end of the text, I shall focus, in addition to Eddison's own imaginings, on the strongest influences: the Icelandic sagas[6] and the *Iliad* of Homer, and Elizabethan drama.

2. The story's origins: "The child is father of the man"

"O, be some other name!"

"What a wonderful talent you have for the invention of names," wrote H. Rider Haggard to Eddison when Eddison sent him a copy of *Ouroboros.*[7] Haggard wrote this praise when he had just begun the book, and perhaps he spoke politely from partial knowledge of it; or, if not, he may be the only admirer of Eddison who has liked Eddison's names. The main trouble with most of Eddison's names is that they hinder our belief in his imagined Mercury: when we read a novel in which the author creates a new world different from our familiar one, we imaginatively enter that world, and, while reading, we believe the events and characters and places and names because they are consistent with and seem appropriate to that created world. If the author puts in something inconsistent with this world's other aspects, we respond with disbelief.[8] Unfortunately, annoyed disbelief has been the response of many readers to Eddison's names for the races that inhabit Mercury: Demons, Witches, Imps, Pixies, Goblins, and Ghouls. Because of their associations in our familiar world, no reader of *Ouroboros* swallows these easily when Eddison uses them to name the magnificent, valiant, and mighty warrior races in his invented world: the term *witch,* to a modern reader, has feminine connotations associated with Halloween and *Macbeth;* and, the terms *imp, pixie,* and *goblin* denote the diminutive, puckish, sprightly, supernatural creatures of faerie tales and *A Midsummer Night's Dream.* Ironically, some of the nonsensical but lyrical names, like "Gaslark" or "Tivarandardale," sound lovely and gain easy acceptance from most readers.

It appears that Eddison had no etymological system for creating names and that he invented many of them in the most capricious sense of the word, for who could contrive to see etymological connections amid names such as Fax Fay Faz, La Fireez, Gro, the Red Foliot, and Spitfire? Predictably, the philologist J.R.R.

Tolkien, whose genesis of Elvish names forms the heart of his mythology in *The Silmarillion* and is based on systematic linguistic patterns, disliked Eddison's names: "I thought his nomenclature slipshod and often inept. In spite of all of which, I still think of him as the greatest and most convincing writer of 'invented worlds' that I have read."[9]

Why did he do it? Why did Eddison use, in some places, strangely charming names, and, in other places, silly and inept names whose semantic associations impair his creation? The factual answer is that many of the characters, episodes, and places of *Ouroboros* were born in Eddison's childhood, and even though he wrote the novel in his late thirties, he maintained the names that he had invented as a boy. That is what he did, but his motives for doing so elude easy analysis. Perhaps he wanted to preserve or to remain true to the memories of his childhood imagination. Perhaps he could not dissociate the childhood names from the characters in his adult mind. Eddison's motives have roots too deep to be plucked up and inspected here, and to make some easy determination would be impertinent. In any case, I can safely say that these names, troublesome as they are for you and me, retained enough value in Eddison's imagination for him to have used them thirty years later.

"You were writing the *Worm* even then"

Arthur Ransome, the man who first earned fame by witnessing and reporting the Russian revolution for the *Daily News* (London) and then earned fame again when he wrote the "Swallows and Amazons" series of children's books, was a lifelong friend of Eddison. Ransome was with Eddison when he first invented many of the names and characters, and Ransome may have contributed to this creation. He wrote to Eddison in 1922 and said that reading *Ouroboros* elicited "throughout odd memories of old exercise books and theatrical designs carried out on the broad nursery window-sills of St. Helens. . . . You were writing the *Worm* even then."[10] Ransome reiterated these thoughts in his autobiography:

> The language, the place-names and the names of the heroes were for me an echo of those ancient days when Ric and I produced plays in a toy theatre with cardboard actors carrying just such names and eloquent with just such rhetoric. Gorice, Lord Goldry Bluszco, Corinius, Brandoch Daha seemed old friends when I met them nearly forty years later.[11]

Young "Ric" and Arthur shared tutors, and they spent many days learning and playing together in St. Helens, the house of Eddison's father, Octavius, in the village of Adel, which is now a suburb of Leeds. The hours they spent in creating puppet plays with eloquent rhetoric perhaps prepared Eddison's temperament for appreciating the Elizabethan drama. In any case, a relationship existed between the plays that Ric and Arthur produced and the drawings in the "exercise books."

"A sad tale's best for winter. I have one of sprites and goblins."

Only one of the "exercise books" has been preserved, under the title *The Book of Drawings* in the Bodleian Library collection of Eddison's papers. *The Book of Drawings,* boldly dated "1892" in pencil on the inside cover, contains fifty-nine drawings in pencil, and many of these are labeled, thankfully for the observer, with captions describing the scene and identifying the figures. These captions contain the following names, which were later to be part of *Ouroboros:* Juss, Spitfire, Goldry Blusoe, Brandoch Daha, Vizz, Voll, Zigg, Gaslark, La Fireez, Gro, Corund, Gorice, Gallandus, Corsus, Fax Fay Faz, Demon, Witch, Imp, Pixie, Demonland, Impland, and Goblinland.

Four of the fifty-nine drawings depict scenes which so closely follow the plot of the novel that they prove indisputably that Eddison began to create the story around age ten. The first, captioned "The murder of Gallandus by Corsus," depicts the central event of Chapter XVIII and shows Corsus, a dagger in one hand and a lantern in the other, stalking upon the sleeping Gallandus like Macbeth in his stealthy pace toward Duncan. The second drawing is labeled "Lord Goldry Blusoe throwing Gorice I of Witchland in the wrestle for Demonland" and depicts the climactic moment of Chapter II when Goldry hurls the King over his head. Also notable is that this drawing shows the first of several Gorice figures and so suggests the dynasty of kings ruling Witchland: there are drawings of Gorice I, II, VI, and four pictures (including two separate deaths) of Gorice IV. The third picture, captioned "Lord Juss & Lord Brandoch Daha imprisoned by Gorice IV, & tormented by a banquet being placed just beyond their reach," shows Juss and Brandoch Daha placed exactly as, thirty years later, Eddison described them in chapter VII. The last picture, a beautifully detailed piece captioned "Lord Brandoch Daha challenging

Lord Corund," depicts a scene from Chapter XI. Even though Eddison may not have had in mind the idea to write a novel in 1892, and even though these four drawings may not have been, at the time, the most important ones to him, their undoubted connection to the novel excuses exalting them into prominence.

Even the drawings not depicting scenes from the novel have many parallels with the characters' appearances. The various active and often violent positions suggest the battle scenes of the book. Also, the facial features of the figures resemble those of the novel's heroes. Eddison drew the faces in profile, and every face has large eyes, fierce eyebrows, a large pointed or hooked nose, wavy and disheveled hair, and either a mustache or a beard or both. Notably, every head also has horns twined with ornamental feathers like those of the novel's heroic Demons. And, the bellicose, weapon-wielding figures in the drawings are adorned with the splendid clothes that drape the novel's aristocrats: hose, ruffs, jerkins, tunics, and capes.

Many captions themselves have significance because they show the young Eddison's verbal abilities, the eloquent rhetoric Ransome mentions. Some of the best captions label pictures of the Lord Goldry "Blusoe":

> A troop of horsemen appeared, & suddenly, Goldry leapt from their midst, &, followed by his soldiers, sprang onto the scaffold, & by running the executioner right through the body, & knocking down one of the soldiers who was near, saved Lord Gro from a terrible death.

> Goldry lunged forward, with feathers all drooping, and his face covered with dust & blood, & struck the Champion Elfin Boxer straight in the face, so that the blood spurted all over the place, & the Champion Elfin Boxer fell, bruised & bleeding in the dirt.

> But before the sword could descend, Goldry rushed down the rugged hill like a whirlwind with drawn sword. But the sword broke on a poplar tree, but he rushed on & with a blow of his fist he laid the Red Elf lifeless on the ground.

Grammatically, these sentences are notable for their dependent phrases and clauses. They not only show young Eddison's ability to construct complicated prose, they show his predilection for complicated sentences. Stylistically, these sentences show Eddison's felicity with vivid and vigorous language, for each sentence tells of rapid and violent action complemented by detailed imagery. Verbally, these sentences show a child who has already begun to read actively, for the vocabulary used is literary and sophisticated.

Looking at *The Book of Drawings* is like looking at a set of slides of Eddison's childhood imagination. You see some figures pictured several times, and you glimpse many different events. Each drawing, like a snapshot, records a moment within a longer episode, and the sheer number of different scenes suggests that although Eddison had a core group of characters, he made up many stories involving them. Considered as a set, the fifty-nine drawings are the tracings of an energetic storytelling faculty developing quickly and fruitfully in young Ric. The childhood plays and stories made up in abundance remained in Eddison's imagination for more than thirty years, and some of them found their way into *Ouroboros*.

3. Icelandic sagas: "the fierce dispute betwixt damnation and impassioned clay"

"my first saga-madness"

Not long after he was inventing puppet plays with Arthur Ransome and filling the pages of *The Book of Drawings*, Eddison was discovering the two bodies of literature that would influence him most: Homer's poems and the Icelandic sagas. Eddison may have begun reading Homer at age eleven, for he was given a copy of the Lang and Butcher translation of *The Odyssey* in 1893, and at about the same time he began to read *The Saga Library* of William Morris and Eirikr Magnusson. Doubtless Eddison loved Homer, but he wore the Icelandic sagas in his heart's core.

When Eddison was setting out upon his second work of fiction, the historical novel *Styrbiorn the Strong* (London: Jonathan Cape, 1926), he remarked to one of his typists that his new novel would be inspired by "the age of the great classic saga literature of the North, which I have studied these twenty years, and which I love more than any other."[12] Eddison wrote for the volume an introductory letter to his brother, Colin, and said he intended to dedicate the book to him because "you, being a smaller boy than I, suffered so gallantly many years ago my first saga-madness."[13] His mad passion for sagas, first fed by *The Saga Library,* moved Eddison to teach himself Old Icelandic during his student years at Eton and Oxford. His continuing study bore its first fruit in *Styrbiorn the Strong* and its full harvest in his translation of *Egil's Saga,* published in 1930 by the Cambridge University Press. Eddison decided to do the translation in 1926, and he stopped to record the moment of his decision: "Walking in a gale over High Peak, Sidmouth, on 3rd January 1926, when I had just finished writing *Styrbiorn the Strong,* I thought suddenly that my next job should be a big saga translation, and that should be *Egil.* This may pay back some of my debt to the sagas, to which I owe more than can ever be counted."[14]

"I will a round unvarnish'd tale deliver"

Influence means more than admiration. What did Eddison owe to the sagas? Where lies his debt to them? Eddison answers these murky questions in his introduction to *Egil's Saga,* where he defines a saga according to its chief features and points of excellence. The definition descries what he values in this body of literature, so by illuminating the sagas he reflects indirect light on the saga influence in *Ouroboros.*

He begins with a simple definition of the form: "A saga may be roughly defined as a prose narrative which deals dramatically with historical material."[15] In the Introduction to his fourth novel, *A Fish Dinner in Memison,* Eddison says of his fiction, "My form is dramatic narrative in prose." Laying aside the historical setting of the sagas, these descriptions of form and style parallel one another like lines. Yet beyond these generalizations, the line of Eddison's style does not run parallel to the style of the sagas because his eclectic allegiance to other loved sources often makes his style bend away from the conventions of saga prose. As in most aspects of *Ouroboros,* in his prose style Eddison is like an alchemist: he mixes saga prose patterns with those of other literary influences to make a prose that contains proportions of several styles.

Eddison describes the saga writing thus: "The best Icelandic prose is deliberate, simple, and laconic, using the rough, salt speech of men of their hands: direct, unselfconscious, farmer's talk, unsophisticated, yet classic and noble, because it is the talk of a people born with a natural instinct for language and for dramatic narrative." The only occasion on which a farmer speaks in *Ouroboros* is in chapter XXVI. Here is one of his statements to his daughter: "Thou'rt a disobedient lass, and but for thee, come sword, come fire, not a straw care I; knowing it shall be but a passing storm, now that my Lord is home again" (p. 300). Except for *disobedient* and *passing* every word has its origin in a northern Germanic tongue, and most of the words are simple, laconic, "rough, salt speech." For comparison, here are words spoken by Lord Gro to Lady Mevrian: "Certes it is an ill thing that thou, who has not been nourished in mendicity or poverty but in superfluity of honour and largesse, shouldst be made fugitive in thine own dominions, to lodge with foxes and beasts of the wild mountain" (p. 293). Here the syntax and the derivations from French and Latin are certainly foreign to the sagas. The farmer at Holt holds the reader's attention for but three pages; the lords, ladies, princes, queens, and kings dominate four hundred. And yet the aristocrats do not always speak with Elizabethan flourish. Zeldornius, for example, speaks sentences that might have been spoken by Icelandic heroes like Gunnar in *Njal's Saga:* "The world comes back to me, and this memory therewith, that they of Demonland were truth-tellers whether to friend or foe, and ever held it shame to cog and lie" (p. 115). The conversation in *Ouroboros* finds its strongest ancestry in Elizabethan drama, but the quiet strain of simple saga speech resounds in voices too, and the combination is something not entirely English in its overtones.

In the pace of the narrated action, a dominant saga influence again cannot be found in Eddison's prose. His definition of the saga illuminates this in *Ouroboros* when he compares the narrative pulse-rate of the sagas to Homer and to another of his inspirations, Sir Richard Burton's translation of *The Book of a Thousand Nights and a Night:*

> . . . swift as is the movement of Homer, the action pauses continually for the introduction of poetic ornament, simile or description. The action of the saga never pauses except for the introduction of genealogical information. [In Burton] . . . the action is slowed down to give leisure for the luxurious contemplation of every form of sensuous beauty. . . . By the beauty of nature, the Northmen (if we may judge from the sagas) set little store; by physical beauty in man and woman he set much, but was content to note it in his terse objective way, "the fairest of men to look on," seldom going into detail and never permitting it to interrupt the stride of his story.

In this aspect Eddison maintains his eclecticism rather than following only the sagas. He can narrate swiftly without "pausing" to introduce "poetic ornament," as he does in most of the battle scenes, or, for example, when Juss fights the mantichore: "So close he grappled it that it might not reach him with its murthering teeth, but its claws sliced off the flesh from his left knee downward to the ankle bone, and it fell on him and crushed him on the rock, breaking in the bones of his breast" (p. 157). More often, though, Eddison's narrative "contemplates every form of sensuous beauty." He can "slow down" the action to record "the beauty of nature" as when the company of Demons rides at a leisurely amble to Krothering: "On the left a lily-paven lake slept cool beneath mighty elms, with a black swan near the bank and her four cygnets dozing in a row, their heads tucked beneath their wings, so that they looked like balls of gray-brown froth floating on the water" (p. 102). Like the Northmen, Eddison "set much store in the physical beauty of men and women," but rather than noting this beauty with "terse objectivity," Eddison usually writes with lengthy and intricate detail, and he permits it to interrupt completely "the stride of his story." In addition, Eddison often halts his active narration to write long paragraphs telling of rooms and clothing and furniture and weapons. Through most of the book Eddison not only abandons the sagas' terse and restrained pattern, he often far exceeds the "poetic ornament" of his other literary influences: Homer's extended similes usually delay the action for less than five lines, but Eddison's extended descriptions can delay the action for pages.

In the general idiom and expression, again no clear saga dominance appears in the prose of *Ouroboros,* as Eddison shows when he compares the sagas to Welsh and Irish legends:

> . . . the old Keltic heroic story is in its processes the direct opposite of the Icelandic; the instinctive idiom and figure of the one is rhetoric and hyperbole; of the other restraint and meiosis. Thus words and phrases to the Kelt, in his great scenes, are material to be poured out in a spate of eloquent emotion; in the saga, on the contrary, the expression becomes more tense and curbed as the situation heightens.

Often, Eddison exactly follows the saga pattern in moments of fierce emotion. When Juss, standing on the narrow mountain ledge, sees the horrible mantichore rushing down the cliff wall upon him and his friends, Eddison spends a paragraph describing his facial expression, but Juss's only words are "There's little sword-room" (p. 156). But more often than not in such moments, Eddison's expression tends toward hyperbole and "pours out in a spate of eloquent emotion." Hanging by his wrists from the wall of the old banquet chamber in Carcë, afflicted with hunger and with aches and bruises from battle, Brandoch Daha can still greet his rescuer with a flurry of alliteration: "La Fireez! . . . methought ye were yonder false fitchews fostered in filth and fen, the spawn of

Witchland, returned again to fleer and flout at us" (p. 92). Prezmyra, grimly set in proud despair and resolved to self-slaughter after her husband's death, can eloquently refuse the Demons' offer of peace before she drinks from the poisoned cup: "Shall the blackening frost, when it hath blasted and starved all the sweet garden flowers, say to the rose, Abide with us; and shall she harken to such a wolfish suit?" (p. 380). And Juss, on the brink of tears when Goldry has been captured by Witchland's sorcery, can yet cry out in a thick voice: "What in the stablished world is mine, that am thus in a moment reived of him that was mine own heartstring, my brother, the might of mine arm, the chiefest citadel of my dominion?" (p. 60) Eddison's comparison of the sagas with Celtic writings and his decision to abandon the saga pattern of terseness and restraint does not mean that he imitates Celtic material. His rhetorical exuberance comes not from the Welsh tales in *The Mabinogion,* or from Irish legends like those of the hero Cuchulain, or even from Malory's *Morte d'Arthur;* rather, it stems from the same rhetorical stalk as *Tamburlaine the Great, Richard II, Henry V,* and *The Duchess of Malfi.*

The language of Elizabethan drama so dominates Eddison's prose that it is hard to see the sagas in the sentences. The saga influence lies deep and can be seen more readily in the tone of the narrator's voice than in the expressions and vocabulary of the characters. Eddison illuminates this aspect of *Ouroboros* when he compares the sagas to novels:

> The novel, through its protean variations from Proust to the detective story, is almost always analytic: it would be truer perhaps to say that it nearly always employs analytic processes from time to time. But the saga is never analytic. The novelist is often introspective: the saga never.

When Eddison says that the saga is not introspective and does not employ analytic processes, he means that in sagas the narrator's voice does not judge characters' personalities and motives, and it does not offer evaluative commentary on action. The narrators of sagas are always omniscient, but they refrain from psychologic examination of the characters: the narrator's voice shows the characters to the reader; it does not tell the reader what a character is doing and thinking. For example, the narrator of *Njal's Saga* focuses many chapters on Njal's family, but he does not favor Njal and his sons when Flosi and his men come to burn Njal's home: he merely tells what happens. The saga narrator is a reporter, not a commentator. The reader's view of the characters depends solely upon her or his evaluation of their words and actions.

Ouroboros has such a narrator. You and I, like Ebenezer Scrooge in the hands of the Christmas ghosts, accompany the narrator everywhere, from the sunny and flower-filled valleys of Demonland to the wastes of Impland to the secretest chamber in the black fortress of Carcë. But the narrator stands darkly aloof like the Ghost of Christmas Yet to Come: he only points and shows the action; he does not judge, analyze, or comment. The narrator shows the Demons most often, but he does not favor them over the Witches, and he makes Corund as noble as Juss. The narrator's impartiality appears most clearly when Lessingham, the earthly observer induced to Mercury, rejects the comments of his Virgilian guide, the martlet. For the first two chapters of the book, the martlet acts as a secondary narrator who answers Lessingham's questions and makes evaluative, authoritative comments about characters. During these chapters, the primary narrator speaks in a voice unperturbed by the jurisdictional trespassings of the martlet:

> "Behold, wonder, and lament," said the martlet, "that the innocent eye of day should be enforced still to look upon the children of night everlasting, Corund of Witchland and his cursed sons."
>
> Lessingham thought, "A most fiery politician is my little martlet: damned fiends and angels and nothing betwixt for her. But I'll dance to none of their tunes, but wait for these things' unfolding" (p. 19).

You and I and Lessingham listen to the martlet, but Lessingham decides that he would rather ponder things for himself: he will watch and listen and then judge the worth of those who hold a place in the story, without help from another who may have more information. When Lessingham makes his decision to reject an analytical guide, he decides for us, too, and from that point onward we must watch and listen and judge for ourselves.

In sagas the omniscient narrator's reticent and inconspicuous voice places the characters in the foreground of the reader's imagining. You and I do not notice the narrator; we notice the characters. They display their personalities through their words and actions. In sagas, says Eddison, "the interest is concentrated upon individual persons, their characters, actions, and destinies," and "the plot depends for its whole life and power upon the personalities of its actors." The greatest part of Eddison's debt to the sagas lies in their impressive characters. Not the prose but the people.

The saga men and women delighted Eddison and held his lifelong admiration. To him the living attitudes that these women and men express show "much that is finest and noblest in the human spirit."

"the pick and flower of the Norse race"

Eddison stands not alone in his opinion because the historical figures whom the sagas celebrate merit admiration. Norwegian vikings learned of Iceland in Ireland, for Irish priests had been there in the 790's. Seeking new lands, these seafaring Northmen came first to the Faroe Islands and then to Iceland in about 860, and they colonized the island during the two subsequent generations. Aside from the usual motives for viking expeditions, ambition and restlessness and greed and overpopulation and land shortage, the main impetus for colonization was King Harald Fairhair's inexorable conquest of Norway. Many leading men of Norway fled the country because they did not have the manpower to resist Harald's armies, and they could not endure subjection to him. Eddison respected these men: "the men who settled Iceland were precisely the pick and flower of the Norse race; precisely those whose fierce spirit of independence and freedom could not abide the new 'enslavement' in Norway, and who chose loss of lands and goods, and banishment in an unknown country, rather than go under King Harald's hand."[16] Professor Gwyn Jones corroborates this view: ". . . the quality of the settlers was demonstrably high, and among them was a notable percentage of well-born lordly men, restless of constraint, vigorous, and self-reliant, the inheritors, sustainers, and transmitters of a strong and distinctive culture."[17] The saga poets themselves held this view, and it was this inspiration combined with the desire to preserve Icelandic history that prompted them four centuries later to compose fictionalized but historically based prose epics about the founding families of Iceland. One scribe, who copied out *Thidrek's Saga* in the thirteenth century, expressed his view of the value of sagas: "Sagas about worthy men are useful to know, because they show us noble deeds and brave feats, whereas ill-deeds are manifestations of indolence."[18] Foremost in the scribe's mind is the human action in the sagas. A special value lives in human conduct, in these "noble deeds and brave feats"; it lives ingenerate in the sagas and has impressed itself upon most of their readers. Gwyn Jones writes:

> ". . . the Icelandic conception of character and action was
> heroic. The men and women of the sagas had a comparatively

uncomplicated view of human destiny. . . . They had, it is
not too much to say, an aesthetic appreciation of conduct.
There was a right way to act: the consequences might be
dreadful, hateful; but the conduct was more important than its
consequences."[19]

Jones echoes a view expressed several years earlier by E. V.
Gordon:

"In no other literature is there such a sense of the beauty of
human conduct; indeed, the authors of Icelandic prose, with
the exception of Snorri, do not seem to have cared for beauty
in anything else than conduct and character. The heroes and
heroines themselves had the aesthetic view of conduct; it was
their chief guide. . . ."[20]

Eddison quotes Gordon's words in the introduction to his translation of *Egil's Saga,* which has as its main character a man whose
actions fulfill the aesthetic of conduct perfectly: Egil's words and
deeds, right or wrong, admirable or hateful, impress and fascinate
the reader, and thus they have a kind of beauty. In *Ouroboros*
Corinius fascinates in the same way.

The importance, for Eddison's fiction, of the sagas' dramatic
emphasis on characters and on the beauty of human conduct cannot be overstated. "All I did was to write the best story I could,
about the people whose company I most delighted in," wrote
Eddison to an admirer of the novel.[21] Like the sagas *Ouroboros*
achieves its power through its characters and their actions. The
question to answer now is a straightforward one: what sort of
people are the characters whom Eddison found so delightful?

4. The Hero Icelandic and Greek and Mercurian: "He doth bestride the narrow world like a Colossus"

"Persons such as my imagination likes to play among"

"Worthy," "lordly," "vigorous," "self-reliant," men with "a fierce
spirit of independence and freedom" and with "a heroic concep-
tion of character and action": these are the terms that Eddison and
others have used to describe the actual Norse colonists of Iceland
whose somewhat historical and somewhat fictive counterparts live
in the pages of the sagas. All of these qualities can be assigned
unhesitatingly to Eddison's Demons, Witches, Goblins, and Pixies.

But, Eddison's characters are not pure imitations of prominent saga characters. Much of their nature comes from Homer too. In his introduction to *Egil's Saga* Eddison says, "the saga is like Homer in that it is heroic in matter and in spirit."[22] All his life he associated saga with epic, so when he came to write his own imaginative prose epic, he naturally drew on both sources. As with the prose, the characters of *Ouroboros* are like an alchemic combination of eclectic matter.

How did the two sources influence his character creation? Where did the saga influence stop, and where did the Homeric influence begin? In a letter to his brother-in-law, Keith Henderson, Eddison offers clues to the nature of the Homeric influence on his characters when he says that his style is "fitted peculiarly to deal with great and tremendous scenes and persons, persons such as my imagination likes to play among." In this same letter Eddison speaks of his ambition for his historical novel, *Styrbiorn the Strong:* "very different from the Worm, in scope and mood and matter, yet like it in that it is a grand story, of tremendous persons and scenes."[23] The repeated phrase, "tremendous persons and scenes," does not directly indicate Homeric inspiration, but it shows that Eddison considered his characters to be grand and magnificent, and it is a descriptive phrase that, for the saga characters, would be excessive and hyperbolic. The men and women of the sagas impress with their heroic nobility, and some of the heroes behave and speak like Achilleus, Agamemnon, and Hektor, but none of them are "tremendous" people whose grandeur equals that of Homer's heroes.

"The saga is like Homer in that it is heroic in matter and in spirit"

Some difference in magnitude between the sagas and the Homeric epic rests in the disparity of divine participation in human events. Although supernatural events occur in the sagas, the gods never speak or show themselves, while in the *Iliad* the gods walk on the plains of Troy. Zeus, Hera, Athena, Aphrodite, Apollo, Ares, and Poseidon take keen interest in the war, and they all participate, some more than others, in the actions of the warriors. This divine attention endows men's thoughts and actions with a cosmic importance absent from the sagas. Achilleus's decisions illustrate this best. After enduring unjust insult from Agamemnon, flinging down his scepter, and resolving to withdraw from the fighting, the bitterly angry Achilleus asks his divine mother, Thetis, to persuade Zeus to bring the Trojans victory and the Achaians suffering until Agamemnon regrets his insulting treatment of the greatest Achaian warrior. Although troubled by the request, Zeus bends his will to it. Thus Achilleus' angry decisions move heaven and earth, as the poem's first verses tell, and have devastating consequences for a multitude of soldiers. Anger and bloodshed occur often enough in the sagas, and these events may unsettle a family or an entire region, but they do not send a clamor echoing through Asgard.

In this aspect Eddison's *Ouroboros* lies somewhere between the sagas and the *Iliad.* The powerful Mercurian peoples worship the Greek gods, and yet, as in the sagas, the gods do not appear. No one doubts the existence of the gods or of the supernatural world. The gods communicate with mortals through portents, omens, and dreams, and through sorcery mortals can converse with spirits. Most important, Eddison's Mercurian men and women share an attitude of fatalism with the women and men of the sagas and the *Iliad:* the gods decree the events and the lengths of mortal lives. Because the gods determine destiny, these women and men proudly consider themselves not the equals but the fellows of the gods as they move toward their fated ends; they do not, in humility or guilt, abase themselves in subservience to the deities. Beyond these generalizations theology grows delicate in *Ouroboros,* for the story contains eclectic ingredients that stand in cloudy relation to these general truths: the Imps worship false gods; sylphs exist; sometimes men's destinies are ruled by Fates, by gods, or by the stars; reincarnation occurs, but only for Witchland's kings; Mercurians sometimes call on the Furies or on Satan; Hell and Heaven are mentioned; Odin appears to Spitfire; and, the earth opens for Helteranius when he wants to end his life.

Much difference in magnitude rests in the disparity of individual political power. The Homeric heroes are aristocratic lords who rule provinces and command armies. Their actions can bring sorrow or happiness to many under their sway. The saga heroes are aristocratic in spirit and temperament but not in tangible political power, and though they often consider themselves the peers of kings and princes, they are pioneer homesteaders without populous provinces or private armies. Their actions do not carry consequences for scores of people.

Eddison's "tremendous" heroes embrace Homer's magnitude, for they rule large provinces, and when they have need, they can raise armies. During a council of war, King Gorice XII stands up and looks upon Corund and Corinius: "his chosen captains, great men of war raised up by him to be kings over two quarters of the world" (p. 352). Further, Eddison's heroes have more than imperial ambitions, for when Juss and King Gorice XII meet, the narrator says that "those two men met together for whose ambition and their pride the world was too little a place to contain them both and peace lying between them" (p. 354). And, their deeds change the world. When Juss and Brandoch Daha escape him at Eshgrar Ogo, Corund says to Gro, "Dost think these can survive on earth and not raise a racket that shall be heard from hence to Carcë?" (p. 144).

Some difference in magnitude is purely material. The saga heroes settled in the empty, primeval plains of Iceland. They built functional structures from wood, stone, and turf: temples, mead halls, farmhouses, stables, and dairies. Though loving luxury, building luxurious palaces was neither in their interest nor in their resources. The saga heroes have not the gorgeous dwellings, the armies, the ships, the land holdings, the wealth, and the ornate armor possessed by Homer's kings.

In grandeur, wealth, and power, Eddison certainly favors Homer's scale of magnitude more than the sagas', but the material "tremendousness" in *Ouroboros* leaves even Homer behind. One need not read far into the novel to see that the gorgeous luxuriance of Galing far exceeds the wealth of Priam and the splendor of his palace in Troy.[24] Eddison begins his lengthy description of the presence chamber with an evaluation of its splendor: "Surely no potentate of earth, not Croesus, not the great King, not Minos in his royal palace in Crete, not all the Pharaohs, not Queen Semiramis, nor all the kings of Babylon and Nineveh had ever a throne room to compare in glory with that high presence chamber of the lords of Demonland" (p. 6). In addition, the clothing of Eddison's aristocrats surpasses the silken garments and the bronze armor of Homer's kings. As one among many possible examples, Corinius's state-banquet garments illustrate the wealth of Witchland: "His ample chest was cased in a jerkin of untanned buckskin plated with silver scales, and he wore a collar of gold that was rough with smaragds [emeralds] and a long cloak of sky-blue silk brocade lined with cloth of silver" (p. 80). Even the armor worn in battle is elaborate and ornate, as this of Lord Zigg: "His armor from chin to toe shone with silver, and jewels blazed on his gorget [plated metal collar] and baldrick [breastplate] and the hilt of his long straight sword" (p. 319). The gem-encrusted armor of Eddison's heroes rivals even the blazing armor which Hephaistos forges for Achilleus when he returns to battle at the end of the *Iliad*.

"We few, we happy few, we band of brothers"

This novel's joint inspiration from the *Iliad* and the sagas emerges more strongly through comparing their societal structures to those of Mercury. Kinship, marriage, and friendly allegiance were the main societal bonds for heroic Greece and colonial Iceland, and these exist in Eddison's Mercury, but not universally. Eddison's "Argument with Dates" tells that, before the story opens, "the polite nations" of Demonland, Witchland, and Goblinland formed an alliance to bring a "Holy War" against the Ghouls. Chapter V tells that Goldry Bluszco is affianced to the cousin of King Gaslark of Goblinland and that this marriage will cement the already amiable relations between Demonland and Goblinland. Kinship appears most clearly in the fraternal unity between Juss and his brothers, Goldry Bluszco and Spitfire.

Aside from these clear examples, placing structural labels is difficult because Eddison does not clearly explain the particular features of Mercury's different societies. Although the main characters are certainly aristocrats, Eddison never discusses class distinctions or distinctions between princes and other nobles. He does not state the nature of any of the governments of the various lands or states, so one does not know if lands have agnatic, primogenitive, or elective kingship.

Witchland has a dynastic tyranny based on the indisputable claims of reincarnation: when one King Gorice dies, his spirit takes another form. In the first chapter King Gorice XI, "whose power and glory is over all the world" (p. 12), sends an ambassador to Demonland to deliver this message: "no ceremony of homage or fealty hath been performed before me by the dwellers in my province of Demonland." At this, Spitfire claps hand to sword and bellows "Province? Are not the Demons a free people?" (p. 13). This exchange comes as close to a political discussion as any conversation in the book. Although Goldry Bluszco fights Gorice XI over this question, Eddison never explains the justification for Witchland's claim. Arguing intuitively from the context, it seems that Witchland has through conquest and forced annexation gained hegemony over many lands, and that Witchland is determined to subdue Demonland at the outset of the story. Witchland rules its "empire" through fear and the brute force of a large fleet and massed armies.

Demonland's society is more opaque than Witchland's. Demonland has no king. It has ruling lords, but no formal hierarchical structure exists among them. Demonland has no parliament or formal assembly. Aside from the affianced Goldry Bluszco, no marriages occur or are proposed during the story, and only Lord Zigg, among the seven principal Demon lords, is married. No existing aristocrats are older than the ruling lords, and no detailed statement is given about anyone's parents.[25] So, without community bonds to a king, without parliamentary bonds, without marital bonds between families and estates, and without patriarchal or matriarchal bonds of kinship, one wonders what holds Demonland and these lordly bachelors together. In the filial bonding that exists among the three most powerful lords, Juss receives brotherly deference, but whether or not his authority rests on his being the oldest is not made clear. It is the second oldest brother, Goldry Bluszco, who proposes the wrestling match with King Gorice XI, and Juss and the other Demon lords accept this because "this seemed good to them all" (p. 15). However, when Juss proposes the plan for the first expedition to Impland, Spitfire says, "Thou beest our oldest brother, and I shall follow and obey thee in all that thou wilt do" (p. 99). The other Demon lords respect Juss for his wisdom and follow his good counsel, but he does not seem to have any authority to command these aristocratic warriors. Brandoch Daha, Volle, Vizz, and Zigg are allied to Juss and his brothers only through friendship. At the final council of war, all of the Demon lords, except Brandoch Daha, believe that they must rescue Goldry Bluszco before they attack Carcë, and Brandoch Daha rises and says as he leaves the chamber, "Juss, friend of my heart, meseemeth y'are all of one mind, and none of my mind. I'll e'en bid you farewell." Juss, watching him go, says, "His own self shall bring him back to me when time is, no other power should do 'gainst his good will; he whose great heart Heaven cannot force with force." When Brandoch Daha returns, he says, "thou'rt a lucky man in thine undertakings, O Juss, when thou hast such an art to draw thy friends to second thee" (p. 318). Friendship is the basic societal bond, but it is a bond indissoluble.

Demonland's anarchical, highly individualized aristocracy resembles the alliance of kings in the *Iliad*. Homer does not clearly state the relationships between the many kings and princes who come together to attack Troy, but aside from Menelaos, who wants to recapture Helen, most of the kings joined the alliance because they hoped to obtain wealth during the conquest, and they valued the friendship of the powerful Atreides. Homer does say that Agamemnon is the chief commander of the alliance. Based on the evidence from the catalog in Book II, it can be argued that Agamemnon was the most powerful king in the Peloponnesian peninsula.[26] However, Agamemnon, like Juss, does not have ultimate authority over the other kings; if he had it, Achilleus' withdrawal in Book I would have been an act of desertion and a punishable offense. Achilleus and the other kings have chosen to participate in the war, and they support one another through friendly alliance and not by compulsion.

Demonland's friendly lords also resemble the tenth-century Icelanders who, with cooperation unique in the world during that age, formed a united group that was as individually aristocratic as Homer's Achaian alliance and Eddison's Demon alliance and yet more organized than both. The first settlers of Iceland simply claimed large expanses of land, often at great distances from one another. As time passed and families grew up and more settlers arrived, the original landholders portioned their lands out into estates for their sons and for their friends. They also built and preserved places for the worship of, usually, Thor or Frey on their own lands, and so eventually these wealthiest landowners obtained for themselves the status and title of *godi* ("godly one"), a kind of secular priest. Within sixty years after the arrival of the first settlers in the 860's, the wealthiest men, the godar of Iceland, founded the institution of the *althing,* an annual general assembly that occurred at a specified place called the *thingvellir* (plain of assembly). The *althing* was an alliance of thirty-six equal *godi,* and they formed a parliament with legislative and judicial power. The *althing* was not an institution for the executive enforcement of laws: the maintenance of law and order rested on the basic societal bonds of kinship, marriage, and friendship. However, family feuds and private vengeance are common events in the sagas.[27] Fortunately, such violent domestic quarrels do not wrack Demonland's internal peace.

"When the blast of war blows in our ears, Then imitate the action of the tiger"

The nonexistence of an elderly generation in Demonland is perhaps the strangest aspect of the Demonland society, especially since the oldest Demon lord, Volle, is only forty when the story opens, and one would expect that some venerable older lords, like old Nestor and King Priam in the *Iliad* or Kveldulf in *Egil's Saga,* would still survive. Eddison's silence on the parentage of his Demons precludes my making any hypothesis about primogenitive or agnatic lordship in Demonland. Consequently, I wonder how these horned men became lords and how they maintain their lord-ships. The novel's evidence suggests that martial prowess makes the foundation for aristocratic power. The first chapter tells that Juss knows the art of sorcery, "yet useth not that art; for it sappeth the life and strength, nor is it held worthy that a Demon should put trust in that art, but rather in his own might and main" (p. 10). Unlike Juss, King Gorice XII does not disdain sorcery as an unwor-thy practice; he puts much strength and trust into it. Yet, Gorice XII delegates his imperial authority on the basis of martial prow-ess: he rewards his victorious generals, Corund and Corinius, with kingdoms when they prove their martial ability through successful conquests that extend Witchland's empire. To the ancient Greeks an aristocracy was a state in which the best citizens rule. Demon-land and Witchland are military aristocracies: the best military leaders rule.

In placing such emphasis on military virtues, Eddison departs from the Icelandic situation and forms societies more bellicose than those in the *Iliad.* The heroes of the sagas were chiefly agricul-tural or dairy farmers. Some of these men led dual lives as vikings during the summer and as farmers during the balance of the year. But in the sagas, fighting is almost never the principal aspect of a man's life: the strength and the identity of the saga men, and their claim to local rulership, came through their landed estates. Hom-er's kings, while doubtless great warriors, held power over their Greek provinces because an accepted agnatic practice had pro-duced ruling dynasties in each part of Peloponnessos, and each king's connection with the dynasty was his justification for possess-ing the kingdom.

Warfare is everything on Mercury, especially for the Demons. Fighting distinguishes and identifies the lords. When the little martlet introduces the Demon lords to Lessingham, it distin-guishes each lord according to his martial skills, deeds, or attri-butes. Volle is "a great sea-captain" and "one that did service to the cause of Demonland, and of the whole world besides, in the late wars against the Ghouls." Zigg is "the far-famed tamer of horses" and "a mighty man of his hands withal when he leadeth his horsemen against the enemy." Spitfire is "impetuous in war." Goldry Bluszco wears the sword "wherewith he slew the sea mon-ster." Brandoch Daha "for years was held for the third best man-at-arms in all Mercury, along with these, Goldry Bluszco and Gorice X. of Witchland. . . . And Gorice he slew, nine summers back, in single combat . . . and now can none surpass Lord Brandoch Daha in feats of arms, save perchance Goldry alone"

(p. 9). Fighting is the foundation of the friendships so important for holding the society of Demon lords together. The deep love between the three brethren and the other lords rests upon mutual admiration for martial skill. Military prowess, when seen in an enemy, elicits admiration as well, and this is proper and necessary in a heroic society, for the Demons and Witches would not contend with one another if they did not respect one another: a warrior cannot gain glory by defeating an enemy he holds in contempt. At the battle before Carcë, Juss looks upon Corund's brave stand and says, "This is the greatest deed of arms that ever I in the days of my life did see, and I have so great an admiration and wonder in my heart for Corund that almost I would give him peace" (p. 366). All loves and loyalties between friends, and all honest hatreds between enemies, are rooted in martial prowess.

> **"Priam aloud called out to Helen**
> **'Come over where I am, dear child, and sit down**
> **beside me, ... tell me of the name of this man**
> **who is so tremendous'"**

The heroic societies of the sagas and the *Iliad* have, compared to other social systems, relatively narrow parameters for the acceptable forms of masculine endeavor. Only a handful of occupations are available to aristocrats. In the *Iliad* all of the prominent Achaians and Trojans are warriors and governing princes. In the sagas the prominent men are wealthy farmers and landowners, priests, lawyers, and vikings; many pursue more than one of these occupations. In each society the prominent men do similar things, hold similar attitudes and values, and think in similar ways. Both societies also have narrow parameters for acceptable moral behavior. The people strictly uphold their moral standards, and the maintenance of a man's position in society depends upon his ability to behave in ways that compare well to the behavioral ideals. These generalizations apply to the societies of *Ouroboros* as well. And yet, Eddison's societies, propelled by a moral system based mainly on military virtues, are simpler and more rigorous than their two sources. To be part of the heroic group, a Witch or Demon must be like the group and behave in the accepted martial ways.

Amid such human uniformity, how can the author define human difference? How can he make individuals have singular personalities and stand apart from the group? The basic method, used in various ways, is characterization through action. The heroes in sagas, in the *Iliad,* and in *Ouroboros* are men of action. Their actions serve to define them as individuals. Even though they must act within a rigorous and often unspoken set of heroic standards, by acting differently within those standards they distinguish themselves from one another.

Certainly unique action sets a man apart from the group. Bolli's killing his best friend, Kjartan, at the end of *Laxdaela Saga,* Diomedes's wounding of Ares in Book V of the *Iliad,* and Goldry Bluszco's victory over Gorice XI in Chapter II of *Ouroboros:* these singular actions distinguish their performers from their fellows because no one else performs a comparable action. But, this method is not restricted to the saga writers, Homer, and Eddison; it is used commonly by dramatists, novelists, and narrative poets. Nevertheless, a second and more particular method is shared by Homer and his disciple Eddison. Making characters different is a harder task for Homer and Eddison than for the saga writers because the *Iliad* and *Ouroboros* have an epic opposition of Trojan against Achaian and Demon against Witch. Where the saga writers deal with contending individuals who, by their quarrel, distinguish themselves within the uniform Icelandic society, Homer and Eddison deal with polarized groups. Both Homer and his disciple frequently use action to create individual personalities by exhibiting several characters' differing responses to a common situation.

At the end of Book XV of the *Iliad,* Hektor leads the Trojans to the climax of their advance when he brings the fighting to the Achaian ships lying beached in a row, grabs the stern of one of the vessels, and calls for a torch to set the ship aflame (1.704). This event, one of the most significant in the poem, provides Homer with the opportunity for developing individual characters because three Achaian heroes respond to it, but each responds differently within the heroic standards. The huge Telemonian Aias refuses to stand back with the other Achaian soldiers, and even before Hektor achieved his triumphant handhold, Aias "went in huge strides up and down the decks of the vessels/He wielded in his hands a great pike for sea fighting" (XV: 676–677). Alone among the Achaians, Aias takes the foremost position as a one-man vanguard, and he singlehandedly holds off the Trojans with a spear exceeding twenty-five feet in length. He maintains this position although he grows weary: "They could not/beat him out of his place, though they piled their missiles upon him" (XVI: 107–108). Aias displays the grim and stalwart courage that characterizes all his fighting and that makes him, after Achilleus, the ablest Achaian warrior. Another warrior, Patroklos, responds in a way that seems somewhat odd to our modern sensibilities of heroic behavior: he weeps "warm tears like a spring dark-running" (XVI: 3), but when he pleads with Achilleus to return to the battle, it appears that his tears mark not his cowardice but his frustration with Achilleus's stubborn refusal to fight and his pity for the men shuddering under Hektor's onslaught. The third warrior, Achilleus, displays both the stubborn resentment stemming from his dispute with Agamemnon and also his thoughtful, sensitive disposition when he responds to Patroklos. He says that Patroklos's words have brought back "bitter sorrow" to him, and "it was not/in my heart to be angry forever" (XVI: 60–61). Achilleus's resolutions, faced with the suffering of warriors he loves, sharply trouble him, and after some thought, he decides to satisfy his honor by continuing his nonparticipation and to relent some of his anger by loaning his excellent armor to Patroklos. At this significant moment three different responses help to create three individual personalities.[28]

An example of Eddison's use of this method is the responses of the Demon lords to King Gorice's "sending of the worm of the pit" and his capture of Goldry Bluszco in Chapter V. King Gaslark finds them on their broken and charred ship, dazed and weeping with grief. Gaslark proposes that they sail quickly and attack Carcë with surprise, for he thinks Goldry has been taken there. Juss disagrees with Gaslark's plan for a surprise attack: "Yet not so is Witchland to be overcome, but after long days of labour only, and laying of schemes and building of ships and gathering of hosts." Juss also thinks it is but "wild fancy" that Goldry has been taken to Carcë, and though he does not tell Gaslark, he thinks Gaslark's Goblins cannot match the strength of Witches. Gaslark presses some more, but "not for all his urging might Gaslark move him any whit." Throughout this crisis Juss's actions display the circumspection and wisdom that mark him as a great commander. Spitfire, however, cannot understand what seems to him cowardly complacency in Juss, and he leaps up cursing: "With Goldry hath all manliness departed out of Demonland, and we be milksops that remain, and objects of scorn and spitting." Spitfire, first characterized by the phrase "impetuous in war" (p. 10), acts with the impassioned rashness that often prevents him from seeing wisdom. Meanwhile, Brandoch Daha, the coolly elegant Demon lord, "fared fore and aft on the gangway, about and about, as a caged panther fareth when feeding time is long overdue." Brandoch Daha then speaks of a "cruel perturbation" and a "tempest in his mind" to Gaslark, and demands that Gaslark fight with him: "The cure of this is only fighting. . . . Fight I must, or this passion will kill me quite out" (p. 63). In response to the capture of Goldry Bluszco, each of the characters has strong feelings, but their feelings are different, and they express them differently in action. The horned men act within the behavioral ideals of their heroic society, but they act differently.

Action for distinguishing character has more potency and importance than its narrative use by writers. To the heroes in the story it is irrevocable necessity. Idleness is not available to them. They must act not only to be heroes but also to have something they may call their own: to have reputation. "I must have more great action . . ." says King Gaslark. "Something I would enact that shall embroil and astonish the world . . . ere I go down into silence" (p. 59). Great pressure for success weighs upon these heroes. As in the *Iliad* earned glory is the most desired thing and earned shame is the most feared thing. These inseparably paired emotions make one propelling motive for success. Shame consequent from failure produces suicidal feelings of worthlessness. Seething with pain and anger after Corinius has defeated him, Spitfire cries out to Volle, "Boasted he not that he is king in Demonland? And yet I had not my sword in his umbles. And thou thinkest I'll live in shame? . . . Better dead than run from Corinius like a beaten puppy" (p. 241). For Spitfire present death is more desirable than a shameful life that includes the constant remembrance of failure in action. And yet, as in the *Iliad,* defeat does not necessarily incur shame. Defeated and captured by the Demons, the Witchland hero Laxus looks proudly at his captors and says, "It may be pain, but no shame to us to be vanquished after so equal and so great a fight" (p. 309). But it takes "so great a fight" to prevent the advent of shame. "O, I have lost my reputation!" cries Michael Cassio in despairing words that would find sympathetic ears among defeated men on Mercury. "I have lost the immortal part of myself, and what remains is bestial."[29] Successful deeds bring glory, and upon that glory hangs reputation, not just the meaning of a warrior's life, but his very soul.

"The Dragon that eateth his own tail"

Glory in victory and shame in defeat: these are like obverse and reverse sides of one coin. If the gods take this coin and flip it high in the air, it will alternately turn one face toward the sun and one face toward the shadow, over and over, but it will eventually fall to the ground and lie still. At the end of all wars is a final battle. Final defeat and final victory, final glory and final shame, and an end of military reputation: these things follow the last battle. When fighting ends in sagas and in the Homeric poems, the men return home and take up domestic occupations or civil offices. Not so on Mercury. There, an end to fighting brings an end to identity. If warfare ended, in Juss's words, "we that were lords of all the world must turn shepherds and hunters, lest we become mere mountebanks and fops" (p. 390–91). It is not the victory that these lords love, it is the fighting. If war becomes obsolete, the patterns of life and the disciplines of every worthy endeavor will pass away, the foundations of civilization will decay, and the lords themselves will lose their fame and power almost to the point at which they will be objects of contempt. War justifies and nourishes all desirable qualities in the civilization on Mercury.

10. and 1. Witchland sends an ambassador to Demonland

9. The death of Gorice XII

2. The death of Gorice XI

8. The second conjuring in the Iron Tower

3. The first conjuring in the Iron Tower

7. The second attack on Carcë

4. The first attack on Carcë

6. The second quest to Impland in search of Goldry Bluzco

5. The first quest to Impland in search of Goldry Bluzco

So war on Mercury cannot stop. Eddison prevents the end of life-giving warfare and the sad decay of Mercurian civilization through an impeccably balanced plot structure based on the ouroboros. Eddison arranges his major events symmetrically so that they occur twice and seem to return to their source.

This story ends where it begins and begins where it ends. The ouroboros structure makes Eddison's Mercury an everlasting world in which the heroic ideals never wane. Lord Juss best expresses this vision of a warrior's utopia when he wishes for an unending struggle with King Gorice: "Let me dream yet awhile," says Juss. "From this time forth to maintain, I and he, his and mine, ageless and deathless for ever, for ever our high contention whether he or we should be great masters of all the earth" (p. 396).

Eddison's last page invites us to turn back to his first and to begin the adventure story again. And so it is with the reading of all great books: we only need to take our favorites from the shelves again, and the characters and stories, dwelling in the dark limbo of ink and paper within closed covers, will jump back to life in our imaginations. But the ouroboros surrounds more than just reading. The ever-renewing dragon that eats its tail symbolizes the pattern of the love of beauty in our minds. Once we experience beauty in any form, we need only to remember it and to go back to it, and it will be reborn for us to love it again by finding new things to love in it: another morning at the gallery, another night at the concert hall, another afternoon in the theater, another trip to the lake, another walk beneath favorite trees, another uncorking of that favorite wine, another smiling glance toward that face you love best.

PAUL EDMUND THOMAS
Minneapolis
October 1990

To W.G.E. *and to my friends* K.H. *and* G.C.L.M.
I dedicate this book

It is neither allegory nor fable but a Story to be read for its own sake.

The proper names I have tried to spell simply. The *e* in Carcë is long, like that in Phryne, the *o* in Krothering short and the accent on that syllable: Corund is accented on the first syllable, Prezmyra on the second, Brandoch Daha on the first and fourth, Gorice on the last syllable, rhyming with thrice: Corinius rhymes with Flaminius, Galing with sailing, La Fireez with desire ease: *ch* is always guttural, as in loch.

E.R.E.

9th January 1922

THE INDUCTION[1]

HERE was a man named Lessingham[2] dwelt in an old low house in Wasdale, set in a gray old garden where yew-trees flourished that had seen Vikings in Copeland in their seedling time. Lily and rose and larkspur bloomed in the borders, and begonias with blossoms big as saucers, red and white and pink and lemon-colour, in the beds before the porch. Climbing roses, honeysuckle, clematis, and the scarlet flame-flower scrambled up the walls. Thick woods were on every side without the garden, with a gap north-eastward opening on the desolate lake and the great fells beyond it: Gable rearing his crag-bound head against the sky from behind the straight clean outline of the Screes.[3]

Cool long shadows stole across the tennis lawn. The air was golden. Doves murmured in the trees; two chaffinches played on the near post of the net; a little water-wagtail scurried along the path. A French window stood open to the garden, showing darkly a dining-room panelled with old oak, its Jacobean table bright with flowers and silver and cut glass and Wedgwood dishes heaped with fruit: greengages, peaches, and green muscat grapes. Lessingham lay back in a hammock-chair watching through the blue smoke of an after-dinner cigar the warm light on the Gloire de Dijon roses that clustered about the bedroom window overhead. He had her hand in his. This was their House.

"Should we finish that chapter of Njal?"[4] she said.

She took the heavy volume with its faded green cover, and read: " 'He went out on the night of the Lord's day, when nine weeks were still to winter; he heard a great crash, so that he

1

thought both heaven and earth shook. Then he looked into the west airt, and he thought he saw thereabouts a ring of fiery hue, and within the ring a man on a gray horse. He passed quickly by him, and rode hard. He had a flaming firebrand in his hand, and he rode so close to him that he could see him plainly. He was black as pitch, and he sung this song with a mighty voice—

> Here I ride swift steed,
> His flank flecked with rime,
> Rain from his mane drips,
> Horse mighty for harm;
> Flames flare at each end,
> Gall glows in the midst,
> So fares it with Flosi's redes
> As this flaming brand flies;
> And so fares it with Flosi's redes
> As this flaming brand flies.

" 'Then he thought he hurled the firebrand east towards the fells before him, and such a blaze of fire leapt up to meet it that he could not see the fells for the blaze. It seemed as though that man rode east among the flames and vanished there.

" 'After that he went to his bed, and was senseless for a long time, but at last he came to himself. He bore in mind all that had happened, and told his father, but he bade him tell it to Hjallti Skeggi's son. So he went and told Hjallti, but he said he had seen "the Wolf's Ride, and that comes ever before great tidings." ' "

They were silent awhile; then Lessingham said suddenly, "Do you mind if we sleep in the east wing to-night?"

"What, in the Lotus Room?"

"Yes."

"I'm too much of a lazy-bones to-night, dear," she answered.

"Do you mind if I go alone, then? I shall be back to breakfast. I like my lady with me; still, we can go again when next moon wanes. My pet is not frightened, is she?"

"No!" she said, laughing. But her eyes were a little big. Her fingers played with his watch-chain. "I'd rather," she said presently, "you went later on and took me. All this is so odd still: the House, and that; and I love it so. And after all, it is a long way and several years too, sometimes, in the Lotus Room, even though it is all over next morning. I'd rather we went together. If anything happened then, well, we'd both be done in, and it wouldn't matter so much, would it?"

"Both be what?" said Lessingham. "I'm afraid your language is not all that might be wished."

"Well, you taught me!" said she; and they laughed.

They sat there till the shadows crept over the lawn and up the trees, and the high rocks of the mountain shoulder beyond burned red in the evening rays. He said, "If you like to stroll a bit of way up the fell-side, Mercury is visible to-night. We might get a glimpse of him just after sunset."

A little later, standing on the open hillside below the hawking bats,[5] they watched for the dim planet that showed at last low down in the west between the sunset and the dark.

He said, "It is as if Mercury had a finger on me tonight, Mary. It's no good my trying to sleep to-night except in the Lotus Room."

Her arm tightened in his. "Mercury?" she said. "It is another world. It is too far."

But he laughed and said, "Nothing is too far."

They turned back as the shadows deepened. As they stood in the dark of the arched gate leading from the open fell into the garden, the soft clear notes of a spinet sounded from the house. She put up a finger. "Hark," she said. "Your daughter playing *Les Barricades.*"

They stood listening. "She loves playing," he whispered. "I'm glad we taught her to play." Presently he whispered again, *"Les Barricades Mystérieuses.*[6] What inspired Couperin with that enchanted name? And only you and I know what it really means. *Les Barricades Mystérieuses.*"

That night Lessingham lay alone in the Lotus Room. Its casements opened eastward on the sleeping woods and the sleeping bare slopes of Illgill Head. He slept soft and deep; for that was the House of Postmeridian,[7] and the House of Peace.

In the deep and dead time of the night, when the waning moon peered over the mountain shoulder, he woke suddenly. The silver beams shone through the open window on a form perched at the foot of the bed: a little bird, black, round-headed, short-beaked, with long sharp wings, and eyes like two stars shining. It spoke and said, "Time is."

So Lessingham got up and muffled himself in a great cloak that lay on a chair beside the bed. He said, "I am ready, my little martlet."[8] For that was the House of Heart's Desire.

Surely the martlet's eyes filled all the room with starlight. It was an old room with lotuses carved on the panels and on the bed and chairs and roof-beams; and in the glamour the carved flowers swayed like waterlilies in a lazy stream. He went to the window, and the little martlet sat on his shoulder. A chariot coloured like the halo about the moon waited by the window, poised in air, harnessed to a strange steed. A horse it seemed,[9] but winged like an eagle, and its fore-legs feathered and armed with eagle's claws instead of hooves. He entered the chariot, and that little martlet sat on his knee.

With a whirr of wings the wild courser sprang skyward. The night about them was like the tumult of bubbles about a diver's ears diving in a deep pool under a smooth steep rock in a mountain cataract. Time was swallowed up in speed; the world reeled; and it was but as the space between two deep breaths till that strange courser spread wide his rainbow wings and slanted down the night over a great island that slumbered on a slumbering sea, with lesser isles about it: a country of rock mountains and hill pastures and many waters, all a-glimmer in the moonshine.

They landed within a gate crowned with golden lions. Lessingham came down from the chariot, and the little black martlet circled about his head, showing him a yew avenue leading from the gates. As in a dream, he followed her.

The Castle of Lord Juss

*Of the rarities that were in the lofty presence
chamber, fair and lovely to behold, and of the
qualities and conditions of the lords of
Demonland: and of the embassy sent unto them by
King Gorice XI., and of the answer thereto.*

 H E eastern stars were paling to the dawn as Lessingham followed his conductor along the grass walk between the shadowy ranks of Irish yews, that stood like soldiers mysterious and expectant in the darkness. The grass was bathed in night-dew, and great white lilies sleeping in the shadows of the yews loaded the air of that garden with fragrance. Lessingham felt no touch of the ground beneath his feet, and when he stretched out his hand to touch a tree his hand passed through branch and leaves as though they were unsubstantial as a moonbeam.

The little martlet, alighting on his shoulder, laughed in his ear. "Child of earth," she said, "dost think we are here in dreamland?"

He answered nothing, and she said, "This is no dream. Thou, first of the children of men, art come to Mercury, where thou and I will journey up and down for a season to show thee the lands and oceans, the forests, plains, and ancient mountains, cities and palaces of this world, Mercury, and the doings of them that dwell therein. But here thou canst not handle aught, neither make the folk ware of thee, not though thou shout thy throat hoarse. For thou and I walk here impalpable and invisible, as it were two dreams walking."[1]

They were now on the marble steps which led from the yew walk to the terrace opposite the great gate of the castle. "No need to unbar gates to thee and me," said the martlet, as they passed beneath the darkness of that ancient portal, carved with strange devices, and clean through the massy timbers of the bolted gate thickly riveted with silver, into the inner court. "Go we into the lofty presence chamber and there tarry awhile. Morning is kindling the upper air, and folk will soon be stirring in the castle, for they lie not long abed when day begins in Demonland. For be it known to thee, O earthborn, that this land is Demonland, and this castle the castle of Lord Juss, and this day now dawning his birthday, when the Demons hold high festival in Juss's castle to do honour unto him and to his brethren, Spitfire and Goldry Bluszco; and these and their fathers before them bear rule from time immemorial in Demonland, and have the lordship over all the Demons."

She spoke, and the first low beams of the sun smote javelin-like through the eastern windows, and the freshness of morning breathed and shimmered in that lofty chamber, chasing the blue and dusky shades of departed night to the corners and recesses, and to the rafters of the vaulted roof. Surely no potentate of earth, not Croesus,[2] not the great King, not Minos[3] in his royal palace in Crete, not all the Pharaohs, not Queen Semiramis,[4] nor all the Kings of Babylon and Nineveh had ever a throne room to compare in glory with that high presence chamber of the lords of Demonland.[5] Its walls and pillars were of snow-white marble, every vein whereof was set with small gems: rubies, corals, garnets, and pink topaz. Seven pillars on either side bore up the shadowy vault of the roof; the roof-tree and the beams were of gold, curiously carved, the roof itself of mother-of-pearl. A side aisle ran behind each row of pillars, and seven paintings on the western side faced seven spacious windows on the east. At the end of the hall upon a dais stood three high seats, the arms of each composed of two hippo-griffs[6] wrought in gold, with wings spread, and the legs of the seats the legs of the hippogriffs; but the body of each high seat was a single jewel of monstrous size: the lefthand seat a black opal, asparkle with steel-blue fire, the next a fire-opal, as it were a burning coal, the third seat an alexandrite, purple like wine by night but deep sea-green by day. Ten more pillars stood in semicircle behind the high seats, bearing up above them and the dais a canopy of gold. The benches that ran from end to end of the lofty chamber were of cedar, inlaid with coral and ivory, and so were the tables that stood before the benches. The floor of the chamber was tessellated, of marble and green tourmaline, and on every square of tourmaline was carven the image of a fish: as the dolphin, the conger,[7] the cat-fish, the salmon, the tunny, the squid, and other wonders of the deep. Hangings of tapestry were behind the high seats, worked with flowers, snake's-head, snapdragon, dragon-mouth, and their kind; and on the dado below the windows were sculptures of birds and beasts and creeping things.

But a great wonder of this chamber, and a marvel to behold, was how the capital of every one of the four-and-twenty pillars was hewn from a single precious stone, carved by the hand of some sculptor of long ago into the living form of a monster: here was a harpy[8] with screaming mouth, so wondrously cut in ochre-tinted jade it was a marvel to hear no scream from her: here in wine-yellow topaz a flying fire-drake:[9] there a cockatrice[10] made of a single ruby: there a star sapphire the colour of moonlight, cut for a cyclops,[11] so that the rays of the star trembled from his single eye: salamanders, mermaids, chimaeras,[12] wild men o' the woods, leviathans,[13] all hewn from faultless gems, thrice the bulk of a big man's body, velvet-dark sapphires, crystolite,[14] beryl,[15] amethyst,[16] and the yellow zircon that is like transparent gold.

To give light to the presence chamber were seven escarbuncles,[17] great as pumpkins, hung in order down the length of it, and nine fair moonstones standing in order on silver pedestals between the pillars on the dais. These jewels, drinking in the sunshine by day, gave it forth during the hours of darkness in a radiance of pink light and a soft effulgence as of moonbeams. And yet another marvel, the nether side of the canopy over the high seats was encrusted with lapis lazuli,[18] and in that feigned dome of heaven burned the twelve signs of the zodiac, every star a diamond that shone with its own light.

Folk now began to be astir in the castle, and there came a score of serving men into the presence chamber with brooms and brushes, cloths and leathers, to sweep and garnish it, and burnish the gold and jewels of the chamber. Lissome they were and sprightly of gait, of fresh complexion and fair-haired. Horns grew on their heads. When their tasks were accomplished they departed, and the presence began to fill with guests. A joy it was to see such a shifting maze of velvets, furs, curious needleworks and cloth of tissue,[19] tiffanies,[20] laces, ruffs, goodly chains and carcanets[21] of gold: such glitter of jewels and weapons: such nodding of the plumes the Demons wore in their hair, half veiling the horns that

grew upon their heads. Some were sitting on the benches or leaning on the polished tables, some walking forth and back upon the
shining floor. Here and there were women among them, women so
fair one had said: it is surely white-armed Helen[22] this one; this,
Arcadian Atalanta;[23] this, Phryne[24] that stood to Praxiteles for
Aphrodite's picture; this, Thaïs, for whom great Alexander to pleasure her fantasy did burn Persepolis like a candle; this, she that was
rapt by the Dark God from the flowering fields of Enna, to be
Queen for ever among the dead that be departed.[25]

Now came a stir near the stately doorway, and Lessingham
beheld a Demon of burly frame and noble port, richly attired. His
face was ruddy and somewhat freckled, his forehead wide, his eyes
calm and blue like the sea. His beard, thick and tawny, was parted
and brushed back and upwards on either side.

"Tell me, my little martlet," said Lessingham, "is this Lord
Juss?"

"This is not Lord Juss," answered the martlet, "nor aught so
worshipful as he. The lord thou seest is Volle, who dwelleth under
Kartadza, by the salt sea. A great sea-captain is he, and one that did
service to the cause of Demonland, and of the whole world besides,
in the late wars against the Ghouls.

"But cast thine eyes again towards the door, where one
standeth amid a knot of friends, tall and somewhat stooping, in a
corselet of silver, and a cloak of old brocaded silk coloured like
tarnished gold; something like to Volle in feature, but swarthy, and
with bristling black moustachios."

"I see him," said Lessingham. "This then is Lord Juss!"

"Not so," said martlet. " 'Tis but Vizz, brother to Volle. He is
wealthiest in goods of all the Demons, save the three brethren only
and Lord Brandoch Daha."

"And who is this?" asked Lessingham, pointing to one of light
and brisk step and humorous eye, who in that moment met Volle
and engaged him in converse apart. Handsome of face he was,
albeit somewhat long-nosed and sharp-nosed: keen and hard and
filled with life and the joy of it.

"Here thou beholdest," answered she, "Lord Zigg, the far-
famed tamer of horses. Well loved is he among the Demons, for he
is merry of mood, and a mighty man of his hands withal when he
leadeth his horsemen against the enemy."

Volle threw up his beard and laughed a great laugh at some
jest that Zigg whispered in his ear, and Lessingham leaned forward
into the hall if haply he might catch what was said. The hum of talk
drowned the words, but leaning forward Lessingham saw where

the arras curtains behind the dais parted for a moment, and one of princely bearing advanced past the high seats down the body of the hall. His gait was delicate, as of some lithe beast of prey newly wakened out of slumber, and he greeted with lazy grace the many friends who hailed his entrance. Very tall was that lord, and slender of build, like a girl. His tunic was of silk coloured like the wild rose, and embroidered in gold with representations of flowers and thunderbolts. Jewels glittered on his left hand and on the golden bracelets on his arms, and on the fillet twined among the golden curls of his hair, set with plumes of the king-bird of Paradise. His horns were dyed with saffron, and inlaid with filigree work of gold. His buskins were laced with gold, and from his belt hung a sword, narrow of blade and keen, the hilt rough with beryls and black diamonds. Strangely light and delicate was his frame and seeming, yet with a sense of slumbering power beneath, as the delicate peak of a snow mountain seen afar in the low red rays of morning. His face was beautiful to look upon, and softly coloured like a girl's face, and his expression one of gentle melancholy, mixed with some disdain; but fiery glints awoke at intervals in his eyes, and the lines of swift determination hovered round the mouth below his curled moustachios.

"At last," murmured Lessingham, "at last, Lord Juss!"

"Little art thou to blame," said the martlet, "for this misprision, for scarce could a lordlier sight have joyed thine eyes. Yet is this not Juss, but Lord Brandoch Daha, to whom all Demonland west of Shalgreth and Stropardon oweth allegiance: the rich vineyards of Krothering, the broad pasture lands of Failze, and all the western islands and their cragbound fastnesses. Think not, because he affecteth silks and jewels like a queen, and carrieth himself light and dainty as a silver birch tree on the mountain, that his hand is light or his courage doubtful in war. For years was he held for the third best man-at-arms in all Mercury, along with these, Goldry Bluszco and Gorice X. of Witchland. And Gorice he slew, nine summers back, in single combat, when the Witches harried in Goblinland and Brandoch Daha led five hundred and fourscore Demons to succour Gaslark, the king of that country. And now can none surpass Lord Brandoch Daha in feats of arms, save perchance Goldry alone.

"Yet, lo," she said, as a sweet and wild music stole on the ear, and the guests turned towards the dais, and the hangings parted, "at last, the triple lordship of Demonland! Strike softly, music: smile, Fates, on this festal day! Joy and safe days shine for this world and Demonland! Turn thy gaze first on him who walks in majesty in the midst, his tunic of olive-green velvet ornamented with devices of hidden meaning in thread of gold and beads of chrysolite. Mark how the buskins, clasping his stalwart calves, glitter with gold and amber. Mark the dusky cloak streamed with gold and lined with blood-red silk: a charmed cloak, made by the sylphs[26] in forgotten days, bringing good hap to the wearer, so he be true of heart and no dastard. Mark him that weareth it, his sweet dark countenance, the violet fire in his eyes, the sombre warmth of his smile, like autumn woods in late sunshine. This is Lord Juss, lord of this age-remembering castle, than whom none hath more worship in wide Demonland. Somewhat he knoweth of art magical, yet useth not that art; for it sappeth the life and strength, nor is it held worthy that a Demon should put trust in that art, but rather in his own might and main.

"Now turn thine eyes to him that leaneth on Juss's left arm, shorter but mayhap sturdier than he, apparelled in black silk that shimmers with gold as he moveth, and crowned with black eagle's feathers among his horns and yellow hair. His face is wild and keen like a sea-eagle's, and from his bristling brows the eyes dart glances sharp as a glancing spear. A faint flame, pallid like the fire of a Will-o'-the-Wisp,[27] breathes ever and anon from his distended nostrils. This is Lord Spitfire, impetuous in war.

"Last, behold on Juss's right hand, yon lord that bulks mighty as Hercules yet steppeth lightly as a heifer. The thews and sinews of his great limbs ripple as he moves beneath a skin whiter than ivory; his cloak of cloth of gold is heavy with jewels, his tunic of black sendaline[28] hath great hearts worked thereon in rubies and red silk thread. Slung from his shoulders clanks a two-handed sword, the pommel a huge star-ruby carven in the image of a heart, for the heart is his sign and symbol. This is that sword forged by the elves, wherewith he slew the sea-monster, as thou mayest see in the painting on the wall. Noble is he of countenance, most like to his brother Juss, but darker brown of hair and ruddier of hue and bigger of cheekbone. Look well on him, for never shall thine eyes behold a greater champion than the Lord Goldry Bluszco, captain of the hosts of Demonland."

Now when the greetings were done and the strains of the lutes and recorders sighed and lost themselves in the shadowy vault of the roof, the cup-bearers did fill great gems made in form of cups with ancient wine, and the Demons caroused to Lord Juss deep draughts in honour of this day of his nativity. And now they were ready to set forth by twos and threes into the parks and pleasaunces, some to take their pleasure about the fair gardens and fishponds, some to hunt wild game among the wooded hills, some to disport themselves at quoits or tennis or riding at the ring or martial exercises; that so they might spend the livelong day as befitteth high holiday, in pleasure and action without care, and thereafter revel in the lofty presence chamber till night grew old with eating and drinking and all delight.

But as they were upon going forth, a trumpet was sounded without, three strident blasts.

"What kill-joy have we here?" said Spitfire. "The trumpet soundeth only for travellers from the outlands. I feel it in my bones some rascal is come to Galing, one that bringeth ill hap in his pocket and a shadow athwart the sun on this our day of festival."

"Speak no word of ill omen," answered Juss. "Whosoe'er it be, we will straight dispatch his business and so fall to pleasure indeed. Some, run to the gate and bring him in."

The serving man hastened and returned, saying, "Lord, it is an Ambassador from Witchland and his train. Their ship made land at Lookinghaven-ness at nightfall. They slept on board, and your soldiers gave them escort to Galing at break of day. He craveth present audience."

"From Witchland, ha?" said Juss. "Such smokes use ever to go before the fire."

"Shall's bid the fellow," said Spitfire, "wait on our pleasure? It is pity such should poison our gladness."

Goldry laughed and said, "Whom hath he sent us? Laxus, think you? to make his peace with us again for that vile part of his practised against us off Kartadza, detestably falsifying his word he had given us?"

Juss said to the serving man, "Thou sawest the Ambassador. Who is he?"

"Lord," answered he, "His face was strange to me. He is little of stature and, by your highness' leave, the most unlike to a great lord of Witchland that ever I saw. And, by your leave, for all the marvellous rich and sumptuous coat a weareth, he is very like a false jewel in a rich casing."

"Well," said Juss, "a sour draught sweetens not in the waiting. Call we in the Ambassador."

Lord Juss sat in the high seat midmost of the dais, with Goldry on his right in the seat of black opal, and on his left Spitfire, throned on the alexandrite. On the dais sat likewise those other lords of Demonland, and the guests of lower degree thronged the benches and the polished tables as the wide doors opened on their silver hinges, and the Ambassador with pomp and ceremony paced up the shining floor of marble and green tourmaline.

"Why, what a beastly fellow is this?" said Lord Goldry in his brother's ear. "His hairy hands reach down to his knees. A shuffleth in his walk like a hobbled jackass."

"I like not the dirty face of the Ambassador," said Lord Zigg. "His nose sitteth flat on the face of him as it were a dab of clay, and I can see pat up his nostrils a summer day's journey into his head. If's upper lip bespeak him not a rare spouter of rank fustian, perdition catch me. Were it a finger's breadth longer, a might tuck it into his collar to keep his chin warm of a winter's night."

"I like not the smell of the Ambassador," said Lord Brandoch Daha. And he called for censers and sprinklers of lavender and rose water to purify the chamber, and let open the crystal windows that the breezes of heaven might enter and make all sweet.

So the Ambassador walked up the shining floor and stood before the lords of Demonland that sat upon the high seats between the golden hippogriffs. He was robed in a long mantle of scarlet lined with ermine, with crabs, woodlice, and centipedes worked thereon in golden thread. His head was covered with a black velvet cap with a peacock's feather fastened with a brooch of silver. Supported by his trainbearers and attendants, and leaning on his golden staff, he with raucous accent delivered his mission:

"Juss, Goldry, and Spitfire, and ye other Demons, I come before you as the Ambassador of Gorice XI., most glorious King of Witchland, Lord and great Duke of Buteny and Estremerine, Commander of Shulan, Thramnë, Mingos, and Permio, and High Warden of the Esamocian Marches, Great Duke of Trace, King Paramount of Beshtria and Nevria and Prince of Ar, Great Lord over the country of Ojedia, Maltraëny, and of Baltary and Toribia, and Lord of many other countries, most glorious and most great, whose power and glory is over all the world and whose name shall endure for all generations. And first I bid you be bound by that reverence for my sacred office of envoy from the King, which is accorded by all people and potentates, save such as be utterly barbarous, to ambassadors and envoys."

"Speak and fear not," answered Juss. "Thou hast mine oath. And that hath never been forsworn, to Witch or other barbarian."

The Ambassador shot out his lips in an O, and threatened with his head; then grinned, laying bare his sharp and misshapen teeth, and proceeded:

"Thus saith King Gorice, great and glorious, and he chargeth me to deliver it to you, neither adding any word nor taking away: 'I have it in mind that no ceremony of homage or fealty hath been performed before me by the dwellers in my province of Demon-land——' "

As the rustling of dry leaves strewn in a flagged court when a sudden wind striketh them, there went a stir among the guests. Nor might the Lord Spitfire contain his wrath, but springing up and clapping hand to swordhilt, as minded to do a hurt to the Ambassador, "Province?" he cried. "Are not the Demons a free people? And is it to be endured that Witchland should commission this slave to cast insults in our teeth, and this in our own castle?"

A murmur went about the hall, and here and there folk rose from their seats. The Ambassador drew down his head between his shoulders like a tortoise, baring his teeth and blinking with his small eyes. But Lord Brandoch Daha, lightly laying his hand on Spitfire's arm, said: "The Ambassador hath not ended his message, cousin, and thou hast frightened him. Have patience and spoil not the comedy. We shall not lack words to answer King Gorice: no, nor swords, if he must have them. But it shall not be said of us of Demonland that it needeth but a boorish message to turn us from our ancient courtesy toward ambassadors and heralds."

So spake Lord Brandoch Daha, in lazy half-mocking tone, as one who but idly returneth the ball of conversation; yet clearly, so that all might hear. And therewith the murmurs died down, and Spitfire said, "I am tame. Say thine errand freely, and imagine not that we shall hold thee answerable for aught thou sayest, but him that sent thee."

"Whose humble mouthpiece I only am," said the Ambassador, somewhat gathering courage; "and who, saving your reverence, lacketh not the will nor the power to take revenge for any outrage done upon his servants. Thus saith the King: 'I therefore summon and command you, Juss, Spitfire, and Goldry Bluszco, to make haste and come to me in Witchland in my fortress of Carcë, and there dutifully kiss my toe, in witness before all the world that I am your Lord and King, and rightful overlord of all Demonland.' "

Gravely and without gesture Lord Juss harkened to the Ambassador, leaning back in his high seat with either arm thrown athwart the arched neck of the hippogriff. Goldry, smiling scornfully, toyed with the hilt of his great sword. Spitfire sat strained and glowering, the sparks crackling at his nostrils.

"Thou hast delivered all?" said Juss.

"All," answered the Ambassador.

"Thou shalt have thine answer," said Juss. "While we take

rede thereon, eat and drink"; and he beckoned the cupbearer to pour out bright wine for the Ambassador. But the Ambassador excused himself, saying that he was not athirst, and that he had store of food and wine aboard of his ship, which should suffice his needs and those of his following.

Then said Lord Spitfire, "No marvel though the spawn of Witchland fear venom in the cup. They who work commonly such villany against their enemies, as witness Recedor of Goblinland whom Corsus murthered[29] with a poisonous draught, shake still in the knees lest themselves be so entertained to their destruction;" and snatching the cup he quaffed it to the dregs, and dashed it on the marble floor before the Ambassador, so that it was shivered into pieces.

And the lords of Demonland rose up and withdrew behind the flowery hangings into a chamber apart, to determine of their answer to the message sent unto them by King Gorice of Witchland.

When they were private together, Spitfire spake and said, "Is it to be borne that the King should put such shame and mockery upon us? Could a not at the least have made a son of Corund or of Corsus his Ambassador to bring us his defiance, 'stead of this filthiest of his domestics, a gibbering dwarf fit only to make them gab and game at their tippling bouts when they be three parts senseless with boosing?"

Lord Juss smiled somewhat scornfully. "With wisdom," he said, "and with foresight hath Witchland made choice of his time to move against us, knowing that thirty and three of our well-built ships are sunken in Kartadza Sound in the battle with the Ghouls,[30] and but fourteen remain to us. Now that the Ghouls are slain, every soul, and utterly abolished from this world, and so the great curse and peril of all this world ended by the sword and great valour of Demonland alone, now seemeth the happy moment unto these late mouth-friends to fall upon us. For have not the Witches a strong fleet of ships, since their whole fleet fled at the beginning of their fight with us against the Ghouls, leaving us to bear the burden? And now are they minded for this new treason, to set upon us traitorously and suddenly in this disadvantage. For the King well judgeth we can carry no army to Witchland nor do aught in his despite, but must be long months a-shipbuilding. And doubt not he holdeth an armament ready aboard at Tenemos to sail hither if he get the answer he knoweth we shall send him."

"Sit we at ease then," said Goldry, "sharpening our swords; and let him ship his armies across the salt sea. Not a Witch shall land in Demonland but shall leave here his blood and bones to make fat our cornfields and our vineyards."

"Rather," said Spitfire, "apprehend this rascal, and put to sea to-day with the fourteen ships left us. We can surprise Witchland in his strong place of Carcë, sack it, and give him to the crows to peck at, or ever he is well awake to the swiftness of our answer. That is my counsel."

"Nay," said Juss, "we shall not take him sleeping. Be certain that his ships are ready and watching in the Witchland seas, prepared against any rash onset. It were folly to set our neck in the noose; and little glory to Demonland to await his coming. This, then, is my rede: I will bid Gorice to the duello, and make offer to him to let lie on the fortune thereof the decision of this quarrel."

"A good rede, if it might be fulfilled," said Goldry. "But never will he dare to stand with weapons in single combat 'gainst thee or 'gainst any of us. Nevertheless the thing shall be brought about. Is not Gorice a mighty wrastler, and hath he not in his palace in Carcë the skulls and bones of ninety and nine great champions whom he hath vanquished and slain in that exercise? Puffed up beyond measure is he in his own conceit, and folk say it is a grief to him that none hath been found this long while that durst wrastle with him, and wofully he pineth for the hundredth. He shall wrastle a fall with me!"

Now this seemed good to them all. So when they had talked on it awhile and concluded what they would do, glad of heart the lords of Demonland turned them back to the lofty presence chamber. And there Lord Juss spake and said: "Demons, ye have heard the words which the King of Witchland in the overweening pride and shamelessness of his heart hath spoken unto us by the mouth of this Ambassador. Now this is our answer which my brother shall give, the Lord Goldry Bluszco; and we charge thee, O Ambassador, to deliver it truly, neither adding any word nor taking away."

And the Lord Goldry spake: "We, the lords of Demonland, do utterly scorn thee, Gorice XI., for the greatest of dastards, in that thou basely fleddest and forsookest us, thy sworn confederates, in the sea battle against the Ghouls. Our swords, which in that battle ended so great a curse and peril to all this world, are not bent nor broken. They shall be sheathed in the bowels of thee and thy minions, Corsus to wit, and Corund, and their sons, and Corinius, and what other evildoers harbour in waterish Witchland, sooner than one little sea-pink growing on the cliffs of Demonland shall do thee obeisance. But, that thou mayest, if so thou wilt, feel our power somewhat, I, Lord Goldry Bluszco, make thee this offer:

that thou and I do match ourselves singly each against other to wrastle three falls at the court of the Red Foliot, who inclineth neither to our side nor to thine in this quarrel. And we will bind ourselves by mighty oaths to these conditions, that if I overcome thee, the Demons shall leave you of Witchland in peace, and ye them, and the Witches shall forswear for ever their impudent claims on Demonland. But if thou, Gorice, win the day, then hast thou the glory of that victory, and withal full liberty to thrust thy claims upon us with the sword."

So spake the Lord Goldry Bluszco, standing in great pride and splendour beneath the starry canopy, and scowling terribly on the Ambassador from Witchland, so that the Ambassador was abashed and his knees smote together. And Goldry called his scribe and made him write the message for Gorice the King in great characters on a roll of parchment, and the lords of Demonland sealed it with their seals, and gave it to the Ambassador.

The Ambassador took it and made haste to depart; but when he was come to the stately doorway of the presence chamber, being near the door and amongst his attendants, and away from the lords of Demonland, he plucked up heart a little and turned and said: "Rashly and to thy certain undoing, O Goldry Bluszco, hast thou bidden our Lord the King to contend with thee in wrastling. For be thou never so mighty of limb, yet hath he overthrown as mighty. And he wrastleth not for sport, but will surely work thy life's decay, and keep the dead bones of thee with the bones of the ninety and nine champions whom he hath heretofore laid low in that exercise."

Therewith, because Goldry and the other lords scowled upon him terribly, and the guests near the door fell to hooting and reviling of the Witches, the Ambassador went forth hastily and hastily down the shining stairs and across the court, as one who fleeth along a lane on a dark and windy night, daring not to turn his head lest his eye behold some fearsome thing prepared to clasp him. So speeding, he was fain to catch up about his knees the folds of his velvet cloak richly worked with crabs and creeping things; and huge whooping and laughter went up among the common lag of people without, to behold his long and nerveless tail thus bared to their unfriendly gaze. Insomuch that they fell to shouting with one accord, "Though his mouth be foul he hath a fair tail! Saw ye not his tail? Hurrah for Gorice who hath sent us a monkey for his Ambassador!"

And with jibe and unmannerly yell the crowd hung lovingly upon the Ambassador and his train all the way down from Galing castle to the quays. So that it was like a sweet homecoming to him to come on board his wellbuilt ship and have her rowed amain out of Lookinghaven. So when they had rounded Lookinghaven-ness and were free of the land, they hoisted sail and voyaged before a favouring breeze eastward over the teeming deep to Witchland.

II

THE WRASTLING FOR DEMONLAND

Of the prognosticks which troubled Lord Gro
concerning the meeting between the king of
Witchland and the Lord Goldry Bluszco; and
how they met, and of the issue of that wrastling.

ow could I have fallen asleep?" cried Lessingham.
"Where is the castle of the Demons, and how did we
leave the great presence chamber where they saw the
Ambassador?" For he stood on rolling uplands that
leaned to the sea, treeless on every side as far as the
eye might reach; and on three sides shimmered the sea, kissed by
the sun and roughened by the salt glad wind that charged over the
downs, charioting clouds without number through the illimitable
heights of air.

The little black martlet answered him, "My hippogriff travel-
leth as well in time as in space. Days and weeks have been left
behind by us, in what seemeth to thee but the twinkling of an eye,
and thou standest in the Foliot Isles, a land happy under the mild
regiment of a peaceful prince, on the day appointed by King
Gorice to wrastle with Lord Goldry Bluszco. Terrible must be the
wrastling betwixt two such champions, and dark the issue thereof.
And my heart is afraid for Goldry Bluszco, big and strong though
he be and unconquered in war; for there hath not arisen in all the
ages such a wrastler as this Gorice, and strong he is, and hard and

18

unwearying, and skilled in every art of attack and defence, and subtle withal,[1] and cruel and fell like a serpent."

Where they stood the down was cut by a combe[2] that descended to the sea, and overhanging the combe was the palace of the Red Foliot, rambling and low, with many little towers and battlements, built of stones hewn from the wall of the combe, so that it was hard from a distance to discern what was palace and what native rock. Behind the palace stretched a meadow, flat and smooth, carpeted with the close wiry turf of the downs. At either end of the meadow were booths set up, to the north the booths of them of Witchland, and to the south the booths of the Demons. In the midst of the meadow was a space marked out with withies[3] sixty paces either way for the wrastling ground.[4]

Only the birds of the air and the sea-wind were abroad as then, save those that walked armed before the Witches' booths, six in company, harnessed as for battle in byrnies[5] of shining bronze, with greaves[6] and shields of bronze and helms that glanced in the sun. Five were proper slender youths, the eldest of whom had not yet beard full grown, black-browed and great of jaw; the sixth, huge as a neat,[7] topped them by half a head. Age had flecked with gray the beard that spread over his big chest to his belt stiffened with studs of iron, but the vigour of youth was in his glance and in his voice, and in the tread of his foot, and in his fist so lightly handling his burly spear.

"Behold, wonder, and lament," said the martlet, "that the innocent eye of day should be enforced still to look upon the children of night everlasting. Corund of Witchland and his cursed sons."

Lessingham thought, "A most fiery politician is my little martlet: damned fiends and angels and nothing betwixt for her. But I'll dance to none of their tunes, but wait for these things' unfolding."[8]

So walked those back and forth as caged lions before the Witches' booths, until Corund halted and leaning on his spear said to one of his sons, "Go in and seek out Gro that I may speak with him." And the son of Corund went, and returned anon with Lord Gro,[9] that came with furtive step yet goodly and fair to behold. The nose of him was hooked like a sickle and his eyes great and fair like the eyes of an ox, inscrutable as they. Lean and spare was his frame. Pale was his face and pale his delicate hands, and his long black beard was tightly curled[10] and bright as the coat of a black retriever.

Corund said, "How is it with the King?"

Gro answered him, "He chafeth to be at it; and to pass away the time he playeth at dice with Corinius, and the luck goeth against the King."

"What makest thou of that?" asked Corund.

And Gro said, "The fortune of the dice jumpeth not commonly with the fortune of war."

Corund grunted in his beard, and laying his large hand on Lord Gro's shoulder, "Speak to me a little apart," he said; and when they were private, "Darken not counsel," said Corund, "to me and my sons. Have I not these four years past been as a brother unto thee, and wilt thou still be secret toward us?"

But Gro smiled a sad smile and said, "Why should we by words of ill omen strike yet another blow where the tree tottereth?"

Corund groaned. "Omens," said he, "increase upon us from that time forth when the King accepted the challenge, evilly, and flatly against thy counsel and mine and the counsel of all the great ones in the land. Surely the Gods have made him fey, having ordained his destruction and our humbling before these Demons." And he said, "Omens thicken upon us, O Gro. First, the night raven that went widdershins[11] round about the palace of Carcë, that night when the King accepted this challenge, and we were all drunken with wine after our great feasting and surfeiting in his halls. Next, the stumbling of the King whenas he went upon the poop of the long ship which bare us on this voyage to these islands. Next, the squint-eyed cup-bearer that poured out unto us yesternight. And throughout, the devilish pride and bragging humour of the King. No more: he is fey. And the dice fall against him."

Gro spake and said, "O Corund, I will not hide it from thee that my heart is heavy as thy heart under shadow of ill to be. For as I lay sleeping betwixt the strokes of night, a dream of the night stood by my bed and beheld me with a glance so fell that I was all adrad and quaking with fear. And it seemed to me that the dream smote the roof above my bed, and the roof opened and disclosed the outer dark, and in the dark travelled a bearded star, and the night was quick with fiery signs. And blood was on the roof, and great gouts of blood on the walls and on the cornice of my bed. And the dream screeched like the screech-owl, and cried, *Witchland from thy hand, O King!* And methought the whole world was lighted in a lowe, and with a great cry I awoke out of the dream."

"Thou art wise," said Corund; "and belike the dream was a

true dream, sent thee through the gate of horn, and belike it forebodeth events great and evil for the King and for Witchland."

Gro said, "Disclose it not to the others, for none can strive with Fate and gain the victory, and it would but cast down their hearts. But it is fitting we be ready against evil hap. If (which yet may the Gods forfend) ill come of this wrastling bout, fail not every one of you ere you act on any enterprise to take counsel of me. 'Bare is back without brother behind it.' Together must we do that we do."

"Thou hast my firm assurance on't," said Corund.

Now began a great company to come forth from the palace and take their stand on either side of the wrastling ground. The Red Foliot sate in his car of polished ebony, drawn by six black horses with flowing manes and tails; before him went his musicians, pipers and minstrels doing their craft, and behind him fifty spearmen, weighed down with armour and ponderous shields that covered them from chin to toe. Their armour was stained with madder,[12] in such wise that they seemed bathed in blood. Mild to look on was the Red Foliot, yet kingly. His skin was scarlet like the head of the green woodpecker. He wore a diadem of silver, and robes of scarlet trimmed with black fur.

So when the Foliots were assembled, one stood forth with a horn at the command of the Red Foliot and blew three blasts. Therewith came forth from their booths the lords of Demonland and their men-at-arms, Juss, Goldry, Spitfire, and Brandoch Daha, all armed as for battle save Goldry, who was muffled in a cloak of cloth of gold with great hearts worked thereon in red silk thread. And from their booths in turn came the lords of Witchland all armed, and their fighting men, and little love there was in the glances they and the Demons cast upon each other. In the midst stalked the King, his great limbs muffled, like Goldry's, in a cloak: and it was of black silk lined with black bearskin, and ornamented with crabs worked in diamonds. The crown of Witchland, fashioned like a hideous crab and encrusted with jewels so thickly that none might discern the iron whereof it was framed, weighed on his beetling brow. His beard was black and bristly, spade-shaped and thick: his hair close cropped. His upper lip was shaved, displaying his sneering mouth, and from the darkness below his eyebrows looked forth eyes that showed a green light, like those of a wolf. Corund walked at the King's left elbow, his giant frame an inch less in stature than the King. Corinius[13] went on the right, wearing a rich cloak of skyblue tissue over his shining armour. Tall and soldierlike was Corinius, and young and goodly to look upon, with swaggering gait and insolent eye, thick-lipped withal and some-what heavy of feature, and the sun shone brightly on his shaven jowl.

Now the Red Foliot let sound the horn again, and standing in his ebony car he read out the conditions, as thus:

"O Gorice XI., most glorious King of Witchland, and O Lord Goldry Bluszco, captain of the hosts of Demonland, it is compact betwixt you, and made fast by mighty oaths whereof I, the Red Foliot, am keeper, that ye shall wrastle three falls together on these conditions, namely, that if Gorice the King be victorious, then hath he that glory and withal full liberty to enforce with the sword his claims of lordship over many-mountained Demonland: but if victory fall to the Lord Goldry Bluszco, then shall the Demons let the Witches abide in peace, and they them, and the Witches shall forswear for ever their claims of lordship over the Demons. And you, O King, and you, O Goldry Bluszco, are likewise bound by oath to wrastle fairly and to abide by the ruling of me, the Red Foliot, whom ye are content to choose as your umpire. And I do swear to judge justly between you. And the laws of your wrastling are that neither shall strangle his adversary with his hands, nor bite him, nor claw nor scratch his flesh, nor poach out his eyes, nor smite him with his fists, nor do any other unfair thing against him, but in all other respects ye shall wrastle freely together. And he that shall be brought to earth with hip or shoulder shall be accounted fallen."

The Red Foliot said, "Have I spoken well, O King, and do you swear to these conditions?"

The King said, "I swear."

The Red Foliot asked in like manner, "Dost thou swear to these conditions, O Lord Goldry Buszco?"

And Goldry answered him, "I swear."

Without more ado the King stepped into the wrastling ground on his side, and Goldry Bluszco on his, and they cast aside their rich mantles and stood forth naked for the wrastling. And folk stood silent for admiration of the thews and sinews of those twain, doubting which were mightier of build and likelier to gain the victory. The King stood taller by a little, and was longer in the arm than Goldry. But the great frame of Goldry showed excellent proportions, each part wedded to each as in the body of a God, and if either were brawnier of chest it was he, and he was thicker of neck than the King.

Now the King mocked Goldry, saying, "Rebellious hound, it is fit that I make demonstration unto thee, and unto these Foliots and

Demons that witness our meeting, that I am thy King and Lord not by virtue only of this my crown of Witchland, which I thus put by for an hour, but even by the power of my body over thine and by my might and main. Be satisfied that I will not have done with thee until I have taken away thy life, and sent thy soul squealing bodiless into the unknown. And thy skull and thy marrow-bones will I have away to Carcë, to my palace, to be a token unto all the world that I have been the bane of an hundredth great champion by my wrastling, and thou not least among them that I have slain in that exercise. Thereafter, when I have eaten and drunken and made merry in my royal palace at Carcë, I will sail with my armies over the teeming deep to many-mountained Demonland. And it shall be my footstool, and these other Demons the slaves of me, yea, and the slaves of my slaves."

But the Lord Goldry Bluszco laughed lightly and said to the Red Foliot, "O Red Foliot; I am not come hither to contend with the King of Witchland in windy railing, but to match my strength against his, sinew against sinew."

Now they stood ready, and the Red Foliot made a sign with his hand, and the cymbals clashed for the first bout.

At the clash the two champions advanced and clasped one another with their strong arms, each with his right arm below and left arm above the other's shoulder, until the flesh shrank beneath the might of their arms that were as brazen bands. They swayed a little this way and that, as great trees swaying in a storm, their legs planted firmly so that they seemed to grow out of the ground like the trunks of oak trees. Nor did either yield ground to other, nor might either win a master hold upon his enemy. So swayed they back and forth for a long time, breathing heavily. And now Goldry, gathering his strength, gat the King lifted a little from the ground, and was minded to swing him round and so dash him to earth. But the King, in that moment when he found himself lifted, leaned forward mightily and smote his heel swiftly round Goldry's leg on the outside, striking him behind and a little above the ankle, in such wise that Goldry was fain to loosen his hold on the King; and greatly folk marvelled that he was able in that plight to save himself from being thrown backward by the King. So they gripped again until red wheals rose on their backs and shoulders by reason of the grievous clasping of their arms. And the King on a sudden twisted his body sideways, with his left side turned from Goldry; and catching with his leg Goldry's leg on the inside below the great muscle of the calf, and hugging him yet closer, he lurched mightily against him, striving to pull Goldry backward and so fall upon him and crush him as they fell to earth. But Goldry leaned violently forward, ever tightening his hold on the King, and so violently bare he forward in his strength that the King was baulked of his design; and clutched together they fell both to earth side by side with a heavy crash, and lay bemused while one might count half a score.

The Red Foliot proclaimed them even in this bout, and each returned to his fellows to take breath and rest for a space.

Now while they rested, a flittermouse[14] flew forth from the Witchland booths and went widdershins round the wrestling ground and so returned silently whence she came. Lord Gro saw her, and his heart waxed heavy within him. He spake to Corund and said, "Needs must that I make trial even at this late hour if there be not any means to turn the King from further adventuring of himself, ere all be lost."

Corund said, "Be it as thou wilt, but it will be in vain."

So Gro stood by the King and said, "Lord, give over this wrestling. Great of growth and mightier of limb than any that you did overcome aforetime is this Demon, yet have you vanquished him. For you did throw him, as we plainly saw, and wrongfully hath the Red Foliot adjudged you evenly matched because in the throwing of him your majesty's self did fall to earth. Tempt not the fates by another bout. Yours is the victory in this wrestling: and now we, your servants, wait but your nod to make a sudden onslaught on these Demons and slay them, as we may lightly overcome them taken at unawares. And for the Foliots, they be peaceful and sheeplike folk, and will be held in awe when we have smitten the Demons with the edge of the sword. So may you depart, O King, with pleasure and great honour, and afterward fare to Demonland and bring it into subjection."

The King looked sourly upon Lord Gro, and said, "Thy counsel is unacceptable and unseasonable. What lieth behind it?"

Gro answered, "There have been omens, O King."

And the King said, "What omens?"

Gro answered and said, "I will not hide it from you, O my Lord the King, that in my sleep about the darkest hour a dream of the night came to my bed and beheld me with a glance so fell that the hairs of my head stood up and pale terror gat hold upon me. And methought the dream smote up the roof above my bed, and the roof yawned to the naked air of the midnight, that laboured with fiery signs, and a bearded star travelling in the houseless dark. And I beheld the roof and the walls one gore of blood. And the dream screeched like the screech-owl, crying, *Witchland from thy hand, O King!* And therewith the whole world seemed lighted in one flame, and with a shout I awoke sweating from the dream."

But the King rolled his eyes in anger upon Lord Gro and said, "Well am I served and faithfully by such false scheming foxes as thou. It ill fits your turn that I should carry this deed to the end with mine own hand only, and in the blindness of your impudent folly ye come to me with tales made for scaring of babes, praying me gently to forgo my glory that thou and thy fellows may make yourselves big in the world's eyes by deeds of arms."

Gro said, "Lord, it is not so."

But the King would not hear him, but said, "Methinks it is for loyal subjects to seek greatness in the greatness of their King, nor desire to shine of their own brightness. As for this Demon, when thou sayest that I have overcome him thou speakest a gross and impudent lie. In this bout I did but measure myself with him. But thereby know I of a surety that when I put forth my might he will not be able to withstand me; and all ye shall shortly behold how, as one shattereth a stalk of angelica,[15] I will break and shatter the limbs of this Goldry Bluszco. As for thee, false friend, subtle fox, unfaithful servant, this long time am I grown weary of thee slinking up and down my palace devising darkly things I know not: thou, that art nought akin to Witchland, but an outlander, a Goblin exile, a serpent warmed in my bosom to my hurt. But these things shall have an end. When I have put down this Goldry Bluszco, then shall I have leisure to put down thee also."

And Gro bowed in sorrow of heart before the anger of the King, and held his peace.

Now was the horn blown for the second bout, and they stepped into the wrestling ground. At the clashing of the cymbals the King sprang at Goldry as the panther springeth, and with the rush bare him backward and well nigh forth of the wrestling ground. But when they were carried almost among the Demons where they stood to behold the contest, Goldry swung to the left and strove as before to get the King lifted off his feet; but the King foiled him and bent his ponderous weight upon him, so that Goldry's spine was like to have been crushed beneath the murthering violence of the King's arms. Then did the Lord Goldry Bluszco show forth his great power as a wrestler, for, even under the murthering clasp of the King, he by the might that was in the muscles of his brawny chest shook the King first to the right and then to the left; and the King's hold was loosened, and all his skill and mastery but narrowly saved him from a grievous fall. Nor did

Goldry delay nor ponder how next to make trial of the King, but sudden as the lightning he slackened his hold and turned, and with his back under the King's belly gave a mighty lift; and they that witnessed it stood amazed in expectancy to see the King thrown over Goldry's head. Yet for all his striving might not Goldry get the King lifted clean off the ground. Twice and three times he strove, and at each trial he seemed further from his aim, and the King bettered his hold. And at the fourth essay that Goldry made to lift the King over his back and fling him headlong, the King thrust him forward and tripped him from behind, so that Goldry was crawled on his hands and knees. And the King clung to him from behind and passed his arms round his body beneath the armpits and so back over the shoulders, being minded to clasp his two hands at the back of Goldry's neck.

Then said Corund, "The Demon is sped already. By this hold hath the King brought to their bane more than three score famous champions. He delayeth only till his fingers be knit together behind the neck of the accursed Demon to draw the head of him forward until the bones of the neck or the breastbone be bursten asunder."

"He delayeth over long for my peace," said Gro.

The King's breath came out of him in great puffs and grunts as he strained to bring his fingers to meet behind Goldry's neck. Nor was it aught else than the hugeness of his neck and burly chest that saved the Lord Goldry Bluszco in that hour from utter destruction. Crawled on his hands and knees he could nowise escape from the hold of the King, neither lay hold on him in turn; howbeit because of the bigness of Goldry's neck and chest it was impossible for the King to fasten that hold upon him, for all his striving.

When the King perceived that this was so, and that he but wasted his strength, he said, "I will loose my hold on thee and let thee up, and we will stand again face to face. For I deem it unworthy to grapple on the ground like dogs."

So they stood up, and wrastled another while in silence. Soon the King made trial once again of the fall whereby he had sought to throw him in the first bout, twisting suddenly his right side against Goldry, and catching with his leg Goldry's leg, and therewith leaning against him with main force. And when, as before, Goldry bare forward with great violence, tightening his grip, the King lurched mightily against him, and, being still ill content to have missed his hold that never heretofore had failed him, he thrust his fingers up Goldry's nose in his cruel anger, scratching and clawing at the delicate inner parts of the nostrils in such wise that Goldry was fain to draw back his head. Therewith the King, lurching against him yet more heavily, gat him thrown a grievous fall on his back, and himself fell atop of him, crushing him and stunning him on the earth.

And the Red Foliot proclaimed Gorice the King victorious in this bout.

Therewithal the King turned him back to his Witches, that loudly acclaimed his mastery over Goldry. He said unto Lord Gro, "It is as I have spoken: the testing first, next the bruising, and in the last bout the breaking and killing." And the King looked evilly on Gro. Gro answered him not a word, for his soul was grieved to see blood on the nails and fingers of the King's left hand, and he thought he knew that the King must have been sore bested in this bout, seeing that he must do this beastly deed or ever he might overcome the might of his adversary.

But the Lord Goldry Bluszco when he was come to his senses and had gotten him up from that great fall, spake to the Red Foliot in mickle[16] wrath, saying, "This devil hath overcome me by craft, doing that which it is a shame to do, in that he clawed me with his fingers up my nose."

The sons of Corund raised an uproar at the words of Goldry, loudly crying that he was the greatest liar and dastard; and all they of Witchland shouted and cursed in like manner. But Goldry shouted in a voice like a brazen trumpet that was plain to hear above the clamour of the Witches, "O Red Foliot, judge now fairly betwixt me and King Gorice, as thou art sworn to do. Let him show his finger nails, if there be not blood on them. This fall is void, and I claim that we wrastle it anew." And the lords of Demonland in like manner shouted that this fall should be wrastled anew.

Now the Red Foliot had seen somewhat of what was done, and well was he minded to call the bout void. Yet had he forborne to do this out of fear of King Gorice that had looked upon him with a basilisk's eye, threatening him. And now, while the Red Foliot was troubled in his mind, uncertain between the angry shouts of the Witches and the Demons whether safety lay rather with his honour or with truckling to King Gorice, the King spake a word to Corinius, who went straightway and standing by the Red Foliot spake privily in his ear. And Corinius menaced the Red Foliot, and said, "Beware lest thy mind be swayed by the brow-beating of the Demons. Rightfully hast thou adjudged the victory in this bout unto our Lord the King, and this talk of thrusting of fingers in the nose is but a pretext and a vile imagination of this Goldry Bluszco, who, being thrown fairly before thine eyes and before us all, and perceiving himself unable to stand against the King, now thinketh with his swaggering he can bear it away, and thinketh by cheats and subtleties to avoid defeat. If, against thine own beholding and the witness of us and the plighted word of the King, thou art so hardy as to harken to the guileful persuading of these Demons, yet bethink thee that the King hath overborne ninety and nine great champions in this exercise, and this shall be the hundredth; and bethink thee, too, that Witchland lieth nearer to thine Isles than Demonland by many days' sailing. Hard shall it be for thee to abide the avenging sword of Witchland if thou do him despite, and against thy sworn oath as umpire incline wrongfully to his enemies in this dispute.''

So spake Corinius; and the Red Foliot was cowed. Albeit he believed in his heart that the King had done what thereof Goldry accused him, yet for terror of the King and of Corinius that stood by and threatened him he durst not speak his thought, but in sore perplexity gave order for the horn to be blown for the third bout.

And it came to pass at the blowing of the horn that the flittermouse fared forth again from the booths of the Witches, and going widdershins round about the wrastling ground returned on silent wing whence she came.

When the Lord Goldry Bluszco understood that the Red Foliot would pay no heed to his accusation, he grew red as blood. A fearsome sight it was to behold how he swelled in his wrath, and his eyes blazed like disastrous stars at midnight, and being wood with anger he gnashed his teeth till the froth stood at his lips and slavered down his chin. Now the cymbals clashed for the onset. Therewith ran Goldry upon the King as one straught of his wits, bellowing as he ran, and gripped him by the right arm with both his hands, one at the wrist and one near the shoulder. And so it was that, before the King might move, Goldry spun round with his back to the King and by his mickle strength and the strength of the anger that was in him he heaved the King over his head,[17] hurling him as one hurleth a ponderous spear, head-foremost to the earth. And the King smote the ground with his head, and the bones of his head and his spine were driven together and smashed, and blood flowed from his ears and nose. With the might of that throw Goldry's wrath departed from him and left him strengthless,[18] in such sort that he reeled as he went from the wrastling ground. His brethren, Juss and Spitfire, bare him up on either side, and put his cloak of cloth of gold worked with red hearts about his mighty limbs.

Meanwhile dismay was fallen upon the Witches to behold

their King so caught up on a sudden and dashed upon the ground, where he lay crumpled in an heap, shattered like the stalk of an hemlock that one breaketh and shattereth. In great agitation the Red Foliot came down from his car of ebony and made haste thither where the King was fallen; and the lords of Witchland came likewise thither stricken at heart, and Corund lifted the King in his burly arms. But the King was stone dead. So those sons of Corund made a litter with their spears and laid the King on the litter, and spread over him his royal mantle of black silk lined with bearskin, and set the crown of Witchland on his head, and without word spoken bare him away to the Witches' booths. And the other lords of Witchland without word spoken followed after.

III

THE RED FOLIOT

*Of the entertainment of the witches in the palace
of the Red Foliot; and of the wiles and subtleties
of Lord Gro; and how the witches departed by
night out of the Foliot Isles.*

HE Red Foliot gat him back into his palace and sat in
his high seat. And he sent unto the lords of Witchland
and of Demonland that they should come and see him.
Nor did they delay, but came straightway and sat on
the long benches, the Witches on the eastern side of
the hall and the Demons on the west; and their fighting men stood
in order on either side behind them. So sat they in the shadowy
hall, and the sun declining to the western ocean shone through the
high windows of the hall on the polished armour and weapons of
the Witches.

The Red Foliot spake among them and said, "A great champion hath been strook to earth this day in fair and equal combat.
And according to the solemn oaths whereby ye are bound, and
whereof I am the keeper, there is here an end to all unpeace
betwixt Witchland and Demonland, and ye of Witchland are to
forswear for ever your claims of lordship over the Demons. Now
for a sealing and making fast of this solemn covenant between you
I see no likelier rede than that ye all join with me here this day in
good friendship to forget your quarrels in drinking of the arvale[1]
of King Gorice XI., than whom hath reigned none mightier nor

30

more worshipful in all this world, and thereafter depart in peace to your native lands."

So spake the Red Foliot, and the lords of Witchland assented thereto.

But Lord Juss answered and said, "O Red Foliot, as to the oaths sworn between us and the King of Witchland, thou hast spoken well; nor shall we depart one tittle from the article of our oaths, and the Witches may abide in peace for ever as for us if, as is clean against their use and nature, they forbear to devise evil against us. For the nature of Witchland was ever as a flea, that attacketh a man in the dark. But we will not eat nor drink with the lords of Witchland, who bewrayed and forsook us their sworn confederates at the sea-fight against the Ghouls. Nor we will not drink the arvale of King Gorice XI., who worked a shameful and unlawful sleight against my kinsman this day when they wrastled together."

So spake Lord Juss, and Corund whispered Gro in the ear, saying, "Were't not for the privilege of this respected company, now were the time to set upon them." But Gro said, "I prithee yet have patience. This were over hazardous, for the luck goeth against Witchland. Let us rather take them in their beds to-night."

Fain would the Red Foliot turn the Demons from their resolve, but without avail; they courteously thanking him for his hospitality which they said they would enjoy that night in their booths, being minded on the morrow to take to their beaked ship and fare over the unvintaged sea to Demonland.

Therewith stood up Lord Juss, and with him the Lord Goldry Bluszco, that went in all his war gear, his horned helm of gold and his golden byrny set with ruby hearts, and bare his two-handed sword forged by the elves wherewith he slew the beast out of the sea in days gone by; and Lord Spitfire that glared upon the lords of Witchland as a falcon glareth, hungering for her prey; and the Lord Brandoch Daha that looked on them, and chiefly on Corinius, with the eye of contemptuous amusement, playing idly with the jewelled hilt of his sword, until Corinius grew ill at ease beneath his gaze and shifted this way and that in his seat, scowling back defiance. For all the rich array and goodly port and countenance of Corinius, he seemed but a very boor beside the Lord Brandoch Daha, and dearly did each hate the other. So the lords of Demonland with their fighting men went forth from the hall.

The Red Foliot sent after them and made them in their own booths to be served of great plenty of wine and good and delicate

meats, and sent them musicians and a minstrel to gladden them
with songs and stories of old time, that they might lack nought of
entertainment. But for his other guests he let bear in the massy
cups of silver, and the great eared wine jars holding two firkins[2]
apiece, and he let pour forth to the Witches and the Foliots, and
they drank the cup of memory unto King Gorice XI., slain that day
by the hand of Goldry Bluszco. Thereafter when their cups were
brimmed anew with foaming wine the Red Foliot spake among
them and said, "O ye lords of Witchland, will you that I speak a
dirge in honour of Gorice the King that the dark reaper hath this
day gathered?" So when they said yea to this, he called to him his
player on the theorbo[3] and his player on the hautboy,[4] and commanded them saying, "Play me a solemn music." And they played
softly in the Aeolian mode[5] a music that was like the wailing of
wind through bare branches on a moonless night, and the Red
Foliot leaned forth from his high seat and recited this lamentation:

> I that in heill was and gladness
> Am trublit[6] now with great sickness
> > And feblit[7] with infirmitie:—
> > *Timor Mortis conturbat me.*[8]
>
> Our plesance[9] here is all vain glory,
> This fals world is but transitory,
> > The flesh is bruckle,[10] the Feynd is slee:[11]—
> > *Timor Mortis conturbat me.*
>
> The state of man does change and vary,
> Now sound, now sick, now blyth, now sary,[12]
> > Now dansand mirry,[13] now like to die:[14]—
> > *Timor Mortis conturbat me.*
>
> No state in Erd here standis sicker;
> As with the wynd wavis the wicker,[15]
> > So wannis[16] this world's vanitie:—
> > *Timor Mortis conturbat me.*
>
> Unto the Death gois all Estatis,[17]
> Princis, Prelattis, and Potestatis,
> > Baith[18] rich and poor of all degree:—
> > *Timor Mortis conturbat me.*
>
> He takis the knichtis in to field
> Enarmit under helm and scheild;

Victor he is at all mellie:[19]—
Timor Mortis conturbat me.

That strong unmerciful tyrand
Takis, on the motheris breast sowkand,[20]
    The babe full of benignitie:—
    Timor Mortis conturbat me.

He takis the campion[21] in the stour,[22]
The captain closit in the tour,[23]
    The lady in bour full of bewtie:—
    Timor Mortis conturbat me.

He spairis no lord for his piscence,[24]
Na clerk for his intelligence;
    His awful straik[25] may no man flee:—
    Timor Mortis conturbat me.

Art-magicianis and astrologis,
Rethoris, logicianis, theologis,
    Them helpis no conclusions slee:—
    Timor Mortis conturbat me.

In medecine the most practicianis,
Leechis, surrigianis, and physicianis,
    Themself from Death may nocht supplee:—
    Timor Mortis conturbat me.

When the Red Foliot had spoken thus far his dirge, he was interrupted by an unseemly brawling betwixt Corinius and one of the sons of Corund. For Corinius, who gave not a fig for music or dirges, but liked well of carding and dicing, had brought forth his dice box to play with the son of Corund. They played awhile to Corinius's great content, for at every throw he won and the other's purse waxed light. But at this eleventh stanza the son of Corund cried out that the dice of Corinius were loaded. And he smote Corinius on his shaven jowl with the dice box, calling him cheat and mangy rascal, whereupon Corinius drew forth a bodkin[26] to smite him in the neck withal; but some went betwixt them, and with much ado and much struggling and cursing they were parted, and it being shown that the dice were not loaded, the son of Corund was fain to make amends to Corinius, and so were they set at one again.

Now was the wine poured forth yet again to the lords of Witchland, and the Red Foliot drank deep unto the glory of that land and the rulers thereof. And he issued command saying, "Let my Kagu come and dance before us, and thereafter my other dancers. For there is no pleasure whereon the Foliots do more dearly dote than this pleasure of the dance, and sweet to us it is to behold delightful dancing, be it the stately splendour of the Pavane[27] which progresseth as large clouds at sun-down that pass by in splendour; or the graceful Allemande;[28] or the Fandango,[29] which goeth by degrees from languorous beauty to the swiftness and passion of Bacchanals[30] dancing on the high lawns under a summer moon that hangeth in the pine trees; or the joyous maze of the Galliard;[31] or the Gigue,[32] dear to the Foliots. Therefore delay not, but let my Kagu come, that she may dance before us."

Therewith hastened the Kagu into the shadowy hall, moving softly and rolling a little in her gait, with her head thrust forward; and a little flurried was she in her bearing as she darted this way and that her large and beautiful eyes, mild and timid, that were like liquid gold heated to redness. Somewhat like a heron she was, but stouter, and shorter of leg, and her beak shorter and thicker than the heron's; and so long and delicate was her pale gray plumage that hard it was to say whether it were hair or feathers. So the wind instruments and the lutes and dulcimers played a Coranto,[33] and the Kagu tripped up the hall betwixt the long tables, jumping a little and bowing a little in her step and keeping excellent time to the music; and when she came near to the dais where the Red Foliot sat ravished with delight at her dancing, the Kagu lengthened her step and glided smoothly and slowly forward toward the Red Foliot; and so gliding she drew herself up in stately wise and opened her mouth and drew back her head till her beak lay tight against her breast, flouncing out her feathers so that they showed like a widecut skirt with a crinoline, and the crest that was on her head rose up erect half again her own height from the ground, and she sailed majestically toward the Red Foliot. On this wise did the Kagu at every turn that she took in the Coranto, forth and back along the length of the Foliots' hall. And they all laughed sweetly at her, being overjoyed at her dancing. When the dance was done, the Red Foliot called the Kagu to him and made her sit on the bench beside him, and stroked her soft gray feathers and made much of her. All bashfully she sat beside the Red Foliot, casting her ruby eyes in wonder upon the Witches and their company.

Next the Red Foliot called for his Cat-bears, that stood before him foxy-red above but with black bellies, round furry faces, and innocent amber eyes, and soft great paws, and tails barred alternately with ruddy rings and creamy; and he said, "O Cat-bears, dance before us, since dearly we delight in your dancing."

They asked, "Lord, will you that we perform the Gigue?"

And he answered them, "The Gigue, and ye love me."

So the stringed instruments began a swift movement, and the tambourines and triangles entered on the beat, and swiftly twinkled the feet of the Cat-bears in the joyous dance. The music rippled and ran and the dancers danced till the hall was awhirl with the rhythm of their dancing, and the Witches roared applause. On a sudden the music ceased, and the dancers were still, and standing side by side, paw in furry paw, they bowed shyly to the company, and the Red Foliot called them to him and kissed them on the mouth and sent them to their seats, that they might rest and view the dances that were to follow.

Next the Red Foliot called for his white Peacocks, coloured like moonlight, that they might lead the Pavane before the lords of Witchland. In glorious wise did they spread their tails for the stately dance, and a fair and lovely sight it was to see their grace and the grandeur of their carriage as they moved to the music chaste and noble. With them were joined the Golden Pheasants, who spread wide their collars of gold, and the Silver Pheasants, and the Peacock Pheasants, and the Estridges,[34] and the Bustards,[35] footing it in pomp, pointing the toes, and bowing and retiring in due time to the solemn strains of the Pavane. Every instrument took part in the stately Pavane: the lutes and the dulcimers, and the theorbos, and the sackbuts,[36] and the hautboys; the flutes sweetly warbling as birds in the upper air, and the silver trumpets, and the horns that breathed deep melodies trembling with mystery and tenderness that shakes the heart; and the drum that beateth to battle, and the wild throb of the harp, and the cymbals clashing as the clash of armies. And a nightingale sitting by the Red Foliot sang the Pavane in passionate tones that dissolved the soul in their sweet, mournful beauty.

The Lord Gro covered his face with his mantle and wept to hear and behold the divine Pavane; for as ghosts rearisen it raised up for him old happy half-forgotten days in Goblinland, before he had conspired against King Gaslark and been driven forth from his dear native land, an exile in waterish Witchland.

Thereafter let the Red Foliot give order for the Galliard. Joyously swept forth the melody from the stringed instruments, and two dormice, fat as butter, spun into the hall. Wilder whirled the music, and the dormice capered ever higher till they bounded from the floor up to the beams of the vaulted roof, and down again, and up again to the roof-beams in the joyful dance. And the Foliots joined in the Galliard, spinning and capering in mad delight of the dance. And into the hall twirled six capripeds, footing it lightly as the music swept ever faster, and a one-footer that leaped hither and thither about and about, as the flea hoppeth, till the Witches grew hoarse with singing and shouting and hounding of him on. Yet ever capered the dormice higher and wilder than any else, and so swiftly flashed their little feet to the galloping music that no eye might follow their motion.

But little enow was Lord Gro gladdened by the merry dance. Sad melancholy sat with him for his companion, darkening his thoughts and making joy hateful to him as sunshine to owls of the night. So that he was well pleased to mark the Red Foliot go softly from his seat on the dais and forth from the hall by a door behind the arras, and seeing this, himself departed softly amid the full tide of the Galliard, forth of that hall of swift movement and gleeful laughter, forth into the quiet evening, where above the smooth downs the wind was lulled to sleep in the vast silent spaces of the sky, and the west was a bower of orange light fading to purple and unfathomable blue in the upper heaven, and nought was heard save the murmur of the sleepless sea, and nought seen save a flight of wildfowl flying against the sunset. In this quietness Gro walked westward above the combe until he came to the land's edge and stood on the lip of a chalk cliff falling to the sea, and was ware of the Red Foliot, alone on that high western cliff, gazing in a study at the dying colours in the west.

When they had stood for a while without speech, gazing over the sea, Gro spake and said, "Consider how as day now dieth in yonder chambers of the west, so hath the glory departed from Witchland."

But the Red Foliot answered him not, being in a study.

Then Gro said, "Though Demonland lieth where thou sawest the sun descend, yet eastward out of Witchland must thou look for the morning splendour. Not more surely shalt thou behold the sun go up thence to-morrow than thou shalt see shine forth in short season the glory and honour and power of Witchland, and beneath her destructive sword her enemies shall be as grass before the sickle."

The Red Foliot said, "I am in love with peace and the soft influence of the evening air. Leave me; or if thou wilt stay, break not the charm."

"O Red Foliot," said Gro, "art thou in love with peace indeed? So should the rising again of Witchland tune sweet music to thy thought, since we of Witchland love peace, nor are we stirrers up of strife, but the Demons only. The war against the Ghouls, whereby the four corners of the earth were shaken, was hatched by Demonland——"

"Thou speakest," said the Red Foliot, "clean against thine intention, a great praise of them. For who ever saw the like of these man-eating Ghouls for corruption of manners, inhuman degeneration, and deluge of iniquities? Who every fifth year from time immemorial have had their grand climacterical year, and but last year brake forth in never-imagined ferocity. But if they sail now, 'tis on the dark lake they sail, grieving no earthly seas nor rivers. Praise Demonland, therefore, who did put them down for ever."

"I make no question of that," answered Lord Gro. "But foul water, as soon as fair, will quench hot fire. Sore against our will did we of Witchland join with the Demons in that war, forseeing (as hath been bloodily approved) that the issue must be but the puffing up of the Demons, who desire no other thing than to be lords and tyrants of all the world."

"Thou," said the Red Foliot, "wast in thy young days King Gaslark's man: a Goblin born and bred: his very foster-brother, nourished at the same breast. Why must I observe thee, a plain traitor against so good a king? Whose perfidy the common people then did openly reprove (as I did well perceive even so lately as last autumn, when I was in the city of Zajë Zaculo at the time of their festivities for the betrothal of the king's cousin german the Princess Armelline unto the Lord Goldry Bluszco), they carrying filthy pictures of thee in the street, singing of thee thus:

> It was pittie
> One so wittie
>   Malcontent:
> Leaving reason
> Should to treason
>   So be bent.
>
> But his gifts
> Were but shifts
>   Void of grace:
> And his braverie
> Was but knaverie
>   Vile and base."

Said Gro, wincing a little, "The art of it agreeth well with the sentiment, and with the condition of those who invented it. I will not think so noble a prince as thou art will set thy sails to the wind of the rabble's most partial hates and envies. For the vile addition of traitor, I do reject and spit upon it. But true it is that, regarding not the god of fools and women, nice opinion, I do steer by mine own lode-star[37] still. Howbeit, I came not to discourse to thee on so small a matter as myself. This I would say unto thee with most sad and serious entertain: Be not lulled to think the Demons will leave the world at peace: that is farthest from their intent. They would not listen to thy comfortable words nor sit at meat with us, so set be they to imagine mischief against us. What said Juss? 'Witchland was ever as a flea': ay, as a flea which he itcheth to crush betwixt his finger-nails. O, if thou be in love with peace, a short way lieth open to thy heart's desire."

Nought spake the Red Foliot, gazing still into the dim reflections of the sunset which lingered below a darkening sky where stars were born. Gro said softly, as a cat purring, "Where softening unctions failed, sharp surgery bringeth speediest ease. Wilt thou not leave it to me?"

But the Red Foliot looked angrily upon him, saying, "What have I to do with your enmities? You are sworn to keep the peace, and I will not abide your violence nor your breaking of oaths in my quiet kingdom."

Gro said, "Oaths be of the heart, and he that breaketh them in open fact is oft, as now, no breaker in truth, for already were they scorned and trampled on by his opposites."

But the Red Foliot said again, "What have I to do with your enmities that set you by the ears like fighting dogs? I am yet to learn that he that hath a righteous heart, and clean hands, and hateth none, must needs be drawn into the brawls and manslayings of such as you and the Demons."

Lord Gro looked narrowly upon him, saying, "Thinkest thou that the strait path of him that affecteth neither side lieth still open for thee? If that were thine aim, thou shouldst have bethought thee ere thou gavest thy judgement on the second bout. For clear as day it was to us and to thine own people, and most of all to the Demons, that the King played foul in that bout, and when thou calledst him victorious thou didst loudly by that word trumpet thyself his friend, and unfriends to Demonland. Markedst thou not, when they left the hall, with what a snake's eye Lord Juss beheld thee? Not with us only but with thee he refused to eat and drink, that so his superstitious scruples may be unhurt when he proceeds to thy destruction. For on this are they determined. Nothing is more certain."

The Red Foliot sank his chin upon his breast, and stood silent for a space. The hues of death and silence spread themselves where late the fires of sunset glowed, and large stars opened like flowers on the illimitable fields of the night sky: Arcturus, Spica, Gemini, and the Little Dog, and Capella and her Kids.

The Red Foliot said, "Witchland lieth at my door. And Demonland: how stand I with Demonland?"

And Gro said, "Also to-morrow's sun goeth up out of Witchland."

For a while they spoke not. Then Lord Gro took forth a scroll from his bosom, and said, "The harvest of this world is to the resolute, and he that is infirm of purpose[38] is ground betwixt the upper and the nether millstone. Thou canst not turn back: so would they scorn and spurn thee, and we Witches likewise. And now by these means only may lasting peace be brought about, namely, by the setting of Gorice of Witchland on the throne of Demonland, and the utter humbling of that brood beneath the heel of the Witches."

The Red Foliot said, "Is not Gorice slain, and drank we not but now his arvale, slain by a Demon? and is he not the second in order of that line who hath so died by a Demon?"

"A twelfth Gorice," said Gro, "at this moment of time sitteth King in Carcë. O Red Foliot, know thou that I am a reader of the planets of the night and of those hidden powers that work out the web of destiny. Whereby I know that this twelfth King of the house of Gorice in Carcë shall be a most crafty warlock, full of guiles and wiles, who by the might of his egromancy[39] and the sword of Witchland shall exceed all earthly powers that be. And ineluctable as the levin-bolt of heaven goeth out his wrath against his enemies." So saying, Gro stooped and took a glowworm from the grass, saying kindly to it, "Sweeting, thy lamp for a moment," and breathed upon it, and held it to the parchment, saying, "Sign now thy royal name to these articles, which require thee not at all to go to war, but only (in case war shall arise) to be of our party, and against these Demons that do privily pursue thy life."

But the Red Foliot said, "Wherein am I certified that thou speakest not a lie?"

Then took Gro a writing from his purse and showed thereon a seal like the seal of Lord Juss; and there was written:[40] "Unto Voll al love and truste: and fayll nat whenas thow saylest upon Wychlande to caste of iij or iv shippes for the Folyott Isles to putt downe those and brenne the Redd Folyott in hys hous. For if wee get nat the lyfe of these wormes chirted owt of them the shame will stikk on us for ever." And Gro said, "My servant stole this from them while they spoke with thee in thine hall to-night."

Which the Red Foliot believed, and took from his belt his ink-horn and his pen, and signed his royal name to the articles of the treaty proposed to him.

Therewith Lord Gro put up the parchment in his bosom and said, "Swift surgery. Needs must that we take them in their beds to-night; so shall to-morrow's dawn bring glory and triumph to Witchland, now fixed in an eclipse, and to the whole world peace and soft contentment."

But the Red Foliot answered him, "My Lord Gro, I have signed these articles, and thereby stand I bound in enmity to Demonland. But I will not bewray my guests that have eaten my salt, be they never so deeply pledged mine enemies. Be it known to thee, I have set guards on your booths this night and on the booths of them of Demonland, that no unpeaceful deeds may be done betwixt you. This which I have done, by this will I stand, and ye shall both depart to-morrow in peace, even as ye came. Because I am your friend and sworn to your party, I and my Foliots will be on your side when war is between Witchland and Demonland. But I will not suffer night-slayings nor murthers in my Isles."

Now with these words of the Red Foliot, Lord Gro was as one that walketh along a flowery path to his rest, and in the last steps a gulf yawneth suddenly athwart the path, and he standeth a-gape and disappointed at the hither side. Yet in his subtlety he made no sign, but straight replied, "Righteously hast thou decreed and wisely, O Red Foliot, for it was truly said:

> Let worthy minds ne'er stagger in distrust
> To suffer death or shame for what is just,

and that which we sow in darkness must unfold in the open light of day, lest it be found withered in the very hour of maturity. Nor would I have urged thee otherwise, but that I do throughly fear these Demons, and all my mind was to take their plotting in re-verse. Do then one thing only for us. If we set sail homeward and they on our heels, they will fall upon us at a disadvantage, for they have the swifter ship; or if they get to sea before us, they will lie in wait for us on the high seas. Suffer us then to sail to-night, and do thou on some pretext delay them here for three days only, that we may get us home or ever they leave the Foliot Isles."

"I will not gainsay thee in this," answered the Red Foliot, "for here is nought but what is fair and just and lieth with mine honour. I will come to your booths at midnight and bring you down to your ship."

When Gro came to the Witches' booths he found them guarded even as the Red Foliot had said, and the booths of them of Demonland in like manner. So went he into the royal booth where the King lay in state on a bier of spear-shafts, robed in his kingly robes over his armour that was painted black and inlaid with gold, and the crown of Witchland on his head. Two candles burned at the head of King Gorice and two at his feet; and the night wind blowing through the crannies of the booth made them flare and flicker, so that shadows danced unceasingly on the wall and roof and floor. On the benches round the walls sat the lords of Witchland sullen of countenance, for the wine was dead in them. Balefully they eyed Lord Gro at his coming in, and Corinius sate upright in his seat and said, "Here is the Goblin, father and fosterer of our misfortunes. Come, let us slay him."

Gro stood among them with head erect and held Corinius with his eye, saying, "We of Witchland are not run lunatic, my Lord Corinius, that we should do this gladness to the Demons, to bite each at the other's throat like wolves. Methinks if Witchland be the land of my adoption only, yet have I not done least among you to ward off sheer destruction from her in this pass we stand in. If ye have aught against me, let me hear it and answer it."

Corinius laughed a bitter laugh. "Harken to the fool! Are we babies and milksops, thinkest thou, and is it not clear as day thou stoodest in the way of our falling on the Demons when we might have done so, urging what silly counsels I know not in favour of doing it by night? And now is night come, and we close prisoned in our booths, and no chance to come at them unless we would bring an hornets' nest of Foliots about our ears and give warning of our intent to the Demons and every living soul in this island. And all this has come about since thy slinking off and plotting with the Red Foliot. But now hath thy guile overreached itself, and now we will kill thee, and so an end of thee and thy plotting."

With that Corinius sprang up and drew his sword, and the other Witches with him. But Lord Gro moved not an eyelid, only he said, "Hear mine answer first. All night lieth before us, and 'tis but a moment's task to murther me."

Therewith stood forth the Lord Corund with his huge bulk betwixt Gro and Corinius, saying in a great voice, "Whoso shall point weapon 'gainst him shall first have to do with me, though it were one of my sons. We will hear him. If he clear not himself, then will we hew him in pieces."

They sat down, muttering. And Gro spake and said, "First behold this parchment, which is the articles of a solemn covenant and alliance, and behold where the Red Foliot hath set his sign manual thereto. True, his is a country of no might in arms, and we might tread him down and ne'er feel the leavings stick to our boot, and little avail can their weak help be unto us in the day of battle. But there is in these Isles a meetly good road and riding-place for ships, which if our enemies should occupy, their fleet were most aptly placed to do us all the ill imaginable. Is then this treaty a light benefit where now we stand? Next, know that when I counselled you take the Demons in their beds 'stead of fall upon them in the Foliots' hall, I did so being advertised that the Red Foliot had commanded his soldiers to turn against us or against the Demons, whichever first should draw sword upon the other. And when I went forth from the hall it was, as Corinius hath so deeply divined, to plot with the Red Foliot; but the aim of my plotting I have shown you, on these articles of alliance. And indeed, had I as Corinius vilely accuseth me practised with the Red Foliot against Witchland, I had hardly been so simple as return into the mouth of destruction when I might have bided safely in his palace."

Now when Gro perceived that the anger of the Witches against him was appeased by his defence, wherein he spake cunningly both true words and lies, he spake again among them saying, "Little gain have I of all my pains and thought expended by me for Witchland. And better it were for Witchland if my counsel were better heeded. Corund knoweth how, to mine own peril, I counselled the King to wrastle no more after the first bout, and if he had ta'en my rede, rather than suspect me and threaten me with death, we should not be now to bear him home dead to the royal catacombs in Carcë."

Corund said, "Truly hast thou spoken."

"In one thing only have I failed," said Gro; "and it can shortly be amended. The Red Foliot, albeit of our party, will not be won to attack the Demons by fraud, nor will he suffer us smite them in these Isles. Some fond simple scruples hang like cobwebs in his mind, and he is stubborn as touching this. But I have prevailed upon him to make them tarry here for three days' space, while we put to sea this very night, telling him, which he most innocently believeth, that we fear the Demons, and would flee home ere they be let loose to take us at a disadvantage on the high seas. And home we will indeed ere they set sail, yet not for fear of them, but rather that we may devise a deadly blow against them or ever they win home to Demonland."

"What blow, Goblin?" said Corinius.

And Gro answered and said, "One that I will devise upon with our Lord the King, Gorice XII., who now awaiteth us in Carcë. And I will not blab it to a wine-bibber and a dicer who hath but now drawn sword against a true lover of Witchland." Whereupon Corinius leaped up in mickle wrath to thrust his sword into Gro. But Corund and his sons restrained him.

In due time the stars revolved to midnight, and the Red Foliot came secretly with his guards to the Witches' booths. The lords of Witchland took their weapons and the men-at-arms bare the goods, and the King went in the midst on his bier of spearshafts. So went they picking their way in the moonless night round the palace and down the winding path that led to the bed of the combe, and so by the stream westward toward the sea. Here they deemed it safe to light a torch to show them the way. Desolate and bleak showed the sides of the combe in the wind-blown flare; and the flare was thrown back from the jewels of the royal crown of Witchland, and from the armoured buskins on the King's feet showing stark with toes pointing upward from below his bear-skin mantle, and from the armour and the weapons of them that bare him and walked beside him, and from the black cold surface of the little river hurrying for ever over its bed of boulders to the sea. The path was rugged and stony, and they fared slowly, lest they should stumble and drop the King.

IV

Conjuring in the Iron Tower

Of the hold of Carcë, and of the midnight practices of King Gorice XII. in the ancient chamber, preparing dole and doom for the lords of Demonland.

H E N the Witches were come aboard of their ship and all stowed, and the rowers set in order on the benches, they bade farewell to the Red Foliot and rowed out to the deep, and there hoisted sail and put up their helm and sailed eastward along the land. The stars wheeled overhead, and the east grew pale, and the sun came out of the sea on the larboard bow. Still sailed they two days and two nights, and on the third day there was land ahead, and morning rose abated by mist and cloud, and the sun was as a ball of red fire over Witchland in the east. So they hung awhile off Tenemos waiting for the tide, and at high water sailed over the bar and up the Druima past the dunes and mud-flats and the Ergaspian mere, till they reached the bend of the river below Carcë. Solitary marsh-land stretched on either side as far as the eye might reach, with clumps of willow and rare homesteads showing above the flats. Northward above the bend a bluff of land fell sharply to the elbow of the river, and on the other side sloped gently away for a few miles till it lost itself in the dead level of the marshes. On the southern face of the bluff, monstrous as a mountain in those low sedge-lands, hung square and black the fortress of Carcë. It was built of black marble, rough-hewn and unpolished, the outworks enclosing many acres. An inner wall with a tower at each corner formed the main stronghold, in the south-west corner of which was the palace, overhanging the river. And on the south-west corner of the palace, towering sheer from the water's edge seventy cubits and more to the battlements, stood the keep, a round tower lined with iron, bearing on the corbel[1] table beneath its parapet in varying form and untold repetition the sculptured figure of the crab of Witchland. The outer ward of the fortress was dark with cypress trees: black flames burning changelessly to heaven from a billowy sea of gloom. East of the keep was the water-gate, and beside it a bridge and bridge-house across the river, strongly fortified with turrets and machico-lations[2] and commanded from on high by the battlements of the keep. Dismal and fearsome to view was this strong place of Carcë, most like to the embodied soul of dreadful night brooding on the waters of that sluggish river: by day a shadow in broad sunshine, the likeness of pitiless violence sitting in the place of power, dark-ening the desolation of the mournful fen,[3] by night, a blackness more black than night herself.

Now was the ship made fast near the water-gate, and the lords of Witchland landed and their fighting men, and the gate opened to them, and mournfully they entered in and climbed the steep ascent to the palace, bearing with them their sad burden of the King. And in the great hall in Carcë was Gorice XI. laid in state for that night; and the day wore to its close. Nor was any word from King Gorice XII.

But when the shades of night were falling, there came a cham-berlain to Lord Gro as he walked upon the terrace without the western wall of the palace; and the chamberlain said, "My lord, the King bids you attend him in the Iron Tower, and he chargeth you bring unto him the royal crown of Witchland."

Gro made haste to fulfil the bidding of the King, and betook himself to the great banqueting hall, and all reverently he lifted the iron crown of Witchland set thick with priceless gems, and went by a winding stair to the tower, and the chamberlain went before him. When they were come to the first landing, the chamberlain knocked on a massive door that was forthwith opened by a guard; and the chamberlain said, "My lord, it is the King's will that you attend his majesty in his secret chamber at the top of the tower." And Gro marvelled, for none had entered that chamber for many years. Long ago had Gorice VII. practised forbidden arts therein, and folk said that in that chamber he raised up those spirits whereby he gat his bane.[4] Sithence [5] was the chamber sealed, nor had the late Kings need of it, since little faith they placed in art magical, relying rather on the might of their hands and the sword of Witchland. But Gro was glad at heart, for the opening of this chamber by the King met his designs half way. Fearlessly he mounted the winding stairs that were dusky with the shadows of approaching night and hung with cobwebs and strewn with the dust of neglect, until he came to the small low door of that chamber, and pausing knocked thereon and harkened for the answer.

And one said from within, "Who knocketh?" and Gro answered, "Lord, it is I, Gro." And the bolts were drawn and the door opened, and the King said, "Enter." And Gro entered and stood in the presence of the King.

Now the fashion of the chamber was that it was round, filling the whole space of the loftiest floor of the round donjon keep.[6] It was now gathering dusk, and weak twilight only entered through the deep embrasures of the windows that pierced the walls of the tower, looking to the four quarters of the heavens. A furnace glowing in the big hearth threw fitful gleams into the recesses of the chamber, lighting up strange shapes of glass and earthenware, flasks and retorts,[7] balances, hour-glasses, crucibles and astrolabes,[8] a monstrous three-necked alembic[9] of phosphorescent glass supported on a bain-marie,[10] and other instruments of doubtful and unlawful aspect. Under the northern window over against the doorway was a massive table blackened with age, whereon lay great books bound in black leather with iron guards and heavy padlocks. And in a mighty chair beside this table was King Gorice XII., robed in his conjuring robe of black and gold, resting his cheek on his hand that was lean as an eagle's claw. The low light, mother of shade and secrecy, that hovered in that chamber moved about the still figure of the King, his nose hooked as the eagle's beak, his cropped hair, his thick close-cut beard and shaven upper lip, his high cheek-bones and cruel heavy jaw, and the dark eaves of his brows whence the glint of green eyes showed as no friendly lamp to them without. The door shut noiselessly, and Gro stood before the King. The dusk deepened, and the firelight pulsed and blinked in that dread chamber, and the King leaned without motion on his hand, bending his brow on Gro; and there was utter silence save for the faint purr of the furnace.

In a while the King said, "I sent for thee, because thou alone wast so hardy as to urge to the uttermost thy counsel upon the King that is now dead, Gorice XI. of memory ever glorious. And because thy counsel was good. Marvellest thou that I wist[11] of thy counsel?"

Gro said, "O my Lord the King, I marvel not of this. For it is known to me that the soul endureth, albeit the body perish."

"Keep thou thy lips from overspeech," said the King. "These be mysteries whereon but to think may snatch thee into peril, and whoso speaketh of them, though in so secret a place as this, and with me only, yet at his most bitter peril speaketh he."

Gro answered, "O King, I spake not lightly; moreover, you did tempt me by your questioning. Nevertheless I am utterly obedient to your majesty's admonition."

The King rose from his chair and walked towards Gro, slowly. He was exceeding tall, and lean as a starved cormorant.[12] Laying his hands upon the shoulders of Gro, and bending his face to Gro's, "Art not afeared," he asked, "to abide me in this chamber, at the close of day? Or hast not thought on't, and on these instruments thou seest, their use and purpose, and the ancient use of this chamber?"

Gro blenched never a whit, but stoutly said, "I am not afeared, O my Lord the King, but rather rejoiced I at your summons. For it jumpeth with mine own designs, when I took counsel secretly in my heart after the woes that the Fates fulfilled for Witchland in the Foliot Isles. For in that day, O King, when I beheld the light of Witchland darkened and her might abated in the fall of King Gorice XI. of glorious memory, I thought on you, Lord, the twelfth Gorice raised up King in Carcë; and there was present to my mind the word of the soothsayer of old, where he singeth:

> Ten, eleven, twelf I see
> In sequent varietie
> Of puissaunce[13] and maistrye
> With swerd, sinwes, and grammarie,[14]
> In the holde of Carcë
> Lordinge it royally.

And being minded that he singleth out you, the twelfth, as potent in grammarie, all my care was that these Demons should be detained within reach of your spells until we should have time to win home to you and to apprise you of their farings, that so you might put forth your power and destroy them by art magic or ever they come safe again to many-mountained Demonland."

The King took Gro to his bosom and kissed him, saying, "Art

thou not a very jewel of wisdom and discretion? Let me embrace thee and love thee for ever."

Then the King stood back from him, keeping his hands on Gro's shoulders, and gazed piercingly upon him for a space in silence. Then kindled he a taper that stood in an iron candlestick by the table where the books lay, and held it to Gro's face. And the King said, "Ay, wise thou art and of good discretion, and some courage hast thou. But if thou be to serve me this night, needs must I try thee first with terrors till thou be inured to them, as tried gold runneth in the crucible; or if thou be base metal only, till that thou be eaten up by them."

Gro said unto the King, "For many years, Lord, or ever I came to Carcë, I fared up and down the world, and I am acquainted with objects of terror as a child with his toys. I have seen in the southern seas, by the light of Achernar and Canopus, giant sea-horses battling with eight-legged cuttle-fishes in the whirlpools of the Korsh. Yet was I unafraid. I was in the isle Ciona when the first of the pit brast forth in that isle and split it as a man's skull is split with an axe, and the green gulfs of the sea swallowed that isle, and the stench and the steam hung in the air for days where the burning rock and earth had sizzled in the ocean. Yet was I unafraid. Also was I with Gaslark in the flight out of Zajë Zaculo, when the Ghouls took the palace over our heads, and portents walked in his halls in broad daylight, and the Ghouls conjured the sun out of heaven. Yet was I unafraid. And for thirty days and thirty nights wandered I alone on the face of the Moruna in Upper Impland, where scarce a living soul hath been: and there the evil wights that people the air of that desert dogged my steps and gibbered at me in darkness. Yet was I unafraid; and came in due time to Morna Moruna, and thence, standing on the lip of the escarpment as it were on the edge of the world, looked southaway where never mortal eye had gazed aforetime, across the untrodden forests of the Bhavinan. And in that skyey distance, pre-eminent beyond range on range of ice-robed mountains, I beheld two peaks throned for ever between firm land and heaven in unearthly loveliness: the spires and airy ridges of Koshtra Pivrarcha, and the wild precipices that soar upward from the abysses to the queenly silent snowdome of Koshtra Belorn."

When Gro had ended, the King turned him away and, taking from a shelf a retort filled with a dark blue fluid, set it on a bain-marie, and a lamp thereunder. Fumes of a faint purple hue came forth from the neck of the retort, and the King gathered them in a flask. He made signs over the flask and shook forth into his hand therefrom a fine powder. Then said he unto Gro, holding out the powder in the open palm of his hand, "Look narrowly at this powder." And Gro looked. The King muttered an incantation, and the powder moved and heaved, and was like a crawling mass of cheesemites in an overripe cheese. It increased in volume in the King's hand, and Gro perceived that each particular grain had legs. The grains grew before his eyes, and became the size of mustard seeds, and then of barleycorns, swiftly crawling each over other. And even as he marvelled, they waxed great as kidney beans, and now was their shape and seeming clear to him, so that he beheld that they were small frogs and paddocks; and they overflowed from the King's hand as they waxed swiftly in size, pouring on to the floor. And they ceased not to increase and grow; and now were they large as little dogs, nor might the King retain more than a single one, holding his hand under its belly while it waved its legs in the air; and they were walking on the tables and jostling on the floor. Pallid they were, and permeable to light like thin horn, and their hue a faint purple, even as the hue of the vapour whence they were engendered. And now was the room filled with them so that they mounted perforce one on another's shoulders, and they were of the bigness of well fatted hogs; and they goggled their eyes at Gro and croaked. The King looked narrowly on Gro, who stood in the presence of that spectacle, the crown of Witchland in his hands; and the King marked that the crown trembled not a whit in Gro's hands that held it. So he said a certain word, and the paddocks and the frogs grew small again, shrinking more swiftly than they had grown, and so vanished.

The King now took from the shelf a ball the size of the egg of an estridge, of dark green glass. He said unto Gro, "Look well at this glass and tell me what thou seest." Gro answered him, "I see a shifting shadow within." The King commanded him saying, "Dash it down with all thy strength upon the floor." The Lord Gro lifted the ball with both hands above his head, and it was ponderous as a ball of lead, and according to the command of Gorice the King he hurled it on the floor, so that it was pashed in pieces. And, behold, a puff of thick smoke burst forth from the fragments of the ball and took the form of one of human shape and dreadful aspect, whose two legs were two writhing snakes; and it stood in the chamber so tall that the head of it touched the vaulted ceiling, viewing the King and Gro malevolently and menacing them. The King caught down a sword that hung against the wall, and put it in Gro's hand, shouting, "Smite off the legs of it! and delay not, or thou art but dead!" Gro smote and cut off the left leg of the evil wight, easily, as it were cutting of butter. But from the stump came forth two fresh snakes awrithing; and so it fared likewise with the right leg, but the King shouted, "Smite and cease not, or thou art but a dead dog!" and ever as Gro hewed a snake in twain forth came two more from the wound, till the chamber was a maze of their wriggling forms. And still Gro hewed with a will, until the sweat stood on his brow, and he said, panting between the strokes, "O King, I have made him many-legged as a centipede: must I make him a myriapod ere night's decline?" And the King smiled, and spake a word of hidden meaning; and therewith the turmoil was gone as a gust of wind departeth, and nought left save the shivered splinters of the green ball on the chamber floor.

"Wast not afeared?" asked the King, and when Gro said nay, "Methinks these sights of terror should much afflict thee," said the King, "since well I know thou art not skilled in art magical."

"Yet am I a philosopher," answered Lord Gro; "and somewhat know I of alchymy and the hidden properties of this material world: the virtues of herbs, plants, stones, and minerals, the ways of the stars in their courses, and the influences of those heavenly bodies. And I have held converse with birds and fishes in their degree, and that generation which creepeth on the earth is not held in scorn by me, but oft talk I in sweet companionship with the eft of the pond, and the glowworm, and the lady-bird, and the pismire,[15] and their kind, making them my little gossips. So have I a certain lore which lighteth me in the outer court of the secret temple of grammarie and art forbid, albeit I have not peered within that temple. And by my philosophy, O King, I am certified concerning these apparitions which you have raised for me, that they be illusions and phantasms only, able to terrify the soul indeed of him that knoweth not divine philosophy, but without bodily power or essence. Nor is aught to fear in such, save the fear itself wherewith they strike the simple."

Then said the King, "By what token knowest thou this?"

And the Lord Gro made answer unto him, "O King, as a child weaveth a daisy-chain, thus easily did you conjure up these shapes of terror. Not in such wise fareth he that calleth out of the deep the deadly terror indeed; but with toil and sweat and with straining of thought, will, heart, and sinew fareth he."

The King smiled. "Thou sayest true. Now, therefore, since phantasmagoria [16] maketh not thy heart to quail, I present thee a more material horror."[17]

And he lighted the candles in the great candlesticks of iron and opened a little secret door in the wall of the chamber near the floor; and Gro beheld iron bars within the little door, and heard a hissing from behind the bars. The King took a key of silver of delicate construction, the handle slender and three spans in length, and opened the iron grated door. And the King said, "Behold and see, that which sprung from the egg of a cock, hatched by the deaf adder. The glance of its eye sufficeth to turn to stone any living thing that standeth before it. Were I but for one instant to loose my spells whereby I hold it in subjection, in that moment would end my life days and thine. So strong in properties of ill is this serpent which the ancient Enemy that dwelleth in darkness hath placed upon this earth, to be a bane unto the children of men, but an instrument of might in the hand of enchanters and sorcerers."

Therewith came forth that offspring of perdition from its hole, strutting erect on its two legs that were the legs of a cock; and a cock's head it had, with rosy comb and wattles, but the face of it like no fowl's face of middle-earth but rather a gorgon's[18] out of Hell. Black shining feathers grew on its neck, but the body of it was the body of a dragon with scales that glittered in the rays of the candles, and a scaly crest stood on its back; and its wings were like bats' wings, and its tail the tail of an aspick[19] with a sting in the end thereof, and from its beak its forked tongue flickered venomously. And the stature of the thing was a little above a cubit. Now because of the spells of King Gorice whereby he held it ensorcelled[20] it might not cast its baneful glance upon him, nor upon Gro, but it walked back and forth in the candle light, averting its eyes from them. The feathers on its neck were fluffed up with anger and wondrous swiftly twirled its scaly tail, and it hissed ever more fiercely, irked by the bonds of the King's enchantment; and the breath of it was noisome, and hung in sluggish wreaths about the chamber. So for a while it walked before them, and as it looked sidelong past him Gro beheld the light of its eyes that were as sick moons burning poisonously through a mist of greenish yellow in the dusk of night. And strong loathing seized him, so that his gorge rose to behold the thing, and his brow and the palms of his hands became clammy, and he said, "My Lord the King, I have looked steadfastly on this cockatrice and it affrighteth me no whit, but it is loathly in my sight, so that my gorge riseth because of it," and with that he fell a-vomiting. And the King commanded that serpent back into its hole, whither it returned, hissing wrathfully.

Now the King poured forth wine, speaking a charm over the cup, and when the bright wine had revived Lord Gro, the King spake saying, "It is well, O Gro, that thou hast shown thyself a philosopher indeed, and of heart intrepid. Yet even as no blade is utterly tried until one try it in very battle, where if it snap woe and doom wait on the hand that wields it, so must thou in this midnight suffer a yet fiercer furnace-heat of terror, wherein if thou be reduced we are both lost eternally, and this Carcë and all Witchland blasted with us for ever in ruin and oblivion. Durst abide this trial?"

Gro answered, "I am hot to obey your word, O King. For well know I that it is idle to hope by phantoms and illusions to appal the Demons, and that against the Demons the deadly eye of thy cockatrice were turned in vain. Stout of heart are they, and instructed in all lore, and Juss a sorcerer of ancient power, who hath charms to blunt the glance of basilisk or cockatrice. He that would strike down the Demons must conjure indeed."

"Great," said the King, "is the strength and cunning of the seed of Demonland. By main strength have they now shown mastery over us, as sadly witnesseth the overthrow of Gorice XI., 'gainst whom no mortal could stand up and wrastle and not die, till cursed Goldry, drunk with spleen and envy, slew him in the Foliot Isles. Nor was there any aforetime to outdo us in feats of arms, and Gorice X., victorious in single combats without number, made our name glorious over all the world. Yet at the last he gat his death, out of all expectation and by what treacherous sleight I know not, standing in single combat against the curled step-dancer from Krothering. But I, that am skilled in grammarie, do bear a mightier engine against the Demons than brawny sinews or the sword that smiteth asunder. Yet is mine engine perilous to him that useth it."

Therewith the King unlocked the greatest of those books that lay by on the massive table, saying in Gro's ear, as one who would not be overheard, "This is that awful book of grammarie wherewith in this same chamber, on such a night, Gorice VII. stirred the vasty deep. And know that from this circumstance alone ensued the ruin of King Gorice VII., in that, having by his hellish science conjured up somewhat from the primaeval dark, and being utterly fordone with the sweat and stress of his conjuring, his mind was clouded for a moment, in such sort that either he forgot the words writ in this grammarie, or the page whereon they were writ, or speech failed him to speak those words that must be spoken, or might to do those things which must be done to complete the charm. Wherefore he kept not his power over that which he had called out of the deep, but it turned upon him and tare him limb from limb. Such like doom will I avoid, renewing in these latter days those self-same spells, if thou durst stand by me undismayed the while I utter my incantations. And shouldst thou mark me fail or waver ere all be accomplished, then shalt thyself lay hand on book and crucible and fulfil whatsoever is needful, as I shall first show thee. Or quailest thou at this?"

Gro said, "Lord, show me my task. And I will carry it, though all the Furies of the pit flock to this chamber to say me nay."

So the King instructed Gro, rehearsing to him those acts that were needful, and making known unto him the divers pages of the grammarie whereon were writ those words which must be spoken each in its due time and sequence. But the King pronounced not yet those words, pointing only to them in the book, for whoso speaketh those words in vain and out of season is lost. And now when the retorts and beakers with their several necks and tubes and the appurtenances thereof were set in order, and the unhallowed processes of fixation, conjunction, deflagration, putrefaction, and rubefication were nearing maturity,[21] and the baleful star Antares standing by the astrolabe within a little of the meridian signified the instant approach of midnight, the King described on the floor with his conjuring rod three pentacles inclosed within a seven-pointed star, with the signs of Cancer and of Scorpio joined by certain runes. And in the midst of the star he limned the image of a green crab eating of the sun. And turning to the seventy-third page of his great black grammarie the King recited in a mighty voice words of hidden meaning, calling on the name that it is a sin to utter.

Now when he had spoken the first spell and was silent, there was a deadly quiet in that chamber, and a chill in the air as of winter. And in the quiet Gro heard the King's breath coming and going, as of one who hath rowed a course. Now the blood rushed back to Gro's heart and his hands and feet became cold and a cold sweat brake forth on his brow. But for all that, he held yet his courage firm and his brain ready. The King motioned to Gro to break off the tail of a certain drop of black glass that lay on the table; and with the snapping of its tail the whole drop fell in pieces in a coarse black powder. Gro by the King's direction gathered that powder and dropped it in the great alembic wherein a green fluid seethed and bubbled above the flame of a lamp; and the fluid became red as blood, and the body of the alembic filled with a tawny smoke, and sparks of sun-like brilliance flashed and crackled through the smoke. Thereupon distilled from the neck of the alembic a white oil incombustible, and the King dipped his rod in that oil and described round the seven-pointed star on the floor the figure of the worm Ouroboros, that eateth his own tail. And he wrote the formula of the crab below the circle, and spake his second spell.

When that was done, yet more biting seemed the night air and yet more like the grave the stillness of the chamber. The King's hand shook as with an ague as he turned the pages of the mighty book. Gro's teeth chattered in his head. He gritted them together and waited. And now through every window came a light into the chamber as of skies paling to the dawn. Yet not wholly so; for never yet came dawn at midnight, nor from all four quarters of the sky at once, nor with such swift strides of increasing light, nor with a light so ghastly. The candle flames burned filmy as the glare waxed strong from without: an evil pallid light of bale and corruption, wherein the hands and faces of the King Gorice and his disciple showed death-pale, and their lips black as the dark skin of a grape where the bloom has been rubbed off from it. The King cried terribly, "The hour approacheth!" And he took a phial[22] of crystal containing a decoction[23] of wolf's jelly and salamander's blood, and dropped seven drops from the alembic into the phial and poured forth that liquor on the figure of the crab drawn on the floor. Gro leaned against the wall, weak in body but with will unbowed. So bitter was the cold that his hands and feet were benumbed, and the liquor from the phial congealed where it fell. Yet the sweat stood in beads on the forehead of the King by reason of the mighty striving that was his, and in the overpowering glare of that light from the underskies he stood stiff and erect, hands clenched and arms outstretched, and spake the words LURO VOPO VIR VOARCHADUMIA.

Now with those words spoken the vivid light departed as a blown-out lamp, and the midnight closed down again without. Nor was any sound heard save the thick panting of the King; but it was as if the night held its breath in expectation of that which was to come. And the candles sputtered and burned blue. The King swayed and clutched the table with his left hand; and again the King pronounced terribly the word VOARCHADUMIA.

Thereafter for the space of ten heart-beats silence hung like a kestrel [24] poised in the listening night. Then went a crash through earth and heaven, and a blinding wildfire through the chamber as it had been a thunderbolt. All Carcë quaked, and the chamber was filled with a beating of wings, like the wings of some monstrous bird. The air that was wintry cold waxed on a sudden hot as the breath of a burning mountain, and Gro was near choking with the smell of soot and the smell of brimstone. And the chamber rocked as a ship riding in a swell with the wind against the tide. But the

King, steadying himself against the table and clutching the edge of it till the veins on his lean hand seemed nigh to bursting, cried in short breaths and with an altered voice, "By these figures drawn and by these spells enchanted, by the unction of wolf and salamander, by the unblest sign of Cancer now leaning to the sun, and by the fiery heart of Scorpio that flameth in this hour on night's meridian, thou art my thrall and instrument. Abase thee and serve me, worm of the pit. Else will I by and by summon out of ancient night intelligences and dominations mightier far than thou, and they shall serve mine ends, and thee shall they chain with chains of quenchless fire and drag thee from torment to torment through the deep."

Therewith the earthquake was stilled, and there remained but a quivering of the walls and floor and the wind of those unseen wings and the hot smell of soot and brimstone burning. And speech came out of the teeming air of that chamber, strangely sweet, saying, "Accursed wretch that troublest our quiet, what is thy will?" The terror of that speech made the throat of Gro dry, and the hairs on his scalp stood up.

The King trembled in all his members like a frightened horse, yet was his voice level and his countenance unruffled as he said hoarsely, "Mine enemies sail at day-break from the Foliot Isles. I loose thee against them as a falcon from my wrist. I give thee them. Turn them to thy will: how or where it skills not, so thou do but break and destroy them off the face of the world. Away!"

But now was the King's endurance clean spent, so that his knees failed him and he sank like a sick man into his mighty chair. But the room was filled with a tumult as of rushing waters, and a laughter above the tumult like to the laughter of souls condemned. And the King was reminded that he had left unspoken that word which should dismiss his sending. But to such weariness was he now come and so utterly was his strength gone out from him in the exercise of his spells, that his tongue clave to the roof of his mouth, so that he might not speak the word; and horribly he rolled up the whites of his eyes beckoning to Gro, the while his nerveless fingers sought to turn the heavy pages of the grammarie. Then sprang Gro forth to the table, and against it sprawling, for now was the great keep of Carcë shaken anew as one shaketh a dice box, and lightnings opened the heavens, and the thunder roared unceasingly, and the sound of waters stunned the ear in that chamber, and still that laughter pealed above the turmoil. And Gro knew that it was now with the King even as it had been with Gorice VII. in years gone by, when his strength gave forth and the spirit tare him and plastered those chamber-walls with his blood. Yet was Gro mindful, even in that hideous storm of terror, of the ninety-seventh page whereon the King had shown him the word of dismissal, and he wrenched the book from the King's palsied grasp and turned to the page. Scarce had his eye found the word, when a whirlwind of hail and sleet swept into the chamber, and the candles were blown out and the tables overset. And in the plunging darkness beneath the crashing of the thunder Gro pitching headlong felt claws clasp his head and body. He cried in his agony the word, that was the word TRIPSARECOPSEM, and so fell a-swooning.

It was high noon when the Lord Gro came to his senses in that chamber. The strong spring sunshine poured through the southern window, lighting up the wreckage of the night. The tables were cast down and the floor strewn and splashed with costly essences[25] and earths spilt from shattered phials and jars and caskets: aphroselmia, shell of gold, saffron of gold, asem, amianth, stypteria of Melos, confounded with mandragora, vinum ardens, sal armoniack, devouring aqua regia, little pools and scattered globules of quicksilver, poisonous decoctions of toadstools and of yewberries, monkshood, thorn-apple, wolf's bane and black hellebore, quintessences of dragon's blood and serpent's bile; and with these, splashed together and wasted, elixirs that wise men have died a-dreaming of: spiritus mundi, and that sovereign alkahest which dissolveth every substance dipped therein, and that aurum potabile[26] which being itself perfect induceth perfection in the living frame. And in this welter of spoiled treasure were the great conjuring books hurled amid the ruin of retorts and aludels of glass and lead and silver, sand-baths, matrasses, spatulae, athanors, and other instruments innumerable of rare design,[27] tossed and broken on the chamber floor. The King's chair was thrown against the furnace, and huddled against the table lay the King, his head thrown back, his black beard pointing skyward, showing his sinewy hairy throat. Gro looked narrowly at him; saw that he seemed unhurt and slept deep; and so, knowing well that sleep is a present remedy for every ill, watched by the King in silence all day till supper time, for all he was sore an-hungered.

When at length the King awoke, he looked about him in amaze. "Methought I tripped at the last step of last night's journey," he said. "And truly strange riot hath left its footprints in my chamber."

Gro answered, "Lord, sorely was I tried; yet fulfilled I your behest."

The King laughed as one whose soul is at ease, and standing upon his feet said unto Gro, "Take up the crown of Witchland and crown me. And that high honour shalt thou have, because I do love thee for this night gone by."

Now without were the lords of Witchland assembled in the courtyard, being bound for the great banqueting hall to eat and drink, unto whom the King came forth from the gate below the keep, robed in his conjuring robe. Wondrous bright sparkled the gems of the iron crown of Witchland above the heavy brow and cheekbones and the fierce disdainful lip of the King, as he stood there in his majesty, and Gro with the guard of honour stood in the shadow of the gate. And the King said, "My lords Corund and Corsus and Corinius and Gallandus, and ye sons of Corsus and of Corund, and ye other Witches, behold your King, the twelfth Gorice, crowned with this crown in Carcë to be King of Witchland and of Demonland. And all countries of the world and the rulers thereof, so many as the sun doth spread his beams over, shall do me obeisance, and call me King and Lord."

All they shouted assent, praising the King and bowing down before him.

Then said the King, "Imagine not that oaths sworn unto the Demons by Gorice XI. of memory ever glorious bind me any whit. I will not be at peace with this Juss and his brethren, but do account them all mine enemies. And this night have I made a sending to take them on the waste of waters as they sail homeward to many-mountained Demonland."

Corund said, "Lord, your words are as wine unto us. And well we guessed that the principalities of darkness were afoot last night, seeing all Carcë rocked and the foundations thereof rose and fell as the breast of the large earth a-breathing."

When they were come into the banqueting hall, the King said, "Gro shall sit at my right hand this night, since manfully hath he served me." And when they scowled at this, and spake each in the other's ear, the King said, "Whoso among you shall so serve me and so water the growth of this Witchland as hath Gro in this night gone by, unto him will I do like honour." But unto Gro he said, "I will bring thee home to Goblinland in triumph, that wentest forth an exile. I will pluck Gaslark from his throne, and make thee king in Zajë Zaculo, and all Goblinland shalt thou hold for me in fee, exercising dominion over it."

V

KING GORICE'S SENDING

*Of King Gaslark, and of the coming of the
sending upon the demons on the high seas; with
how the Lord Juss by the egging on of his
companions was persuaded to an unadvised
rashness.*

HE next morning following that night when King
Gorice XII. sat crowned in Carcë as is aforesaid, was
Gaslark a-sailing on the middle sea, homeward from
the east. Seven ships of war he had, and they steered
in column south-westward close hauled on the starboard tack. Greatest and fairest among them was she who led the
line, a great dragon of war painted azure of the summer sea with
towering head of a worm, plated with gold and wrought with
overlapping scales, gaping defiance from her bows, and a worm's
tail erect at the poop. Seventy and five picked men of Goblinland
sailed on that ship, clad in gay kirtles[1] and byrnies of mail and
armed with axes, spears, and swords. Their shields, each with his
device, hung at the bulwarks. On the high poop sat King Gaslark,
his sturdy hands grasping the great steering paddle. Goodly of
mien and well knit were all they of Goblinland that went on that
great ship, yet did Gaslark outdo them all in goodliness and
strength and all kingliness. He wore a silken kirtle of Tyrian purple.[2] Broad wristlets of woven gold were on his wrists. Dark-
skinned was he as one that hath lived all his days in the hot sunshine: clean-cut of feature, somewhat hooky-nosed, with great eyes

and white teeth and tightcurled black moustachios. Nought restful was there in his presence and bearing, but rashness and impetuous fire; and he was wild to look on, swift and beautiful as a stag in autumn.

Teshmar, that was the skipper of his ship, stood at his elbow. Gaslark said to him, "Is it not one of the three gallant spectacles of the world, a good ship treading the hastening furrows of the sea like a queen in grace and beauty, scattering up the wave-crests before her stem in a glittering rain?"

"Yea, Lord," answered he; "and what be the other two?"

"One that I most unhappily did miss, whereof but yesterday we had tidings: to behold such a battling of great champions and such a victory as Lord Goldry obtained upon yonder vaunting tyrant."

"The third shall be seen, I think," said Teshmar, "when the Lord Goldry Bluszco shall in your royal palace of Zajë Zaculo, amid pomp and high rejoicing, wed the young princess your cousin: most fortunate lord, that must be lord of her whom all just censure doth acknowledge the ornament of earth, the model of heaven, the queen of beauty."

"Kind Gods hasten the day," said Gaslark. "For truly 'tis a most sweet lass, and those kinsmen of Demonland my dearest friends. But for whose great upholding time and again, Teshmar, in days gone by, where were I today and my kingdom, and where thou and all of you?" The king's brow darkened a little with thought. After a time he began to say, "I must have more great action: these trivial harryings, spoils of Nevria, chasing of Esamocian black-a-moors, [3] be toys not worthy of our great name and renown among the nations. Something I would enact that shall embroil and astonish the world, even as the Demons when they purged earth of the Ghouls, ere I go down into silence."

Teshmar was staring toward the southern bourne. He pointed with his hand: "There rideth a great ship, O king. And methinks she hath a strange look."

Gaslark gazed earnestly at her for an instant, then straightway shifted his helm and steered towards her. He spake no more, staring ever as he sailed, marking ever as the distance lessened more and more particulars of that ship. Her silken sail fluttered in tatters from the yard; she rowed feebly, as one groping in darkness, with barely strength to stay her from drifting stern-foremost before the wind. So hung she on the sea, as one struck stupid by some blow, doubting which way her harbour lay or which way her course. As a thing which hath been held in the flame of a mon-

strous candle, so seemed she, singed and besmirched with soot.
Smashed was her proud figure-head, and smashed was her high
forecastle, and burned and shattered the carved timbers of the
poop and the fair seats that were thereon. She leaked, so that a
score of her crew must be still a-baling to keep her afloat. Of her
fifty oars, half were broken or gone adrift, and many of the ship's
company lay wounded and some slain under her thwarts.

And now was King Gaslark ware as he drew near that here was
the Lord Juss on her ruined poop a-steering, and by him Spitfire
and Brandoch Daha. Their jewelled arms and gear and rich attire
were black with most stinking soot, and it was as though admiration and grief and anger were so locked and twined within them
that none of these passions might win forth to outward showing on
their frozen countenances.

When they were within hailing distance, Gaslark hailed them.
They answered him not, only beholding him with alien eyes. But
they stopped the ship, and Gaslark lay aboard of her and came on
board and went up on the poop and greeted them. And he said,
"Well met in an ill hour. What's the matter?"

The Lord Juss made as if to speak, but no word came. Only he
took Gaslark by both hands and sat down with a great groan on the
poop, averting his face. Gaslark said, "O Juss, for so many a time as
thou hast borne part in my evils and succoured me, surely right
requireth I have part of thine?"

But Juss answered in a thick, strange voice all unlike himself,
"Mine, sayest thou, O Gaslark? What in the stablished world is
mine, that am thus in a moment reived of him that was mine own
heartstring, my brother, the might of mine arm, the chiefest citadel
of my dominion?" And he burst into a great passion of weeping.

King Gaslark's rings were driven into the flesh of his fingers by
the grip of Juss's strong hands on his. But he scarce wist of the
pain, such agony of mind was in him for the loss of his friend, and
for the bitterness and wonder that it was to behold these three
great lords of Demonland weep like frightened women, and all
their ship's company of tried men of war weeping and wailing
besides. And Gaslark saw well that their lordly souls were unseated
for a season because of some dreadful fact, the havoc whereof his
eyes most woefully beheld, while its particulars were yet dark to
him, yet with a terror in darkness that might well make his heart to
quail.

By much questioning he was at last well advertised of what had
befallen: how they the day before, in broad noon, on such a summer sea, had heard a noise like the flapping of wings outstretched

from one edge of the sky to another, and in a moment the calm sea was lifted up and fell again and the whole sea clashed together and roared, yet was the ship not sunken. And there was a tumult about them of thunder and raging waters and black night and wildfire in the night; which presently passing away and the darkness lifting, the sea lay solitary as far as eye might reach. "And nothing is more certain," said Juss, "than that this is a sending of King Gorice XII. spoken of by the prophets as a great clerk of necromancy beyond all other this world hath seen. And this is his vengeance for the woes we wrought for Witchland in the Foliot Isles. Against such a peril I had provided certain amulets made of the stone alectorian,[4] which groweth in the gizzard of a cock hatched on a moonless night when Saturn burneth in a human sign and the lord of the third house is in the ascendant. These saved us, albeit sorely buffeted, from destruction: all save Goldry alone. He, by some cursed chance, whether he neglected to wear the charm I gave him, or the chain of it was broken in the plunging of the ship, or by some other means 'twas lost: when daylight came again, we stood but three on this poop where four had stood. More I know not."

"O Gaslark," said Spitfire, "our brother that is stolen from us, with us it surely lieth to find him and set him free."

But Juss groaned and said, "In which star of the unclimbed sky wilt thou begin our search? Or in which of the secret streams of ocean where the last green rays are quenched in oozy darkness?"

Gaslark was silent for a while. Then he said, "I think nought likelier than this, that Gorice hath caught away Goldry Bluszco into Carcë, where he holdeth him in duress. And thither must we straightway to deliver him."

Juss answered no word. But Gaslark seized his hand, saying, "Our ancient love and your oft succouring of Goblinland in days gone by make this my quarrel. Hear now my rede. As I fared from the east through the Straits of Rinath I beheld a mighty company of forty sail, bound eastward to the Beshtrian sea. Well it was they marked us not as we lay under the isles of Ellien in the dusk of evening. For touching later at Norvasp in Pixyland we learned that there sailed Laxus with the whole Witchland fleet, being minded to work evil deeds among the peaceful cities of the Beshtrian seaboard. And as well met were an antelope with a devouring lion, as I and my seven ships with those ill-doers in such strength on the high seas. But now, behold how wide standeth the door to our wishes. Laxus and that great armament are safe harrying eastward-ho. I make question whether at this moment more than nine score or ten score fighting men be left in Carcë. I have here of mine own nigh on five hundred. Never was fairer chance to take Witchland with his claws beneath the table, and royally may we scratch his face ere he get them forth again.'' And Gaslark laughed for joy of battle, and cried, "O Juss, smiles it not to thee, this rede of mine?''

"Gaslark,'' said Lord Juss, "nobly and with that open hand and heart that I have loved in thee from of old hast thou made this offer. Yet not so is Witchland to be overcome, but after long days of labour only, and laying of schemes and building of ships and gathering of hosts answerable to the strength we bare of late against the Ghouls when we destroyed them.''

Nor for all his urging might Gaslark move him any whit.

But Spitfire sat by his brother and spake privately to him: "Kinsman, what ails thee? Is all high heart and swiftness to action crushed out of Demonland, and doth but the unserviceable juice-less skin remain to us? Thou art clean unlike that thou hast ever been, and could Witchland behold us now well might he judge that base fear had ta'en hold upon us, seeing that with the odds of strength so fortunately of our side we shrink from striking at him.''

Juss said in Spitfire's ear, "This it is, that I do misdoubt me of the steadfastness of the Goblins. Too like to fire among dead leaves is the sudden flame of their valour, a poor thing to rely on if once they be checked. So do I count it folly trusting in them for our main strength to go up against Carcë. Also it is but a wild fancy that Goldry hath been transported into Carcë.''

But Spitfire leaped up a-cursing, and cried out, "O Gaslark, thou wert best fare home to Goblinland. But we will sail openly to Carcë and crave audience of the great King, entreating him suffer us to kiss his toe, and acknowledging him to be our King and us his ill-conditioned, disobedient children. So may he haply restore unto us our brother, when he hath chastised us, and haply of his mercy send us home to Demonland, there to fawn upon Corsus or vile Corinius, or whomsoever he shall set up in Galing for his Viceroy. For with Goldry hath all manliness departed out of Demonland, and we be milksops that remain, and objects of scorn and spitting.''

Now while Spitfire spake thus in wrath and sorrow of heart, the Lord Brandoch Daha fared fore and aft on the gangway about and about, as a caged panther fareth when feeding time is long overdue. And at whiles he clapped hand to the hilt of his long and glittering sword and rattled it in the scabbard. At length, standing over against Gaslark, and eyeing him with a mocking glance, "O Gaslark,'' he said, "this that hath befallen breedeth in me a cruel perturbation which carries my spirits outwards, stirring up a tempest in my mind and preparing my body to melancholy, and madness itself.[5] The cure of this is only fighting. Wherefore if thou love me, Gaslark, out with thy sword and ward thyself. Fight I must, or this passion will kill me quite out. 'Tis pity to draw upon my friend, but sith we be banned from fighting with our enemies, what choice remaineth?"

Gaslark laughed and seized him playfully by the arms, saying, "I will not fight with thee, how prettily soe'er thou ask it, Brandoch Daha, that savedst Goblinland from the Witches"; but straight grew grave again and said to Juss, "O Juss, be ruled. Thou seest what temper thy friends are in. All we be as hounds tugging against the leash to be loosed against Carcë in this happy hour, that likely cometh not again."

Now when Lord Juss perceived them all against him, and hot-mouthed for that attempt, he smiled scornfully and said, "O my brother and my friends, what echoes and quailpipes are you become who seem to catch wisdom by imitating her voice? But ye be mad like March hares, every man of you, and myself too. Break ice in one place, 'twill crack in more. And truly I care not greatly for my life now that Goldry is gone from me. Cast we lots, then, which of us three shall fare home to Demonland with this our ship, that is but a lame duck since this sending. And he on whom the lot shall fall must fare home to concert the raising of a mighty fleet and armament to carry on our war against the Witches."

So spake Lord Juss, and all they who had but a short hour ago felt themselves in such point that there was in them no hope of convalescence nor of life, had now their spirits raised in a seeming drunkenness, and thought only on the gladness of battle.

The lords of Demonland marked each his lot and cast it in the helm of Gaslark, and Gaslark shook the helm, and there leapt forth the lot of the Lord Spitfire. Right wrathful was he. So the lords of Demonland did off their armour and their costly apparel that was black with soot, and let cleanse it. Sixty of their fighting men that were unscathed by the sending went aboard one of Gaslark's ships, and the crew of that ship manned the ship of Demonland, and Spitfire took the steering paddle, and the Demons that were hurt lay in the hold of the hollow ship. They brought forth a spare sail and hoisted it in place of that that was destroyed; so in sore discontent, yet with a cheerful countenance, the Lord Spitfire set sail for the west. And Gaslark the king sat by the steering paddle of his fair dragon of war, and by him the Lord Juss and the Lord Brandoch Daha, who was like a war-horse impatient for battle. Her prow swung north and so round eastaway, and her sail broidered with flower-de-luces [6] smote the mast and filled to the northwest wind, and those other six fared after her in line ahead with white sails unfurled, striding majestic over the full broad billows.

VI

THE CLAWS OF WITCHLAND

*Of King Gaslark's leading in the attempt on
Carcë in the dark, and how he prospered therein,
and of the great stand of Lord Juss and Lord
Brandoch Daha.*

N the evening of the third day, whenas they drew near
to within sight of the Witchland coast, they brailed up[1]
their sails and waited for the night, that so they might
make the landfall after dark; for little to their mind it
was that the King should have news of their farings.
This was their plan, to beach their ships on the lonely shore some
two leagues north of Tenemos, whence it was but two hours' march
across the fen to Carcë. So when the sun set and all the ways were
darkened they muffled their oars and rowed silently to the low
shore that showed strangely near in the darkness, yet ever seemed
to flee and keep its distance as they rowed toward it. Coming at
length ashore, they drew their ships up on the beach. Some fifty
men of the Goblins they left to guard the ships, while the rest took
their weapons. And when they were marshalled they marched inland over the sanddunes and so on to the open fen; and seeing that
the most of them by far were of Goblinland, it was agreed between
those three, Juss, Brandoch Daha, and Gaslark, that Gaslark
should have command of this emprise. So fared they silently across
the marshes, that were firm enough for marching so it were done
circumspectly, rounding the worst moss-hags and the small lochs
that were scattered here and there. For the weather had been fine

for a season, and little new water stood on the marsh. But as they drew near to Carcë the weather worsened and fine rain began to fall. And albeit there was little comfort marching through the drizzling murk of night towards that fortress of evil name, yet was Lord Juss glad at the rain, since it favoured surprise, and on surprise hung all their hopes.

About the middle night they halted within four hundred paces of the outer walls of Carcë, that loomed ghostly through the watery curtain, silent as it had been a tomb where Witchland lay in death, rather than the mailed shell wherein so great a power sat waiting. The sight of that vast bulk couched shadowy in the rain lighted the fire of battle in the breast of Gaslark, nor would aught please him save that they should go forthwith up to the walls with all their force, and so march round them seeking where they might break suddenly in and seize the place. Nor would he listen to the counsel of Lord Juss, who would send forth detachments to select a spot for assault and bring back word before the whole force advanced. "Be sure," said Gaslark, "that they within are all foxed and cup-shotten[2] the third night with swilling of wine, in honour of such triumph as he hath gotten by his sending, and but a sorry watch is kept on such night. For who, say they, shall come up against Carcë now that the power of Demonland is stricken in pieces? The scorned Goblins, ha? A motion for laughter and derision. But thine advance guard might give them warning or ever our main force could seize the occasion. Nay, but as the Ghouls in an evil day coming suddenly upon me in Zajë Zaculo gat my palace taken ere we were well ware of their coming, so must we take this hold of Carcë. And if thou fearest a sally, right hotly do I desire it. For if they open the gate we are enough to force an entry in despite of any numbers they are like to have within."

Now Juss thought ill of this counsel, yet, for a strange languor that still hung about his wits, he would not gainsay Gaslark. So crept they in stealth near to the great walls of Carcë. Softly ever fell the rain, and breathless stood the cypresses within the outer ward, and blank and dumb and untenanted frowned the black marble walls of that sleeping castle. And dour midnight waited over all.

Now Gaslark issued command, bidding them march warily round the walls northward, for no way was betwixt the lofty walls and the river on the south and east, but to the north-east was he hopeful to find a likely place to win into the hold. In such order went they that Gaslark with an hundred of his ablest men led the van, and after him came the Demons. The main strength of the Goblins followed after, with Teshmar for their captain. Warily they

marched, and now were they on the rising ground that ran back
north and west from the bluff of Carcë to the fen. Full eager were
they of Goblinland and flown with the intoxication of impending
battle, and they of the vanguard fared apace, outstripping the
Demons, so that Juss was fain to hasten after them lest they should
lose touch and fall to confusion. But Teshmar's men feared greatly
to be left behind, nor might he hold them back, but they must run
betwixt the Demons and the walls, meaning to join with Gaslark.
Juss swore under his breath, saying, "See the unruly rabble of
Goblinland. And they will yet be our undoing."

In such case stood they, nor were Teshmar's folk more than
twenty paces from the walls, when, sudden as nightlightning, flares
were kindled along the walls, dazzling the Goblins and the Demons
and brightly lighting them for those that manned the walls, who
fell a-shooting at them with spears and arrows and a-slinging of
stones. In the same moment opened a postern gate, whence sallied
forth the Lord Corinius with an hundred and fifty stout lads of
Witchland, shouting, "He that would sup of the crab of Witchland
must deal with the nippers ere he essay the shell"; and charging
Gaslark's army in the flank he cut them clean in two. As one wood[3]
fared forth Corinius, smiting on either hand with a two-edged axe
with heft lapped with bronze; and greatly though the folk of Gaslark outnumbered him, yet were they so taken at unawares and
confounded by the sudden onslaught of Corinius that they might
not abide him but everywhere gave ground before his onslaught.
And many were wounded and some were slain; and with these
Teshmar of Goblinland, the master of Gaslark's ship. For smiting
at Corinius and missing of his aim he louted forward with the blow,
and Corinius hewed at him with his axe and the blow came on
Teshmar's neck and so hewed off his head. Now Gaslark with the
best of his fighting men was come some way past the postern, but
whenas they fell to fighting he turned back straightway to meet
Corinius, calling loudly on his men to rally against the Witches and
drive them back within the walls. So when Gaslark was gotten
through the press to within reach of Corinius, he thrust at Corinius
with a spear, wounding him in the arm. But Corinius smote the
spear-shaft asunder with his axe, and leapt upon Gaslark, giving
him a great wound on the shoulder. And Gaslark took to his sword,
and many blows they bandied that made either stagger, till
Corinius struck Gaslark on the helm a great down-stroke of his axe,
as one driveth a pile with a wooden mallet. And because of the
good helm he wore, given by Lord Juss in days gone by as a gift of
love and friendship, was Gaslark saved and his head not cloven

asunder; for on that helm Corinius's axe might not bite. Yet with that great stroke were Gaslark's senses driven forth of him for a season, so that he fell senseless to the earth. And with his fall came dismay upon them of Goblinland.

All this befell in the first brunt of the battle, nor were the lords of Demonland yet fully joined in the mellay,[4] for the great press of Gaslark's men were between them and the Witches; but now Juss and Brandoch Daha went forth mightily with their following, and took up Gaslark that lay like one dead, and Juss bade a company of the Goblins bear him to the ships, and there was he bestowed safe and sound. But the Witches shouted loudly that King Gaslark was slain; and at this chosen time Corund, that was come privily forth of a hidden door on the western side of Carcë with fifty men, took the Goblins mightily in the rear. So they, still falling back before Corinius and Corund, and their hearts sick at the supposed slaying of Gaslark, waxed full of doubt and dejection; for in the watery darkness they might nowise perceive by how much they outwent in numbers the men of Witchland. And panic took them, so that they broke and fled before the Witches, that came after them resolute, as a stoat[5] holdeth by a rabbit, and slew them by scores and by fifties as they fled from Carcë. Scarce three score men of that brave company of Goblinland that went up with Gaslark against Carcë won away into the marshes and came to their ships, escaping pitiless destruction.

But Corund and Corinius and their main force turned without more ado against the Demons, and bitter was the battle that befell betwixt them, and great the clatter of their blows. And now were the odds clean changed about with the putting of the Goblins out of the battle, since but few of Witchland were fallen, and they were as four to one against the Demons, hemming them in and having at them from every side. And some shot at them from the wall, until a chance shot came that was like to have stove in Corund's helm, who straightway sent word that when the rout was ended he would make lark-pies of the cow-headed doddipole whosoever he might be that had set them thus a-shooting, spoiling sport for their comrades and endangering their lives. Therewith ceased the shooting from the wall.

And now grim and woundsome grew the battle, for the Demons mightily withstood the onset of the Witches, and the Lord Brandoch Daha rushed with an onslaught ever and anon upon Corund or upon Corinius, nor might either of these great captains bear up long against him, but every time gave back before Lord Brandoch Daha; and bitterly cursed they one another as each in turn was fain to save himself amid the press of their fighting men. Nor could one hope in one night's space to behold such deeds of derring-do as were done that night by Lord Brandoch Daha, that played his sword lightly as one handleth a willow wand; yet death sat on the point thereof. In such wise that eleven stout sworders of Witchland were slain by him, and fifteen besides were sorely wounded. And at the last, Corinius, stung by Corund's taunts as by a gadfly, and well nigh bursting for grief and shame at his ill speeding, leapt upon Lord Brandoch Daha as one reft of his wits, aiming at him a great two-handed blow that was apt enough to cleave him to the brisket. But Brandoch Daha slipped from the blow lightly as a kingfisher flying above an alder-shadowed stream avoideth a branch in his flight, and ran Corinius through the right wrist with his sword. And straight was Corinius put out of the fight. Nor had they greater satisfaction that went against Lord Juss, who mowed at them with great swashing blows, beheading some and hewing some asunder in the midst, till they were fain to keep clear of his reaping. So fought the Demons in the glare and watery mist, greatly against great odds, until all were smitten to earth save those two lords alone, Juss and Brandoch Daha.

Now stood King Gorice on the outer battlements of Carcë, all armed in his black armour inlaid with gold; and he beheld those twain how they fought back to back, and how the Witches beset them on every side yet nowise might prevail against them. And the King said unto Gro that was by him on the wall, "Mine eyes dazzle[6] in the mist and torchlight. What be these that maintain so bloody an advantage upon my kemperie-men?"[7]

Gro answered him, "Surely, O King, these be none other than Lord Juss and Lord Brandoch Daha of Krothering."

The King said, "So by degrees cometh my sending home to me. For by my art I have intelligence, albeit not certainly, that Goldry was taken by my sending; so have I my desire on him I hold most in hate. And these, saved by their enchantments from like ruin, have been driven mad to rush into the open mouth of my vengeance." And when he had gazed awhile, the King sneered and said unto Gro, "A sweet sight, to behold an hundred of my ablest men flinch and duck before these twain. Till now methought there was a sword in Witchland, and methought Corinius and Corund not simple braggarts without power or heart, as here appeareth, since like boys well birched[8] they do cringe from the shining swords of Juss and the vile upstart from Krothering."

But Corinius, who stood no longer in the battle but by the King, full of spleen and his wrist all bloody, cried out, "You do us wrong, O King. Juster it were to praise my great deed in ambushing this mighty company of our enemies and putting them all to the slaughter. And if I prevailed not against this Brandoch Daha your majesty needs not to marvel, since a greater than I, Gorice X. of memory ever glorious, was lightly conquered by him. Wherin methinks I am the luckier, to have but a gored wrist and not my death. As for these twain, they be stickfrees, on whom no point or edge may bite. And nought were more to be looked for, since we deal with such a sorcerer as this Juss."

"Rather," said the King, "are ye all grown milksops. But I have no further stomach for this interlude, but straight will end it."

Therewith the King called to him the old Duke Corsus, bidding him take nets and catch the Demons therein. And Corsus, faring forth with nets, by sheer weight of numbers and with the death of near a score of the Witches at length gat this performed, and Lord Juss and Lord Brandoch Daha well tangled in the nets, and lapped about as silkworms in their cocoons, and so drawn into Carcë. Soundly were they bumped along the ground, and glad enow were the Witches to have gotten those great fighters scotched[9] at last. For utterly spent were Corund and his men, and fain to drop for very weariness.

So when they were gotten into Carcë, the King let search with torches and bring in them of Witchland that lay hurt before the walls; and any Demons or Goblins that were happed upon in like case he let slay with the sword. And the Lord Juss and the Lord Brandoch Daha, still lapped tightly in their nets, he let fling into a corner of the inner court of the palace like two bales of damaged goods, and set a guard upon them until morning.

As the lords of Witchland were upon going to bed they beheld westward by the sea a red glow, and tongues of fire burning in the night. Corinius said unto Lord Gro, "Lo where thy Goblins burn their ships, lest we pursue them as they flee shamefully homeward in the ship they keep from the burning. One ship sufficeth, for most of them be dead."

And Corinius betook him sleepily to bed, pausing on the way to kick at the Lord Brandoch Daha, that lay safely swathed in his net powerless as then to do him harm.

VII

GUESTS OF THE KING
IN CARCË

*Of the two banquet halls that were in Carcë, the
old and the new, and of the entertainment given
by King Gorice XII. in the one hall to Lord Juss
and Lord Brandoch Daha and in the other to the
Prince La Fireez; and of their leave-taking when
the banquet was done.*

HE morrow of that battle dawned fair on Carcë. Folk
lay long abed after their toil, and until the sun was
high nought stirred before the walls. But towards
noon came forth a band sent by King Gorice to bring
in the spoil; and they took up the bodies of the slain
and laid them in howe[1] on the right bank of the river Druima half a
mile below Carcë, Witches, Demons, and Goblins in one grave
together, and raised up a great howe over them.

Now was the sun's heat strong, but the shadow of the great
keep rested still on the terrace without the western wall of the
palace. Cool and redolent of ease and soft repose was that terrace,
paved with flagstones of red jasper, with spleenwort,[2] assafoetida,[3]
livid toadstools, dragons' teeth, and bitter moon-seed growing in
the joints. On the outer edge of the terrace were bushes of arbor
vitae[4] planted in a row, squat and round like sleeping dormice,
with clumps of choke-pard aconite[5] in the interspaces. Many hundred feet in length was the terrace from north to south, and at

71

either end a flight of black marble steps led down to the level of the
inner ward and its embattled wall.

Benches of green jasper massily built and laden with velvet
cushions of many colours stood against the palace wall facing to
the west, and on the bench nearest the Iron Tower a lady sat at
ease, eating cream wafers and a quince [6] tart served by her waiting-
women in dishes of pale gold for her morning meal. Tall was that
lady and slender, and beauty dwelt in her as the sunshine dwells in
the red floor and gray-green trunks of a beech wood in early
spring. Her tawny hair was gathered in deep folds upon her head
and made fast by great silver pins, their heads set with anachite
diamonds. Her gown was of cloth of silver with a knotted cord-
work of black silk embroidery everywhere decked with little moonstones, and over it she wore a mantle of figured satin the colour of
the woodpigeon's wing, tinselled[7] and overcast with silver threads.
White-skinned she was, and graceful as an antelope. Her eyes were
green, with yellow fiery gleams. Daintily she ate the tart and wafers,
sipping at whiles from a cup of amber, artificially carved, white
wine cool from the cellars below Carcë, and a maiden sitting at her
feet played on a seven-stringed lute, singing very sweetly this song:

> Aske me no more where Jove bestowes,
> When June is past, the fading rose;
> For in your beautie's orient deepe,
> These flowers, as in their causes, sleepe.
>
> Aske me no more whither do stray
> The golden atomes of the day;
> For in pure love heaven did prepare
> Those powders to enrich your haire.
>
> Aske me no more whither doth haste
> The nightingale when May is past;
> For in your sweet dividing throat
> She winters and keepes warme her note.
>
> Aske me no more where those starres alight,
> That downewards fall in dead of night;
> For in your eyes they sit, and there
> Fixed become as in their sphere.
>
> Aske me no more if east or west
> The Phoenix builds her spicy nest;
> For unto you at last shee flies,
> And in your fragrant bosome dyes.

"No more," said the lady; "thy voice is cracked this morning. Is none abroad yet thou canst find to tell me of last night's doings? Or are all gone my lord's gate,[8] that I left sleeping still as though all the poppies of all earth's gardens breathed drowsiness about his head?"

"One cometh, madam," said the damosel.

The lady said, "The Lord Gro. He may resolve me. Though were he in the stour last night, that were a wonder indeed."

Therewith came Gro along the terrace from the north, clad in a mantle of dun-coloured velvet with a collar of raised work of gold upon silver purl; [9] and his long black curly beard was perfumed with orange-flower water and angelica. When they had greeted one another and the lady had bidden her women stand apart, she said, "My lord, I thirst for tidings. Recount to me all that befell since sundown. For I slept soundly till the streaks of morning showed through my chamber windows, and then I awoke from a flying dream of sennets[10] sounding to the onset, and torches in the night, and war's alarums.[11] And there were torches indeed in my chamber lighting my lord to bed, that answered me no word but straightway fell asleep as in utter weariness. Some slight scratches he hath, but else unhurt. I would not wake him, for balm is in slumber; also is he ill to do with if one wake him so. But the tattle and wild surmise of the servants bloweth as ever to all points of wonder: as that a great armament of Demonland is disembarked at Tenemos, and all routed last night by my lord and by Corinius, and Goldry Bluszco slain in single combat with the King. Or that Juss hath set a charm on Laxus and all our fleet, making them sail like parricides against this land, Juss and the other Demons leading them; and all slain save Laxus and Goldry Bluszco, but these brought bound into Carcë, stark mad and frothing at the lips, and Corinius dead of his wounds after slaying of Brandoch Daha. Or, foolishly," and her green eyes lightened dangerously, "that it was my brother risen in revolt to wrest Pixyland from the overlordship of Gorice, and joined with Gaslark to that end, and their army overthrown and both ta'en prisoner."

Gro laughed and said, "Surely, O my Lady Prezmyra, truth masketh in many a strange disguise when she rideth rumour's broomstick through kings' palaces. But somewhat of herself hath she shown thee, if thou conclude that an event was brought to birth betwixt dark and sunrise to stagger the world, and that the power of Witchland bloomed forth this night into unbeholden glory."

"Thou speakest big, my lord," said the lady. "Were the Demons in it?"

"Ay, madam," he said.

"And triumphed on? and slain?"

"All slain save Juss and Brandoch Daha, and they taken," said Gro.

"Was this my lord's doing?" she asked.

"Greatly, as I think," said Gro; "though Corinius claimeth for himself, as commonly, the main honour of it."

Prezmyra said, "He claimeth overmuch." And she said, "There were none in it save Demons?"

Gro, knowing her thought, smiled and made answer, "Madam, there were Witches."

"My Lord Gro," she cried, "thou dost ill to mock me. Thou art my friend. Thou knowest the Prince my brother proud and sudden to anger. Thou knowest it chafeth him to have Witchland over him. Thou knowest the time is many days overpast when he should bring his yearly tribute to the King."

Gro's great ox-eyes were soft as he looked upon the Lady Prezmyra, saying, "Most assuredly am I thy friend, madam. Belike, if truth were told, thou and thy lord are all the true friends I have in waterish Witchland: you two, and the King: but who sleepeth safe in the favour of kings? Ah, madam, none of Pixyland stood in the battle yesternight. Therefore let thy soul be at ease. But my task it was, standing on the battlements beside the King, to smile and smile while Corinius and our fighting men made a bloody havoc of four or five hundred of mine own kinsfolk."

Prezmyra caught her breath and was silent a moment. Then, "Gaslark?"

"The main force was his, it appeareth," answered Lord Gro. "Corinius braggeth himself his banesman, and certain it is he felled him to earth. But I am secretly advertised he was not among the dead taken up this morning."

"My lord," she said, "my desire for news drinks deep while thou art fasting. Some, bring meat and wine for my Lord Gro." And two damosels ran and returned with sparkling golden wine in a beaker, and a dish of lampreys with hippocras[12] sauce. So Gro sat him down on the jasper bench and, while he ate and drank, rehearsed to the Lady Prezmyra the doings of the night.

When he had ended she said, "How hath the King dealt with those twain, Lord Juss and Lord Brandoch Daha?"

Gro answered, "He hath them clapped up in the old banqueting hall in the Iron Tower." And his brow darkened, and he said, " 'Tis pity thy lord lay thus long abed, and so came not to the council, where Corsus and Corinius, backed by thy step-sons and

the sons of Corsus, egged on the King to use shamefully these
lords of Demonland. True is that distich which admonisheth us—

> Know when to speak, for many times it brings
> Danger to give the best advice to Kings;

and little for my health, and little gain withal, had it been had I then
openly withstood them. Corinius is ever watchful to fling Goblin in
my teeth. But Corund weigheth in their councils as his hand
weigheth in battle.''

Now as Gro spake came the Lord Corund on the terrace,
calling for still wine to cool his throat withal. Prezmyra poured
forth to him: ''Thou art blamed to me for keeping thy bed, my lord,
that shouldst have been devising with the King touching our enemies ta'en captive in this night gone by.''

Corund sat by his lady on the bench and drank. ''If that be all,
madam,'' said he, ''then have I little to charge my conscience
withal. For nought lies readier than strike off their heads, and so
bring all to a fit and happy ending.''

''Far otherwise,'' said Gro, ''hath the King determined. He let
drag before him Lord Juss and Lord Brandoch Daha, and with
many fleers and jibes, 'Welcome,' he saith, 'to Carcë. Your table
shall not lack store of delicates while ye are my guests; albeit ye
come unbidden.' Therewith he let drag them to the old banquet
hall. And he bade his smiths drive great iron staples into the wall,
whereon he let hang up the Demons by their wrists, spread-eagled
against the wall, making both wrists and ankles fast to the staples
with gyves[13] of iron. And the King let dight[14] the table before their
feet as for a banquet, that the sight and the savour might torment
them. And he called all us to his council thither that we might
praise his conceit and mock them anew.''

Said Prezmyra, ''A great king should rather be a dog that
killeth clean, than a cat that patteth and sporteth with his prey.''

''True it is,'' said Corund, ''that they were safer slain.'' He rose
from his seat. '' 'Twere not amiss,'' he said, ''that I had word with
the King.''

''Wherefore so?'' asked Prezmyra.

''He that sleepeth late,'' said Corund, eyeing her humorously,
''sometimes hath news for her that riseth betimes to sit on the
western terrace. And this was I come to tell thee, that I but now
beheld eastward from our chamber window, riding toward Carcë
out of Pixyland down the Way of Kings——''

''La Fireez?'' she said.

"Mine eyes be strong enow and clear enow," said Corund, "but thou'dst scarce require me swear to mine own brother at three miles' distance. And as for thine, I leave thee the swearing."

"Who should ride down the Way of Kings from Pixyland," cried Prezmyra, "but La Fireez?"

"That, madam, let Echo answer thee," said Corund. "And it sticketh in my mind, that the Prince my brother-in-law is one that tieth to his heartstrings the remembrance of past benefits. This too, that none did him ever a greater benefit than Juss, that saved his life six winters back in Impland the More.[15] Wherefore, if La Fireez be to share our revels this night, needful it is that the King command these gabblers to keep silence touching our entertainment of these lords in the old banquet hall, and in general touching the share of Demonland in this fighting."

Prezmyra said, "Come, I'll go with thee."

They found the King on the topmost battlements above the water-gate with his lords about him, gazing eastaway toward the long low hills beyond which lay Pixyland. But when Corund began to open his mind to the King, the King said, "Thou growest old, O Corund, and like a good-for-nothing chapman bringest not thy wares to market ere the market be done. I have already ta'en order for this, and straitly charged my people that nought befell last night save a faring of the Goblins against Carcë, and their overthrow, and my chasing of them with a great slaughter into the sea. Whoso by speech or sign shall reveal to La Fireez that the Demons were in it, or that these enemies of mine are thus entertained by me to their discomfort in the old banquet hall, he shall lose nothing but his life."

Corund said, "It is well, O King."

The King said, "Captain general, what is our strength?"

Corinius answered, "Seventy and three were slain, and the others for the most part hurt: I among them, that am thus one-handed for the while. I will not engage to find you, O King, fifty sound men in Carcë."

"My Lord Corund," said the King, "thine eyes pierced ever a league beyond the best among us, young or old. How many makest thou yon company?"

Corund leaned on the parapet and shaded his eyes with his hand that was broad as a smoked haddock and covered on the back with yellow hairs growing somewhat sparsely, as the hairs on the skin of a young elephant. "He rideth with three score horse, O King. One or two more I give you for good luck, but if a have a horseman fewer than sixty, never love me more."

The King muttered an imprecation. "It is the curse of chance bringeth him thus pat when I have my powers abroad and am left with too little strength to awe him if he prove irksome. One of thy sons, O Corund, shall take horse and ride south to Zorn and Permio and muster a few score fighting men from the herdsmen and farmers with what speed he may. It is commanded."

Now was the afternoon wearing to evening when the Prince La Fireez was come in with all his company, and greetings done, and the tribute safe bestowed, and sleeping room appointed for him and his. And now ere all gathered together in the great banquet hall that was built by Gorice XI., when he was first made King, in the southeast corner of the palace; and it far exceeded in greatness and magnificence the old hall where Lord Juss and Lord Brandoch Daha were held in duress. Seven equal walls it had, of dark green jasper, specked with bloody spots. In the midst of one wall was the lofty doorway, and in the walls right and left of this and in those that inclosed the angle opposite the door were great windows placed high, giving light to the banquet hall. In each of the seven angles of the wall a caryatide,[16] cut in the likeness of a three-headed giant from ponderous blocks of black serpentine, bowed beneath the mass of a monstrous crab hewn out of the same stone. The mighty claws of those seven crabs spreading upwards bare up the dome of the roof, that was smooth and covered all over with paintings of battles and hunting scenes and wrastling bouts in dark and smoky colours answerable to the gloomy grandeur of that chamber. On the walls beneath the windows gleamed weapons of war and of the chase, and on the two blind walls were nailed up all orderly the skulls and dead bones of those champions which had wrastled aforetime with King Gorice XI. or ever he appointed in an evil hour to wrastle with Goldry Bluszco. Across the innermost angle facing the door was a long table and a carven bench behind it, and from the two ends of that table, set square with it, two other tables yet longer and benches by them on the sides next the wall stretched to within a short space of the door. Midmost of the table to the right of the door was a high seat of old cypress wood, great and fair, with cushions of black velvet broidered with gold, and facing it at the opposite table another high seat, smaller, and the cushions of it sewn with silver. In the space betwixt the tables five iron braziers, massive and footed with claws like an eagle's, stood in a row, and behind the benches on either side were nine great stands for flamboys to light the hall by night, and seven behind the cross bench, set at equal distances and even with the walls. The floor was paved with steatite, white and creamy, with veins of rich brown and black and purples and splashes of scarlet. The tables resting on great trestles were massy slabs of a dusky polished stone, powdered with sparks of gold as small as atoms.

The women sat on the cross-bench, and midmost of them the Lady Prezmyra, who outwent the rest in beauty and queenliness as Venus the lesser planets of the night. Zenambria, wife to Duke Corsus, sat on her left, and on her right Sriva, daughter to Corsus, strangely fair for such a father. On the upper bench, to the right of the door, the lords of Witchland sat above and below the King's high seat, clad in holiday attire, and they of Pixyland had place over against them on the lower bench. The high seat on the lower bench was set apart for La Fireez. Great plates and dishes of gold and silver and painted porcelain were set in order on the tables, laden with delicacies. Harps and bagpipes struck up a barbaric music,[17] and the guests rose to their feet, as the shining doors swung open and Gorice the King followed by the Prince his guest entered that hall.

Like a black eagle surveying earth from some high mountain the King passed by in his majesty. His byrny was of black chain mail, its collar, sleeves, and skirt edged with plates of dull gold set with hyacinths and black opals. His hose were black, cross-gartered with bands of sealskin trimmed with diamonds. On his left thumb was his great signet ring fashioned in gold in the semblance of the worm Ouroboros that eateth his own tail: the bezel of the ring the head of the worm, made of a peach-coloured ruby of the bigness of a sparrow's egg. His cloak was woven of the skins of black cobras stitched together with gold wire, its lining of black silk sprinkled with dust of gold. The iron crown of Witchland weighed on his brow, the claws of the crab erect like horns; and the sheen of its jewels was many-coloured like the rays of Sirius on a clear night of frost and wind at Yule-tide.

The Prince La Fireez went in a mantle of black sendaline sprinkled everywhere with spangles of gold, and the tunic beneath it of rich figured silk dyed deep purple of the Pasque flower.[18] From the golden circlet on his head two wings sprung aloft exquisitely fashioned in plates of beaten copper veneered with jewels and enamels and plated with precious metals to the semblance of the wings of the oleander hawk-moth.[19] He was something below the common height, but stout and strong and sturdily knit, with red crisp curly hair, broad-faced and ruddy, cleanshaved, with high wide-nostrilled nose and bushy red heavy eyebrows, whence his eyes, most like his lady sister's, sea-green and fiery, shot glances like a lion's.

When the King was come into his high seat, with Corund and Corinius on his left and right in honour of their great deeds of arms, and La Fireez facing him in the high seat on the lower bench, the thralls made haste to set forth dishes of pickled grigs[20] and oysters in the shell, and whilks,[21] snails, and cockles fried in olive oil and swimming in red and white hippocras. And the feasters delayed not to fall to on these dainties, while the cupbearer bore round a mighty bowl of beaten gold filled with sparkling wine the hue of the yellow sapphire, and furnished with six golden ladles resting their handles in six half-moon shaped nicks in the rim of that great bowl. Each guest when the bowl was brought to him must brim his goblet with the ladle, and drink unto the glory of Witchland and the rulers thereof.

Somewhat greenly looked Corinius on the Prince, and whispering Heming, Corund's son, in the ear, who sat next him, he said, "True it is that La Fireez is the showiest of men in all that belongeth to gear and costly array. Mark with what ridiculous excess he affecteth Demonland in the great store of jewels he flaunteth, and with what an apish insolence he sitteth at the board. Yet this lobcock liveth only by our sufferance, and I see a hath not forgot to bring with him to Witchland the price of our hand withheld from twisting of his neck."

Now were borne round dishes of carp, pilchards,[22] and lobsters, and thereafter store enow of meats: a fat kid roasted whole and garnished with peas on a spacious silver charger, kid pasties, plates of neats' tongues and sweetbreads, sucking rabbits in jellies, hedgehogs baked in their skins, hogs' haslets,[23] carbonadoes,[24] chitterlings,[25] and dormouse pies. These and other luscious meats were borne round continually by thralls who moved silent on bare feet; and merry waxed the talk as the edge of hunger became blunted a little, and the cockles of men's hearts were warmed with wine.

"What news in Witchland?" asked La Fireez.

"I have heard nought newer," said the King, "than the slaying of Gaslark." And the King recounted the battle in the night, setting forth as in a frank and open honesty every particular of numbers, times, and comings and goings; save that none might have guessed from his tale that any of Demonland had part or interest in that battle.

La Fireez said, "Strange it is that he should so attack you. An enemy might smell some cause behind it."

"Our greatness," said Corinius, looking haughtily at him, "is a lamp whereat other moths than he have been burnt. I count it no strange matter at all."

Prezmyra said, "Strange indeed, were it any but Gaslark. But sure with him no wild sudden fancy were too light but it should chariot him like thistle-down[26] to storm heaven itself."

"A bubble of the air, madam: all fine colours without and empty wind within. I have known other such," said Corinius, still resting his gaze with studied insolence on the Prince.

Prezmyra's eye danced. "O my Lord Corinius," said she, "change first thine own fashion, I pray thee, ere thou convince gay attire of inward folly, lest beholding thee we misdoubt thy precept —or thy wisdom."

Corinius drank his cup to the drains and laughed. Somewhat reddened was his insolent handsome face about the cheeks and shaven jowl, for surely was none in that hall more richly apparelled than he. His ample chest was cased in a jerkin[27] of untanned buckskin plated with silver scales, and he wore a collar of gold that was rough with smaragds and a long cloak of sky-blue silk brocade lined with cloth of silver. On his left wrist was a mighty ring of gold, and on his head a wreath of black bryony[28] and sleeping nightshade.[29] Gro whispered Corund in the ear, "He bibbeth it down apace, and the hour is yet early. This presageth trouble, since ever with him indiscretion treadeth hard on the heels of surliness as he waxeth drunken."

Corund grunted assent, saying aloud, "To all peaks of fame might Gaslark have climbed, but for this same rashness. Nought more pitiful hath been heard to tell of than his great sending into Impland, ten years ago, when, on a sudden conceit that a should lay all Impland under him and become the greatest king in all the world, he hired Zeldornius and Helteranius and Jalcanaius Fostus——"

"The three most notable captains found on earth," said La Fireez.

"Nothing is more true," said Corund. "These he hired, and brought 'em ships and soldiers and horses and such a clutter of engines of war as hath not been seen these hundred years, and sent 'em—whither? To the rich and pleasant lands of Beshtria? No. To Demonland? Not a whit. To this Witchland, where with a twentieth part the power a hath now risked all and suffered death and doom? No! but to yonder hell-besmitten wilderness of Upper Impland, treeless, waterless, not a soul to pay him tribute had he laid it under him save wandering bands of savage Imps, with more bugs on their bodies than pence in their purses, I warrant you. Or was he minded to be king among the divels of the air, ghosts, and hob-thrushes that be found in that desert?"

"Without controversy there be seventeen several sorts of divels on the Moruna," said Corsus, very loud and sudden, so that all turned to look on him; "fiery divels, divels of the air, terrestrial divels, as you may say, and watery divels, and subterranean divels. Without controversy there be seven seen sorts, seventeen several sorts of hob-thrushes, and several sorts of divels, and if the humour took me I could name them all by rote."

Wondrous solemn was the heavy face of Corsus, his eyes, baggy underneath and somewhat bloodshed, his pendulous cheeks, thick blubber upper-lip, and bristly gray moustachios and whiskers. He had eaten, mainly to provoke thirst, pickled olives, capers, salted almonds, anchovies, fumadoes,[30] and pilchards fried with mustard, and now awaited the salt chine[31] of beef to be a pillow and a resting place for new potations.[32]

The Lady Zenambria asked, "Knoweth any for certain what fate befell Jalcanaius and Helteranius and Zeldornius and their armies?"

"Heard I not," said Prezmyra, "that they were led by Will-o'-the-Wisps to the regions Hyperborean,[33] and there made kings?"

"Told thee by the madge-howlet,[34] I fear me, sister," said La Fireez. "Whenas I fared through Impland the More, six years ago, there was many a wild tale told me hereof, but nought within credit."

Now was the chine served in amid shallots on a great dish of gold, borne by four serving men, so weighty was the dish and its burden. Some light there glowed in the dull eye of Corsus to see it come, and Corund rose up with brimming goblet, and the Witches cried, "The song of the chine, O Corund!" Great as a neat stood Corund in his russet velvet kirtle, girt about with a broad belt of crocodile hide edged with gold. From his shoulders hung a cloak of wolf's skin with the hair inside, the outside tanned and diapered with purple silk. Daylight was nigh gone, and through a haze of savours rising from the feast the flamboys shone on his bald head set about with thick grizzled curls, and on his keen gray eyes, and his long and bushy beard. He cried, "Give me a rouse, my lords! and if any fail to bear me out in the refrain, I'll ne'er love him more." And he sang this song of the chine in a voice like the sounding of a gong; and all they roared in the refrain till the piled dishes on the service tables rang:

Bring out the Old Chyne, the Cold Chyne to me,
And how Ile charge him come and see,
Brawn[35] tusked, Brawn well sowst[36] and fine,
With a precious cup of Muscadine:

> *How shall I sing, how shall I look,*
> *In honour of the Master-Cook?*

The Pig shall turn round and answer me,
Canst thou spare me a shoulder? a wy, a wy.
The Duck, Goose, and Capon, good fellows all three,
Shall dance thee an antick, so shall the Turkey:
But O! the Cold Chyne, the Cold Chyne for me:

> *How shall I sing, how shall I look,*
> *In honour of the Master-Cook?*

With brewis Ile noynt[37] thee from head to th' heel,
Shal make thee run nimbler than the new oyld wheel;
With Pye-crust wee'l make thee
The eighth wise man to be;
But O! the Old Chyne, the Cold Chyne for me:

> *How shall I sing, how shall I look,*
> *In honour of the Master-Cook?*

When the chine was carved and the cups replenished, the King issued command saying, "Call hither my dwarf, and let him act his antick gestures before us."

Therewith came the dwarf into the hall, mopping and mowing, clad in a sleeveless jerkin of striped yellow and red mockado.[38] And his long and nerveless tail dragged on the floor behind him.

"Somewhat fulsome is this dwarf," said La Fireez.

"Speak within door, Prince," said Corinius. "Know'st not his quality? A hath been envoy extraordinary from King Gorice XI. of memory ever glorious unto Lord Juss in Galing and the lords of Demonland. And 'twas the greatest courtesy we could study to do them, to send 'em this looby for our ambassador."

The dwarf practised before them to the great content of the lords of Witchland and their guests, save for his japing upon Corinius and the Prince, calling them two peacocks, so like in their bright plumage that none might tell either from other; which somewhat galled them both.

And now was the King's heart waxen glad with wine, and he pledged Gro, saying, "Be merry, Gro, and doubt not that I will fulfil my word I spake unto thee, and make thee king in Zajë Zaculo."

"Lord, I am yours for ever," answered Gro. "But methinks I am little fitted to be a king. Methinks I was ever a better steward of other men's fortunes than of mine own."

Whereat the Duke Corsus, that was sprawled on the table well nigh asleep, cried out in a great voice but husky withal, "A brace of divels broil me if thou sayest not sooth! If thine own fortunes come off but bluely, care not a rush. Give me some wine, a full weeping goblet. Ha! Ha! whip i' away! Ha! Ha! Witchland! When wear you the crown of Demonland, O King?"

"How now, Corsus," said the King, "art thou drunk?"

But La Fireez said, "Ye sware peace with the Demons in the Foliot Isles, and by mighty oaths are ye bound to put by for ever your claims of lordship over Demonland. I hoped your quarrels were ended."

"Why so they are," said the King.

Corsus chuckled weakly. "Ye say well: very well, O King, very well, La Fireez. Our quarrels are ended. No room for more. For, look you, Demonland is a ripe fruit ready to drop me thus in our mouth." Leaning back he gaped his mouth wide open, suspending by one leg above it an hortolan[39] basted with its own dripping. The bird slipped through his fingers, and fell against his cheek, and so on to his bosom, and so on the floor, and his brazen byrny and the sleeves of his pale green kirtle were splashed with the gravy.

Whereat Corinius let fly a great peal of laughter; but La Fireez flushed with anger and said, scowling, "Drunkenness, my lord, is a jest for thralls to laugh at."

"Then sit thou mum, Prince," said Corinius, "lest thy quality be called in question. For my part I laugh at my thoughts, and they be very choice."

But Corsus wiped his face and fell a-singing:

> Whene'er I bib the wine down,
>   Asleepe drop all my cares.
>   A fig for fret,
>   A fig for sweat,
>
>   A fig care I for cares.
>   Sith death must come, though I say nay,
>   Why grieve my life's days with affaires?

> Come, bib we then the wine down
> Of Bacchus faire to see;
> For alway while we bibbing be,
> Asleepe drop all our cares.

With that, Corsus sank heavily forward again on the table. And the dwarf, whose japes all else in that company had taken well even when themselves were the mark thereof, leaped up and down, crying, "Hear a wonder! This pudding singeth. When with two platters, thralls! ye have served it o' the board without a dish. One were too little to contain so vast a deal of bullock's blood and lard. Swift, and carve it ere the vapours burst the skin."

"I will carve thee, filth," said Corsus, lurching to his feet; and catching the dwarf by the wrist with one hand he gave him a great box on the ear with the other. The dwarf squealed and bit Corsus's thumb to the bone, so that he loosed his hold; and the dwarf fled from the hall, while the company laughed pleasantly.

"So flieth folly before wisdom which is in wine," said the King. "The night is young: bring me botargoes,[40] and caviare and toast. Drink, Prince. The red Thramnian wine that is thick like honey wooeth the soul to divine philosophy. How vain a thing is ambition. This was Gaslark's bane, whose enterprises of such pitch and moment have ended thus, in a kind of nothing. [41] Or what thinkest thou, Gro, thou which art a philosopher?"

"Alas, poor Gaslark," said Gro. "Had all grown to his mind, and had he 'gainst all expectation gotten us overthrown, even so had he been no nearer to his heart's desire than when he first set forth. For he had of old in Zajë Zaculo eating and drinking and gardens and treasure and musicians and a fair wife, all soft ease and contentment all his days. And at the last, howsoe'er we shape our course, cometh the poppy that abideth all of us by the harbour of oblivion hard to cleanse. Dry withered leaves of laurel or of cypress tree, and a little dust. Nought else remaineth."

"With a sad brow I say it," said the King: "I hold him wise that resteth happy, even as the Red Foliot, and tempteth not the Gods by over-mounting ambition to his dejection."

La Fireez had thrown himself back in his high seat with his elbows resting on its lofty arms and his hands dangling idly on either side. With head held high and incredulous smile he harkened to the words of Gorice the King.

Gro said in Corund's ear, "The King hath found strange kindness in the cup."

"I think thou and I be clean out o' fashion," answered

Corund, whispering, "that we be not yet drunken; the cause whereof is that thou drinkest within measure, which is good, and me this amethyst at my belt keepeth sober, were I never so surfeit-swelled with wine."

La Fireez said, "You are pleased to jest, O King. For my part, I had as lief have this musk-million on my shoulders as a head so blockish as to want ambition."

"If thou wert not our princely guest," said Corinius, "I had called that spoke in the right fashion of a little man. Witchland affecteth not such vaunts, but can afford to speak as our Lord the King in proud humility. Turkey cocks do strut and gobble; not so the eagle, who holdeth the world at his discretion."

"Pity on thee," cried the Prince, "if this cheap victory turn thee so giddy. Goblins!"

Corinius scowled. Corsus chuckled, saying to himself but loud enough for all to hear, "Goblins, quotha? They were small game had they been all. Ay, there it is: had they been all."

The King's brow was like a foul black cloud. The women held their breath. But Corsus, blandly insensible of these gathering thunders, beat time on the table with his cup, drowsily chanting to a most mournful air:

> When birds in water deepe do lie,
> And fishes in the air doe flie,
> When water burns and fire doth freeze,
> And oysters grow as fruits on trees—

A resounding hecup brought him to a full close.

The talk had died down, the lords of Witchland, ill at ease, studying to wear their faces to the bent of the King's looks. But Prezmyra spake, and the music of her voice came like a refreshing shower. "This song of my Lord Corsus," she said, "made me hopeful for an answer to a question in philosophy; but Bacchus, you see, hath ta'en his soul into Elysium for a season, and I fear me nor truth nor wisdom cometh from his mouth to-night. And this was my question, whether it be true that all animals of the land are in their kind in the sea? My Lord Corinius, or thou, my princely brother, can you resolve me?"

"Why, so it is received, madam," said La Fireez. "And inquiry will show thee many pretty instances: as the sea-frog, the sea-fox, the sea-dog, the sea-horse, the sea-lion, the sea-bear. And I have known the barbarous people of Esamocia eat of a conserve of sea-mice mashed and brayed in a mortar with the flesh of that beast named *bos marinus,* seasoned with salt and garlic."

"Foh! speak to me somewhat quickly," cried the Lady Sriva, "ere in imagination I taste such nasty meat. Prithee, yonder gold peaches and raisins of the sun as an antidote."

"Lord Gro will instruct thee better than I," said La Fireez. "For my part, albeit I think nobly of philosophy, yet have I little leisure to study it. Oft have I hunted the badger, yet never answered that question of the doctors whether he hath the legs of one side shorter than of the other. Neither know I, for all the lampreys I have eat, how many eyes the lamprey hath, whether it be nine or two."

Prezmyra smiled: "O my brother, thou art too too smoored,[42] I fear me, in the dust of action and the field to be at accord with these nice searchings. But be there birds under the sea, my Lord Gro?"

Gro made answer, "In rivers, certainly, though it be but birds of the air sojourning for a season. As I myself have found them in Outer Impland, asleep in winter time at the bottom of lakes and rivers, two together, mouth to mouth, wing to wing. But in the spring they revive again, and by and by are the woods full of their singing. And for the sea, there be true sea-cuckows, sea-thrushes, and sea-sparrows, and many more."

"It is passing strange," said Zenambria.

Corsus sang:

> When sorcerers do leave their charme,
> When spiders do the fly no harme.

Prezmyra turned to Corund saying, "Was there not a merry dispute betwixt you, my lord, concerning the toad and the spider,[43] thou maintaining that they do poisonously destroy one another, and my Lord Gro that he would show thee to the contrary?"

" 'Twas even so, lady," said Corund, "and it is yet in controversy."

Corsus sang:

> And when the blackbird leaves to sing,
> And likewise serpents for to sting,
>   Then you may saye, and justly too,
>   The old world now is turned anew:

and so sank back into bloated silence.

"My Lord the King," cried Prezmyra, "I beseech you give order for the ending of this difference between two of your council, ere it wax to dangerous heat. Let them be given a toad, O King, and spiders without delay, that they may make experiment before this goodly company."

Therewith all fell a-laughing, and the King commanded a thrall, who shortly brought fat spiders to the number of seven and a crystal wine-cup, and inclosed with them beneath the cup a toad, and set all before the King. And all beheld them eagerly.

"I will wager two firkins of pale Permian wine to a bunch of radishes," said Corund, "that victory shall be given unto the spiders. Behold how without resistance they do sit upon his head and pass all over his body."

Gro said, "Done."

"Thou wilt lose the wager, Corund," said the King. "This toad taketh no hurt from the spiders, but sitteth quiet out of policy, tempting them to security, that upon advantage he may swallow them down."

While they watched, fruits were borne in: queen-apples, almonds, pomegranates and pistick nuts;[44] and fresh bowls and jars of wine, and among them a crystal flagon of the peach-coloured wine of Krothering vintaged many summers ago in the vineyards that stretch southward toward the sea from below the castle of Lord Brandoch Daha.

Corinius drank deep, and cried, " 'Tis a royal drink, this wine of Krothering! Folk say it will be good cheap this summer."

Whereat La Fireez shot a glance at him, and the King marking it said in Corinius's ear, "Wilt thou be prudent? Let not thy pride flatter thee to think aught shall avail thee, any more than my vilest thrall, if by thy doing this Prince smell out my secrets."

By then was the hour waxing late, and the women took their leave, lighted to the doors in great state by thralls with flamboys. In a while, when they were gone. "A plague of all spiders!" cried Corund. "Thy toad hath swallowed one already."

"Two more!" said Gro. "Thy theoric crumbleth apace,[45] O Corund. He hath two at a gulp, and but four remain."

The Lord Corinius, whose countenance was now aflame with furious drinking, held high his cup and catching the Prince's eye, "Mark well, La Fireez," he cried, "a sign and a prophecy. First one; next two at a mouthful; and early after that, as I think, the four that remain. Art not afeared lest thou be found a spider when the brunt shall come?"

"Hast drunk thyself horn-mad,[46] Corinius?" said the King under his breath, his voice shaken with anger.

"He is as witty a marmalade-eater as ever I conversed with," said La Fireez, "but I cannot tell what the dickens he means."

"That," answered Corinius, "which should make thy smirking face turn serious. I mean our ancient enemies, the haskardly[47] mongrels of Demonland. First gulp, Goldry, taken heaven knows whither by the King's sending in a deadly scud of wind[48]——"

"The devil damn thee!" cried the King, "what drunken brabble is this?"

But the Prince La Fireez waxed red as blood, saying, "This it is then that lieth behind this hudder mudder, and ye go to war with Demonland? Think not to have my help therein."

"We shall not sleep the worse for that," said Corinius. "Our mouth is big enough for such a morsel of marchpane[49] as thou, if thou turn irksome."

"Thy mouth is big enough to blab the secretest intelligence, as we now most laughably approve," said La Fireez. "Were I the King, I would draw lobster's whiskers on thy skin, for a tipsy and a prattling popinjay."[50]

"An insult!" cried the Lord Corinius, leaping up. "I would not take an insult from the Gods in heaven. Reach me a sword, boy! I will make Beshtrian cutworks in his guts."[51]

"Peace, on your lives!" said the King in a great voice, while Corund went to Corinius and Gro to the Prince to quiet them. "Corinius is wounded in the wrist and cannot fight, and belike his brain is fevered by the wound."

"Heal him, then, of this carving the Goblins gave him, and I will carve him like a capon,"[52] said the Prince.

"Goblins!" said Corinius fiercely. "Know, vile fellow, the best swordsman in the world gave me this wound. Had it been thou that stood before me, I had cut thee into steaks, that art caponed already."

But the King stood up in his majesty, saying, "Silence, on your lives!" And the King's eyes glittered with wrath, and he said, "For thee, Corinius, not thy hot youth and rebellious blood nor yet the wine thou hast swilled into that greedy belly of thine shall mitigate the rigour of my displeasure. Thy punishment I reserve unto to-morrow. And thou, La Fireez, look thou bear thyself more humbly in my halls. Over pert was the message brought me by thine herald at thy coming hither this morning, and too much it smacked of a greeting from an equal to an equal, calling thy tribute a gift, though it, and thou, and all thy principality are mine by right to deal with as seems me good. Yet did I bear with thee: unwisely, as I think, since thy pertness nourished by my forbearance springeth up yet ranker at my table, and thou insultest and brawlest in my halls. Be advised, lest my wrath forge thunderbolts against thee."

The Prince La Fireez answered and said, "Keep frowns and threats for thine offending thralls, O King, since me they affright not, and I laugh them to scorn. Nor am I careful to answer thine injurious words; since well thou knowest my old friendship unto thine house, O King, and unto Witchland, and by what bands of marriage I am bound in love to the Lord Corund, to whom I gave my lady sister. If it suit not my stomach to proclaim like a servile minister thy suzerainty, yet needest thou not to carp at this, since thy tribute is paid thee, ay, and in over-measure. But unto Demonland am I bound, as all the world knoweth, and sooner shalt thou prevail upon the lamps of heaven to come down and fight for thee against the Demons than upon me. And unto Corinius that so boasteth I say that Demonland hath ever been too hard for you Witches. Goldry Bluszco and Brandoch Daha have shown you this. This is my counsel unto thee, O King, to make peace with Demonland: my reasons, first that thou hast no just cause of quarrel with them, next (and this should sway thee more) that if thou persist in fighting against them it will be the ruin of thee and of all Witchland."

The King bit his fingers with signs of wonderful anger, and for a minute's time no sound was in that hall. Only Corund spake privately to the King saying, "Lord, O for all sakes swallow your royal rage. You may whip him when my son Hacmon returneth, but till then he outnumbers us, and your own party so overwhelmed with wine that, trust me, I would not adventure the price of a turnip on our chances if it come to fighting."

Troubled at heart was Corund, for well he knew how dear beyond account his lady wife held the keeping of the peace betwixt La Fireez and the Witches.

In this moment Corsus, somewhat roused in an evil hour out of lethargy by the loud talk and movement, began to sing:

> When all the prisons hereabout
> Have justled all their prisoners out,
> Because indeed they have no cause
> To keepe 'em in by common laws.

Whereat Corinius, in whom wine and quarrelling and the King's rebukes had lighted a fire of reckless and outrageous malice before which all counsels of prudence or policy were dissipated like wax in a furnace, shouted loudly, "Wilt see our prisoners, Prince, i' the old banquet hall, to prove thyself an ass?"

"What prisoners?" cried the Prince, springing to his feet. "Hell's furies! I am weary of these dark equivocations and will know the truth."

"Why wilt thou rage so beastly?" said the King. "The man is drunk. No more wild words."

"Thou canst not daff me so. I will know the truth," said La Fireez.

"So thou shalt," said Corinius. "This it is, that we Witches be better men than thou and thy hen-hearted Pixies, and better men than the accursed Demons. No need to hide it further. Two of that brood we have laid by the heels, and nailed 'em up on the wall of the old banquet hall, as farmers nail up weasels and polecats on a barn door. And there shall they bide till they be dead: Juss and Brandoch Daha."

"O most villanous lie!" said the King. "I'll have thee hewn in pieces."

But Corinius said, "I nurse your honour, O King. We must no longer skulk before these Pixies."

"Thou diest for it," said the King, "and it is a lie."

Now was dead silence for a space. At last the Prince sat down slowly. His face was white and drawn, and he spake unto the King, slowly and in a quiet voice: "O King, that I was somewhat hot with you, forgive me. And if I have omitted any form of allegiance due to you, think rather that in my blood it is to chafe at such ceremonies than that I had any lack of friendship unto you or ever dreamed of questioning your over-lordship. Aught that you shall require of me and that lieth with mine honour, aught of ceremony or fealty, will I with joy perform. And, save against Demonland, is my sword ready against your enemies. But here, O King, tottereth a tower ready to fall athwart our friendship and pash it in pieces. It is known to you, O King, and to all the lords of Witchland, that my bones were whitening these six years in Impland the More if Lord Juss had not saved me from the barbarous Imps that followed Fax Fay Faz, who besieged me four months with my small following shut up in Lida Nanguna. My friendship shall you have, O King, if you yield me up my friends."

But the King said, "I have not thy friends."

"Show me then the old banquet hall," said the Prince.

The King said, "I will show it thee anon."

"I will see it now," said the Prince, and he rose from his seat.

"I will dissemble with thee no longer," said the King. "I do love thee well. But when thou askest me to yield up to thee Juss and Brandoch Daha, thou askest a thing all Pixyland and thy dear heart's blood were unable to purchase from me. These be my worst enemies. Thou knowest not at what cost of toil and danger I have at last laid hand on them. And now let not thy hopes make thee an unbeliever, when I swear to thee that Juss and Brandoch Daha shall rot and die in prison."

And for all his gentle speeches, and offers of wealth and rich advantage and upholding in peace and war, might not La Fireez shake the King. And the King said, "Forbear, La Fireez, or thou wilt vex me. They must rot."

So when the Prince La Fireez saw that he might not move the King by soft words, he took up his fair crystal goblet, egg-shaped with three claws of gold to stand withal welded to a collar of gold about its middle bossed with topazes, and hurled it at Gorice the King, so that the goblet smote him on the forehead, and the crystal was brast asunder with the force of the blow, and the King's forehead laid open, and the King strook senseless.

Therewith was huge uproar in the banquet hall; nor would Corund that any should have speedier hand therein than he, but catching up his two-edged sword and crying, "Look to the King, Gro! Here's distressful revels!" he leaped upon the table. And his sons likewise and Gallandus and the other Witches seized their weapons, and in like manner did La Fireez and his men; and there was battle in the great hall in Carcë. Corinius, whose left hand only might as now wield weapon, even so sprang forth in most gallant wise, calling upon the Prince with many vile words to abide his onset. But the fumes of unbridled potations, that being flown to his brain had made him frantic mad, wrought in his legs more foggily, dulling their wonted nimbleness. And his foot sliding in a puddle of spilt wine he fell backward a grievous fall, striking his head against the polished table. And Corsus that was now well nigh speechless and quite stupefied with drink, so that a baby might tell as well as he what meant this hubbub, reeled cup in hand, shouting, "Drunkenness is better for the body than physic! Drink always, and you shall never die!" So shouting he was smitten square in the mouth by a breast of veal flung at him by Elaron of Pixyland, the captain of the Prince's bodyguard, and so fell like a hog athwart Corinius, and there lay without sense or motion. Then were the tables overset, and wounds given and taken, and swiftly ran the tide of vantage against the Witches. For albeit the Pixies were none such great soldiers as they of Witchland, yet this served them mightily that they were well nigh sober and their foes as so many casks filled with wine, staggering and raving for the most part from their long tippling and quaffing. Nor did Corund's amethyst avail him throughly, but the wine clogged his veins so that he waxed scant of breath and his strokes lighter and slower than they were wont.

Now for the love he bare his sister Prezmyra and for his old kindness sake for Witchland, the Prince charged his men to fight only for the overpowering of the Witches, slaying none if so it might be, and on their lives to look to it that the Lord Corund took no hurt. And when they had fairly gotten the mastery, La Fireez made certain of his folk take jars of wine and therewith souse Corund and his men most lustily in the face, while others held them at weapon's point, until by the power of the wine both within and without they were well brought under. And they barricaded the great doorway of the hall with the benches and table tops and heavy oaken trestles, and La Fireez charged Elaron hold the door with the most of his following, and set guards without each window that none might come forth from the hall.

But the Prince himself took flamboys[53] and went six in company to the old banquet hall, overpowered the guard, brake open the doors, and so stood before Lord Juss and Lord Brandoch Daha that hung shackled to the wall side by side. Something dazzled they were in the sudden torch-light, but Lord Brandoch Daha spake and hailed the Prince, and his mocking haughty lazy accents were scarcely touched with hollowness, for all his hunger-starving and long watching and the cark[54] and care of his affliction. "La Fireez!" he said. "Day ne'er broke up till now.[55] And methought ye were yonder false fitchews [56] fostered in filth and fen, the spawn of Witchland, returned again to fleer[57] and flout at us."

La Fireez told them how things had gone, and he said, "Occasion gallopeth apace. Upon this bargain do I loose you, that ye come incontinently with me out of Carcë, and seek no revenge to-night upon the Witches."

Juss said yea to this; and Brandoch Daha laughed, saying, "Prince, I so love thee, I could refuse thee nothing, were it shave half my beard and go in fustian till harvest-time, sleep in my clothes, and discourse pious nothings seven hours a day with my lady's lap-dog. This night we be utterly thine. An instant only bear with us: this fare shows too good to rest untasted after so much looking on. It were discourteous too to leave it so." Therewith, their chains being now stricken off, he eat a great slice of turkey and three quails boned and served in jelly, and Juss a dozen plovers' eggs and a cold partridge. Lord Brandoch Daha said, "I prithee break the egg-shells, Juss, when the meat is out, lest some sorcerer should prick or write thy name thereon, and so mischief thy person." And pouring out a stoup of wine, he quaffed it off, and filling it again, "Perdition catch me if it be not mine own wine of Krothering! Saw any a carefuller host than King Gorice?" And he pledged Lord Juss in the second cup, saying, "I will drink with thee next in Carcë when the King of Witchland and all the lords thereof are slain."

Thereafter they took their weapons that lay by on the table, set there to distress their souls and with little expectation they should so take them up again; and glad at heart albeit somewhat stiff of limb they went forth with La Fireez from that banquet hall.

When they were come into the court-yard Juss spake and said, "Herein might honour hold us back even hadst thou made no bargain with us, La Fireez. For great shame it were to us and we fell upon the lords of Witchland when they were drunk and unable to meet us in equal battle. But let us ere we be gone from Carcë ransack this hold for my kinsman Goldry Bluszco, since for his sake only and in hope to find him here we fared on this journey."

"So you touch no other thing but only Goldry if ye shall find him, I am content," said the Prince.

So when they had found keys they ransacked all Carcë, even to the dread chamber where the King had conjured and the vaults and cellars below the river. But it availed not.

And as they stood in the court-yard in the torchlight there came forth on a balcony the Lady Prezmyra in her nightgown, disturbed by this ransacking. Ethereal as a cloud she seemed, pavilioned in the balmy night, as a cloud touched by the exhalations of the unrisen moon. "What transformation is this?" said she. "Demons loose in the court?"

"Content thee, dear heart," said the Prince. "Thy man is safe, and all else beside as I think; save that the King hath a broken head, the which I lament, and will without question soon be healed. They lie all in the banquet hall to-night, being too sleepy-sodden with the feast to take their chambers."

Prezmyra cried, "My fears are fallen upon me. Art thou broken with Witchland?"

"That may I not forejudge," he answered. "Tell them to-morrow that nought I did in hatred, and nought but what I was by circumstance enforced to. For I am not such a coward nor so great a villain as leave my friends caged up while strength is left me to work for their setting free."

"You must straightway forth from Carcë," said Prezmyra, "and that o' the instant. My step-son Hacmon, which was sent to gather strength to awe thee if need were, rideth by now from the south with a great company. Thy horses are fresh, and ye may well outdistance the

King's men if they ride after you. If thou wilt not yet raise up a river of blood betwixt us, begone."

"Why fare thee well, then, sister. And doubt it not, these rifts 'tween me and Witchland shall soon be patched up and forgot." So spake the Prince with a merry voice, yet grieved at heart. For well he weened the King should never pardon him that blow, nor his robbing him of his prey.

But she said, sadly, "Farewell, my brother. And my heart tells me I shall never see thee more. When thou took'st these from prison, thou didst dig up two mandrakes shall bring sorrow and death[58] to thee and to me and to all Witchland."

The Prince was silent, but Lord Juss bowed to Prezmyra saying, "Madam, these things be on the knees of Fate. But imagine not that while life and breath be in us we shall leave to uphold the Prince thy brother. His foes be our foes for this night sake."

"Thou swearest it?" she said.

He answered, "Madam, I swear it unto thee and unto him."

The Lady Prezmyra withdrew sadly to her chamber. And in short space she heard their horse-hooves on the bridge, and looking forth beheld where they galloped on the Way of Kings dim in the coppery light of a waning moon rising over Pixyland. So sate she by the window of Corund's lofty bed-chamber gazing through the night, long after her brother and the lords of Demonland and her brother's men were ridden beyond her seeing, long after their last hoof-beat had ceased to echo on the road. In a while fresh horse-hooves sounded from the south, and a noise as of many riding in company; and she knew it was young Hacmon back from Permio.

VIII

THE FIRST EXPEDITION
TO IMPLAND

*Of the home-coming of the Demons, and how
Lord Juss was taught in a dream whither he must
seek for tidings of his dear brother, and how they
took counsel at Krothering, and determined of
their expedition to Impland.*

IDSUMMER night, ambrosial, starry-kirtled, walked
on the sea, as the ship that brought the Demons home
drew nigh to her journey's end. The cloaks of Lord
Juss and Lord Brandoch Daha, who slept on the poop,
were wet with dew. Smoothly they had passage
through that charmed night, where winds were hushed asleep and
nought was heard save the waves talking beneath the bows of the
ship, the lilting changeless song of the steersman, and the creak,
dip, and swash of oars keeping time to his singing. Vega burned
like a sapphire near the zenith, and Arcturus low in the north-west,
beaconing over Demonland. In the remote south-east Fomalhaut
rose from the sea, a lonely splendour in the dim region of Capri-
corn and the Fishes.

So rowed they till day broke, and a light wind sprang up fresh
and keen. Juss waked, and stood up to scan the gray glassy surface
of the sea spread to vast distances where sky and water faded into
one. Astern, great clouds bridged the gates of day, boiling upwards into crags of wine-dark vapour and burning plumes of sun-

rise. In the stainless spaces of the sky above these sailed the horned moon, frail and wan as a white foam-flower blown from the waves.[1] Westward, facing the thunder-smoke of dawn, the fine far ridge of Kartadza was like cut crystal against the sky: the first island sentinel of many-mountained Demonland, his topmost cliffs dawn-illumined with pale gold and amethyst while yet the lesser heights lay obscure, lapped in the folds of night. And with the opening day the mists swathing the mountain's skirts were lifted up in billowy masses that grew and shrank and grew again, made restless by the wayward winds which morning waked in the hollow mountain side, and torn by them into wisps and streamers. Some were blown upward, steaming up the great gullies in the rocks below the peak, while now and then a puff of cloud swam free for a minute, floated a minute's space as ready to sail skyward, then indolently stooped again to the mountain wall to veil it in an unsubstantial fleece of golden vapour. And now all the western seaboard of Demonland lay clear to view, stretching fifty miles and more from Northhouse Skerries past the Drakeholms and the low downs of Kestawick and Byland, beyond which tower the mountains of the Scarf, past the jagged sky-line of the Thornbacks and the far Neverdale peaks overhanging the wooded shores of Onwardlithe and Lower Tivarandardale, to the extreme southern headland, filmy-pale in the distance, where the great range of Rimon Armon plunges its last wild bastion in the sea.

As a lover gazing on his mistress, so gazed Lord Juss on Demonland rising from the sea. No word spake he till they came off Lookinghaven-ness and could see where beyond the beaked promontory the sound opened between Kartadza and the mainland. Albeit the outer sea was calm, the air in the sound was thick with spray from the churning of the waters among the reefs and swallowing shoals. For the tide ran like a mill-race through that sound, and the roaring of it was plain to hear at two miles' distance where they sailed. Juss said, "Mindest thou my shepherding of the Ghoul fleet into yonder jaws? I would not tell thee for shame whenas the fit was on me. But this is the first day since the sending came upon us that I have not wished in my heart that the Races of Kartadza had gulped me down also and given me one ending with the accursed Ghouls."

Lord Brandoch Daha looked swiftly upon him and was silent.

Now in a short while was the ship come into Lookinghaven and alongside of the marble quay. There amid his folk stood Spitfire, who greeted them, saying, "I made all ready to bring three of you home in triumph from your ship, but Volle counselled against it. Glad am I that I took his counsel, and put by those things I had prepared. They had cut me to the heart to see them now."

Juss answered him, "O my brother, this noise of hammers in Lookinghaven, and these ten keels laid on the slips, show me ye have been busied on things nearer our needs than bay-leaves and the instruments of joy since thou camest home."

So they took horse, and while they rode they related to Spitfire all that had befallen since their faring to Carcë. In such wise came they north past the harbour, and so over Havershaw Tongue to Beckfoot where they took the upper path that climbs into Evendale close under the screes of Starksty Pike, and so came a little before noon to Galing.

The black rock of Galing stands at the end of the spur that runs down from the south ridge of Little Drakeholm, dividing Brankdale from Evendale. On three sides the cliffs fall sheer from the castle walls to the deep woods of oak and birch and rowan tree which carpet the flats of Moongarth Bottom and feather the walls of the gill through which the Brankdale beck plunges in waterfall after waterfall. Only on the north-east may aught save a winged thing come at the castle across a smooth grass-grown saddle less than a stone's throw in width. Over that saddle runs the paven way leading from the Brankdale road to the Lion Gate, and within the gate is that garden of the grass walk between the yews where Lessingham stood with the martlet nine weeks before, when first he came to Demonland.

When night fell and supper was done, Juss walked alone on the walls of his castle, watching the constellations burn in the moonless sky above the mighty shadows of the mountains, listening to the hooting of the owls in the woods below and the faint distant tinkle of cow-bells, and breathing the fragrance borne up from the garden on the night wind that even in high summer tasted keen of the mountains and the sea. These sights and scents and voices of the holy night so held him in thrall that it wanted but an hour of midnight when he left the battlements, and called the sleepy house-carles[2] to light him to his chamber in the south tower of Galing.

Wondrous fair was the great four-posted bed of the Lord Juss, builded of solid gold, and hung with curtains of dark-blue tapestry whereon were figured sleep-flowers. The canopy above the bed was a mosaic of tiny stones,[3] jet, serpentine, dark hyacinth, black marble, bloodstone, and lapis lazuli, so confounded in a maze of altering hue and lustre that they might mock the palpitating sky of night. And therein was the likeness of the constellation of Orion, held by Juss for guardian of his fortunes, the stars whereof, like those beneath the golden canopy in the presence chamber, were jewels shining of their own light, yet dead wood glimmering in the dark. For Betelgeuze was a ruby shining, and a diamond for Rigel, and pale topazes for the other stars. The four posts of the bed were of the thickness of a man's arm in their upper parts, but their lower parts great as his waist and carven in the image of birds and beasts: at the foot of the bed a lion for courage and an owl for wisdom, and at the head an alaunt[4] for faithfulness of heart and a kingfisher for happiness. On the cornice of the bed and on the panels above the pillow against the wall were carved Juss's deeds of derring-do; and the latest carving was of the sea-fight with the Ghouls. To the right of the bed stood a table with old books of songs and books of the stars and of herbs and beasts and travellers' tales, and there was Juss wont to lay his sword beside him while he slept. All the walls were panelled with dark sweet-smelling wood, and armour and weapons hung thereon. Mighty chests and almeries hasped[5] and bound with gold stood against the wall, wherein he kept his rich apparel. Windows opened to the west and south, and on each window-ledge stood a bowl of palest jade filled with white roses; and the air entering the bed-chamber was laden with their scent.

About cock-crow came a dream unto Lord Juss, standing by his head and touching his eyes so that he seemed to wake and look about the chamber. And he seemed to behold an evil beast all burning as a drake, busy in his chamber, with many heads, the most venomous that ever he the days of his life had seen, and about it its five fawns, like to itself but smaller. It seemed to Juss that in place of his sword there lay a great spear of fair workmanship on the table by his bed; and it seemed to him in his dream that this spear had been his all his life, and was his greatest treasure, and that with it he might accomplish all things and without it scarcely aught to his mind. He laboured to reach out his hand to the spear, but some power withheld him so that for all his striving he might not stir. But that beast took up the spear in its jaws, and went with it forth from the chamber. It seemed to Juss that the power that held him departed with the departing of the beast, so that he leaped up and snatched down weapons from the wall and made an onslaught on the fawns of that fell beast that were tearing down the woven hangings and marring with their fiery breath the figure of the kingfisher at the head of his bed. All the chamber was full of the reek of burning, and he thought his friends were with him in the chamber, Volle and Vizz and Zigg and Spitfire and Brandoch Daha, fighting with the beasts, and the beasts prevailed against them. Then it seemed to him that the bedpost carven in the likeness of an owl spake to him in his dream in human speech; and the owl said, "O fool, that shalt justly be put in great misery without end, except thou bring back the spear. Hast thou forgot that this only is thy greatest treasure and most worthiest thy care?"

Therewith came back that grim and grisful beast into the chamber, and Juss assailed it, crying to the owl, "Uncivil owl, where then must I find my spear that this beast hath hidden?"

And it seemed to him that the owl made answer, "Inquire in Koshtra Belorn."

So tumultuous was Lord Juss's dream that he was flung at waking out of bed on to the deerskin carpets of the floor, and his right hand clutched the hilt of his great sword where it lay on the table by his bed, whereas in his dream he had beheld the spear. Mightily moved was he; and forthwith clothed himself, and faring through the dim corridors came to Spitfire's chamber, and sat on the bed and waked him. And Juss told him his dream, and said, "I hold myself clean of all blame hereabout, for from that day forth this only hath been my care, how to find my dear brother and fetch him home, and only then to wreak myself on the Witches. And what was this spear in my dream if not Goldry? This vision of the night kindleth for us a beacon fire we needs must seek to. It bade me inquire in Koshtra Belorn, and till that be done never will I rest nor so much as think on aught besides."

Spitfire answered and said, "Thou beest our oldest brother, and I shall follow and obey thee in all that thou wilt do or shalt ordain hereof."

Then fared Juss to the guest-chamber, where Lord Brandoch Daha lay a-sleeping, and waked him and told him all. Brandoch Daha snuggled him under the bedclothes and said, "Let me be and let me sleep yet two hours. Then will I rise and bathe and array myself and eat my morning meal, and thereafter will I take rede with thee and tell thee somewhat for thine advantage. I have not slept in a goose-feather bed and sheets of lawn these many weeks. If thou plague me now, by God, I will incontinently take horse over the Stile to Krothering, and let thee and thine affairs go to the devil."

So Juss laughed and left him in peace. And later when they had eaten they walked in a plashed alley, where the air was cool and the purple shadow on the path was dappled with bright flecks of sunshine. Lord Brandoch Daha said, "Thou knowest that Koshtra Belorn is a great mountain, beside which our mountains of Demonland would seem but little hills unremarked, and that it standeth in the uttermost parts of earth beyond the wastes of Upper Impland, and thou mightest search a year through all the peopled countries of the world and not find one living soul who had so much as beheld it from afar."

"This much I know," said Lord Juss.

"Is thine heart utterly bent on this journey?" said Brandoch Daha. "Or is it not preposterous, and a thing to comfort our enemies, that we should thus at the bidding of a dream fly to far and perilous lands, rather than pay Witchland presently for the shame he hath done us?"

Juss answered him, "My bed is hallowed by spells of such a virtue that no naughty dream flown through the ivory gate nor no noisome wizardry hath power to trouble his sleep who sleepeth there. This dream is true. For Witchland there is time enow. If thou wilt not go with me to Koshtra Belorn, I must go without thee."

"Enough," said Lord Brandoch Daha. "Thou knowest for thee I tie my purse with a spider's thread. Then fare we must to Impland, and herein may I help thee. For listen while I tell thee a thing. Whenas I slew Gorice X. in Goblinland, Gaslark gave me along with other good gifts, a great curiosity: a treatise or book copied out on parchment by Bhorreon his secretary, wherein it speaketh of all the ways to Impland and what countries and kingdoms lie next to the Moruna and the fronts thereof, and the marvels that he found in those lands. And all that is writ in this book was set down faithfully by Bhorreon after the telling of Gro, the same which now hath part with the Witchlanders. Great honour had Gro as then from Gaslark for his far journeyings and for that which is written in this book of wonders; and this it was that had first put in Gaslark's mind to send that expedition into Impland, which so reduced him and came so wretchedly to nought. If then thou wilt seek to Koshtra Belorn, come home with me to-day and I will show thee my book."

So spake Lord Brandoch Daha, and Lord Juss straightway ordered forth the horses, and sent messengers to Volle under Kartadza and to Vizz at Darklairstead bidding them meet him at Krothering with what speed they might. It was four hours before noon when Juss, Spitfire, and Brandoch Daha rode down from Galing and through the woods of Moongarth Bottom at the foot of the lake, taking the main bridle road up Breakingdale, that runs by the western margin of Moonmere under the buttresses of the Scarf. They rode slowly, for the sun was strong on their backs. Glassy was the lake and like a turquoise, and the birch-clad slopes to the east and north and the bare rugged ridges of Stathfell and Budrafell beyond were mirrored in its depths. On the left as they rode, the spurs of the Scarf impended from on high in piled bastions of black porphyry like giants' castles; and little valleys choked with monstrous boulders, among which the silver birches crowding showed like tiny garden plants, ran steeply back between the spurs. Up those valleys appeared successively the main summits of the Scarf, savage and remote, frowning downward as it were between their own knees: Glaumry Pike, Micklescarf, and Illstack. By noon they had climbed to the extreme head of Breakingdale, and halted on the Stile, a little beyond the watershed, under the sheer northern wall of Ill Drennock. Before them the pass plunged steeply into Amadardale. The lower reach of Switchwater shone fifteen miles or more to the west, well nigh hidden in the heat-haze. Nearer at hand in the northwest lay Rammerick Mere, bosomed among the smooth-backed Kelialand hills and the easternmost Uplands of Shalgreth Heath, with the sea beyond; and on the valley floor, near the watersmeet where Transdale runs into Amadardale, it was possible to descry the roofs of Zigg's house at Many Bushes.

When they came down thither, Zigg was out a-hunting. So they left word with his lady wife and drank a stirrup cup and rode on, up Switchwater Way, and for twelve miles and more along the southern shore of Switchwater. So dropped they into Gashterndale, and thence rounding the western slopes of Erngate End came up on the Krothering Side when the shadows were lengthening in the golden summer evening. The Side ran gently west for a league or more to where Thunderfirth lay like beaten gold beneath the sun. Across the Firth the pine-forests of Westmark, old as the world, rose toward Brocksty Edge and Gemsar Edge: a far-flung amphitheatre of bare cliff and scree shutting in the prospect to the north. High on the left towered the precipices of Erngate End; southward and south-eastward lay the sea. So rode they down the Side, through deep peaceful meadows fair with white ox-eye daisies, bluebells and yellow goatsbeard and sea campion, deep-blue gentians, agrimony and wild marjoram, and pink clover and bindweed and great yellow buttercups feasting on the sun.[6] And on an eminence beyond which the land fell away more steeply toward the sea, the onyx[7] towers of Krothering standing above woods and gardens showed milk-white against heaven and the clear hyaline.[8]

When they were now but half a mile from the castle Juss said, "Behold and see. The Lady Mevrian hath espied us from afar, and rideth forth to bring thee home."

Brandoch Daha cantered ahead to meet her: a lady light of build and exceeding fair to look upon, brave of carriage like a war-horse, soft of feature, clear-browed, gray-eyed and proud-eyed: sweet-mouthed, but not as one who can speak nought but sweetness. Her robe was of pale buff-coloured silk, with corsage[9] covered as by a spider's web with fine golden threads; and she wore a point-lace ruffle stiffened with gold and silver wire and spangled with little diamonds. Her deep hair, black as the raven's wing, was fastened with pins of gold, and a yellow rose that nestled in its coils was as the moon looking forth among thick clouds of night.

"Doings be afoot, my lady sister," said Lord Brandoch Daha. "One King of Witchland have we done down since we sailed hence; and guested in Carcë with another, little to our content. All which things I'll tell thee anon. Now lieth our road south for Impland, and Krothering is but our caravanserai."[10]

She turned her horse, and they rode all in company into the shadow of the ancient cedars that clustered to the north of the home-meads and pleasure gardens, stately, gaunt-limbed, flat-browed, bleak against the sky. On the left a lily-paven lake slept cool beneath mighty elms, with a black swan near the bank and her four cygnets dozing in a row, their heads tucked beneath their wings, so that they looked like balls of gray-brown froth floating on the water. The path leading to the bridge-gate zig-zagged steeply up the mound between low broad balustrades[11] of white onyx bearing at intervals square onyx pots, planted some with yellow roses and some with wondrous flowers, great and delicate, with frail white shell-like petals. Deep, mysterious centres had those flowers, thick with soft hairs within, and dark within with velvety purple streaked with black and blood colour and dust of gold.

The castle of Lord Brandoch Daha standing at the top of the mound was circled by a ditch both broad and deep. The gate before the drawbridge was of iron gilded and richly wrought. The towers and gatehouse were of white onyx like the castle itself, and on either hand before the gate was a colossal marble hippogriff, standing more than thirty feet high at the withers;[12] and the wings and hooves and talons of the hippogriffs and their manes and forelocks were overlaid with gold, and their eyes carbuncles of purest lustre. Over the gate was written in letters of gold:[13]

Ye braggers an 'a',
Be skeered and awa'
Frae Brandoch Daha.

But to tell even a tenth part of the marvels rich and beautiful that were in the house of Krothering: its cool courts and colonnades rich with gems and fragrant with costly spices and strange blooms: its bed-chambers where, caught like Aphrodite in her golden net, the spirit of sleep seemed ever to shake slumber from its plumes, and none might be waking long in those chambers but sweet sleep overcame their eyelids: the Chamber of the Sun and the Chamber of the Moon, and the great middle hall with its high gallery and ivory stair: to tell of all these were but to cloy imagination with picturing in one while of over-much glory and splendour.

Nought befell that night save the coming of Zigg before sundown, and of those brethren Volle and Vizz in the night, having ridden hard in obedience to the word of Juss. In the morning when they had eaten their day-meal the lords of Demonland went down into pleasaunces, and with them the Lady Mevrian. And in an alley that was roofed with beams of cedar resting on marble pillars, the beams and pillars smothered with dark-red roses, they sat looking eastward across a sunk garden. The weather was sweet and gracious, and thick dew lay on the pale terraced lawns that led down among flower beds to the fish-pond in the midst. The water made a cool mirror whereon floated yellow and crimson waterlilies opening to the sky. All the greens and flower-colours glowed warm and clean, but soft withal and shadowy, veiled in the gray haze of the summer morning.

They sat here and there as they listed on chairs and benches, near a huge tank or vase of dark green jade where sulphur-coloured lilies grew in languorous beauty, their back-curled petals showing the scarlet anthers; and all the air was heavy with their sweetness. The great jade vase was round and flat like the body of a tortoise, open at the top where the lilies grew. It was carved with scales, as it were the body of a dragon, and a dragon's head a-gaping reared itself at one end, and at the other the tail curved up and over like the handle of a basket, and the tail had little fore and hind feet with claws, and a smaller head at the end of the tail gaped downwards biting at the large head. Four legs supported the body, and each leg was a small dragon standing on its hind feet, its head growing into the parent body as the thigh or shoulder joint should join the trunk. In the curve of the creature's neck, his back propped against its head, sat the Lord Brandoch Daha in graceful ease, one foot touching the ground, the other swinging free; and in his hands was the book, bound in dark puce-coloured goatskin and gold, given him by Gaslark in years gone by. Zigg watched him idly turn the pages while the others talked. Leaning toward Mevrian he whispered in her ear, "Is not he able and shapen for to subdue and put under him all the world: thy brother? A man of blood and peril, and yet so fair to behold that it is a marvel?"

Her eyes danced. She said, "It is pure truth, my lord."

Now spake Spitfire saying, "Read forth to us, I pray thee, the book of Gro; for my soul is afire to set forth on this faring."

" 'Tis writ somewhat crabbedly,"[14] said Brandoch Daha, "and most damnably long. I spent half last night a-searching on't, and 'tis most apparent no other way lieth to these mountains save by the Moruna, and across the Moruna is (if Gro say true) but one way, and that from the Gulf of Muelva: 'a xx dayes journeye from northe by south-est.' For here he telleth of watersprings by the way, but he saith in other parts of the desert be no watersprings, save only springs venomous, where 'The water riketh like a sething potte continually, having sumwhat a sulphureous and sumwhat onpleasant savor,' and, 'The grownd nurysheth here no plante nor herbe except yt bee venomous champinions or tode stooles.' "

"If he say true?" said Spitfire. "He is a turncoat and a renegado. Wherefore not therefore a liar?"

"But a philosopher," answered Juss. "I knew him well of old in Goblinland, and I judge him to be one who is not false save only in policy. Subtle of mind he is, and dearly loveth plotting and scheming, and, as I think, perversely affecteth ever the losing side if he be brought into any quarrel; and this hath dragged him ofttimes to misfortune. But in this book of his travels he must needs speak truth, as it seemeth to me, to be true to his own self."

The Lady Mevrian looked approvingly on Lord Juss and her eye twinkled. For well it liked her humour to hear men's natures so divined.

"O Juss, friend of my heart," said Lord Brandoch Daha, "thy words proceed, as ever they did, from the true fount of wisdom, and I embrace them and thee. This book is a guide which we shall follow not helter-skelter but as old men of war. If then the right road to Morna Moruna lie from the Gulf of Muelva, were we not best sail straight thitherward and lay up our ships in that Gulf where the coast and the country side be without habitation, rather than fare to some nearer haven of Outer Impland such as Arlan Mouth whither thou and Spitfire fared six summers ago?"

"Not Arlan Mouth, o' this journey," said Juss. "Some sport perchance we might obtain there had we leisure for fighting with the accursed inhabitants, but every day's delay we now do make holdeth my brother another day in bondage. The princes and Fazes of the Imps have many strong walled towns and towers in all those coastlands, and hard by in a mediamnis[15] of the river Arlan, in Orpish, is the great castle of Fax Fay Faz, whereto Goldry and I drave him home from Lida Nanguna."

" 'Tis an ill coast too, to find a landing," said Brandoch Daha, turning the leaves of the book. "As he saith, 'Ymplande the More beginnith at the west syde of the mowth of Arlan and occupiethe all the lond unto the hedeland Sibrion, and therefro sowth awaye to the Corshe, by gesse a vij hundered myles, wherby the se is not ther of nature favorable nor no haven is or cumming yn meete for shippes.' "

So after some talk and searching of that book of Gro they determined this should be their plan: to fare to Impland by way of the Straits of Melikaphkhaz and the Didornian Sea, and so lay up their ships in the Gulf of Muelva, and landing there start straightway across the wilderness to Morna Moruna, even as Gro had described the way.

"Ere we leave it," said Brandoch Daha, "hear what he speaketh concerning Koshtra Belorn. This he beheld from Morna Moruna, whereof he saith: 'The contery is hylly, sandy, and baren of wood and corne, as forest ful of lynge, mores,[16] and mosses, with stony hilles. Here is a mighty stronge and usid[17] borow for flying serpens in sum baren, hethy, and sandy grownd, and thereby the litle round castel of Morna Moruna stondith on Omprenne Edge, as on the limit of the worlde, sore wether beten and yn ruine. This castelle was brent in tyme of warre, spoyled and razyd by Kynge Goriyse the fourt of Wytchlande in ancient dayes. And they say there was blamelesse folke dwellid therein and ryghte gentle, nor was ther any need for Goriyse to have usid them so cruellie, when hee cawsyd the hole howsholde there to appere before hym and then slawe sum owt of hande, and the residew he throughe all downe the steep cliffe. And but few supervivid[18] after the gret falle, and these fled awaye thorough the untrodden forests of Bavvynaune and withoute question perysht ther yn great sorwe and miserie. Sum fable that it was for thys cruel facte sake that King Goriyse was eat by divels on the Moruna with al hys hoste, one man onely cumming home again to tell of these thynges bifallen.' Now mark: 'From Morna Moruna I behelde sowthawaye two grete mowntaynes standing over Bavvinane as two Queenes in bewty

seted in the skye by estimacion xx legues fro hence above meny
more ise robed mowntaines supereminente. The wyche as I lernyd
was Coshtre Belourne the one and the othere Koshtre Pivrarca.
And I veuyed them continuallie unto the going downe of the sun,
and that was the fayrest sighte and the most bewtifullest and gallant marvaille that mine eyen hath sene. Therewith talkid I with the
smaule thynges that dwell there in the ruines and in the busschis
growing round abowte as it ys my wonte, and amongst them one of
those byrdes cawld martlettes that have feete so litle that they
seime to have none. And thys litle martlette sittynge in a
frambousier[19] or raspis busche tolde mee that none may come
alive unto Coschtra Beloorn, for the mantycores of the
mowntaines will certeynely ete his brains ere he come thither. And
were he so fortunate as scape these mantycores, yet cowlde hee
never climbe up the gret cragges of yce and rocke on Koschtre
Beloorn, for none is so stronge as to scale them but by art magicall,
and such is the vertue of that mowntayne that no magick avayleth
there, but onlie strength and wisdome alone, and as I seye these
woulde not avayl to climbe those cliffes and yce ryvers.' "

"What be these mantichores[20] of the mountains that eat men's
brains?" asked the Lady Mevrian.

"This book is so excellent well writ," said her brother, "that
thine answer appeareth on this same page: 'The beeste Mantichora, whych is as muche as to saye devorer of menne, rennith as
I herde tell, on the skirt of the mowntaynes below the snow feldes.
These be monstrous bestes, ghastlie and ful of horrour, enemies to
mankinde, of a red coloure, with ij rowes of huge grete tethe in
their mouthes. It hath the head of a man, his eyen like a ghoot, and
the bodie of a lyon lancing owt sharpe prickles fro behinde. And
hys tayl is the tail of a scorpioun. And is more delyverer to goo than
is fowle to flee. And hys voys is as the roaryng of x lyons.' "

"These beasts," said Spitfire, "were alone enough to draw me
thither. I shall bring thee home a small one, madam, to keep
chained in the court."

"That should dash me from thy friendship for ever, cousin,"
said Mevrian, stroking the feathery ears of her little marmoset that
cuddled in her lap. "That which feedeth on brains were overnour-
ished in Demonland, and belike would overrun the whole countryside."

"Send it to Witchland," said Zigg. "Where when it hath eat up
Gro and Corund it may sup lightly on the King, and then most
fortunately starve for lack of its proper nutriment."

Juss stood up from his seat. "Thou and I and Spitfire," said he to Brandoch Daha, "must to work roundly and gather strength, for 'tis already midsummer. You, Vizz, Volle, and Zigg, must have the warding of our homes whiles we be gone. We cannot be less than two thousand swords on this faring."

"How many ships, Volle," asked Lord Brandoch Daha, "canst thou give us, busked and boun, ere this moon wane?"

"There be fourteen afloat," said Volle. "Besides these, ten keels lie on the slips at Lookinghaven, and nine more hath Spitfire but now laid down on the beach before his house at Owlswick."

"Thirty and three in sum," said Spitfire. "You see we have not twiddled our thumbs whilst ye were gone."

Juss paced back and forth with great strides, his brow clouded and his jaw clenched. In a while he said, "Laxus hath forty sail, dragons of war. I am not so idle-headed as fare without an army into Impland, but certain it is that if our ill-willers would move war against us we stand in apparent weakness, here or abroad, to throw back their onset."

Volle said, "Of these nineteen ships a-building no more than two can take the water before a month be past, and but seven more ere six months' time, push we never so mightily the work."

"The season weareth, and my brother wasteth in duress. We must sail ere another moon grow old," said Juss.

Volle said, "Then with sixteen sail thou sailest, O Juss; and then thou leavest us not one ship at home till more be finished and launched."

"How can we leave you so?" cried Spitfire.

But Brandoch Daha looked towards his lady sister, met her glance, and was satisfied. "The choice lieth fair before us," said he. "If we will eat the egg, little need to debate whether the shell must go."

Mevrian rose from her seat laughing, and said, "Then let the council rise, my lords." And her eyes grew serious, and she said, "Shall they make rhymes upon us that we of Demonland, whom men repute and hold the mightiest lords in all the world, hung sheepishly back from this high needful enterprise lest, our greatest captains being abroad, our enemies might haply take us at home at disadvantage? It shall not be said of the women of Demonland that they upheld such counsels."

IX

Salapanta Hills

*Of the landing of Lord Juss and his companions
in outer Impland and their meeting with
Zeldornius, Helteranius, and Jalcanaius Fostus;
and of the tidings told by Mivarsh, and the
dealings of the three great captains on the hills
of Salapanta.*

N the thirty and first day after that council held in
Krothering, the fleet of Demonland put to sea from
Lookinghaven: eleven dragons of war and two great
ships of burthen, bound for the uttermost seas of
earth in quest of the Lord Goldry Bluszco. Eighteen
hundred Demons fared on that expedition, and not a man among
them that was not a complete soldier. For five days they rowed
southaway on a windless sea, and on the sixth the sea-cliffs of
Goblinland came out of the haze on their starboard bow. They
rowed south along the land, and on the tenth day out from
Lookinghaven passed under the Ness of Ozam, journeying thence
four days with a favouring wind over the open seas to Sibrion. But
now, when they had rounded that dark promontory and were
about steering east along the coast of Impland the More, and less
than ten days' journey lay betwixt them and their haven in Muelva,
a dismal tempest suddenly surprised them. For forty days it swept
them in hail and sleet over wide-wallowing ocean, without a star,
without a course; till, on a fierce midnight of wind and darkness
and roaring waters was Juss's and Spitfire's ship and other four in

her company driven on the rocks on a lee shore and broken in pieces. Hardly, and after long battling among great waves, those brethren won ashore, weary and hurt. In the inhospitable light of a wet and windy dawn they mustered on the beach such of their folk as had escaped out of the mouth of destruction; and they were three hundred and thirty and three.

Spitfire, beholding these things, spake and said, "This land hath a villanous look stirreth my remembrance, as but to behold verjuice[1] soureth the mouth of him who once tasted thereof. Rememberest thou this land?"

Juss scanned the low long coast-line that swept north and west to an estuary, and beyond ran westwards till it was lost in the scud and driving spray. Desolate birds flew above the welter of the surges. He said, "Certainly this is Arlan Mouth, where least of all I had chosen to come a-land with so small a head of men. Yet shalt thou prove here, as it hath ever been, how all occasions are but steps for us to climb fame by."

"Our ship is lost," cried Spitfire, "and the more part of our men, and worst of all, Brandoch Daha that is worth ten thousand. Easilier shall a little ant bib this ocean dry, than shall we in this taking perform our enterprise." And he cursed and blasphemed, saying, "Cursed be the malice of the sea, which, having broke our power, now speweth us ashore here to our mere undoing; and so hath done great succour to the King of Witchland, and unto all the world beside great damage."

But Juss answered him, "Think not that these contrary winds come of fortune or by the influence of malignant and combustive stars. This weather bloweth out of Carcë. Even as these very waves thou beholdest have each his back-wash or undertow, so followeth after every sending an undertow of evil hap, whereby, albeit in essence a less deadly thing, many have been drowned and washed away who stood unremoved against the main stroke of the breaker. So were we twice since that day brought near to our bane: first, when our judgement being darkened with a strange distraction we went up with Gaslark against Carcë; next, when this storm wrecked us here by Arlan Mouth. Though by mine art I rebated the King's sending, yet against the maleficial undertow that followed it my charms avail not, nor the virtues of all sorcerous herbs that grow."

"Are these things so, and wilt thou yet be temperate?" said Spitfire.

"Content thee," said Juss. "The sands run down. A certain time only runneth this stream for our hurt; it must now have well nigh spent itself, and it were too perilous for him to conjure a second time, as last May he conjured in Carcë."

"Who told thee that?" asked Spitfire.

"I do but conjecture it," answered he, "from my studying of certain prophetic writings touching the princes of that blood and line. Whereby it appeareth (yet not clearly, but riddle-wise) that if one and the same King, essaying a second time in his own person an enterprise in that kind, should fail, and the powers of darkness destroy him, then is not his life spilt alone (as it fortuned aforetime unto Gorice VII. at his first attempt), but there shall be an end for ever of the whole house of Gorice which hath for so many generations reigned in Carcë."

"Well," said Spitfire, "so stand we to our chance. Old muckhills² will bloom at last."

Now for nineteen days fared those brethren and their company eastward through Outer Impland: first across a country of winding sleepy rivers and reedy lakes innumerable, then by rolling uplands and champaign ground. At length, on an even, they came upon a heath running up eastward to a range of tumbled hills. The hills were not lofty nor steep, but rugged of outline and their surface rough with crags and boulders, so that it was a maze of little eminences and valleys grown upon by heather and fern and rank sad-coloured grass, with stunted thorn trees and junipers harbouring in the clefts of the rocks. On the water-shed, as on an horse's withers, looking west to the red October sunset and south to the far line of the Didornian Sea, they came upon a spy-fortalice,³ old and desolate, and one sitting in the gate. For very joy their hearts melted within them, when they knew him for none other than Brandoch Daha.

So they embraced him as one beyond hope risen from the grave. And he said, "Through the Straits of Melikaphkhaz was I borne, and wrecked at last on the lonely shore ten leagues southward from this spot, whither I won alone, having lost my ship and all my dear companions. In my mind it was that ye must fare by this road to Muelva if ye suffered shipwreck in the outer coasts of Impland.

"Harken," he said, "and I will tell you a wonder. A seven-night have I awaited you in this roosting-stead of daws and owls. And it is a caravanserai of great armies that pass by in the wilderness, and having parleyed with two I await the third. For well I think that here I have made discovery of a great mystery, one that hath engaged the speculations of wise men for years. For on that day of my coming hither, when sunset was red, as now you see it, behold an army marching up from the east with great flags a-flaunting in the wind and all kinds of music. Which I beholding, methought if these be enemies, then goeth down my life's days with honour, and if friends, then cometh provender from those waggons of burthen that follow this army. A weighty argument; since not so much as the smell of victuals had I, save nasty nuts and berries of the open field, since I came forth of the sea. So went I, taking my weapons, on the walls of this spy-fortalice and hailed them, bidding them say forth their quality. And he that was their captain rode up under the walls, and hailed me with all courtesy and noble port. And who think ye 'twas?"

They answered nought.

"One that hath been famous," said he, "up and down the earth for a marvellous valorous and brave soldier of fortune. Have ye forgot that enterprise of Gaslark that had its burying in Impland?"

"Was he little and dark," asked Juss, "like a keen dagger suddenly unsheathed at midnight? Or bright with the splendour of a pennoned spear[4] at a jousting on high holiday? Or was he dangerous of aspect like an old sword, rusty in the midst but bright at point and edge, brought forth for deeds of destiny at the fated day?"

"Thine arrow striketh in the triple ring o' the mark," said Lord Brandoch Daha. "Great of growth he was, and a very peacock of splendour in his panoply of war; and a great pitch-black stallion bare him. So I spake him fair, saying, 'O most magnificent and godlike Helteranius, conqueror in an hundred fights, what makest thou these long years in Outer Impland with this great head of men? And what dark lodestone[5] draws you these nine years, since with great sound of trumpets and tramp of horses thou and Zeldornius and Jalcanaius Fostus went forth to make Impland Gaslark's footstool; since which time all the world believeth you lost and dead?' And he beheld me with alien eyes, and made answer, 'O Brandoch Daha, the world journeyeth to its silly will, but I fare alway with my purpose before me. Be it nine years, or but nine moons, or nine ages, what care I? Zeldornius would I encounter and engage him in battle, that still fleeth before my face. Eat and drink with me to-night; but think not to detain me nor to turn me to idle thoughts beside my purpose. For with the dawning of the day I must forth again in quest of Zeldornius.'

"So I ate and drank and was merry that night with Helteranius in his pavilion of silk and gold. And with the dawn he marshalled his army and marched westward toward the plains.

"And on the third day, as I sat without this wall, cursing your slow coming, behold an army marching from the east and one leading them mounted on a small dun horse; and he was clad in black armour shining like the raven's wing, with black eagle's plumes in his helm, and eyes like the eyes of a cat-a-mountain, full of sparkling flame. Little was he, and fierce of face, and lithe, and hard to look on and tireless to look on like a stoat. And I hailed him from where I sat, saying, 'O most notable and puissant Jalcanaius Fostus, shatterer of the hosts of men, whitherward over the lonely heaths forlorn, thou and thy great armament?' And he lighted down from his horse, and took me by the arms with both his hands, and said, 'If a man dream, to speak with dead men betokens profit. And art not thou of the dead, O Brandoch Daha? For in forgotten days, that now spring up in my mind as flowers in a weed-choked garden after many years, so bloomest thou in my memory: great among the great ones of the world that was, thou and thine house in Krothering above the sea-lochs in many-mountained Demonland. But oblivion, like a sounding sea, soundeth betwixt me and those days; and the noise of the surf stoppeth mine ears, and the mist of the sea darkeneth mine eyes that strain for a sight of those far times and the deeds thereof. Yet for those dead days' sake, eat with me and drink with me to-night, since here for a night once more I pitch my moving tent on Salapanta Hills. And to-morrow I fare onward. For never may rest bring balm to my soul until I find out Helteranius and smite his head from his shoulders. Great shame to him but little marvel is it, that he still courseth before me as an hare. For traitors were ever dastards. And who ever heard tell of a more hellish devilish damned traitor than he? Nine years ago, when Zeldornius and I made ready to decide our quarrels by battle, word came to me in a lucky hour how that this Helteranius with cunning colubrine and malice viperine and sleights serpentine went about to attack me in the rear. So turned I right about to crush him, but the fat chuff-cat was fled.'

"So spake Jalcanaius Fostus; and I ate and drank with him that night, and caroused with him in his tent. And at break of day he struck camp and rode westaway with his army."

Brandoch Daha ceased, and looked eastward toward the gates of night. And lo, an army faring up from the lower moor-lands, toward them on the ridge, horsemen and footmen in dense array, and their captain on a great brown horse riding in the van. Long-limbed he was and lean, all armed in dusty rusty armour hacked and dinted in an hundred fights, with worn leather gauntlets on his hands and a faded campaigning cloak thrown back from his shoulders. He carried his casque[6] at his saddle-bow and his head was bare: the head of an old lean hunting-dog, with white hair swept back from a rugged brow where blue veins showed; great-nosed and bony-faced, with huge bushy white moustachios and eyebrows, and blue eyes gleaming from cavernous eye-sockets. His horse was curst-looking, with ears laid back and blood-shed dangerous eyes, and he in the saddle sat erect and unyielding as a lance.

When he and his army came up upon the ridge, he drew rein and hailed the Demons. And he said, "On every ninth day these nine years have I beheld this lonely place of earth, as I pursued after Jalcanaius Fostus that still eludeth me and still fleeth before me; and this is strange, since he was ever a great fighter and engaged these nine years past to do battle with me. And now fear cometh upon me that eld[7] draweth a veil of illusion athwart mine eyes, portending the approach of death or[8] ever I perform my will. For here in the uncertain light of evening rise up before me shapes and semblances as of guests of Gaslark the king in Zajë Zaculo in days gone by: old friends of Gaslark's out of many-mountained Demonland: Brandoch Daha, that slew the King of Witchland, and Spitfire of Owlswick, and Juss his brother, the same which had lordship over all the Demons ere we fared to Impland. Ghosts and back-comers of a world forgot. But if ye be right flesh and blood, speak and discover yourselves."

Juss answered him, "O most redoubtable Zeldornius and in war invincible, well might a man expect spirits of the dead on these quiet hills about cockshut time. And if thou deem us such, how much more shall we, that be wanderers new-shipwrecked out of hungry seas, suppose thee but a shade, and these great hosts of thine but fetches of the dead that be departed, steaming up from Erebus[9] as daylight dies?"

"O most renowned and redoubtable Zeldornius," said Brandoch Daha, "thou wast once my guest in Krothering. To resolve thy doubts and ours, bid us to supper. It were matter indeed if spirits bodiless were able to bib wine and eat up earthly bake-meats."

So Zeldornius let pitch his tents, and appointed the fifth hour before midnight for those lords of Demonland to sup with him. Ere they forgathered in Zeldornius's tent they spake among themselves, and Spitfire said, "Was ever such a wonder or such a pitiful trick o' the Fates as bringeth these three great captains to waste the remnant of their days in this remote wilderness? Doubt not but there's practice in it, that maketh them march these long years this changeless round, each fleeing one that would fain encounter him, and still seeking another that flies before him."

"Never went man with that look of the eyes Zeldornius hath," said Juss, "but he was a man ensorcelled."[10]

"With such a look," said Brandoch Daha, "went Helteranius and Jalcanaius. But mark our interest. 'Twere good to break the charm and claim their help for our pains. Shall's show the old lion all the truth of this fact to-night?"

So spake Lord Brandoch Daha, and those brethren deemed his counsel good. So at supper, when men's hearts were gladdened with good cheer, the Lord Juss sate him down by Zeldornius and opened to him this matter, saying, "O renowned Zeldornius, how befalleth it that these nine years thou pursuest after Jalcanaius Fostus, shatterer of hosts, and what was your difference betwixt you that set you by the ears?"

Zeldornius said, "O Juss, must I answer thee by reasons in this matter that is ruled by the high stars and Fate that lays men at their length? Enough for thee that unpeace befell betwixt me and Jalcanaius mighty in war, and it was confirmed between us that by the arbitrament of the bloody field we should end our difference. But he abode me not; and these nine years I seek to meet with him in vain."

"There was a third of you," said Juss. "What tidings hast thou of Helteranius?"

Zeldornius answered him, "No tidings."

"Wilt thou," said Juss, "that I enlighten thee hereon?"

Zeldornius said, "Thou and thy fellows alone of the children of men have spoken with me since these things began. For they that dwelt in this region fled years ago, accounting the place accursed. A paltry crew they were, and mean meat enow[11] for our swords. Speak then, if thou meanest me well, and show me all."

"Helteranius," said Lord Juss, "pursueth thee these nine years, as thou pursuest Jalcanaius Fostus. My cousin here hath seen him but six days ago, in this same place, and talked with him, and shook him by the hand, and knew his mind. Surely ye be all three holden by some enchantment, that being old comrades in arms so strangely and to so little purpose do pursue each the other's life. I prithee let us be a mean betwixt you all to set you at one again, and free you from so strange a thraldom."

But with those words spoken was Zeldornius grown red as

blood. In a while he said, "It were black treachery. I'll not credit it."

But Lord Brandoch Daha answered him, "From his own lips I received it, O Zeldornius. And thereto I plight my troth. This besides, that Jalcanaius Fostus was turned from battling with thee nine years ago (as he himself hath told me, and made firm his saying with most fearful oaths), by intelligence brought him that Helteranius was in that hour minded to take him in the rear."

"Ay," said Spitfire, "and unto this day he marcheth on Helteranius's track as thou on his."

With those words spoken was Zeldornius grown yellow as old parchment, and his white moustachios bristled like a lion's. He sat silent awhile, then, resting upon Juss the cold and steady gaze of his blue eyes, "The world comes back to me," he said, "and this memory therewith, that they of Demonland were truth-tellers whether to friend or foe, and ever held it shame to cog and lie." All they bowed gravely and he said with a great lowe of anger in his eyes, "This Helteranius deviseth against me, it well appeareth, the self-same treachery whereof he was falsely accused to Jalcanaius Fostus. There were no likelier place to crush him than here on Salapanta ridge. If I stand here to abide his onset, the lie of the ground befriendeth me, and Jalcanaius cometh at his heels to gather the broken meats after I have made my feast."

Brandoch Daha said in Juss's ear, "Our peacemaking taketh a pretty turn. Heels i' the air: monstrous unladylike!"

But nought they could say would move Zeldornius. So in the end they offered him their backing in this adventure. "And when the day is won, then shalt thou lend us thy might in our enterprise, and aid us in our wars with Witchland that be for to come."

But Zeldornius said, "O Juss and ye lords of Demonland, I yield you thanks; but ye shall not meddle in this battle. For we came three captains with our hosts unto this land, and beheld the land, and laid it under us. Ours it is, and if any meddle or make with us, were we never so set at enmity one with another, we must join together in his despite and bring him to bane. Be still then, and behold and see what birth fate shall bring forth on Salapanta Hills. But if I live, thereafter shall ye have my friendship and my help in all your enterprises whatsoever."

For awhile he sat without speech, his stark veined hands clenched on the board before him; then rising, went without word to the door of his pavilion to study the night. Then turned he back to Lord Juss, and spake to him: "Know that when this moon now past was but three days old I began to be troubled with a catarrh or

rheum[12] which yet troubleth me; and well thou wottest[13] that
whoso falleth sick on the third day of the moon's age, he will die.
To-night also is a new moon, and of a Saturday; and that
betokeneth fighting and bloodshed. Also the wind bloweth from
the south; and he that beginneth that game with a south wind shall
have the victory. With such uncertain blackness and brightness
openeth the door of Fate before me."

Juss bowed his head, and said, "O Zeldornius, thy speech is
sooth."

"I was ever a fighter," said Zeldornius.

Far into the night sat they in the tent of renowned Zeldornius,
drinking and talking of life and destiny and old wars and the
chances of war and great adventure; and an hour after midnight
they parted, and Juss and Spitfire and Brandoch Daha betook them
to their rest in the watch-tower on the ridge of Salapanta.

On such wise passed three days by, Zeldornius waiting with his
army on the hill, and the Demons supping with him nightly. And
on the third day he drew out his army as for battle, expecting
Helteranius. But neither that day nor the next nor the next day
following brought sight nor tidings of Helteranius, and strange it
seemed to them and hard to guess what turn of fortune had delayed his coming. The sixth night was overcast, and mirk darkness
covered the earth. When supper was done, as the Demons betook
themselves to their sleeping place, they heard a scuffle and the
voice of Brandoch Daha, who went foremost of them, crying,
"Here have I caught a heath-dog's whelp. Give me a light. What
shall I do with him?"

Men were roused and lights brought, and Brandoch Daha
surveyed that which he held pinioned by the arms, caught by the
entrance to the fortalice: one with scared wild-beast eyes in a swart
face, golden ear-rings in his ears, and a thick close-cropped beard
interlaced with gold wire twisted among its curls; bare-armed, with
a tunic of otter-skin and wide hairy trousers cross-stitched with
silver thread, a circlet of gold on his head, and frizzed dark hair
plaited in two thick tails that hung forward over his shoulders. His
lips were drawn back, like a cross-grained dog's snarling betwixt
fear and fierceness, and his white pointed teeth and the whites of
his eyes flashed in the torch-light.

So they had him with them into the tower, and set him before
them, and Juss said, "Fear not, but tell forth unto us thy name and
lineage, and what brings thee lurking in the night about our lodging. We mean thee no hurt, so thou practise not against us and our

safety. Art thou a dweller in this Impland, or a wanderer, like as we be, from countries beyond the seas? Hast thou companions, and if so, where be they, and what, and how many?"

And the stranger gnashed upon them with his teeth, and said, "O devils transmarine, mock not but slay."

Juss entreated him kindly, giving him meat and drink, and in a while made question of him once more, "What is thy name?"

Whereto he replied, "O devil transmarine, pity of thine ignorance sith thou know'st not Mivarsh Faz." And he fell into a great passion of weeping, crying aloud, "Woe worth the woe that is fallen upon all the land of Impland!"

"What's the matter?" said Juss.

But Mivarsh ceased not to wail and to lament, saying, "Out harrow and alas for Fax Fay Faz and Illarosh Faz and Lurmesh Faz and Gandassa Faz and all the great ones in the land!" And when they would have questioned him he cried again, "Curse ye bitterly Philpritz Faz, which betrayed us into the hand of the devil ultramontane in the castle of Orpish."

"What devil is this thou speakest of?" asked Juss.

"He hath come," he answered, "over the mountains out of the north country, that alone was able to answer Fax Fay Faz. And the voice of his speech is like unto the roaring of a bull."

"Out of the north?" said Juss, giving him more wine, and exchanging glances with Spitfire and Brandoch Daha. "I would hear more of this."

Mivarsh drank, and said, "O devils transmarine, ye give me strong waters which comfort my soul, and ye speak me soft words. But shall I not fear soft words? Soft words were spoke by this devil ultramontane, when he and cursed Philpritz spake soft words unto us in Orpish: unto me, and unto Fax Fay Faz, and Gandassa, and Illarosh, and unto all of us, after our overthrow in battle against him by the banks of Arlan."

Juss asked, "Of what fashion is he to look on?"

"He hath a great yellow beard beflecked with gray," said Mivarsh, "and a bald shiny pate, and standeth big as a neat."

Juss spake apart to Brandoch Daha, "There's matter in it if this be true." And Brandoch Daha poured forth unto Mivarsh and bade him drink again, saying, "O Mivarsh Faz, we be strangers and guests in wide-flung Impland. Be it known to thee that our power is beyond ken, and our wealth transcendeth the imagination of man. Yet is our benevolence of like measure with our power and riches, overflowing as honey from our hearts unto such as receive us openly and tell us that which is. Only be warned, that if any lie to us or assay craftily to delude us, not the mantichores that lodge beyond the Moruna were more dreadful to that man than we."

Mivarsh quailed, but answered him, "Use me well, you were best, and you shall hear from me nought but what is true. First with the sword he vanquished us, and then with subtle words invited us to talk with him in Orpish, pretending friendship. But they are all dead that harkened to him. For when he held them closed up in the council room in Orpish, himself went secretly forth, while his men laid hands on Gandassa Faz and on Illarosh Faz, and on Fax Fay Faz that was greatest amongst us, and on Lurmesh Faz, and cut off their heads and set them up on poles without the gate. And our armies that waited without were dismayed to see the heads of the Fazes of Impland so set on poles, and the armies of the devils ultramontane still threatening us with death. And this big bald bearded devil spake them of Impland fair, saying these that he had slain were their oppressors and he would give them their hearts' desire if they would be his men, and he would make them free, every man, and share out all Impland amongst them. So were the common sort befooled and brought under by this bald devil from beyond the mountains, and now none withstandeth him in all Impland. But I that had held back from his council in Orpish, fearing his guile, hardly escaped from my folk that rose against me. And I fled into the woods and wildernesses."

"Where last saw ye him?" asked Juss.

Mivarsh answered him, "A three days' journey northwest of this, at Tormerish in Achery."

"What made he there?" asked Juss.

Mivarsh answered, "Still devising evil."

"Against whom?" asked Juss.

Mivarsh answered, "Against Zeldornius, which is a devil transmarine."

"Give me some more wine," said Juss, "and fill again a beaker for Mivarsh Faz. I do love nought so much as tale-telling a-nights. With whom devised he against Zeldornius?"

Mivarsh answered, "With another devil from beyond seas; I have forgot his name."

"Drink and remember," said Juss; "or if 'tis gone from thee, paint me his picture."

"He hath about my bigness," said Mivarsh, that was little of stature. "His eyes be bright, and he somewhat favoureth this one," pointing at Spitfire, "though belike he hath not all so fierce a face. He is lean-faced and dark of skin. He goeth in black iron."

"Is he Jalcanaius Fostus?" asked Juss.

And Mivarsh answered, "Ay."

"There's musk and amber in thy speech," said Juss. "I must have more of it. What mean they to do?"

"This," said Mivarsh: "As I sat listening in the dark without their tent, it was made absolute that this Jalcanaius had been deceived in supposing that another devil transmarine, whom men call Helteranius, had been minded to do treacherously against him; whereas, as the bald devil made him believe, 'twas no such thing. And so it was concluded that Jalcanaius should send riders after Helteranius to make peace between them, and that they two should forthwith join to kill Zeldornius, one falling on him in the front and the other in the rear."

"So 'tis come to this?" said Spitfire.

"And when they have Zeldornius slain," said Mivarsh, "then must they help this bald-pate in his undertakings."

"And so pay him for his redes?" said Juss.

And Mivarsh answered, "Even so."

"One thing more I would know," said Juss. "How great a following hath he in Impland?"

"The greatest strength that he can make," answered Mivarsh, "of devils ultramontane is as I think two score hundred. Many Imps beside will follow him, but they have but our country weapons."

Lord Brandoch Daha took Juss by the arm and went forth with him into the night. The frosted grass crunched under their tread: strange stars blinked in the south in a windy space betwixt cloud and sleeping earth, Achernar near the meridian bedimming all lesser fires with his pure radiance.

"So cometh Corund upon us as an eagle out of the sightless blue," said Brandoch Daha, "with twelve times our forces to let us the way to the Moruna, and all Impland like a spaniel smiling at his heel; if indeed this simple soul say true, as I think he doth."

"Thou fallest all of a holiday mood," said Juss, "at the first scenting of this great hazard."

"O Juss," cried Brandoch Daha, "thine own breath lighteneth at it, and thy words come more sprightly forth. Are not all lands, all airs, one country unto us, so there be great doings afoot to keep bright our swords?"

Juss said, "Ere we sleep I will inform Zeldornius how the wind shifteth. He must face both ways now, till this field be cut. This battle must not go against him, for his enemies be engaged (if Mivarsh say true) to give the help of their swords to Corund."

So fared they to Zeldornius's tent, and Juss said by the way,

"Of this be satisfied: Corund bareth not blade on the hills of Salapanta. The King hath intelligencers to keep him advertised of all enchanted circles of the world, and well he knoweth what influences move here, and with what danger to themselves outlanders draw sword here, as witness the doom fulfilled these nine years by these three captains. Therefore will Corund, instructed in these things by his master that sent him, look to deal with us otherwhere than in this charmed corner of the earth. And he were as well take a bear by the tooth as meddle in the fight that now impendeth, and so bring upon him these three seasoned armies joined in one for his destruction."

They passed the guard with the watchword, and waked Zeldornius and told him all. And he, muffled in his great faded cloak, went forth to see guards were set and all sure against an onslaught from either side. And standing by his tent to give good night to those lords of Demonland, he said, "It likes me better so. I ever was a fighter; so, one fight more."

The morrow dawned and passed uneventful, and the morrow's morrow. But on the third morning after the coming of Mivarsh, behold, east and west, great armies marching from the plains, and Zeldornius's array drawn up to meet them on the ridge, with weapons gleaming and horses champing and trumpets blowing the call of battle. No greetings were betwixt them, nor so much as a message of challenge or defiance, but Jalcanaius with his black riders rushed to the onset from the west and Helteranius from the east. But Zeldornius, like a gray old wolf, snapping now this way now that, stemmed the tide of their onslaught. So began the battle great and fell, and continued the livelong day. Thrice on either side Zeldornius went forth with a great strength of chosen men, in so much that his enemies fled before him as the partridge doth before the sparrow-hawk; and thrice did Helteranius and thrice Jalcanaius Fostus rally and hurl him back, mounting the ridge anew.

But when it drew near to evening, and the dark day darkened toward night, the battle ceased, dying down suddenly into silence. Those lords of Demonland came down from their tower, and walked among the heaps of dead men slain toward a place of slabby rock in the neck of the ridge. Here, alone on that field, Zeldornius leaned upon his spear, gazing downward in a study, his arm cast about the neck of his old brown horse who hung his head and sniffed the ground. Through a rift in the western clouds the sun glared forth; but his beams were not so red as the ling and bent[14] of Salapanta field.

As Juss and his companions drew near, no sound was heard save from the fortalice behind them: a discordant plucking of a harp, and the voice of Mivarsh where he walked and harped before the walls, singing this ditty:

> The hag is astride
> This night for to ride;
> The devill and shee together:
> Through thick and through thin,
> Now out and then in,
> Though ne'er so foule be the weather.

> A thorn or a burr
> She takes for a spurre,
> With a lash of a bramble she rides now;
> Through brakes and through bryars,
> O're ditches and mires,
> She followes the spirit that guides now.

> No beast for his food
> Dares now range the wood,
> But husht in his laire he lies lurking;
> While mischiefs, by these,
> On land and on seas,
> At noone of night are a working.

> The storme will arise
> And trouble the skies;
> This night, and more for the wonder,
> The ghost from the tomb
> Affrighted shall come,
> Cal'd out by the clap of the thunder.

When they were come to Zeldornius, the Lord Juss spake saying, "O most redoubtable Zeldornius, renowned in war, surely thy prognostications by the moon were true. Behold the noble victory thou hast obtained upon thine enemies."

But Zeldornius answered him not, still gazing downwards before his feet. And there was Helteranius fallen, the sword of Jalcanaius Fostus standing in his heart, and his right hand grasping still his own sword that had given Jalcanaius his bane-sore.

So looked they awhile on those two great captains slain. And

Zeldornius said, "Speak not comfortably to me of victory, O Juss. So long as that sword, and that, had his master alive, I did not more desire mine own safety than their destruction who with me in days gone by made conquest of wide Impland. And see with what a poisoned violence they laboured my undoing, and in what an unexpected ruin are they suddenly broken and gone." And as one grown into a deep sadness he said, "Where were all heroical parts but in Helteranius? and a man might make a garment for the moon sooner than fit the o'er-leaping actions of great Jalcanaius, who now leaveth but his body to bedung that earth that was lately shaken at his terror. I have waded in red blood to the knee; and in this hour, in my old years, the world is become for me a vision only and a mock-show."

Therewith he looked on the Demons, and there was that in his eyes that stayed their speech.

In a while he spake again, saying, "I sware unto you my furtherance if I prevailed. But now is mine army passed away as wax wasteth before the fire, and I wait the dark ferryman who tarrieth for no man.[15] Yet, since never have I wrote mine obligations in sandy but in marble memories, and since victory is mine, receive these gifts: and first thou, O Brandoch Daha, my sword, since before thou wast of years eighteen thou wast accounted the mightiest among men-at-arms. Mightily may it avail thee, as me in time gone by. And unto thee, O Spitfire, I give this cloak. Old it is, yet may it stand thee in good stead, since this virtue it hath that he who weareth it shall not fall alive into the hand of his enemies. Wear it for my sake. But unto thee, O Juss, give I no gift, for rich thou art of all good gifts: only my good will give I unto thee, ere earth gape for me."

So they thanked him well. And he said, "Depart from me, since now approacheth that which must complete this day's undoing."

So they fared back to the spy-fortalice, and night came down on the hills. A great wind moaning out of the hueless west tore the clouds as a ragged garment, revealing the lonely moon that fled naked betwixt them. As the Demons looked backward in the moonlight to where Zeldornius stood gazing on the dead, a noise as of thunder made the firm land tremble and drowned the howling of the wind. And they beheld how earth gaped for Zeldornius.

After that, the dark shut down athwart the moon, and night and silence hung on the field of Salapanta.

THE MARCHLANDS OF
THE MORUNA

*Of the journey of the demons from Salapanta to
Eshgrar Ogo: wherein is set down concerning
the Lady of Ishnain Nemartra, and other
notable matters.*

IVARSH FAZ came betimes on the morrow to the
lords of Demonland, and found them ready for the
road. So he asked them where their journey lay, and
they answered, "East."

"Eastward," said Mivarsh, "all ways lead to the
Moruna. None may go thither and not die."

But they laughed and answered him, "Do not too narrowly
define our power, sweet Mivarsh, restraining it to thy capacities.
Know that our journey is a matter determined of, and it is fixed
with nails of diamond[1] to the wall of inevitable necessity."

They took leave of him and went their ways with their small
army. For four days they journeyed through deep woods carpeted
with the leaves of a thousand autumns, where at midmost noon
twilight dwelt among hushed woodland noises, and solemn eyeballs glared nightly between the tree-trunks, gazing on the Demons as they marched or took their rest.

The fifth day, and the sixth and the seventh, they journeyed by
the southern margin of a gravelly sea, made all of sand and gravel
and no drop of water, yet ebbing and flowing away with great

123

waves as another sea doth, never standing still and never at rest. And always by day and night as they came through the desert was a great noise very hideous and a sound as it were of tambourines and trumpets; yet was the place solitary to the eye, and no living thing afoot there save their company faring to the east.

On the eighth day they left the shore of that waterless sea and came by broken rocky ground to the descent to a wide vale, shelterless and unfruitful, with the broad stony bed of a little river winding in the strath.[2] Here, looking eastward, they beheld in the lustre of a late bright-shining sun a castle of red stone on a terrace of the fell-side beyond the valley. Juss said, "We can be there before nightfall, and there will we take guesting." When they drew near they were ware, betwixt sunset and moonlight, of one sitting on a boulder in their path about a furlong from the castle, as if gazing on them and awaiting their coming. But when they came to the boulder there was no such person. So they passed on their way toward the castle, and when they looked behind them, lo, there was he sitting on the boulder bearing his head in his hands: a strange thing, which would cause any man to abhor.

The castle gate stood open, and they entered in, and so by the court-yard to a great hall, with the board set as for a banquet, and bright fires and an hundred candles burning in the still air; but no living thing was there to be seen, nor voice heard in all that castle. Lord Brandoch Daha said, "In this land to fail of marvels only for an hour were the strangest marvel. Banquet we lightly and so to bed." So they sat down and ate, and drank of the honey-sweet wine, till all thoughts of war and hardship and the unimagined perils of the wilderness and Corund's great army preparing their destruction faded from their minds, and the spirit of slumber wooed their weary frames.

Then a faint music, troublous in its voluptuous wild sweetness, floated on the air, and they beheld a lady enter on the dais. Beautiful she seemed beyond the beauty of mortal women. In her dark hair was the likeness of the horned moon in honey-coloured cymophanes[3] every stone whereof held a straight beam of light imprisoned that quivered and gleamed as sunbeams quiver wading in the clear deeps of a summer sea. She wore a coat-hardy of soft crimson silk, close fitting, so that she did truly apparel her apparel and with her own loveliness made it more sumptuous. She said, "My lords and guests in Ishnain Nemartra, there be beds of down and sheets of lawn for all of you that be aweary. But know that I keep a sparrow-hawk sitting on a perch in the eastern tower, and he that will wake my sparrow-hawk this night long, alone without any company and without sleep, I shall come to him at the night's end and shall grant unto him the first thing that he will ask me of earthly things." So saying she departed like a dream.

Brandoch Daha said, "Cast we lots for this adventure."

But Juss spake against it, saying, "There's likely some guile herein. We must not in this accursed land suffer aught to seduce our minds, but follow our set purpose. We must not be of those who go forth for wool and come home shorn."

Brandoch Daha and Spitfire mocked at this, and cast lots between themselves. And the lot fell upon Lord Brandoch Daha. "Thou shalt not deny me this," said he to Lord Juss, "else will I never more do thee good."

"I never could yet deny thee anything," answered Juss. "Art not thou and I finger and thumb? Only forget not, whatsoe'er betide, wherefore we be come hither."

"Art not thou and I finger and thumb?" said Brandoch Daha. "Fear nothing, O friend of my heart. I'll not forget it."

So while the others slept, Brandoch Daha waked the sparrow-hawk, night-long in the eastern chamber. For all that the cold hillside without was rough with hoar-frost the air was warm in that chamber and heavy, disposing strongly to sleep. Yet he closed not an eye, but still beheld the sparrow-hawk, telling it stories and tweaking it by the tail ever and anon as it grew drowsy. And it answered shortly and boorishly, looking upon him malevolently.

And with the golden dawn, behold that lady in the shadowy doorway. At her entering in, the sparrow-hawk clicked its wings as in anger, and without more ado tucked its beak beneath its wing and went to sleep. But that bright lady, looking on the Lord Brandoch Daha, spake and said, "Require it of me, my Lord Brandoch Daha, that which thou most desirest of earthly things."

But he, as one bedazzled, stood up saying, "O lady, is not thy beauty at the dawn of day an irradiation that might dispel the mists of hell? My heart is ravished with thy loveliness and only fed with thy sight. Therefore thy body will I have, and none other thing earthly."

"Thou art a fool," she cried, "that knowest not what thou askest. Of all things earthly mightest thou have taken choose; but I am not earthly."

He answered, "I will have nought else."

"Thou dost embrace then a great danger," said she, "and loss of all thy good luck, for thee and thy friends beside."

But Brandoch Daha, seeing how her face became on a sudden such as are new-blown roses at the dawning, and her eyes wide and dark with love-longing, came to her and took her in his arms and fell to kissing and embracing of her. On such wise they abode for awhile, that he was ware of no thing else on earth save only the sense-maddening caress of that lady's hair, the perfume of it, the kiss of her mouth, the swell and fall of that lady's breast straining against his. She said in his ear softly, "I see thou art too masterful. I see thou art one who will be denied nothing, on whatsoever thine heart is set. Come." And they passed by a heavy-curtained doorway into an inner chamber, where the air was filled with the breath of myrrh and nard and ambergris,[4] a fragrancy as of sleeping loveliness. Here, amid the darkness of rich hangings and subdued glints of gold, a warm radiance of shaded lamps watched above a couch, great and broad and downy-pillowed. And here for a long time they solaced them with love and all delight.

Even as all things have an end, he said at the last, "O my lady, mistress of hearts, here would I abide ever, abandoning all else for thy love sake. But my companions tarry for me in thine halls below, and great matters wait on my direction. Give me thy divine mouth once again, and bid me adieu."

She was lying as if asleep across his breast: smooth-skinned, white, warm, with shapely throat leaned backward against the spice-odorous darknesses of her unbound hair; one tress, heavy and splendid like a python, coiled between white arm and bosom. Swift as a snake she turned, clinging fiercely about him, pressing fiercely again to his her insatiable sweet fervent lips, crying that here must he dwell unto eternity in the intoxication of perfect love and pleasure.

But when in the end, gently constraining her to loose him and let him go, he arose and clothed and armed him, that lady caught about her a translucent robe of silvery sheen, as when the summer moon veils but not hides with a filmy cloud her beauties' splendour, and so standing before him spake and said, "Go then. This is got by casting of pearls to hogs. I may not slay thee, since over thy body I have no other power. But because thou shalt not laugh overmuch, having required me of that which was beyond the pact and being enjoyed is now slighted of thee and abused, therefore know, proud man, that three gifts I here will grant thee thereto of mine own choosing. Thou shalt have war and not peace. He that thou worst hatest shall throw down and ruin thy fair lordship, Krothering Castle and the mains thereof. And though vengeance shall overtake him at the last, by another's hand than thine shall it come, and to thine hand shall it be denied."

Therewith she fell a-weeping. And the Lord Brandoch Daha,

with great resolution, went forth from the chamber.[5] And looking back from the threshold he beheld both that and the outer chamber void of lady and sparrow-hawk both. And a great weariness came suddenly upon him. So, going down, he found Lord Juss and his companions sleeping on the cold stones, and the banquet hall empty of all gear and dank with moss and cobwebs, and bats sleeping head-downward among the crumbling roofbeams; nor was any sign of last night's banqueting. So Brandoch Daha roused his companions, and told Juss how he had fared, and of the weird[6] laid on him by that lady.

And they went greatly wondering forth of the accursed castle of Ishnain Nemartra, glad to come off so scatheless.

On that ninth day of their journey from Salapanta they came through waste lands of stone and living rock, where not so much as an earth-louse stirred with life. Gorges split the earth here and there: rock-walled labyrinths of gloom, unvisited for ever by sunbeam or moonbeam, turbulent in their depths with waters that leaped and churned for ever, never still and never silent. So was that day's journey tortuous, turning now up now down along those river banks to find crossing places.

When they were halted at noon by the deepest rift they had yet beheld, there came one hastening to them and fell down by Juss and lay panting face to earth as breathless from long running. And when they raised him up, behold Mivarsh Faz, harnessed in the gear of a black rider of Jalcanaius Fostus and armed with axe and sword. Great was his agitation, and he speechless for lack of breath. They used him kindly, and gave him to drink from a great skin of wine, Zeldornius's gift, and anon he said, "He hath armed countless hundreds of our folk with weapons taken from Salapanta field. These, led by the devils his sons, with Philpritz cursed of the gods, be gone before to hold all the ways be-east of you. Night and day have I ridden and run to warn you. Himself, with his main strength of devils ultramontane, rideth hot on your tracks."

They thanked him well, marvelling much that he should be at such pains to advertise them of their danger. "I have eat your salt," answered he, "and moreover ye are against this naughty wicked baldhead that came over the mountains to oppress us. Therefore I would do you good. But I can little. For I am poor, that was rich in land and fee. And I am alone, that had formerly five hundred spearmen lodging in my halls to do my pleasure."

"There's need to do quickly that we do," said Lord Brandoch Daha. "How great start of him hadst thou?"

"He must be upon you in an hour or twain," said Mivarsh, and fell a-weeping.

"To cope him in the open," said Juss, "were great glory, and our certain death."

"Give me to think, but a minute's while," said Brandoch Daha. And while they busked them he walked musing by the lip of that ravine, switching pebbles over the edge with his sword. Then he said, "This is without doubt that stream Athrashah spoken of by Gro. O Mivarsh, runneth not this flood of Athrashah south to the salt lakes of Ogo Morveo, and was there not thereabout a hold named Eshgrar Ogo?"

Mivarsh answered, "This is so. But never heard I of any so witless as go thither. Here where we stand is the land fearsome enough; but Eshgrar Ogo standeth at the very edge of the Moruna. No man hath harboured there these hundred years."

"Standeth it yet?" said Brandoch Daha.

"For all I wot of," answered Mivarsh.

"Is it strong?" he asked.

"In old times it was thought no place stronger," answered Mivarsh. "But ye were as well die here by the hand of the devils ultramontane, as there be torn in pieces by bad spirits."

Brandoch Daha turned him about to Juss. "It is resolved?" said he. Juss answered, "Yea;" and forthwith they started at a great pace south along the river.

"Methought you should have been gotten clean away ere this," said Mivarsh as they went. "This is but nine or ten days' journey, and 'tis now the sixteenth day since ye did leave me on Salapanta Hills."

Brandoch Daha laughed. "Sixteenth!" said he. "Thou'lt be rich, Mivarsh, if thou reckon gold pieces o' this fashion thou dost days. This is but our ninth day's journey."

But Mivarsh stood stoutly to it, saying that was the seventh day after their departure when Corund first came to Salapanta, "And I fleeing now nine days before his face chanced on your tracks, and now out of all expectation on you." Nor for all their mocking would he be turned from this. And when, as they still pressed through the desert southward, the sun declined and set in a clear sky, behold the moon a little past her full: and Juss saw that she was seven days older than on that night she was when they came to Ishnain Nemartra. So he showed this wonder to Brandoch Daha and Spitfire, and much they marvelled.

"You are much to thank me," said Brandoch Daha, "that I

kept you not a full year awaiting of me. Beshrew me, but that seven days' space seemed to me but an hour!"

"Likely enow, to thee," said Spitfire somewhat greenly. "But all we slept the week out on the cold stones, and I am half lamed yet with the ache on't."

"Nay," said Juss, laughing; "I will not have thee blame him."

The moon was high when they came to the salt lakes that lay one a little above the other in rocky basins. Their waters were like rough silver, and the harsh face of the wilderness was black and silver in the moonlight; and it was as a country of dead bones, blind and sterile beneath the moon. Betwixt the lakes a rib of rock rose monstrous to an eminence crag-begirt on every side, with dark walls ringing it round above the cliffs. Thither they hastened, and as they climbed and stumbled among the crags a she-owl squeaked on the battlements and took wing ghost-like above their heads. The teeth of Mivarsh Faz chattered, but right glad were the Demons as they won up the rocks and entered at last into that deserted burg. Without, the night was still; but fires were burning in the desert eastward, and others as they watched were kindled in the west, and soon was the circle joined of twinkling points of red round about Eshgrar Ogo and the lakes.

Juss said, "By an hour have we forestalled them. And behold how he ringeth us about as men ring a scorpion in flame."

So they made all sure, and set the guard, and slept until past dawn. But Mivarsh slept not, for terror of hob-thrushes from the Moruna.

XI

THE BURG OF ESHGRAR OGO

*Of the Lord Corund's besieging of the burg above
the lakes of Ogo Morveo, and what befell there
betwixt him and the demons; wherein is also an
example how the subtle of heart standeth at whiles
in great danger of his death.*

HEN the Lord Corund knew of a surety that he held them of Demonland shut up in Eshgrar Ogo, he let dight supper[1] in his tent, and made a surfeit of venison pasties and heath-cocks and lobsters from the lakes. Therewith he drank nigh a skinful of sweet dark Thramnian wine, in such sort that an hour before midnight, becoming speechless, he was holpen by Gro to his couch and slept a great deep sleep till morning.

Gro watched in the tent, his right elbow propped on the table, his cheek resting on his hand, his left hand reaching forward with delicate fingers toying now with the sleek heavy perfumed masses of his beard, now with the goblet whence he sipped ever and anon pale wine of Permio. His thoughts inconstant as insects in a summer garden flitted ever round and round, resting now on the scene before him, the great form of his general wrapt in slumber, now on other scenes sundered by great gulfs of time or weary leagues of perilous ways. So that in one instant he saw in fancy that lady in Carcë welcoming her lord returned in triumph, and him, may be, crowned king of new-vanquished Impland; and in the next, swept from the future to the past, beheld again the great sending-off in

130

Zajë Zaculo, Gaslark in his splendour on the golden stairs saying adieu to those three captains and their matchless armament foredoomed to dogs and crows on Salapanta Hills; and always, like a gloomy background darkening his mind, loomed the yawning void, featureless and vast, beyond the investing circle of Corund's armies: the blind blasted emptiness of the Moruna.

With such fancies, melancholy like a great bird settled upon his soul. The lights flickered in their sockets, and for very weariness Gro's eyelids closed at length over his large liquid eyes; and, too tired to stir from his seat to seek his couch, he sank forward on the table, his head pillowed on his arms. The red glow of the brazier slumbered ever dimmer and dimmer on the slender form and black shining curls of Gro, and on the mighty frame of Corund where he lay with one great spurred booted leg stretched along the couch, and the other flung out sideways resting its heel on the ground.

It wanted but two hours of noon when a sunbeam striking through an opening in the hangings of the tent shone upon Corund's eyelids, and he awoke fresh and brisk as a youth on a hunting morn. He waked Gro, and giving him a clap on the shoulder, "Thou wrongest a fair morn," he said. "The devil damn me black as buttermilk[2] if it be not great shame in thee; and I, that was born this day six and forty years as the years come about, busy with mine affairs since sunrise."

Gro yawned and smiled and stretched himself. "O Corund," he said, "counterfeit a livelier wonder in thine eyes if thou wilt persuade me thou sawest the sunrise. For I think that were as new and unexampled a sight for thee as any I could produce to thee in Impland."

Corund answered, "Truly I was seldom so uncivil as surprise Madam Aurora in her nightgown. And the thrice or four times I have been forced thereto, taught me it is an hour of crude airs and mists which breed cold dark humours in the body,[3] an hour when the torch of life burns weakest. Within there! bring me my morning draught."

The boy brought two cups of white wine, and while they drank, "A thin ungracious drink is the well-spring," said Corund: "a drink for queasy-stomached skipjacks:[4] for sand-levericks,[5] not for men. And like it is the dayspring: an ungrateful sapless hour, an hour for stab-i'-the-backs and cold-blooded betrayers. Ah, give me wine," he cried, "and noon-day vices, and brazen-browed iniquities."

"Yet there's many a deed of profit done by owl-light," said Gro.

"Ay," said Corund: "deeds of darkness: and there, my lord, I'm still thy scholar. Come, let's be doing." And taking his helm and weapons, and buckling about him his great wolfskin cloak, for the air was eager and frosty without, he strode forth. Gro wrapped himself in his fur mantle, drew on his lambskin gloves, and followed him.

"If thou wilt take my rede," said Lord Gro, as they looked on Eshgrar Ogo stark in the barren sunlight, "thou'lt do this honour to Philpritz, which I question not he much desireth, to suffer him and his folk take first knock at this nut. It hath a hard look. Pity it were to waste good Witchland blood in a first assault, when these vile instruments stand ready to our purpose."

Corund grunted in his beard, and with Gro at his elbow paced in silence through the lines, his keen eyes searching ever the cliffs and walls of Eshgrar Ogo, till in some half-hour's space he halted again before his tent, having made a complete circuit of the burg. Then he spake: "Put me in yonder fighting-stead, and if it were only but I and fifty able lads to man the walls, yet would I hold it against ten thousand."

Gro held his peace awhile, and then said, "Thou speakest this in all sadness?"

"In sober sadness," answered Corund, squaring his shoulders at the burg.

"Then thou'lt not assault it?"

Corund laughed. "Not assault it, quotha! That were a sweet tale 'twixt the boiled and the roast in Carcë: I'd not assault it!"

"Yet consider," said Gro, taking him by the arm. "So shapeth the matter in my mind: they be few and shut up in a little place, in this far land, out of reach and out of mind of all succour. Were they devils and not men, the multitude of our armies and thine own tried qualities must daunt them. Be the place never so cocksure,[6] doubt not some doubts thereof must poison their security. Therefore before thou risk a repulse which must dispel those doubts use thine advantage. Bid Juss to a parley. Offer him conditions: it skills not what.[7] Bribe them out into the open."

"A pretty plan," said Corund. "Thou'lt merit wisdom's crown if thou canst tell me what conditions we can offer that they would take. And whilst thou riddlest that, remember that though thou and I be masters hereabout, another reigns in Carcë."

Lord Gro laughed gently. "Leave jesting," he said, "O Corund, and never hope to gull me to believe thee such a babe in policy. Shall the King blame us though we sign away Demonland, ay and the wide world besides, to Juss to lure him forth? Unless indeed we were so neglectful of our interest as suffer him, once forth, to elude our clutches."

"Gro," said Corund, "I love thee. But hardly canst thou receive things as I receive them that have dealt all my days in great stripes, given and taken in the open field. I sticked not to take part in thy notable treason against these poor snakes of Impland that we trapped in Orpish. All's fair against such dirt. Besides, great need was upon us then, and hard it is for an empty sack to stand straight. But here is far other matter. All's won here but the plucking of the apple: it is the very main of my ambition to humble these Demons openly by the terror of my sword: wherefore I will not use upon them cogs and stops[8] and all thy devilish tricks, such as should bring me more of scorn than of glory in the eyes of aftercomers."

So speaking, he issued command and sent an herald to go forth beneath the battlements with a flag of truce. And the herald cried aloud and said: "From Corund of Witchland unto the lords of Demonland: thus saith the Lord Corund, 'I hold this burg of Eshgrar Ogo as a nut betwixt the crackers. Come down and speak with me in the batable land before the burg, and I swear to you peace and grith[9] while we parley, and thereto pledge I mine honour as a man of war."

So when the due ceremonies were performed, the Lord Juss came down from Eshgrar Ogo and with him the lords Spitfire and Brandoch Daha and twenty men to be their bodyguard. Corund went to meet them with his guard about him, and his four sons that fared with him to Impland, Hacmon, namely, and Heming and Viglus and Dormanes: sullen and dark young men, likely of look, of a little less fierceness than their father. Gro, fair to see and slender as a racehorse, went at his side, muffled to the ears in a cloak of ermine; and behind came Philpritz Faz helmed with a winged helm of iron and gold. A gilded corselet had Philpritz, and trousers of panther's skin, and he came a-slinking at Corund's heel as the jackal slinks behind the lion.

When they were met, Juss spake and said, "This would I know first, my Lord Corund, how thou comest hither, and why, and by what right thou disputest with us the ways eastward out of Impland."

Corund answered, leaning on his spear, "I need not answer thee in this. And yet I will. How came I? I answer thee, over the cold mountain wall of Akra Skabranth. And 'tis a feat hath not his fellow in man's remembrance until now, with so great a force and in so short a space of time."

" 'Tis well enough," said Juss. "I'll grant thee thou hast outrun mine expectations of thee."

"Next thou demandest why," said Corund. "Suffice it for thee that the King hath had advertisement of your farings into Impland and your designs therein. For to bring these to nought am I come."

"There was many firkins[10] of wine drunk dry in Carcë," said Hacmon, "and many a noble person senseless and spewing on the ground ere morn for pure delight, when cursed Goldry was made away. We were little minded these healths should be proved vain at last."

"Was that ere thou rodest from Permio?" said Lord Brandoch Daha. "The merry god wrought of our side that night, if my memory cheat not."

"Thou demandest last," said Corund, "my Lord Juss, by what right I bar your passage eastaway. Know, therefore, that not of mine own self speak I unto you, but as vicar in wide-fronted Impland of our Lord Gorice XII., King of Kings, most glorious and most great. There remaineth no way out for you from this place save into the rigour of mine hands. Therefore let us, according to the nature of great men, agree to honourable conditions. And this is mine offer, O Juss. Yield up this burg of Eshgrar Ogo, and therewith thy sealed word in a writing acknowledging our Lord the King to be King of Demonland and all ye his quiet and obedient subjects, even as we be. And I will swear unto you of my part, and in the name of our Lord the King, and give you hostages thereto, that ye shall depart in peace whither you list with all love and safety."

The Lord Juss scowled fiercely on him. "O Corund," he said, "as little as we do understand the senseless wind, so little we understand thy word. Oft enow hath gray silver been in the fire betwixt us and you Witchlanders; for the house of Gorice fared ever like the foul toad, that may not endure to smell the sweet savour of the vine when it flourisheth. So for this time we will abide in this hold, and withstand your most grievous attempts."

"With free honesty and open heart," said Corund, "I made thee this offer; which if thou refuse I am not thy lackey to renew it."

Gro said, "It is writ and sealed, and wanteth but thy signmanual, my Lord Juss," and with the word he made sign to Philpritz Faz that went to Lord Juss with a parchment. Juss put the parchment by, saying, "No more: ye are answered," and he was turning on his heel when Philpritz, louting forward suddenly, gave him a great yerk beneath the ribs[11] with a dagger slipped from his sleeve. But Juss wore a privy coat that turned the dagger. Howbeit with the greatness of that stroke he staggered aback.

Now Spitfire clapped hand to sword, and the other Demons with him, but Juss loudly shouted that they should not be truce-breakers but know first what Corund would do. And Corund said, "Dost hear me, Juss? I had neither hand nor part in this."

Brandoch Daha drew up his lip and said, "This is nought but what was to be looked for. It is a wonder, O Juss, that thou shouldst hold out to such mucky dogs a hand without a whip in it."

"Such strokes come home or miss merely," said Gro softly in Corund's ear, and he hugged himself beneath his cloak, looking with furtive amusement on the Demons. But Corund with a face red in anger said, "It is thine answer, O Juss?" And when Juss said, "It is our answer, O Corund," Corund said violently, "Then red war I give you; and this withal to testify our honour." And he let lay hands on Philpritz Faz and with his own hand hacked the head from his body before the eyes of both their armies. Then in a great voice he said, "As bloodily as I have revenged the honour of Witchland on this Philpritz, so will I revenge it on all of you or ever I draw off mine armies from these lakes of Ogo Morveo."

So the Demons went up into the burg, and Gro and Corund home to their tents. "This was well thought on," said Gro, "to flaunt the flag of seeming honesty, and with the motion rid us of this fellow that promised ever to grow thorns to make uneasy our seat in Impland."

Corund answered him not a word.

In that same hour Corund marshalled his folk and assaulted Eshgrar Ogo, placing those of Impland in the van.[12] They prospered not at all. Many a score lay slain without the walls that night; and the obscene beasts from the desert feasted on their bodies by the light of the moon.[13]

Next morning the Lord Corund sent an herald and bade the Demons again to a parley. And now he spake only to Brandoch Daha, bidding him deliver up those brethren Juss and Spitfire, "And if thou wilt yield them to my pleasure, then shalt thou and all thy people else depart in peace without conditions."

"An offer indeed," said Lord Brandoch Daha; "if it be not in mockery. Say it loud, that my folk may hear."

Corund did so, and the Demons heard it from the walls of the burg.

Lord Brandoch Daha stood somewhat apart from Juss and

Spitfire and their guard. "Libel it me out,"[14] he said. "For good as I now must deem thy word, thine hand and seal must I have to show my followers ere they consent with me in such a thing."

"Write thou," said Corund to Gro. "To write my name is all my scholarship." And Gro took forth his ink-horn and wrote in a great fair hand this offer on a parchment. "The most fearfullest oaths thou knowest," said Corund; and Gro wrote them, whispering, "He mocketh us only." But Corund said, "No matter: 'tis a chance worth our chancing," and slowly and with labour signed his name to the writing, and gave it to Lord Brandoch Daha.

Brandoch Daha read it attentively, and tucked it in his bosom beneath his byrny. "This," he said, "shall be a keepsake for me of thee, my Lord Corund. Reminding me," and here his eyes grew terrible, "so long as there surviveth a soul of you in Witchland, that I am still to teach the world throughly what that man must abide that durst affront me with such an offer."

Corund answered him, "Thou art a dapper fellow. It is a wonder that thou wilt strut in the tented field with all this womanish gear. Thy shield: how many of these sparkling baubles thinkest thou I'd leave in it were we once come to knocks?"

"I'll tell thee," answered Lord Brandoch Daha. "For every jewel that hath been beat out of my shield in battle, never yet went I to war that I brought not home an hundredfold to set it fair again, from the spoils I obtained from mine enemies. Now this will I bid thee, O Corund, for thy scornful words: I will bid thee to single combat, here and in this hour. Which if thou deny, then art thou an open and apparent dastard."[15]

Corund chuckled in his beard, but his brow darkened somewhat. "I pray what age dost thou take me of?" said he. "I bare a sword when thou was yet in swaddling clothes. Behold mine armies, and what advantage I hold upon you. Oh, my sword is enchanted, my lord: it will not out of the scabbard."

Brandoch Daha smiled disdainfully, and said to Spitfire, "Mark well, I pray thee, this great lord of Witchland. How many true fingers hath a Witch on his left hand?"

"As many as on his right," said Spitfire.

"Good. And how many on both?"

"Two less than a deuce," said Spitfire; "for they be false fazarts[16] to the fingers' ends."

"Very well answered," said Lord Brandoch Daha.

"You're pleasant," Corund said. "But your fusty jibes move me not a whit. It were a simple part indeed to take thine offer when all wise counsels bid me use my power and crush you."

"Thou'dst kill me soon with thy mouth," said Brandoch Daha. "In sum, thou art a brave man when it comes to roaring and swearing: a big bubber of wine, as men say to drink drunk is an ordinary matter with thee every day in the week; but I fear thou durst not fight."

"Doth not thy nose swell at that?" said Spitfire.

But Corund shrugged his shoulders. "A footra for your baits!" he answered. "I am scarce bounden to do such a kindness to you of Demonland as lay down mine advantage and fight alone, against a sworder.[17] Your old foxes are seldom taken in springes."[18]

"I thought so," said Lord Brandoch Daha. "Surely the frog will have hair sooner than any of you Witchlanders shall dare to stand me."

So ended the second parley before Eshgrar Ogo. The same day Corund essayed again to storm the hold, and grievous was the battle and hard put to it were they of Demonland to hold the walls. Yet in the end were Corund's men thrown back with great slaughter. And night fell, and they returned to their tents.

"Mine invention," said Gro, when on the next day they took counsel together, "hath yet some contrivance in her purse which shall do us good, if it fall but out to our mind. But I doubt much it will dislike thee."

"Well, say it out, and I'll give thee my censure on't," said Corund.

Gro spake: "It hath been shown we may not have down this tree by hewing above ground. Let's dig about the roots. And first give them a seven-night's space for reckoning up their chances, that they may see morning and evening from the burg thine armies set down to invest them. Then, when their hopes are something sobered by that sight, and want of action hath trained their minds to sad reflection, call them to parley, going straight beneath the wall; and this time shalt thou address thyself only to the common sort, offering them all generous and free conditions thou canst think on. There's little they can ask that we'd not blithely grant them if they'll but yield us up their captains."

"It mislikes me," answered Corund. "Yet it may serve. But thou shalt be my spokesman herein. For never yet went I cap in hand to ask favour of the common muck o' the world, nor I will not do it now."

"O but thou must," said Gro. "Of thee they will receive in good faith what in me they would account but practice."

"That's true enough," said Corund. "But I cannot stomach it. Withal, I am too rough spoken."

Gro smiled. "He that hath need of a dog," he said, "calleth him 'Sir Dog.' Come, come, I'll school thee to it. Is it not a smaller thing than months of tedious hardship in this frozen desert? Bethink thee too what honour it were to thee to ride home to Carcë with Juss and Spitfire and Brandoch Daha bounden in a string."

Not without much persuasion was Corund won to this. Yet at the last he consented. For seven days and seven nights his armies sat before the burg without sign; and on the eighth day he bade the Demons to a parley, and when that was granted went with his sons and twenty men-at-arms up the great rib of rock between the lakes, and stood below the east wall of the burg. Bitter chill was the air that day. Powdery snow light-fallen blew in little wisps along the ground, and the rocks were slippery with an invisible coat of ice. Lord Gro, being troubled with an ague, excused himself from that faring and kept his tent.

Corund stood beneath the walls with his folk about him. "I have matter of import," he cried, "and 'tis needful it be heard both by the highest and the lowest amongst you. Ere I begin, summon them all to this part of the walls: a look-out is enow to shield you of the other parts from any sudden onslaught, which besides I swear to you is clean without my purpose." So when they were thick on the wall above him, he began to say, "Soldiers of Demonland, against you had I never quarrel. Behold how in this Impland I have made freedom flourish as a flower. I have strook off the heads of Philpritz Faz, and Illarosh, and Lurmesh, and Gandassa, and Fax Fay Faz, that were the lords and governors here aforetime, abounding in all the bloody and crying sins, oppression, gluttony, idleness, cruelty, and extortion. And of my clemency I delivered all their possessions unto their subjects to hold and order after their own will alone, who before did put on patience and endured with much heartburning the tyranny of these Fazes, until by me they found a remedy for their more freedom. In like manner, not against you do I war, O men of Demonland; but against the tyrants that enforced you for their private gain to suffer hardship and death in this remote country: namely, against Juss and Spitfire that came hither in quest of their cursed brother whom the might of the great King hath happily removed. And against Brandoch Daha am I come, of insolence untamed, who liveth a chambering idle life eating and drinking and exercising tyranny, while the pleasant lands of Krothering and Failze and Stropardon, and the dwellers in the isles, Sorbey, Morvey, Strufey, Dalney, and Kenarvey, and they of Westmark and all the western parts of Demonland groan and wax lean to feed his luxury. To your hurt only have these three led you, as cattle to the slaughter. Deliver them to me, that I may chastise them, and I, that am great viceroy of Impland, will make you free and grant you lordships: a lordship for every man of you in this my realm of Impland."

While Corund spake, the Lord Brandoch Daha went among the soldiers bidding them hold their peace and not murmur against Corund. But those that were most hot for action he sent about an errand preparing what he had in mind. So that when the Lord Corund ceased from his declaiming, all was ready to hand, and with one voice the soldiers of Lord Juss that stood upon the wall cried out and said, "This is thy word, O Corund, and this our answer," and therewith flung down upon him from pots and buckets and every kind of vessel a deluge of slops and offal and all filth that came to hand. A bucketful took Corund in the mouth, befouling all his great beard, so that he gave back spitting. And he and his, standing close beneath the wall, and little expecting so sudden and ill an answer, fared shamefully, being all well soused and bemerded with filth and lye.

Therewith went up great shouts of laughter from the walls. But Corund cried out, "O filth of Demonland, this is my latest word with you. And though 'twere ten years I must besiege this hold, yet will I take it over your heads. And very ill to do with shall ye find me in the end, and very puissant, proud, mighty, cruel, and bloody in my conquest."

"What, lads?" said Lord Brandoch Daha, standing on the battlements, "have we not fed this beast with pigwash enow, but he must still be snuffing and snouking at our gate? Give me another pailful."

So the Witches returned to their tents with great shame. So hot was Corund in anger against the Demons, that he stayed not to eat nor drink at his coming down from Eshgrar Ogo, but straight gathered force and made an assault upon the burg, the mightiest he had yet essayed; and his picked men of Witchland were in that assault, and he himself to lead them. Thrice by main fury they won up into the hold, but all were slain who set foot therein, and Corund's young son Dormanes wounded to the death. And at even they drew off from the battle. There fell in that fight an hundred and four-score Demons, and of the Imps five hundred, and of the Witches three hundred and ninety and nine. And many were hurt of either side.

*   *   *

Wrath sat like thunder on Corund's brow at suppertime. He ate his meat savagely, thrusting great gobbets in his mouth, crunching the bones like a beast, taking deep draughts of wine with every mouthful, which yet dispelled not his black mood. Over against him Gro sat silent, shivering now and then for all that he kept his ermine cloak about him and the brazier stood at his elbow. He made but a poor meal, drinking mulled wine in little sips and dipping little pieces of bread in it.

So wore without speech that cheerless and unkindly meal, until the Lord Corund, looking suddenly across the board at Gro and catching his eye studying him, said, "That was a bright star of thine and then shined clear upon thee when thou tookest this bout of shivering fits and so wentest not with me to be soused with muck before the burg."

"Who would have dreamed," answered Gro, "of their using so base and shameful a part?"

"Not thou, I'll swear," said Corund, looking evilly upon him and marking, as he thought, a twinkling light in Gro's eyes. Gro shivered again, sipped his wine, and shifted his glance uneasily under that unfriendly stare.

Corund drank awhile in silence, then flushing suddenly a darker red, said, leaning heavily across the board at him, "Dost know why I said 'not thou'?"

" 'Twas scarce needful, to thy friend," said Gro.

"I said it," said Corund, "because I know thou didst look for another thing when thou didst skulk shamming here."

"Another thing?"

"Sit not there like some prim-mouthed miss feigning an innocence all know well thou hast not," said Corund, "or I'll kill thee. Thou plottedst my death with the Demons. And because thyself hast no shred of honour in thy soul, thou hadst not the wit to perceive that their nobility would shrink from such a betrayal as thy hopes entertained."

Gro said, "This is a jest I cannot laugh at; or else 'tis madman's brabble."

"Dissembling cur," said Corund, "be sure that I hold him not less guilty that holds the ladder than him that mounts the wall. It was thy design they should smite us at unawares when we went up to them with this proposal thou didst urge on me so hotly."

Gro made as if to rise. "Sit down!" said Corund. "Answer me; didst not thou egg on the poor snipe Philpritz to that attempt on Juss?"

"He told me on't," said Gro.

"O, thou art cunning," said Corund. "There too I see thy treachery. Had they fallen upon us, thou mightest have thrown thyself safely upon their mercy."

"This is foolishness," said Gro. "We were far stronger."

" 'Tis so," said Corund. "When did I charge thee with wisdom and sober judgement? With treachery I know thou art soaked wet."

"And thou art my friend!" said Gro.

Corund said in a while, "I have long known thee to be both a subtle and dissembling fox, and now I durst trust thee no more, for fear I should fall further into thy danger. I am resolved to murther thee."

Gro fell back in his chair and flung out his arms. "I have been here before," he said. "I have beheld it, in moonlight and in the barren glare of day, in fair weather and in hail and snow, with the great winds charging over the wastes. And I knew it was accursed. From Morna Moruna, ere I was born or thou, O Corund, or any of us, treason and cruelty blacker than night herself had birth, and brought death to their begetter and all his folk. From Morna Moruna bloweth this wind about the waste to blast our love and bring us destruction. Ay, kill me; I'll not ward myself, not i' the smallest."

" 'Tis small matter, Goblin," said Corund, "whether thou shouldst or no. Thou art but a louse between my fingers, to kill or cast away as shall seem me good."

"I was King Gaslark's man," said Gro, as if talking in a dream; "and between a man and a boy near fifteen years I served him true and costly. Yet it was my fortune in all that time and at the ending thereof only to get a beard on my chin and remorse at heart. To what scorned purpose must I plot against him? Pity of Witchland, of Witchland sliding as then into the pit of adverse luck, 'twas that made force upon me. And I served Witchland well: but fate ever fought o' the other side. I it was that counselled King Gorice XI. to draw out from the fight at Kartadza. Yet wanton Fortune trod down the scale for Demonland. I prayed him not wrastle with Goldry in the Foliot Isles. Thou didst back me. Nought but rebukes and threats of death gat I therefrom; but because my redes were set at nought, evil fell upon Witchland. I helped our Lord the King when he conjured and made a sending against the Demons. He loved me therefor and upheld me, but great envy was raised up against me in Carcë for that fact. Yet I bare up, for thy friendship and thy lady wife's were as bright fires to warm me against all the frosts of their ill-will. And now, for love of thee, I fared with thee to Impland.

And here by the Moruna where in old days I wandered in danger and in sorrow, it is fitting I behold at length the emptiness of all my days."

Therewith Gro fell silent a minute, and then began to say: "O Corund, I'll strip bare my soul to thee before thou kill me. It is most true that until now, sitting before Eshgrar Ogo, it hath been present to my heart how great an advantage we held against the Demons, and the glory of their defence, so little a strength against us so many, and the great glory of their flinging of us back, these things were a splendour to my soul beholding them. Such glamour hath ever shone to me all my life's days when I behold great men battling still beneath the bludgeonings of adverse fortune that, howsoever they be mine enemies, it lieth not in my virtue to withhold from admiration of them and well nigh love. But never was I false to thee, nor much less ever thought, as thou most unkindly accusest me, to compass thy destruction."

"Thou dost whine like a woman for thy life," said Corund. "Cowardly hounds never stirred pity in me." Yet he moved not, only looking dourly on Gro.

Gro plucked forth his own sword, and pushed it towards Corund hilt-foremost across the board. "Such words are worse than sword-thrusts betwixt us twain," said he. "Thou shalt see how I'll welcome death. The King will praise thee, when thou showest the cause. And it will be sweet news to Corinius and them that have held me in their hate, that thy love hath cast me off, and thou hast rid them of me at last."

But Corund stirred not. After a space, he filled another cup, and drank, and sat on. And Gro sat motionless before him. At last Corund rose heavily from his seat, and pushing Gro's sword back across the table, "Thou'dst best to bed," said he. "But the night air's o'er shrewd for thine ague. Sleep on my couch to-night."

The day dawned cold and gray, and with the dawn Corund ordered his lines round about Eshgrar Ogo and sat down for a siege. For ten days he sat before the burg, and nought befell from dawn till night, from night till dawn: only the sentinels walked on the walls and Corund's folk guarded their lines. On the eleventh day came a bank of fog rolling westward from the Moruna, chill and dank, blotting out the features of the land. Snow fell, and the fog hung on the land, and night came of such a pitchy blackness that even by torch-light a man might not see his hand stretched forth at arm's length before him. Five days the fog held. On the fifth night, it being the twenty-fourth of November, in the darkness of the third hour after midnight, the alarm was sounded and Corund summoned by a runner from the north with word that a sally was made from Eshgrar Ogo, and the lines bursten through in that quarter, and fighting going forward in the mirk. Corund was scarce harnessed and gotten forth into the night, when a second runner came hot-foot from the south with tidings of a great fight thereaway. All was confounded in the dark, and nought certain, save that the Demons were broken out from Eshgrar Ogo. In a space, as Corund came with his folk to the northern quarter and joined in the fight, came a message from his son Heming that Spitfire and a number with him were broken out at the other side and gotten away westward, and a great band chasing him back towards Outer Impland; and therewith that more than an hundred Demons were surrounded and penned in by the shore of the lakes, and the burg entered and taken by Corund's folk; but of Juss and Brandoch Daha no certain news, save that they were not of Spitfire's company, but were with those against whom Corund went in person, having fared forth northaway. So went the battle through the night. Corund himself had sight of Juss, and exchanged shots with him with twirl-spears in a lifting of the fog toward dawn, and a son of his bare witness of Brandoch Daha in that same quarter, and had gotten a great wound from him.

When night was past, and the Witches returned from the pursuit, Corund straitly questioned his officers, and went himself about the battlefield hearing each man's story and viewing the slain. Those Demons that were hemmed against the lakes had all lost their lives, and some were taken up dead in other parts, and some few alive. These would his officers let slay, but Corund said, "Since I am king in Impland, till that the King receive it of me, it is not this handful of earth-lice shall shake my safety here; and I may well give them their lives, that fought sturdily against us." So he gave them peace. And he said unto Gro, "Better that for every Demon dead in Ogo Morveo ten should rise up against us, if but Juss only and Brandoch Daha were slain."

"I'll be in the tale with thee, if thou wilt proclaim them dead," said Gro. "And nothing is likelier, if they be gone with but two or three on to the Moruna, than that such a tale should come true ere it were told in Carcë."

"Pshaw!" said Corund, "to the devil with such false feathers. What's done shows brave enow without them: Impland conquered, Juss's army minced to a gallimaufry,[19] himself and

Brandoch Daha chased like runaway thralls up on the Moruna. Where if devils tear them, 'tis my best wish come true. If not, thou'lt hear of them, be sure. Dost think these can survive on earth and not raise a racket that shall be heard from hence to Carcë?"

XII

KOSHTRA PIVRARCHA

*Of the coming of the Lords of Demonland to
Morna Moruna, whence they beheld the
Zimiamvian Mountains, seen also by Gro in years
gone by; and of the wonders seen by them and
perils undergone and deeds done in their attempt
on Koshtra Pivrarcha, the which alone of all
Earth's mountains looketh down upon Koshtra
Belorn; and none shall ascend up into Koshtra
Belorn that hath not first looked down upon her.*

OW it is to be said of Lord Juss and Lord Brandoch
Daha that they, finding themselves parted from their
people in the fog, and utterly unable to find them,
when the last sound of battle had died away wiped and
put up their bloody swords and set forth at a great
pace eastward. Only Mivarsh fared with them of all their following.
His lips were drawn back a little, showing his teeth, but he carried
himself proudly as one who being resolved to die walks with a quiet
mind to his destruction. Day after day they journeyed, sometimes
in clear weather, sometimes in mist or sleet, over the changeless
desert, without a landmark, save here a little sluggish river, or here
a piece of rising ground, or a pond, or a clump of rocks: small
things which faded from sight amid the waste ere they were passed
by a half-mile's distance. So was each day like yesterday, drawing to
a morrow like to it again. And always fear walked at their heel and

145

sat beside them sleeping: clanking of wings heard above the wind, a brooding hush of menace in the sunshine, and noises out of the void of darkness as of teeth chattering. So came they on the twentieth day to Morna Moruna, and stood at even in the sorrowful twilight by the little round castle, silent on Omprenne Edge.

From their feet the cliffs dropped sheer. Strange it was, standing on that frozen lip of the Moruna, as on the limit of the world, to gaze southward on a land of summer, and to breathe faint summer airs blowing up from blossoming trees and flower-clad alps. In the depths a carpet of huge tree-tops clothed a vast stretch of country, through the midst of which, seen here and there in a bend of silver among the woods, the Bhavinan bore the waters of a thousand secret mountain solitudes down to an unknown sea. Beyond the river the deep woods, blue with distance, swelled to feathery hill-tops with some sharper-featured loftier heights bodying cloudily beyond them. The Demons strained their eyes searching the curtain of mystery behind and above those foot-hills; but the great peaks, like great ladies, shrouded themselves against their curious gaze, and no glimpse was shown them of the snows.

Surely to be in Morna Moruna was to be in the death chamber of some once lovely presence. Stains of fire were on the walls. The fair gallery of open wood-work that ran above the main hall was burnt through and partly fallen in ruin, the blackened ends of the beams that held it jutting blindly in the gap. Among the wreck of carved chairs and benches, broken and worm-eaten, some shreds of figured tapestries rotted, the home now of beetles and spiders. Patches of colour, faded lines, mildewed and damp with the corruption of two hundred years, lingered to be the memorials, like the mummied skeleton of a king's daughter long ago untimely dead, of sweet gracious paintings on the walls. Five nights and five days the Demons and Mivarsh dwelt in Morna Moruna, inured to portents till they marked them as little as men mark swallows at their window. In the still night were flames seen, and flying forms dim in the moonlit air; and in moonless nights unstarred, moans heard and gibbering accents: prodigies beside their beds, and ridings in the sky, and fleshless fingers plucking at Juss unseen when he went forth to make question of the night.

Cloud and mist abode ever in the south, and only the foot-hills showed of the great ranges beyond Bhavinan. But on the evening of the sixth day before Yule, it being the nineteenth of December when Betelgeuze stands at midnight on the meridian, a wind blew out of the northwest with changing fits of sleet and sunshine. Day was fading as they stood above the cliff. All the forest land was blue with shades of approaching night: the river was dull silver: the wooded heights afar mingled their outlines with the towers and banks of turbulent deep blue vapour that hurtled in ceaseless passage through the upper air. Suddenly a window opened in the clouds to a space of clean wan wind-swept sky high above the shaggy hills. Surely Juss caught his breath in that moment, to see those deathless ones where they shone pavilioned in the pellucid air, far, vast, and lonely, most like to creatures of unascended heaven, of wind and of fire all compact, too pure to have aught of the gross elements of earth or water. It was as if the rose-red light of sundown had been frozen to crystal and these hewn from it to abide to everlasting, strong and unchangeable amid the welter of earthborn mists below and tumultuous sky above them. The rift ran wider, eastward and westward, opening on more peaks and sunset-kindled snows. And a rainbow leaning to the south was like a sword of glory across the vision.

Motionless, like hawks staring from that high place of prospect, Juss and Brandoch Daha looked on the mountains of their desire.

Juss spake, haltingly as one talking in a dream. "The sweet smell, this gusty wind, the very stone thy foot standeth on: I know them all before. There's not a night since we sailed out of Lookinghaven that I have not beheld in sleep these mountains and known their names."

"Who told thee their names?" asked Lord Brandoch Daha.

"My dream," Juss answered. "And first I dreamed it in mine own bed in Galing when I came home from guesting with thee last June. And they be true dreams that are dreamed there." And he said, "Seest thou where the foothills part to a dark valley that runneth deep into the chain, and the mountains are bare to view from crown to foot? Mark where, beyond the nearer range, bleak-visaged precipices, cobweb-streaked with huge snow corridors, rise to a rampart where the rock towers stand against the sky. This is the great ridge of Koshtra Pivrarcha, and the loftiest of those spires his secret mountaintop."

As he spoke, his eye followed the line of the eastern ridge, where the towers, like dark gods going down from heaven, plunge to a parapet which runs level above a curtain of avalanche-fluted snow. He fell silent as his gaze rested on the sister peak that east of the gap flamed skyward in wild cliffs to an airy snowy summit, softlined as a maiden's cheek, purer than dew, lovelier than a dream.

While they looked the sunset fires died out upon the mountains, leaving only pale hues of death and silence. "If thy dream," said Lord Brandoch Daha, "conducted thee down this Edge, over the Bhavinan, through yonder woods and hills, up through the leagues of ice and frozen rock that stand betwixt us and the main ridge, up by the right road to the topmost snows of Koshtra Belorn: that were a dream indeed."

"All this it showed me," said Juss, "up to the lowest rocks of the great north buttress of Koshtra Pivrarcha, that must first be scaled by him that would go up to Koshtra Belorn. But beyond those rocks not even a dream hath ever climbed. Ere the light fades, I'll show thee our pass over the nearer range." He pointed where a glacier crawled betwixt shadowy walls down from a torn snow-field that rose steeply to a saddle. East of it stood two white peaks, and west of it a sheer-faced and long-backed mountain like a citadel, squat and dark beneath the wild sky-line of Koshtra Pivrarcha that hung in air beyond it.

"The Zia valley," said Juss, "that runneth into Bhavinan. There lieth our way: under that dark bastion called by the Gods Tetrachnampf."

On the morrow Lord Brandoch Daha came to Mivarsh Faz and said, "It is needful that this day we go down from Omprenne Edge. I would for no sake leave thee on the Moruna, but 'tis no walking matter to descend this wall. Art thou a cragsman?"

"I was born," answered he, "in the high valley of Perarshyn by the upper waters of the Beirun in Impland. There boys scarce toddle ere they can climb a rock. This climb affrights me not, nor those mountains. But the land is unknown and terrible, and many loathly ones inhabit it, ghosts and eaters of men. O devils transmarine, and my friends, is it not enough? Let us turn again, and if the Gods save our lives we shall be famous for ever, that came unto Morna Moruna and returned alive."

But Juss answered and said, "O Mivarsh Faz, know that not for fame are we come on this journey. Our greatness already shadoweth all the world, as a great cedar tree spreading his shadow in a garden; and this enterprise, mighty though it be, shall add to our glory only so much as thou mightest add to these forests of the Bhavinan by planting of one more tree. But so it is, that the great King of Witchland, practising in darkness in his royal palace of Carcë such arts of grammarie and sendings magical as the world hath not been grieved with until now, sent an ill thing to take my brother, the Lord Goldry Bluszco, who is dear to me as mine own soul. And They that dwell in secret sent me word in a dream, bidding me, if I would have tidings of my dear brother, inquire in Koshtra Belorn. Therefore, O Mivarsh, go with us if thou wilt, but if thou wilt not, why, fare thee well. For nought but my death shall stay me from going thither."

And Mivarsh, bethinking him that if the mantichores of the mountains should devour him along with those two lords, that were yet a kindlier fate than all alone to abide those things he wist of on the Moruna, put on the rope, and after commending himself to the protection of his gods followed Lord Brandoch Daha down the rotten slopes of rock and frozen earth at the head of a gully leading down the cliff.

For all that they were early afoot, yet was it high noon ere they were off the rocks. For the peril of falling stones drove them out from the gully's bed first on to the eastern buttress and after, when that grew too sheer, back to the western wall. And in an hour or twain the gully's bed grew shallow and it narrowed to an end, whence Brandoch Daha gazed between his feet to where, a few spear's lengths below, the smooth slabs curved downward out of sight and the eye leapt straight from their clean-cut edge to shimmering tree-tops that showed tiny as mosses beyond the unseen gulf of air. So they rested awhile; then returning a little up the gully forced a way out on to the face and made a hazardous traverse to a new gully westward of the first, and so at last plunged down a long fan of scree and rested on soft fine turf at the foot of the cliffs.

Little mountain gentians grew at their feet; the pathless forest lay like the sea below them; before them the mountains of the Zia stood supreme: the white gables of Islargyn, the lean dark finger of Tetrachnampf nan Tshark lying back above the Zia Pass pointing to the sky, and west of it, jutting above the valley, the square bastion of Tetrachnampf nan Tsurm. The greater mountains were for the most part sunk behind this nearer range, but Koshtra Belorn still towered above the Pass. As a queen looking down from her high window, so she overlooked those green woods sleeping in the noon-day; and on her forehead was beauty like a star. Behind them where they sat, the escarpment reared back in cramped perspective, a pile of massive buttresses cleft with ravines leading upward from that land of leaves and waters to the hidden wintry flats of the Moruna.

That night they slept on the fell under the stars, and next day, going down into the woods, came at dusk to an open glade by the waters of the broad-bosomed Bhavinan. The turf was like a cushion, a place for elves to dance in. The far bank full half a mile away was wooded to the water with silver birches, dainty as mountain nymphs, their limbs gleaming through the twilight, their reflections quivering in the depths of the mighty river. In the high air day lingered yet, a faint warmth tingeing the great outlines of the mountains, and westward up the river the young moon stooped above the trees. East of the glade a little wooded eminence, no higher than a house, ran back from the river bank, and in its shoulder a hollow cave.

"How smiles it to thee?" said Juss. "Be sure we shall find no better place than this thou seest to dwell in until the snows melt and we may on. For though it be summer all the year round in this fortunate valley, it is winter on the great hills, and until the spring we were mad to essay our enterprise."

"Why then," said Brandoch Daha, "turn we shepherds awhile. Thou shalt pipe to me, and I'll foot thee measures shall make the dryads think they ne'er went to school. And Mivarsh shall be a goat-foot god to chase them; for to tell thee truth country wenches are long grown tedious to me. O, 'tis a sweet life. But ere we fall to it, bethink thee, O Juss: time marcheth, and the world waggeth: what goeth forward in Demonland till summer be come and we home again?"

"Also my heart is heavy because of my brother Spitfire," said Juss. "Oh, 'twas an ill storm, and ill delays."

"Away with vain regrettings," said Lord Brandoch Daha. "For thy sake and thy brother's fared I on this journey, and it is known to thee that never yet stretched I out mine hand upon aught that I have not taken it, and had my will of it."

So they made their dwelling in that cave beside deep-eddying Bhavinan, and before that cave they ate their Yule feast, the strangest they had eaten all the days of their lives: seated, not as of old, on their high seats of ruby or of opal, but on mossy banks where daisies slept and creeping thyme; lighted not by the charmed escarbuncle of the high presence chamber in Galing, but by the shifting beams of a brushwood fire that shone not on those pillars crowned with monsters that were the wonder of the world but on the mightier pillars of the sleeping beechwoods. And in place of that feigned heaven of jewels self-effulgent beneath the golden canopy at Galing, they ate pavilioned under a charmed summer night, where the great stars of winter, Orion, Sirius, and the Little Dog, were raised up near the zenith, yielding their known courses in the southern sky to Canopus and the strange stars of the south. When the trees spake, it was not with their winter voice of bare boughs creaking, but with whisper of leaves and beetles droning in the fragrant air. The bushes were white with blossom, not with hoar-frost, and the dim white patches under the trees were not snow, but wild lilies and wood anemones sleeping in the night.

All the creatures of the forest came to that feast, for they were without fear, having never looked upon the face of man. Little tree-apes, and popinjays, and titmouses, and coalmouses, and wrens, and gentle roundeyed lemurs, and rabbits, and badgers, and dor-mice, and pied squirrels, and beavers from the streams, and storks, and ravens, and bustards, and wombats, and the spider-monkey with her baby at her breast: all these came to gaze with curious eye upon those travellers. And not these alone, but fierce beasts of the woods and wildernesses: the wild buffalo, the wolf, the tiger with monstrous paws, the bear, the fiery-eyed unicorn, the elephant, the lion and she-lion in their majesty, came to behold them in the firelight in that quiet glade.

"It seems we hold court in the woods to-night," said Lord Brandoch Daha. "It is very pleasant. Yet hold thee ready with me to put some fire-brands amongst 'em if need befall. 'Tis likely some of these great beasts are little schooled in court ceremonies."

Juss answered, "And thou lovest me, do no such thing. There lieth this curse upon all this land of the Bhavinan, that whoso, whether he be man or beast, slayeth in this land or doeth here any deed of violence, there cometh down a curse upon him that in that instant must destroy and blast him for ever off the face of the earth. Therefore it was I took away from Mivarsh his bow and arrows when we came down from Omprenne Edge, lest he should kill game for us and so a worse thing befall him."

Mivarsh harkened not, but sat all a-quake, looking intently on a crocodile that came ponderously out upon the bank. And now he began to scream with terror, crying, "Save me! let me fly! give me my weapons! It was foretold me by a wise woman that a cocadrill-serpent must devour me at last!" Whereat the beasts drew back uneasily, and the crocodile, his small eyes wide, startled by Mivarsh's cries and violent gestures, lurched with what speed he might back into the water.

Now in that place Lord Juss and Lord Brandoch Daha and Mivarsh Faz abode for four moons' space. Nothing they lacked of meat and drink, for the beasts of the forest, finding them well disposed, brought them of their store. Moreover, there came flying from the south, about the ending of the year, a martlet which alighted in Juss's bosom and said to him, "The gentle Queen Sophonisba,[1] fosterling of the Gods, had news of your coming.

And because she knoweth you both mighty men of your hands and high of heart, therefore by me she sent you greeting."

Juss said, "O little martlet, we would see thy Queen face to face, and thank her."

"Ye must thank her," said the bird, "in Koshtra Belorn."

Brandoch Daha said, "That shall we fulfil. Thither only do our thoughts intend."

"Your greatness," said the martlet, "must approve that word. And know that it is easier to lay under you all the world in arms than to ascend up afoot into that mountain."

"Thy wings were too weak to lift me, else I'd borrow them," said Brandoch Daha.

But the martlet answered, "Not the eagle that flieth against the sun may alight on Koshtra Belorn. No foot may tread her, save of those blessed ones to whom the Gods gave leave ages ago, till they be come that the patient years await: men like unto the Gods in beauty and in power, who of their own might and main, unholpen by magic arts, shall force a passage up to her silent snows."

Brandoch Daha laughed. "Not the eagle?" he cried, "but thou, little flitter-jack?"

"Nought that hath feet," said the martlet. "I have none."

The Lord Brandoch Daha took it tenderly in his hand and held it high in the air, looking to the high lands in the south. The birches swaying by the Bhavinan were not more graceful nor the distant mountain-crags behind them more untameable to behold than he. "Fly to thy Queen," he said, "and say thou spakest with Lord Juss beside the Bhavinan and with Lord Brandoch Daha of Demonland. Say unto her that we be they that were for to come; and that we, of our own might and main, ere spring be well turned summer, will come up to her in Koshtra Belorn to thank her for her gracious sendings."

Now when it was April, and the sun moving among the signs of heaven was about departing out of Aries and entering into Taurus, and the melting of the snows in the high mountains had swollen all the streams to spate, filling the mighty river so that he brimmed his banks and swept by like a tide-race, Lord Juss said, "Now is the season propitious for our crossing of the flood of Bhavinan and setting forth into the mountains."

"Willingly," said Lord Brandoch Daha. "But shall's walk it, or swim it, or take to us wings? To me, that have many a time swum back and forth over Thunderfirth to whet mine appetite ere I brake my fast, 'tis a small matter of this river stream howso swift it runneth. But with our harness and weapons and all our gear, that were far other matter."

"Is it for nought we are grown friends with them that do inhabit these woods?" said Juss. "The crocodile shall bear us over Bhavinan for the asking."

"It is an ill fish," said Mivarsh; "and it sore dislikes me."

"Then here thou must abide," said Brandoch Daha. "But be not dismayed, I will go with thee. The fish may bear us both at a draught and not founder."

"It was a wise woman foretold it me," answered Mivarsh, "that such a kind of serpent must be my bane. Yet be it according to your will."

So they whistled them up the crocodile; and first the Lord Juss fared over Bhavinan, riding on the back of that serpent with all his gear and weapons of war, and landed several hundred paces down stream for the stream was very strong; and thereafter the crocodile returning to the north bank took the Lord Brandoch Daha and Mivarsh Faz and put them across in like manner. Mivarsh put on a gallant face, but rode as near the tail as might be, fingering certain herbs from his wallet that were good against serpents, his lips moving in urgent supplication to his gods. When they were come ashore they thanked the crocodile and bade him farewell and went their way swiftly through the woods. And Mivarsh, as one new loosed from prison, went before them with a light step, singing and snapping his fingers.

Now had they for three days or four a devious journey through the foot-hills, and thereafter made their dwelling for forty days' space in the Zia valley, above the gorges. Here the valley widens to a flat-floored amphitheatre, and lean limestone crags tower heavenward on every side. High in the south, couched above great gray moraines, the Zia glacier, wrinkle-backed like some dragon survived out of the elder chaos, thrusts his snout into the valley. Here out of his caves of ice the young river thunders, casting up a spray where rainbows hover in bright weather. The air blows sharp from the glacier, and alpine flowers and shrubs feed on the sunlight.

Here they gathered them good store of food. And every morning they were afoot before the sunrise, to ascend the mountains and make sure their practice ere they should attempt the greater peaks. So they explored all the spurs of Tetrachnampf and Islargyn, and those peaks themselves; the rock peaks of the lower Nuanner range overlooking Bhavinan; the snow peaks east of Islargyn: Avsek, Kiurmsur, Myrsu, Byrshnargyn, and Borch Mehephtharsk, loftiest of the range, by all his ridges, dwelling a

week on the moraines of the Mehephtharsk glacier above the upland valley of Foana; and westward the dolomite group of
Burdjazarshra and the great wall of Shilack.

Now were their muscles by these exercises grown like bands of
iron, and they hardy as mountain bears and sure of foot as mountain goats. So on the ninth day of May they crossed the Zia Pass and
camped on the rocks under the south wall of Tetrachnampf nan
Tshark. The sun went down, like blood, in a cloudless sky. On
either hand and before them, the snows stretched blue and silent.
The air of those high snowfields was bitter cold. A league and more
to the south a line of black cliffs bounded the glacier-basin. Over
that black wall, twelve miles away, Koshtra Belorn and Koshtra
Pivrarcha towered against an opal heaven.

While they supped in the fading light, Juss said, "The wall
thou seest is called the Barriers of Emshir. Though over it lieth the
straight way to Koshtra Pivrarcha, yet is it not our way, but an ill
way. For, first, that barrier hath till now been held unclimbable,
and so proven even by half-gods that alone assayed it."

"I await not thy second reason," said Brandoch Daha. "Thou
hast had thy way until now, and now thou shalt give me mine in
this, to come with me to-morrow and show how thou and I make of
such barriers a puff of smoke if they stand in the path between us
and our fixed ends."

"Were it only this," answered Juss, "I would not gainsay thee.
But not senseless rocks alone are we set to deal with if we take this
road. Seest thou where the Barriers end in the east against yonder
monstrous pyramid of tumbled crags and hanging glaciers that
shuts out our prospect east-away? Menksur men call it, but in
heaven it hath a more dreadful name: Ela Mantissera, which is to
say, the Bed of the Mantichores. O Brandoch Daha, I will climb
with thee what unscaled cliff thou list, and I will fight with thee
against the most grisfullest beasts that ever grazed by the Tartarian[2] streams. But both these things in one moment of time, that
were a rash part and a foolish."

But Brandoch Daha laughed, and answered him, "To nought
else may I liken thee, O Juss, but to the sparrow-camel. To whom
they said, 'Fly,' and it answered, 'I cannot, for I am a camel'; and
when they said, 'Carry,' it answered, 'I cannot, for I am a bird.' "

"Wilt thou egg me on so much?" said Juss.

"Ay," said Brandoch Daha, "if thou wilt be assish."

"Wilt thou quarrel?" said Juss.

"Thou knowest me," said Brandoch Daha.

"Well," said Juss, "thy counsel hath been right once and saved us, for nine times that it hath been wrong, and my counsel saved thee from an evil end. If ill behap us, it shall be set down that it had from thy peevish will original." And they wrapped them in their cloaks and slept.

On the morrow they rose betimes and set forth south across the snows that were crisp and hard from the frosts of the night. The Barriers, as it were but a stone's-throw removed, stood black before them; starlight swallowed up size and distance that showed only by walking, as still they walked and still that wall seemed no nearer nor no larger. Twice and thrice they dipped into a valley or crossed a raised-up fold of the glacier; till they stood at break of day below the smooth blank wall frozen and bleak, with never a ledge in sight great enough to bear snow, barring their passage southward.

They halted and ate and scanned the wall before them. And ill to do with it seemed. So they searched for an ascent, and found at last a spot where the glacier swelled higher, a mile or less from the western shoulder of Ela Mantissera. Here the cliff was but four or five hundred feet high; yet smooth enow and ill enow to look on; yet their likeliest choice.

Some while it was ere they might get a footing on that wall, but at length Brandoch Daha, standing on Juss's shoulder, found him a hold where no hold showed from below, and with great travail fought a passage up the rock to a stance some hundred feet above them, whence sitting sure on a broad ledge great enough to hold six or seven folk at a time he played up Lord Juss on the rope and after him Mivarsh. An hour and a half it cost them for that short climb.

"The north-east buttress of Ill Stack was children's gruel to this," said Lord Juss.

"There's more aloft," said Lord Brandoch Daha, lying back against the precipice, his hands clasped behind his head, his feet a-dangle over the ledge. "In thine ear, Juss: I would not go first on the rope again on such a pitch for all the wealth of Impland."

"Wilt repent and return?" said Juss.

"If thou'lt be last down," he answered. "If not, I'd liever risk what waits untried above us. If it prove worse, I am confirmed atheist."

Lord Juss leaned out, holding by the rock with his right hand, scanning the wall beside and above them. An instant he hung so, then drew back. His square jaw was set, and his teeth glinted under his dark moustachios something fiercely, as a thunder-beam betwixt dark sky and sea in a night of thunder. His nostrils widened, as of a war-horse at the call of battle; his eyes were like the violet levin-brand, and all his body hardened like a bowstring drawn as he grasped his sharp sword and pulled it forth grating and singing from its sheath.

Brandoch Daha sprang afoot and drew his sword, Zeldornius's loom. "What stirreth?" he cried. "Thou look'st ghastly. That look thou hadst when thou tookest the helm and our prows swung westward toward Kartadza Sound, and the fate of Demonland and all the world beside hung in thine hand for wail or bliss."

"There's little sword-room," said Juss. And again he looked forth eastward and upward along the cliff. Brandoch Daha looked over his shoulder. Mivarsh took his bow and set an arrow on the string.

"It hath scented us down the wind," said Brandoch Daha.

Small time was there to ponder. Swinging from hold to hold across the dizzy precipice, as an ape swingeth from bough to bough, the beast drew near. The shape of it was as a lion, but bigger and taller, the colour a dull red, and it had prickles lancing out behind, as of a porcupine; its face a man's face, if aught so hideous might be conceived of human kind, with staring eyeballs, low wrinkled brow, elephant ears, some wispy mangy likeness of a lion's mane, huge bony chaps, brown blood-stained gubber-tushes grinning betwixt bristly lips. Straight for the ledge it made, and as they braced them to receive it, with a great swing heaved a man's height above them and leaped down upon their ledge from aloft betwixt Juss and Brandoch Daha ere they were well aware of its changed course. Brandoch Daha smote at it a great swashing blow and cut off its scorpion tail; but it clawed Juss's shoulder, smote down Mivarsh, and charged like a lion upon Brandoch Daha, who, missing his footing on the narrow edge of rock, fell backwards a great fall, clear of the cliff, down to the snow an hundred feet beneath them.

As it craned over, minded to follow and make an end of him, Juss smote it in the hinder parts and on the ham, shearing away the flesh from the thigh bone, and his sword came with a clank against the brazen claws of its foot. So with a horrid bellow it turned on Juss, rearing like a horse; and it was three heads greater than a tall man in stature when it reared aloft, and the breadth of its chest like the chest of a bear. The stench of its breath choked Juss's mouth and his senses sickened, but he slashed it athwart the belly, a great round-armed blow, cutting open its belly so that the guts fell out. Again he hewed at it, but missed, and his sword came against the rock, and was shivered into pieces. So when that noisome vermin fell forward on him roaring like a thousand lions, Juss grappled with it, running in beneath its body and clasping it and thrusting his arms into its inward parts, to rip out its vitals if so he might. So close he grappled it that it might not reach him with its murthering teeth, but its claws sliced off the flesh from his left knee downward to the ankle bone, and it fell on him and crushed him on the rock, breaking in the bones of his breast. And Juss, for all his bitter pain and torment, and for all he was well nigh stifled by the sore stink of the creature's breath and the stink of its blood and puddings blubbering about his face and breast, yet by his great strength wrastled with that fell and filthy man-eater. And ever he thrust his right hand, armed with the hilt and stump of his broken sword, yet deeper into its belly until he searched out its heart and did his will upon it, slicing the heart asunder like a lemon and severing and tearing all the great vessels about the heart until the blood gushed about him like a spring. And like a caterpillar the beast curled up and straightened out in its death spasms, and it rolled and fell from that ledge, a great fall, and lay by Brandoch Daha, the foulest beside the fairest of all earthly beings, reddening the pure snow with its blood. And the spines that grew on the hinder parts of the beast went out and in like the sting of a new-dead wasp that goes out and in continually. It fell not clean to the snow, as by the care of heaven was fallen Brandoch Daha, but smote an edge of rock near the bottom, and that strook out its brains. There it lay in its blood, gaping to the sky.

Now was Juss stretched face downward as one dead, on that giddy edge of rock. Mivarsh had saved him, seizing him by the foot and drawing him back to safety when the beast fell. A sight of terror he was, clotted from head to toe with the beast's blood and his own. Mivarsh bound his wounds and laid him tenderly as he might back against the cliff, then peered down a long while to know if the beast were dead indeed.

When he had gazed downward earnestly so long that his eyes watered with the strain, and still the beast stirred not, Mivarsh prostrated himself and made supplication saying aloud, "O Shlimphli, Shlamphi, and Shebamri, gods of my father and my father's fathers, have pity of your child, if as I dearly trow your power extendeth over this far and forbidden country no less than over Impland, where your child hath ever worshipped you in your holy places, and taught my sons and my daughters to revere your holy names, and made an altar in mine house, pointed by the stars in manner ordained from of old, and offered up my seventh-born son and was minded to offer up my seventh-born daughter thereon, in meekness and righteousness according to your holy will; but this I might not do, since you vouchsafed me not a seventh daughter, but six only. Wherefore I beseech you, of your holy names' sake, strengthen my hand to let down this my companion safely by the rope, and thereafter bring me safely down from this rock, howsoever he be a devil and an unbeliever; O save his life, save both their lives. For I am sure that if these be not saved alive, never shall your child return, but in this far land starve and die like an insect that dureth but for a day."

So prayed Mivarsh. And belike the high Gods were moved to pity of his innocence, hearing him so cry for help unto his mumbo-jumbos, where no help was; and belike they were not minded that those lords of Demonland should there die evilly before their time, unhonoured, unsung. Howsoever, Mivarsh arose and made fast the rope about Lord Juss, knotting it cunningly beneath the arms that it might not tighten in the lowering and crush his breast and ribs, and so with much ado lowered him down to the foot of the cliff. Thereafter came Mivarsh himself down that perilous wall, and albeit for many a time he thought his bane was upon him, yet by good cragsmanship spurred by cold necessity he gat him down at last. Being down, he delayed not to minister to his companions, who came to themselves with heavy groaning. But when Lord Juss was come to himself he did his healing art both on himself and on Lord Brandoch Daha, so that in a while they were able to stand upon their feet, albeit something stiff and weary and like to vomit. And it was by then the third hour past noon.

While they rested, beholding where the beast mantichora lay in his blood, Juss spake and said, "It is to be said of thee, O Brandoch Daha, that thou to-day hast done both the worst and the best. The worst, when thou wast so stubborn set to fare upon this climb which hath come within a little of spilling both thee and me. The best, whenas thou didst smite off his tail. Was that by policy or by chance?"

"Why," said he, "I was never so poor a man of my hands that I need turn braggart. 'Twas handiest to my sword, and it disliked me to see it wagging. Did aught lie on it?"

"The sting of his tail," answered Juss, "were competent for thine or my destruction, and it grazed but our little finger."

"Thou speakest like a book," said Brandoch Daha. "Else might I scarce know thee for my noble friend, being betrayed with blood as a buffalo with mire. Be not angry with me, if I am most at ease to windward of thee."

Juss laughed. "If thou be not too nice," he said, "go to the beast and dabble thyself too with the blood of his bowels. Nay, I mock not; it is most needful. These be enemies not of mankind only, but each of other; walking every one by himself, loathing every one his kind living or dead, so that in all the world there abideth nought loathlier unto them than the blood of their own kind, the least smell whereof they do abhor as a mad dog abhorreth water. And 'tis a clinging smell. So are we after this encounter most sure against them."

That night they camped at the foot of a spur of Avsek, and set forth at dawn down the long valley eastward. All day they heard the roaring of mantichores from the desolate flanks of Ela Mantissera that showed now no longer as a pyramid but as a long-backed screen, making the southern rampart of that valley. It was ill going, and they somewhat shaken. Day was nigh gone when beyond the eastern slopes of Ela they came where the white waters of the river they followed thundered together with a black water rushing down from the south-west. Below, the river ran east in a wide valley dropping afar to treeclad depths. In the fork above the watersmeet the rocks enclosed a high green knoll, like some fragment of a kindlier clime that over-lived into an age of ruin.

"Here, too," said Juss, "my dream walked with me. And if it be ill crossing there where this stream breaketh into a dozen branching cataracts a little above the watersmeet, yet well I think 'tis our only crossing." So, ere the light should fade, they crossed that perilous edge above the water-falls, and slept on the green knoll.

That knoll Juss named Throstlegarth, after a thrush that waked them next morning, singing in a little windstunted mountain thorn that grew among the rocks. Strangely sounded that homely song on the cold mountain side, under the unhallowed heights of Ela, close to the confines of those enchanted snows which guard Koshtra Belorn.

No sight of the high mountains had they from Throstlegarth, nor, for a long while, from the bed of that straight steep glen of the black waters up which now their journey lay. Rugged spurs and buttresses shut them in. High on the left bank above the cataracts they made their way, buffeted by the wind that leaped and charged among the crags, their ears sated with the roaring sound of waters, their eyes filled with the spray blown upward. And Mivarsh followed after them. Silent they fared, for the way was steep and in such a wind and such a noise of torrents a man must shout lustily if he would be heard. Very desolate was that valley, having a dark aspect and a ghastful, such as a man might look for in the infernal glens of Pyriphlegethon or Acheron.[3] No living thing they saw, save at whiles high above them an eagle sailing down the wind, and once a beast's form running in the hollow mountain side. This stood at gaze, lifting up its foul human platter-face with glittering eyes bloody and great as saucers; scented its fellow's blood, started, and fled among the crags.

So fared they for the space of three hours, and so, coming suddenly round a shoulder of the hill, stood on the upper threshold of that glen at the gates of a flat upland valley. Here they beheld a sight to darken all earth's glories and strike dumb all her singers with its grandeur. Framed in the crags of the hillsides, canopied by blue heaven, Koshtra Pivrarcha stood before them. So huge he was that even here at six miles' distance the eye might not at a glance behold him, but must sweep back and forth as over a broad landscape from the ponderous roots of the mountain where they sprang black and sheer from the glacier, up the vast face, where buttress was piled upon buttress and tower upon tower in a blinding radiance of ice-hung precipice and snow-filled gully, to the lone heights where like spears menacing high heaven the white teeth of the summit-ridge cleft the sky. From right to left he filled nigh a quarter of the heavens, from the graceful peak of Ailinon looking over his western shoulder, to where on the east the snowy slopes of Jalchi shut in the prospect, hiding Koshtra Belorn.

They camped that evening on the left moraine of the High Glacier of Temarm. Long spidery streamers of cloud, filmy as the gauze of a lady's veil, blew eastward from the spires on the ridge, signs of wild weather aloft.

Juss said, "Glassy clear is the air. That forerunneth not fair weather."

"Well, time shall wait for us if need be," said Brandoch Daha. "So mightily my desire crieth unto me from those horns of ice that, having once looked on them, I had as lief die as leave them unclimbed. But of thee, O Juss, I make some marvel. Thou wast bidden inquire in Koshtra Belorn, and sure she were easier won than Koshtra Pivrarcha, going behind Jalchi by the snowfields and so avoiding her great western cliffs."

"There is a saw in Impland," answered Juss, " 'Ware of a tall wife.' Even so there lieth a curse on any that shall attempt Koshtra Belorn that hath not first looked down upon her; and he shall have his death or ever he have his will. And from one point only of earth may a man look down on Koshtra Belorn; and 'tis from yonder unascended tooth of ice where thou seest the last beam burn. For that is the topmost pinnacle of Koshtra Pivrarcha. And it is the highest point of the stablished earth."

They were silent a minute's space. Then Juss spake: "Thou wast ever greatest amongst us as a mountaineer. Which way likes thee best for our climbing up him?"

"O Juss," said Brandoch Daha, "on ice and snow thou art my master. Therefore give me thy rede. For mine own choice and pleasure, I have settled it this hour and more: namely to ascend into the gap between the two mountains, and thence turn westward up the east ridge of Pivrarcha."

"It is the fearsomest climb to look on," said Juss, "and belike the grandest, and for both counts I had wagered it thy choice. That gap hight the Gates of Zimiamvia.[4] It, and the Koshtra glacier that runneth up to it, lieth under the weird I told thee of. It were our death to adventure there ere we had looked down upon Koshtra Belorn; which done, the charm is broke for us, and from that time forth it needeth but our own might and skill and a high heart to accomplish whatsoever we desire."

"Why then, the great north buttress," cried Brandoch Daha. "So shall she not behold us as we climb, until we come forth on the highest tooth and overlook her and tame her to our will."

So they supped and slept. But the wind cried among the crags all night long, and in the morning snow and sleet blotted out the mountains. All day the storm held, and in a lull they struck camp and came down again to Throstlegarth, and there abode nine days and nine nights in wind and rain and battering hail.

On the tenth day the weather abated, and they went up and crossed the glacier and lodged them in a cave in the rock at the foot of the great north buttress of Koshtra Pivrarcha. At dawn Juss and Brandoch Daha went forth to survey the prospect. They crossed the mouth of the steep snow-choked valley that ran up to the main ridge betwixt Ashnilan on the west and Koshtra Pivrarcha on the east, rounded the base of Ailinon, and climbed from the west to a snow saddle some three thousand feet up the ridge of that mountain, whence they might view the buttress and choose their way for their attempt.

" 'Tis a two days' journey to the top," said Lord Brandoch Daha. "If night on the ridge freeze us not to death, I dread no other hindrance. That black rib that riseth half a mile above our camp, shall take us clean up to the crest of the buttress, striking it above the great tower at the northern end. If the rocks be like those we camped on, hard as diamond and rough as a sponge, they shall not fail us but by our own neglect. As I live, I ne'er saw their like for climbing."

"So far, well," said Juss.

"Above," said Brandoch Daha, "I'd drive thee a chariot until we come to the first great kick o' the ridge. That must we round, or ne'er go further, and on this side it showeth ill enough, for the rocks shelve outward. If they be iced, there's work indeed. Beyond that, I'll prophesy nought, O Juss, for I can see nought clear save that the ridge is hacked into clefts and steeples. How we may overcome them must be put to the proof. It is too high and too far to know. This only: where we would go, there have we gone until now. And by that ridge lieth, if any way there lieth, the way to this mountain top that we crossed the world to climb."

Next day with the first paling of the skies they arose all three and set forth southward over the crisp snows. They roped at the foot of the glacier that came down from the saddle, some five thousand feet above them, where the main ridge dips between Ashnilan and Koshtra Pivrarcha. Ere the brighter stars were swallowed in the light of morning they were cutting their way among the labyrinthine towers and chasms of the ice-fall. Soon the new daylight flooded the snowfields of the High Glacier of Temarm, dyeing them green and saffron and palest rose. The snows of Islargyn glowed far away in the north to the right of the white dome of Emshir. Ela Mantissera blocked the view north-eastward. The buttress that bounded their valley on the east plunged it in shadow blue as a summer sea. High on the other side the great twin peaks of Ailinon and Ashnilan, roused by the warm beams out of their frozen silence of the night, growled at whiles with avalanches and falling stones.

Juss was their leader in the ice-fall, guiding them now along high knife-edges that fell away on either hand to unsounded depths, now within the very lips of those chasms, along the bases of the ice-towers. These, five times a man's height, some square, some pinnacled, some shattered or piled with the ruins of their kind, leaned above the path, as ready to fall and overwhelm the climbers and dash their bones for ever down to those blue-green secret places of frost and silence where the chips of ice chinked hollow as Juss pressed onward, cutting his steps with Mivarsh's axe. At length the slope eased and they walked out on the unbroken surface of the glacier, and passing by a snow-bridge over the great rift betwixt the glacier and the mountain side came two hours before noon to the foot of the rock-rib that they had scanned from Ailinon.

Now was Brandoch Daha to lead them. They climbed face to the rock, slowly and without rest, for sound and firm as the rocks were the holds were small and few and the cliffs steep. Here and there a chimney gave them passage upward, but the climb was mainly by cracks and open faces of rock, a trial of main strength and endurance such as few might sustain for a short while only: but this wall was three thousand feet in height. By noon they gained the crest, and there rested on the rocks too weary to speak, looking across the avalanche-swept face of Koshtra Pivrarcha to the corniced parapet that ended against the western precipices of Koshtra Belorn.

For some way the ridge of the buttress was broad and level. Then it narrowed suddenly to the width of a horse's back, and sprang skyward two thousand feet and more. Brandoch Daha went forward and climbed a few feet up the cliff. It bulged out above him, smooth and holdless. He tried it once and again, then came down saying, "Nought without wings."

Then he went to the left. Here hanging glaciers overlooked the face from on high, and while he gazed an avalanche of ice-blocks roared down it. Then he went to the right, and here the rocks sloped outward, and the sloping ledges were piled with rubbish and the rocks rotten and slippery with snow and ice. So having gone a little way he returned, and, "O Juss," he said, "wilt take it right forth, and that must be by flying, for hold there is none: or wilt go east and dodge the avalanche: or west, where all is rotten and slither and a slip were our destruction?"

So they debated, and at length decided on the eastern road. It was an ill step round the jutting corner of the tower, for little hold there was, and the rocks were undercut below, so that a stone or a man loosed from that place must fall clear at a bound three or four thousand feet to the Koshtra glacier and there be dashed in pieces. Beyond, wide ledges gave them passage along the wall of the tower, that now swept inward, facing south. Far overhead, dazzling white in the sunshine, the broken glacier-edges and splinters jutted against the blue, and icicles greater than a man hung glittering from every ledge: a sight heavenly fair, whereof they yet had little joy, hastening as they had not hastened in their lives before to be out of the danger of that ice-swept face.

Suddenly was a noise above them like the crack of a giant whip, and looking up they beheld against the sky a dark mass which opened like a flower and spread into a hundred fragments. The

Demons and Mivarsh hugged the cliffs where they stood, but there was little cover. All the air was filled with the shrieking of the stones, as they swept downwards like fiends returning to the pit, and with the crash of them as they dashed against the cliffs and burst in pieces. The echoes rolled and reverberated from cliff to distant cliff, and the limbs of the mountain seemed to writhe as under a scourge. When it was done, Mivarsh was groaning for pain of his left wrist sore hurt with a stone. The others were scatheless.

Juss said to Brandoch Daha, "Back, howsoever it dislike thee."

Back they went; and an avalanche of ice crashed down the face which must have destroyed them had they proceeded. "Thou dost misjudge me," said Brandoch Daha, laughing. "Give me where my life lieth on mine own might and main; then is danger meat and drink to me, and nought shall turn me back. But here on this cursed cliff, on the ledges whereof a cripple might walk at ease, we be the toys of chance. And it were pure folly to abide upon it a moment longer."

"Two ways be left us," said Juss. "To turn back, and that were our shame for ever; and to essay the western traverse."

"And that should be the bane of any save of me and thee," said Brandoch Daha. "And if our bane, why, we shall sleep sound."

"Mivarsh," said Juss, "is nought so bounden to this adventure. He hath bravely held by us, and bravely stood our friend. Yet here we be come to such a pass, I sore misdoubt me if it were less danger of his life to come with us than seek safety alone."

But Mivarsh put on a hardy face. Never a word he spake, but nodded his head, as who should say, "Forward."

"First I must be thy leech,[5]" said Juss. And he bound up Mivarsh's wrist. And because the day was now far spent, they camped under the great tower, hoping next day to reach the top of Koshtra Pivrarcha that stood unseen some six thousand feet above them.

Next morning, when it was light enough to climb, they set forth. For two hours' space on that traverse not a moment passed but they were in instant peril of death. They were not roped, for on those slabbery rocks one man had dragged a dozen to perdition had he made a slip. The ledges sloped outward; they were piled with broken rock and mud; the soft red rock broke away at a hand's touch and plunged at a leap to the glacier below. Down and up and along, and down and up and up again they wound their way, rounding the base of that great tower, and came at last by a rotten gully safe to the ridge above it.

While they climbed, white wispy clouds which had gathered in the high gullies of Ailinon in the morning had grown to a mass of blackness that hid all the mountains to the west. Great streamers ran from it across the gulf below, joined and boiled upward, lifting and sinking like a full-tided sea, rising at last to the high ridge where the Demons stood and wrapping them in a cloak of vapour with a chill wind in its folds, and darkness in broad noon-day. They halted, for they might not see the rocks before them. The wind grew boisterous, shouting among the splintered towers. Snow swept powdery and keen across the ridge. The cloud lifted and plunged again like some great bird shadowing them with its wings. From its bosom the lightning flared above and below. Thunder crashed on the heels of the lightning, sending the echoes rolling among the distant cliffs. Their weapons, planted in the snow, sizzled with blue flame; Juss had counselled laying them aside lest they should perish holding them. Crouched in a hollow of the snow among the rocks of that high ridge of Koshtra Pivrarcha, Lord Juss and Lord Brandoch Daha and Mivarsh Faz weathered that night of terror. When night came they knew not, for the storm brought darkness on them hours before sun-down. Blinding snow and sleet and fire and thunder, and wild winds shrieking in the gullies till the firm mountain seemed to rock, kept them awake. They were near frozen, and scarce desired aught but death, which might bring them ease from that hellish roundelay.

Day broke with a weak gray light, and the storm died down. Juss stood up weary beyond speech. Mivarsh said, "Ye be devils, but of myself I marvel. For I have dwelt by snow mountains all my days, and many I wot of that have been benighted on the snows in wild weather. And not one but was starved by reason of the cold. I speak of them that were found. Many were not found, for the spirits devoured them."

Whereat Lord Brandoch Daha laughed aloud, saying, "O Mivarsh, I fear me that in thee I have but a graceless dog. Look on him, that in hardihood and bodily endurance against all hardships of frost or fire surpasseth me as greatly as I surpass thee. Yet is he weariest of the three. Wouldst know why? I'll tell thee: all night he hath striven against the cold, chafing not himself only but me and thee to save us from frost-bite. And be sure nought else had saved thy carcase."

By then was the mist grown lighter, so that they might see the ridge for an hundred paces or more where it went up before them, each pinnacle standing out shadowy and unsubstantial against the next succeeding one more shadowy still. And the pinnacles showed monstrous huge through the mist, like mountain peaks in stature.

They roped and set forth, scaling the towers or turning them, now on this side now on that; sometimes standing on teeth of rock that seemed cut off from all earth else, solitary in a sea of shifting vapour; sometimes descending into a deep gash in the ridge with a blank wall rearing aloft on the further side and empty air yawning to left and right. The rocks were firm and good, like those they had first climbed from the glacier. But they went but a slow pace, for the climbing was difficult and made dangerous by new snow and by the ice that glazed the rocks.

As the day wore the wind was fallen, and all was still when they stood at length before a ridge of hard ice that shot steeply up before them like the edge of a sword. The east side of it on their left was almost sheer, ending in a blank precipice that dropped out of sight without a break. The western slope, scarcely less steep, ran down in a white even sheet of frozen snow till the clouds engulfed it.

Brandoch Daha waited on the last blunt tooth of rock at the foot of the ice-ridge. "The rest is thine," he cried to Lord Juss. "I would not that any save thou should tread him first, for he is thy mountain."

"Without thee I had never won up hither," answered Juss; "and it is not fitting that I should have that glory to stand first upon the peak when thine was the main achievement. Go thou before."

"I will not," said Lord Brandoch Daha. "And it is not so."

So Juss went forward, smiting with his axe great steps just below the backbone of the ridge on the western side, and Lord Brandoch Daha and Mivarsh Faz followed in the steps.

Presently a wind arose in the unseen spaces of the sky, and tore the mist like a rotten garment. Spears of sunlight blazed through the rifts. Distant sunny lands shimmered in the unimaginable depths to the southward, seen over the crest of a tremendous wall that stood beyond the abyss: a screen of black rock buttresses seamed with a thousand gullies of glistening snow, and crowned as with battlements with a row of mountain peaks, savage and fierce of form, that made the eye blink for their brightness: the lean spires of the summit-ridge of Koshtra Pivrarcha. These, that the Demons had so long looked up to as in distant heaven, now lay beneath their feet. Only the peak they climbed still reared itself above them, clear now and near to view, showing a bare beetling cliff on the north-east, overhung by a cornice of snow. Juss marked the cornice, turned him again to his step-cutting, and in half an hour from the breaking of the clouds stood on that unascended pinnacle, with all earth beneath him.

They went down a few feet on the southern side and sat on some rocks. A fair lake studded with islands lay bosomed in wooded and crag-girt hills at the foot of a deep-cut valley which ran down from the Gates of Zimiamvia. Ailinon and Ashnilan rose near by in the west, with the delicate white peak of Akra Garsh showing between them. Beyond, mountain beyond mountain like the sea.

Juss looked southward where the blue land stretched in fold upon fold of rolling country, soft and misty, till it melted in the sky. "Thou and I," said he, "first of the children of men, now behold with living eyes the fabled land of Zimiamvia. Is that true, thinkest thou, which philosophers tell us of that fortunate land: that no mortal foot may tread it, but the blessed souls do inhabit it of the dead that be departed, even they that were great upon earth and did great deeds when they were living, that scorned not earth and the delights and the glories thereof, and yet did justly and were not dastards nor yet oppressors?"

"Who knoweth?" said Brandoch Daha, resting his chin in his hand and gazing south as in a dream. "Who shall say he knoweth?"

They were silent awhile. Then Juss spake saying, "If thou and I come thither at last, O my friend, shall we remember Demonland?" And when he answered him not, Juss said, "I had rather row on Moonmere under the stars of a summer's night, than be a King of all the land of Zimiamvia. And I had rather watch the sunrise on the Scarf, than dwell in gladness all my days on an island of that enchanted Lake of Ravary, under Koshtra Belorn."

Now the curtain of cloud that had hung till now about the eastern heights was rent into shreds, and Koshtra Belorn stood like a maiden before them, two or three miles to eastward, facing the slanting rays of the sun. On all her vast precipices scarce a rock showed bare, so encrusted were they with a dazzling robe of snow. More lovely she seemed and more graceful in her airy poise than they had yet beheld her. Juss and Brandoch Daha rose up, as men arise to greet a queen in her majesty. In silence they looked on her for some minutes.

Then Brandoch Daha spake, saying, "Behold thy bride, O Juss."

XIII

KOSHTRA BELORN

*How the Lord Juss accomplished at length his
dream's behest, to inquire in Koshtra Belorn; and
what manner of answer he received.*

THAT night they spent safely, by favour of the Gods,
under the highest crags of Koshtra Pivrarcha, in a
sheltered hollow piled round with snow. Dawn came
like a lily, saffron-hued, smirched with smoke-gray
streaks that slanted from the north. The great peaks
stood as islands above a main of level cloud, out of which the sun
walked flaming, a ball of red-gold fire. An hour before his face
appeared, the Demons and Mivarsh were roped and started on
their eastward journey. Ill to do with as was the crest of the great
north buttress by which they had climbed the mountain, seven
times worse was this eastern ridge, leading to Koshtra Belorn.
Leaner of back it was, flanked by more profound abysses, deeplier
gashed, too treacherous and too sudden in its changes from sure
rock to rotten and perilous: piled with tottering crags, hung about
with cornices of uncertain snow, girt with cliffs smooth and holdless as a castle wall. Small marvel that it cost them thirteen hours to
come down that ridge. The sun wheeled towards the west when
they reached at length that frozen edge, sharp as a sickle, that was
in the Gates of Zimiamvia. Weary they were, and ropeless; for by
no means else might they come down from the last great tower
save by the rope made fast from above. A fierce north-easter had
swept the ridges all day, bringing snow-storms on its wings. Their

fingers were numbed with cold, and the beards of Lord Brandoch Daha and Mivarsh Faz stiff with ice.

Too weary to halt, they set forth again, Juss leading. It was many hundred paces along that ice-edge, and the sun was near setting when they stood at last within a stone's throw of the cliffs of Koshtra Belorn. Since before noon avalanches had thundered ceaselessly down those cliffs. Now, in the cool of the evening, all was still. The wind was fallen. The deep blue sky was without a cloud. The fires of sunset crept down the vast white precipices before them till every ledge and fold and frozen pinnacle glowed pink colour, and every shadow became an emerald. The shadow of Koshtra Pivrarcha lay cold across the lower stretches of the face on the Zimiamvian side. The edge of that shadow was as the division betwixt the living and the dead.

"What dost think on?" said Juss to Brandoch Daha, that leaned upon his sword surveying that glory.

Brandoch Daha started and looked on him. "Why," said he, "on this: that it is likely thy dream was but a lure, sent thee by the King to tempt us on to mighty actions reserved for our destruction. On this side at least 'tis very certain there lieth no way up Koshtra Belorn."

"What of the little martlet," said Juss, "who, whiles we were yet a great way off, flew out of the south to greet us with a gracious message?"

"Well if it were not a devil of his," said Brandoch Daha.

"I will not turn back," said Juss. "Thou needest not to come with me." And he turned again to look on those frozen cliffs.

"No?" said Brandoch Daha. "Nor thou with me. Thou'lt make me angry if thou wilt so vilely wrest my words. Only fare not too securely; and let that axe still be ready in thine hand, as is my sword, for kindlier work than step-cutting. And if thou embrace the hope to climb her by this wall before us, then hath the King's enchantery made thee fey."

By then was the sun gone down. Under the wings of night uplifted from the east, the unfathomable heights of air turned a richer blue; and here and there, most dim and hard to see, throbbed a tiny point of light: the greater stars opening their eyelids to the gathering dark. Gloom crept upward, brimming the valleys far below like a rising tide of the sea. Frost and stillness waited on the eternal night to resume her reign. The solemn cliffs of Koshtra Belorn stood in tremendous silence, death-pale against the sky.

Juss came backward a step along the ridge, and laying his hand on Brandoch Daha's, "Be still," he said, "and behold this marvel." A little up the face of the mountain on the Zimiamvian side, it was as if some leavings of the after-glow had been entangled among the crags and frozen curtains of snow. As the gloom deepened, that glow brightened and spread, filling a rift that seemed to go into the mountain.

"It is because of us," said Juss, in a low voice. "She is afire with expectation of us."

No sound was there save of their breath coming and going, and of the strokes of Juss's axe, and of the chips of ice chinking downwards into silence as he cut their way along the ridge. And ever brighter, as night fell, burned that strange sunset light above them. Perilous climbing it was for fifty feet or more from the ridge, for they had no rope, the way was hard to see, and the rocks were steep and iced and every ledge deep in snow. Yet came they safe at length up by a steep short gully to the gully's head where it widened to that rift of the wondrous light. Here might two walk abreast, and Lord Juss and Lord Brandoch Daha took their weapons and entered abreast into the rift. Mivarsh was fain to call to them, but he was speechless. He came after, close at their heels like a dog.

For some way the bed of the cave ran upwards, then dipped at a gentle slope deep into the mountain. The air was cold, yet warm after the frozen air without. The rose-red light shone warm on the walls and floor of that passage, but none might say whence it shone. Strange sculptures glimmered overhead, bull-headed men, stags with human faces, mammoths, and behemoths of the flood: vast forms and uncertain carved in the living rock. For hours Juss and his companions pursued their way, winding downward, losing all sense of north and south. Little by little the light faded, and after an hour or two they went in darkness: yet not in utter darkness, but as of a starless night in summer where all night long twilight lingers. They went a soft pace, for fear of pitfalls in the way.

After a while Juss halted and sniffed the air. "I smell new-mown hay," he said, "and flower-scents. Is this my fantasy, or canst thou smell them too?"

"Ay, and have smelt it this half-hour past," answered Brandoch Daha; "also the passage wideneth before us, and the roof of it goeth higher as we journey."

"This," said Juss, "is a great wonder."

They fared onward, and in a while the slope slackened, and they felt loose stones and grit beneath their feet, and in a while soft earth. They bent down and touched the earth, and there was grass growing, and night-dew on the grass, and daisies folded up asleep. A brook tinkled on the right. So they crossed that meadow in the dark, until they stood below a shadowy mass that bulked big above them. In a blind wall so high the top was swallowed up in the darkness a gate stood open. They crossed that threshold and passed through a paved court that clanked under their tread. Before them a flight of steps went up to folding doors under an archway.

Lord Brandoch Daha felt Mivarsh pluck him by the sleeve. The little man's teeth were chattering together in his head for terror. Brandoch Daha smiled and put an arm about him. Juss had his foot on the lowest step.

In that instant came a sound of music playing, but of what instruments they might not guess. Great thundering chords began it, like trumpets calling to battle, first high, then low, then shuddering down to silence; then that great call again, sounding defiance. Then the keys took new voices, groping in darkness, rising to passionate lament, hovering and dying away on the wind, until nought remained but a roll as of muffled thunder, long, low, quiet, but menacing ill. And now out of the darkness of that induction burst a mighty form, three ponderous blows, as of breakers that plunge and strike on a desolate shore; a pause; those blows again; a grinding pause; a rushing of wings, as of Furies steaming up from the pit;[1] another flight of them dreadful in its deliberation; then a wild rush upward and a swooping again; confusion of hell, raging serpents blazing through night sky. Then on a sudden out of a distant key, a sweet melody, long-drawn and clear, like a blaze of low sunshine piercing the dust-clouds above a battle-field. This was but an interlude to the terror of the great main theme that came in tumultuous strides up again from the deeps, storming to a grand climacteric of fury and passing away into silence. Now came a majestic figure, stately and calm, born of that terror, leading to it again: battlings of these themes in many keys, and at last the great triple blow, thundering in new strength, crushing all joy and sweetness as with a mace of iron, battering the roots of life into a general ruin. But even in the main stride of its outrage and terror, that great power seemed to shrivel. The thunder-blasts crashed weaklier, the harsh blows rattled awry, and the vast frame of conquest and destroying violence sank down panting, tottered and rumbled ingloriously into silence.

Like men held in a trance those lords of Demonland listened to the last echoes of the great sad chord where that music had breathed out its heart, as if the very heart of wrath were broken. But this was not the end. Cold and serene as some chaste virgin vowed to the Gods, with clear eyes which see nought below high heaven, a quiet melody rose from that grave of terror. Weak it seemed at first, a little thing after that cataclysm; a little thing, like spring's first bud peeping after the blasting reign of cold and ice. Yet it walked undismayed, gathering as it went beauty and power. And on a sudden the folding doors swung open, shedding a flood of radiance down the stairs.

Lord Juss and Lord Brandoch Daha watched, as men watch for a star to rise, that radiant portal. And like a star indeed, or like the tranquil moon appearing, they beheld after a while one crowned like a Queen with a diadem of little clouds that seemed stolen from the mountain sunset, scattering soft beams of rosy brightness. She stood alone under that mighty portico with its vast shadowy forms of winged lions in shining stone black as jet. Youthful she seemed, as one that hath but just bidden adieu to childhood, with grave sweet lips and grave black eyes and hair like the night. Little black martlets perched on her either shoulder, and a dozen more skimmed the air above her head, so swift of wing that scarcely the eye might follow them. Meantime, that delicate and simple melody mounted from height to height, until in a while it burned with all the fires of summer, burned as summer to the uttermost ember, fierce and compulsive in its riot of love and beauty. So that, before the last triumphant chords died down in silence, that music had brought back to Juss all the glories of the mountains, the sunset fires on Koshtra Belorn, the first great revelation of the peaks from Morna Moruna; and over all these, as the spirit of that music to the eye made manifest, the image of that Queen so blessed-fair in her youth and her clear brow's sweet solemn respect and promise: in every line and pose of her fair form, virginal dainty as a flower, and kindled from withinward as never flower was with that divinity before the face of which speech and song fall silent and men may but catch their breath and worship.

When she spoke, it was with a voice like crystal: "Thanks be and praise to the blessed Gods. For lo, the years depart, and the fated years bring forth as the Gods ordain. And ye be those that were for to come."

Surely those great lords of Demonland stood like little boys before her. She said again, "Are not ye Lord Juss and Lord Brandoch Daha of Demonland, come up to me by the way banned to all mortals else, come up into Koshtra Belorn?"

Then answered Lord Juss for them both and said, "Surely, O Queen Sophonisba, we be they thou namest."

Now the Queen carried them into her palace, and into a great hall where was her throne and state. The pillars of the hall were as vast towers, and there were galleries above them, tier upon tier, rising higher than sight could reach or the light of the gentle lamps in their stands that lighted the tables and the floor. The walls and the pillars were of a sombre stone unpolished, and on the walls strange portraitures: lions, dragons, nickers of the sea,[2] spread-eagles, elephants, swans, unicorns, and other, lively made and richly set forth with curious colours of painting: all of giant size beyond the experience of human kind so that to be in that hall was as it were to shelter in a small spot of light and life, canopied, vaulted, and embraced by the circumambient unknown.

The Queen sate on her throne that was bright like the face of a river ruffled with wind under a silver moon. Save for those little martlets she was unattended. She made those lords of Demonland sit down before her face, and there were brought forth by the agency of unseen hands tables before them and precious dishes filled with unknown viands.[3] And there played a soft music, made in the air by what unseen art they knew not.

The Queen said, "Behold, ambrosia which the Gods do eat and nectar which they drink; on which meat and wine myself do feed, by the bounty of the blessed Gods. And the savour thereof wearieth not, and the glow thereof and the perfume thereof dieth not for ever."

So they tasted of the ambrosia, that was white to look on and crisp to the tooth and sweet, and being eaten revived strength in the body more than a surfeit of bullock's flesh, and of the nectar that was all afoam and coloured like the inmost fires of sunset. Surely somewhat of the peace of the Gods was in that nectar divine.

The Queen said, "Tell me, why are ye come?"

Juss answered, "Surely there was a dream sent me, O Queen Sophonisba, through the gate of horn,[4] and it bade me inquire hither after him I most desire, for want of whom my whole soul languisheth in sorrow this year gone by: even after my dear brother, the Lord Goldry Bluszco."

His words ceased in his throat. For with the speaking of that name the firm fabric of the palace quivered like the leaves of a forest under a sudden squall. Colour went from the scene, like the blood chased from a man's face by fear, and all was of a pallid hue, like the landscape which one beholds of a bright summer day after lying with eyes closed for a space face-upward under the blazing sun: all gray and cold, the warm colours burnt to ashes. Withal, followed the appearance of hateful little creatures issuing from the joints of the paving stones and the great blocks of the walls and pillars: some like grasshoppers with human heads and wings of flies, some like fishes with stings in their tails, some fat like toads, some like eels a-wriggling with puppy-dogs' heads and asses' ears: loathly ones, exiles of glory, scaly and obscene.

The horror passed. Colour returned. The Queen sat like a graven statue, her lips parted. After a while she said with a shaken voice, low and with downcast eyes, "Sirs, you demand of me a very strange matter, such as wherewith never hitherto I have been acquainted. As you are noble, I beseech you speak not that name again. In the name of the blessed Gods, speak it not again."

Lord Juss was silent. Nought good were his thoughts within him.

In due time a little martlet by the Queen's command brought them to their bed-chambers. And there in great beds soft and fragrant they went to rest.

Juss waked long in the doubtful light, troubled at heart. At length he fell into a troubled sleep. The glimmer of the lamps mingled with his dreams and his dreams with it, so that scarce he wist whether asleep or waking he beheld the walls of the bed-chamber dispart in sunder,[5] disclosing a prospect of vast paths of moonlight, and a solitary mountain peak standing naked out of a sea of cloud that gleamed white beneath the moon. It seemed to him that the power of flight was upon him, and that he flew to that mountain and hung in air beholding it near at hand, and a circle as the appearance of fire round about it, and on the summit of the mountain the likeness of a burg or citadel of brass that was green with eld and surface-battered by the frosts and winds of ages. On the battlements was the appearance of a great company both men and women, never still, now walking on the wall with hands lifted up as in supplication to the crystal lamps of heaven, now flinging themselves on their knees or leaning against the brazen battlements to bury their faces in their hands, or standing at gaze as nightwalkers gazing into the void. Some seemed men of war, and some great courtiers by their costly apparel, rulers and kings and kings' daughters, grave bearded counsellors, youths and maidens and crowned queens. And when they went, and when they stood, and when they seemed to cry aloud bitterly, all was noiseless even as the tomb, and the faces of those mourners pallid as a dead corpse is pallid.

Then it seemed to Juss that he beheld a keep of brass flat-roofed standing on the right, a little higher than the walls, with battlements about the roof. He strove to cry aloud, but it was as if some devil gripped his throat stifling him, for no sound came. For in the midst of the roof, as it were on a bench of stone, was the appearance of one reclining; his chin resting in his great right hand, his elbow on an arm of the bench, his cloak about him gorgeous with cloth of gold, his ponderous two-handed sword beside him with its heart-shaped ruby pommel darkly resplendent in the moonlight. Nought otherwise looked he than when Juss last beheld him, on their ship before the darkness swallowed them; only the ruddy hues of life seemed departed from him, and his brow seemed clouded with sorrow. His eye met his brother's, but with no look of recognition, gazing as if on some far point in the deeps beyond the star-shine. It seemed to Juss that even so would he have looked to find his brother Goldry as he now found him; his head unbent for all the tyranny of those dark powers that held him in captivity: keeping like a God his patient vigil, heedless alike of the laments of them that shared his prison and of the menace of the houseless night about him.

The vision passed; and Lord Juss perceived himself in his bed again, the cold morning light stealing between the hangings of the windows and dimming the soft radiance of the lamps.

Now for seven days they dwelt in that palace. No living thing they encountered save only the Queen and her little martlets, but all things desirous were ministered unto them by unseen hands and all royal entertainment. Yet was Lord Juss heavy at heart, for as often as he would question the Queen of Goldry, so she would ever put him by, praying him earnestly not a second time to pronounce that name of terror. At last, walking with her alone in the cool of the evening on a trodden path of a meadow where asphodel grew and other holy flowers beside a quiet stream, he said, "So it is, O Queen Sophonisba, that when first I came hither and spake with thee I well thought that by thee my matter should be well sped. And didst not thou then promise me thy goodness and grace from thee thereafter?"

"This is very true," said the Queen.

"Then why," said he, "when I would question thee of that I make most store of, wilt thou always daff me and put me by?"

She was silent, hanging her head. He looked sidelong for a minute at her sweet profile, the grave clear lines of her mouth and chin. "Of whom must I inquire," he said, "if not of thee, which art Queen in Koshtra Belorn and must know this thing?"

She stopped and faced him with dark eyes that were like a child's for innocence and like a God's for splendour. "My lord, that I have put thee off, ascribe it not to evil intent. That were an unnatural part indeed in me unto you of Demonland who have fulfilled the weird and set me free again to visit again the world of men which I so much desire, despite all my sorrows I there fulfilled in elder time. Or shall I forget you are at enmity with the wicked house of Witchland, and therefore doubly pledged my friends?"

"That the event must prove, O Queen," said Lord Juss.

"O saw ye Morna Moruna?" cried she. "Saw ye it in the wilderness?" And when he looked on her still dark and mistrustful, she said, "Is this forgot? And methought it should be mention and remembrance made thereof unto the end of the world. I pray thee, my lord, what age art thou?"

"I have looked upon this world," answered Lord Juss, "for thrice ten years."

"And I," said the Queen, "but seventeen summers. Yet that same age had I when thou wast born, and thy grandsire before thee, and his before him. For the Gods gave me youth for ever more, when they brought me hither after the realm-rape that befell our house, and lodged me in this mountain."

She paused, and stood motionless, her hands clasped lightly before her, her head bent, her face turned a little away so that he saw only the white curve of her neck and her cheek's soft outline. All the air was full of sunset, though no sun was there, but a scattered splendour only, shed from the high roof of rock that was like a sky above them, self-effulgent. Very softly she began again to speak, the crystal accents of her voice sounding like the faint notes of a bell borne from a great way off on the quiet air of a summer evening. "Surely time past is gone by like a shadow since those days, when I was Queen in Morna Moruna, dwelling there with my lady mother and the princes my cousins in peace and joy. Until Gorice III. came out of the north, the great King of Witchland, desiring to explore these mountains, for his pride's sake and his insolent heart; which cost him dear. 'Twas on an evening of early summer we beheld him and his folk ride over the flowering meadows of the Moruna. Nobly was he entertained by us, and when we knew what way he meant to go, we counselled him turn back, and the mantichores must tear him if he went. But he mocked at our advisoes, and on the morrow departed, he and his, by way of Omprenne Edge. And never again were they seen of living man.

"That had been small loss; but hereof there befell a great and horrible mischief. For in the spring of the year came Gorice IV. with a great army out of waterish Witchland, saying with open mouth of defamation that we were the dead King's murtherers: we that were peaceful folk, and would not entertain an action should call us villain for all the wealth of Impland. In the night they came, when all we save the sentinels upon the walls were in our beds secure in a quiet conscience. They took the princes my cousins and all our men, and before our eyes most cruelly murthered them. So that my mother seeing these things fell suddenly into deadly swoonings and was presently dead. And the King commanded them burn the house with fire, and he brake down the holy altars of the Gods, and defiled their high places. And unto me that was young and fair to look on he gave this choice: to go with him and be his slave, other else to be cast down from the Edge and all my bones be broken. Surely I chose this rather. But the Gods, that do help every rightful true cause, made light my fall, and guided me hither safe through all perils of height and cold and ravening beasts, granting me youth and peaceful days for ever, here on the borderland between the living and the dead.

"And the Gods blew upon all the land of the Moruna in the fire of their wrath, to make it desolate, and man and beast cut off therefrom, for a witness of the wicked deeds of Gorice the King, even as Gorice the King made desolate our little castle and our pleasant places. The face of the land was lifted up to high airs where frosts do dwell, so that the cliffs of Omprenne Edge down which ye came are ten times the height they were when Gorice III. came down them. So was an end of flowers on the Moruna, and an end there of spring and of summer days for ever."

The Queen ceased speaking, and Lord Juss was silent for a space, greatly marvelling.

"Judge now," said she, "if your foes be not my foes. It is not hidden from me, my lord, that you deem me but a lukewarm friend and no helper at all in your enterprise. Yet have I ceased not since ye were here to search and to inquire, and sent my little martlets west and east and south and north after tidings of him thou namedst. They are swift, even as wingy thoughts circling the stablished world; and they returned to me on weary wings, yet with never a word of thy great kinsman."

Juss looked at her eyes that were moist with tears. Truth sat in them like an angel. "O Queen," he cried, "why need thy little minions scour the world, when my brother is here in Koshtra Belorn?"

She shook her head, saying, "This I will swear to thee, there hath no mortal come up into Koshtra Belorn save only thee and thy companions these two hundred years."

But Juss said again, "My brother is here in Koshtra Belorn. Mine eyes beheld him that first night, hedged about with fires. And he is held captive on a tower of brass on a peak of a mountain."

"There be no mountains here," said she, "save this in whose womb we have our dwelling."

"Yet so I beheld my brother," said Juss, "under the white beams of the full moon."

"There is no moon here," said the Queen.

So Lord Juss rehearsed to her his vision of the night, telling her point to point of everything. She harkened gravely, and when he had done, trembled a little and said, "This is a mystery, my lord, beyond my resolution."

She fell silent awhile. Then she began to say in a hushed voice, as if the very words and breath might breed some dreadful matter: "Taken up in a sending maleficial by King Gorice XII. So it hath ever been, that whensoever there dieth one of the house of Gorice there riseth up another in his stead, and so from strength to strength. And death weakeneth not this house of Witchland, but like the dandelion weed being cut down and bruised it springeth up the stronger. Dost thou know why?"

He answered, "No."

"The blessed Gods," said she, speaking yet lower, "have shown me many hidden matters which the sons of men know not neither imagine. Behold this mystery. There is but One Gorice. And by the favour of heaven (that moveth sometimes in a manner our weak judgement seeketh in vain to justify) this cruel and evil One, every time whether by the sword or in the fulness of his years he cometh to die, departeth the living soul and spirit of him into a new and sound body, and liveth yet another lifetime to vex and to oppress the world, until that body die, and the next in his turn, and so continually; having thus in a manner life eternal."

Juss said, "Thy discourse, O Queen Sophonisba, is in a strain above mortality. This is a great wonder thou tellest me; whereof some little part I guessed aforetime, but the main I knew not. Rightfully, having such a timeless life, this King weareth on his thumb that worm Ouroboros which doctors have from of old made for an ensample of eternity, whereof the end is ever at the beginning and the beginning at the end for ever more."

"See then the hardness of the thing," said the Queen. "But I forget not, my lord, that thou hast a matter nearer thine heart than this: to set free him (name him not!) concerning whom thou didst inquire of me. Touching this, know it for thy comfort, some ray of light I see. Question me no more till I have made trial thereof, lest it prove but a false dawn. If it be as I think, 'tis a trial yet abideth thee should make the stoutest blench."

XIV

The Lake of Ravary

*Of the furtherance given by Queen Sophonisba,
fosterling of the Gods, to Lord Juss and Lord
Brandoch Daha; with how the Hippogriff's egg
was hatched beside the enchanted lake, and
what ensued therefrom.*

 EXT day the Queen came to Lord Juss and Lord
Brandoch Daha and made them go with her, and
Mivarsh with them to serve them, over the meadows
and down a passage like that whereby they had entered the mountain, but this led downward. "Ye may
marvel," she said, "to see daylight in the heart of this great mountain. Yet it is but the hidden work of Nature. For the rays of the sun,
striking all day upon Koshtra Belorn and upon her robe of snow,
sink into the snow like water, and so soaking through the secret
places of the rocks shine again in this hollow chamber where we
dwell and in these passages cleft by the Gods to give us our goings
out and our comings in. And as sunset followeth broad day with
coloured fires, and moonlight or darkness followeth sunset, and
dawn followeth night ushering the bright day once more, so these
changes of the dark and light succeed one another within the
mountain."

They passed on, ever downward, till after many hours they
came suddenly forth into dazzling sunlight. They stood at a cave's
mouth on a beach of sand white and clean, that was lapped by the
ripples of a sapphire lake: a great lake, sown with islets craggy and

luxuriant with trees and flowering growths. Many-armed was the lake, winding everywhere in secret reaches behind promontories that were spurs of the mountains that held it in their bosom: some wooded or green with lush flower-spangled turf to the water's edge, some with bare rocks abrupt from the water, some crowned with rugged lines of crag that sent down scree-slopes into the lake below. It was mid-afternoon, sweet-aired, a day of dappled cloud-shadows and changing lights. White birds circled above the lake, and now and then a kingfisher flashed by like a streak of azure flame. That was a westward facing beach, at the end of a headland that ran down clothed with pine-forests with open primrose glades from a spur of Koshtra Belorn. Northward the two great mountains stood at the head of a straight narrow valley that ran up to the Gates of Zimiamvia. Vaster they seemed than the Demons had yet beheld them, showing at but six or seven miles' distance a clear sixteen thousand feet above the lake. Nor from any other point of prospect were they more lovely to behold: Koshtra Pivrarcha like an eagle armed, shadowing with wings, and Koshtra Belorn as a Goddess fallen a-dreaming, gracious as the morning star of heaven. Wondrous bright were their snows in the sunshine, yet ghostly and unsubstantial to view seen through the hazy summer air. Olive trees, gray and soft-outlined like embodied mist, grew in the lower valleys; woods of oak and birch and every forest tree clothed the slopes; and in the warmer folds of the mountain sides belts of creamy rhododendrons straggled upwards even to the moraines above the lower glaciers and the very margin of the snows.

The Queen watched Lord Juss as his gaze moved to the left past Koshtra Pivrarcha, past the blunt lower crest of Gôglio, to a great lonely peak many miles distant that frowned over the rich maze of nearer ridges which stood above the lake. Its southern shoulder swept in a long majestic line of cliffs up to a clean sharp summit; northward it fell steeplier away. Little snow hung on the sheer rock faces, save where the gullies cleft them. For grace and beauty scarce might Koshtra Belorn herself surpass that peak: but terrible it looked, and as a mansion of old night, that not high noon-day could wholly dispossess of darkness.

"There standeth a mountain great and fair," said Lord Brandoch Daha, "which was hid in a cloud when we were on the high ridges. It hath the look of a great beast couchant."[1]

Still the Queen watched Lord Juss, who looked still on that peak. Then he turned to her, his hands clenched on the buckles of his breast-plates. She said, "Was it as I think?"

He took a great breath. "It was so I beheld it in the beginning," he said, "as from this place. But here are we too far off to see the citadel of brass, or know if it be truly there." And he said to Brandoch Daha, "This remaineth, that we climb that mountain."

"That can ye never do," said the Queen.

"That shall be shown," said Brandoch Daha.

"List," said she. "Nameless is yonder mountain upon earth, for until this hour, save only for me and you, the eye of living man hath not looked upon it. But unto the Gods it hath a name, and unto the spirits of the blest that do inhabit this land, and unto those unhappy souls that are held in captivity on that cold mountain top: Zora Rach nam Psarrion, standing apart above the noiseless lifeless snow-fields that feed the Psarrion glaciers; loneliest and secretest of all earth's mountains, and most accursed. O my lords," she said, "think not to climb up Zora. Enchantments ring round Zora, so that ye should not get so near as to the edges of the snow-fields at her feet ere ruin gathered you."

Juss smiled. "O Queen Sophonisba, little thou knowest our mind, if thou think this shall turn us back."

"I say it," said the Queen, "with no such vain purpose; but to show you the necessity of that way I shall now tell you of, since well I know ye will not give over this attempt. To none save to a Demon durst I have told it, lest heaven should hold me answerable for his death. But unto you I may with the less danger commit this dangerous counsel if it be true, as I was taught long ago, that the hippogriff was seen of old in Demonland."

"The hippogriff?" said Lord Brandoch Daha. "What else is it than the emblem of our greatness? A thousand years ago they nested on Neverdale Hause, and there abide unto this day in the rocks the prints of their hooves and talons. He that rode it was a forefather of mine and of Lord Juss."

"He that shall ride it again," said Queen Sophonisba, "he only of mortal men may win to Zora Rach, and if he be man enough of his hands may deliver him we wot of [2] out of bondage."

"O Queen," said Juss, "somewhat I know of grammarie and divine philosophy, yet must I bow to thee for such learning, that dwellest here from generation to generation and dost commune with the dead. How shall we find this steed? Few they be, and high they fly above the world, and come to birth but one in three hundred years."

She answered, "I have an egg. In all lands else must such an egg lie barren and sterile, save in this land of Zimiamvia which is sacred to the lordly races of the dead. And thus cometh this steed to the birth: when one of might and heart beyond the wont of man sleepeth in this land with the egg in his bosom, greatly desiring some high achievement, the fire of his great longing hatcheth the egg, and the hippogriff cometh out therefrom, weak-winged at first as thou hast seen a butterfly new-hatched out his chrysalis. Then only mayst thou mount him, and if thou be man enow to turn him to thy will he shall bear thee to the uttermost parts of earth unto thine heart's desire. But if thou be aught less than greatest, beware that steed, and mount only earthly coursers. For if there be aught of dross[3] within thee, and thine heart falter, or thy purpose cool,[4] or thou forget the level aim of thy glory, then will he toss thee to thy ruin."

"Thou hast this thing, O Queen?" said Lord Juss.

"My lord," she said softly, "more than an hundred years ago I found it, while I rambled on the cliffs that are about this charmed Lake of Ravary. And here I hid it, being taught by the Gods what thing I had found and knowing what was foreordained, that certain of earth should come at last to Koshtra Belorn. Thinking in my heart that he that should come might be of those who bare some great unfulfilled desire, and might be of such might as could ride to his desire on such a steed."

They abode, talking little, by the charmed lake's shore till evening. Then they arose, and went with her to a pavilion by the lake, built in a grove of flowering trees. Ere they went to rest, she brought them the hippogriff's egg, great as a man's body, yet light of weight, rough and coloured like gold. And she said, "Which of you, my lords?"

Juss answered, "He, if might and a high heart should only count; but I, because my brother it is that we must free from his dismal place."

So the Queen gave the egg to Lord Juss; and he, bearing it in his arms, bade her good-night, saying, "I need no other laudanum than this to make me sleep."

And the ambrosial night came down. And gentle sleep, softer than sleep is on earth, closed their eyes in that pavilion beside the enchanted lake.

Mivarsh slept not. Small joy had he of that Lake of Ravary, caring for none of its beauties but mindful still of certain lewd bulks he had seen basking by its shores all through the golden afternoon. He had questioned one of the Queen's martlets concerning them, who laughed at him and let him know that these were crocodiles, wardens of the lake, tame and gentle toward the heroes of bliss who resorted thither to bathe and disport themselves. "But should such an one as thou," she said, "adventure there, they would chop thee up at a mouthful." This saddened him. And indeed, little ease of heart had he since he came out of Impland, and dearly he desired his home, though it were sacked and burnt, and the men of his own blood, though they should prove his foes. And well he thought that if Juss should fly with Brandoch Daha mounted on hippogriff to that cold mountain top where souls of the great were held in bondage, he should never win back alone to the world of men, past the frozen mountains, and the mantichores, and past the crocodile that dwelt beside Bhavinan.

He lay awake an hour or twain, weeping quietly, until out of the giant heart of midnight came to him with fiery clearness the words of the Queen, saying that by the heat of great longing in his heart that claspeth it must that egg be hatched, and that that man should then mount and ride on the wind unto his heart's desire. Therewith Mivarsh sat up, his hands clammy with mixed fear and longing. It seemed to him, awake and alone among the sleepers in that breathless night, that no longing could be greater than his longing. He said in his heart, "I will arise, and take the egg privily from the devil transmarine and clasp it myself. I do him no wrong thereby, for said she not it was perilous? Also every man raketh the embers to his own cake."

So he arose, and came secretly to Juss where he lay with his strong arms circling the egg. A beam of the moon came in by a window, shining on the face of Juss, that was as the face of a God. Mivarsh bent over him and teased the egg gently from his embrace, praying fervently the while. And, for Juss was in a profound slumber, his soul mounting in vision far from earth, far from that shore divine, to lone regions where Goldry watched still in frozen mournful patience on the heights of Zora, at last Mivarsh gat the egg and bare it to his bed. Very warm it was, crackling to his ear as he embraced it, as of a power moving from withinwards.

In such wise Mivarsh fell asleep, clasping the egg as a man should clasp his dearest. And a little before dawn it hatched in his arms and fell asunder, and he started awake, his arms about the neck of a strange steed. It went forth into the pale light before the sunrise, and he with it, holding it fast. The sheen of its hair was like the peacock's neck; its eyes like the changing fires of a star of a windy night. Its nostrils widened to the breath of the dawn. Its wings unfolded and grew stiff, their feathers like the tail-feathers of the peacock pheasant, white with purple eyes, and hard to the touch as iron blades. Mivarsh was mounted on its back, seizing the shining mane with both hands, trembling. And now was he fain to descend, but the hippogriff snorted and reared, and he, fearing a great fall, clung closer. It stamped with its silver hoofs, flapping its wings, ramping like a lioness, tearing up the grass with its claws. Mivarsh screamed, torn between hope and fear. It plunged forward and leaped into the air and flew.

The Demons, waked by the whirring of wings, rushed from the pavilion, to behold that marvel flown against the obscure west. Wild was its flight, like a snipe dipping and plunging. And while they looked, they saw the rider flung from his seat and heard, some moments after, a dull flop and splash of a body fallen in the lake.

The wild steed vanished, winging toward the upper air. Rings ran outward from the splash, troubling the surface of the lake, marring the dark reflection of Zora Rach mirrored in the sleeping waters.

"Poor Mivarsh!" cried Lord Brandoch Daha. "After all the weary leagues I made him go with me." And he threw off his cloak, took a dagger in his teeth, and swam with great overarm strokes out to the spot where Mivarsh fell. But nought he found of Mivarsh. Only he saw near by on an island beach a crocodile, big and bloated, that eyed him guiltily and stayed not for his coming, but lumbering into the water dived and disappeared. So Brandoch Daha turned and swam ashore again.

Lord Juss stood as a man stricken to stone. As one despaired he turned to the Queen, who now came forth to them wrapped in a mantle of swansdown; yet high he held his head. "O Queen Sophonisba, here is that secret glome or bottom of our days,[5] come when we sniffed the sweetness of the morning."

"My lord," said she, "the flies hemerae take life with the sun and die with the dew.[6] But thou, if thou be truly great, join not hands with desperation. Let the sad ending of this poor servant of thine be to thee a monument against such folly. Earth is not ruined for a single shower. Come back with me to Koshtra Belorn."

He looked at the grand peak of Zora, dark against the wakening east. "Madam," he said, "thou hast little more than half my years, and yet by another computation thou art seven times mine age. I am not light of will, nor thou shalt not find me a fool to thee. Let us go back to Koshtra Belorn."

They brake their fast quietly and returned by the way they came. And the Queen said, "My lords Juss and Brandoch Daha, there be few steeds of such a kind to carry you to Zora Rach nam Psarrion, and not ye, though ye be beyond the half-gods in your might and virtue, might have power to ride them but if ye take them from the egg. So high they fly, so shy they are, ye should not catch them though ye waited ten men's lifetimes. I will send my martlets to see if there be another egg in the world."

So she despatched them, north and west and south and east. And in due time those little birds returned on weary wing, all save one, without tidings.

"All have come back to me," said the Queen, "save Arabella alone. Dangers attend them in the world: birds of prey, men that slay little birds for their sport. Yet hope with me that she may come back at last."

But the Lord Juss spake and said, "O Queen Sophonisba, to hope and wait lieth not in my nature, but to be swift, resolute, and exact whensoever I see my way before me. This have I ever approved, that the strawberry groweth underneath the nettle still. I will assay the ascent of Zora."

Nor might all her prayers turn him from this rashness, wherein the Lord Brandoch Daha besides did most eagerly second him.

Two nights and two days they were gone, and the Queen abode them in great trouble of heart in her pavilion by the enchanted lake. The third evening came Brandoch Daha back to the pavilion, bringing with him Juss that was like a man at point of death, and himself besides deadly sick.

"Tell me not anything," said the Queen. "Forgetfulness is the only sovran[7] remedy, which with all my art I will strive to induce in thy mind and in his. Surely I despaired ever to see you in life again, so rashly entered into those regions forbid."

Brandoch Daha smiled, but his look was ghastly. "Blame us not overmuch, dear Queen. Who shoots at the mid-day sun, though he be sure he shall never hit the mark, yet as sure he is he shall shoot higher than who aims but at a bush." His voice broke in his throat; the whites of his eyes rolled up; he caught at the Queen's hand like a frightened child. Then with a mighty effort mastering himself, "I pray bear with me a little," he said. "After a little good meats and drinks taken 'twill pass. I pray look to Juss: is a dead, think you?"

Days passed, and months, and the Lord Juss lay yet as it were in the article of death tended by his friend and by the Queen in that pavilion by the lake. At length when winter was gone in middle earth,[8] and the spring far spent, back came that last little martlet on weary wing, she they had long given up for lost. She sank in her mistress's bosom, almost dead indeed for weariness. But the

Queen cherished her, and gave her nectar, so that she gathered strength and said, "O Queen Sophonisba, fosterling of the Gods, I flew for thee east and south and west and north, by sea and by land, in heat and frost, unto the frozen poles, about and about. And at the last came to Demonland, to the range of Neverdale. There is a tarn among the mountains, that men call Dule Tarn. Very deep it is, and men that live by bread do hold it for bottomless. Yet hath it a bottom, and on the bottom lieth an hippogriff's egg, seen by me, for I flew at a great height above it."

"In Demonland!" said the Queen. And she said to Lord Brandoch Daha, "It is the only one. Ye must go home to fetch it."

Brandoch Daha said, "Home to Demonland? After we spent our powers and crossed the world to find the way?"

But when Lord Juss knew of it, straightway with hope so renewed began his sickness to depart from him, so that he was in a few weeks' space very well recovered.

And it was now a full year gone by since first the Demons came up into Koshtra Belorn.

QUEEN PREZMYRA

*How the Lady Prezmyra discovered to Lord Gro
what she would have brought about for
Demonland, in which should also appear her
Lord's yet more greatness and advancement: and
how her too loud speaking of her purpose was the
occasion whereby the Lord Corinius was to learn
the sweetness of bliss deferred.*

N that same twenty-sixth night of May, when Lord Juss
and Lord Brandoch Daha beheld from earth's loftiest
pinnacle the land of Zimiamvia and Koshtra Belorn,
Gro walked with the Lady Prezmyra on the western
terrace in Carcë. It wanted yet two hours of midnight.
The air was warm, the sky a bower of moonbeam and starbeam.
Now and then a faint breeze stirred as if night turned in her sleep.
The walls of the palace and the Iron Tower cut off the terrace from
the direct moonlight, and flamboys spreading their wobbling light
made alternating regions of brightness and gloom. Galloping
strains of music and the noise of revelry came from within the
palace.

Gro spake: "If thy question, O Queen, overlie a wish to have
me gone, I am as lightning to obey thee howsoe'er it grieve me."

" 'Twas an idle wonder only," she said. "Stay and it like thee."

"It is but a native part of wisdom," said he, "to follow the
light. When thou wast departed from the hall methought all the

bright lights were bedimmed." He looked at her sidelong as they passed into the radiance of a flamboy, studying her countenance that seemed clouded with grievous thought. Fair of all fairs she seemed, stately and splendid; crowned with a golden crown set about with dark amethysts. A figure of a crab-fish topped it above the brow, curiously wrought in silver and bearing in either claw a ball of chrysolite[1] the bigness of a thrush's egg.

Lord Gro said, "This too was part of my mind, to behold those stars in heaven that men call Berenice's Hair, and know if they can outshine in glory thine hair, O Queen."

They paced on in silence. Then, "These phrases of forced gallantry," she said, "sort ill with our friendship, my Lord Gro. If I be not angry, think it is because I father them on the deep healths thou hast caroused unto our Lord the King on this night of nights, when the returning year bringeth back the date of his sending, and our vengeance upon Demonland."

"Madam," he said, "I would but have thee give over this melancholy. Seemeth it to thee a little thing that the King hath pleased so singularly to honour Corund thy husband as give him a king's style and dignity and all Impland to hold in fee? All took notice of it how uncheerfully thou didst receive this royal crown when the King gave it thee to-night, in honour of thy great lord, to wear in his stead till he come home to claim it; this, and the great praise spoke by the King of Corund, which methinks should bring the warmth of pride to thy cheeks. Yet are all these things of as little avail against thy frozen scornful melancholy as the weak winter sun availeth against congealed pools in a black frost."

"Crowns are cheap trash to-day," said Prezmyra; "whenas the King, with twenty kings to be his lackeys, raiseth up now his lackeys to be kings of the earth. Canst wonder if my joyance in this crown were dashed some little when I looked on that other given by the King to Laxus?"

"Madam," said Gro, "thou must forgive Laxus in his own particular. Thou knowest he set not so much as a foot in Pixyland; and if now he must be called king thereof, that should rather please thee, being in despite of Corinius that carried war there and by whatsoever means of skill or fortune overcame thy noble brother and drave him into exile."

"Corinius," she answered, "tasteth in that miss that bane or ill-hap which I dearly pray all they may groan under who would fatten by my brother's ruin."

"Then should Corinius's grief lift up thy joy," said Gro. "Yet certain it is, Fate is a blind puppy: build not on her next turn."

"Am not I a Queen?" said Prezmyra. "Is not this Witchland? Have we not strength to make curses strong, if Fate be blind indeed?"

They halted at the head of a flight of steps leading down to the inner ward. The Lady Prezmyra leaned awhile on the black marble balustrade, gazing seaward over the level marshes rough with moonlight. "What care I for Laxus?" she said at last. "What care I for Corinius? A cast of hawks flown by the King against a quarry that in dearworthiness and nobility outshineth an hundred such as they. Nor I will not suffer mine indignation so to witwanton with fair justice as persuade me to put the wite on Witchland.[2] It is most true the Prince my brother practised with our enemies the downthrow of our fortunes, breaking open, had he but known it, the gate of destruction for himself and us, that night when our banquet was turned by him to a battle and our winey mirths to bloody rages." She was silent for a time, then said, "Oathbreakers: a most odious name, flat against all humanity. Two faces in one hood. O that earth would start up and strike the sins that tread on her!"

"I see thou lookest west over sea," said Gro.

"There's somewhat thou canst see, then, my Lord Gro, by owl-light," said Prezmyra.

"Thou didst tell me at the time," he said, "with what compliments in vows and strange well-studied promises of friendship the Lord Juss took leave of thee at their escaping out of Carcë. Yet art thou to blame, O Queen, if thou take in too ill part the breaking of such promises given in extremity, which prove commonly like fish, new, stale, and stinking in three days."

"Sure, 'tis a small matter," said she, "that my brother should cast aside all ties of interest and alliance to save these great ones from an evil death; and they, being delivered, should toss him a light grammercy[3] and go their ways, leaving him to be exterminated out of his own country and, for all they know or reck, to lose his life. May the great Devil of Hell torture their souls!"

"Madam," said Lord Gro, "I would have thee view the matter soberly, and leave these bitter flashes. The Demons did save thy brother once in Lida Nanguna, and his delivering of them out of the hand of our Lord the King was but just payment therefor. The scales hang equal."

She answered, "Do not defile mine ears with their excuses. They have shamefully abused us; and the guilt of their black deed planteth them day by day more firmlier in my deeper-settled hate. Art thou so deeply read in nature and her large philosophy, and I am yet to teach thee that deadliest hellebore or the vomit of a toad are qualified poison to the malice of a woman?"

The darkness of a great cloud-bank spreading from the south swallowed up the moonlight. Prezmyra turned to resume her slow pacing down the terrace. The yellow fiery sparkles in her eyes glinted in the flamboys' flare. She looked dangerous as a lioness, and delicate and graceful like an antelope. Gro walked beside her, saying, "Did not Corund drive them forth in winter on to the Moruna, and can they continue there in life, alone amid so many devouring perils?"

"O my lord," she cried, "say these good tidings to the kitchen wenches, not to me. Why, thyself didst enter in past years the very heart of the Moruna and yet camest off, else art thou the greatest liar. This only cankerfrets my soul: that days go by, and months, and Witchland beateth down all peoples under him, and yet he suffereth the crown of pride, these rebels of Demonland, to go yet untrodden under feet. Doth he deem it the better part to spare a foe and spoil a friend? That were an unhappy and unnatural conclusion. Or is he fey,[4] even as was Gorice XI.? Heaven foreshield it, yet as ill an end may bechance him and utter ruin come on all of us if he will withhold his scourge from Demonland until Juss and Brandoch Daha come home again to meet with him."

"Madam," said Lord Gro, "in these few words thou hast given me the picture of mine own mind in small. And forgive me that I bespake thee warily at the first, for these are matters of heavy moment, and ere I opened my mind to thee I would know that it agreed with thine. Let the King smite now, in the happy absence of their greatest champions. So shall we be in strength against them if they return again, and perchance Goldry with them."

She smiled, and it seemed as if all the sultry night freshened and sweetened at that lady's smile. "Thou art a dear companion to me," she said. "Thy melancholy is to me as some shady wood in summer, where I may dance if I will, and that is often, or be sad if I will, and that is in these days oftener than I would: and never thou crossest my mood. Save but now thou didst so, to plague me with thy precious flattering jargon, till I had thought thee skin-changed with Laxus or young Corinius, seeking such lures as gallants spread their wings to, to stoop in ladies' bosoms."

"For I would shake thee from this late-received sadness," said Gro. And he said, "Thou art to commend me too, since I spake nought but truth."

"Oh, have done, my lord," she cried, "or I'll dismiss thee hence." And as they walked Prezmyra sang softly:

> He that cannot chuse but love,
> And strives against it still,
> Never shall my fancy move,
> For he loves 'gaynst his will;
> Nor he which is all his own,
> And can att pleasure chuse;
> When I am caught he can be gone,
> And when he list refuse.
> Nor he that loves none but faire,
> For such by all are sought;
> Nor he that can for foul ones care,
> For his Judgement then is naught;
> Nor he——

She broke off suddenly, saying, "Come, I have shook off the ill disposition the sight of Laxus bred in me and of his tawdry crown. Let's think on action. And first, I will tell thee a thing. This we spoke of hath been in my mind these two or three moons, ever since Corinius's campaigning in Pixyland. So when word came of my lord's destroying of the Demon host, and his driving of Juss and Brandoch Daha like runaway thralls on the Moruna, I sent him a letter by the hand of Viglus that bare him from our Lord the King the king's name in Impland. Therein I expressed how that the crown of Demonland should be a braver crown for us than this of Impland, howsoe'er it sparkle, praying him urge upon the King his sending of an armament to Demonland, and my lord the leader thereof; or, if he could not as then come home to ask it, then I entreated him make me his ambassador to lay this counsel before the King and crave the enterprise for Corund."

"Is not his answer in those letters I brought thee?" said Gro.

"Ay," said she, "and a very scurvy beggarly lickspittle answer for a great lord to send to such a matter as I propounded. Alack, it puffs away all my wifely duty but to speak on't, and makes me rail like a gangrel-woman."[5]

"I'll walk apart, madam," said Gro, "if thou wouldst have privateness to deliver thy mind."

Prezmyra laughed. " 'Tis not all so bad," she said, "and yet it makes me angry. The enterprise he commends, up to the hilt, and I have his leave to broach it to the King, as his mouth-piece, and press it with him out of all ho.[6] But for the leading on't, he will not have it, he. Corsus must have it, or Corinius. Stay, let me read it out," and standing near one of the lights she took a parchment from her bosom. "Pooh! 'tis too fond; I will not shame my lord to read it, even to thee."

"Well," said Gro, "were I the King, Corund should be my general to put down Demonland. Corsus he may send, for he hath done great work in his day, but in mine own judgement I like him not for such an errand. Corinius he hath not yet forgiven for his fault at the banquet a year ago."

"Corinius!" said Prezmyra. "So his butchery of mine own dear land goeth not only without reward, but hath not so much as bought him back to favour, thou thinkest?"

"I think not," said Lord Gro. "Besides, he is mad wroth to have plucked that prickly fruit but for another's eating. He bare himself so presumptuous-ill in the hall to-night, gleeking and galling[7] at Laxus, slapping of his sword, and with so many more shameless braves and wanton fashions, and worst of all his most openly seeking to toy with Sriva, i' this first month of her betrothal unto Laxus, it will be a wonder if blood be not spilt betwixt them ere the night be done. Methinks he is not i' the mood to take the field again without some sure reward; and methinks the King, guessing his mind, would not offer him a new enterprise and so give him the glory of refusing it."

They stood near the arched gateway that opened on the terrace from the inner court. Music still sounded from the great banquet hall of Gorice XI. Under the archway and in the shadows of the huge buttresses of the walls it was as though the elements of gloom, expelled from the bright circles round the flamboys, huddled with sister glooms to make a double darkness.

"Well, my lord," said Prezmyra, "doth thy wisdom bless my resolve?"

"Whate'er it be, yes, because it is thine, O Queen."

"Whate'er it be!" she cried. "Dost hang in doubt on't? What else, but seek audience with the King as my first care in the morning. Have I not my lord's bidding so far?"

"And if thy zeal outrun his bidding in one particular?" said Gro.

"Why, just!" said she. "And if I bring thee not word ere to-morrow's noon that order is given for Demonland, and my Lord Corund named his general for that sailing, ay, and letters sealed for his straight recall from Orpish——"

"Hist!" said Gro. "Steps i' the court."

They turned towards the archway, Prezmyra singing under her breath:

> Nor he that still his Mistresse payes,
> For she is thrall'd therefore;
> Nor he that payes not, for he sayes
> Within, shee's worth no more.
> Is there then no kinde of men
> Whom I may freely prove?
> I will vent that humour then
> In mine own selfe love.

Corinius met them in the gateway, coming from the banquet house. He halted full in their path to peer closely through the darkness at Prezmyra, so that she felt the heat of his breath, heavy with wine. It was too dark to know faces but he knew her by her stature and bearing.

"Cry thee mercy, madam," he said. "Methought an instant 'twas—but no matter. Your best of rest."

So saying he made way for her with a deep obeisance, jostling roughly against Gro with the same motion. Gro, little minded for a quarrel, gave him the wall, and followed Prezmyra into the inner court.

The Lord Corinius sat him down on the nearest of the benches, leaned his stalwart back luxuriously upon the cushions and there rested, thripping his fingers and singing to himself:

> What an Ass is he
>   Waits a woman's leisure
>   For a minute's pleasure,
> And perhaps may be
>   Gull'd at last, and lose her;
> What an ass is he?
>
> What need I to care
>   For a woman's favour?
>   If another have her,
> Why should I despair?
>   When for gold and labour
> I can have my share.

> If I chance to see
> > One that's brown, I love her,
> > Till I see another
> Browner is than she;
> > For I am a lover
> Of my liberty.

A rustle behind him on his left made him turn his head. A figure stole out of the deep shadow of the buttress nearest the archway. He leapt up and was first in the gate, blocking it with open arms. "Ah," he cried, "so titmice roost i' the shade, ha? What ransom shall I have of thee for making me keep empty tryst last night? Ay, and wast creeping hence to make me a fool once more the night-long and I had not caught thee."

The lady laughed. "Last night my father kept me by him; and to-night, my lord, wouldst thou not have been fitly served for thy shameless ditty? Is that a sweet serenade for ladies' ears? Sing it again, to thy liberty, and show thyself an ass."

"Thou art very bold to provoke me, madam, with not even a star to be thy witness if I quite thee for't. These flamboys are old roisterers,[8] grown gray in scenes of riot. They shall not blab."

"Nay, if thou speakest in wine I'm gone, my lord;" and as he took a step towards her, "and I return not, here or otherwise, but fling thee off for ever," she said. "I will not be entreated like a serving-maid. I have borne too long with thy forced soldier fashions."

Corinius caught his arms about her, lifting her against his broad chest so that her toes scarce kept footing on the ground. "O Sriva," he said thickly, bending his face to hers, "dost think to light so great a fire, and after walk through it and not be scorched thereat?"

Her arms were close pinioned at her sides in that strong embrace. She seemed to swoon, as a lily swooning in the flaming noon-day. Corinius bent down his face and kissed her fiercely, saying, "By all the sweets that ever darkness tasted, thou art mine to-night."

"To-morrow," she said, as if stifled.

But Corinius said, "My dearest happiness, to-night."

"My dear lord," said the Lady Sriva softly, "sith thou hast made such a conquest of my love, be not a harsh and forward conqueror. I swear to thee by all the dreadful powers that clip the earth about, there's matter in it I should to my father this night, nay more, now on the instant. 'Twas this only made me avoid thee but now: this, and no light conceit to vex thee."

"He can attend our pleasure," said Corinius. " 'Tis an old man, and oft sitteth late at his book."

"How? and thou leftest him carousing?" said she. "There's that I must impart to him ere the wine quite o'erflow his wits. Even this delay, how sweet soe'er to us, is dangerous."

But Corinius said, "I will not let thee go."

"Well," said she, "be a beast, then. But know I'll cry on a rescue shall make all Carcë run to find us, and my brothers, ay, and Laxus, if he be a man, shall deal thee bitter payment for thy violence toward me. But if thou wilt be thy noble self, and respect my love with friendship, let me go. And if thou come secretly to my chamber door, an hour past midnight; I think thou'lt find no bolt to it."

"Ha, thou swearest it?" he said.

She answered, "Else may steep destruction swallow me quick."

"An hour past midnight. And until then 'tis a year in my desires," said he.

"There spoke my noble lover," said Sriva, giving him her mouth once more. And swiftly she fared through the shadowy archway and across the court to where in the north gallery her father Corsus had his chamber.

The Lord Corinius went back to his seat, and there reclined for a space in slothful ease, humming to an old tune:

> My Mistris is a shittle-cock,[9]
>   Compos'd of Cork and feather;
> Each Battledore[10] sets on her dock,[11]
>   And bumps her on the leather.
>   But cast her off which way you Will,
>   She will requoile to another still—
>   Fa, la, la, la, la, la.

He stretched his arms and yawned. "Well, Laxus, my chub-faced meacock,[12] this medicine hath eased powerfully my discontent. 'Tis but fair, sith I must miss my crown, that I should have thy mistress. And to say true, seeing how base, little, and ordinary a kingdom is this of Pixyland, and what a delectable sweet wagtail this Sriva, whom besides I have these two years past ne'er looked on but my mouth watered: why, I may hold me part paid for the nonce;[13] until I weary of her.

> Love is all my life,
>> For it keeps me doing:
>> Yet my love and wooing
> Is not for a Wife—

"An hour past midnight, ha? What wine's best for lovers? I'll go drink a stoup, and so to dice with some of these lads to pass away the time till then."

XVI

THE LADY SRIVA'S
EMBASSAGE

*How the Duke Corsus thought it proper to
commit an errand of state unto his daughter: and
how she prospered therein.*

 RIVA fared swiftly to her father's closet, and finding her lady mother sewing in her chair, nodding towards sleep, two candles at her left and right, she said, "My lady mother, there's a queen's crown waits the pluck-ing. 'Twill drop into the foreign woman's lap if thou and my father bestir you not. Where is he? Still i' the banquet house? Thou or I must fetch him on the instant."

"Fie!" cried Zenambria. "How thou'st startled me! Fall some-what into a slower speech, my girl. With such wild sudden talk I know not what thou meanest nor what's the matter."

But Sriva answered, "Matter of state. Thou goest not? Good, then I fetch him. Thou shalt hear all anon, mother;" and so turned towards the door. Nor might all her mother's crying out upon the scandal of their so returning to the banquet long past the hour of the women's withdrawal turn her from this. So that the Lady Zenambria, seeing her so wilful, thought it less evil to go herself; and so went, and in awhile returned with Corsus.

Corsus sat in his great chair over against his lady wife, while his daughter told her tale.

"Twice and thrice," said she, "they passed me by, as near as I

198

stand to thee, O my father, she leaning most familiarly on the arm of her curled philosopher. 'Twas plain they had never a thought that any was by to overhear them. She said so and so;" and therewith Sriva told all that was spoke by the Lady Prezmyra as to an expedition to Demonland, and as to her purposed speaking with the King, and as to her design that Corund should be his general for that sailing, and letters sealed on the morrow for his straight recall from Orpish.

The Duke listened unmoved, breathing heavily, leaning heavily forward, his elbow on his knees, one great fat hand twisting and pushing back the sparse gray growth of his moustachios. His eyes shifted with sullen glance about the chamber, and his blabber cheeks, scarlet from the feast, flushed to a deeper hue.

Zenambria said, "Alas, and did not I tell thee long ago, my lord, that Corund did ill to wed with a young wife? And thence cometh now that shame that was but to be looked for. It is pity indeed of so goodly a man, now past his prime age, she should so play at fast and loose with his honour, and he at the far end of the world. Indeed and indeed, I hope he will revenge it on her at his coming home. For sure I am, Corund is too high-minded to buy advancement at so shameful a price."

"Thy talk, wife," said Corsus, "showeth long hair and a short wit. In brief, thou art a fool."

He was silent for a space, then raised his gaze to Sriva, where she rested, her back to the massive table, half standing, half sitting, a dainty jewel-besparkled hand planted on the table's edge at her either side, her arms like delicate white pillars supporting that fair frame. Somewhat his dull eye brightened, resting on her. "Come hither," he said, "on my knee: so."

When she was seated, " 'Tis a brave gown," said he, "thou wearest to-night, my pretty pug. Red, for a sanguine humour." His great arm gave her a back, and his hand, huge as a platter, lay like a buckler beneath her breast. "Thou smell'st passing sweet."

" 'Tis malabathrum in the leaf," answered she.

"I'm glad it likes thee, my lord," said Zenambria. "My woman still protesteth that such, being boiled with wine, yieldeth a perfume that passeth all other."

Corsus still looked on Sriva. After a while he asked, "What madest thou on the terrace i' the dark, ha?"

She looked down, saying, "It was Laxus prayed me meet him there."

"Hum!" said Corsus. " 'Tis strange then he should await thee this hour gone by in the paved alley of the privy court."

"He did mistake me," said Sriva. "And well is he served, for such neglect."

"So. And thou turnest politician to-night, my little puss-cat?" said Corsus. "And thou smellest an expedition to Demonland? 'Tis like enow. But methinks the King will send Corinius."

"Corinius?" said Sriva. "It is not thought so. 'Tis Corund must have it, if thou push not the matter to a decision with the King to-night, O my father, ere my lady fox be private with him to-morrow."

"Bah!" said Corsus. "Thou art but a girl, and knowest nought. She hath not the full blood nor the resolution to carry it thus. No, 'tis not Corund stands i' the light, it is Corinius. It is therefore the King withheld from him Pixyland, which was his due, and tossed the bauble to Laxus."

"Why, 'tis a monstrous thing," said Zenambria, "if Corinius shall have Demonland, which surely much surpasseth this crown of Pixyland. Shall this novice have all the meat, and thou, because thou art old, have nought but the bones and the parings?"

"Hold thy tongue, mistress," said Corsus, looking upon her as one looketh on a sour mixture. "Why hadst not the wit to angle for him for thy daughter?"

"Truly, husband, I'm sorry for it," said Zenambria.

The Lady Sriva laughed, placing her arm about her father's bullock-neck and playing with his whiskers. "Content thee," she said, "my lady mother. I have my choice, and that is very certain, of these and of all other in Carcë. And now I bethink me on the Lord Corinius, why, there's a proper man indeed: weareth a shaven lip too, which, as experienced opinion shall tell thee, far exceedeth your nasty moustachios."

"Well," said Corsus, kissing her, "howe'er it shape, I'll to the King to-night to move my matter with him. Meanwhile, madam," he said to Zenambria, "I'll have thee take thy chamber straight. Bolt well the door, and for more safety I will lock it myself o' the outer side. There's much mirth toward to-night, and I'd not have these staggering drunken swads offend thee, as full well might befall, whiles I am on mine errand of state."

Zenambria bade him good-night, and would have taken her daughter with her, but Corsus said nay to this, saying, "I'll see her safe bestowed."

When they were alone, and the Lady Zenambria locked away in her chamber, Corsus took forth from an oaken cupboard a great silver flagon and two chased goblets. These he brimmed with a sparkling yellow wine from the flagon and made Sriva drink with him not once only but twice, emptying each time her goblet. Then he drew up his chair and sinking heavily into it folded his arms upon the table and buried his head upon them.

Sriva paced back and forth, impatient at her father's strange posture and silence. Surely the wine lighted riot in her veins; surely in that silent room came back to her Corinius's kisses hot upon her mouth, the strength of his arms like bands of bronze holding her embraced. Midnight tolled. Her bones seemed to melt within her as she bethought of her promise, due in an hour.

"Father," said she at last, "midnight hath stricken. Wilt thou not go ere it be too late?"

The Duke raised his face and looked at her. He answered "No." "No," he said again, "where's the profit? I wax old, my daughter, and must wither. The world is to the young. To Corinius; to Laxus; to thee. But most of all to Corund, who if a be old yet hath his mess of sons, and mightiest of all his wife, to be his ladder to climb thrones withal."

"But thou saidst but now—" said Sriva.

"Ay, when thy mammy was by. She cometh to her second childhood before her time, so as to a child I speak to her. Corund did ill to wed with a young wife, ha? Phrut! Is not this the very bulwark and rampire of his fortune? Didst ever see a fellow so spurted up in a moment? My secretary when I managed the old wars against the Ghouls, and now climbed clean over me, that am yet nine year his elder. Called king, forsooth, and like to be ta'en soon (under the King) for Dominus fac totum throughout all the land if a play this woman as a should. Will not the King, for such payment as she intends, give Demonland upon Impland and all the world beside? Hell's dignity, that would I, and 'twere offered me."

He stood up, reaching unsteadily for the wine jug. Furtively he watched his daughter, shifting his gaze ever as her eye met his.

"Corund," said he, pouring out some wine, "would split his sides for laughter to hear thy mother's prim-mouthed brabble: he that hath enjoined upon his wife, there's ne'er a doubt on't, this very errand, and if he visit it on her at his coming home 'twill but be with hotter love and gratitude for that she wins him in our despite. Trust me, 'tis not every lady of quality shall find favour with a King."

The casement stood open, and while they stood without speech sounds of a lute trembled upward from the court below, and a man's voice, soft and deep, singing this song:

Hornes to the bull,
   Hooves to the steede,
To little hayres
   Light feete for speed,
And unto lions she giveth tethe
   A-gaping dangerouslye.

Fishes to swim,
   And birds to flye,
And men to judge
   And reeson why,
She teacheth. Yet for womankind
   None of these thinges hath she.

For women beautie
   She hath made
Their onely shielde
   Their onely blade.
O'er sword and fire they triumph stille,
   Soe they but beautious be.

The Lady Sriva knew it was Laxus singing to her chamber
window. Her blood beat wildly, the spirit of enterprise winging her
imagination not toward him, nor yet Corinius, but into paths
strangely and perilously inviting, undreamed of until now. The
Duke her father came towards her, thrusting the chairs from his
way, and saying, "Corund and his mess of sons! Corund and his
young Queen! If he conjure with the white rose, why not thou and I
with the red? It hath as fair a look, the devil damn me else, and
savoureth as excellent sweet perfume."

She stared at him big-eyed, with blushing cheeks. He took her
hands in his.

"Shall this outland woman," he said, "and her sallow-cheeked
gallant still ruffle it over us? Long beards, whether they be white or
black, are too huge a blemish in our eye, methinks. The thing
seemeth not supportable, that this precise madam with her foreign
fashions—Dost fear to stand i' the field against her?"

Sriva put her forehead on his shoulder and said, scarce to be
heard, "And it come to that, I'll show thee."

"It must be now," said Corsus. "Prezmyra, thou hast told me,
seeketh audience betimes i' the morning. Women are best at night-
time, too."

"If Laxus should hear thee!" she said.

He answered, "Tush, he need never blame thee, even if he

knew on't, and we can manage that. Thy silly mother prated but now of honour. 'Tis but a school-name; and if 'twere other, tell me whence springeth the fount of honour if not from the King of Kings? If he receive thee, then art thou honoured, and all they that have to do with thee. I am yet to learn dishonour lieth on that man or woman whom the King doth honour."

She laughed, turning from him toward the window, her hands still held in his. "Foh, thou hast given me a strong potion! and I think that swayeth me more than thy many arguments, O my father, which to say truth I cannot well remember because I did not much believe."

Duke Corsus took her by the shoulders. His face overlooked her by a little, for she was not tall of build. "By the Gods," he said, " 'tis a stronger sweet scent of the red rose to make a great man drunk withal than of the white, though that be a bigger flower." And he said, "Why not, for a game, for a madcap jest? A mantle and hood, a mask if thou wilt, and my ring to prove thee mine ambassador. I'll attend thee through the court-yard to the foot o' the stairs."

She said nothing, smiling at him as she turned for him to put the great velvet mantle about her shoulders.

"Ha," said he, " 'tis well seen a daughter is worth ten sons."

In the meanwhile Gorice the King sate in his private chamber writing at a parchment spread before him on the table of polished marmolite.[1] A silver lamp burned at his left elbow. The window stood open to the night. The King had laid aside his crown, that sparkled darkly in the shadow below the lamp. He put down his pen and read again what he had writ, in manner following:

Fram Me, Gorice the Twelft, Greate Kyng of Wychlande and of Ympelande and of Daemonlande and of al kyngdomes the sonne dothe spread hys bemes over, unto Corsus My servaunte: Thys is to signifye to the that thoue shalt with all convenient spede repaire with a suffycyaunt strengthe of menne and schyppes to Daemonlande, bycause that untowarde and traytorly cattell that doe there inhabyt are to fele by the the sharpnes of My correctioun. I wyll the, as holdynge the place of My generalle ther, that thow enter forcybly ynto the sayd cuntrie and doe with al dilygence spoyl ravysche and depopulate that lande, enslavying oppressyng and puttyng to the dethe as thow shalt thynke moost servychable al them that shal fall ynto thy powre, and in pertyculer pullyng downe and ruinating all thayr stronge houlds or castels, as Galinge, Dreppabie, Crothryng, Owleswyke, and othere. Thys enterpryse in head is one of the gretest that ever was since yt is to trampe downe Daemonlande and once and for al to cutt thayr coames whose crestes may daunger us, and thow art toe onderstande that withowt extraordinair experiens of thy former merrits I wolde not commyt to the so greate a chairge, and especially in such a tyme. And since al gret enterpryses oughte to bee sodeynly and resolutely prose-quuted, therefore thys oughte to bee done and executed at fur-thest in harveste nexte. Therefore yt is My commaundemente that thow Corsus take order for the instant furnesshynge of shippes, seamen, souldiers, horsemen, officiers, and pertyculer personnes, wepons, municions, and al other necessaries whych is thought to be needfull for the armie and hoast whych shalbe levied for the sayd entrepryse, for whyche this letter shalbe thy suffycyaunt war-rant under My hande. Given under My signeth of Ouroboros in My pallaice of Carcie thys xxix daie of may, beynge the vij daie of My yeare II.

The King took wax and a taper from the great gold inkstand, and sealed the warrant with the ruby head of the worm Ouroboros, saying, "The ruby, most comfortable to the heart, brain, vigour, and memory of man. So, 'tis confirmed."

In that instant when the wax was yet soft of the King's seal sealing that commission for Corsus, one tapped gently at the chamber door. The King bade enter, and there came the captain of his bodyguard and stood before the King, with word that one waited without, praying instant audience, "And showed me for a token, O my Lord the King, a bull's head with fiery nostrils graven in a black opal in the bezel of a ring, which I knew for the signet of my Lord Corsus that his lordship beareth alway on his left thumb. And 'twas this, O King, that only persuaded me to deliver the message unto your Majesty in this unseasonable hour. Which if it be a fault in me, I do humbly hope your Majesty will pardon."

"Knowest thou the man?" said the King.

He answered, "I might not know him, dread Lord, for the mask and great hooded cloak he weareth. It is a little man, and speaketh a husky whisper."

"Admit him," said King Gorice; and when Sriva was come in, masked and hooded and holding forth the ring, he said, "Thou lookest questionable, albeit this token opened a way for thee. Put off these trappings and let me know thee."

But she, speaking still in a husky whisper, prayed that they might be private ere she disclosed herself. So the King bade leave them private.

"Dread Lord," said the soldier, "is it your will that I stand ready without the door?"

"No," said the King. "Void the ante-chamber, set the guard, and let none disturb me." And to Sriva he said, "If thine errand prove not more honester than thy looks, this is an ill night's journey for thee. At the lifting of my finger I am able to metamorphose thee to a mandrake. If indeed thou beest aught else already."

When they were alone the Lady Sriva doffed her mask and put back her hood, uncovering her head that was crowned with two heavy trammels of her dark brown hair bound up and interwoven above her brow and ears and pinned with silver pins headed with garnets coloured like burning coals. The King beheld her from under the great shadow of his brows, darkly, not by so much as the moving of an eyelid or a lineament of his lean visage betraying aught that passed in his mind at this disclosing.

She trembled and said, "O my Lord the King, I hope you will indulge and pardon in me this trespass. Truly I marvel at mine own boldness how I durst come to you."

With a gesture of his hand the King bade her be seated in a chair on his right beside the table. "Thou needest not be afraid, madam," he said. "That I admit thee, let it make thee assured of welcome. Let me know thine errand."

The fire of her father's wine shuddered down within her like a low-lit flame in a gust of wind as she sat there alone with King Gorice XII. in the circle of the lamplight. She took a deep breath to still her heart's fluttering and said, "O King, I was much afeared to come, and it was to ask you a boon: a little thing for you to give, Lord, and yet to me that am the least of your handmaids a great thing to receive. But now I am come indeed, I durst not ask it."

The glitter of his eyes looking out from their eaves of darkness dismayed her; and little comfort had she of the iron crown at his elbow, bright with gems and fierce with uplifted claws, or of the copper serpents interlaced that made the arms of his chair, or of the bright image of the lamp reflected in the table top where were red streaks like streaks of blood and black streaks like edges of swords streaking the green shining surface of the stone.

Yet she took heart to say, "Were I a great lord had done your majesty service as my father hath, or these others you did honour to-night, O King, it had been otherwise." He said nothing, and still gathering courage she said, "I too would serve you, O King. And I came to ask you how."

The King smiled. "I am much beholden to thee, madam. Do as thou hast done, and thou shalt please me well. Feast and be merry, and charge not thine head with these midnight questionings, lest too much carefulness make thee grow lean."

"Grow I so, O King? You shall judge." So speaking the Lady Sriva rose up and stood before him in the lamplight. Slowly she opened her arms upwards right and left, putting back her velvet cloak from her shoulders, until the dark cloak hanging in folds from either uplifted hand was like the wings of a bird lifted up for flight. Dazzling fair shone her bare shoulders and bare arms and throat and bosom. One great hyacinth stone, hanging by a gold chain about her neck, rested above the hollow of her breasts. It flashed and slept with her breathing's alternate fall and swell.

"You did threaten me, Lord, but now," she said, "to transmew me to a mandrake. Would you might change me to a man."

She could read nothing in the crag-like darkness of his countenance, the iron lip, the eyes that were like pulsing firelight out of hollow caves.

"I should serve you better so, Lord, than my poor beauty may. Were I a man, I had come to you to-night and said, 'O King, let us not suffer any longer of that hound Juss. Give me a sword, O King, and I will put down Demonland for you and tread them under feet.'"

She sank softly into her chair again, suffering her velvet cloak to fall over its back. The King ran his finger thoughtfully along the upstanding claws of the crown beside him on the table.

"Is this the boon thou askest me?" he said at length. "An expedition to Demonland?"

She answered it was.

"Must they sail to-night?" said the King, still watching her.

She smiled foolishly.

"Only," he said, "I would know what gadfly of urgency stung thee on to come so strangely and suddenly and after midnight."

She paused a minute, then summoning courage: "Lest another should first come to you, O King," she answered. "Believe me, I know of preparations, and one that shall come to you in the morning praying this thing for another. What intelligence soever some hath, I am sure of that to be true that I have."

"Another?" said the King.

Sriva answered, "Lord, I'll say no names. But there be some, O King, be dangerous sweet suppliants, hanging their hopes belike on other strings than we may tune."

She had bent her head above the polished table, looking curiously down into its depths. Her corsage and gown of scarlet silk brocade[2] were like the chalice[3] of a great flower; her white arms and shoulders like the petals of the flower above it. At length she looked up.

"Thou smilest, my Lady Sriva," said the King.

"I smiled at mine own thought," she said. "You'll laugh to hear it, O my Lord the King, being so different from what we spoke on. But sure, of women's thoughts is no more surety nor rest than is in a vane that turneth at all winds."

"Let me hear it," said the King, bending forward, his lean hairy hand flung idly across the table's edge.

"Why thus it was, Lord," said she. "There came me in mind of a sudden that saying of the Lady Prezmyra when first she was wed to Corund and dwelt here in Carcë. She said all the right part of her body was of Witchland but the left Pixy. Whereupon our people that were by rejoiced much that she had given the right part of her body to Witchland. Whereupon she said, but her heart was on the left side."

"And where wearest thou thine?" asked the King. She durst not look at him, and so saw not the comic light go like summer lightning across his dark countenance as she spoke Prezmyra's name.

His hand had dropped from the table edge; Sriva felt it touch her knee. She trembled like a full sail that suddenly for an instant the wind leaves. Very still she sat, saying in a low voice, "There's a word, my Lord the King, if you'd but speak it, should beam a light to show you mine answer."

But he leaned closer, saying, "Dost think I'll chaffer with thee? I'll know the answer first i' the dark."

"Lord," she whispered, "I would not have come to you in this deep and dead time of the night but that I knew you noble and the great King, and no amorous surfeiter that should deal false with me."

Her body breathed spices: soft warm scents to make the senses reel: perfume of malabathrum bruised in wine, essences of sulphur-coloured lilies planted in Aphrodite's garden. The King drew her to him. She cast her arms about his neck, saying close to his ear, "Lord, I may not sleep till you tell me they must sail, and Corsus must be their captain."

The King held her gathered up like a child in his embrace. He kissed her on the mouth, a long deep kiss. Then he sprang to his feet, set her down like a doll before him upon the table by the lamp, and so sat back in his own chair again and sat regarding her with a strange and disturbing smile.

On a sudden his brow darkened, and thrusting his face towards hers, his thick black square-cut beard jutting beneath the curl of his shaven upper lip, "Girl," he said, "who sent thee o' this errand?"

He rolled his eye upon her with such a gorgon look that her blood ran back with a great leap towards her heart, and she answered, scarce to be heard, "Truly, O King, my father sent me."

"Was he drunk when he sent thee?" asked the King.

"Truly, Lord, I think he was," said she.

"That cup that he was drunken withal," said King Gorice, "let him prize and cherish it all his life natural. For if in his sober senses he should make no more estimation of me than think to bribe my favours with a bona roba;⁴ by my soul, in his evil health he had sought to do it, for it should cost him nothing but his life."

Sriva began to weep, saying, "O King, your gentle pardon."

But the King paced the room like a prowling lion. "Did he fear I should supply Corund in his place?" said he. "This was a cock-sure way to make me do it, if indeed his practice had might to move me at all. Let him learn to come to me with his own mouth if he hope to get good of me. Other else, out of Carcë let him go and avoid my sight, that all the great masters of Hell may conduct him thither."

The King paused at length beside Sriva, that was perched still upon the table, showing a kind of sweetness in tears, sobbing very pitifully, her face hidden in her two hands. So for a time he beheld her, then lifted her down, and while he sat in his great chair, holding her on his knee with one hand, with the other drew hers gently from before her face. "Come," he said, "I blame it not on thee. Give over all thy weeping. Reach me that writing from the table."

She turned in his arms and stretched a hand out for the parchment.

"Thou knowest my signet?" said the King.

She nodded, ay.

"Read," said he, letting her go. She stood by the lamp, and read.

The King was behind her. He took her beneath the arms, bending to speak hot-breathed in her ear. "Thou seest, I had already chose my general. Therefore I let thee know it, because I mean not to let thee go till morning; and I would not have thee think thy loveliness, howe'er it please me, moveth such deep-commanding spells as to sway my policy."

She lay back against his breast, limp and strengthless, while he kissed her neck and eyes and throat; then her lips met his in a long voluptuous kiss. Surely the King's hands upon her were like live coals.

Bethinking her of Corinius, fuming at an open door and an empty chamber, the Lady Sriva was yet content.

XVII

THE KING FLIES
HIS HAGGARD

*How the Lady Prezmyra came to the King on
an errand of state, and how she prospered therein:
wherein is also seen why the King would send
the Duke Corsus into Demonland; and how on
the fifteenth day of July these Lords, Corsus,
Laxus, Gro, and Gallandus, sailed with a
fleet from Tenemos.*

N the morn came the Lady Prezmyra to pray audience
of the King, and being admitted to his private chamber stood before him in great beauty and splendour,
saying, "Lord, I came to thank you as occasion served
not for me fitly so to do last night i' the banquet hall.
Sure, 'tis no easy task, since when I thank you as I would, I must
seem too unmindful of Corund's deserving who hath won this
kingdom: but if I speak too large of that, I shall seem to minish[1]
your bounty, O King. And ingratitude is a vice abhorred."

"Madam," said the King, "thou needest not to thank me. And
to mine ears great deeds have their own trumpets."

So now she told him of her letters received from Corund out
of Impland. "It is well seen, Lord," said she, "how in these days
you do beat down all peoples under you, and do set up new
tributary kings to add to your great praise in Carcë. O King, how

long must this ill weed of Demonland offend us, going still untrodden under feet?"

The King answered her not a word. Only his lip showed a gleam of teeth, as of a tiger's troubled at his meal.

But Prezmyra said with great hardiness, "Lord, be not angry with me. Methinks it is the part of a faithful servant honoured by his master to seek new service. And where lieth likelier service Corund should do you than west over seas, to lead presently an army naval thither and make an end of them, ere their greatness stand up again from the blow wherewith last May you did strike them?"

"Madam," said the King, "this charge is mine. I'll tell thee when I need thy counsel, which is not now." And standing up as if to end the matter, he said, "I do intend some sport to-day. They tell me thou hast a falcon gentle towereth[2] so well she passeth the best Corinius hath. 'Tis clear calm weather. Wilt thou take her out to-day and show us the mounty[3] at a heron?"

She answered, "Joyfully, O King. Yet I beseech you add this favour to all your former goodness, to hear me yet one word. Something persuades me you have already determined of this enterprise, and by your putting of me off I do fear your majesty meaneth not Corund shall undertake it but some other."

Dark and immovable as his own dark fortress facing the bright morning, Gorice the King stood and beheld her. Sunshine streaming through the eastern casement lighted red-gold smouldering splendours in the heavy coils of that lady's hair, and flew back in dazzling showers from the diamonds fastened among those coils. After a space he said, "Suppose I am a gardener. I go not to the butterfly for counsel. Let her be glad that there be rose-trees there and red stonecrops for her delight; which if any be lacking I'll give her more for the asking, as I'll give thee more masques and revels and all brave pleasures in Carcë. But war and policy is not for women."

"You have forgot, O King," said the Lady Prezmyra, "Corund made me his ambassador." But seeing a blackness fall upon the King's countenance she said in haste, "But not in all, O King. I will be open as day to you. The expedition he strongly urged, but not for himself the leading on't."

The King looked evilly upon her. "I am glad to hear it," he said. Then, his brow clearing, "Know thou it for thy good, madam, order is ta'en for this already. Ere winter-nights return again, Demonland shall be my footstool. Therefore write to thy lord I gave him his wish beforehand."

Prezmyra's eyes danced triumph. "O the glad day!" she cried. "Mine also, O King?"

"If thine be his," said the King.

"Ah," said she, "you know mine outgallops it."

"Then school thine, madam," said the King, "to run in harness. Why think'st thou I sent Corund into Impland, but that I knew he had excellent wit and noble courage to govern a great kingdom? Wouldst have me a wilful child snatch Impland from him like a sampler half stitched?"

Then, taking leave of her with more gracious courtesy, "We shall look to see thee then, madam, o' the third hour before noon," he said, and smote on a gong, summoning the captain of his guard. "Soldier," he said, "conduct the Queen of Impland. And bid the Duke Corsus straight attend me."

The third hour before noon the Lord Gro met with Prezmyra in the gate of the inner court. She had a riding-habit of dark green tiffany⁴ and a narrow ruff edged with margery-pearls. She said, "Thou comest with us, my lord? Surely I am beholden to thee. I know thou lovest not the sport, yet to save me from Corinius I must have thee. He plagueth me much this morning with strange courtesies; though why thus on a sudden I cannot tell."

"In this," said Lord Gro, "as in greater matters, I am thy servant, O Queen. 'Tis yet time enough, though. This half hour the King will not be ready. I left him closeted with Corsus, that setteth presently about his arming against the Demons. Thou hast heard?"

"Am I deaf," said Prezmyra, "to a bell clangeth through all Carcë?"

"Alas," said Gro, "that we waked too long last night, and lay too long abed i' the morning!"

Prezmyra answered, "That did not I. And yet I'm angry with myself now that I did not so."

"How? Thou sawest the King before the council?"

She bent her head for yes.

"And he nay-said thee?"

"With infinite patience," said she, "but most irrevocably. My lord must hold by Impland till it be well broke to the saddle. And truly, when I think on't, there's reason in that."

Gro said, "Thou takest it, madam, with that clear brow of nobleness and reason I had looked for in thee."

She laughed. "I have the main of my desire, if Demonland shall be put down. Natheless, it maketh a great wonder the King picketh for this work so rude a bludgeon when so many goodly blades lie ready to his hand. Behold but his armoury."

For, standing in the gateway at the head of the steep descent to the river, they beheld where the lords of Witchland were met beyond the bridge-gate to ride forth to the hawking. And Prezmyra said, "Is it not brave, my Lord Gro, to dwell in Carcë? Is it not passing brave to be in Carcë, that lordeth it over all the earth?"[5]

Now came they down and by the bridge to the Way of Kings to meet with them on the open mead on the left bank of Druima. Prezmyra said to Laxus that rode on a black gelding full of silver hairs, "I see thou hast thy goshawks[6] forth to-day, my lord."

"Ay, madam," said he. "There is not a stronger hawk than these. Withal they are very fierce and crabbed, and I must keep them private lest they slay all other sort."

Sriva, that was by, put forth a hand to stroke them. "Truly," she said, "I love them well, thy goshawks. They be stout and kingly." And she laughed and said, "Truly to-day I look not lower than on a King."

"Thou mayst look on me, then," said Laxus, "albeit I bear not my crown i' the field."

" 'Tis therefore I'll mark thee not," said she.

Laxus said to Prezmyra, "Wilt thou not praise my hawks, O Queen?"

"I praise them," answered she, "circumspectly. For methinks they fit thy temper better than mine. These be good hawks, my lord, for flying at the bush. I am for the high mountee."

Her step-son Heming, black-browed and sullen-eyed, laughed in his throat, knowing she mocked and thought on Demonland.

Meanwhile Corinius, mounted on a great white liard like silver with black ear-tips, mane, and tail, and all four feet black as coal, drew up to the Lady Sriva and spoke with her apart, saying secretly so that none but she might hear, "Next time thou shalt not carry it so, but I will have thee when and where I would. Thou mayst gull the Devil with thy perfidiousness, but not me a second time, thou lying cozening vixen."

She answered softly, "Beastly man, I did perform the very article of mine oath, and left thee an open door last night. If thou didst look to find me within, that were beyond aught I promised. And know for that I'll seek a greater than thou, and a nicer to my liking: one less ready to swap each kitchen slut on the lips. I know thy practice, my lord, and thy conditions."

His face flamed red. "Were that my custom, I'd now amend it.

Thou art so true a runt of their same litter, they shall all be loathly to me as thou art loathly."

"Mew!" said she, "wittily spoke, i' faith; and right in the manner of a common horse-boy. Which indeed thou art."

Corinius struck spurs into his horse so that it bounded aloft; then cried out and said to Prezmyra, "Incomparable lady, I shall show thee my new horse, what rounds, what bounds, what stop he makes i' the full course of the gallop galliard."[7] And therewith, trotting up to her, made his horse fetch a close turn in a flying manner upon one foot, and so away, rising to a racking pace, an amble, and thence after some double turns returning at the gallop and coming to a full stop by Prezmyra.

" 'Tis very pretty, my lord," said she. "Yet I would not be thy horse."

"So, madam?" he cried. "Thy reason?"

"Why," said she, "were I the most temperate, strongest, and of the gentlest nature i' the world, of the heat of the ginger, most swift to all high curvets and caprioles,[8] I'd fear my crest should fall i' the end, tired with thy spur-galling."

Whereat the Lady Sriva fell a-laughing.

Now came Gorice the King among them with his austringers[9] and falconers and his huntsmen with setters and spaniels and great fierce boar-hounds drawn in a string. He rode upon a black mare with eyes fire-red, so tall a tall man's head scarce topped her withers. He wore a leather gauntlet on his right hand, on the wrist whereof an eagle sat, hooded and motionless, gripping with her claws. He said, "It is met. Corsus goeth not with us: I fly him at higher game. His sons attend him, losing not an hour in preparation for this journey. The rest, take pleasure in the chase."

So they praised the King, and rode forth with him eastaway. The Lady Sriva whispered Corinius in the ear, "Enchantery, my lord, ruleth in Carcë, and this it must be bringeth it about that none may see nor touch me 'twixt midnight hour and cock-crow save he that must be King in Demonland."

But Corinius made as not to hear her, turning toward the Lady Prezmyra, that turned thence toward Gro. Sriva laughed. Merry of heart she seemed that day, eager as the small merlin[10] sitting on her fist, and willing at every turn to have speech with King Gorice. But the King heeded her not at all, and gave her not a look nor a word.

So rode they awhile, jesting and discoursing, toward the Pixyland border, rousing herons by the way whereat none made better sport than Prezmyra's falcons, flown from her fist at many hundred paces as the quarry rose, and mounting with it to the clouds in corkscrew flights, ring upon ring, up and up till the fowl was but a speck in the upper sky, and her falcons two lesser specks beside it.

But when they were come to the higher ground and the scrub and underwood, then the King whistled his eagle off his fist. She flew from him as if she would never have turned head again, yet presently upon his shout came in; then soaring aloft waited on above his head, till the hounds started a wolf out of the brake. Thereon she swooped sudden as a thunderbolt; and the King lighted down and helped her with his hunting-knife; and so again, thrice and four times till four wolves were slain. And that was the greatest sport.

The King made much of his eagle, giving her the last wolf's lights and liver to gorge herself withal. And he gave her over to his falconer, and said, "Ride we now into the flats of Armany, for I will fly my haggard: my haggard eagle[11] caught this March in the hills of Largos. Many a good night's rest hath she cost me, to wake her and man her and teach her to know my call and be obedient. I will fly her now at the big black boar of Largos that afflicteth the farmers hereabout these two years past and bringeth them death and loss. So shall we see good sport, if she be not too coy and wild."

So the King's falconer brought the haggard and the King took her on his fist. A black eagle she was, red-beaked and glorious to look on. Her jesses were of red leather with little silver varvels whereon the crab of Witchland was engraved in small. Her hood[12] was of red leather tasselled with silver. First she bated from the fist of the King, screaming and flapping her wings, but soon was quiet. And the King rode forth, sending his great brindled hounds before him to put up the boar; and all his company followed after.

In no long time they roused the boar, that turned red-eyed and moody-mad on the King's hounds, and charged among them ripping up the foremost so that her bowels gushed out. The King unhooded his eagle and flew her off his fist. But she, wild and ungentle, fastened not upon the boar but on a hound that held him by the ear. She fixed her cruel claws in the hound's neck and picked his eyes out ere a man might speak two curses on her.

Gro, that was by the King, muttered, "O, I like not that. 'Tis ominous."

By then was the King ridden up, and thrust the boar through with his spear, piercing him above and a little behind the shoulder so that the blade went through the heart of him and he sank down dying in his blood. Then the King smote his eagle in his wrath with the butt of his spear-shaft, but smote her lightly and with a glancing blow, and away she flew and was lost to sight. And the King was angry, for all that the boar was slain, for the loss of his hound and his haggard, and for her ill behaviour. So he bade his huntsmen skin the boar and bring home his skin to be a trophy, and so turned homeward.

After a while the King called to him the Lord Gro to ride forward a little with him and out of earshot of the rest. The King said to him, "Thou hast a discontented look. Is it that I send not Corund into Demonland to crown the work he began at Eshgrar Ogo? Thou babblest besides of omens."

Gro answered, "My Lord the King, pardon my fears. For omens, indeed 'tis oft as the saw sayeth, 'As the fool thinketh, so the bell blinketh.' I spake in haste. Who shall weep Fate from her determined purpose? But since you did name Corund's name——"

"I named him," said the King, "because I am still ringing in the ears with women's talk. Whereto also I doubt not thou art privy."

"Only so much," answered he, "that this is my thought: he were our best, O King."

"Haply so," said the King. "But wouldst have me therefore hold my stroke in the air while occasion knocketh at the gate? I'll tell thee, I am potent in art magical, but scarce may I stay time's wing the while I fetch Corund out of Impland and pack him west-away."

Gro held his peace. "Well," said the King, "I will hear more from thee."

"Lord," he answered, "I like not Corsus."

The King gave him a frump[13] to his face. Gro held his peace again awhile, but seeing the King would have more, he said, "Since it likes your majesty to demand my counsel, I will speak. You know, Lord, of all your men in Carcë Corinius is least my friend, and if I back him you will be little apt to think me moved by interest. In my clear judgement, if Corund be barred from this journey (as reason is, I freely embrace it, he must bide in Impland, both to harvest there his victories and to deny the road to Juss and Brandoch Daha if haply they return from the Moruna, and besides, time, as you most justly say, O King, calleth for speedy action): if he be barred, you have no better than Corinius. A complete soldier, a tried captain, young, fierce, and resolute, and one that sitteth not down again when once he standeth up till that his will be accomplished. Send him to Demonland."

"No," said the King. "I will not send Corinius. Hast thou not seen hawks that be in their prime and full pride for beauty and goodness, but must be tamed ere they be flown at the quarry? Such an one is he, and I will tame him with harshness and duress till I be certain of him. Also I have sworn and told him, last year when in his drunkenness he betrayed my counsel and o'erset all our plans, broke me from Pixyland and set my prisoners free, that Corund and Corsus and Laxus should be preferred and advanced before him until by quiet service he shall purchase my good will again."

"Give then the glory to Corsus, but to Corinius the rude work on't for a tiring. Send him as Corsus's secretary, and your work shall be better performed, O King."

But the King said, "No. Thou art a fool to think he would receive it, that being in disgrace could not humble himself but look bigger than before. And certainly I will not ask him, and so give him the glory to refuse it."

"My Lord the King," said Gro, "when I said unto you, I like not Corsus, you did scoff. Yet 'tis no simple niceness made me say it, but because I do fear he shall prove a false cloth: he will shrink in the wetting and can abide no trial."

"By the blight of Sathanas,"[14] said the King, "what crazy talk is this? Hast forgot the Ghouls twelve years ago? True, thou wast not here. And yet, what skills it? When the fame hath gone back and forth through all the world of their great spill when Witchland stood i' the greatest strait that ever she stood, and more than any other Corsus was to praise for our delivering. And since then, five years later, when he held Harquem against Goldry Bluszco, and made him at last to give over the siege and go home most ingloriously, and else had all the Sibrion coast been the Demons' appanage[15] not ours."

Gro bowed his head, having nought to say. The King was silent awhile, then bared his teeth. "When I would burn mine enemy's house," he said, "I choose me a good brand, full of pitch and rosin, apt to sputter well i' the fire and fry them. Such an one is Corsus, since he fared to Goblinland ten years ago, on that ill faring which, had I been King, I never had agreed to; when Brandoch Daha took him prisoner on Lormeron field and despitefully used him, stripped him stark naked, shaved him all of one side smooth as a tennis ball and painted him yellow and sent him home with mickle shame to Witchland. Hell devour me, but I think his heart is in this enterprise. I think thou'lt see brave doings in Demonland when he comes thither."

Still Gro was silent, and the King said after awhile, "I have given thee reasons enow, I think, why I send Corsus into Demonland. There is yet this other, that by itself weigheth not one doit,[16] yet with the others beareth down the balance if more thou lookest for. Unto mine other servants great tasks have I given, and great rewards: to Corund Impland and a king's crown therefor, to Laxus the like in Pixyland, to thee by anticipation Goblinland, for so I do intend. But this old hunting-dog of mine sitteth yet in's kennel with ne'er a bone to busy his teeth withal. That is not well, and shall no longer be neither, since there's no reason for't."

"Lord," said Gro, "in all argument and wise prevision you have quite o'erset me. Yet my heart misgives me. You would ride to Galing. You have ta'en an horse therefor with never a star in's forehead. Instead, I see there is a cloud in's face; and such prove commonly furious, dogged, full of mischief and misfortune."

They came down now upon the Way of Kings. Westward before them lay the marshes, with the great bulk of Carcë eight or ten miles distant their chiefest landmark, and the towers of Tenemos breaking the level horizon line beyond it. The King, after a long silence, looked down on Gro. His lean rugged countenance was outlined darkly against the sky, terrible and proud. "Thou too," said he, "shalt be in this faring to Demonland. Laxus shall have sway afloat, since that is his element of water. Gallandus shall be secretary to Corsus, and thou shalt be with them in their counsels. But the main command, as I have decreed, lieth in Corsus. I'll not crop his authority, no, not by an hair's breadth. Sith Juss hath called the main, I will go hazard[17] with Corsus. If I throw out with him, Hell rot him for a false die. But 'tis not such a cast shall cast away all my fortune. I have a langret[18] in my purse shall cross-bite for me i' the end and win me all, howsoe'er the Demons cog against me."

So ended that day's sporting. And that day, and the next, and near a month thereafter was the Duke Corsus busied up and down the land preparing his great armament. And on the fifteenth day of July was the fleet busked and boun in Tenemos Roads, and that great army of five thousand men-at-arms, with horses and all instruments of war, marched from their camp without Carcë down to the sea.

First of them went Laxus with his guard of mariners, he wearing the crown of Pixyland and they loudly acclaiming him as king and Gorice of Witchland as his overlord. A gallant man he seemed, ready-looking and hard, well-armed, with open countenance and bright seaman's eyes, and brown, crisp, curly beard and hair. Next came the main foot army heavy-armed with axe and spear and the short Witchland hanger, yeomen and farmers from the low lands about Carcë or from the southern vineyards or the hill country against Pixyland: burly swashing fellows, rough as bears, hardy as wild oxen, agile as an ape; four thousand fighting men chose out by Corsus up and down the land as best for this great conquest. The sons of Corsus, Dekalajus and Gorius, rode abreast before them with twenty pipers piping a battle song. Surely the tramp of that great army on the paven way was like the tramp of Fate moving from the east. Gorice the King, sitting in state on the battlements above the water-gate, sniffed with his nostrils as a lion at the scent of blood. It was early morn, and the wind hung southerly, and the great banners, blue and green and purple and gold, each with an iron crab displayed above it, flaunted in the sun.

Now came four or five companies of horse, four hundred or more in all, with brazen armour and bucklers and glancing spears; and last of all, Corsus himself with his picked legion of five hundred veterans to bring up the rear, fierce soldiers of the coastlands that followed him of old to the eastern main and Goblinland, and had stood beside him in the great days when he smote the Ghouls in Witchland. On Corsus's left and right, a little behind him, rode Gro and Gallandus. Ruddy of countenance was Gallandus, gay of carriage and likely-looking, long of limb, with long brown moustachios and large kind eyes like a dog.

Prezmyra stood beside the King, and with her the ladies Zenambria and Sriva, watching the long column marching toward the sea. Heming the son of Corund leaned on the battlements. Behind him stood Corinius, scornful-lipped, with folded arms, most glorious in holiday attire, a wreath of dwale[19] about his brows, and wearing on his mighty breast the gold badge of the King's captain general in Carcë.

Corsus, as he rode by beneath them, planted on the point of his sword his great helm of bronze plumed with green-dyed estridge-plumes and raised it high above his head in homage to the King. The sparse gray locks of his hair lifted in the breeze, and pride flamed on the heavy face of him like a November sunset. He rode a dark bay, heavily built like a bear, that stepped ponderously as weighed down by his rider's bulk and the great weight of gear and battle-harness. His veterans marching at his heel lifted their helms on spear and sword and bill,[20] singing their old marching song in time to the clank of their mailed feet marching down the Way of Kings:

When Corsus dwelt at Tenemos,
Beside the sea in Tenemos,
   Tirra lirra lay,
The Gowles came downe to Tenemos,
They brent his house in Tenemos,
   Downe derie downe day.

But Corsus carved the Gowls
   The coarsest meat
   They ere did ete,
He made him garters with their bowels.
When hee came home to Tenemos,
Came home agayn to Tenemos,
   With a roundelaye.

The King held aloft his staff-royal, returning Corsus his salute, and all Carcë shouted from the walls.

In such wise rode the Lord Corsus down to the ships with his great army that should bring bale and woe to Demonland.

XVIII

THE MURTHER OF
GALLANDUS BY CORSUS

*Of the uprising of the wars of King Gorice XII.
in Demonland; wherein is seen how in an old
man of war stiffneckedness and tyranny may
overlive good generalship, and how a great king's
displeasure dureth only so long as it agreeth with
his policy.*

OUGHT befell to tell of after the sailing of the fleet
from Tenemos till August was nigh spent. Then came
a ship of Witchland from the west and sailed up the
river to Carcë and moored by the water-gate. Her
skipper went straight aland and up into the royal palace in Carcë and the new banquet hall, whereas was King Gorice
XII. eating and drinking with his folk. And the skipper gave letters
into the hand of the King.

By then was night fallen, and all the bright lights kindled in the
hall. The feast was three parts done, and thralls poured forth unto
the King and unto them that sat at meat with him dark wines that
crown the banquet. And they set before the feasters sweetmeats
wondrous fair: bulls and pigs and gryphons and other, made all of
sugar paste, some wines and spigots in their bellies to taste of,
every one with his silver fork. Mirth and pleasure was that night in
the great hall in Carcë; but now were all fallen silent, looking on
the King's countenance while he read his letters. But none might

221

read the countenance of the King, that was inscrutable as the high blind walls of Carcë brooding on the fen. So in that waiting silence, sitting in his great high seat, he read his letters, which were sent by Corsus, and writ in manner following:

"Renouned Kinge and moste highe Prince and Lorde, Goreiyse Twelft of Wychlonde and of Daemounlonde and of all kingdomes the sonne dothe spread his bemes over, Corsus your servaunte dothe prosterate miself befoare your Greateness, evene befoare the face of the erthe. The Goddes graunte unto you moste nowble Lorde helthe and continewance and saffetie meny yeres. After that I hadde receaved my dispache and leave fram your Majestie wherby you did of your Royall goodnes geave and graunt unto mee to be cheefe commaundere of al the warlyke foarces furneshed and sent by you into Daemonlond, hit may please your Majestie I did with haiste carry mine armie and all wepons municions vittualls and othere provicions accordingly toward those partes of Daemonlonde that lye coasted against the estern seas. Here with xxvij schyppes and the moare partt of my peopell I sayling upp ynto the Frith Mickelfrith did fynde x or xi Daemouns schyppes asayling whereof had Vol the commaundemente withowt the herborough of Lookingehaven, and by and by did mak syncke all schyppes of the sayd Voll withowt excepcioun and did sleay the maist paart of them that were with hym and hys ashipboard.

"Nowe I lette you onderstande O my Lorde the Kyng that or ever wee made the landfalle I severinge my armye ynto ij trowpes had dispatched Gallandus with xiij schyppes north-abowt to lande with xv honderede menne at Eccanois, with commande that hee shoulde thenceawaye fare upp ynto the hylles thorow Celyalonde and soe sease the passe calld the Style because none schoulde cum overe fram the west; for that is a gode fyghtynge stede as a man myghte verry convenably hould ageynst gret nomberes yf he bee nat an asse.

"So havinge ridd me wel of Vol, and by my hoep and secreat intilligence these were thayr entire flete that was nowe al sonken and putt to distruccioun by mee, and trewly hit was a paltry werk and light, so few they were agaynst my foarce agaynst them, I dyd comme alande att the place hyghte Grunda by the northe perte of the frith wher the watere owt of Breakingdal falleth into the se. Here I made make my campe with the rampyres thereof reachynge to the schore of the salt se baithe befoare and behynde of me, and drew in supplies and brent and slawe and sent forth hoarsmen to bryng mee in intelligence. And on the iv daie hadd notise of a gret

powre and strengtht cumming at me from sowth out of Owleswyke
to assaille mee in Grunda. And dyd fyghte agaynst them and dyd
flinge them backe beinge iv or v thowsand souldiers. Who returning nexte daie towarde Owlswyke I dyd followe aftir, and so
toke them facynge me in a plaise cauled Crosbie Owtsykes where
they did make shifte to kepe the phords and passages of Ethrey
river very stronge. Heare was bifaln an horable great murtheringe
battell where Thy Servaunte dyd oppresse and over-throwe with
mitch dexteritee those Daemons, makynge of them so bluddie and
creuell a slawghter as hathe not been sene afore not once nor twice
in mans memorye, and blythely I tel you of Vizze theyr cheefe
capitaine kild and ded of strips taken at Crosby felde.

"Soe have I nowe in the holow of my hand by thys victorie the
conquest and possession of al thys lande of Daemonlande, and doe
nowe purpose to dele with thayr castels villages riches cattell how-
ssys and poepell in my waye on al thys estren seaborde within L
miells compas with rapes and murtheres and burnyngs and all
harsche dyscypline according to your Majesties wille. And do
stande with mine armie befoare Owleswyke, bluddie Spitfyer's
notable great castel and forteres that alone yet liveth in this lande
of your daungerous grivious and malitious arche enymies, and the
same Spitfire being att my cominge fledde into the mowntaynes all
do submytt and become your Majesties vassalls. But I wyll nat
conclud nor determyn of peace no not with man weoman nor chyld
of them but kyll them al, havinge always befoare my minde the
satisfactioun of your Princely Pleasure.

"Lest I be too large I leve here to tel you of many rare and
remarcable occurants and observacions whych never the less I laye
by in my mynde to aquent you with agaynst my coming home or by
further writinge. Laxus bearing a kings name do puffe himself up
alledging he wan the sefight but I shall satisfy your Majestie to the
contrary. Gro followeth the wars in as goode sort as his lean spare
bodey will wel beare. Of Gallandus I nedes must saye he do meddyl
too much in my counsailles, still desyring me do thus and thus but I
will nat. Heretofore in the like unrespective manner he hath now
and then used mee which I have swolewed but will not no more.
Who if hee go about to calumniate me in any thinge I praye you
Lorde let mee know it though I despise baithe him and all such.
And in acknowledgement of Your highe favors unto meward do
kiss your Majesties hand.

"Most humbly and reverently untoe my Lorde the Kynge,
undir my seal.   CORSUS."

＊ ＊ ＊

The King put up the writing in his bosom. "Bring me Corsus's cup," said he.

They did so, and the King said, "Fill it with Thramnian wine. Drop me an emerald in it to spawn luck i' the cup, and drink him fortune and wisdom in victory."

Prezmyra, that had watched the King till now as a mother watches her child in the crisis of a fever, rose up radiant in her seat, crying, "Victory!" And all they fell a-shouting and smiting on the boards till the roof-beams shook with their great shouting, while the King drank first and passed on the cup that all might drink in turn.

But Gorice the King sat dark among them as a cliff of serpentine[1] that frowns above dancing surges of a springtide summer sea.

When the women left the banquet hall the Lady Prezmyra came to the King and said, "Your brow is too dark, Lord, if indeed this news is all good that lights your heart and mind from withinward."

The King answered and said, "Madam, it is very good news. Yet remember that hard it is to lift a full cup without spilling."

Now was summer worn and harvest brought in, and on the twenty-seventh day after these tidings afore-writ came another ship of Witchland out of the west sailing over the teeming deep, and rowed on a full tide up Druima and through the Ergaspian Mere, and so anchored below Carcë an hour before supper time. That was a calm clear sunshine evening, and King Gorice rode home from his hunting at that instant when the ship made fast by the water-gate. And there was the Lord Gro aboard of her; and the face of him as he came up out of the ship and stood to greet the King was the colour of quicklime a-slaking.[2]

The King looked narrowly at him, then greeting him with much outward show of carelessness and pleasure made him go with him to the King's own lodgings. There the King made Gro drink a great stoup of red wine, and said to him, "I am all of a muck sweat from the hunting. Go in with me to my baths and tell me all while I bathe me before supper. Princes of all men be in greatest danger, for that men dare not acquaint them with their own peril. Thou look'st prodigious. Know that shouldst thou proclaim to me all my fleet and army in Demonland brought to sheer destruction, that should not dull my stomach for the feast to-night. Witchland is not so poor I might not pay back such a loss thrice and four times and yet have money in my purse."

So speaking, the King was come with Gro into his great bath

chamber, walled and floored with green serpentine, with dolphins carved in the same stone to belch water into the baths that were lined with white marble and sunken in the floor, both wide and deep, the hot bath on the left and the cold bath, many times greater, on the right as they entered the chamber. The King dismissed all his attendants, and made Gro sit on a bench piled with cushions above the hot bath, and drink more wine. And the King stripped off his jerkin of black cowhide and his hose and his shirt of white Beshtrian wool and went down into the steaming bath. Gro looked with wonder on the mighty limbs of Gorice the King, so lean and yet so strong to behold, as if he were built all of iron; and a great marvel it was how the King, when he had put off his raiment and royal apparel and went down stark naked into the bath, yet seemed to have put off not one whit of his kingliness and the majesty and dread which belonged to him.

So when he had plunged awhile in the swirling waters of the bath, and soaped himself from head to foot and plunged again, the King lay back luxuriously in the water and said to Gro, "Tell me of Corsus and his sons, and of Laxus and Gallandus, and of all my men west over seas, as thou shouldest tell of those whose life or death in our conceit importeth as much as that of a scarab fly.[3] Speak and fear not, keeping nothing back nor glozing over nothing. Only that should make me dreadful to thee if thou shouldst practise to deceive me."

Gro spake and said, "My Lord the King, you have letters, I think, from Corsus that have told you how we came to Demonland, and how we gat a victory over Volle in the sea-fight, and landed at Grunda, and fought two battles against Vizz and overthrew him in the last, and he is dead."

"Didst thou see these letters?" asked the King.

Gro answered, "Ay."

"Is it a true tale they tell me?"

Gro answered, "Mainly true, O King, though somewhat now and then he windeth truth to his turn, swelling overmuch his own achievement. As at Grunda, where he maketh too great the Demons' army, that by a just computation were fewer than us, and the battle was not ours nor theirs, for while our left held them by the sea they stormed our camp on the right. And well I think 'twas to enveagle us into country that should be likelier to his purpose that Vizz fell back toward Owlswick in the night. But as touching the battle of Crossby Outsikes Corsus braggeth not too much. That was greatly fought and greatly devised by him, who also slew Vizz with his own hands in the thick of the battle, and made a great victory over them and scattered all their strength, coming upon them at unawares and taking them upon advantage."

So saying Gro stretched forth his delicate white fingers to the goblet at his side and drank. "And now, O King," said he, leaning forward over his knees and running his fingers through the black perfumed curls above his ears, "I am to tell you the uprising of those discontents that infected all our fortunes and confounded us all. Now came Gallandus with some few men down from Break-ingdale, leaving his main force of fourteen hundred men or so to hold the Stile as was agreed upon aforetime. Now Gallandus had advertisement of Spitfire come out of the west country where he was sojourning when we came into Demonland, disporting himself in the mountains with hunting of the bears that do there inhabit, but now come hot-foot eastward and agathering of men at Galing. And on Gallandus's urgent asking, was held a council of war three days after Crossby Outsikes, wherein Gallandus set forth his coun-sel that we should fare north to Galing and disperse them.

"All thought well of this counsel, save Corsus. But he took it mighty ill, being stubborn set to carry out his predetermined pur-pose, which was to follow up this victory of Crossby Outsikes by so many cruel murthers, rapes, and burnings, up and down the coun-try side in Upper and Lower Tivarandardale and down by Onward-lithe and the southern seaboard, as should show those vermin he was their master whom they did require, and the scourge in your hand, O King, that must scourge them to the bare bone.

"To which Gallandus making answer that the preparations at Galing did argue something to be done and not afar off, and that 'This were a pretty matter, if Owlswick and Drepaby shall be able to enforce us cast our eyes over our shoulders while those before us' (meaning in Galing) 'strike us in the brains'; Corsus answereth most unhandsomely, 'I will not satisfy myself with this intelligence until I find it more soundly seconded.' Nor would he listen, but said that this was his mind, and all we should abide by it or an ill thing should else befall us: that this south-eastern corner of the land being gained with great terror and cruelty the neck of the wars in Demonland should then be broken, and all the others whether in Galing or otherwhere could not choose but die like dogs; that 'twas pure folly, because of the hardness and naughty ways of the country, to set upon Galing; and that he would quickly show Gal-landus he was lord there. So was the council broke up in great discontent. And Gallandus abode before Owlswick, which as thou knowest, O King, is a mighty strong place, seated on an arm of the land that runneth out into the sea beside the harbour, and a paven way goeth thereto that is covered with the sea save at low tide of a spring-tide. And we drew great store of provisions thither against a siege if such should befall us. But Corsus with his main forces went south about the country, murthering and ravishing, on his way to the new house of Goldry Bluszco at Drepaby, giving out that from henceforth should folk speak no more of Drepaby Mire and Drepaby Combust that the Ghouls did burn, but both should shortly be burnt alike as two cinders."

"Ay," said the King, coming out of the bath, "and did he burn it so?"

Gro answered, "He did, O King."

The King lifted his arms above his head and plunged head foremost into the great cold swimming bath. Coming forth anon, he took a towel to dry himself, and holding an end of it in either hand came and stood by Gro, the towel rushing back and forth behind his shoulders, and said, "Proceed, tell me more."

"Lord," said Gro, "so it was that they in Owlswick gave up the place at last unto Gallandus, and Corsus came back from the burning of Drepaby Mire. All the folk in that part of Demonland had he brought to misery in her most sharp condition. But now was he to find by sour experience what that neglect had bred him when he went not north to Galing as Gallandus had counselled him to do.

"For now was word of Spitfire marching out from Galing with an hundred and ten score foot and two hundred and fifty horse. Upon which tidings we placed ourselves in very warlike fashion and moved north to meet them, and on the last morn of August fell in with their army in a place called the Rapes of Brima in the open parts of Lower Tivarandardale. All we were blithe at heart, for we held them at an advantage both in numbers (for we were more than three thousand four hundred fighting men, whereof were four hundred a-horseback), and in the goodness of our fighting stead, being perched on the edge of a little valley looking down on Spitfire and his folk. There we abode for a time, watching what he would do, till Corsus grew weary of this and said, 'We are more than they. I will march north and then east across the head of the valley and so cut them off, that they escape not north again to Galing after the battle when they are worsted by us.'

"Now Gallandus nay-said this strongly, willing him to stand and abide their onset; for being mountaineers they must certainly choose at length, if we kept quiet, to attack us up the slope, and that were mightily to our advantage. But Corsus, that still grew from day to day more hard to deal with, would not hear him, and at last sticked not to accuse him before them all (which was most false) that he did practise to gain the command for himself, and had caused Corsus to be set upon to have him and his sons murthered as they went from his lodging the night before.

"And Corsus gave order for the march across their front as I have told it you, O King; which indeed was the counsel of a madman. For Spitfire, when he saw our column crossing the dale-head on his right, gave order for the charge, took us i' the flank, cut us in two, and in two hours had our army smashed like an egg that is dropped from a watch-tower on pavement of hard granite. Never saw I so evil a destruction wrought on a great army. Hardly and in evil case we won back to Owlswick with but seventeen hundred men, and of them some hundreds wounded sore. And if two hundred fell o' the other side, 'tis a wonder and past expectation, so great was Spitfire's victory upon us at the Rapes of Brima. And now was our woe worsened by fugitives coming from the north, telling how Zigg had fallen upon the small force that was left to hold the Stile and clean o'erwhelmed them. So were we now shut up in Owlswick and close besieged by Spitfire and his army, who but for the devilish folly of Corsus, had ne'er made head against us.

"An ill night was that, O my Lord the King, in Owlswick by the sea. Corsus was drunk, and both his sons, guzzling down goblet upon goblet of the wine from Spitfire's cellars in Owlswick. Till at last he was fallen spewing on the floor betwixt the tables, and Gallandus standing amongst us all, galled to the quick after this shame and ruin of our fortunes, cried out and said, 'Soldiers of Witchland, I am aweary of this Corsus: a rioter, a lecher, a surfeiter, a brawler, a spiller of armies, our own not our enemies', who must bring us all to hell and we take not order to prevent him.' And he said, 'I will go home again to Witchland, and have no more share nor part in this shame.' But all they cried, 'To the devil with Corsus! Be thou our general.' "

Gro was silent a minute. "O King," he said at last, "if so it be that the malice of the Gods and mine unfortune have brought me to that case that I am part guilty of that which came about, blame me not overmuch. Little I thought any word of mine should help Corsus and the going forward of his bad enterprise. When all they called still upon Gallandus, saying, 'Ha, ha, Gallandus! weed out the weeds, lest the best corn fester! Be thou our general,' he took me aside to speak with him; because he said he would take further judgement of me before he would consent in so great a matter. And I, seeing deadly danger in these disorders, and thinking that there only lay our safety if he should have command who was both a soldier and whose mind was bent to high attempts and noble enterprises, did egg him forward to accept it. So that he, albeit unwilling, said yea to them at last. Which all applauded; and Corsus said nought against it, being too sleepy-sodden as we thought with drunkenness to speak or move.

"So for that night we went to bed. But in the morn, O King, was a great clamour betimes in the main court in Owlswick. And I, running forth in my shirt in the misty gray of dawn, beheld Corsus standing forth in a gallery before Gallandus's lodgings that were in an upper chamber. He was naked to the waist, his hairy breast and arms to the armpits clotted and adrip with blood, and in his hands two bloody daggers. He cried in a great voice, 'Treason in the camp, but I have scotched it.[4] He that will have Gallandus to his general, come up and I shall mix his blood with his and make them familiar.' "

By then had the King drawn on his silken hose, and a clean silken shirt, and was about lacing his black doublet trimmed with diamonds. "Thou tellest me," said he, "two faults committed by Corsus. That first he lost me a battle and nigh half his men, and next did murther Gallandus in a spleen against him when he would have amended this."

"Killing Gallandus in his sleep," said Gro, "and sending him from the shade into the house of darkness."

"Well," said the King, "there be two days in every month when whatever is begun will never reach completion. And I think it was on such a day he did execute his purpose upon Gallandus."

"The whole camp," said Lord Gro, "is up in a mutiny against him, being marvellously offended at the murther of so worthy a man in arms. Yet durst they not openly go against him; for his veterans guard his person, and he hath let slice the guts out of some dozen or more that were foremost in murmuring at him, so that the rest are afeared to make open rebellion. I tell you, O King, your army of Demonland is in great danger and peril. Spitfire sitteth down before Owlswick in mickle strength, and there is no expectation that we shall hold out long without supply of men. There is danger too lest Corsus do some desperate act. I see not how, with so mutinous an army as his, he can dare to attempt anything at all. Yet hath he his ears filled with the continual sound of reputation, and the contempt which will be spread to the disgrace of him if he repair not soon his fault on the Rapes of Brima. It is thought that the Demons have no ships, and Laxus commandeth the sea. Yet hard it is to make any going between betwixt the fleet and Owlswick, and there be many goodly harbours and places for building of ships in Demonland. If they can stop our relieving of Corsus, and prevent Laxus with a fleet at spring, may be we shall be driven to a great calamity."

"How camest thou off?" said the King.

"O King," answered Lord Gro, "after this murther in Owls-wick I did daily fear a fig or a knife, so for mine own health and Witchland's devised all the ways I could to come away. And gat at last to the fleet by stealth and there took rede with Laxus, who is most hot upon Corsus for this ill deed of his, whereby all our hopes may end in smoke, and prayed me come to you for him as for myself and for all true hearts of Witchland that do seek your greatness, O King, and not decay, that you might send them succour ere all be shent.[5] For surely in Corsus some wild distraction hath overturned his old condition and spilt the goodness you once did know in him. His luck hath gone from him, and he is now one that would fall on his back and break his nose. I pray you strike, ere Fate strike first and strike us into the hazard."[6]

"Tush!" said the King. "Do not lift me before I fall. 'Tis supper time. Attend me to the banquet."

By now was Gorice the King in full festival attire, with his doublet of black tiffany slashed with black velvet and broidered o'er with diamonds, black velvet hose cross-gartered with silver-spangled bands of silk, and a great black bear-skin mantle and collar of ponderous gold. The Iron crown was on his head. He took down from his chamber wall, as they went by, a sword hafted of blue steel with a pommel of bloodstone[7] carved like a dead man's skull. This he bare naked in his hand, and they came into the banquet hall.

They that were there rose to their feet in silence, gazing expectant on the King where he stood between the pillars of the door with that sharp sword held on high, and the jewelled crab of Witchland ablaze above his brow. But most they marked his eyes. Surely the light in the eyes of the King under his beetle brows was like a light from the under-skies shed upward from the pit of hell.

He said no word, but with a gesture beckoned Corinius. Corinius stood up and came to the King, slowly, as a night-walker, obedient to that dread gaze. His cloak of sky-blue silk was flung back from his shoulders. His chest, broad as a bull's, swelled beneath the shining silver scales of his byrny, that was short-sleeved, leaving his strong arms bare to view with golden rings about the wrists. Proudly he stood before the King, his head firm planted above his mighty throat and neck; his proud luxurious mouth, made for wine-cups and for ladies' lips, firm set above the square shaven chin and jaw; the thick fair curls of his hair bound with black bryony;[8] the insolence that dwelt in his dark blue eyes tamed for the while in face of that green bale-light that rose and fell in the steadfast gaze of the King.

When they had so stood silent while men might count twenty breaths, the King spake saying: "Corinius, receive the name of the kingdom of Demonland which thy Lord and King give thee, and make homage to me thereof."

The breath of amazement went about the hall. Corinius kneeled. The King gave him that sword which he held in his hand, bare for the slaughter, saying, "With this sword, O Corinius, shalt thou wear out this blemish and blot that until now rested upon thee in mine eye. Corsus hath proved haggard.[9] He hath made miss in Demonland. His sottish folly hath shut him up in Owlswick and lost me half his force. His jealousy, too maliciously and bloodily bent against my friends 'stead of mine enemies, hath lost me a good captain. The wonderful disorder and distresses of his army must, if thou amend it not, swing all our fortune at one chop from bliss to bale. If this be rightly handled by thee, one great stroke shall change every deal. Go thou, and prove thy demerits."

The Lord Corinius stood up, holding the sword point-downward in his hand. His face flamed red as an autumn sky when leaden clouds break apart on a sudden westward and the sun looks out between. "My Lord the King," said he, "give me where I may sit down: I will make where I may lie down. Ere another moon shall wax again to the full I will set forth from Tenemos. If I do not shortly remedy for you our fortunes which this bloody fool hath laboured to ruinate, spit in my face, O King, withhold from me the light of your countenance, and put spells upon me shall destroy and blast me for ever."

THREMNIR'S HEUGH

*Of the Lord Spitfire's besieging of the witches in
his own castle of Owlswick; and how he did
battle against Corinius under Thremnir's Heugh,
and the men of Witchland won the day.*

 ORD Spitfire sat in his pavilion before Owlswick in
mickle discontent. A brazier of hot coals made a pleasant warmth within, and lights filled the rich tent with
splendour. From without came the noise of rain steadily falling in the dark autumn night, splashing in the
puddles, pattering on the silken roof. Zigg sat by Spitfire on the
bed, his hawk-like countenance shadowed with an unwonted look
of care. His sword stood between his knees point downward on the
floor. He tipped it gently with either hand now to the left now to
the right, watching with pensive gaze the warm light shift and
gleam in the ball of balas[1] ruby that made the pommel of the
sword.

"Fell it out so accursedly?" said Spitfire. "All ten, thou saidst,
on Rammerick Strands?"

Zigg nodded assent.

"Where was he that he saved them not?" said Spitfire. "O, it
was vilely miscarried!"

Zigg answered, " 'Twas a swift and secret landing in the dark a
mile east of the harbour. Thou must not blame him unheard."

"What more remain to us?" said Spitfire. "Content: I'll hear
him. What ships remain to us, is more to the purpose. Three by

Northsands Eres, below Elmerstead: five on Throwater: two by Lychness: two more at Aurwath: six by my direction on Stropardon Firth: seven here on the beach."

"Besides four at the firth head in Westmark," said Zigg. "And order is ta'en for more in the Isles."

"Twenty and nine," said Spitfire, "and those in the Isles beside. And not one afloat, nor can be ere spring. If Laxus smell them out and take them as lightly as these he burned under Volle's nose on Rammerick Strands, we do but plough the desert building them."

He rose to pace the tent. "Thou must raise me new forces for to break into Owlswick. 'Fore heaven!" he said, "this vexes me to the guts, to sit at mine own gate full two months like a beggar, whiles Corsus and those two cubs his sons drink themselves drunk within, and play at cockshies with my treasures."

"O' the wrong side of the wall," said Zigg, "the masterbuilder may judge the excellence of his own building."

Spitfire stood by the brazier, spreading his strong hands above the glow. After a time he spake more soberly. "It is not these few ships burnt in the north should trouble me; and indeed Laxus hath not five hundred men to man his whole fleet withal. But he holdeth the sea, and ever since his putting out into the deep with thirty sail from Lookinghaven I do expect fresh succours out of Witchland. 'Tis that maketh me champ still on the bit till this hold be won again; for then were we free at least to meet their landing. But 'twere most unfit at this time of the year to carry on a siege in low and watery grounds, the enemy's army being on foot and unengaged. Wherefore, this is my mind, O my friend, that thou go with haste over the Stile and fetch me supply of men. Leave force to ward our ships a-building, wheresoever they be; and a good force in Krothering and thereabout, for I will not be found a false steward of his lady sister's safety. And in thine own house make sure. But these things being provided, shear up the war-arrow[2] and bring me out of the west fifteen or eighteen hundred men-at-arms. For I do think that by me and thee and such a head of men of Demonland as we shall then command Owlswick gates may be brast open and Corsus plucked out of Owlswick like a whilk out of his shell."

Zigg answered him, "I'll be gone at point of day."

Now they rose up and took their weapons and muffled themselves in their great campaigning cloaks and went forth with torch-bearers to walk through the lines, as every night ere he went to rest it was Spitfire's wont to do, visiting his captains and setting the guard. The rain fell gentlier. The night was without a star. The wet sands gleamed with the lights of Owlswick Castle, and from the castle came by fits the sound of feasting heard above the wash and moan of the sullen sleepless sea.

When they had made all sure and were come nigh again to Spitfire's tent and Zigg was upon saying goodnight, there rose up out of the shadow of the tent an ancient man and came betwixt them into the glare of the torches. Shrivelled and wrinkled and bowed he seemed as with extreme age. His hair and his beard hung down in elf-locks adrip with rain. His mouth was toothless, his eyes like a dead fish's eyes. He touched Spitfire's cloak with his skinny hand, saying in a voice like the nightraven's, "Spitfire, beware of Thremnir's Heugh."[3]

Spitfire said, "What have we here? And which way the devil came he into my camp?"

But that aged man still held him by the cloak, saying, "Spitfire, is not this thine house of Owlswick? And is it not the most strong and fair place that ever man saw in this countree?"

"Filth, unhand me," said Spitfire, "else shall I presently thrust thee through with my sword, and send thee to the Tartarus of hell, where I doubt not the devils there too long await thee."

But that aged man said again, "Hot stirring heads are too easily entrapped. Hold fast, Spitfire, to that which is thine, and beware of Thremnir's Heugh."

Now was Lord Spitfire wood angry, and because the old carle[4] still held him by the cloak and would not let him go, plucked forth his sword, thinking to have stricken him about the head with the flat of his sword. But with that stroke went a gust of wind about them, so that the torch-flames were nigh blown out. And that was strange, of a still windless night. And in that gust was the old man vanished away like a cloud passing in the night.

Zigg spake: "The thin habit of spirits is beyond the force of weapons."

"Pish!" said Spitfire. "Was this a spirit? I hold it rather a simulacrum or illusion prepared for us by Witchland's cunning, to darken our counsel and shake our resolution."

On the morrow while yet sunrise was red, Lord Zigg went down to the sea-shore to bathe in the great rock pools that face southward across the little bay of Owlswick. The salt air was fresh after the rain. The wind that had veered to the east blew in cold and pinching gusts. In a rift between slate-blue clouds the low sun flamed blood-red. Far to the south-east where the waters of

Micklefirth open on the main, the low cliffs of Lookinghaven-ness loomed shadowy as a bank of cloud.

Zigg laid down his sword and spear and looked south-east across the firth; and behold, a ship in full sail rounding the ness and steering northward on the larboard tack.[5] And when he had put off his kirtle he looked again, and behold, two more ships a-steering round the ness and sailing hard in the wake of the first. So he donned his kirtle again and took his weapons, and by then were fifteen sail a-steering up the firth in line ahead, dragons of war.

So he fared hastily to Spitfire's tent, and found him yet abed, for sweet sleep yet nursed in her bosom impetuous Spitfire; his head was thrown back on the broidered pillow, displaying his strong shaven throat and chin; his fierce mouth beneath his bristling fair moustachios was relaxed in slumber, and his fierce eyes closed in slumber beneath their yellow bristling eyebrows.

Zigg took him by the foot and waked him and told him all the matter: "Fifteen ships, and every ship (as I might plainly see as they drew nigh) as full of men as there be eggs in a herring's roe. So cometh our expectation to the birth."

"And so," said Spitfire, leaping from the couch, "cometh Laxus again to Demonland, with fresh meat to glut our swords withal."

He caught up his weapons and ran to a little knoll that stood above the beach over against Owlswick Castle. And all the host ran to behold those dragons of war sail up the firth at dawn of day.

"They dowse sail," said Spitfire, "and put in for Scaramsey. 'Tis not for nothing I taught these Witchlanders on the Rapes of Brima. Laxus, since he witnessed that down-throw of their army, now accounteth islands more wholesomer than the mainland, well knowing we have nor sails nor wings to strike across the firth at him. Yet scarcely by skulking in the islands shall he break up the siege of Owlswick."

Zigg said, "I would know where be his fifteen other ships."

"In fifteen ships," said Spitfire, "it is not possible he beareth more than sixteen hundred or seventeen hundred men of war. Against so many I am strong enough to-day, should they adventure a landing, to throw 'em into the sea and still contain Corsus if he make a sally. If more be added, I am the less secure. Therefore occasion calleth but the louder for thy purposed faring to the west."

So the Lord Zigg called him out a dozen men-at-arms and went a-horseback. By then were all the ships rowed ashore under

236 ❖ E. R. Eddison

the southern spit of Scaramsey, where is good anchorage for ships. They were there hidden from view, all save their masts that showed over the spit, so that the Demons might observe nought of their disembarking.

Spitfire rode with Zigg three miles or four, as far as the brow of the descent to the fords of Ethreywater, and there bade him farewell. "Lightning shall be slow to my hasting," said Zigg, "till I be back again. Meantime, I would have thee be not too scornfully unmindful of that old man."

"Chirking of sparrows!" said Spitfire. "I have forgot his brabble." Nevertheless his glance shifted southward beyond Owlswick to the great bluff of tree-hung precipice that stands like a sentinel above the meadows of Lower Tivarandardale, leaving but a narrow way betwixt its lowest crags and the sea. He laughed: "O my friend, I am yet a boy in thine eyes it seemeth, albeit I am well-nigh twenty-nine years old."

"Laugh at me and thou wilt," said Zigg. "Without this word said I could not leave thee."

"Well," said Spitfire, "to lull thy fears, I'll not go a-birdsnesting on Thremnir's Heugh till thou come back again."

Now for a week or more was nought to tell of save that Spitfire's army sat before Owlswick, and they on the island sent ever and again three or four ships to land suddenly about Lookinghaven or at the head of the firth, or southaway beyond Drepaby, as far as the coastlands under Rimon Armon, harrying and burning. And as oft as force was gathered against them, they fared aboard again and sailed back to Scaramsey. In those days came Volle from the west with an hundred men and joined him with Spitfire.

The eighth day of November the weather worsened, and clouds gathered from the west and south, till all the sky was a welter of huge watery leaden clouds, separated one from another by oily streaks of white. The wind grew fitful as the day wore. The sea was dark like dull iron. Rain began to fall in big drops. The mountains showed monstrous and shadowy: some dark inky blue, others in the west like walls and bastions of clotted mist against the hueless mist of heaven behind them. Evening closed with thunder and rain and lightning-torn banks of vapour. All night long the thunder roared in sullen intermission, and all night long new banks of thunder-cloud swung together and parted and swung together again. And the light of the moon was abated, and no light seen save the levin-brand, and the camp-fires before Owlswick, and the light of revelry within. So that the Demons camped before the castle were not ware of those fifteen ships that put out from Scaramsey on that wild sea and landed two or three miles to the southward by the great bluff on Thremnir's Heugh. Nor were they ware at all of them that landed from the ships: fifteen or sixteen hundred men-at-arms with Heming of Witchland and his young brother Cargo for their leaders. And the ships rowed back to Scaramsey through the loud storm and fury of the weather, all save one that foundered in Bothrey Sound.

But on the morn, when the tempest was abated, might all behold the putting forth of fourteen ships of war from Scaramsey, every ship of them laden with men-at-arms. They had passage swiftly over the firth, and came aland two miles south of Owlswick. And the ships stood off again from the land, but the army marshalled for battle on the meads above Mingarn Hope.

Now Lord Spitfire let draw up his men and moved out southward from the lines before Owlswick. When they were come within some half mile's distance of the Witchland army, so that they might see clearly their russet kirtles and their shields and body-armour of bronze, and the dull glint of their sword-blades and the heads of their spears, Volle, that rode by Spitfire, spake and said, "Markest thou him, O Spitfire, that rideth back and forth before their battle, marshalling them? So ever rode Corinius; and well mayst thou know him even afar off by his showiness and jaunting carriage. Yet see a great wonder now: for who ever heard tell of this young hotspur giving back from the fight? And now, or ever we be gotten within spear-shot——"

"By the bright eye of day," cried Spitfire, " 'tis so! Will he baulk me quite of a battle? I'll loose a handful of horse upon them to delay their haste ere they be flown beyond sight and finding."

Therewith he gave command to his horsemen to ride forth upon the enemy. And they rode forth with Astar of Rettray, that was brother-in-law to Lord Zigg, for their leader. But the Witchland horse met them by the shallows of Aron Pow and held them in the shallows while Corinius with his main army won across the river. And when the main body of the Demons were come up and the passage forced, the Witchlanders were gotten clean away across the water-meadows to the pass betwixt the shore and the steeps of Thremnir's Heugh.

Then said Spitfire, "They stay not to form even i' the narrow way 'twixt the sea and the Heugh. And that were their safety, if they had but the heart to turn and stand us." And he shouted with a great shout upon his men to charge the enemy, and suffer not a Witch to overlive that slaughter.

So the footmen caught hold of the stirrup-leathers of the horsemen, and running and riding they poured into the narrow pass; and ever was Spitfire foremost among his men, hewing to left and to right among the press, riding on that whelming battle-tide that seemed to bear him on to triumph.

But now on a sudden was he, who with but twelve hundred men had so hotly followed fifteen hundred into the strait passage under Thremnir's Heugh, made ware too late that he must have to do with three thousand: Corinius rallying his folk and turning like a wolf in the pass, while Corund's sons, that had landed as aforesaid in the storm in the mirk of night, swept down with their battalions from the wooded slopes behind the Heugh. In such wise that Spitfire wist not sooner of any foreshadowing of disaster than of disaster's self: the thunder of the blow in flank and front and rear.

Then befell great manslaying between the sea-cliffs and the sea. The Demons, taken at that advantage, were like a man tripped in mid-stride by a rope across the way. By the sore onset of the Witches they were driven down into the shallows of the sea, and the spume of the sea was red with blood. And the Lord Corinius, now that he had done with feigned retreat, fared through the battle like a stream of unquenchable wildfire, that none might sustain his strokes that were about him.

Now was Spitfire's horse slain under him with a spear-thrust, as riding fetlock-deep in the yielding sand he rallied his men to fling back Heming. But Bremery of Shaws brought him another horse, and so mightily went he forth against the Witches that the sons of Corund were fain to give back before his onslaught, and that wing of the Witchland army was pressed back against the broken ground below the Heugh. Yet was that of little avail, for Corinius brake through from the north, thrusting the Demons with great slaughter back from the sea, so that they were penned betwixt him and Heming. Therewith Spitfire turned with some picked companies against Corinius; and well it seemed for awhile that a great force of the Witches must be whelmed or drowned in the salt waves. And Corinius himself stood now in great peril of his life, for his horse was bogued in the soft sands and might not win free for all his plunging.

In that nick of time came Spitfire through the stour, with a band of Demons about him, slaying as he came. He shouted with a terrible voice, "O Corinius, hateful to me and mine as are the gates of Hell, now will I kill thee, and thy dead carcase shall fatten the sweet meads of Owlswick."

Corinius answered him, "Bloody Spitfire, last of three whelps, for thy brothers are by now dead and rotten, I shall give thee a choke-pear."[6]

Therewith Spitfire shot a twirl-spear at him. It missed the man but smote the great horse in the shoulder so that he plunged and fell in a heap, hurt to the death. But the Lord Corinius lighting nimbly on his feet caught Spitfire's horse by the bridle rein and smote it on the muzzle, even as he rode at him, so that the horse reared up and swerved. Spitfire made a great blow at him with an axe, but it came slantwise on the helmet ridge and glented aside in air. Then Corinius thrust up under Spitfire's shield with his sword, and the point entered the big muscle of the arm near the armpit, and glancing against the bone tore up through the muscles of the shoulder. And that was a great wound.

Nevertheless Spitfire slacked not from the fight, but smote at him again, thinking to have hewn off his arm the hand whereof still clutched the bridle-rein. Corinius caught the axe on his shield, but his fingers loosed the rein, and almost he fell to earth under that mighty stroke, and the good bronze shield was dented and battered in.

Now with the loosing of the reins was Spitfire's horse plunged forward, carrying him past Corinius toward the sea. But he turned and hailed him, crying, "Get thee an horse. For I count it unworthy to fight with thee bearing this advantage over thee, I a-horseback and thou on foot."

Corinius cried out and answered, "Come down from thine horse then, and meet me foot to foot. And know it, my pretty throstle-cock,[7] that I am king in Demonland, which dignity I hold of the King of Kings, Gorice of Witchland, mine only overlord. Meet it is that I show thee in combat singular, that vauntest thyself greatest among the rebels yet left alive in this my kingdom, how much greater is my might than thine."

"These be great and thumping words," said Spitfire. "I shall thrust them down thy throat again."

Therewith he made as if to light down from his horse; but as he strove to light down, a mist went before his eyes and he reeled in his saddle. His men rushed in betwixt him and Corinius, and the captain of his bodyguard bare him up, saying, "You are hurt, my lord. You must not fight no more with Corinius, for your highness is unmeet for fighting and may not stand alone."

So they that were about him bare up great Spitfire. And the

mellay that was stayed while those lords dealt together in single combat brake forth afresh in that place. But all the while had furious war swung and ravened below Thremnir's Heugh, and wondrous was the valour of the Demons; for many hundred were slain or wounded to the death, and but a small force were they that yet remained to bear up the battle against the Witches.

Now those that were with Spitfire departed with him in the secretest manner that they could out of the fight, wrapping about him a watchet-coloured cloak[8] to hide his shining armour. They stanched the blood that ran from the great wound in his shoulder and bound it up carefully, and carried him a-horseback by Volle's command into Tremmerdale by secret mountain paths up to a desolate corrie[9] east of Sterry Gap, under the great scree-shoot[10] that flanks the precipices of the south summit of Dina. A long time he lay there senseless, like to one dead. For many hurts had he taken in the unequal fight, and greatly was he bruised and battered, but worst of all was the sore hurt Corinius gave him ere they parted betwixt the limits of land and sea.

And when night was fallen and all the ways were darkened, came the Lord Volle with a few companions utterly wearied to that lonely corrie. The night was still and cloudless, and the maiden moon walked high heaven, blackening the shadows of the great peaks that were like sharks' teeth against the night. Spitfire lay on a bed of ling and cloaks in the lee of a great boulder. Ghastly pale was his face in the silver moonlight.

Volle leaned upon his spear looking earnestly upon him. They asked him tidings. And Volle answered, "All lost," and still looked upon Spitfire.

They said, "My lord, we have stanched the blood and bound up the wound, but his lordship abideth yet senseless. And greatly we fear for his life, lest this great hurt yet prove his bane-sore."[11]

Volle kneeled beside him on the cold sharp stones and tended him as a mother might her sick child, applying to the wound leaves of black horehound and millefoil[12] and other healing simples, and giving him to drink out of a flask of precious wine of Arshalmar, ripened for an age in the deep cellars below Krothering. So that in a while Spitfire opened his eyes and said, "Draw back the curtains of the bed, for 'tis many a day since I woke up in Owlswick. Or is it night indeed? How went the fight, then?"

His eyes stared at the naked rocks and the naked sky beyond them. Then with a great groan he lifted himself on his right elbow.

Volle put a strong arm about him, saying, "Drink the good wine, and have patience. There be great doings toward."

Spitfire stared round him awhile, then said violently, "Shall we be foxes and fugitive men to dwell in holes o' the hollow mountain side? So the bright day is done, ha? Then off with these trammels." And he fell a-tearing at the bandage on his wounds.

But Volle prevented him with strong hands, saying, "Bethink thee how on thee alone, O glorious Spitfire, and on thy wise heart and valiant soul that delighteth in furious war, resteth all our hope to ward off from our lady wives and dear children and all our good land and fee the fury of the men of Witchland, and to save alive the great name of Demonland. Let not thy proud heart be capable of despair."

But Spitfire groaned and said, "Certain it was that woe and evil hap must be to Demonland until my kinsmen be gotten home again. And that day I think shall never dawn." And he cried, "Boasted he not that he is king in Demonland? and yet I had not my sword in his umbles.[13] And thou thinkest I'll live in shame?"

Therewithal he strove again to tear off the bandages, but Volle prevented him. And he raved and said, "Who was it forced me from the battle? 'Tis pity of his life, to have abused me so. Better dead than run from Corinius like a beaten puppy. Let me go, false traitors! I will amend this. I will die fighting. Let me go back."

Volle said, "Lift up thine eyes, great Spitfire, and behold the lady moon, how virgin free she walketh the wide fields of heaven, and the glory of the stars of heaven which in their multitudes attend her. And as little as earthly mists and storms do dim her, but though she be hid awhile yet when the tempest is abated and the sky swept bare of clouds there she appeareth again in her steadfast course, mistress of tides and seasons and swayer of the fates of mortal men: even such is the glory of sea-girt Demonland, and the glory of thine house, O Spitfire. And as little as commotions in the heavens should avail to remove these everlasting mountains, so little availeth disastrous war, though it be a great fight lost as was to-day, to shake down our greatness, that are mightiest with the spear from of old and able to make all earth bow to our glory."

So said Volle. And the Lord Spitfire looked out across the mist-choked sleeping valley to the great rock-faces dim in the moonlight and the lean peaks grand and silent beneath the moon. He spake not, whether for strengthlessness or as charmed to silence by the mighty influences of night and the mountain solitudes and by Volle's voice speaking deep and quiet in his ear, like the voice of night herself calming earth-born tumults and despairs.

After a time Volle spake once more: "Thy brethren shall come home again: doubt it not. But till then art thou our strength. Therefore have patience; heal thy wounds; and raise forces again. But shouldst thou in desperate madness destroy thy life, then were we shent indeed."

XX

KING CORINIUS

*Of the entry of the Lord Corinius into Owlswick
and how he was crowned in Spitfire's sapphire
chair as viceroy of Gorice the King and King in
Demonland: and how all that were in Owlswick
Castle did so receive and acknowledge him.*

ORINIUS, having completed this great victory, came
with his army north again to Owlswick as daylight
began to fade. The drawbridge was let down for him
and the great gates flung wide, that were studded with
silver and ribbed with adamant;[1] and in great pomp
rode he and his into Owlswick Castle, over the causey builded of
the living rock and great blocks of hewn granite out of Tremmerdale. The more part of his army lay in Spitfire's camp before
the castle, but a thousand were with him in his entry into Owlswick
with Corund's sons and the lords Gro and Laxus besides, for the
fleet had put across to anchor there when they saw the day was
won.

Corsus greeted them well, and would have brought them to
their lodgings near his own chamber, that they might put off their
harness and don clean linen and festival garments before supper.
But Corinius excused himself, saying he had eat nought since
breakfast-time: "Let us therefore not pass for ceremony, but bring
us I pray you forthright to the banquet house."

Corinius went in with Corsus before them all, putting lovingly
about his shoulder his arm all befouled with dust and clotted

243

blood. For he had not so much as stayed for washing of his hands. And that was scarce good for the broidered cloak of purple taffety[2] the Duke Corsus wore about his shoulders. Howbeit, Corsus made as if he marked it not.

When they were come into the hall, Corsus looked about him and said, "So it is, my Lord Corinius, that this hall is something little for the great press that here befalleth. Many of mine own folk that be of some account should by long custom sit down with us. And here be no seats left for them. Prithee command some of the common sort that came in with thee to give place, that all may be done orderly. Mine officers must not scramble in the buttery."

"I'm sorry, my lord," answered Corinius, "but needs must that we bethink us o' these lads of mine which have chiefly borne the toil of battle, and well I weet[3] thou'lt not deny them this honour to sit at meat with us: these that thou hast most to thank for opening Owlswick gates and raising the siege our enemies held so long against you."

So they took their seats, and supper was set before them: kids stuffed with walnuts and almonds and pistachios; herons in sauce cameline,[4] chines of beef; geese and bustards; and great beakers and jars of ruby-hearted wine. Right fain of the good banquet were Corinius and his folk, and silence was in the hall for awhile save for the clatter of dishes and the champing of the mouths of the feasters.

At length Corinius, quaffing down at one draught a mighty goblet of wine, spake and said, "There was battle in the meads by Thremnir's Heugh to-day, my lord Duke. Wast thou at that battle?"

Corsus's heavy cheeks flushed somewhat red. He answered, "Thou knowest I was not. And I should account it most blameable hotheadedness to have sallied forth when it seemed Spitfire had the victory."

"O my lord," said Corinius, "think not I made this a quarrel to thee. The rather let me show thee how much I hold thee in honour."

Therewith he called his boy that stood behind his chair, and the boy returned anon with a diadem of polished gold set all about with topazes that had passed through the fire; and on the frontlet of that diadem was the small figure of a crab-fish in dull iron, the eyes of it two green beryls on stalks of silver. The boy set it down on the table before the Lord Corinius, as it had been a dish of meat before him. Corinius took a writing from his purse, and laid it on the table for Corsus to see. And there was the signet upon it of the worm Ouroboros in scarlet wax, and the sign manual of Gorice the King.

"My Lord Corsus," said he, "and ye sons of Corsus, and ye other Witches, I do you to wit[5] that our Lord the King made me by these tokens his viceroy for his province of Demonland, and willed that I should bear a king's name in this land and that under him all should render me obedience."

Corsus, looking on the crown and the royal warrant of the King, waxed in one instant deadly pale, and in the next red as blood.

Corinius said, "To thee, O Corsus, out of all these great ones that here be gathered together in Owlswick, will I submit me for thee to crown me with this crown, as king in Demonland. This, that thou mayst see and know how most I honour thee."

Now were all silent, waiting on Corsus to speak. But he spake not a word. Dekalajus said privily in his ear, "O my father, if the monkey reigns, dance before him. Time shall bring us occasion to right you."

And Corsus, disregarding not this wholesome rede, for all he might not wholly rule his countenance, yet ruled himself to bite in the injuries he was fain to utter. And with no ill grace he did that office, to set on Corinius's head the new crown of Demonland.

Corinius sat now in Spitfire's seat, whence Corsus had moved to make place for him: in Spitfire's high seat of smoke-coloured jade, curiously carved and set with velvet-lustred sapphires, and right and left of him were two high candlesticks of fine gold. The breadth of his shoulders filled all the space between the pillars of the spacious seat. A hard man he looked to deal with, clothed upon with youth and strength and all armed and yet smoking from the battle.[6]

Corsus, sitting between his sons, said under his breath, "Rhubarb! bring me rhubarb to purge away this choler!"[7]

But Dekalajus whispered him, "Softly, tread easy. Let not our counsels walk in a net, thinking they are hidden. Nurse him to security, which shall be our safety and the mean to our wiping out this shaming. Was not Gallandus as big a man?"

Corsus's dull eye gleamed. He lifted a brimming winecup to toast Corinius. And Corinius hailed him and said, "My lord Duke, call in thine officers I pray thee and proclaim me, that they in turn may proclaim me king unto all the army that is in Owlswick."

Which Corsus did, albeit sore against his liking, knowing not where to find a reason against it.

When the plaudits[8] were heard in the courts without, acclaiming him as king, Corinius spake again and said, "I and my folk be a-weary, my lord, and would betimes to our rest. Give order, I pray thee, that they make ready my lodgings. And let them be those same lodgings Gallandus had whenas he was in Owlswick."

Whereat Corsus might scarce forbear a start. But Corinius's eye was on him, and he gave the order.

While he waited for his lodgings to be made ready, the Lord Corinius made great good cheer, calling for more wine and fresh dainties to set before those lords of Witchland: olives, and botargoes, and conserves of goose's liver richly seasoned, taken from Spitfire's plenteous store.

In the meantime Corsus spake softly to his sons: "I like not his naming of Gallandus. Yet seemeth he careless, as one that feareth no guile."

And Dekalajus answered in his ear, "Peradventure the Gods ordained his destruction, to make him choose that chamber."

So they laughed. And the banquet drew to a close with much pleasure and merrymaking.

Now came serving men with torches to light them to their chambers. As they stood up to bid good-night, Corinius said, "I'm sorry, my lord, if, after thy pleasant usage, I should do aught that is not convenable to thee. But I doubt not Owlswick Castle must be irksome to thee and thy sons, that were so long mewed up within it, and I doubt not ye are wearied by this siege and long warfare. Therefore it is my will that you do instantly depart home to Witchland. Laxus hath a ship manned ready to transport you thither. To put a fit and friendly term to our festivities, we'll bring you down to the ship."

Corsus's jaw fell. Yet he schooled his tongue to say, "My lord, so as it shall please thee. Yet let me know thy reasons. Surely the swords of me and my sons avail not so little for Witchland in this country of our evil-willers that we should sheathe 'em and go home. Howbeit, 'tis a matter demandeth no sweaty haste. We will take rede hereon in the morning."

But Corinius answered him, "Cry you mercy, needful it is that this very night you go ashipboard." And he gave him an ill look, saying, "Sith I lie to-night in Gallandus's lodgings, I think it fit my bodyguard should have thy chamber, my lord Duke, which, as I lately learned, adjoineth it."

Corsus said no word. But Gorius, his younger son, that was drunk with wine, leaped up and said, "Corinius, in an evil hour art thou come into this land to demand servitude of us. And thou art informed of my father right maliciously if thou art afeared of us because of Gallandus. 'Tis this viper sitteth beside thee, the Goblin swabber, told thee falsely this bad tale of us. And 'tis pity he is still inward with thee, for still he plotteth evil 'gainst Witchland."

Dekalajus thrust him aside, saying to Corinius, "Heed not my brother though he be hasty and rude of speech; for in wine he speaketh, and wine is another man. But most true it is, O Corinius, and this shall the Duke my father and all we swear and confirm to thee with the mightiest oaths thou wilt, that Gallandus sought to usurp authority for this sake only, to betray our whole army to the enemy. And 'twas only therefore Corsus slew him."

"That is a flat lie," said Laxus.

Gro laughed lightly.

But Corinius's sword leaped half naked from the scabbard, and he made a stride toward Corsus and his sons. "Give me the king's name when ye speak to me," he said, scowling upon them. "You sons of Corsus are not men to make me a stalk to catch birds with or to serve your own turn. And thou," he said, looking fiercely on Corsus, "wert best go meekly, and not bandy words with me. Thou fool! think'st thou I am Gallandus come again? Thou that didst murther him shalt not murther me. Or think'st I delivered thee out of the toils thine own folly and thrawart ways[9] had bound thee in, only to suffer thee lord it again here and cast all amiss again by the unquietness of thy malice? Here is the guard to bring you down to the ship. And well it is for thee if I slash not off thy head."

Now Corsus and his sons stood for a little doubting in their hearts whether it were fitter to leap with their weapons upon Corinius, putting their fortunes to the hazard of battle in Owlswick hall, or to embrace necessity and go down to the ship. And this seemed to them the better choice, to go quietly ashipboard; for there stood Corinius and Laxus and their men, and but few to face them of Corsus's own people, that should be sure for his party if it came to fighting; and withal they were not eager to have to do with Corinius, not though it had been on more even terms. So at the last, in anger and bitterness of heart, they submitted them to obey his will; and in that same hour Laxus brought them to the ship, and put them across the firth to Scaramsey.

There were they safe as a mouse in a mill. For Cadarus was skipper of that ship, a trusted liegeman of Lord Laxus, and her crew men leal[10] and true to Corinius and Laxus. She lay at anchor as for that night in the lee of the island, and with the first streak of dawn sailed down the firth, bearing Corsus and his sons homeward from Demonland.

XXI

THE PARLEY BEFORE KROTHERING

*Wherein is shown how warlike policy and a
picture painted drew the war westward: and how
the Lord Gro went on an embassage to
Krothering Gates, and of the answer he gat there.*

N o w it is to be said of Zigg that he failed not to fulfil Spitfire's behest, but gathered hastily an army of more than fifteen hundred horse and foot out of the northern dales and the habitations about Shalgreth Heath and the pasture-lands of Kelialand and Switchwater Way and the region of Rammerick, and came in haste over the Stile. But when Corinius knew of this faring from the west, he marched three thousand strong to meet them above Moonmere Head, to deny them the way to Galing. But Zigg, being yet in the upper defiles of Breakingdale, now for the first time had advertisement of the great slaughter at Thremnir's Heugh, and how the forces of Spitfire and Volle were broken and scattered and themselves fled up into the mountains; and so deeming it small gain with so little an army to give battle to Corinius, he turned back without more ado and returned hastily over the Stile whence he came. Corinius sent light forces to harry his retreat, but being not minded as then to follow them into the west country, let build a burg in the throat of the pass in a place of vantage, and stationed there sufficient men to ward it, and so came again to Owlswick.

They that were with Corinius in Demonland numbered now more than five thousand fighting men: a great and redoubtable army. With these, the weather being fine and open, he in a short time laid under him all eastern Demonland, gave Galing alone. Bremery of Shaws with but seventy men held Galing for Lord Juss against all assaults. So that Corinius, thinking this fruit should ripen later and drop into his hand when the rest had been gathered, resolved at winter's end to march with his main army into the west country, leaving a small force to hold down the eastlands and contain Bremery in Galing. To this determination he was led by all arguments of sound soldiership, most happily seconding his own inclinations. For besides this of warlike policy two scarce weaker lodestones drew him westward: first the old cankered malice he bare in his heart against the Lord Brandoch Daha, that made Krothering his dearest prey; and next, his own lustful desires most outrageously burning for the Lady Mevrian. And this only for the sight of her picture, found by him in Spitfire's closet among his pens and inkstands and other trinkets, which once looked on he swore that with Heaven's will (ay, or without if so it must be) she should be his paramour.

So on the fourteenth day of March, of a bright frosty morn, he with his main army marched up Breakingdale and over the Stile, by that same road that Lord Juss fared by and Lord Brandoch Daha, that summer's day when they went to take counsel in Krothering before the Impland expedition. So came the Witches down to the watersmeet and turned aside to Many Bushes. There they found not Zigg nor his lady wife nor any of his folk, but found the house desolate. So they robbed and burned and went their way. And a famous castle of Juss's they sacked and burned in the confines of Kelialand, and another on Switchwater Way, and a summer palace of Spitfire's on a little hill above Rammerick Mere. In such wise they marched victoriously down Switchwater Way, and there was none to dispute their progress but all fled at the approach of that great army and hid themselves in the secret places of the mountains, avoiding death and fate.

When he was come through the straits of Gashterndale up on to Krothering Side, Corinius let pitch his camp under Erngate End, at the foot of the scree-strewn slopes that rise steeply to the high western face of the mountain, where the lean embattled crags far aloft stand like a wall against high heaven.

Corinius came to Lord Gro and said to him, "To thee will I entrust mine embassage to this Mevrian. Thou shalt go with a flag of truce to gain thee entry to the castle; or if they will not admit thee, then bid her parley with thee without the wall. Then shalt thou use what fantastic courtier's jargon nature and thine invention shall lightliest counsel thee, and say, 'Corinius, by the grace of the great King and the might of his own hand king of Demonland, sitteth as thou well mayst see in power invincible before this castle. But he willed me let thee know that he is not come for to make war against ladies and damosels, and be thou of this sure, that neither to thee nor to none of thy fortress he will nought say nor hurt. Only this honour he proffereth thee, to wed thee in sweet marriage and make thee his queen in Demonland.' Whereto if she say yea, well and good, and we will go up peaceably into Krothering and possess it and the woman. But if she deny me this, then shalt thou say unto her right fiercely that I will set on against the castle like a lion, and neither rest nor give over until I have beaten it all to a ruin about her ears and slain the folk with the edge of the sword. And that which she refuseth me to have in peaceful love and kindness I will have of my own violent deed, that she and her stiff-necked Demons may know that I am their king, and master of all that is theirs, and their own bodies but chattels to serve my pleasure."

Gro said, "My Lord Corinius, choose I pray thee another who shall be fitter than I to do this errand for thee;" and so for a long time most earnestly besought him. But Corinius, the more he perceived the duty hateful to Gro, the firmer became his resolution that none but Gro should undertake it. So that in the end Gro perforce consented, and in the same hour went with eleven up to the gates of Krothering, and a white flag of truce was borne before him.

He sent his herald up to the gate to desire speech of the Lady Mevrian. And in a while the gates were opened, and she came down attended to meet Lord Gro in the open garden before the bridge-gate. It was by then late afternoon, and the burning sun swam low amid streaked level clouds incarnadine, setting aflame the waters of Thunderfirth with the reflection of his beams. From the horizon, high beyond the pine-clad hills of Westmark, a range of clouds reared themselves, solid and of an iron hue; so hard-edged against the vapoury sky of sunset, that they seemed substantial mountains, not clouds: unearthly mountains (a man might fancy) divinely raised up for Demonland, for whom not all her ancient hills gave any longer refuge against her enemies. Here, in Krothering gates, wintersweet and the little purple daphne bush that blooms before the leaf breathed fragrance abroad. Yet was it not this sweetness in the air that troubled the Lord Gro, nor that western glory burning that dazzled his eyes; but to look upon that lady standing in the gate, white-skinned and dark, like the divine Huntress,[1] tall and proud and lovely.

Mevrian, seeing him speechless, said at last, "My lord, I heard thou hadst some errand to declare unto me. And seeing a great camp of war gathered under Erngate End, and having heard of robbers and evil-doers rife about the land these many moons, I look not for soft speech. Take heart, therefore, and declare plainly what ill thou meanest."

Gro answered and said, "Tell me first if thou that speakest art in truth the Lady Mevrian, that I may know whether to human kind I speak or to some Goddess come down from the shining floor of heaven."

She answered, "Of thy compliments I have nought to do. I am she thou namest."

"Madam," said Lord Gro, "I would not have brought your highness this message nor delivered it, but that I know full well that did I refuse it another should bear it thee full speedily, and with less compliment and less sorrow than I."

She nodded gravely, as who should say, Proceed. So, with what countenance he might, he rehearsed his message, saying when it was ended, "Thus, madam, saith Corinius the king: and thus he charged me deliver it unto your highness."

Mevrian heard him attentively with head erect. When he had done she was silent a little, still studying him. Then she spake: "Methinks I know thee now. Thou art Lord Gro of Goblinland that bearest me this message."

Gro answered, "Madam, he thou namest went years ago from this earth. I am Lord Gro of Witchland."

"So it seemeth, from thy talk," said she; and was silent again.

The steady contemplation from that lady's eyes was like a knife scraping his tender skin, so that he was ill at ease well nigh past bearing.

After a little she said, "I remember thee, my lord. Let me stir thy memory. Eleven years ago, my brother went to war in Goblinland against the Witches, and overcame them on Lormeron field. There slew he the great King of Witchland in single combat, Gorice X., that until that day was held for the mightiest man-at-arms in all the world. My brother was as then but eighteen winters old, and that was the first blazing up of his great fame and glory. So King Gaslark made great feasting and great rejoicing in Zajë Zaculo because of the ridding of his land of the oppressors. I was at those revels. I saw thee there, my lord; and being but a little maid of eleven summers, sat on thy knee in Gaslark's halls. Thou didst show me books, with pictures in strange colours of gold and green and scarlet, of birds and beasts and distant countries and wonders of the world. And I, being a little harmless maid, thought thee good and kind of heart, and loved thee."

She ceased, and Gro, like a man hath taken some drowsy drug, stood looking on her confounded.

"Tell me," said she, "of this Corinius. Is he such a fighter as men say?"

"He is," said Gro, "one of the most famousest captains that ever was. That might not his worst enemies gainsay."

Mevrian said, "A likely consort, think'st thou, for a lady of Demonland? Remember, I have said nay to crowned kings. I would know thy mind, for doubtless he is thy very familiar friend, since he made thee his go-between."

Gro saw that she mocked, and he was troubled at heart. "Madam," said he, and his voice shook somewhat, "take not in too great scorn this vile part in me. Verily this I brought thee is the most shamefullest message, and flatly against my will did I deliver it unto thee. Yet with such constraint upon me, how could I choose but strike my forehead into dauntless marble and word by word deliver my charge?"

"Thy tongue," said Mevrian, "hath struck hot irons in my face. Go back to thy master. If he look for an answer, tell him he may read it in letters of gold above the gates."

"Thy noble brother, madam," said Gro, "is not here to make good that answer." And he came near to her, saying in a low voice so that only they two should hear it, "Be not deceived. This Corinius is a naughty, wicked, and luxurious youth, that will use thee without any respect if once he break in by force into Krothering Castle. It were wiselier carried to make some open show to receive him; so by fair words and putting of him off thou mayst yet escape."

But Mevrian said, "Thou hast mine answer. I have no ears to his request. Say too that my cousin the Lord Spitfire hath healed his wounds, and hath an army afoot shall whip these Witches from my gates ere many days be passed by."

So saying she returned in great scorn within the castle.

But the Lord Gro returned again to the camp and to Corinius, who asked him how he had sped.

He answered, she did utterly refuse it.

"So," said Corinius; "doth the puss thump me off? Then pause my hot desires an instant, only the more thunderingly to clap it on. For I will have her. And this coyness and pert rejection hath the more fixedly confirmed me."

XXII

Aurwath and Switchwater

*How the Lady Mevrian beheld from Krothering
Walls the Witchland Army and the Captains
thereof: and of the tidings brought her there of the
war in the west country, of Aurwath Field and
the great slaughter on Switchwater Way.*

HE fourth day after these doings aforewrit, the Lady
Mevrian walked on the battlements of Krothering
keep. A blustering wind blew from the north-west.
The sky was cloudless: clear blue overhead, all else
pearl-gray, and the air a little misty. Her old steward,
stalwart and soldier-like, greaved and helmed and clad in a plated
jerkin of bull's hide, walked with her.

"The hour should be about striking," said she. " 'Tis to-day or
to-morrow my Lord Zigg named to me when they were here
a-guesting. If but Goblinland keep tryst it were the prettiest feat, to
take them so pat."

"As your ladyship might clap a gnat 'twixt the palms of your
two hands," said the old man; and he gazed again southward over
the sea.

Mevrian set her gaze in the same quarter. "Nothing but mist
and spray," she said after a few minutes' searching. "I'm glad I
sent Lord Spitfire those two hundred horse. He must have every
man can be scraped up, for such a day. How thinkest thou, Ravnor:

if King Gaslark come not, hath Lord Spitfire force enow to cope them alone?"

Ravnor chuckled in his beard. "I think and my lord your brother were here he should tell your highness 'ay' to that. Since first I bowled a hoop,[1] they taught me a Demon was undermatched against five Witches."

She looked at him a little wistfully. "Ah," she said, "were he at home. And were Juss at home." Then on a sudden she faced round northward, pointing to the camp. "Were they at home," she cried, "thou shouldst not see outlanders insulting in arms on Krothering Side, sending me shameful offers, caging me like a bird in this castle. Have such things been in Demonland, until now?"

Now came a boy running along the battlements from the far side of the tower, crying that ships were hove in sight sailing from the south and east, "And they make for the firth."

"Of what land?" said Mevrian, while they hastened back to look.

"What but Goblinland?" said Ravnor.

"O say not so too hastily!" cried she. They came round the turret wall, and the sea and Stropardon Firth opened wide and void before them. "I see nought," she said; "or is yon flight of sea-mews the fleet thou sawest?"

"He meaneth Thunderfirth," said Ravnor, who had gone on ahead, pointing to the west. "They shape their course toward Aurwath. 'Tis King Gaslark for sure. Mark but the blue and gold of his sails."

Mevrian watched them, her gloved hand drumming nervously on the marble battlement. Very stately she seemed, muffled in a flowing cloak of white watered silk collared and lined with ermine. "Eighteen ships!" she said. "I dreamed not Goblinland might make so great a force."

"Your ladyship may see," said Ravnor, walking back along the wall, "whether the Witchlanders have slept while these ships sailed to port."

She followed and looked. Great stir there was in the Witchland army, marshalling before the camp; there was coming and going and leaping on horseback, and faintly on the wind their trumpets' blare was borne to Mevrian's ears as she beheld them from her high watch-tower. The host moved forth down the meadows, all orderly, aglitter with bronze and steel. Southward they came, passing at length through the home-meads of Krothering, so near that each man was plainly seen from the battlements, as they rode beneath.

Mevrian leaned forward in an embrasure, one hand on either battlement at her left and right. "I would know their names,"[2] said she. "Thou, that hast oft fared to the wars, mayst teach me. Gro I know, with a long beard; and heart-heaviness it is to see a lord of Goblinland in such a fellowship. What's he beside him, yon bearded gallant, with a winged helm and a diadem about it, like a king's, and beareth a glaive crimson-hafted?[3] He looketh a proud one."

The old man answered, "Laxus of Witchland: the same that was admiral of their fleet against the Ghouls."

" 'Tis a brave man to look on, and worthy a better cause. What's he rideth now below us, heading their horse: ruddy and swarthy and light of build, hath a brow like the thunder-cloud, and weareth armour from neck to toe?"

Ravnor answered, "Highness, I know him not certainly, the sons of Corund so favour one another. But methinks 'tis the young prince Heming."

Mevrian laughed. "Prince quotha?"

"So moveth the world, your highness. Since Gorice set Corund in kingdom in Impland——"

Said Mevrian, "Name him prithee Heming Faz: I warrant they trap them now with barbarous additions. Heming Faz, good lack! lording it now in Demonland.

"The prime huff-cap of all," said she after a little, "holdeth aback it seemeth. O here he comes. Sweet heaven, what furious horsemanship! Troth, and he can sit a horse, Ravnor, and hath the great figure of an athlete. Look where he gallopeth bare-headed down the line. I ween he'll need more than golden curls to keep his head whole ere he have done with Gaslark, ay, and our own folk gathering from the north. I see he beareth his helm at the saddle-bow. To ape us so!" she cried as he drew nearer. "All silks and silver. Thou'dst have sworn none but a Demon went to battle so costly apparelled. O, for a scissors to cut his comb withal!"

So speaking she leaned forward all she might, to watch him. And he, galloping by below, looked up; and marking her so watching, reined mightily his great chestnut horse, throwing him with the check well nigh on his haunches. And while the horse plunged and reared, Corinius hailed her in a great voice, crying, "Mistress, good-morrow!" crying, "Wish me victory, and swift to thine arms!"

So near below was he a-riding, she might scan the very lineaments of his face and read it as he looked up and shouted to her that greeting. He saluted with his sword, and spurred onward to overtake Gro and Laxus in the van.

As if sickened on a sudden, or as if she had been ready to tread on a deadly stinging adder, the Lady Mevrian leaned against the marble of the battlements. Ravnor stepped towards her: "Is your ladyship ill? Why, what's the matter?"

"A silly qualm," said Mevrian faintly. "If thou'dst medicine it, show me the sheen of Spitfire's spears to the northward. The blank land dazzles me."

So wore the afternoon. Twice and thrice Mevrian went upon the walls, but could see nought save the sea and the firths and the mountain-bosomed plain fair and peaceful in the spring-time: no sign of men or of war's alarums, save only the masts of Gaslark's ships seen over the land's brow three miles or more to the south-west. Yet she knew surely that near those ships beside Aurwath harbour must be desperate fighting toward,[4] Gaslark the king engaged at heavy odds against Laxus and Corinius and the spears of Witchland. And the sun wheeled low over the dark pines of Westmark, and still no sign from the north.

"Thou didst send one forth for tidings?" she said to Ravnor, the third time she went on the wall.

He answered, "Betimes this morning, your highness. But 'tis slow faring until a be a mile or twain clear of the castle, for a must elude their small bands that go up and down guarding the country-side."

"Bring him to me o' the instant of his return," said she.

With a foot on the stair, she turned back. "Ravnor," she said. He came to her.

"Thou," she said, "hast been years enow my brother's steward in Krothering, and our father's before him, to know what mind and spirit dwelleth in them of our line. Tell me, truly and sadly, what thou makest of this. Lord Spitfire is too late: other else, Goblinland too sudden-early (and that was his fault from of old). What seest thou in it? Speak to me as thou shouldst to my Lord Brandoch Daha were it he that asked thee."

"Highness," said the old man Ravnor, "I will answer you my very thought: and it is, woe to Goblinland. Since my Lord Spitfire cometh not yet from the north, only the deathless Gods descending out of heaven can save the king. The Witches number at an humble reckoning twice his strength; and man to man you were as well pit a hound against a bear, as against Witches Goblins. For all that these be fierce and full of fiery courage, the bear hath it at the last."

Mevrian listened, looking on him with sorrowful steady eyes. "And he so generous-noble flown to comfort Demonland in the blackness of her days," she said at last. "Can fate be so ungallant? O Ravnor, the shame of it! First La Fireez, now Gaslark. How shall any love us any more? The shame of it, Ravnor!"

"I would not have your highness," said Ravnor, "too hasty to blame us. If their plan and compact have gone amiss, 'tis likelier King Gaslark's misprision[5] than Lord Spitfire's. We know not for sure which day was set for this landing."

While he so spake, he was looking past her seaward, a little south of the reddest part of the sunset. His eyes widened. He touched her arm and pointed. Sails were hoisted among the masts at Aurwath. Smoke, as of burning, reeked up against the sky. As they watched, the most part of the ships moved out to sea. From those that remained, some five or six, fire leaped and black clouds of smoke. The rest as they came out of the lee of the land, made southward for the open sea under oar and sail.

Neither spake; and the Lady Mevrian leaning her elbows on the parapet of the wall hid her face in her hands.

Now came Ravnor's messenger at length back from his faring, and the old man brought him in to Mevrian in her bower in the south part of Krothering. The messenger said, "Highness, I bring no writing, since that were too perilous had I fallen in my way among Witches. But I had audience of my Lord Spitfire and my Lord Zigg in the gates of Gashterndale. And thus their lordships commanded me deliver it unto you, that your highness should be at ease and secure, seeing that they do in such sort hold all the ways to Krothering, that the Witchland army cannot escape out of this countryside that is betwixt Thunderfirth and Stropardon Firth and the sea, but and if they will give battle unto their lordships. But if they choose rather to abide here by Krothering, then may our armies close on them and oppress them, since our forces do exceed theirs by near a thousand spears. Which to-morrow will be done whate'er betide, since that is the day appointed for Gaslark the king to land with a force at Aurwath."

Mevrian said, "They know nought then of this direful miscarriage, and Gaslark here already before his time and thrown back into the sea?" And she said, "We must apprise them on't, and that hastily and to-night."

When the man understood this, he answered, "Ten minutes for a bite and a stirrup-cup, and I am at your ladyship's service."

And in a short while, that man went forth again secretly out of Krothering in the dusk of night to bring word to Lord Spitfire of what was befallen. And the watchmen watching in the night from Krothering walls beheld northward under Erngate End the camp-fires of the Witches like the stars.

Night passed and day dawned, and the camp of the Witches showed empty as an empty shell.

Mevrian said, "They have moved in the night."

"Then shall your highness hear great tidings ere long," said Ravnor.

" 'Tis like we may have guests in Krothering to-night," said Mevrian. And she gave order for all to be made ready against their coming, and the choicest bed-chambers for Spitfire and Zigg to welcome them. So, with busy preparations, the day went by. But as evening came, and still no riding from the north, some shadows of impatience and anxious doubt crept with night's shades creeping across heaven across their eager expectancy in Krothering. For Mevrian's messenger returned not. Late to rest went the Lady Mevrian; and with the first peeping light she was abroad, muffled in her great mantle of velvet and swansdown against the eager winds of morning. Up to the battlements she went, and with old Ravnor searched the blank prospect. For pale morning rose on an empty landscape; and so all day until the evening: watching, and waiting, and questioning in their hearts.

So went they at length to supper on this third night after Aurwath field. And ere supper was half done was a stir in the outer courts, and the rattle of the bridge let down, and a clatter of horse-hooves on the bridge and the jasper[6] pavements. Mevrian sat erect and expectant. She nodded to Ravnor who wanting no further sign went hastily out, and returned in an instant hastily and with heavy brow. He spake in her ear, "News, my Lady. It were well you bade him to private audience. Drink this cup first," pouring out some wine for her.

She rose up, saying to the steward, "Come thou, and bring him with thee."

As they went he whispered her, "Astar of Rettray, sent by the Lord Zigg with matter of urgent import for your highness's ear."

The Lady Mevrian sat in her ivory chair cushioned with rich stuffed silks of Beshtria, with little golden birds and strawberry leaves with the flowers and rich red fruits all figured thereon in gorgeous colours of needlework. She reached out her hand to Astar who stood before her in his battle harness, muddy and bebloodied from head to foot. He bowed and kissed her hand: then stood silent. He held his head high and looked her in the face, but his eyes were bloodshot and his look was ghastly like a messenger of ill.

"Sir," said Mevrian, "stand not in doubt, but declare all. Thou knowest it is not in our blood to quail under dangers and misfortune."

Astar said, "Zigg, my brother-in-law, gave me this in charge, madam, to tell thee all truly."

"Proceed," said she. "Thou knowest our last news. Hour by hour since then, we watched on victory. I have no mean welcome feast prepared against your coming."

Astar groaned. "My Lady Mevrian," said he, "you must now prepare a sword, not a banquet. You did send a runner to Lord Spitfire."

"Ay," said she.

"He brought us advertisement that night," said Astar, "of Gaslark's overthrow. Alas, that Goblinland was a day too soon, and so bare alone the brunt. Yet was vengeance ready to our hand, as we supposed. For every pass and way was guarded, and ours the greater force. So for that night we waited, seeing Corinius's fires alight in his camp on Krothering Side, meaning to smite him at dawn of day. Now in the night were mists abroad, and the moon early sunken. And true it is as ill it is, that the whole Witchland army marched away past us in the dark."

"What?" cried Mevrian, "and slept ye all to let them by?"

"In the middle night," answered he, "we had sure tidings he was afoot, and the fires yet burning in his camp a show to mock us withal. By all sure signs, we might know he was broke forth northwestward, where he must take the upper road into Mealand over Brocksty Hause. Zigg with seven hundred horse galloped to Heathby to head him off, whiles our main force fared their swiftest up Little Ravendale. Thou seest, madam, Corinius must march along the bow and we along the bowstring."

"Yes," said Mevrian. "Ye had but to check him with the horse at Heathby, and he must fight or fall back toward Justdale where he was like to lose half his folk in Memmery Moss. Outlanders shall scarce find a firm way there in a dark night."

"Certain it is we should have had him," said Astar. "Yet certain it is he doubled like a hare and fooled us all to the top of our bent:[7] turned in his tracks, as later we concluded, somewhere by

Goosesand, and with all his army slipped back eastward under our rear. And that was the wonderfullest feat heard tell of in all chronicles of war."

"Tush, noble Astar," said Mevrian. "Labour not Witchland's praises, nor imagine not I'll deem less of Spitfire's nor Zigg's generalship because Corinius, by art or fortune's favour, dodged 'em in the dark."

"Dear Lady," said he, "even look for the worst and prepare yourself for the same."

Her gray eyes steadily beheld him. "Certain intelligence," said he, "was brought us of their faring with all speed they might eastaway past Switchwater; and ere the sun looked well over Gemsar Edge we were hot on the track of them, knowing our force the stronger and our only hope to bring them to battle ere they reached the Stile, where they have made a fortress of great strength we might scarce hope to howster[8] them out from if they should win thither."

He paused. "Well," said she.

"Madam," he said, "that we of Demonland are great and invincible in war, 'tis most certain. But in these days fight we as a man that fighteth hobbled, or with half his gear laid by, or as a man half roused from sleep. For we be reft of our greatest. Bereft of these, such sorrows befall us and such doom as at Thremnir's Heugh last autumn shattered our strength in pieces, and now this very day yet more terribly hath put us down on Switchwater Way."

Mevrian's cheek turned white, but she said no word, waiting.

"We were eager in the chase," said Astar. "I have told thee why, madam. Thou knowest how near to the mountains runneth the road past Switchwater, and the shores of the lake hem in the way for miles against the mountain spurs, and woods clothe the lower slopes, and dells and gorges run up betwixt the spurs into the mountain side. The day was misty, and the mists hung by the shores of Switchwater. When we had marched so far that our van was about over against the stead of Highbank that stands on the farther shore, the battle began: greatly to their advantage, since Corinius had placed strong forces in the hills on our right flank, and so ambushed us and took us at unawares. Not to grieve thee with a woful tale, madam, we were most bloodily overthrown, and our army merely brought to not-being. And in the mid rout, Zigg stole an instant to charge me by my love for him ride to Krothering as if my life lay on it and the weal of all of us, and bid you fly hence to Westmark or the isles or whither you will, ere the Witches come again and here entrap you. Since save for these walls and these few brave soldiers you have to ward them, no help standeth any more 'twixt you and these devilish Witches."

Still she was silent. He said, "Let me not be too hateful to you, most gracious Lady, for this rude tale of disaster. The suddenness of the times bar any pleasant glozing. And indeed I thought I should satisfy you more with plainness, than should opinion of I know not what false courtliness bind me to show you comfort where comfort is not."

The Lady Mevrian stood up and took him by both hands. Surely the light of that lady's eyes was like the new light of morning glancing through mists on the gray still surface of a mountain tarn, and the accent of her voice sweet as the voices of the morning as she said, "O Astar, think me not so unhandsome, nor yet so foolish. Thanks, gentle Astar. But thou hast not supped, and sure in a great soldier battle and swift far riding should breed hunger, how ill soever the news he beareth. Thy welcome shall not be the colder because we looked for more than thee, alas, and for far other tidings. A chamber is prepared for thee. Eat and drink; and when night is done is time enough to speak more of these things."

"Madam," he said, "you must come now or 'tis too late."

But she answered him, "No, noble Astar. This is my brother's house. So long as I may keep it for him against his coming home I will not creep out of Krothering like a rat, but stand to my watch. And this is certain, I shall not open Krothering gates to Witches whiles I and my folk yet live to bar them against them."

So she made him go to supper; but herself sat late that night alone in the Chamber of the Moon, that was in the donjon keep above the inner court in Krothering. This was Lord Brandoch Daha's banquet chamber, devised and furnished by him in years gone by; and here he and she commonly sat at meat, using not the banquet hall across the court save when great company was present. Round was that chamber, following the round walls of the tower that held it. All the pillars and the walls and the vaulted roof were of a strange stone, white and smooth, and yielding such a glistering show of pallid gold in it as was like the golden sheen of the full moon of a warm night in midsummer. Lamps that were milky opals self-effulgent filled all the chamber with a soft radiance, in which the bas-reliefs of the high dado,[9] delicately carved, portraying those immortal blooms of amaranth and nepenthe and moly and Elysian asphodel, were seen in all their delicate beauty,[10] and the fair painted pictures of the Lord of Krothering and his lady sister, and of Lord Juss above the great open fireplace with Goldry and Spitfire on his left and right. A few other pictures there were, smaller than these: the Princess Armelline of Goblinland, Zigg and his lady wife, and others; wondrous beautiful.

Here a long while sat the Lady Mevrian. She had a little lute wrought of sweet sandalwood and ivory inlaid with gems. While she sat a-thinking, her fingers strayed idly on the strings, and she sang in a low sweet voice:

> There were three ravens sat on a tree,
> They were as black as they might be.
> *With a downe, derrie down.*
>
> The one of them said to his make,
> Where shall we our breakefast take?
>
> Downe in yonder greene field,
> There lies a knight slain under his shield.
>
> His hounds they lie downe at his feete,
> So well they can their master keepe.
>
> His haukes they flie so eagerly,
> There's no fowle dare him come nie.[11]
>
> Downe there comes a fallow doe[12]
> As great with yong as she might goe.
>
> She lift up his bloudy hed,
> And kist his wounds that were so red.
>
> She gat him up upon her backe,
> And carried him to earthen lake.
>
> She buried him before the prime;
> She was dead herselfe ere even-song time.
>
> God send every gentleman
> Such haukes, such hounds, and such a leman.[13]
> *With a downe, derrie down.*

With the last sighing sweetness trembling from the strings, she laid aside the lute, saying, "The discord of my thoughts, my lute, doth ill agree with the harmonies of thy strings. Put it by."

She fell to gazing on her brother's picture, the Lord Brandoch Daha, standing in his jewelled hauberk[14] laced about with gold, his hand upon his sword. And that lazy laughter-loving yet imperious look of the eyes which in life he had was there, wondrous lively caught by the painter's art, and the lovely lines of his brow and lip and jaw, where power and masterful determination slumbered, as brazen Ares might slumber in the arms of the Queen of Love.[15]

A long while Mevrian looked on that picture, musing. Then, burying her face in the cushions of the long low seat she sat on, she burst into a great passion of tears.

XXIII

THE WEIRD BEGUN OF ISHNAIN NEMARTRA

Of the counsel taken by the witches touching the
conduct of the war: whereafter in the fifth assault
the castle of Lord Brandoch Daha was made a
prey unto Corinius.

OW was little time for debate or conjecture, but with the morrow's morn came the Witchland army once more before Krothering, and a herald sent by Corinius to bid Mevrian yield up the castle and her own proper person lest a worse thing befall them. Which she stoutly refusing, Corinius let straight assault the castle, but won it not. And in the next three days following he thrice assaulted Krothering, and, failing with some loss of men to win an entry, closely invested it.[1]

And now summoned he those other lords of Witchland to talk with him. "How say ye? Or what rede shall we take? They be few only within to man the walls; and great shame it is to us and to all Witchland if we get not this hold taken, so many as we be here gone up against it, and so great captains."

Laxus said, "Thou art king in Demonland. Thine it is to take order what shall be done. But if thou desire my rede, then shall I give it thee."

"I desire each one of you," said Corinius, "to show forth to me frankly and freely his rede. And well ye know I strive for nought

266

else but for Witchland's glory and to make firm our conquest here."

"Well," said Laxus, "I told thee once already my counsel, and thou wast angry with me. Thou madest a mighty victory on Switchwater Way; which had we followed up, pushing home the sword of our advantage till the hilts came clap against the breast-plate of our adversary, we might now have exterminated from the land the whole nest of them, Spitfire, Zigg, and Volle. But now are they gotten away the devil knows whither, for the preparing of fresh thorns to prick our sides withal."

Corinius said, "Claim not wisdom after the event, my lord. 'Twas not so thou didst advise. Thou didst bid me let go Krothering: a thing I will not do, once I have set mine hand to it."

Laxus answered him, "Not only did I so advise thee as I have said, but Heming was by, and will bear me out, that I did offer that he or I with a small force should keep this comfit-box² shut for thee till thou shouldst have done the main business."

" 'Tis so," said Heming.

But Corinius said, " 'Tis not so, Heming. And were it so, 'tis easily seen why he or thou shouldst hanker for first suck at this luscious fruit. Yet not so easy to see why I should yield it you."

"That," said Laxus, "is very ill said. I see thy memory needs jogging, and thou art sliding into ingratitude. How many such like fruits hast thou enjoyed since we came out hither, that we had all the pains and plucking of?"

"O cry thee mercy, my lord," said Corinius, "I should have remembered, dreams of Sriva's moist lips keep thee from straying. But enough of this fooling: to the matter."

Lord Laxus flushed. "By my faith," said he, "this is very much to the matter. 'Twere well, Corinius, if thy loose thoughts were kept from straying. Spend men on a fortress? Better assay Galing, then: that were a prize worth more to our safety and our lordship here."

"Ay," said Heming. "Seek out the enemy. 'Tis therefore we came hither: not to find women for thee."

Thereupon the Lord Corinius struck him across the table a great buffet in the face. Heming, mad wroth, snatched out a dagger; but Gro and Laxus catching him one by either hand restrained him. Gro said, "My lords, my lords, you must not word it so dangerous ill. We have but one heart and mind here, to magnify our Lord the King and his glory. Thou, Heming, forget not the King hath put authority in the hand of Corinius, so that thy dagger set against him setteth most treasonably against the King's majesty. And thou, my lord, I pray be temperate in thy power. Sure, for want of open war it is that our hands be so ready for these private brawls."

When by fair words this stew was cooled again, Corinius bade Gro say forth his mind, what he thought lay next to do. Gro answered, "My lord, I am of Laxus's opinion. Abiding here by Krothering, we fare as idle cooks toying with sweetmeats while the roast spoils. We should seek out power and destroy it where still it fareth free, lest it swell again to a growth may danger us: wheresoever these lords be fled, think not they'll be slack to prepare a mischief for us."

"I see," said Corinius, "ye be all three of an accord against me. But there is no one beam of these thoughts your discourse hath planted in me, but is able to discern a greater cloud than you do go in."

"It is very true," said Laxus, "that we do think somewhat scornfully of this war against women."

"Ay, there's the cover off the dish!" said Corinius, "and a pretty mess within. Y'are woman-mad, every jack of you, and this blears your eyes to think me sick o' the same folly. Thou and thy little dark-eyed baggage, that I dare swear hath months ago forgot thee for another. Heming here and I know not what sweet maid his young heart doteth on. Gro, ha! ha!" and he fell a-laughing. "Wherefore the King saddled me with this Goblin, he only knoweth, and his secretary the Devil: not I. By Satan, thou hast a starved look i' the eyes giveth me to think the errand I sent thee to Krothering gates did thee no good. My cat's leering look showeth me that my cat goeth a catterwawing. Dost now find the raven's wing a seemlier hue in a wench's hair to set they cold blood aleaping than tawny red? Or dost think this one hath a softer breast than thy Queen's to cushion thy perfumed locks?"

With that word spoken, all three of them leaped from their seats. Gro, with a face ashen gray, said, "At me thou mayst spit what filth thou wilt. I am schooled to bear with it for Witchland's sake and until thine own venom choke thee. But this shalt thou not do whiles I live, thou or any other: to let thy bawdy tongue meddle with Queen Prezmyra's name."

Corinius sat still in his chair in a posture of studied ease, but his sword was ready. His great jowl was set, his insolent blue eyes scornfully looked from one to another of those lords where they stood menacing him. "Pshaw!" said he, at last. "Who brought her name into it but thyself, my Lord Gro? not I."

"Thou wert best not bring it in again, Corinius," said Heming.

"Have we not well followed thee and upheld thee? And so shall we do henceforth. But remember, I am King Corund's son. And if thou speak this wicked lie again, it shall cost thee thy life if I may."

Corinius threw out his arms and laughed. "Come," said he, standing up, with much show of jolly friendliness, " 'twas but a jest; and, I freely acknowledge, an ill jest. I'm sorry for it, my lords.

"And now," said he, "come we again to the matter. Krothering Castle will I not forgo, since 'tis not my way to turn back for any man on earth, no not for the Gods almighty, once I have ta'en my course. But I will make a bargain with you, and this it is: that we to-morrow do assault the hold a last time, using all our men and all our might. And if, as I think is most unlikely and most shameful, we get it not, then shall we fare away and do according to thy counsel, O Laxus."

" 'Tis now four days lost," said Laxus. "Thou canst not retrieve them. Howso, be it as thou wilt."

So brake up their council. But the mind and heart of the Lord Gro was nought peaceful within him, but tumultuous with manifold imaginings of hopes and fears and old desires, that intertwined like serpents twisting and contending. So that nought was clear to him save the unclear trouble of his discontent; and it was as if the conscience of a secret grant his inward mind made had suddenly cast a vail betwixt his thoughts and him that he durst not pluck aside.

Betimes on the morrow Corinius let fare against Krothering with all his host, Laxus from the south, Heming and Cargo from the east against the main gates, and himself from the west where the walls and towers showed strongest but the natural strength of the place weaker than elsewhere. Now they within were few, because of Mevrian's sending of those two hundred horse to follow Zigg and those came not back after Switchwater; and as the day wore, and still the battle went forward, and still were wounds given and taken, the odds swung yet heavier against them of Demonland, and more and more must the castle hold of its own strength only, for there were not whole men left enow to man the walls. And now had Corinius well nigh won the castle, faring up on the walls west of the donjon tower where he and his fell to clearing the battlements, rushing on like wolves. But Astar of Rettray stayed him there with so great a sword-stroke on the helm that he overthrew him all astonied[3] down without the wall and into the ditch; but his men drew him forth and saved him. So was the Lord Corinius put out of the fight; but greatly still he egged on his men. And about the fifth hour after noon the sons of Corund gat the main gate.

Lady Mevrian bare in that hour with her own hand a stoup of wine to Astar in a lull of the battle. While he drank, she said, "Astar, the hour demandeth that I pledge thee to obedience, even as I pledged mine own folk and Ravnor that here commandeth my garrison in Krothering."

"My Lady Mevrian," answered he, "under your safety, I shall obey you."

She said, "No conditions, sir. Harken and know. First I will thank thee and these valiant men that so mightily warded us and golden Krothering against our enemies. This was my mind, to ward it unto the last, because it is my dear brother's house, and I count it unworthy Corinius should stable his horses in our chambers, and carousing amid his drunkards do hurt to our fair banquet hall. But now, by hard necessity of disastrous war, hath this thing come to pass, and all fallen into his hand save only this keep alone."

"Alas, madam," said he, "to our shame I may not deny it."

"O trample out any thought of shame," said she. "A score of them against every one of us: the glory of our defence shall be for ever. But not 'tis for me mainly he still beareth against Krothering so great and peisant[4] strokes as thick as rain falleth from the sky. And now must ye obey me and do my commandment; else must we perish, for even this tower we are not enough to hold against him many days."

"Divine Lady," said Astar, "but once shall one pass the cruel pass of death. I and your folk will defend you unto that end."

"Sir," said she, standing like a queen before him, "I shall now defend myself and our precious things in Krothering more certainly than ye men of war may do." And she showed him shortly that this was her design, to yield up the keep unto Corinius under promise of a safe conduct for Astar and Ravnor and all her men.

"And submit thee to this Corinius?" said Astar. But she answered, "Thy sword hath likely cut his claws for awhile. I fear him not."

Of all this would Astar at first have nought to do, and the old steward withal was well nigh mutinous. But so firm of purpose was she, and withal showed them so plainly that this was the only hope to save herself and Krothering, and the Witches must else sack the house of Krothering and in a few days win the keep, "and then, snaky despair; and the fault on't not in fortune but in ourselves, that could not frame ourselves to our fortune"; that at last with heavy hearts they consented to do her bidding.

Without more ado, was a parley called, Mevrian speaking for herself from a high window opening on the court and Gro for Corinius. In which parley it was articled that she should render up the tower; and that the fighting men which were within should have peace and safe passage whither they would; and that there should be no scathe nor outrage done to Krothering neither to the lands thereof; and that all this should be writ down and sealed under the hands of Corinius, Gro, and Laxus, and the gates opened to the Witches and all keys delivered up within an half hour of the giving of the sealed writing into Mevrian's hand.

Now was all this performed accordingly, and Krothering keep rendered to the Lord Corinius. Astar and Ravnor and their men would have abided as prisoners for Mevrian's sake, but Corinius would not suffer it, vowing with bloody imprecations that he would let slay out of hand any man of them he should take after an hour's space within three miles of Krothering. So, under Mevrian's strait commands, they departed.

A KING IN KROTHERING

How the Lord Corinius would take unto himself
a queen in Demonland, and made him a bridal
feast thereto: wherein is a notable instance how
unto them which the gods do love helpers are
raised up and comforters even in the midst of
their enemies.

HAT same evening Corinius let dight a banquet[1] in the Chamber of the Moon for some two score of his chiefest men, a very pompous and kingly entertainment; and conceiving that he might now very well avail to accomplish his pleasure touching the Lady Mevrian, he sent her word by one of his gentlemen that she should attend him there. And she sending answer to tell him gently all else in the castle was at his service, but for herself she was quite fordone[2] and greatly desired rest and sleep that night, he fell a-laughing immoderately and saying, "A most unseasonable desire, and one that smacketh[3] besides of mockery, since well she knoweth what this night I do intend. Wish her to repair to us, and that right swiftly, lest I fetch her."

To that message sent her came she in a short while herself to answer, dressed all in funereal black, her gown and close-fitting bodice of black sendal slashed with black sarcenett,[4] and about her throat a chain of sapphires darkly lustrous. Very nobly she carried her head. Framed with the piled and braided masses of her night-dark hair, her face showed pale indeed, but unruffled and undismayed.

All at her coming in stood up to greet her; and Corinius said, "Lady, thou didst change thy mind quickly since thou didst first affirm thou never wouldst yield up Krothering unto me."

"As quickly as I might, my lord," said she, "for I saw I was wrong."

He abode silent a minute, his eyes like amorous surfeiters over-running her fair form. Then said he, "Thou didst wish to purchase safety for thy friends?"

She answered, "Yes."

"For thine own self," said Corinius, "it had made no jot of difference. Be witness unto me the omnisciency of the Gods, whereunto is nothing concealable, I mean thee only good."

"My lord," said she, "I embrace the comfort of that word. And know that good to me is mine own freedom: not conditions of any man's choosing."

Whereto he, being well tippled with wine, framing the most lovely countenance he might, made answer, "I doubt not but tonight, madam, thou shalt be well advised to choose that highest condition, and till to-day unknown, which I shall proffer thee: to be Queen of Demonland."

She thanked him in her best manner, but said she was minded to forgo that supposedly pleasing eminence.

"How?" said he. "Is it too little a thing for thee? Or is it as I think, that thou laughest?"

She said, "My lord, it should little beseem me that am of the seed of men of war since long generations to trap my mind with the false shows of a greatness that is gone. Yet I pray you forget not this: the dominion of the Demons hath used to soar a pitch above common royalty, and like the eye of day regarded kings from above. And for this style of Queen thou offerest me, I say unto thee it is an addition I desire not, who am sister unto him that writ that writing above the gate that all ye had tasted the truth thereof had he been here to meet with you."

Corinius said, "True it is, some have out-bragged the world, yet I ere this have used them like knaves. My jackboot hath known things in Carcë, madam, I'll not gall thy heart to tell thee of." But perceiving a great lowe of disdainful anger blaze in Mevrian's eye, "Cry you mercy," said he, "incomparable lady; this was beside the mark. I would not sully our new friendship with memories of—— Ho there! a chair beside me for the Queen."

But Mevrian made them set it on the far side of the board, and there sat her down, saying, "I pray thee, my Lord Corinius, unsay that word. Thou knowest it dislikes me."

He looked on her in silence for a minute, leaned forward across the board, his lips parted a little and between them his breath coming and going thick and swift. "Well," he said, "sit there, and it like thee, madam, and manage my delights by stages. Last year the wide world betwixt us: this year the mountains: yestereve Krothering walls: to-night a table's breadth: and ere night be done, not so much as——"

Gro saw the wild-deer look in Lady Mevrian's eyes. She said, "This is talk I have not learned to understand, my lord."

"I shall learn it thee," said Corinius, his face aflame. "Lovers live by love as larks by leeks. By Satan, I do love thee as thou wert the heart out of my body."

"My Lord Corinius," said she, "we ladies of the north have little stomach for these fashions, howe'er they commend them in waterish Witchland. If thou'lt have my friendship, bring me service therefor, and that in season. This is no fit table-talk."

"Why there," said he, "we're in fast agreement. I'll blithely show thee all this, and a quainter thing beside, in thine own chamber. But 'twas beyond my hopes thou'dst grant me that so suddenly. Are we so happy?"

In great shame and anger the Lady Mevrian stood up from the table. Corinius, something unsteadily, leaped to his feet. For all his bigness, so tall she was she looked him level in the eye. And he, as when in the face of a night-ranging beast suddenly a man brandishes a bright light, stood stupid under that gaze, the springs of action strangely frozen in him on a sudden, and said sullenly, "Madam, I am a soldier. Truly mine affection standeth not upon compliment. That I am impatient, put the wite on thy beauty not on me. Pray you, be seated."

But Mevrian answered, "Thy language, my lord, is too bold and vicious. Come to me to-morrow if thou wilt; but I'll have thee know, patience only and courtesy shall get good of me."

She turned to the door. He, as if with the turning away of that lady's eyes the spell was broke, cried loudly upon his folk to stay her. But there was none stirred. Therewith he, as one that cannot command his own indecent appetites, o'ersetting bench and board in eager haste to lay hands on her, it so betided that he tripped up with one of these and fell a-sprawling. And ere he was gotten again on his feet, the Lady Mevrian was gone from the hall.

He rose up painfully, proffering from his lips a mudspring of barbarous and filthy imprecations; so that Laxus who helped raise him up was fain to chide him, saying, "My lord, unman not thyself by such a bestial transformation.[5] Are not we yet with harness on our backs[6] in a kingdom newly gained, the old lords thereof discomfited in deed but not yet ta'en nor slain, studying belike to raise new powers against us? And above such and so many affairs wilt thou make place for the allurements of love?"

"Ay!" answered he. "Nor shall such a sapless ninny as thou avail to cross me therein. Ask thy little gamesome Sriva, when thou comest home to wed her, if I be not better able than thou to please a woman. She'll tell thee! I' the main season meddle not in matters that be too high for such as thou."

Both Gro and the sons of Corund were by and heard those words. The Lord Laxus schooled himself to laugh. He turned toward Gro, saying, "The general is far gone in wine."

Gro, marking Laxus's face flushed red to the ears for all his studied carelessness, answered him softly, " 'Tis so, my lord. And in wine is truth."

Now Corinius, bethinking him that it was yet early and the feast barely well begun, let set a guard on all the passages which led to Mevrian's lodgings, to the end that she might not issue therefrom but there wait on his pleasure. That done, he bade renew their feasting.

No stint of luscious meats and wines was there, and the lords of Witchland sat them down again right eagerly to the good banquet. Laxus spoke secretly to Gro: "I wot well thou takest in very ill part these doings. Let it stand firm in thy mind that if thou shouldst deem it fitting to play him a trick and steal the lady from him, I'll not stand i' the way on't."

"In a bunch of cards," said Gro, "knaves wait upon the kings. It were not so ill done and we made it so here. I heard a bird sing lately thou hadst a quarrel to him."

"Thou must not think so," answered Laxus. "I'll give thee still a Roland for thine Oliver,[7] and tell thee 'tis most apparent thyself dost love this lady."

Gro said, "Thou chargest me with a sweet folly is foreign to my nature, being a grave scholar that if ever I did frequent such toys have long eschewed them. Only meseems 'tis an ill thing if she must be given over unto him against her will. Thou knowest him of a rough and mere soldierly mind, besides his dissolute company with other women."

"Tush," said Laxus, "he may go his gate[8] for me, and be as close as a butterfly with the lady. But out of policy, 'twere best rid her hence. I'd not be seen in't. That provided, I'll second thee all ways. If he lie here the summer long in amorous dalliance, justly might the King abraid us that midst o' the day's sport we gave his good hawk a gorge, and so lost him the game."

"I see," said Gro, smiling in himself, "thou art a man of sober government and understanding, and thinkest first of Witchland. And that is both just and right."

Now went the feast forward with great surfeiting and swigging of wine. Mevrian's women that were there, much against their own good will, to serve the banquet, set ever fresh dishes before the feasters and poured forth fresh wines, golden and tawny and ruby-red, in the goblets of jade and crystal and hammered gold. The air in the fair chamber was thick with the steam of bake-meats and the vinous breath of the feasters, so that the lustre of the opal lamps burned coppery, and about each lamp was a bush of coppery beams like the beams about a torch that burns in a fog. Great was the clatter of cups, and great the clinking of glass as in their drunkenness the Witches cast down the priceless beakers on the floor, smashing them in shivers. And huge din there was of laughter and song; and amidst of it, women's voices singing, albeit near drowned in the hurly burly. For they constrained Mevrian's damosels in Krothering to sing and dance before them, howsoever woeful at heart. And to other entertainment than this of dance and song was many a black-bearded reveller willing to constrain them; and sought occasion thereto, but this by stealth only, and out of eye-shot of their general. For heavily enow was his wrath fallen on some who rashly flaunted in his face their light disports, presuming to hunt in such fields while their lord went still a-fasting.

After a while Heming, who sat next to Gro, began to say to him in a whisper, "This is an ill banquet."

"Meseems rather 'tis a very good banquet," said Gro.

"Would I saw some other issue thereof," said Heming, "than that he purposeth. Or how thinkest thou?"

"I scarce can blame him," answered Gro. " 'Tis a most lovesome lady."

"Is not the man a most horrible open swine? And is it to be endured that he should work his lewd purpose on so sweet a lady?"

"What have I to do with it?" said Gro.

"What less than I?" said Heming.

"It dislikes thee?" said Gro.

"Art thou a man?" said Heming. "And she that hateth him besides as bloody Atropos!"[9]

Gro looked him a swift searching look in the eye. Then he whispered, his head bowed over some raisins he was a-picking: "If this is thy mind, 'tis well." And speaking softly, with here and there some snatch of louder discourse or jest between whiles lest he should seem too earnestly engaged in secret talk, he taught Heming orderly and clearly what he had to do, discovering to him that Laxus also, being bit with jealousy, was of their accord. "Thy brother Cargo is aptest for this. He standeth about her height, and by reason of his youth is yet beardless. Go find him out. Rehearse unto him word by word all this talking that hath been between me and thee. Corinius holdeth me too deep suspect to suffer me out of his eye to-night. Unto you sons of Corund therefore is the task; and I biding at his elbow may avail to hold him here i' the hall till it be performed. Go; and wise counsel and good speed wait on your attempts."

The Lady Mevrian, being escaped to her own chamber in the south tower, sat by an eastern window that looked across the gardens and the lake, past the sea-lochs of Stropardon and the dark hills of Eastmark, to the stately ranges afar which overhang in mid-air Mosedale and Murkdale and Swartriverdale and the inland sea of Throwater. The last lights of day still lingered on their loftier summits: on Ironbeak, on the gaunt wall of Skarta, and on the distant twin towers of Dina seen beyond the lower Mosedale range in the depression of Neverdale Hause. Behind them rolled up the ascent of heaven the wheels of quiet Night: holy Night, mother of the Gods, mother of sleep, tender nurse of all little birds and beasts that dwell in the field and all tired hearts and weary: mother besides of strange children, affrights, and rapes, and midnight murders bold.

Mevrian sat there till all the earth was blurred in darkness and the sky a-throb with starlight, for it was yet an hour until the rising of the moon. And she prayed to Lady Artemis, calling her by her secret names and saying, "Goddess and Maiden chaste and holy; triune Goddess, Which in heaven art, and on the earth Huntress divine, and also hast in the veiled sunless places below earth Thy dwelling, viewing the large stations of the dead: save me and keep me that am Thy maiden still."

She turned the ring upon her finger and scanned in the gathering gloom the bezel thereof, which was of that chrysoprase that is hid in light and seen in darkness, being as a flame by night but in the day-time yellow or wan. And behold, it palpitated with splendour from withinward, and was as if a thousand golden sparks danced and swirled within the stone.

While she pondered what interpretation lay likeliest on this

sudden flowering of unaccustomed splendour within the chrysoprase, behold, one of her women of the bedchamber who brought
lights said, standing before her, "Twain of those lords of Witchland would speak with your ladyship in private."

"Two?" said Mevrian. "There's safety yet in numbers. Which
be they?"

"Highness, they be tall and slim of body. They be black-
advised. They bear them discreet as dormice, and most commend-
ably sober."

Mevrian asked, "Is it the Lord Gro? Hath he a great black
beard, much curled and perfumed?"

"Highness, I marked not that either weareth a beard," said the
woman, "nor their names I know not."

"Well," said Mevrian, "admit them. And do thou and thy
fellows attend me while I give them audience."

So it was done according to her bidding. And there entered in
those two sons of Corund.

They greeted her with respectful salutations, and Heming
said, "Our errand, most worshipful lady, was for thine own ear
only if it please thee."

Mevrian said to her women, "Make fast the doors, and attend
me in the ante-chamber. And now, my lords," said she, and waited
for them to begin.

She was seated sideways in the window, betwixt the light and
the dark. The crystal lamps shining from within the room showed
deeper darknesses in her hair than night's darkness without. The
curve of her white arms resting in her lap was like the young moon
cradled above the sunset. A falling breeze out of the south came
laden with the murmur of the sea, far away beyond fields and
vineyards, restlessly surging even in that calm weather amid the
sea-caves of Stropardon. It was as if the sea and the night enfolding
Demonland gasped in indignation at such things as Corinius, holding himself already an undoubted possessor of his desires, devised
for that night in Krothering.

Those brethren stood abashed in the presence of such rare
beauty. Heming with a deep breath spake and said, "Madam, what
slender opinion soever thou hast held of us of Witchland, I pray
thee be satisfied that I and my kinsman have sought to thee now
with a clean heart to do thee service."

"Princes," said she, "scarce might ye blame me did I misdoubt
you. Yet, seeing that my life's days have been not among
ambidexters and coney-catchers but lovers of clean hands and
open dealing, not even after that which I this night endured will

mine heart believe that all civility is worn away in Witchland. Did I
not freely receive Corinius's self when I did open my gates to him,
firmly believing him to be a king and not a ravening wolf?"

Then said Heming, "Canst thou wear armour, madam? Thou
art something of an height with my brother. To bring thee past the
guard, if thou go armed, as I shall conduct thee, the wine they have
drunken shall be thy minister. I have provided an horse. In the
likeness of my young brother mayst thou ride forth to-night out of
this castle, and win clean away. But in thine own shape thou mayst
never pass from these thy lodgings, for he hath set a guard
thereon; being resolved, come thereof what may, to visit thee here
this night: in thine own chamber, madam."

The sounds of furious revelry floated up from the banquet
chamber. Mevrian heard by snatches the voice of Corinius singing
an unseemly song. As in the presence of some dark influence that
threatened an ill she might not comprehend, yet felt her blood
quail and her heart grow sick because of it, she looked on those
brethren.

She said at last, "Was this your plan?"

Heming answered, "It was the Lord Gro did most ingeniously
conceive it. But Corinius, as he hath ever held him in distrust, and
most of all when he hath drunken overmuch, keepeth him most
firmly at his elbow."

Cargo now did off his armour, and Mevrian calling in her
women to take this and other gear fared straightway to an inner
chamber to change her fashion.

Heming said to his brother, "Thou shalt need to go about it
with great circumspection, to come off when we are gone so as
thou be not aspied. Were I thou, I should be tempted for the
rareness of the jest to await his coming, and assay whether thou
couldst not make as good a counterfeit Mevrian as she a counterfeit Cargo."

"Thou," said Cargo, "mayst well laugh and be gay, thou that
must conduct her. And art resolved, I dare lay my head to a turnip,
to do thy utmost endeavour to despoil Corinius of that felicity he
hath to-night decreed him, and bless thyself therewith."

"Thou hast fallen," answered Heming, "into a most barbarous thought. Shall my tongue be so false a traitor to mine heart as
to say I love not this lady? Compare but her beauty and my youth
together, how should it other be? But with such a height of fervour
I do love her that I'd as lief offer violence to a star of heaven, as
require of her aught but honest."

Said Cargo, "What said the wise little boy to's elder brother?

'Sith thou'st gotten the cake, brother, I must e'en make shift with the crumbs.' When you are gone, and all whisht and quiet, and I left here amid the waiting women, it shall go hard but I'll teach 'em somewhat afore good-night."

Now opened the door of the inner chamber, and there stood before them the Lady Mevrian armed and helmed. She said, " 'Tis no light matter to halt before a cripple. Think you this will pass i' the dark, my lords?"

They answered, 'twas beyond all commendation excellent.

"I'll thank thee now, Prince Cargo," said she, stretching out her hand. He bowed and kissed it in silence. "This harness," she said, "shall be a keepsake unto me of a noble enemy. Would some-day I might call thee friend, for suchwise hast thou borne thee this night."

Therewith, bidding young Cargo adieu, she with his brother went forth from the chamber and through the ante-chamber to that shadowy stairway where Corinius's soldiers stood sentinel. These (as many more be drowned in the beaker than in the ocean), not over-heedful after their tipplings, seeing two go by together with clanking armour and knowing Heming's voice when he an-swered the challenge, made no question but here were Corund's sons returning to the banquet.

So passed he and she lightly by the sentinels. But as they fared by the lofty corridor without the Chamber of the Moon, the doors of that chamber opening suddenly left and right there came forth torch-bearers and minstrels two by two as in a progress, with cymbals clashing and flutes and tambourines, so that the corridor was fulfilled with the flare of flamboys and the din. In the midst walked the Lord Corinius. The lusty blood within him burned scarlet in all his shining face, and made stand the veins like cords on the strong neck and arms and hands of him. The thick curls above his brow where they strayed below his coronal of sleeping nightshade were a-drip with sweat. Plain it was he was in no good trim, after that shrewd knock on the head Astar that day had given him, to withstand deep quaffings. He went between Gro and Laxus, swaying heavily now on the arm of this one now of the other, his right hand beating time to the music of the bridal song.

Mevrian whispered to Heming, "Let us bear out a good face so long as we be alive."

They stood aside, hoping to be passed by unnoticed, for re-treat nor concealment was there none. But Corinius his eye light-ing on them stopped and hailed them, catching them each by an arm, and crying, "Heming, thou'rt drunk! Cargo, thou'rt drunk, sweet youth! 'Tis a damnable folly, drink as drunk as you be, and these bonny wenches I've provided you. How shall I satisfy 'em, think ye, when they come to me with their plaints to-morn, that each must sit with a snoring drunkard's head in her lap the night long?"

Mevrian, as if she had all her part by rote, was leaned this while heavily upon Heming, hanging her head.

Heming could think on nought likelier to say, than, "Truly, O Corinius, we be sober."

"Thou liest," said Corinius. " 'Twas ever sign manifest of drunkenness to deny it. Look you, my lords, I deny not I am drunk. Therefore is sign manifest I am drunk, I mean, sign manifest I am sober. But the hour calleth to other work than questioning of these high matters. Set on!"

So speaking he reeled heavily against Gro, and (as if moved by some airy influence that, whispering him of schemings afoot, yet conspired with the wine that he had drunken to make him look all otherwhere for treason than where it lay under his hand to dis-cover it) gripped Gro by the arm, saying, "Bide by me, Goblin, thou wert best. I do love thee very discreetly, and will still hold thee by the ears, to see thou bite me not, nor go no more a-gad-ding."

Being by such happy fortune delivered out of this peril, Hem-ing and Mevrian with what prudent haste they might, and without mishap or hindrance, got them their horses and fared forth of the main gate between the marble hippogriffs, whose mighty forms shone above them stark in the low beams of the rising moon. So they rode silently through the gardens and the home-meads and thence to the wild woods beyond, quickening now their pace to a gallop on the yielding turf. So hard they rode, the air of the wind-less April night was lashed into storm about their faces. The tram-ple and thunder of hoofbeats and the flying glimpses of the trees were to young Heming but an undertone to the thunder of his blood which night and speed and that lady galloping beside him knee to knee set a-gallop within him. But to Mevrian's soul, as she galloped along those woodland rides, those moonlight glades, these things and night and the steadfast stars attuned a heavenlier music; so that she waxed momently wondrous peaceful at heart, as with the most firm assurance that not without the abiding glory of Demonland must the great mutations of the world be acted, and but for a little should their evil-willers usurp her dear brother's seat in Krothering.

They drew rein in a clearing beside a broad stretch of water.

Pine-woods rose from its further edge, shadowy in the moonshine. Mevrian rode to a little eminence that stood above the water and turned her eyes toward Krothering. Save by her instructed and loving eye scarce might it be seen, many miles away be-east of them, dimmed in the obscure soft radiance under the moon. So sat she awhile looking on golden Krothering, while her horse grazed quietly, and Heming at her elbow held his peace, only beholding her.

At last, looking back and meeting his gaze, "Prince Heming," she said, "from this place goeth a hidden path north-about beside the firth, and a dry road over the marsh, and a ford and an upland horse-way leadeth into Westmark. Here and all-wheres in Demonland I might fare blindfold. And here I'll say farewell. My tongue is a poor orator. But I mind me of the words of the poet where he saith:

> My mind is like to the asbeston stone,
> Which if it once be heat in flames of fire,
> Denieth to becomen cold again.

Be the latter issue of these wars in my great kinsmen's victory, as I most firmly trow it shall be, or in Gorice's his, I shall not forget this experiment of your nobility manifested unto me this night."

But Heming, still beholding her, answered not a word.

She said, "How fares the Queen thy step-mother? Seven summers ago this summer I was in Norvasp at Lord Corund's wedding feast, and stood by her at the bridal. Is she yet so fair?"

He answered, "Madam, as June bringeth the golden rose unto perfection, so waxeth her beauty with the years."

"She and I," said Mevrian, "were playmates, she the elder by two summers. Is she yet so masterful?"

"Madam, she is a Queen," said Heming, nailing his very eyes on Mevrian. Her face half turned towards him, sweet mouth half closed, clear eyes uplifted toward the east, showed dim in the glamour of the moon, and the lilt of her body was as a lily fallen a-dreaming beside some enchanted lake at midnight. With a dry throat he said, "Lady, until to-night I had not supposed there lived on earth a woman more beautiful than she."

Therewith the love that was in him went like a wind and like an up-swooping darkness athwart his brain. As one who has too long, unbold, unresolved, delayed to lift that door's latch which must open on his heart's true home, he caught his arms about her. Her cheek was soft to his kiss, but deadly cold: her eyes like a wild bird's caught in a purse-net. His brother's armour that cased her body was not so dead nor so hard under his hand, as to his love that yielding cheek, that alien look. He said, as one a-stagger for his wits in the presence of some unlooked-for chance, "Thou dost not love me?"

Mevrian shook her head, putting him gently away.

Like the passing of a fire on a dry heath in summer the flame of his passion was passed by, leaving but a smouldering desolation of scornful sullen wrath: wrath at himself and fate.

He said, in a low shamed voice, "I pray you forgive me, madam."

Mevrian said, "Prince, the Gods give thee good-night. Be kind to Krothering. I have left there an evil steward."

So saying, she reined up her horse's head and turned down westward towards the firth. Heming watched her an instant, his brain a-reel. Then, striking spurs to his horse's flanks so that the horse reared and plunged, he rode away at a great pace east again through the woods to Krothering.

XXV

LORD GRO AND THE
LADY MEVRIAN

How the Lord Gro, conducted by a strange
enamourment with lost causes, fared with none
save this to be his guide into the regions of
Neverdale, and there beheld wonders, and tasted
again for a season the goodness of those things
he did most desire.

INETY days and a day after these doings aforesaid, in
the last hour before the dawn, was the Lord Gro a-riding toward the paling east down from the hills of
Eastmark to the fords of Mardardale. At a walking
pace his horse came down to the water-side, and
halted with fetlocks awash: his flanks were wet and his wind gone,
as from swift faring on the open fell since midnight. He stretched
down his neck, sniffed the fresh river-water, and drank. Gro turned
in the saddle, listening, his left hand thrown forward to slack the
reins, his right flat-planted on the crupper. But nought there was
to hear save the babble of waters in the shallows, the sucking noise
of the horse drinking, and the plash and crunch of his hooves when
he shifted feet among the pebbles. Before and behind and on
either hand the woods and strath[1] and circling hills showed dim in
the obscure gray betwixt darkness and twilight. A light mist hid the
stars. Nought stirred save an owl that flitted like a phantom out
from a hollybush in a craggy bluff a bow-shot or more down

284

stream, crossing Gro's path and lighting on a branch of a dead tree above him on the left, where she sat as if to observe the goings of this man and horse that trespassed in this valley of quiet night.

Gro leaned forward to pat his horse's neck. "Come, gossip,[2] we must on," he said; "and marvel not if thou find no rest, going with me which could never find any steadfast stay under the moon's globe." So they forded that river, and fared through low rough grass-lands beyond, and by the skirts of a wood up to an open heath, and so a mile or two, still eastward, till they turned to the right down a broad valley and crossed a river above a waters-meet, and so east again up the bed of a stony stream and over this to a rough mountain track that crossed some boggy ground and then climbed higher and higher above the floor of the narrowing valley to a pass between the hills. At length the slope slackened, and they passing, as through a gateway, between two high moun-tains which impended sheer and stark on either hand, came forth upon a moor of ling and bog-myrtle, strewn with lakelets[3] and abounding in streams and mosshags and outcrops of the living rock; and the mountain peaks afar stood round that moorland waste like warrior kings. Now was colour waking in the eastern heavens, the bright shining morning beginning to clear the earth. Conies[4] scurried to cover before the horse's feet: small birds flew up from the heather: some red deer stood at gaze in the fern, then tripped away southward: a moorcock[5] called.

Gro said in himself, "How shall not common opinion account me mad, so rash and presumptuous dangerously to put my life in hazard? Nay, against all sound judgement; and this folly I enact in that very season when by patience and courage and my politic wisdom I had won that in despite of fortune's teeth which obsti-nately hitherto she had denied me: when after the brunts of divers tragical fortunes I had marvellously gained the favour and grace of the King, who very honourably placed me in his court, and tender-eth me, I well think, so dearly as he doth the balls of his two eyes."

He put off his helm, baring his white forehead and smooth black curling locks to the airs of morning, flinging back his head to drink deep through his nostrils the sweet strong air and its peaty smell. "Yet is common opinion the fool, not I," he said. "He that imagineth after his labours to attain unto lasting joy, as well may he beat water in a mortar. Is there not in the wild benefit of nature instances enow to laugh this folly out of fashion? A fable of great men that arise and conquer the nations: Day goeth up against the tyrant night. How delicate a spirit is she, how like a fawn she footeth it upon the mountains: pale pitiful light matched with the primeval dark. But every sweet hovers in her battalions, and every heavenly influence: coolth[6] of the wayward little winds of morning, flowers awakening, birds a-carol, dews a-sparkle on the fine-drawn webs the tiny spinners hang from fern-frond to thorn, from thorn to wet dainty leaf of the silver birch; the young day laughing in her strength, wild with her own beauty; fire and life and every scent and colour born anew to triumph over chaos and slow darkness and the kinless night.

"But because day at her dawning hours hath so bewitched me, must I yet love her when glutted with triumph she settles to garish noon? Rather turn as now I turn to Demonland, in the sad sunset of her pride. And who dares call me turncoat, who do but follow now as I have followed this rare wisdom all my days: to love the sunrise and the sundown and the morning and the evening star? Since there only abideth the soul of nobility, true love, and wonder, and the glory of hope and fear."

So brooding he rode at an easy pace bearing east and a little north across the moor, falling because of the strange harmony that was between outward things and the inward thoughts of his heart into a deep study. So came he to the moor's end, and entered among the skirts of the mountains beyond, crossing low passes, threading a way among woods and water-courses, up and down, about and about. The horse led him which way that he would, for no heed nor advice had he of aught about him, for cause of the deep contemplation that he had within himself.

It was now high noon. The horse and his rider were come to a little dell of green grass with a beck[7] winding in the midst with cool water flowing over a bed of shingle. About the dell grew many trees both tall and straight. Above the trees high mountain crags a-bake in the sun showed ethereal through the shimmering heat. A murmur of waters, a hum of tiny wings flitting from flower to flower, the sound of the horse grazing on the lush pasture: there was nought else to hear. Not a leaf moved, not a bird. The hush of the summer noon-day, breathless, burnt through with the sun, more awful than any shape of night, paused above that lonely dell.

Gro, as if waked by the very silence, looked quickly about him. The horse felt belike in his bones his rider's unease; he gave over his feeding and stood alert with wild eye and quivering flanks. Gro patted and made much of him; then, guided by some inward prompting the reason whereof he knew not, turned west by a small tributary beck and rode softly toward the wood. Here he was stopped with a number of trees so thickly placed together that he was afraid he should with riding through be swept from the saddle.

So he lighted down, tied his horse to an oak, and climbed the bed of the little stream till he was come whence he might look north over the tree-tops to a green terrace about at a level with him and some fifty paces distant along the hillside, shielded from the north by three or four great rowan trees on the far side of it, and on the terrace a little tarn or rock cistern of fair water very cool and deep.

He paused, steadying himself with his left hand by a jutting rock overgrown with rose-campion. Surely no children of men were these, footing it on that secret lawn beside that fountain's brink, nor no creatures of mortal kind. Such it may be were the goats and kids and soft-eyed does that on their hind-legs merrily danced among them; but never such those others of manly shape and with pointed hairy ears, shaggy legs, and cloven hooves, nor those maidens white of limb beneath the tread of whose feet the blue gentian and the little golden cinque-foil bent not their blossoms, so airy-light was their dancing. To make them music, little goat-footed children with long pointed ears sat on a hummock of turf-clad rock piping on pan-pipes, their bodies burnt to the hue of red earth by the wind and the sun. But, whether because their music was too fine for mortal ears, or for some other reason, Gro might hear no sound of that piping. The heavy silence of the waste white noon was lord of the scene, while the mountain nymphs and the simple genii of sedge and stream and crag and moorland solitude threaded the mazes of the dance.

The Lord Gro stood still in great admiration, saying in himself, "What means my drowsy head to dream such fancies? Spirits of ill have I heretofore beheld in their manifestations; I have seen fantasticoes framed and presented by art magic; I have dreamed strange dreams anights. But till this hour I did account it an idle tale of poets' faining, that amid woods, forests, fertile fields, seacoasts, shores of great rivers and fountain brinks, and also upon the tops of huge and high mountains, do still appear unto certain favoured eyes the sundry-sorted nymphs and fieldish demigods. Which thing if I now verily behold, 'tis a great marvel, and sorteth well with the strange allurements whereby this oppressed land hath so lately found a means to govern mine affections." And he thought awhile, reasoning thus in his mind: "If this be but an apparition, it hath no essence to do me a hurt. If o' the contrary these be very essential beings, needs must they joyfully welcome me and use me well, being themselves the true vital spirits of many-mountained Demonland; unto whose comfort and the restorement of her old renown and praise I have with such a strange determination bent all my painful thoughts and resolution."

So on the motion he discovered himself and hailed them. The wild things bounded away and were lost among the flanks of the hill. The capripeds,[8] leaving on the instant their piping or their dancing, crouched watching him with distrustful startled eyes. Only the Oreads[9] still in a dazzling drift pursued their round: quiet maiden mouths, beautiful breasts, slender lithe limbs, hand joined to delicate hand, parting and closing and parting again, in rhythms of unstaled variety; here one that, with white arms clasped behind her head where her braided hair was as burnished gold, circled and swayed with a langourous motion; here another, that leaped and paused hovering a-tiptoe, like an arrow of the sun shot through the leafy roof of an old pine-forest when the warm hill-wind stirs the tree-tops and opens a tiny window to the sky.

Gro went toward them along the grassy hillside. When he was come a dozen paces the strength was gone from his limbs. He kneeled down crying out and saying, "Divinities of earth! deny me not, neither reject me, albeit cruelly have I till now oppressed your land, but will do so no more. The footsteps of mine overtrodden virtue lie still as bitter accusations unto me. Bring me of your mercy where I may find out them that possessed this land and offer them atonement, who were driven forth because of me and mine to be outlaws in the woods and mountains."

So spake he, bowing his head in sorrow. And he heard, like the trembling of a silver lute-string, a voice in the air that cried:

> North 'tis and north 'tis!
> Why need we further?

He raised his eyes. The vision was gone. Only the noon and the woodland, silent, solitary, dazzling, were about and above him.

Lord Gro came now to his horse again, and mounted and rode northaway through the fells all that summer afternoon, full of cloudy fancies. When it was eventide his way was high up along the steep side of a mountain between the screes and the grass, following a little path made by the wild sheep. Far beneath in the valley was a small river tortuously flowing along a bouldery bed amid hillocks of old moraines which were like waves of a sea of grass-clad earth. The July sun wheeled low, flinging the shadows of the hills far up the westward-facing slopes where Gro was a-riding, but where he rode and above him the hillside was yet aglow with the warm low sunshine; and the distant peak that shut in the head of the valley, rearing his huge front like the gable of a house, with sweeping ribs of bare rock and scree and a crest of crag like a great breaker frozen to stone in mid career, bathed yet in a radiance of opalescent light.

Turning the shoulder of the hillside at a place where the hill was cut by a shallow gully, he saw before him a hollow or sheltered nook. There, protected by the great body of the hill from the blasts of the east and north, two rowan trees and some hollies grew in the clefts of the rock above the watercourse. Under their shadow was a cave, not large but so big as a man might well abide in and be dry in wild weather, and beyond it on the right a little waterfall, so beautiful it was a wonder to behold. This was the fashion of it: a slab of rock, twice a man's height, tilted a little forward from the hill, so that the water fell clear from its upper edge in a thin stream into a rocky basin. The water in the basin was clear and deep, but a-churn always with bubbles from the plunging jet from above; and over all the rocks about it grew mosses and lichens and little water-flowers, nourished by the stream at root and refreshed by the spray.

The Lord Gro said in his heart, "Here would I dwell for ever had I but the art to make myself little as an eft.[10] And I would build me an house a span high beside yonder cushion of moss emerald-hued, with those pink foxgloves to shade my door which balance their bells above the foaming waters. This shy grass of Parnassus[11] should be my drinking cup, with pure white chalice poised on a hair-thin stem; and the curtains of my bed that little thirsty sand-wort which, like a green heaven sown with milk-white stars, curtains the shady sides of these rocks."

Resting in this imagination he abode long time looking on that fairy place, so secretly bestowed in the fold of the naked mountain. Then, unwilling to depart from so fair a spot, and bethinking him, besides, that after so many hours his horse was weary, he dismounted and lay down beside the stream. And in a short while, having his spirits sublimed with the sweet imagination of those wonders he had beheld, he was fain to suffer the long dark lashes to droop over his large and liquid eyes. And deep sleep overcame him.

When he awoke, all the sky was afire with the red of sunset. A shadow was betwixt him and the western light: the shape of one bending over him and saying in masterful wise, yet in accents wherein the echoes and memories of all sweet sounds seemed mingled and laid up at rest for ever, "Lie still, my lord, nor cry not a rescue. Behold, thine own sword; and I took it from thee sleeping." And he was ware of a sharp sword pointed against his throat where the big veins lie beneath the tongue.

He stirred not at all, neither spake aught, only looking up at her as at some vision of delight strayed from the fugitive flock of dreams.

The lady said, "Where by thy company? And how many? Answer me swiftly."

He answered her like a dreamer, "How shall I answer thee? How shall I number them that be beyond all count? Or how name unto your grace their habitation which are even very now closer to me than hand or feet, yet o' the next instant are able to transcend a main wilder belike than even a starbeam hath journeyed o'er?"

She said, "Riddle me no riddles. Answer me, thou wert best."

"Madam," said Gro, "these that I told thee of be the company of mine own silent thoughts. And, but for mine horse, this is all the company that came hither with me."

"Alone?" said she. "And sleep so securely in thine enemies' country? That showed a strange confidence."

"Not enemies, if I may," said he.

But she cried, "And thou Lord Gro of Witchland?"

"That one sickened long since," he answered, "of a mortal sickness; and 'tis now a day and a night since he is dead thereof."

"What art thou, then?" said she.

He answered, "If your grace would so receive me, Lord Gro of Demonland."

"A very practised turncoat," said she. "Belike they also are wearied of thee and thy ways. Alas," she said in an altered voice, "thy gentle pardon! when doubtless it was for thy generous deeds to me-ward they fell out with thee, when thou didst so nobly befriend me."

"I will tell your highness," answered he, "the pure truth. Never stood matters better 'twixt me and all of them than when yesternight I resolved to leave them."

The Lady Mevrian was silent, a cloud in her face. Then, "I am alone," she said. "Therefore think it not little-hearted in me, nor forgetful of past benefits, if I will be further certified of thee ere I suffer thee to rise. Swear to me thou wilt not betray me."

But Gro said, "How should an oath from me avail thee, madam? Oaths bind not an ill man. Were I minded to do thee wrong, lightly should I swear thee all oaths thou mightest require, and lightly o' the next instant be forsworn."

"That is not well said," said Mevrian. "Nor helpeth not thy safety. You men do say that women's hearts be faint and feeble, but

I shall show thee the contrary is in me. Study to satisfy me. Else will I assuredly smite thee to death with thine own sword."

The Lord Gro lay back, clasping his slender hands behind his head. "Stand, I pray thee," said he, "o' the other side of me, that I may see thy face."

She did so, still threatening him with the sword. And he said smiling, "Divine lady, all my days have I had danger for my bedfellow, and peril of death for my familiar friend; whilom leading a delicate life in princely court, where murther sitteth in the wine-cup and in the alcove; whilom journeying alone in more perilous lands than this, as witness the Moruna, where the country is full of venomous beasts and crawling poisoned serpents, and the divels be as abundant there as grasshoppers on a hot hillside in summer. He that feareth is a slave, were he never so rich, were he never so powerful. But he that is without fear is king of all the world. Thou hast my sword. Strike. Death shall be a sweet rest to me. Thraldom, not death, should terrify me."

She paused awhile, then said unto him, "My Lord Gro, thou didst do me once a right great good turn. Surely I may build my safety on this, that never yet did kite bring forth a good flying hawk."[12] She shifted her hold on his sword, and very prettily gave it him hilt-foremost, saying, "I give it thee back, my lord, nothing doubting that that which was given in honour thou wilt honourably use."

But he, rising up, said, "Madam, this and thy noble words hath given such rootfastness to the pact of faith betwixt us that it may now unfold what blossom of oaths thou wilt; for oaths are the blossom of friendship, not the root. And thou shalt find me a true holder of my vowed amity unto thee without spot or wrinkle."

For sundry nights and days abode Gro and Mevrian in that place, hunting at whiles to get their sustenance, drinking of the sweet spring-water, sleeping a-nights, she in her cave beneath the holly bushes and the rowans beside the waterfall, he in a cleft of the rocks a little below in the gully, where the moss made cushions soft and resilient as the great stuffed beds in Carcë. In those days she told him of her farings since that night of April when she escaped out of Krothering: how first she found harbourage at By in Westmark, but hearing in a day or two of a hue and cry fled east again, and sojourning awhile beside Throwater came at length about a month ago upon this cave beside the little fountain, and here abode. Her mind had been to win over the mountains to Galing, but she had after the first attempt given over that design, for fear of companies of the enemy whose hands she barely escaped when she came forth into the lower valleys that open on the eastern coast-lands. So she had turned again to this hiding place in the hills, as secret and remote as any in Demonland. For this dale she let him know was Neverdale, where no road ran save the way of the deer and the mountain goats, and no garth[13] opened on that dale, and the reek of no man's hearthstone burdened the winds that blew thither. And that gable-crested peak at the head of the dale was the southernmost of the Forks of Nantreganon, nursery of the vulture and the eagle. And a hidden way was round the right shoulder of that peak, over the toothed ridge by Neverdale Hause to the upper waters of Tivarandardale.

On an afternoon of sultry summer heat it so befell that they rested below the hause on a bastion of rock that jutted from the south-western slope. Beneath their feet precipices fell suddenly away from a giddy verge, sweeping round in a grand cirque above which the mountain rose like some Tartarian fortress, ponderous, cruel as the sea and sad, scarred and gashed with great lines of cleavage as though the face of the mountain had been slashed away by the axe-stroke of a giant. In the depths the waters of Dule Tarn slept placid and fathomless.

Gro was stretched on the brink of the cliff, face downward, propped on his two elbows, studying those dark waters. "Surely," he said, "the great mountains of the world are a present remedy if men did but know it against our modern discontent and ambitions. In the hills is wisdom's fount. They are deep in time. They know the ways of the sun and the wind, the lightning's fiery feet, the frost that shattereth, the rain that shroudeth, the snow that putteth about their nakedness a softer coverlet than fine lawn: which if their large philosophy question not if it be a bridal sheet or a shroud, hath not this unpolicied calm his justification ever in the returning year, and is it not an instance to laugh our carefulness out of fashion? of us, little children of the dust, children of a day, who with so many burdens do burden us with taking thought and with fears and desires and devious schemings of the mind, so that we wax old before our time and fall weary ere the brief day be spent and one reaping-hook gather us home at last for all our pains."

He looked up and she met the gaze of his great eyes; deep pools of night they seemed, where strange matters might move unseen, disturbing to look on, yet filled with a soft slumbrous charm that lulled and soothed.

"Thou'st fallen a-dreaming, my lord," said Mevrian. "And for me 'tis a hard thing to walk with thee in thy dreams, who am awake in the broad daylight and would be a-doing."

"Certes it is an ill thing," said Lord Gro, "that thou, who hast not been nourished in mendicity or poverty but in superfluity of honour and largesse, shouldst be made fugitive in thine own dominions, to lodge with foxes and beasts of the wild mountain."

Said she, "It is yet a sweeter lodging than is to-day in Krothering. It is therefore I chafe to do somewhat. To win through to Galing, that were something."

"What profit is in Galing," said Gro, "without Lord Juss?"

She answered, "Thou wilt tell me it is even as Krothering without my brother."

Looking sidelong up at her, where she sat armed beside him, he beheld a tear a-tremble on her eyelid. He said gently, "Who shall foreknow the ways of Fate? Your highness is better here belike."

Lady Mevrian stood up. She pointed to a print in the living rock before her feet. "The hippogriff's hoofmark!" she cried, "stricken in the rock ages ago by that high bird which presideth from of old over the predestined glory of our line, to point us on to a fame advanced above the region of the glittering stars. True is the word that that land which is in the governance of a woman only is not surely kept. I will abide idly here no more."

Gro, beholding her so stand all armed on that high brink of crag, setting with so much perfection in womanly beauty manlike valour, bethought him that here was that true embodiment of morn and eve, that charm which called him from Krothering, and for which the prophetic spirits of mountain and wood and field had pointed his path with a heavenly benison, meaning to bid him go northward to his heart's true home. He kneeled down and caught her hand in his, embracing and kissing it as of her in whom all his hopes were placed, and saying passionately, "Mevrian, Mevrian, let me but be armed in thy good grace and I defy whatever there is or can be against me. Even as the sun lighteth broad heaven at noon-day, and that giveth light unto this dreary earth, so art thou the true light of Demonland which because of thee maketh the whole world glorious. Welcome unto me be all miseries, so only unto thee I may be welcome."

She sprang back, snatching away her hand. Her sword leapt singing from the scabbard. But Gro, that was so ravished and abused that he remembered of nothing worldly but only that he beheld his lady's face, abode motionless. She cried, "Back to back! Swift, or 'tis too late!"

He leaped up, barely in time. Six stout fellows, soldiers of Witchland stolen softly upon them at unawares, closed now upon them. No breath to waste in parley, but the clank of steel: he and Mevrian back to back on a table of rock, those six setting on from either side. "Kill the Goblin," said they. "Take the lady unhurt: 'tis death to all if she be touched."

So for a time those two defended them of all their power. Yet at such odds could not the issue stand long in doubt, nor Gro's high mettle make up what he lacked of strength bodily and skill in arms. Cunning of fence indeed was the Lady Mevrian, as they guessed not to their hurt; for the first of them, a great chuff-headed fellow that thought to bear her down with rushing in upon her, she with a deft thrust passing his guard ran clean through the throat; by whose taking off, his fellows took some lesson of caution. But Gro being at length brought to earth with many wounds, they had the next instant caught Mevrian from behind whiles others engaged her in the face, when in the nick of time as by the intervention of heaven was all their business taken in reverse, and all five in a moment laid bleeding on the stones beside their fellows.

Mevrian, looking about and seeing what she saw, fell weak and faint in her brother's arms, overcome with so much radiant joy after that stress of action and peril; beholding now with her own eyes that home-coming whereof the genii of that land had had foreknowledge and in Gro's sight shown themselves wild with joy thereof: Brandoch Daha and Juss come home to Demonland, like men arisen from the dead.

"Not touched," she answered them. "But look to my Lord Gro: I fear he be hurt. Look to him well, for he hath approved him our friend indeed."

XXVI

THE BATTLE OF KROTHERING SIDE

*How word was brought unto the Lord Corinius
that the Lords Juss and Brandoch Daha were
come again into the land, and how he resolved to
give them battle on the side, under Erngate End;
and of the great flank march of Lord Brandoch
Daha over the mountains from Transdale; and of
the great battle, and of the issue thereof.*

AXUS and those sons of Corund walked on an afternoon in Krothering home mead. The sky above them was hot and coloured of lead, presaging thunder. No wind stirred in the trees that were livid-green against that leaden pall. The noise of mattock and crow-bar came without intermission from the castle. Where gardens had been and arbours of shade and sweetness, was now but wreck: broken columns and smashed porphyry vases of rare workmanship, mounds of earth and rotting vegetation. And those great cedars, emblems of their lord's estate and pride, lay prostrate now with their roots exposed, a tangle of sere foliage and branches broken, withered and lifeless. Over this death-bed of ruined loveliness the towers of onyx showed ghastly against the sky.

"Is there not a virtue in seven?" said Cargo. "Last week was the sixth time we thought we had gotten the eel by the tail in yon

295

fly-blown hills of Mealand and came empty home. When think'st, Laxus, shall's run 'em to earth indeed?"

"When egg-pies shall grow on apple-trees," answered Laxus. "Nay, the general setteth greater store by his proclamations concerning the young woman (who likely never heareth of them, and assuredly will not be by them 'ticed home again), and by these toys of revenge, than by sound soldiership. Hark! there goeth this day's work."

They turned at a shout from the gates, to behold the northern of those two golden hippogriffs totter and crash down the steeps into the moat, sending up a great smoke from the stones and rubble which poured in its wake.

Lord Laxus's brow was dark. He laid hand on Heming's arm, saying, "The times need all sage counsel we can reach unto, O ye sons of Corund, if our Lord the King shall have indeed from this expedition into Demonland the victory at last of all his evil-willers. Remember, that was a great miss to our strength when the Goblin went."

"Out upon the viper!" said Cargo. "Corinius was right in this, not to warrant him the honesty of such slippery cattle. He had not served above a month or two, but that he ran to the enemy."

"Corinius," said Laxus, "is yet but green in his estate. Doth he suppose the rest of his reign shall be but play and the enjoying of a kingdom? Those left-handed strokes of fortune may yet o'erthrow him, the while that he streameth out his youth in wine and venery and manageth his private spite against this lady. Slippery youth must be under-propped with elder counsel, lest all go amiss."

"A most reverend old counsellor art thou!" said Cargo; "of six-and-thirty years of age."

Said Heming, "We be three. Take command thyself. I and my brother will back thee."

"I will that thou swallow back those words," said Laxus, "as though they had never been spoke. Remember Corsus and Gallandus. Besides, albeit he seemeth now rather to be a man straught than one that hath his wits, yet is Corinius in his sober self a valiant and puissant soldier, a politic and provident captain as is not found besides in Demonland, no, nor in Witchland neither, and it were not your noble father; and this one in his youthly age."

"That is true," said Heming. "Thou hast justly reproved me."

Now while they were a-talking, came one from the castle and made obeisance unto Laxus saying, "You are inquired for, O king, so please you to walk into the north chamber."

Said Laxus, "Is it he that was newly ridden from the east country?"

"So it is, so please you," with a low leg he made answer.

"Hath he not had audience with King Corinius?"

"He hath sought audience," said the man, "but was denied. The matter presseth, and he urged me therefore seek unto your lordship."

As they walked toward the castle Heming said in Laxus's ear, "Knowest thou not this brave new piece of court ceremony? O' these days, when he hath 'stroyed an hostage to spite the Lady Mevrian, as to-day was 'stroyed the horse-headed eagle, he giveth not audience till sundown. For, the deed of vengeance done, a retireth himself to his own chamber and a wench with him, the daintiest and gamesomest he may procure; and so, for two hours or three drowned in the main sea of his own pleasures, he abateth some little deal for a season the pang of love."

Now when Laxus was come forth from talking with the messenger from the east, he fared without delay to Corinius's chamber. There, thrusting aside the guards, he flung wide the shining doors, and found the Lord Corinius merrily disposed. He was reclined on a couch deep-cushioned with dark green three-pile velvet. An ivory table inlaid with silver and ebony stood at his elbow bearing a crystal flagon already two parts emptied of the foaming wine, and a fair gold goblet beside it. He wore a long loose sleeveless gown of white silk edged with a gold fringe; this, fallen open at the neck, left naked his chest and one strong arm that in that moment when Laxus entered reached out to grasp the wine cup. Upon his knee he held a damosel of some seventeen years, fair and fresh as a rose, with whom he was plainly on the point to pass from friendly converse to amorous privacy. He looked angrily upon Laxus, who without ceremony spoke and said, "The whole east is in a tumult. The burg is forced which we built astride the Stile. Spitfire hath passed into Breakingdale to victual Galing, and hath overthrown our army that sat in siege thereof."

Corinius drank a draught and spat. "Phrut!" said he. "Much bruit, little fruit. I would know by what warrant thou troublest me with this tittle-tattle, and I pleasantly disposing myself to mirth and recreation. Could it not wait till supper time?"

Ere Laxus might say more, was a great clatter heard without on the stairs, and in came those sons of Corund.

"Am I a king?" said Corinius, gathering his robe about him, "and shall I be forced? Avoid the chamber." Then marking them stand silent with disordered looks, "What's the matter?" he said.

"Are ye ta'en with the swindle or the turn-sickness? Or are ye out of your wits?"

Heming answered and said, "Not mad, my lord. Here's Didarus that held the Stile-burg for us, ridden from the east as fast as his horse might wallop, and gotten here hard o' the heels of the former messenger with fresh and more certain advertisement, fresher by four days than that one's. I pray you hear him."

"I'll hear him," said Corinius, "at supper time. Nought sooner, if the roof were afire."

"The land beneath thy feet's afire!" cried Heming. "Juss and Brandoch Daha home again, and half the country lost thee ere thou heard'st on't. These devils are home again! Shall we hear that and still be swill-bowls?"

Corinius listened with folded arms. His great jaw was lifted up. His nostrils widened. For a minute he abode in silence, his cold blue eyes fixed as it were on somewhat afar. Then, "Home again?" said he. "And the east in a hubbub? And not unlikely. Thank Didarus for his tidings. He shall sweeten mine ears with some more at supper. Till then, leave me, unless ye mean to be stretched."

But Laxus, with sad and serious brow, stood beside him and said, "My lord, forget not that you are here the vicar and legate of the King. Let the crown upon your head put perils in your thoughts, so as you may harken peaceably to them that are willing to lesson you with sound and sage advice. If we take order to-night to march by Switchwater, we may very well shut back this danger and stifle it ere it wax to too much bigness. If o' the contrary we suffer them to enter into these western parts, like enough without let or stay they will overrun the whole country."

Corinius rolled his eye upon him. "Can nothing," he said, "prescribe unto thee obedience? Look to thine own charge. Is the fleet in proper trim? For there's the strength, ease, and anchor of our power, whether for victualling, or to shift our weight against 'em which way we choose, or to give us sure asylum if it were come to that. What ails thee? Have we not these four months desired nought better than that these Demons should take heart to strike a field with us? If it be true that Juss himself and Brandoch Daha have thrown down the castles and strengths which I had i' the east and move with an army against us, why then I have them in the forge already, and shall now bring them to the hammer.[1] And be satisfied, I'll choose mine own ground to fight them."

"There's yet matter for haste in this," said Laxus. "A day's march, and we oppose 'em not, will bring them before Krothering."

"That," answered Corinius, "jumpeth pat with mine own design. I'll not go a league to bar their way, but receive 'em here where the ground lieth most favourable to meet an enemy. Which advantage I'll employ to the greatest stretch of service, standing on Krothering Side, resting my flank against the mountain. The fleet shall ride in Aurwath haven."

Laxus stroked his beard and was silent a minute, considering this. Then he looked up and said, "This is sound generalship, I may not gainsay it."

"It is a purpose, my lord," said Corinius, "I have long had in myself, stored by for the event. Let me alone, therefore, to do that my right is. There's this good in it, too, as it befalleth: 'twill suffer that dive-dapper[2] to behold his home again afore I kill him. A shall find it a sight for sore eyes, I think, after my tending on't."

The third day after these doings, the farmer at Holt[3] stood in his porch that opened westward on Tivarandardale. An old man was he, crooked like a mountain thorn. But a bright black eye he had, and the hair curled crisp yet above his brow. It was late afternoon and the sky overcast. Tousle-haired sheep-dogs slept before the door. Swallows gathered in the sky. Near to him sat a damosel, dainty as a meadow-pipit,[4] lithe as an antelope; and she was grinding grain in a hand-mill, singing the while:

> Grind, mill, grind,
> Corinius grinds us all;
> Kinging it in widowed Krothering.

The old man was furbishing a shield and morion-cap,[5] and other tackle of war lay at his feet.

"I wonder thou wilt still be busy with thy tackle, O my father," said she, looking up from her singing and grinding. "If ill tide ill again what should an old man do but grieve and be silent?"

"There shall be time for that hereafter," said the old man. "But a little while is hand fain of blow."[6]

"They'll be for firing the roof-tree, likely, if they come back," said she, still grinding.

"Thou'rt a disobedient lass. If thou'dst but flit as I bade thee to the shiel-house[7] up the dale, I'd force not a bean for their burnings."

"Let it burn," said she, "if he be taken. What avail then for thee or for me to be a-tarrying? Thou that art an old man and full of good days, and I that will not be left so."

A great dog awoke beside her and shook himself, then drew near and laid his nose in her lap, looking up at her with kind solemn eyes.

The old man said, "Thou'rt a disobedient lass, and but for thee, come sword, come fire, not a straw care I; knowing it shall be but a passing storm, now that my Lord is home again."

"They took the land from Lord Spitfire," said she.

"Ay, hinny," said the old man, "and thou shalt see my Lord shall take it back again."

"Ay?" said she. And still she ground and still she sang:

> Grind, mill, grind,
> Corinius grinds us all.

After a time, "Hist!" said the old man, "was not that a horse-tread i' the lane? Get thee within-doors till I know if all be friendly." And he stooped painfully to take up his weapon. Woefully it shook in his feeble hand.

But she, as one that knew the step, heeding nought else, leapt up with face first red then pale then flushed again, and ran to the gate of the garth. And the sheepdogs bounded before her. There in the gate she was met with a young man riding a weary horse. He was garbed like a soldier, and horse and man were so bedraggled with mire and dust and all manner of defilement they were a sorry sight to see, and so jaded both that scarce it seemed they had might to journey another furlong. They halted within the gate, and all those dogs jumped up upon them, whining and barking for joy.

Ere the soldier was well down from the saddle he had a sweet armful. "Softly, my heart," said he, "my shoulder's somewhat raw. Nay, 'tis nought to speak on. I've brought thee all my limbs home."

"Was there a battle?" said the old man.

"Was there a battle, father?" cried he. "I'll tell thee, Krothering Side is thicker with dead men slain than our garth with sheep i' the shearing time."

"Alack and alack, 'tis a most horrid wound, dear," said the girl. "Go in, and I'll wash it and lay to it millefoil[8] pounded with honey; 'tis most sovran against pain and loss of blood, and drieth up the lips of the wound and maketh whole thou'dst no credit how soon. Thou hast bled over-much, thou foolish one. And how couldst thou thrive without thy wife to tend thee?"

The farmer put an arm about him, saying, "Was the field ours, lad?"

"I'll tell you all orderly, old man," answered he, "but I must stable him first," and the horse nuzzled his breast. "And ye must ballast me first. God shield us, 'tis not a tale for an empty man to tell."

" 'Las, father," said the damosel, "have we not one sweet sippet i' the mouth, that we hold him here once more? And, sweet or sour, let him take his time to fetch us the next."

So they washed his hurt and laid kindly herbs thereto, and bound it with clean linen, and put fresh raiment upon him, and made him sit on the bench without the porch and gave him to eat and drink: cakes of barley meal and dark heather-honey, and rough white wine of Tivarandardale. The dogs lay close about him as if there was warmth there and safety whereas he was. His young wife held his hand in hers, as if that were enough if it should last for aye. And that old man, eating down his impatience like a schoolboy chafing for the bell, fingered his partisan[9] with trembling hand.

"Thou hadst the word I sent thee, father, after the fight below Galing?"

"Ay. 'Twas good."

"There was a council held that night," said the soldier. "All the great men together in the high hall in Galing, so as it was a heaven to see. I was one of their cupbearers, 'cause I'd killed the standard-bearer of the Witches, in that same battle below Galing. Methought 'twas no great thing I did; till after the battle, look you, my Lord's self standing beside me; and saith he, 'Arnod' (ay, by my name, father), 'Arnod,' a saith, 'thou'st done down the pennon o' Witchland that 'gainst our freedom streamed so proud. 'Tis thy like shall best stead Demonland i' these dog-days,' saith he. 'Bear my cup to-night, for thine honour.' I would, lass, thou'dst seen his eyes that tide. 'Tis a lord to put marrow in the sword-arm, our Lord.

"They had forth the great map o' the world, of this Demon-land, to study their business. I was by, pouring the wine, and I heard their disputations. 'Tis a wondrous map wrought in crystal and bronze, most artificial, with waters a-glistering and mountains standing substantial to the touch. My Lord points with's sword. 'Here,' a saith, 'standeth Corinius, by all sure tellings, and budgeth not from Krothering. And, by the Gods, 'a saith, ''tis a wise disposition. For, mark, if we go by Gashterndale, as go we must to come at him, he striketh down on us as hammer on anvil. And if we will pass by toward the head of Thunderfirth,' and here a pointeth it out with's sword, 'down a cometh on our flank; and every-gate the land's slope serveth his turn and fighteth against us.'

"I mind me o' those words," said the young man, " 'cause my

Lord Brandoch Daha laughed and said, 'Are we grown so strange by our travels, our own land fighteth o' the opposite party? Let me study it again.'

"I filled his cup. Dear Gods, but I'd fill him a bowl of mine own heart's blood if he required it of me, after our times together, father. But more o' that anon. The stoutest gentleman and captain without peer.

"But Lord Spitfire, that was this while vaunting up and down the chamber, cried out and said, ''Twere folly to travel his road prepared us. Take him o' that side he looketh least to see us: south through the mountains, and upon him in his rear up from Mardardale.'

" 'Ah,' saith my Lord, 'and be pressed back into Murkdale Hags if we miss of our first spring. 'Tis too perilous. 'Tis worse than Gashterndale.'

"So went it: a nay for every yea, and nought to please 'em. Till i' the end my Lord Brandoch Daha, that had been long time busy with the map, said: 'Now that y' have threshed the whole stack and found not the needle, I will show you my rede, 'cause ye shall not say I counselled you rashly.'

"So they bade him say his rede. And he said unto my Lord, 'Thou and our main power shall go by Switchwater Way. And let the whole land's face blaze your coming before you. Ye shall lie to-morrow night in some good fighting-stead whither it shall not be to his vantage to move against you: haply[10] in the old shielings[11] above Wrenthwaite, or at any likely spot afore the road dippeth south into Gashterndale. But at point of day strike camp and go by Gashterndale and so up on to the Side to do battle with him. So shall all fall out even as his own hopes and expectations do desire it. But I,' saith my Lord Brandoch Daha, 'with seven hundred chosen horse, will have fared by then clean along the mountain ridge from Transdale even to Erngate End; so as when he turneth all his battle northward down the Side to whelm you, there shall hang above the security of his flank and rear that which he ne'er dreamed on. If he support my charging of his flank at unawares, with you in front to cope him, and he with so small an advantage upon us in strength of men: if he stand that, why then, good-night! the Witches are our masters in arms, and we may off cap to 'em and strive no more to right us.'

"So said my Lord Brandoch Daha. But all called him daft to think on't. Carry an army a-horseback in so small time 'cross such curst ground? It might not be. 'Well,' quoth he, 'sith you count it not possible, so much the more shall he. Cautious counsels never will serve us this tide. Give me but my pick of man and horse to the number of seven hundred, and I'll so set this masque[12] you shall not desire a better master of the revels.'

"So i' the end he had his way. And past midnight they were at it, I wis, planning and studying.

"At dawn was the whole army marshalled in the meadows below Moonmere, and my Lord spake among them and told us he was minded to march into the west country and exterminate the Witches out of Demonland; and he bade any man that deemed he had now his fill of furious war and deemed it a sweeter thing to go home to his own place, say forth his mind without fear, and he would let him go, yea, and give him good gifts thereto, seeing that all had done manful service; but he would have no man in this enterprise who went not to it with his whole heart and mind."[13]

The damosel said, "I wis there was not a man would take that offer."

"There went up," said the soldier, "such a shout, with such a stamping, and such a clashing together of weapons, the land shook with't, and the echoes rolled in the high corries of the Scarf like thunder, of them shouting 'Krothering!' 'Juss!' 'Brandoch Daha!' 'Lead us to Krothering!' Without more ado was the stuff packed up, and ere noon was the whole army gotten over the Stile. While we halted for daymeal hard by Blackwood in Amadardale, came my Lord Brandoch Daha a-riding among the ranks for to take his pick of seven hundred of our ablest horse. Nor a would not commit this to his officer, but himself called on each lad by name whenso he saw a likely one, and speered[14] would a ride with him. I trow he gat never a nay to that speering. My heart was a-cold lest he'd o'erlook me, watching him ride by as jaunty as a king. But a reined in's horse and saith, 'Arnod, 'tis a bonny horse thou ridest. Could he carry thee to a swine-hunt down from Erngate End i' the morning?' I saluted him and said, 'Not so far only, Lord, but to burning Hell so thou but lead us.' 'Come on,' saith he. ''Tis a better gate I shall lead thee: to Krothering hall ere eventide.'

"So now was our strength sundered, and the main army made ready to march westward down Switchwater Way; with the Lord Zigg to lead the horse, and the Lord Volle and my Lord's self and his brother the Lord Spitfire faring in the midst amongst 'em all. And with them yonder outland traitor, Lord Gro; but I do think him more a stick of sugar-paste than a man of war. And many gentlemen of worth went with them: Gismor Gleam of Justdale, Astar of Rettray, and Bremery of Shaws, and many more men of mark. But there abode with my Lord Brandoch Daha, Arnund of

By, and Tharmrod of Kenarvey, Kamerar of Stropardon, Emeron Galt, Hesper Golthring of Elmerstead, Styrkmir of Blackwood, Melchar of Strufey, Quazz's three sons from Dalney, and Stypmar of Failze: fierce and choleric young gentlemen, after his own heart, methinks; great horsemen, not very forecasting of future things afar off but entertainers of fortune by the day; too rash to govern an army, but best of all to obey and follow him in so glorious an enterprise.

"Ere we parted, came my Lord to speak with my Lord Brandoch Daha. And my Lord looked into the lift that was all dark cloud and wind; and quoth he, 'Fail not at the tryst, cousin. 'Tis thy word, that thou and I be finger and thumb; and never more surely than to-morrow shall this be seen.'

" 'O friend of my heart, content thee,' answereth my Lord Brandoch Daha. 'Didst ever know me neglect my guests? And have I not bidden you to breakfast with me to-morrow morn in Krothering meads?'

"Now we of the seven hundred turned leftward at the waters-meet up Transdale into the mountains. And now came ill weather upon us, the worst that ever I knew. 'Tis soft enow and little road enow in Transdale, as thou knowest, father, and weary work it was with every deer-track turned a water-course and underfoot all slush and mire, and nought for a man to see save white mist and rain above and about him, and soppy bent and water under's horse-hooves. Little there was to tell us we were won at last to the top of the pass, and 'twere not the cloud blew thicker and the wind wilder about us. Every man was wet to the breech, and bare a pint o' water in's two shoes.

"Whiles we were halted on the Saddle my Lord Brandoch Daha rested not at all, but gave his horse to his man to hold and himself fared back and forth among us. And for every man he had a jest or a merry look, so as 'twas meat and drink but to hear or to behold him. But a little while only would he suffer us to halt; then right we turned, up along the ridge, where the way was yet worse than in the dale had been, with rocks and pits hidden in the heather, and slithery slabs of granite. By my faith, I think no horse that was not born and bred to't might cross such country, wet or fine; he should be foundered or should break his legs and his rider's neck ere he should be gotten two hours' journey along those ridges; but we that rode with my Lord Brandoch Daha to Krothering Side were ten hours riding so, besides our halts to water our horses and longer halts to feed 'em, and the last part o' the way through murk night, and all the way i' the wind's teeth with rain blown on the wind like spray, and hail at whiles. And when the rain was done, the wind veered to the north-west and blew the ridges dry. And then the little bits of rotten granite blew in our faces like hailstones on the wind. There was no shelter, not o' the lee side of the rocks, but everywhere the storm-wind baffled and buffeted us, and clapped his wings among the crags like thunder. Dear Heaven, weary we were and like to drop, cold to the marrow, nigh blinded man and horse, yet with a dreadful industry pressed on. And my Lord Brandoch Daha was now in the van now in the rear-guard, cheering men's hearts who marked with what blithe countenance himself did suffer the same hardships as his meanest trooper: like to one riding at ease to some great wedding-feast; crying, 'What, lads, merrily on! These fen-toads of the Druima shall learn too late what way our mountain ponies do go like stags upon the mountain.'

"When it began to be morning we came to our last halt, and there was our seven hundred horse hid in the corrie under the tall cliffs of Erngate End. I warrant you we went carefully about it, so as no prying swine of Witchland looking up from below should aspy a glimpse of man or horse o' the skyline. His highness first set his sentinels and let call the muster, and saw that every man had his morning meal and every horse his feed. Then he took his stand behind a crag of rock whence he could overlook the land below. He had me by him to do his errands. In the first light we looked down westward over the mountain's edge and saw Krothering and the arms of the sea, not so dark but we might behold their fleet at anchor in Aurwath roads, and their camp like a batch of beehives so as a man might think to cast a stone into't below us. That was the first time I'd e'er gone to the wars with him. Faith, he's a pretty man to see: leaned forward there on the heather with's chin on his folded arms, his helm laid aside so they should not see it glint from below; quiet like a cat: half asleep you'd say; but his eyes were awake, looking down on Krothering. 'Twas well seen even from so far away how vilely they had used it.

"The great red sun leaped out o' the eastern cloudbanks. A stir began in their camp below: standards set up, men gathering thereto, ranks forming, bugles sounding; then a score of horse galloping up the road from Gashterndale into the camp. His highness, without turning his head, beckoned with's hand to me to call his captains. I ran and fetched 'em. He gave 'em swift commands, pointing down where the Witchland swine rolled out their battle; thieves and pirates who robbed his highness' subjects within his streams; with standard and pennons and glistering naked spears, moving northward from the tents. Then in the quiet came a sound made a man's heart leap within him: faint out of the far hollows of Gashterndale, the trumpet of my Lord Juss's battlecall.

"My Lord Brandoch Daha paused a minute, looking down. Then a turned him about with face that shone like the morning, 'Fair lords,' a saith, 'now lightly on horseback, for Juss fighteth against his enemies.' I think he was well content. I think he was sure he would that day get his heart's syth[15] of every one that had wronged him.

"That was a long ride down from Erngate End. With all our hearts' blood drumming us to haste, we must yet go warily, picking our way i' that tricky ground, steep as a roof-slope, uneven and with no sure foothold, with sikes in wet moss and rocks outcropping and shifting screes. There was nought but leave it to the horses, and bravely they brought us down the steeps. We were not half way down ere we heard and saw how battle was joined. So intent were the Witchlanders on my Lord's main army, I think we were off the steep ground and forming for the charge ere they were ware of us. Our trumpeters sounded his battle challenge, *Who meddles wi' Brandoch Daha?* and we came down on to Krothering Side like a rock-fall.

"I scarce know what way the battle went, father. 'Twas like a meeting of streams in spate.[16] I think they opened to us right and left to ease the shock. They that were before us went down like standing corn under a hailstorm. We wheeled both ways, some 'gainst their right that was thrown back toward the camp, the more part with my Lord Brandoch Daha to our own right. I was with these in the main battle. His highness rode a hot stirring horse very fierce and dogged; knee to knee with him went Styrkmir of Blackwood o' the one side and Tharmrod o' the other. Neither man nor horse might stand up before 'em, and they faring as in a maze now this way now that, amid the thrumbling and thrasting o' the footmen, heads and arms smitten off, men hewn in sunder from crown to belly,[17] ay, to the saddle, riderless horses maddened, blood splashed up from the ground like the slush from a marsh.

"So for a time, till we had spent the vantage of our onset and felt for the first time the weight of their strength. For Corinius, as it appeareth, was now himself ridden from the vanward where he had beat back for a time our main army, and set on against my Lord Brandoch Daha with horsemen and spearmen; and commanded his sling-casters besides to let freely at us and drive us toward the camp.

"And now in the great swing of the battle were we carried back to the camp again; and there was a sweet devils' holiday: horses and men tripping over tent-ropes, tents torn down, crashes of broken crockery, and King Laxus come thither with sailors from the fleet, hamstringing our horses while Corinius charged us from the north and east. That Corinius beareth him in battle more like a devil from Hell than a mortal man. I' the first two strokes of's sword he overthrew two of our best captains, Romenard of Dalney and Emeron Galt. Styrkmir, that stood in's way to stop him, a flung down with's spear, horse and man. They say he met twice with my Lord Brandoch Daha that day, but each time were they parted in the press ere they might rightly square together.

"I have stood in some goodly battles, father, as well thou knowest: first following my Lord and my Lord Goldry Bluszco in foreign parts, and last year in the great rout at Crossby Outsikes, and again with my Lord Spitfire when he smote the Witches on Brima Rapes, and in the murthering great battle under Thremnir's Heugh. But never was I in fight like to this of yesterday.

"Never saw I such feats of arms. As witness Kamerar of Stropardon, who with a great two-handed sword hewed off his enemy's leg close to the hip, so huge a blow the blade sheared through leg and saddle and horse and all. And Styrkmir of Blackwood, rising like a devil out of a heap of slain men, and though's helm was lossen and a was bleeding from three or four great wounds a held off a dozen o' the Witches with's deadly thrusts and swordstrokes, till they had enough and gave back before him: twelve before one, and he given over for dead a while before. But all great deeds seemed trash beside the deeds of my Lord Brandoch Daha. In one short while had he three times a horse slain stark dead under him, yet gat never a wound himself, which was a marvel. For without care he rode through and about, smiting down their champions. I mind me of him once, with's horse ripped and killed under him, and one of those Witchland lords that tilted at him on the ground as he leaped to's feet again; how a caught the spear with's two hands and by main strength yerked his enemy out o' the saddle. Prince Cargo it was, youngest of Corund's sons. Long may the Witchland ladies strain their dear eyes, they'll ne'er see yon hendy lad come sailing home again.[18] His highness swapt him such a swipe o' the neck-bone as he pitched to earth, the head of him flew i' the air like a tennis ball. And i' the twinkling of an eye was my Lord Brandoch Daha horsed again on's enemy's horse, and turned to charge 'em anew. You'd say his arm must fail at last for weariness, of a man so lithe and jimp[19] to look on. Yet I think his last stroke i' that battle was not lighter than the first. And stones and spears and sword-strokes seemed to come upon him with no more impression than blows with a straw would give to an adamant.

"I know not how long was that fight among the tents. Only 'twas the best fight I ever was at, and the bloodiest. And by all tellings 'twas as great work o' the other part, where my Lord and his folk fought their way up on to the Side. But of that we knew nothing. Yet certain it is we had all been dead men had my Lord not there prevailed, as certain 'tis he had never so prevailed but for our charging of their flank when they first advanced against him. But in that last hour all we that fought among the tents thought each man only of this, how he might slay yet one more Witch, and yet again one more, afore he should die. For Corinius in that hour put forth his might to crush us; and for every enemy there felled to earth two more seemed to be raised up against us. And our own folk fell fast, and the tents that were so white were one gore of blood.

"When I was a little tiny boy, father, we had a sport, swimming in the deep pools of Tivarandarwater, that one boy would catch 'tother[20] and hold him under till he could no more for want of breath. Methinks there's no longing i' the world so sore as the longing for air when he that is stronger than thou grippeth thee still under the water, nor no gladness i' the world like the bonny sweet air i' thy lungs again when a letteth thee shoot up to the free daylight. 'Twas right so with us, who had now said adieu to hope and saw all lost save life itself, and that not like to tarry long; when we heard suddenly the thunder of my Lord's trumpet sounding to the charge. And ere our startled wits might rightly think what that portended, was the whole surging battle whipped and scattered like the water of a lake caught up in a white squall; and that massed strength of the enemy which had invested us round with so great a stream of shot and steel reeled first forward then backward then forward again upon us, confounded in a vast confusion. I trow new strength came to our arms; I trow our swords opened their mouths. For northward we beheld the ensign of Galing streaming like a blazing star; and my Lord's self in a moment, high advanced above the rout, and Zigg, and Astar, and hundreds of our horse, hewing their way toward us whiles we hewed towards them. And now was reaping time for us, and time of payment for all those weary bloody hours we had held on to life with our teeth among the tents on Krothering Side, while they o' the other part, my Lord and his, had with all the odds of the ground against them painfully and yard by yard fought out the fight to victory. And now, ere we well wist of it, the day was won, and the victory ours, and the enemy broken and put to so great a rout as hath not been seen by living man.

"That false king Corinius, after he had tarried to see the end of the battle, fled with a few of his men out of the great slaughter, and as it later appeared gat him ashipboard in Aurwath harbour and with three ships or four escaped to sea. But the most of their fleet was burned there in the harbour to save it from our hands.

"My Lord gave command to take up the wounded and tend 'em, friend and foe alike. Among them was King Laxus ta'en up, stunned with a mace-blow or some such. So they brought him before the lords where they rested a little way down the Side above the home meads of Krothering.

"He looked 'em all in the eye, most proud and soldier-like. Then a saith unto my Lord, 'It may be pain, but no shame to us to be vanquished after so equal and so great a fight. Herein only do I blame my ill luck, that it denied me fall in battle. Thou mayst now, O Juss, strike off my head for the treason I wrought you three years ago. And since I know thee of a courteous and noble nature, I'll not scorn to ask of thee this courtesy, not to tarry but take it now.'

"My Lord stood there like a war-horse after a breather. He took him by the hand. 'O Laxus,' saith he, 'I give thee not thy head only, but thy sword;' and here a gave it him hilt-foremost. 'For thy dealings with us in the battle of Kartadza, let time that hath an art to make dust of all things so do with the memory of these. Since then, thou hast shown thyself still our noble enemy; and so shall we account thee still.'

"Therewith my Lord commanded bring King Laxus down to the sea, and ship him aboard of a boat, for Corinius still held off the land with his ships, waiting no doubt to see if he or any other of his folk could yet be saved.

"But as King Laxus was upon parting, my Lord Brandoch Daha, speaking with great show of carelessness as of some trifling matter a had by chance called to mind, 'My lord,' saith he, 'I ne'er ask favour of any man. Only in a manner of return of courtesies, methought thou mightest be willing to bear my salutations to Corinius, sith I've no other messenger.'

"Laxus answereth he would freely do it. Then saith his highness, 'Say to him I will not blame him that he abode us not i' the field after the battle was lost, for that had been a simple part, flatly 'gainst all maxims of right soldiership, and but to cast his life away. But freakish Fortune I blame, that twined[21] us one from the other when we should have dealt together this day. He hath borne him in my halls, I am let to know, more i' the fashion of a swine or a beastly ape than a man. Pray him come ashore ere you sail home, that I and he, with no man else to make betwixt us, may cast up our account. We swear him peace and grith[22] and a safe conduct back to's ships if he prevail against me or if I so use him that he cry for mercy. If he'll not take this offer, then is he a dastard; and the whole world shall so acclaim him.'

" 'Sir,' saith Laxus, 'I'll punctually discharge thy message.'

"Whether he did so or no, father, I know not. But if he did, it seemeth it was little to Corinius's liking. For no sooner had his ship ta'en Laxus aboard, than she hoised sail and put out into the deep, and so good-bye."

The young man ceased, and they were all three silent awhile. A faint breeze rippled the foliage of the oakwoods of Tivarandardale. The sun was down behind the stately Thornbacks, and the whole sky from bourne to bourne was alight with the sunset glory. Dappled clouds, with sky showing here and there between, covered the heavens, save in the west where a great archway of clear air opened between clouds and earth: air of an azure that seemed to burn, so pure it was, so deep, so charged with warmth: not the harsh blue of noon-day nor the sumptuous deep eastern blue of approaching night, but a bright heavenly blue bordering on green, deep, tender, and delicate as the spirit of evening. Athwart the midst of that window of the west a blade of cloud, hard-edged and jagged with teeth coloured as of live coals and dead, fiery and iron-dark in turn, stretched like a battered sword. The clouds above the arch were pale rose: the zenith like black opal, dark blue and thunderous gray dappled with fire.

XXVII

THE SECOND EXPEDITION
TO IMPLAND

*How the Lord Juss, not to be persuaded from his
set purpose, found, where least it was to be looked
for, upholding in that resolve; and of the sailing
of the armament to Muelva by way of the Straits
of Melikaphkhaz.*

HAT was the last ember of red summer burning when
they cut them that harvest on Krothering Side. Autumn came, and winter months, and the lengthening
days of the returning year. And with the first breath of
spring were the harbours filled with ships of war, so
many as had never in former days been seen in the land, and in
every countryside from the western Isles to Byland, from Shalgreth and Kelialand to the headlands under Rimon Armon, were
soldiers gathered with their horses and all instruments of war.

Lord Brandoch Daha rode from the west, the day the Pasque
flowers first opened on the bluffs below Erngate End and prim-
roses made sweet the birch-forests in Gashterndale. He set forth
betimes,[1] and hard he rode, and he rode into Galing by the Lion
Gate about the hour of noon. There was Lord Juss in his private
chamber, and greeted him with great joy and love. So Brandoch
Daha asked, "What speed?" And Juss answered, "Thirty ships and
five afloat in Lookinghaven, whereof all save four be dragons of
war. Zigg I expect tomorrow with the Kelialand levies; Spitfire lieth

at Owlswick with fifteen hundred men from the southlands; Volle came in but three hours since with four hundred more. In sum, I'll have four thousand, reckoning ships' companies and our own bodyguards."

"Eight ships of war have I," said Lord Brandoch Daha, "in Stropardon Firth, all busked and boun.[2] Five more at Aurwath, five at Lornagay in Morvey, and three on the Mealand coast at Stackray Oyce, besides four more in the Isles. And I have sixteen hundred spearmen and six hundred horse. All these shall come together to join with thine in Lookinghaven at the snapping of my fingers, give me but seven days' notice."

Juss gripped him by the hand. "Bare were my back without thee," he said.

"In Krothering I've shifted not a stone nor swept not a chamber clean," said Brandoch Daha. " 'Tis a muck-pit. Every man's hand I might command I set only to this. And now 'tis ready." He turned sharp toward Juss and looked at him a minute in silence. Then with a gravity that sat not often on his lips he said, "Let me be urgent with thee once more: strike and delay not. Do him not again that kindness we did him aforetime, fribbling our strength away on the cursed shores of Impland, and by the charmed waters of Ravary, so as he might as secure as sleep send Corsus hither and Corinius to work havoc i' the land; and so put on us the greatest shame was ever laid on mortal men, and we not bred up to suffer shame."

"Thou saidst seven days," said Juss. "Snap thy fingers and call up thy armies. I'll delay thee not an hour."

"Ay, but I mean to Carcë," said he.

"To Carcë, whither else?" said Juss. "But I'll take my brother Goldry with us."

"But I mean first to Carcë," said Brandoch Daha. "Let my opinion sway thee once. Why, a schoolboy should tell thee, clear thy flank and rear ere thou go forward."

Juss smiled. "I love this new garb of caution, cousin," said he; "it doth most prettily become thee. I question though whether this be not the true cause: that Corinius took not up thy challenge last summer, but let it lie, and that hath left thee hungry still."

Brandoch Daha looked him sidelong in the eye, and laughed. "O Juss," he said, "thou hast touched me near. But 'tis not that. That was in the weird that bright lady laid on me, in the sparrow-hawk castle in Impland forlorn: that he I held most in hate should ruin my fair lordship, and that to my hand should vengeance be denied. That I e'en must brook. O no. Think only, delays are dangerous. Come, be advised. Be not mulish."

But the Lord Juss's face was grave. "Urge me no more, dear friend," said he. "Thou sleep'st soft. But to me, when I am cast in my first sleep, cometh many a time the likeness of Goldry Bluszco, held by a maleficial charm on the mountain top of Zora Rach, that standeth apart, out of the sunlight, out of all sound or warmth of life. Long ago I made vow to turn neither to the right nor to the left, until I set him free."

"He is thy brother," said Lord Brandoch Daha. "Also is he mine own familiar friend, whom I love scarce less than thee. But when thou speakest of oaths, remember there's La Fireez too. What shall he think on us after our oaths to him three years ago, that night in Carcë? Yet this one blow should right him too."

"He will understand," said Juss.

"He is to come with Gaslark, and thou told'st me thou dost e'en now expect them," said Brandoch Daha. "I'll leave you. I cannot for shame say to him, 'Patience, friend, truly 'tis not to-day convenient. Thou shalt be paid in time.' By heavens, I'd scorn to entreat my mantle-maker so. And this our friend that lost all and languisheth in exile because he saved our lives."

So saying, he stood up in great discontent and ire as if to leave the chamber. But Juss caught him by the wrist. "Thou dost upbraid me most unjustly, and well thou knowest it in thy heart, and 'tis that makes thee so angry. Hark, the horn soundeth at the gate, and 'tis for Gaslark. I'll not let thee go."

"Well," said Lord Brandoch Daha, "have thy will. Only ask not me to plead thy rotten case to them. If I speak it shall be to shame thee. Now thou'rt warned."

Now went they into the high presence chamber, where were bright ladies not a few, and captains and noble persons from up and down the land, and stood on the dais. Gaslark the king walked up the shining floor, and behind him his captains and councillors of Goblinland walked two by two. The Prince La Fireez strode at his elbow, proud as a lion.

Blithely they greeted those lords of Demonland that rose up to greet them beneath the starry canopy, and the Lady Mevrian that stood betwixt her brother and Lord Juss so as 'twere hard to say which of the three was fairest to look on, so much they differed in their beauty's glory. Gro, standing near, said in himself, "I know a fourth. And were she but joined with these, then were the crown of the whole earth's loveliness fitted in this one chamber: in a right casket surely. And the Gods in heaven (if there be Gods indeed) should go pale for envy, having in their starry gallery no fair to match with these; not Phoebus Apollo, not the chaste Huntress, nor the foam-born Queen[3] herself."

But Gaslark, when his eye lighted on the long black beard, the lean figure slightly stooping, the pallid brow, the curls smoothed with perfumed unguents, the sickle-like nose, the great liquid eyes, the lily hand; he, beholding and knowing these of old, waxed in a moment dark as thunder with the blood-rush beneath his sun-browned skin, and with a great sweep snatched out his sword, as if without gare or beware to thrust him through. Gro stepped hastily back. But the Lord Juss came between them.

"Let alone, Juss," cried Gaslark. "Know'st not this fellow, what a vile enemy and viper we have here? A pretty perfumed villain! who for so many years did spin me a thread of many seditions and troubles, while his smooth tongue gat money from me still. Blessed occasion! Now will I let his soul out."

But the Lord Juss laid his hand on Gaslark's sword-arm. "Gaslark," said he, "leave off thy rages, and put up thy sword. A year ago thou'dst done me no wrong. But to-day thou'dst have slain me a man of mine own men, and a lord of Demonland."

Now when they had done their greetings, they washed their hands and sate at dinner and were nobly served and feasted. And the Lord Juss made peace betwixt Gro and Gaslark, albeit 'twas no light task to prevail upon Gaslark to forgive him. Thereafter they retired them with Gaslark and La Fireez into a chamber apart.

Gaslark the king spake and said, "None can gainsay it, O Juss, that this fight ye won last harvest tide was the greatest seen on land these many years, and of greatest consequence. But I have heard a bird sing there shall be yet greater deeds done ere many moons be past. Therefore it is we came hither to thee, I and La Fireez that be your friends from of old, to pray thee let us go with thee on thy quest across the world after thy brother, for sorrow of whose loss the whole world languisheth; and thereafter let us go with you on your going up to Carcë."

"O Juss," said the Prince, "we would not in after-days that men should say, On such a time fared the Demons into perilous lands enchanted and by their strength and valorousness set free the Lord Goldry Bluszco (or haply, there ended their life's days in that glorious quest); but Gaslark and La Fireez were not in it, they bade their friends farewell, hung up their swords, and lived a quiet and merry life in Zajë Zaculo. So let their memory be forgot."

Lord Juss sat silent a minute, as one much moved. "O Gaslark," he said at length, "I'll take thine offer without another word.

But unto thee, dear Prince, I must bare mine heart somewhat. For thou here art come not strest[4] in our quarrel to spend thy blood, only to put us yet deeper in thy debt. And yet small blame it were to thee shouldst thou in dishonourable sort revile me, as many shall cry out against me, for a false friend unto thee and a friend forsworn."

But the Prince La Fireez brake in upon him, saying, "I prithee have done, or thou'lt shame me quite. Whate'er I did in Carcë, 'twas but equal payment for your saving of my life in Lida Nanguna. So was all evened up betwixt us. Think then no more on't, but deny me not to go with you to Impland. But up to Carcë I'll not go with you: for albeit I am clean broke with Witchland, against Corund and his kin I will not draw sword nor against my lady sister. A black curse on the day I gave her white hand to Corund! She holdeth too much of our stock, methinks: her heraldry is hearts not hands. And giving her hand she gave her heart.[5] 'Tis a strange world."

"La Fireez," said Juss, "we weigh not so lightly our obligation unto thee. Yet must I hold my course; having sworn a strong oath that I would turn aside neither to the right nor to the left until I had delivered my dear brother Goldry out of bondage. So sware I or ever I went that ill journey to Carcë and was closed in prison fast and by thee delivered. Nor shall blame of friends nor wrongful misprison nor any power that is shake me in this determination. But when that is done, no rest remaineth unto us till we win back for thee thy rightful realm of Pixyland, and many good things besides to be a token of our love."

Said the Prince, "Thou doest right. If thou didst other thou'dst have my blame."

"And mine thereto," said Gaslark. "Do not I grieve, think'st thou, to see the Princess Armelline, my sweet young cousin, grow every day more wan o' the cheek and pale? And all for sorrow and teen[6] for her own true love, the Lord Goldry Bluszco. And she so carefully brought up by her mother as nothing was too dear or hard to be brought to pass for her desire, thinking that a creature so noble and perfect could not be trained up too delicately. I deem to-day better than to-morrow, and to-morrow better than his morrow, to set sail for wide-fronted Impland."

All this while the Lord Brandoch Daha said never a word. He sat back in his chair of ivory and chrysoprase,[7] now toying with his golden finger-rings, now twisting and untwisting the yellow curls of his moustachios and beard. In a while he yawned, rose from his seat and fell to pacing lazily up and down. He had hitched up his sword across his back under his two elbows, so that the shoe of the scabbard stood out under one arm and the jewelled hilt under the other. His fingers strummed little tunes on the front of the rich rose velvet doublet that cased his chest. The spring sunlight as he paced from shine to shade and to shine again, passing the tall windows, seemed to caress his face and form. It was as if spring laughed for joy beholding in him one that was her own child, clothed to outward view with so much loveliness and grace, but full besides to the eyes and finger-tips with fire and vital sap, like her own buds bursting in the Brankdale coppices.[8]

In a while he ceased his walking, and stood by the Lord Gro who sat a little apart from the rest. "How thinkest thou, Gro, of our counsels? Art thou for the straight road or the crooked? For Carcë or Zora Rach?"

"Of the roads," answered Gro, "a wise man will choose ever that one which is indirect. For but consider the matter, thou that art a great cragsman: think our life's course a lofty cliff. I am to climb it, sometime up, sometime down. I pray, whither leadeth the straight road on such a cliff? Why, nowhither. For if I will go up by the straight way, 'tis not possible; I am left gaping whiles thou by crooked courses hast gained the top. Or if down, why 'tis easy and swift; but then, no more climbing ever more for me. And thou, clambering down by the crooked way, shalt find me a dead and unsightly corpse at the bottom."

"Grammercy for thy me's and thee's," said Lord Brandoch Daha. "Well, 'tis a most weighty principle, backed with a most just and lively exposition. How dost thou interpret thy maxim in our present question?"

Lord Gro looked up at him. "My lord, you have used me well, and to deserve your love and advance your fortunes I have pondered much how you of Demonland might best obtain revenge upon your enemies. And I daily thinking hereupon, and conceiving in my head divers imaginations, can devise no means but one that in my fancy seemeth best, which is this."

"Let me hear it," said Lord Brandoch Daha.

Said Gro, " 'Twas ever a fault in you Demons that you would not perceive how 'tis oft-times good to draw the snake from her hole by another man's hand. Consider now your matter. You have a great force both for land and sea. Trust not too much in that. Oft hath he of the little force o'ercome most powerful enemies, going about to entrap them by sleight and policy. But consider yet again. You have a thing is mightier far than all your horses and spearmen and dragons of war, mightier than thine own sword, my lord, and thou accounted the best swordsman in all the world."

"What thing is that?" asked he.

Gro answered, "Reputation, my Lord Brandoch Daha. This reputation of you Demons for open dealings even to your worst enemies."

"Tush," said he. " 'Tis but our way i' the world. Moreover, 'tis, I think, a thing natural in great persons, of whatsoever country they be born. Treachery and double dealing proceed commonly from fear, and that is a thing which I think no man in this land comprehendeth. Myself, I do think that when the high Gods made a person of my quality they traced tween his two eyes something, I know not what, which the common sort durst not look upon without trembling."

"Give me but leave," said Lord Gro, "and I'll pluck you a braver triumph in a little hour than your swords should win you in two years. Speak smooth words to Witchland, offer him composition, bring him to a council and all his great men along with him. I'll so devise it, they shall all be suddenly taken off in a night, haply by setting upon them in their beds, or as we may find most convenient. All save Corund and his sons; them we may wisely spare, and conclude peace with them. It shall not by ten days delay your sailing to Impland, whither you might then proceed with light hearts and minds at ease."

"Very prettily conceived, upon my soul," said Brandoch Daha. "Might I advise thee, thou'dst best not talk to Juss i' this manner. Not now, I mean, while his mind's so bent on matters of weight and moment. Nor I should not say it to my sister Mevrian. Women will oft-times take in sad earnest such a conceit,[9] though it be but talk and discourse. With me 'tis otherwise. I am something of a philosopher myself, and thy jest ambleth with my humour very pleasantly."

"Thou art pleased to be merry," said Lord Gro. "Many ere now, as the event hath proved, rejected my wholesome counsels to their own great hurt."

But Brandoch Daha said lightly, "Fear not, my Lord Gro, we'll reject no honest redes of so wise a counsellor as thou. But," and here was a light in the eye of him made Gro startle, "did any man with serious intent dare bid me do a dastard deed, he should have my sword through the dearest part of's body."

Lord Brandoch Daha now turned him to the rest of them. "Juss," said he, "friend of my heart, meseemeth y'are all of one mind, and none of my mind. I'll e'en bid you farewell. Farewell, Gaslark; farewell, La Fireez."

"But whither away?" said Juss, standing up from his chair. "Thou must not leave us."

"Whither but to mine own place?" said he, and was gone from the chamber.

Gaslark said, "He's much incensed. What hast thou done to anger him?"

Mevrian said to Juss, "I'll follow and cool him." She went, but soon returned saying, "No avail, my lords. He is ridden forth from Galing and away as fast as his horse might carry him."

Now were they all in a great stew, some conjecturing one thing and some another. Only the Lord Juss kept silence and a calm countenance, and the Lady Mevrian. And Juss said at length to Gaslark, "This it is, that he chafeth at every day's delay that letteth him from having at Corinius. Certes,[10] I'll not blame him, knowing the vile injuries the fellow did him and his insolence toward thee, madam. Be not troubled. His own self shall bring him back to me when time is, as no other power should do 'gainst his good will; he whose great heart Heaven cannot force with force."

And even so, the next night after, when folk were abed and asleep, Juss, in his high bed-chamber sitting late at his book, heard a bridle ring. So he called his boys to go with him with torches to the gate. And there in the dancing torch-light came the Lord Brandoch Daha a-riding into Galing Castle, and somewhat of the bigness of a great pumpkin tied in a silken cloth hung at his saddle-bow. Juss met him in the gate alone. "Let me down from my horse," he said, "and receive from me thy bed-fellow that thou must sleep with by the Lake of Ravary."

"Thou hast gotten it?" said Juss. "The hippogriff's egg, out of Dule Tarn, by thyself alone?" and he took the bundle right tenderly in his two hands.

"Ay," answered he. " 'Twas where thou and I made sure of it last summer, according to the word of her little martlet that first found it for us. The tarn was frozen and 'twas tricky work diving and most villanous cold. It is small marvel thou'rt a lucky man in thine undertakings, O Juss, when thou hast such an art to draw thy friends to second thee."

"I thought thou'dst not leave me," said Juss.

"Thought?" cried Brandoch Daha. "Didst ever dream I'd suffer thee to do thy foolishness alone? Nay, I'll come first to the enchanted lake with thee, and let be Carcë i' the meantime. Howbeit I'll do it 'gainst the stream of my resolution quite."

* * *

Now was but six days more of preparation, and on the second day of April was all ready in Lookinghaven for the sailing of that mighty armament: fifty and nine ships of war and five ships of burthen and thrice two thousand fighting men.

Lady Mevrian sat on her milk-white mare overlooking the harbour where the ships all orderly rode at anchor, shadowy gray against the sun-bright shimmer of the sea, with here and there a splash of colour, crimson or blue or grass-green, from their painted hulls or a beam of the sun glancing from their golden masts or figureheads. Gro stood at her bridle-rein. The Galing road, winding down from Havershaw Tongue, ran close below them and so along the sea-shore to the quays at Lookinghaven. Along that road the hard earth rang with the tramp of armed men and the tramp of horses, and the light west wind wafted to Gro and Mevrian on their grassy hill snatches of deep-voiced battle-chants or the galloping notes of trumpet and pipe and the drum that sets men's hearts a-throb.

In the van rode the Lord Zigg, four trumpeters walking before him in gold and purple. His armour from chin to toe shone with silver, and jewels blazed on his gorget and baldrick[11] and the hilt of his long straight sword. He rode a black stallion savage-eyed with ears laid back and a tail that swept the earth. A great company of horse followed him, and half as many tall spearmen, in russet leather jerkins plated with brass and silver. "These," said Mevrian, "be of Kelialand and the shore-steads of Arrowfirth, and his own vassalage from Rammerick and Amadardale. That is Hesper Golthring rideth a little behind him on his right hand; he loveth two things in this world, a good horse and a swift ship. He on the left, he o' the helm of dull silver set with raven's wings, so long of the leg thou'dst say if he rode a little horse he might straddle and walk it: Styrkmir of Blackwood. He is of our kin; not yet twenty years old, yet since Krothering Side accounted one of our ablest."

So she showed him all as they rode by,[12] Peridor of Sule, captain of the Mealanders, and his nephew Stypmar. Fendor of Shalgreth with Emeron Galt his young brother that was newly healed from the great wound Corinius gave him at Krothering Side; these leading the shepherds and herdsmen from the great heaths north of Switchwater, who will hold by the stirrup and so with their light bucklers and little brown swords go into battle with the horsemen full gallop against the enemy. Bremery in his ram's-horn helm of gold and broidered surcoat[13] of scarlet velvet, leading the dalesmen from Onwardlithe and Tivarandardale.

Trentmar of Scorradale with the northeastern levies from Byland and the Strands and Breakingdale. Astar of Rettray, lean and lithe, bony-faced, gallant-eyed, white of skin, with bright red hair and beard, riding his lovely roan at the head of two companies of spearmen with huge iron-studded shields: men from about Drepaby and the south-eastern dales, landed men and home-men of Lord Goldry Bluszco. Then the island dwellers from the west, with old Quazz of Dalney riding in the place of honour, noble to look on with his snowy beard and shining armour, but younger men their true leaders in war: Melchar of Strufey, great-chested, fierce-eyed, with thick brown curling hair, horsed on a plunging chestnut, his byrny bright with gold, a rich mantle of creamy silk brocade flung about his ample shoulders, and Tharmrod on his little black mare with silver byrny and bats-winged helm, he that held Kenarvey in fee for Lord Brandoch Daha, keen and ready like an arrow drawn to the barbs. And after them the Westmark men, with Arnund of By their captain. And after them, four hundred horse, not to be surpassed for beauty or ordered array by any in that great army, and young Kamerar riding at their head, burly as a giant, straight as a lance, apparelled like a king, bearing on his mighty spear the pennon of the Lord of Krothering.

"Look well on these," said Mevrian as they passed by. "Our own men of the Side and Thunderfirth and Stropardon. Thou may'st search the wide world and not find their like for speed and fire and all warlike goodliness and readiness to the word of command. Thou look'st sad, my lord."

"Madam," said Lord Gro, "to the ear of one that useth, as I use, to consider the vanity of all high earthly pomps, the music of these powers and glories hath a deep underdrone of sadness. Kings and governors that do exult in strength and beauty and lustihood[14] and rich apparel, showing themselves for awhile upon the stage of the world and open dominion of high heaven, what are they but the gilded summer fly that decayeth with the dying day?"

"My brother and the rest must not stay for us," said the lady. "They meant to go aboard as soon as the army should be come down to the harbour, for their ships be to sail out first down the firth. Is it determined indeed that thou goest with them on this journey?"

"I had so determined, madam," answered he. She was beginning to move down towards the road and the harbour, but Gro put a hand on the rein and stopped her. "Dear lady," he said, "these three nights together I have dreamed a dream: a strange dream, and all the particulars thereof betokening heavy anxiety, increase of peril, and savage mischief; promising some terrible issue. Methinks if I go on this journey thou shalt see my face no more."

"O fie, my lord," cried she, reaching him her hand, "give never a thought to such fond imaginings. 'Twas the moon but glancing in thine eye. Or if not, stay with us here and cheat Fate."

Gro kissed her hand, and kept it in his. "My Lady Mevrian," he said, "Fate will not be cheated, cog[15] we never so wisely. I do think there be not many extant that in a noble way fear the face of death less than myself. I'll go o' this journey. There is but one thing should turn me back."

"And 'tis?" said she, for he fell silent on a sudden.

He paused, looking down at her gloved hand resting in his. "A man becometh hoarse and dumb," said he, "if a wolf hath the advantage first to eye him. Didst thou procure thee a wolf to dumb me when I would tell thee? But I did once; enough to let thee know. O Mevrian, dost thou remember Neverdale?"

He looked up at her. But Mevrian sat with head erect, like her Patroness divine, with sweet cool lips set firm and steady eyes fixed on the haven and the riding ships. Gently she drew her hand from Gro's, and he strove not to retain it. She eased forward the reins. Gro mounted and followed her. They rode quietly down to the road and so southward side by side to the harbour. Ere they came within earshot of the quay, Mevrian spake and said, "Thou'lt not think me graceless nor forgetful, my lord. All that is mine, O ask it, and I'll give it thee with both hands. But ask me not that I have not to give, or if I gave should give but false gold. For that's a thing not good for thee nor me, nor I would not do it to an enemy, far less to thee my friend."

Now was the army all gotten ashipboard, and farewells said to Volle and those who should abide at home with him. The ships rowed out into the firth all orderly, their silken sails unfurled, and that great armament sailed southward into the open seas under a clear sky. All the way the wind favoured them, and they made a swift passage, so that on the thirtieth morning from their sailing out of Lookinghaven they sighted the long gray cliff-line of Impland the More dim in the low blown spray of the sea, and sailed through the Straits of Melikaphkhaz in column ahead, for scarce might two ships pass abreast through that narrow way. Black precipices shut in the straits on either hand, and the sea-birds in their thousands whitened every little ledge of those cliffs like snow. Great flights of them rose and circled overhead as the ships sped by, and the air was full of their plaints. And right and left, as of young whales blowing, columns of white spray shot up continually from the surface of the sea. For these were the stately-winged gannets fishing that sea-strait. By threes and fours they flew, each following other in ordered line, many mast-heights high; and ever and anon one checked in her flight as if a bolt had smitten her, and swooped head-foremost with wings half-spread, like a broad-barbed dart of dazzling whiteness, till at a few feet above the surface she clapped close her wings and cleft the water with a noise as of a great stone cast into the sea. Then in a moment up she bobbed, white and spruce with her prey in her gullet; rode the waves a minute to rest and consider; then with great sweeping wing-strokes up again to resume her flight.

After a mile or two the narrows opened and the cliffs grew lower, and the fleet sped past the red reefs of Uaimnaz and the lofty stacks of Pashnemarthra white with sea-gulls on to the blue solitude of the Didornian Sea. All day they sailed south-east with a failing wind. The coastline of Melikaphkhaz fell away astern, paled in the mists of distance, and was lost to sight, until only the square cloven outline of the Pashnemarthran islands broke the level horizon of the sea. Then these too sank out of sight, and the ships rowed on south-eastward in a dead calm. The sun stooped to the western waves, entering his bath of blood-red fire. He sank, and all the ways were darkened. All night they rowed gently on under the strange southern stars, and the broken waters of that sea at every oar-stroke were like fire burning. Then out of the sea to eastward came the day-star, ushering the dawn, brighter than all night's stars, tracing a little path of gold along the waters. Then dawn, filling the low eastern skies with a fleet of tiny cockle-shells of bright gold fire; then the great face of the sun ablaze. And with the going up of the sun a light wind sprang up, bellying their sails on the starboard tack; so that ere day declined the sea-cliffs of Muelva hung white above the spray-mist on their larboard bow. They beached the ships on a white shell-strand behind a headland that sheltered it from the east and north. Here the barrier of cliffs stood back a little from the shore, giving place for a fertile dell of green pasture, and woods clustering at the foot of the cliffs, and a little spring of water in the midst.

So for that night they slept on board, and next day made their camp, discharging the ships of burthen that were laden with the horses and stuff. But the Lord Juss was minded not to tarry an hour more in Muelva than should suffice to give all needful orders to Gaslark and La Fireez what they should do and when expect him again, and to make provision for himself and those who must fare with him beyond these shadowing cliffs into the haunted wastes of the Moruna. Ere noon was all this accomplished and farewells said, and these lords, Juss, Spitfire, and Brandoch Daha, set forth along the beach southward towards a point where it seemed most hopeful to scale the cliffs. With them went the Lord Gro, both by his own wish and because he had known the Moruna aforetime and these particular parts thereof; and with them went besides those two brothers-in-law, Zigg and Astar, bearing the precious burden of the egg, for that honour and trust had Juss laid on them at their earnest seeking. So with some pains after an hour or more they won up the barrier, and halted for a minute on the cliff's edge.

The skin of Gro's hands was hurt with the sharp rocks. Tenderly he drew on his lambswool gloves, and shivered a little; for the breath of that desert blew snell and frore[16] and there seemed a shadow in the air southward, for all it was bright and gentle weather below whence they were come. Yet albeit his frail body quailed, even so were his spirits within him raised with high and noble imaginings as he stood on the lip of that rocky cliff. The cloudless vault of heaven; the unnumbered laughter of the sea; that quiet cove beneath, and those ships of war and that army camping by the ships; the emptiness of the blasted wolds[17] to southward, where every rock seemed like a dead man's skull and every rank tuft of grass hag-ridden; the bearing of those lords of Demonland who stood beside him, as if nought should be of commoner course to them pursuing their resolve than to turn their backs on living land and enter those regions of the dead; these things with a power as of a mighty music made Gro's breath catch in his throat and the tear spring in his eye.

In such wise after more than two years did Lord Juss begin his second crossing of the Moruna in quest of his dear brother the Lord Goldry Bluszco.

XXVIII

Zora Rach Nam Psarrion

Of the Lord Juss's riding of the hippogriff to Zora Rach, and of the ills encountered by him in that accursed place, and the manner of his performing his great enterprise to deliver his brother out of bondage.

 ULLED with light-stirring airs too gentle-soft to ruffle her glassy surface, warm incense-laden airs sweet with the perfume of immortal flowers, the charmed Lake of Ravary dreamed under the moon. It was the last hour before the dawn. Enchanted boats, that seemed builded of the glow-worm's light, drifted on the starry bosom of the lake. Over the sloping woods the limbs of the mountains lowered, unmeasured, vast, mysterious in the moon's glamour. In remote high spaces of night beyond glimmered the spires of Koshtra Pivrarcha and the virgin snows of Romshir and Koshtra Belorn. No bird or beast moved in the stillness: only a nightingale singing to the stars from a coppice of olive-trees near the Queen's pavilion on the eastern shore. And that was a note not like a bird's of middle earth, but a note to charm down spirits out of the air, or to witch[1] the imperishable senses of the Gods when they would hold communion with holy Night and make her perfect, and all her lamps and voices perfect in their eyes.

The silken hangings of the pavilion door, parting as in the

portal of a vision, made way for that Queen, fosterling of the most high Gods. She paused a step or two beyond the threshold, looking down where those lords of Demonland, Spitfire and Brandoch Daha, with Gro and Zigg and Astar, wrapped in their cloaks, lay on the gowany² dewy banks that sloped down to the water's edge.

"Asleep," she whispered. "Even as he within sleepeth against the dawn. I do think it is only in a great man's breast sleep hath so gentle a bed when great events are toward."

Like a lily, or like a moonbeam strayed through the leafy roof into a silent wood, she stood there, her face uplifted to the starry night where all the air was drenched with the silver radiance of the moon. And now in a soft voice she began supplication to the Gods which are from everlasting, calling upon them in turn by their holy names, upon gray-eyed Pallas, and Apollo, and Artemis the fleet Huntress, upon Aphrodite, and Hera, Queen of Heaven, and Ares, and Hermes, and the dark-tressed Earthshaker.³ Nor was she afraid to address her holy prayers to him⁴ who from his veiled porch beside Acheron and Lethe Lake binds to his will the devils of the under-gloom, nor to the great Father of All⁵ in Whose sight time from the beginning until to-day is but the dipping of a wand into the boundless ocean of eternity. So prayed she to the blessed Gods, most earnestly requiring them that under their countenance might be that ride, the like whereof earth had not known: the riding of the hippogriff, not rashly and by an ass as heretofore to his own destruction, but by the man of men who with clean purpose and resolution undismayed should enforce it carry him to his heart's desire.

Now in the east beyond the feathery hilltops and the great snow wall of Romshir the gates were opening to the day. The sleepers wakened and stood up. There was a great noise from within the pavilion. They turned wide-eyed, and forth of the hangings of the doorway came that young thing new-hatched, pale and doubtful as the new light which trembled in the sky. Juss walked beside it, his hand on the sapphire mane. High and resolute was his look, as he gave good-morrow to the Queen, to his brother and his friends. No word they said, only in turn gripped him by the hand. The hour was upon them. For even as day striding on the eastern snow-fields stormed night out of high heaven, so and with such swift increase of splendour was might bodily and the desire of the upper air born in that wild steed. It shone as if lighted by a moving lamp from withinward, sniffed the sweet morning air and whinnied, pawing the grass of the waterside and tearing it up with its claws of gold. Juss patted the creature's arching neck, looked to the

HIPPOGRIFF IN FLIGHT

bridle he had fitted to its mouth, made sure of the fastenings of his armour, and loosened in the scabbard his great sword. And now up sprang the sun.

The Queen said, "Remember: when thou shalt see the lord thy brother in his own shape, that is no illusion. Mistrust all else. And the almighty Gods preserve and comfort thee."

Therewith the hippogriff, as if maddened with the day-beams, plunged like a wild horse, spread wide its rainbow pinions, reared, and took wing. But the Lord Juss was sprung astride of it, and the grip of his knees on the ribs of it was like brazen clamps. The firm land seemed to rush away beneath him to the rear; the lake and the shore and islands thereof showed in a moment small and remote, and the figures of the Queen and his companions like toys, then dots, then shrunken to nothingness, and the vast silence of the upper air opened and received him into utter loneliness. In that silence earth and sky swirled like the wine in a shaken goblet as the wild steed rocketed higher and higher in great spirals. A cloud billowy-white shut in the sky before them; brighter and brighter it grew in its dazzling whiteness as they sped towards it, until they touched it and the glory was dissolved in a gray mist that grew still darker and colder as they flew till suddenly they emerged from the further side of the cloud into a radiance of blue and gold blinding in its glory. So for a while they flew with no set direction, only ever higher, till at length obedient to Juss's mastery the hippogriff ceased from his sports and turned obediently westward, and so in a swift straight course, mounting ever, sped over Ravary towards the departing night. And now indeed it was as if they had verily over-taken night in her western caves. For the air waxed darker about them and always darker, until the great peaks that stood round Ravary were hidden, and all the green land of Zimiamvia, with its plains and winding waters and hills and uplands and enchanted woods, hidden and lost in an evil twilight. And the upper heaven was ateem[6] with portents: whole armies of men skirmishing in the air, dragons, wild beasts, bloody streamers, blazing comets, fiery strakes,[7] with other apparitions innumerable. But all silent, and all cold, so that Juss's hands and feet were numbed with the cold and his moustachios stiff with hoar-frost.

Before them now, invisible till now, loomed the gaunt peak of Zora Rach, black, wintry, and vast, still towering above them for all they soared even higher, grand and lonely above the frozen wastes of the Psarrion Glaciers. Juss stared at that peak till the wind of their flight blinded his eyes with tears; but it was yet too far for any glimpse of that which he hungered to behold: no brazen citadel, no coronal of flame, no watcher on the heights. Zora, like some dark queen of Hell that disdains that presumptuous mortal eyes should dare to look lovely on her dread beauties, drew across her brow a veil of thundercloud. They flew on, and that steel-blue pall of thunderous vapour rolled forth till it canopied all the sky above them. Juss tucked his two hands for warmth into the feathery armpits of the hippogriff's wings where the wings joined the creature's body. So bitter cold it was, his very eyeballs were frozen and fixed; but that pain was a light thing beside somewhat he now felt within him the like whereof he never before had known: a death-like horror as of the houseless loneliness of naked space, which gripped him at the heart.

They landed at last on a crag of black obsidian stone a little below the cloud that hid the highest rocks. The hippogriff, crouched on the steep slope, turned its head to look on Juss. He felt the creature's body beneath him quiver. Its ears were laid back, its eye wide with terror. "Poor child," he said. "I have brought thee an ill journey, and thou but one hour hatched from the egg."

He dismounted; and in that same instant was bereaved. For the hippogriff with a horse-scream of terror took wing and vanished down the mirk air, diving headlong away to eastward, back to the world of life and sunlight.

And the Lord Juss stood alone in that region of fear and frost and the soul-quailing gloom, under the black summit-rocks of Zora Rach.

Setting, as the Queen had counselled him to do, his whole heart and mind on the dread goal he intended, he turned to the icy cliff. As he climbed the cold cloud covered him, yet not so thick but he might see ten paces' distance before and about him as he went. Ill sights enow, and enow to quail a strong man's resolution, showed in his path: shapes of damned fiends and gorgons of the pit running in the way, threatening him with death and doom. But Juss, gritting his teeth, climbed on and through them, they being unsubstantial. Then up rose an eldritch[8] cry, "What man of middle-earth is this that troubleth our quiet? Make an end! Call up the basilisks. Call up the Golden Basilisk, which bloweth upon and setteth on fire whatsoever he seeth. Call up the Starry Basilisk, and whatso he seeth it immediately shrinks up and perisheth. Call up the Bloody Basilisk, who if he see or touch any living thing it floweth away so that nought there remaineth but the bones!"

That was a voice to freeze the marrow, yet he pressed on, saying in himself, "All is illusion, save that alone she told me of." And nought appeared: only the silence and the cold, and the rocks grew ever steeper and their ice-glaze more dangerous, and the difficulty like the difficulty of those Barriers of Emshir, up which more than two years ago he had followed Brandoch Daha and on which he had encountered and slain the beast mantichora. The leaden hours drifted by, and now night shut down, bitter and black and silent. Sore weariness bodily was come upon Juss, and his whole soul weary withal and near to death as he entered a snow-bedded gully that cut deep into the face of the mountain, there to await the day. He durst not sleep in that freezing night; scarcely dared he rest lest the cold should master him, but must keep for ever moving and stamping and chafing hands and feet. And yet, as the slow night crept by, death seemed a desirable thing that should end such utter weariness.

Morning came with but a cold alteration of the mist from black to gray, disclosing the snow-bound rocks silent, dreary, and dead. Juss, enforcing his half frozen limbs to resume the ascent, beheld a sight of woe too terrible for the eye: a young man, helmed and graithed[9] in dark iron, a black-a-moor with goggle-eyes and white teeth agrin, who held by the neck a fair young lady kneeling on her knees and clasping his as in supplication, and he most bloodily brandishing aloft his spear of six foot of length as minded to reave her of her life. This lady, seeing the Lord Juss, cried out on him for succour very piteously, calling him by his name and saying, "Lord Juss of Demonland, have mercy, and in your triumph over the powers of night pause for an instant to deliver me, poor afflicted damosel, from this cruel tyrant. Can your towering spirit, which hath quarried upon kingdoms, make a stoop at him? O that should approve you noble indeed, and bless you for ever!"

Surely the very heart of him groaned, and he clapped hand to sword wishing to right so cruel a wrong. But on the motion he bethought him of the wiles of evil that dwelt in that place, and of his brother, and with a great groan passed on. In which instant he beheld sidelong how the cruel murtherer smote with his spear that delicate lady, and detrenched and cut the two master-veins of her neck, so as she fell dying in her blood. Juss mounted with a great pace to the head of the gully, and looking back beheld how black-a-moor and lady both were changed to two coiling serpents. And he laboured on, shaken at heart, yet glad to have so escaped the powers that would have limed him so.

Darker grew the mist, and heavier the brooding dread which seemed elemental of the airs about that mountain. Pausing well nigh exhausted on a small stance of snow, Juss beheld the appearance of a man armed who rolled prostrate in the way, tearing with his nails at the hard rock and frozen snow, and the snow was all one gore of blood beneath the man; and the man besought him in a stifled voice to go no further but raise him up and bring him down the mountain. And when Juss, after an instant's doubt betwixt pity and his resolve, would have passed by, the man cried and said, "Hold, for I am thy very brother thou seekest, albeit the King hath by his art framed me to another likeness, hoping so to delude thee. For thy love sake be not deluded!" Now the voice was like to the voice of his brother Goldry, howbeit weak. But the Lord Juss bethought him again of the words of Sophonisba the Queen, that he should see his brother in his own shape and nought else must he trust; and he thought, "It is an illusion, this also." So he said, "If that thou be truly my dear brother, take thy shape." But the man cried as with the voice of the Lord Goldry Bluszco, "I may not, till that I be brought down from the mountain. Bring me down, or my curse be upon thee for ever."

The Lord Juss was torn with pity and doubt and wonder, to hear that voice again of his dear brother so beseeching him. Yet he answered and said, "Brother, if that it be thou indeed, then bide till I have won to this mountain top and the citadel of brass which in a dream I saw, that I may know truly thou art not there, but here. Then will I turn again and succour thee. But until I see thee in thine own shape I will mistrust all. For hither I came from the ends of the earth to deliver thee, and I will set my good on no doubtful cast, having spent so much and put so much in danger for thy dear sake."

So with a heavy heart he set hand again to those black rocks, iced and slippery to the touch. Therewith up rose an eldritch cry, "Rejoice, for this earth-born is mad! Rejoice, for that was not perfect friend, that relinquished his brother at his need!" But Juss climbed on, and by and by looking back beheld how in that seeming man's place writhed a grisful[10] serpent. And he was glad, so much as gladness might be in that mountain of affliction and despair.

Now was his strength near gone, as day drew again toward night and he climbed the last crags under the peak of Zora. And he, who had all his days drunk deep of the fountain of the joy of life and the glory and the wonder of being, felt ever deadlier and darker in his soul that lonely horror which he first had tasted the day before at his first near sight of Zora, while he flew through the cold air portent-laden; and his whole heart grew sick because of it.

And now he was come to the ring of fire that was about the summit of the mountain. He was beyond terror or the desire of life,

and trod the fire as it had been his own home's threshold. The blue
tongues of flame died under his foot-tread, making a way before
him. The brazen gates stood wide. He entered in, he passed up the
brazen stair, he stood on that high roof-floor which he had beheld
in dreams, he looked as in a dream on him he had crossed the
confines of the dead to find: Lord Goldry Bluszco keeping his lone
watch on the unhallowed heights of Zora. Not otherwise was the
Lord Goldry, not by an hairsbreadth, than as Juss had aforetime
seen him on that first night in Koshtra Belorn, so long ago. He
reclined propped on one elbow on that bench of brass, his head
erect, his eyes fixed as on distant space, viewing the depths beyond
the star-shine, as one waiting till time should have an end.

He turned not at his brother's greeting. Juss went to him and
stood beside him. The Lord Goldry Bluszco moved not an eyelid.
Juss spoke again, and touched his hand. It was stiff and like dank
earth. The cold of it struck through Juss's body and smote him at
the heart. He said in himself, "He is dead."

With that, the horror shut down upon Juss's soul like madness. Fearfully he stared about him. The cloud had lifted from the
mountain's peak and hung like a pall above its nakedness. Chill air
that was like the breath of the whole world's grave: vast blank
cloud-barriers: dim far forms of snow and ice, silent, solitary, pale,
like mountains of the dead: it was as if the bottom of the world
were opened and truth laid bare: the ultimate Nothing.

To hold off the horror from his soul, Juss turned in memory to
the dear life of earth, those things he had most set his heart on,
men and women he loved dearest in his life's days; battles and
triumphs of his opening manhood, high festivals in Galing, golden
summer noons under the Westmark pines, hunting morns on the
high heaths of Mealand; the day he first backed a horse, of a spring
morning in a primrose glade that opened on Moonmere, when his
small brown legs were scarce the length of his fore-arm now, and
his dear father held him by the foot as he trotted, and showed him
where the squirrel had her nest in the old oak tree.

He bowed his head as if to avoid a blow, so plain he seemed to
hear somewhat within him crying with a high voice and loud,
"Thou art nothing. And all thy desires and memories and loves
and dreams, nothing. The little dead earth-louse were of greater
avail than thou, were it not nothing as thou art nothing. For all is
nothing: earth and sky and sea and they that dwell therein. Nor
shall this illusion comfort thee, if it might, that when thou art
abolished these things shall endure for a season, stars and months
return, and men grow old and die, and new men and women live

and love and die and be forgotten. For what is it to thee, that shalt be as a blown-out flame? and all things in earth and heaven, and things past and things for to come, and life and death, and the mere elements of space and time, of being and not being, all shall be nothing unto thee; because thou shalt be nothing, for ever."

And the Lord Juss cried aloud in his agony, "Fling me to Tartarus, deliver me to the black infernal Furies, let them blind me, seethe me in the burning lake. For so should there yet be hope. But in this horror of Nothing is neither hope nor life nor death nor sleep nor waking, for ever. For ever."

In this black mood of horror he abode for awhile, until a sound of weeping and wailing made him raise his head, and he beheld a company of mourners walking one behind another about the brazen floor, all cloaked in funeral black, mourning the death of Lord Goldry Bluszco. And they rehearsed his glorious deeds and praised his beauty and prowess and goodliness and strength: soft women's voices lamenting, so that the Lord Juss's soul seemed as he listened to arise again out of annihilation's waste, and his heart grew soft again, even unto tears. He felt a touch on his arm and looking up met the gaze of two eyes gentle as a dove's, suffused with tears, looking into his from under the darkness of that hood of mourning; and a woman's voice spake and said, "This is the observable day of the death of the Lord Goldry Bluszco, which hath been dead now a year; and we his fellows in bondage do bewail him, as thou mayst see, and shall so bewail him again year by year whiles we are on life. And for thee, great lord, must we yet more sorrowfully lament, since of all thy great works done this is the empty guerdon,[11] and this the period of thine ambition. But come, take comfort for a season, since unto all dominions Fate hath set their end, and there is no king on the road of death."

So the Lord Juss, his heart dead within him for grief and despair, suffered her take him by the hand and conduct him down a winding stairway that led from that brazen floor to an inner chamber fragrant and delicious, lighted with flickering lamps. Surely life and its turmoils seemed faded to a distant and futile murmur, and the horror of the void seemed there but a vain imagination, under the heavy sweetness of that chamber. His senses swooned; he turned towards his veiled conductress. She with a sudden motion cast off her mourning cloak, and stood there, her whole fair body bared to his gaze, open-armed, a sight to ravish the soul with love and all delight.

Well nigh had he clasped to his bosom that vision of dazzling loveliness. But fortune, or the high Gods, or his own soul's might, woke yet again in his drugged brain remembrance of his purpose, so that he turned violently from that bait prepared for his destruction, and strode from the chamber up to that roof where his dear brother sat as in death. Juss caught him by the hand: "Speak to me, kinsman. It is I, Juss. It is Juss, thy brother."

But Goldry moved not, neither answered any word.

Juss looked at the hand resting in his, so like his own to the very shape of the finger nails and the growth of the hairs on the back of the hand and fingers. He let it go, and the arm dropped lifeless. "It is very certain," said he, "thou art in a manner frozen, and thy spirits and understanding frozen and congealed within thee."

So saying, he bent to gaze close in Goldry's eyes, touching his arm and shoulder. Not a limb stirred, not an eyelid flickered. He caught him by the hand and sleeve as if to force him up from the bench, calling him loudly by his name, shaking him roughly, crying, "Speak to me, thy brother, that crossed the world to find thee;" but he abode a dead weight in Juss's grasp.

"If thou be dead," said Juss, "then am I dead with thee. But till then I'll ne'er think thee dead." And he sat down on the bench beside his brother, taking his hand in his, and looked about him. Nought but utter silence. Night had fallen, and the moon's calm radiance and the twinkling stars mingled with the pale fires that hedged that mountain top in an uncertain light. Hell loosed no more her denizens in the air, and since the moment when Juss had in that inner chamber shaken himself free of that last illusion no presence had he seen nor simulacrum of man or devil save only Goldry his brother; nor might that horror any more master his high heart, but the memory of it was but as the bitter chill of a winter sea that takes the swimmer's breath for an instant as he plunges first into the icy waters.

So with a calm and a steadfast mind the Lord Juss abode there, his second night without sleep, for sleep he dared not in that accursed place. But for joy of his found brother, albeit it seemed there was in him neither speech nor sight nor hearing, Juss scarce wist of his great weariness. And he nourished himself with that ambrosia given him by the Queen, for well he thought the uttermost strength of his body should now be tried in the task he now decreed him.

When it was day, he arose and taking his brother Goldry bodily on his back set forth. Past the gates of brass Juss bore him, and past the barriers of flame, and painfully and by slow degrees down the long northern ridge which overhangs the Psarrion Glaciers. All that day, and the night following, and all the next day after were they on the mountain, and well nigh dead was Juss for weariness when on the second day an hour or two before sundown they reached the moraine. Yet was triumph in his heart, and gladness of a great deed done. They lay that night in a grove of strawberry trees under the steep foot of a mountain some ten miles beyond the western shore of Ravary, and met Spitfire and Brandoch Daha who had waited with their boat two nights at the appointed spot, about eventide of the following day.

Now as soon as Juss had brought him off the mountain, this frozen condition of the Lord Goldry was so far thawed that he was able to stand upon his feet and walk; but never a word might he speak, and never a look they gat from him, but still his gaze was set and unchanging, seeming when it rested on his companions to look through and beyond them as at some far thing seen in a mist. So that each was secretly troubled, fearing lest this condition of the Lord Goldry Bluszco should prove remediless, and this that they now received back from prison but the poor remain of him they had so much desired.

They came aland and brought him to Sophonisba the Queen where she made haste to meet them on the fair lawn before her pavilion. The Queen, as if knowing beforehand both their case and the remedy thereof, took by the hand the Lord Juss and said, "O my lord, there yet remaineth a thing for thee to do to free him throughly, that hast outfaced terrors beyond the use of man to bring him back: a little stone indeed to crown this building of thine, and yet without it all were in vain, as itself were vain without the rest that was all thine: and mine is this last, and with a pure heart I give it thee."

So saying she made the Lord Juss bow down till she might kiss his mouth, sweetly and soberly, one light kiss. And she said, "This give unto the lord thy brother." And Juss did so, kissing his dear brother in like manner on the mouth; and she said, "Take him, dear my lords. And I have utterly put out the remembrance of these things from his heart. Take him, and give thanks unto the high Gods because of him."

Therewith the Lord Goldry Bluszco looked upon them and upon that fair Queen and the mountains and the woods and the cool lake's loveliness, as a man awakened out of a deep slumber.

Surely there was joy in all their hearts that day.

XXIX

THE FLEET AT MUELVA

*How the Lords of Demonland came again to
their ships at Muelva, and the tidings they
learned there.*

O R nine days' space the lords of Demonland abode
with Queen Sophonisba in Koshtra Belorn and beside
the Lake of Ravary tasting such high and pure delights
as belike none else hath tasted, if it were not the spirits
of the blest in Elysium. When they bade her farewell,
the Queen said, "My little martlets shall bring me tidings of you.
And when you shall have brought to mere perdition the wicked
regiment of Witchland and returned again to your dear native
land, then is my time for that, my Lord Juss, whereof I have often
talked to thee and often gladded my dreams with the thought
thereof: to visit earth again and the habitations of men, and be
your guest in many-mountained Demonland."

Juss kissed her hand and said, "Fail not in this, dear Queen,
whatsoe'er betide."

So the Queen let bring them by a secret way out upon the high
snow-fields that are betwixt Koshtra Belorn and Romshir, whence
they came down into the glen of the dark water that descends from
the glacier of Temarm, and so through many perilous scapes after
many days back by way of the Moruna to Muelva and the ships.

There Gaslark and La Fireez, when their greetings were done
and their rejoicings, said to the Lord Juss, "We abide too long time
here. We have entered the barrel and the bung-hole is stopped."

Therewithal they brought him Hesper Golthring, who three days ago sailing to the Straits for forage came back again but yesterday with a hot alarum that he met certain ships of Witchland: and brought them to battle: and gat one sunken ere they brake off the fight: and took up certain prisoners. "By whose examination," saith he, "as well as from mine own perceiving and knowing, it appeareth Laxus holdeth the Straits with eight score ships of war, the greatest ships that ever the sea bare until this day, come hither of purpose to destroy us."

"Eight score ships?" said Lord Brandoch Daha. "Witchland commandeth not the half, nor the third part, of such a strength since we did them down last harvest-tide in Aurwath haven. It is not leveable,[1] Hesper."

Hesper answered him, "Your highness shall find it truth; and more the sorrow on't and the wonder."

" 'Tis the scourings of his subject-allies," said Spitfire. "We shall find them no such hard matter to dispatch after the others."

Juss said to the Lord Gro, "What makest thou of these news, my lord?"

"I think no wonder in it," answered he. "Witchland is of good memory and mindeth him of your seamanship off Kartadza. He useth not to idle, nor to set all on one hazard. Nor comfort not thyself, my Lord Spitfire, that these be pleasure-galleys borrowed from the soft Beshtrians or the simple Foliots. They be new ships builded for us, my lords, and our undoing: it is by no conjecture I say it unto you, but of mine own knowledge, albeit the number appeareth far greater than ere I dreamed of. But or ever I sailed with Corinius to Demonland, great buildings of an army naval was begun at Tenemos."

"I do very well believe," said King Gaslark, "that none knoweth all this better than thou, because thyself didst counsel it."

"O Gaslark," said Lord Brandoch Daha, "must thou still itch to play at chop-cherry when cherry-time is past? Let him alone. He is our friend now."

"Eight score ships i' the Straits," said Juss. "And ours an hundred. 'Tis well seen what great difference and odds there is betwixt us. Which we must needs encounter, or else ne'er sail home again, let alone to Carcë. For out of this sea is no sea-way for ships, but only by these Straits of Melikaphkhaz."

"We shall do of Laxus," said Lord Brandoch Daha, "that he troweth to do of us."

But Juss was fallen silent, his chin in his hand.

Goldry Bluszco said, "I would allow him odds and beat him."

"It is a great shame in thee, O Juss," said Brandoch Daha, "if thou wilt be abashed at this. If that they be in number more than we, what then? They are in hope, quarrel, and strength far inferior."

But Juss, still in a study, reached out and caught him by the sleeve, holding him so a moment or two, and then looked up at him and said, "Thou art the greatest quarreller, of a friend, that ever I knew, and if I were an angry man I could not abear thee. May I not three minutes study the means, but thou shalt cry out upon me for a milksop?"

They laughed, and the Lord Juss rose up and said, "Call we a council of war. And let Hesper Golthring be at it, and his skippers that were with him o' that voyage. And pack up the stuff, for we will away o' the morn. If we like not these lettuce, we may pull back our lips. But no choice remaineth. If Laxus will deny us sea-room through Melikaphkhaz Straits, I trow there shall go up thence a crash which when the King heareth it he shall know it for our first banging on the gates of Carcë."

XXX

TIDINGS OF MELIKAPHKHAZ

*Of news brought unto Gorice the King in Carcë
out of the south, where the Lord Laxus lying in
the straits with his armada held the fleet of
Demonland prisoned in the Midland Sea.*

O N a night of late summer leaning towards autumn, eight weeks after the sailing of the Demons out of Muelva as is aforewrit, the Lady Prezmyra sate before her mirror in Corund's lofty bed-chamber in Carcë. The night without was mild and full of stars. Within, yellow flames of candles burning steadily on either side of the mirror rayed forth tresses of tinselling brightness in twin glories or luminous spheres of warmth. In that soft radiance grains as of golden fire swam and circled, losing themselves on the confines of the gloom where the massy furniture and the arras[1] and the figured hangings of the bed were but cloudier divisions and congestions of the general dark. Prezmyra's hair caught the beams and imprisoned them in a tawny tangle of splendour that swept about her head and shoulders down to the emerald clasps of her girdle. Her eyes resting idly on her own fair image in the shining mirror, she talked light nothings with her woman of the bed-chamber who, plying the comb, stood behind her chair of gold and tortoise-shell.

"Reach me yonder book, nurse, that I may read again the words of that serenade the Lord Gro made for me the night when first we had tidings from my lord out of Impland of his conquest of that land, and the King did make him king thereof."

338

The old woman gave her the book, that was bound in goat-skin chiselled and ornamented by the gilder's art, fitted with clasps of gold, and enriched with little gems, smaragds[2] and margery-pearls, inlaid in the panels of its covers. Prezmyra turned the page and read:

> You meaner Beauties of the Night,
>   That poorly satisfie our Eies,
> More by your number than your light,
>   You Common-people of the Skies;
>   What are you when the Moone shall rise?
>
> You Curious Chanters of the Wood,
>   That warble forth Dame Natures layes,[3]
> Thinking your Passions understood
>   By your weake accents; what's your praise
>   When Philomell[4] her voyce shall raise?
>
> You Violets that first apeare,
>   By your pure purpel mantles knowne,
> Like the proud Virgins of the yeare,
>   As if the Spring were all your own;
>   What are you when the Rose is blowne?
>
> So, when my Princess shall be seene
>   In form and Beauty of her mind,
> By Vertue first, then Choyce a Queen,
>   Tell me, if she were not design'd
>   Th' Eclipse and Glory of her kind.

She abode silent awhile. Then, in a low sweet voice where all the chords of music seemed to slumber: "Three years will be gone next Yule-tide," she said, "since first I heard that song. And not yet am I grown customed to the style of Queen."

" 'Tis pity of my Lord Gro," said the nurse.

"Thou thinkest?"

"Mirth sat oftener on your face, O Queen, when he was here, and you were used to charm his melancholy and make a pish of his phantastical humorous forebodings."

"Oft doubting not his forejudgement," said Prezmyra, "even the while I thripped my fingers at it. But never saw I yet that the louring thunder hath that partiality of a tyrant, to blast him that faced it and pass by him that quailed before it."

"He was most deeply bound servant to your beauty," said the

old woman. "And yet," she said, viewing her mistress sidelong to see how she would receive it, "that were a miss easily made good."

She busied herself with the comb awhile in silence. After a time she said, "O Queen, mistress of the hearts of men, there is not a lord in Witchland, nor in earth beside, you might not bind your servant with one thread of this hair of yours. The likeliest and the goodliest were yours at an eye-glance."

The Lady Prezmyra looked dreamily into her own sea-green eyes imaged in the glass. Then she smiled mockingly and said, "Whom then accountest thou the likeliest and the goodliest man in all the stablished earth?"

The old woman smiled. "O Queen," answered she, "this was the very matter in dispute amongst us at supper only this evening."

"A pretty disputation!" said Prezmyra. "Let me be merry. Who was adjudged the fairest and gallantest by your high court of censure?"

"It was not generally determined of, O Queen. Some would have my Lord Gro."

"Alack, he is too feminine," said Prezmyra.

"Others our Lord the King."

"There is none greater," said Prezmyra, "nor more worshipful. But for an husband, thou shouldst as well wed with a thunderstorm or the hungry sea. Give me some more."

"Some chose the lord Admiral."

"That," said Prezmyra, "was a nearer stroke. No skip-jack nor soft marmalady courtier, but a brave, tall, gallant gentleman. Ay, but too watery a planet burned at his nativity. He is too like a statua of a man. No, nurse, thou must bring me better than he."

The nurse said, "True it is, O Queen, that most were of my thinking when I gave 'em my choice: the king of Demonland."

"Fie on thee!" cried Prezmyra. "Name him not so that was too unmighty to hold that land against our enemies."

"Folk say it was by foxish arts and practices magical a was spilt on Krothering Side. Folk say 'twas divels and not horses carried the Demons down the mountain at us."

"They say!" cried Prezmyra. "I say to thee, he hath found it apter to his bent to flaunt his crown in Witchland than make 'em give him the knee in Galing. For a true king both knee and heart do truly bow before him. But this one, if he had their knee 'twas in the back side of him he had it, to kick him home again."

"Fie, madam!" said the nurse.

"Hold thy tongue, nurse," said Prezmyra. "It were good ye

were all well whipped for a bunch of silly mares that know not a
horse from an ass."

The old woman watching her in the glass counted it best keep
silence. Prezmyra said under her breath as if talking to herself, "I
know a man should not have miscarried it thus." The old nurse
that loved not Lord Corund and his haughty fashions and rough
speech and wine-bibbing, and was besides jealous that so rude a
stock should wear so rich a jewel as was her mistress, followed not
her meaning.

After some time, the old woman spake softly and said, "You
are full of thoughts to-night, madam."

Prezmyra's eyes met hers in the mirror. "Why may I not be so
and it likes me?" said she.

That stony look of the eyes struck like a gong some twenty-
year-old memory in the nurse's heart: the little wilful maiden, ill to
goad but good to guide, looking out from that Queen's face across
the years. She knelt down suddenly and caught her arms about her
mistress's waist. "Why must you wed then, dear heart?" said she,
"if you were minded to do what likes you? Men love not sad looks
in their wives. You may ride a lover on the curb, madam, but once
you wed him 'tis all t'other way: all his way, madam, and beware of
'had I wist.' "

Her mistress looked down at her mockingly. "I have been wed
seven years to-night. I should know these things."

"And this night!" said the nurse. "And but an hour till midnight, and yet he sitteth at board."

The Lady Prezmyra leaned back to look again on her own
mirrored loveliness. Her proud mouth sweetened to a smile. "Wilt
thou learn me common women's wisdom?" said she, and there was
yet more voluptuous sweetness trembling in her voice. "I will tell
thee a story, as thou hast told them me in the old days in Norvasp
to wile me to bed. Hast thou not heard tell how old Duke Hilmanes
of Maltraëny, among some other fantasies such as appear by night
unto many in divers places, had one in likeness of a woman with
old face of low and little stature or body, which did scour his pots
and pans and did such things as a maid servant ought to do,
liberally and without doing of any harm? And by his art he knew
this thing should be his servant still, and bring unto him whatsoever he would, so long time as he should be glad of the things it
brought him. But this duke, being a foolish man and a greedy,
made his familiar bring him at once all the year's seasons and their
several goods and pleasures, and all good things of earth at one
time. So as in six months' space, he being sated with these and all

good things, and having no good thing remaining unto him to expect or to desire, for very weariness did hang himself. I would never have ta'en me an husband, nurse, and I had not known that I was able to give him every time I would a new heaven and a new earth, and never the same thing twice."

She took the old woman's hands in hers and gathered them to her breast, as if to let them learn, rocked for a minute in the bountiful infinite sweetness of that place, what foolish fears were these. Suddenly Prezmyra clasped the hands tighter in her own, and shuddered a little. She bent down to whisper in the nurse's ear, "I would not wish to die. The world without me should be summer without roses. Carcë without me should be a night without the star-shine."

Her voice died away like the night breeze in a summer garden. In the silence they heard the dip and wash of oar-blades from the river without; the sentinel's challenge, the answer from the ship.

Prezmyra stood up quickly and went to the window. She could see the ship's dark bulk by the water-gate, and comings and goings, but nought clearly. "Tidings from the fleet," she said. "Put up my hair."

And ere that was done, came a little page running to her chamber door, and when it was opened to him, stood panting from his running and said, "The king your husband bade me tell you, madam, and pray you go down to him i' the great hall. It may be ill news, I fear."

"Thou fearest, pap-face?" said the Queen. "I'll have thee whipped if thou bringest thy fears to me. Dost know aught? What's the matter?"

"The ship's much battered, O Queen. He is closeted with our Lord the King, the skipper. None dare speak else. 'Tis feared the high Admiral——"

"Feared!" cried she, swinging round for the nurse to put about her white shoulders her mantle of sendaline and cloth of silver, that shimmered at the collar with purple amethysts and was scented with cedar and galbanum[5] and myrrh. She was forth in the dark corridor, down by the winding marble stair, through the mid-court, hasting to the banquet hall. The court was full of folk talking; but nought certain, nought save suspense and wonder; rumour of a great sea-fight in the south, a mighty victory won by Laxus upon the Demons: Juss and those lords of Demonland dead and gone, the captives following with the morning's tide. And here and there like an undertone to these triumphant tidings, contrary rumours, whispered low, like the hissing of an adder from her shadowy lair: all not well, the lord Admiral wounded, half his ships lost, the battle doubtful, the Demons escaped. So came that lady into the great hall; and there were the lords and captains of the Witches all in a restless quiet of expectation. Duke Corsus lolled forward in his seat down by the cross-bench, his breath stertorous, his small eyes fixed in a drunken stare. On the other side Corund sate huge and motionless, his elbow propped on the table, his chin in his hand, sombre and silent, staring at the wall. Others gathered in knots, talking in low tones. The Lord Corinius walked up and down behind the cross-bench, his hands clasped behind him, his fingers snapping impatiently at whiles, his heavy jaw held high, his glance high and defiant. Prezmyra came to Heming where he stood among three or four and touched him on the arm. "We know nothing, madam," he said. "He is with the King."

She came to her lord. "Thou didst send for me."

Corund looked up at her. "Why, so I did, madam. Tidings from the fleet. Maybe somewhat, maybe nought. But thou'dst best be here for't."

"Good tidings or ill: that shaketh not Carcë walls," said she.

Suddenly the low buzz of talk was hushed. The King stood in the curtained doorway. They rose up all to meet him, all save Corsus that sat drunk in his chair. The crown of Witchland shed baleful sparkles above the darkness of the dark fortress-face of Gorice the King, the glitter of his dread eyeballs, the deadly line of his mouth, the square black beard jutting beneath. Like a tower he stood, and behind him in the shadow was the messenger from the fleet with countenance the colour of wet mortar.

The King spake and said, "My lords, here's tidings touching the truth whereof I have well satisfied myself. And it importeth the mere perdition of my fleet. There hath been battle off Melikaphkhaz in the Impland seas. Juss hath sunken our ships, every ship save that which brought the tidings, sunk, with Laxus and all his men that were with him." He paused: then, "These be heavy news," he said, "and I'll have you bear 'em in the old Witchland fashion: the heavier hit the heavier strike again."

In the strange deformed silence came a little gasping cry, and the Lady Sriva fell a-swooning.

The King said, "Let the kings of Impland and of Demonland attend me. The rest, it is commanded that all do get them to bed o' the instant."

The Lord Corund said in his lady's ear as he went by, taking her with his hand about the shoulder. "What, lass? if the broth's split, the meat remaineth. To bed with thee, and never doubt we'll pay them yet."

And he with Corinius followed the King.

It was past middle night when the council brake up, and Corund sought his chamber in the eastern gallery above the inner court. He found his lady sitting yet at the window, watching the false dawn over Pixyland. Dismissing his lamp-bearers that lighted him to bed, he bolted and barred the great iron-studded door. The breadth of his shoulders when he turned filled the shadowy doorway; his head well nigh touched the lintel. It was hard to read his countenance in the uncertain gloom where he stood beyond the bright region made by the candle-light, but Prezmyra's eyes could mark how care sat on his brow, and there was in the carriage of his ponderous frame kingliness and the strength of some strong determination.

She stood up, looking up at him as on a mate to whom she could be true and be true to her own self. "Well?" she said.

"The tables are set," said he, without moving.

"The King hath named me his captain general in Carcë."

"Is it come to that?" said Prezmyra.

"They have hewn a limb from us," answered he. "They have wit to know the next stroke should be at the heart."

"Is it truly so?" said she. "Eight thousand men? twice thine army's strength that won Impland for us? all drowned?"

" 'Twas the devilish seamanship of these accursed Demons," said Corund. "It appeareth Laxus held the Straits where they must go if ever they should win home again, meaning to fight 'em in the narrows and so crush 'em with the weight of 's ships as easy as kill flies, having by a great odds the bigger strength both in ships and men. They o' their part kept the sea without, trying their best to 'tice him forth so they might do their sailor tricks i' the open. A week or more he withstood it, till o' the ninth day (the devil curse him for a fool, wherefore could a not have had patience?) o' the ninth morning, weary of inaction and having wind and tide something in his favour"; the Lord Corund groaned and snapped his fingers contemptuously. "O I'll tell thee the tale to-morrow, madam. I'm surfeited with it to-night. The sum is, Laxus drownded and all that were with him, and Juss with his whole great armament northward bound for Witchland."

"And the wide seas his. And we expect him any day?"

"The wind hangeth easterly. Any day," said Corund.

Prezmyra said, "That was well done to rest the command in

thee. But what of our qualified young gentleman who had that office aforetime. Will he play o' these terms?"

Corund answered, "Hungry dogs will eat dirty puddings. I think he'll play, albeit he showed his teeth i' the first while."

"Let him keep his teeth for the Demons," said she.

"This very ship was ta'en," said Corund, "and sent home by them in a bravado to tell us what betid: a stupid insolent part, shall cost 'em dear, for it hath forewarned us. The skipper had this letter for thee: gave it me monstrous secretly."

Prezmyra took away the wax and opened the letter, and knew the writer of it. She held it out to Corund: "Read it to me, my lord. I am tired with watching; I read ill by this flickering candle-light."

But he said, "I am too poor a scholar, madam. I prithee read it."

And in the light of the guttering candles, vexed with an east wind that blew before the dawn, she read this letter, that was conceived in manner following:

"Unto the right high mighti and doubtid Prynsace the Quen of Implande, one that was your Servaunt but now beinge both a Traitor and a manifald parjured Traitor, which Heaven above doth abhorre, the erth below detest, the sun moone and starres be eschamed of, and all Creatures doo curse and ajudge unworthy of breth and life, do wish onelie to die your Penytent. In hevye sorrowe doo send you these advisoes which I requyre your Mageste in umblest manner to pondur wel, seeinge ells your manyfest Overthrowe and Rwyn att hand. And albeit in Carcee you reste in securitie, it is serten you are there as saife as he that hingeth by the Leves of a Tree in the end of Autumpne when as the Leves begin to fall. For in this late Battaile in Mellicafhaz Sea hath the whole powre of Wychlande on the sea been beat downe and ruwyned, and the highe Admirall of our whole Navie loste and ded and the names of the great men of accownte that were slayen at the battaile I may not numbre nor the common sorte much lesse by reaisoun that the more part were dround in the sea which came not to Syght. But of Daemounlande not ij schips companies were lossit, but with great puissaunce they doo buske them for Carsee. Havinge with them this Gowldri Bleusco, strangely reskewed from his preassoun-house beyond the toombe, and a great Armey of the moste strangg and fell folke that ever I saw or herd speke of. Such is the Die of Warre. Most Nowble Prynsace I will speke unto you not by a Ryddle or Darck Fygure but playnly that you let not slipp this Occasioun. For I have drempt an evill Dreeme and one pourtend-

346 ❖ E. R. Eddison

ing ruwyn unto Wychlande, beinge in my slepe on the verie eve of this same bataille terrified and smytten with an appeering schape of Laxus armde cryinge in an hyghe voise and lowd, An Ende an Ende an ende of All. Therefore most aernestly I do beseek your Magestie and your nowble Lorde that was my Frend before that by my venemous tresun I loste both you and him and alle, take order for your proper saffetie, and the thinge requyers Haste of your Magestes. And this must you doo, to fare strayght way into your owne cuntrie of Picselande and there raise Force. Be you before these rebalds and obstynates of Demounlande in their Prowd Attempts to strike at Wychlande and so purchas their Frenshyp who it is verie sertan will in powre invintiable stand before Carsee or ever Wychlande shall have time to putt you downe. This Counsell I give you knowinge full well that the Power and Domynyon of the Demouns standeth now preheminent and not to be withstode. So tarry not by a Sinckinge Schippe, but do as I saye lest all bee loste.

"One thinge more I telle you, that shall haply enforce my counsell unto you, the hevyeste Newes of alle."

" 'Tis heavy news that such a false troker as he is should yet supervive so many honest men," said Corund.

The Lady Prezmyra held out the letter to her lord. "Mine eyes dazzle," she said. "Read thou the rest." Corund put his great arm about her as he sat down to the table before the mirror and pored over the writing, spelling it out with one finger. He had little book-learning, and it was some time ere he had the meaning clear. He did not read it out; his lady's face told him she had read all ere he began.

This was the last news Gro's letter told her: the Prince her brother dead in the sea-fight, fighting for Demonland; dead and drowned in the sea off Melikaphkhaz.

Prezmyra went to the window. Dawn was beginning, bleak and gray. After a minute she turned her head. Like a she-lion she looked, proud and dangerous-eyed. She was very pale. Her accents, level and quiet, called to the blood like the roll of a distant drum, as she said, "Succours of Demonland: late or never."

Corund beheld her uneasily.

"Their oaths to me and to him!" said she, "sworn to us that night in Carcë. False friends! O, I could eat their hearts with garlic."

He put his great hands on her two shoulders. She threw them off. "In one thing," she cried, "Gro counselleth us well: to tarry no more on this sinking ship. We must raise forces. But not as he would have it, to uphold these Demons, these oath-breakers. We must away this night."

Her lord had cast aside his great wolfskin mantle. "Come, madam," said he, "to bed's our nearest journey."

Prezmyra answered, "I'll not to bed. It shall be seen now, O Corund, if that thou be a king indeed."

He sat down on the bed's edge and fell to doing off his boots. "Well," he said, "every one as he likes, as the goodman said when he kissed his cow. Day's near dawning; I must be up betimes, and a sleepless night's a poor breeder of invention."

But she stood over him, saying, "It shall be seen if thou be a true king. And be not deceived: if thou fail me here I'll have no more of thee. This night we must away. Thou shalt raise Pixyland, which is now mine by right: raise power in thine own vast kingdom of Impland. Fling Witchland to the winds. What care I if she sink or swim? This only is the matter: to punish these vile perjured Demons, enemies of ours and enemies of all the world."

"We need ride o' no journey for that," said Corund, still putting off his boots. "Thou shalt shortly see Juss and his brethren before Carcë with three score hundred fighting men at's back. Then cometh the metal to the anvil. Come, come, thou must not weep."

"I do not weep," said she. "Nor I shall not weep. But I'll not be ta'en in Carcë like a mouse in a trap."

"I'm glad thou'lt not weep, madam. It is as great pity to see a woman weep as a goose to go barefoot. Come, be not foolish. We must not part forces now. We must bide this storm in Carcë."

But she cried, "There is a curse on Carcë. Gro is lost to us and his good counsel. Dear my lord, I see something wicked that like a thick dark shadow shadoweth all the sky above us. What place is there not subject to the power and regiment of Gorice the King? but he is too proud: we be all too insolent overweeners of our own works. Carcë hath grown too great, and the Gods be offended at us. The insolent vileness of Corinius, the old dotard Corsus that must still be at his boosing-can, these and our own private quarrels in Carcë must be our bane. Repugn not therefore against the will of the Gods, but take the helm in thine own hand ere it be too late."

"Tush, madam," said he, "these be but fray-bugs.[6] Day-light shall make thee laugh at 'em."

But Prezmyra, queening it no longer, caught her arms about his neck. "The odd man to perform all perfectly is thou. Wilt thou see us rushing on this whirlpool and not swim for it ere it be too late?" And she said in a choked voice, "My heart is near broke already. Do not break it utterly. Only thou art left now."

The chill dawn, the silent room, the guttering candles, and that high-hearted lady of his, daunted for an instant from her noble and equal courage, cowering like a bird in his embrace: these things were like an icy breath that passed by and quailed him for a moment. He took her by her two hands and held her off from him. She held her head high again, albeit her cheek was blanched; he felt the brave comrade-grip of her hands in his.

"Dear lass," he said, "I cast me not to be odd with none of these spawn of Demonland. Here is my hand, and the hand of my sons, heavy while breath remaineth us against Demonland for thee and for the King. But sith our lord the King hath made me a king, come wind, come weet, we must weather it in Carcë. True is that saw, 'For fame one maketh a king, not for long living.'"

Prezmyra thought in her heart that these were fey words. But having now put behind her hope and fear, she was resolved to kick against the wind no more, but stand firm and see what Destiny would do.

XXXI

The Demons Before Carcë

*How Gorice the King, albeit so strong a sorcerer,
elected that by the sword, and chiefly by the Lord
Corund his Captain General, should be
determined as for this time the event of these
high matters; and how those twain, the King and
the Lord Juss, spake face to face at last; and of
the bloody battle before Carcë, and what fruit
was garnered there and what made ripe
against harvest.*

ORICE the king sate in his chamber the thirteenth morning after these tidings brought to Carcë. On the table under his hand were papers of account and schedules of his armies and their equipment. Corund sate at the King's right hand, and over against him Corinius.

Corund's great hairy hands were clasped before him on the table. He spoke without book, resting his gaze on the steady clouds that sailed across the square of sky seen through the high window that faced him. "Of Witchland and the home provinces, O King, nought but good. All the companies of soldiers which were appointed to repair to this part by the tenth of the month are now come hither, save some bands of spearmen from the south, and

some from Estreganzia. These last I expect to-day; Viglus writeth
they come with him with the heavy troops from Baltary I sent him
to assemble. So is the muster full as for these parts: Thramnë,
Zorn, Permio, the land of Ar, Trace, Buteny, and Estremerine. Of
the subject allies, there's less good there. The kings of Mynia and
Gilta: Olis of Tecapan: County Escobrine of Tzeusha: the king of
Ellien: all be here with their contingents. But there's mightier
names we miss. Duke Maxtlin of Azumel hath flung off's allegiance
and cut off your envoy's ears, O King; 'tis thought for some supposed light part of the sons of Corsus done to his sister. That
docketh us thirty score stout fighters. The lord of Eushtlan sendeth
no answer, and now are we advertised by Mynia and Gilta of his
open malice and treason, who did stubbornly let them the way
hither through his country while they hastened to do your majesty's commands. Then there's the Ojedian levies, should be nigh a
thousand spears, ten days overdue. Heming, that raiseth Pixyland
in Prezmyra's name, will bring them in if he may. Who also hath
order, being on his way, to rouse Maltraëny to action, from whom
no word as yet; and I do fear treachery in 'em. Maltraëny and
Ojedia both, they have been so long of coming. King Barsht of
Toribia sendeth flat refusal."

"It is known to you besides, O King," said Corinius, "that the
king of Nevria came in last night, many days past the day appointed, and but half his just complement."

The King drew back his lips. "I will not dash his spirits by
blaming him at this present. Later, I'll have that king's head for
this."

"This is the sum," said Corund. "Nay, then, I had forgot the
Red Foliot with's folk, three hundred perchance, came in this
morning."

Corinius thrust out his tongue and laughed: "One hen-lobster
such as he shall scarce afford a course for this banquet."

"He keepeth faith," said Corund, "where bigger men turn
dastards. 'Tis seen now that these forced leagues be as sure as they
were sealed with butter. Your majesty will doubtless give him audience."

The King was silent awhile, studying his papers. "What
strength to-day in Carcë?" he asked.

Corund answered him, "As near as may be two score hundred
foot and fifty score horse: five thousand in all. And, that I weigh
most, O King, big broad strong set lads of Witchland nigh every
jack of 'em."

The King said, " 'Twas not well done, O Corund, to bid thy

son delay for Ojedia and Maltraëny. He might else have been in Carcë now with a thousand Pixylanders to swell our strength."

"I did that I did," answered Corund, "seeking only your good, O King. A few days' delay might buy us a thousand spears."

"Delay," said the King, "hath favoured mine enemy. This we should have done: at his first landing give him no time but wink, set on him with all our forces, and throw him into the sea."

"If luck go with us that may yet be," said Corund.

The King's nostrils widened. He crouched forward, glaring at Corund and Corinius, his jaw thrust out so that the stiff black beard on it brushed the papers on the table before him. "The Demons," said he, "landed i' the night at Ralpa. They come on with great journeys northward. Will be here ere three days be spent."

Both they grew red as blood. Corund spake: "Who told you these tidings, O King?"

"Care not thou for that," said the King. "Enough for thee, I know it. Hath it ta'en you napping?"

"No," answered he. "These ten days past we have been ready, with what strength we might make, to receive 'em, come they from what quarter they will. So it is, though, that while we lack the Pixyland succours Juss hath by some odds the advantage over us, if, as our intelligence saith, six thousand fighting men do follow him, and these forced besides with some that should be ours."[1]

"Thou wouldst," said the King, "await these out of Pixyland, with that else Heming may gather, afore we offer them battle?"

Said Corund, "That would I. We must look beyond the next turn of the road, O my Lord the King."

"That would not I," said Corinius.

"That is stoutly said, Corinius," said the King. "Yet remember, thou hadst the greater force on Krothering Side, yet wast overborne."

" 'Tis that standeth in my mind, Lord," said Corund. "For well I know, had I been there I'd a fared no better."

The Lord Corinius, whose brow had darkened with the naming of his defeat, looked cheerfully now and said, "I pray you but consider, O my Lord the King, that here at home is no room for such a sleight or gin as that whereby in their own country they took me. When Juss and Brandoch Daha and their stinking gaberlunzies[2] do cry huff at us on Witchland soil, 'tis time to give 'em a choke-pear. Which with your leave, Lord, I will promise now to do, other else to lose my life."

"Give me thy hand," said Corund. "Of all men else would I a chosen thee for such a day as this, and (were't to-day to meet the whole power of Demonland in arms) to stand perdue[3] with thee for this bloody service. But let us hear the King's commands: which way soe'er he choose, we shall do it right gladly."

Gorice the King sat silent. One lean hand rested on the iron serpent-head of his chair's arm, the other, with finger outstretched against the jutting cheekbone, supported his chin. Only in the deep shadow of his eye-sockets a lambent light moved. At length he started, as if the spirit, flown to some unsounded gulfs of time or space, had in that instant returned to its mortal dwelling. He gathered the papers in a heap and tossed them to Corund.

"Too much lieth on it," said he. "He that hath many peas may put more in the pot. But now the day approacheth when I and Juss must cast up our account together, and one or all shall be brought to death and bane." He stood up from his chair and looked down on those two, his chosen captains, great men of war raised up by him to be kings over two quarters of the world. They watched him like little birds under the eye of a snake. "The country hereabout," said the King, "is not good for horsemanship, and the Demons be great horsemen. Carcë is strong, and never can it be forced by assault. Also under mine eye should my men of Witchland acquit[4] themselves to do the greatest deeds. Therefore will we abide them here in Carcë, until young Heming come and his levies out of Pixyland. Then shall ye fall upon them and never make an end till the land be utterly purged of them, and all the lords of Demonland be slain."

Corinius said, "To hear is to obey, O King. Howsoever, not to dissemble with you, I'd liever[5] at 'em at once, 'stead of let them sit awhile and refresh their army. Occasion is a wanton wench, O King, that is quick to beckon another man if one look coldly on her. Moreover, Lord, could you not by your art, in small time, with certain compositions?——"

But the King brake in upon him saying, "Thou knowest not what thou speakest. There is thy sword; there thy men; these my commands. See thou perform them punctually when time shall come."

"Lord," said Corinius, "you shall not find me wanting." Therewith he did obeisance and went forth from before the King.

The King said unto Corund, "Thou hast manned him well, this tassel-gentle.[6] There was some danger he should so mislike subjection unto thee in these acts martial as it should breed some quarrel should little speed our enterprise."

"Think not you that, O King," answered Corund. " 'Tis

grown like an almanac for the past year, past date. A will feed out of my hand now."

"Because thou hast carried it with him," said the King, "in so honourable and open plainness. Hold on the road thou hast begun, and be mindful still that into thine hand is given the sword of Witchland, and therein have I put my trust for this great hour."

Corund looked upon the King with gray and quick eyes shining like unto the eagle's. He slapped his heavy sword with the flat of his hand: " 'Tis a tough fox, O my Lord the King; will not fail his master."

Therewith, glad at the King's gracious words, he did obeisance unto the King and went forth from the chamber.

The same night there appeared in the sky impending over Carcë a blazing star with two bushes. Corund beheld it in an open space betwixt the clouds as he went to his chamber. He said nought of it to his lady wife, lest it should trouble her; but she too had from her window seen that star, yet spake not of it to her lord for a like reason.

And King Gorice, sitting in his chamber with his baleful books, beheld that star and its fiery streamers, which the King rather noted than liked. For albeit he might not know of a certain what way that sign intended, yet was it apparent to one so deeply learned in nigromancy and secrets astronomical that this thing was fatal, being of those prodigies and ominous prognosticks which fore-run the tragical ends of noble persons and the ruins of states.

The third day following, watchmen beheld from Carcë walls in the pale morning the armies of the Demons that filled the whole plain to southward. But of the succours out of Pixyland was as yet no sign at all. Gorice the King, according as he had determined, held all his power quiet within the fortress. But for passing of the time, and because it pleased his mind to speak yet face to face with the Lord Juss before this last mortal trial in arms should be begun betwixt them, the King sent Cadarus as his herald with flags of truce and olive-branches into the Demons' lines. By which mission it was concluded that the Demons should withdraw their armies three bowshots from the walls, and they of Witchland should abide all within the hold; only the King with fourteen of his folk unarmed and Juss with a like number unarmed should come forth into the midst of the bateable ground and there speak together. And this meeting must be at the third hour after noon.

So either party came to this parley at the hour appointed. Juss went bare-headed but, save for that, all armed in his shining byrny with gorget and shoulder-plates demasked and embossed[7] with wires of gold, and golden leg-harness, and rings of red gold upon his wrists. His kirtle was of wine-dark silken tissue, and he wore that dusky cloak the sylphs had made for him, the collar whereof was stiff with broidery and strange beasts worked thereon in silver thread. According to the compact he bare no weapon; only in his hand a short ivory staff inlaid with precious stones, and the head of it a ball of that stone which men call Belus' eye, that is white and hath within it a black apple, the midst whereof a man shall see to glitter like gold. Very masterful and proud he stood before the King, carrying his head like a stag that sniffs the morning. His brethren and Brandoch Daha remained a pace or two behind him, with King Gaslark and the lords Zigg and Gro, and Melchar and Tharmrod and Styrkmir, Quazz with his two sons, and Astar, and Bremery of Shaws: goodly men and lordly to look on, unweaponed all; and wondrous was the sparkle of their jewels that were on them.

Over against them, attending on the King, were these: Corund king of Impland, and Corinius called king of Demonland, Hacmon and Viglus Corund's sons, Duke Corsus and his sons Dekalajus and Gorius, Eulien king of Mynia, Olis lord of Tecapan, Duke Avel of Estreganzia, the Red Foliot, Erp the king of Ellien, and the counts of Thramnë and Tzeusha; unweaponed, but armoured to the throat, big men and strong the most of them and of lordly bearing, yet none to match with Corinius and Corund.

The King, in his mantle of cobra-skins, his staff-royal in his hand, topped by half a head all those tall men about him, friend and foe alike. Lean and black he towered amongst them, like a thunder-blasted pine-tree seen against the sunset.

So, in the golden autumn afternoon, in the midst of that sad main of sedgelands where between slimy banks the weed-choked Druima deviously winds toward the sea, were those two men met together for whose ambition and their pride the world was too little a place to contain them both and peace lying between them. And like some drowsy dragon of the elder slime, squat, sinister, and monstrous, the citadel of Carcë slept over all.

By and by the King spake and said: "I sent for thee because I think it good I and thou should talk together while yet is time for talking."

Juss answered, "I quarrel not with that, O King."

"Thou," said the King, bending his brow upon him, "art a man wise and fearless. I counsel thee, and all these that be with thee, turn back from Carcë. Well I see the blood thou didst drink in Melikaphkhaz will not allay thy thirst, and war is to thee thy pearl and thy paramour. Yet, if it be, turn back from Carcë. Thou standest now on the pinnacle of thine ambition; wilt leap higher, thou fall'st in the abyss. Let the four corners of the earth be shaken with our wars, but not this centre. For here shall no man gather fruit, but and if it be death he gather; or if, then this fruit only, that Zoacum, that fruit of bitterness, which when he shall have tasted of, all the bright lights of heaven shall become as darkness and all earth's goodness as ashes in his mouth all his life's days until he die."

He paused. The Lord Juss stood still, quailing not at all beneath that dreadful gaze. His company behind him stirred and whispered. Lord Brandoch Daha, with mockery in his eye, said somewhat to Goldry Bluszco under his breath.

But the King spake again to the Lord Juss, "Be not deceived. These things I say unto thee not as labouring to scare you from your set purpose with frights and fairy-babes: I know your quality too well. But I have read signs in heaven: nought clear, but threatful unto both you and me. For thy good I say it, O Juss, and again (for that our last speech leaveth the firmest print) be advised: turn back from Carcë or it be too late."

Lord Juss harkened attentively to the words of Gorice the King, and when he had ended, answered and said, "O King, thou hast given us terrible good counsel. But it was riddlewise. And hearing thee, mine eye was still on the crown thou wearest, made in the figure of a crab-fish,[8] which, because it looks one way and goes another, methought did fitly pattern out thy looking to our perils but seeking the while thine own advantage."

The King gave him an ill look, saying, "I am thy lord paramount. With subjects it sits not to use this familiar style unto their King."

Juss answered, "Thou dost thee and thou me.[9] And indeed it were folly in either of us twain to bend knee to t'other, when the lordship of all the earth waiteth on the victor in our great contention. Thou hast been open with me, Witchland, to let me know thou art uneager to strike a field with us. I will be open too, and I will make an offer unto thee, and this it is: that we will depart out of thy country and do no more unpeaceful deeds against thee (till thou provoke us again); and thou, of thy part, of all the land of Demonland shalt give up thy quarrel, and of Pixyland and Impland beside, and shalt yield me up Corsus and Corinius thy servants that

I may punish them for the beastly deeds they did in our land whenas we were not there to guard it."

He ceased, and for a minute they beheld each other in silence. Then the King lifted up his chin and smiled a dreadful smile.

Corinius whispered mockingly in his ear, "Lord, you may lightly give 'em Corsus. That were easy composition, and false coin too methinks."

"Stand back i' thy place," said the King, "and hold thy peace." And unto Lord Juss he said, "Of all ensuing harm the cause is in thee; for I am now resolved never to put up my sword until of thy bleeding head I may make a football. And now, let the earth be afraid, and Cynthia obscure her shine: no more words but mum. Thunder and blood and night must usurp our parts, to complete and make up the catastrophe of this great piece."

That night the King walked late in his chamber in the Iron Tower alone. These three years past he had seldom resorted thither, and then commonly but to bear away some or other of his books to study in his own lodging. His jars and flasks and bottles of blue and green and purple glass wherein he kept his cursed drugs and electuaries[10] of secret composition, his athals and athanors, his crucibles, his horsebellied retorts and alembics and bainsmaries, stood arow on shelves coated with dust and hung about with the dull spider's weavings; the furnace was cold; the glass of the windows was clouded with dirt; the walls were mildewed; the air of the chamber fusty and stagnant. The King was deep in his contemplation, with a big black book open before him on the six-sided reading-stand: the damnablest of all his books, the same which had taught him aforetime what he must do when by the wicked power of enchantment he had wanted but a little to have confounded Demonland and all the lords thereof in death and ruin.

The open page under his hand was of parchment discoloured with age, and the writing on the page was in characters of ancient out-of-fashion crabbedness, heavy and black, and the great initial letters and the illuminated borders were painted and gilded in dark and fiery hues with representations of dreadful faces and forms of serpents and toad-faced men and apes and mantichores and succubi and incubi[11] and obscene representations and figures of unlawful meaning. These were the words of the writing on the page which the King conned[12] over and over, falling again into a deep study betweenwhiles, and then conning these words again of an age-old prophetic writing touching the preordinate destinies of the royal house of Gorice in Carcë:

Soo schel your hous stonde and bee
Unto eternytee
Yet walke warilie
Wyttinge ful sarteynlee
That if impiouslie
The secounde tyme in the bodie
Practisinge grammarie
One of ye katched shulle be
By the feyndis subtiltee
And hys liffe lossit bee
Broke ys thenne this serye
Dampned are you thenne eternallie
Yerth shuldestow thenne never more se
Scarsly the Goddes mought reskue ye
Owt of the Helle where you woll lie
Unto eternytee
The sterres tealde hit mee.

Gorice the King stood up and went to the south window. The casement bolts were rusted: he forced them and they flew back with a shriek and a clatter and a thin shower of dust and grit. He opened the window and looked out. The heavy night grew to her depth of quiet. There were lights far out in the marshes, the lights of Lord Juss's camp-fires of his armies gathered against Carcë. Scarcely without a chill might a man have looked upon that King standing by the window; for there was in the tall lean frame of him an iron aspect as of no natural flesh and blood but some harder colder element; and his countenance, like the picture of some dark divinity graven ages ago by men long dead, bore the imprint of those old qualities of unrelenting power, scorn, violence, and oppression, ancient as night herself yet untouched by age, young as each night when it shuts down and old and elemental as the primaeval dark.

A long while he stood there, then came again to his book. "Gorice VII.," he said in himself. "That was once in the body. And I have done better than that, but not yet well enough. 'Tis too hazardous, the second time, alone. Corund is a man undaunted in war, but the man is too superstitious and quaketh at that which hath not flesh and blood. Apparitions and urchin-shows[13] can quite unman him. There's Corinius, careth not for God or man a point. But he is too rash and unadvised: I were mad to trust him in it. Were the Goblin here, it might be carried. Damnable both-sides villain, he's cast off from me." He scanned the page as if his piercing eyes would thrust beyond the barriers of time and death and discover some new meaning in the words which should agree better with the thing his mind desired while his judgement forbade it. "He says 'damned eternally:' he says that breaketh the series, and 'earth shouldst thou then never more see.' Put him by."

And the King slowly shut up his book, and locked it with three padlocks, and put back the key in his bosom. "The need is not yet," he said. "The sword shall have his day, and Corund. But if that fail me, then even this shall not turn me back but I will do that I will do."

In the same hour when the King was but now entered again into his own lodgings, came through a runner of Heming's to let them know that he, fifteen hundred strong, marched down the Way of Kings from Pixyland. Moreover they were advertised that the Demon fleet lay in the river that night, and it was not unlike the attack should be in the morning by land and water.

All night the King sate in his chamber holding council with his generals and ordering all things for the morrow. All night long he closed not his eyes an instant, but the others he made sleep by turns because they should be brisk and ready for the battle. For this was their counsel, to draw out their whole army on the left bank before the bridge-gate and there offer battle to the Demons at point of day. For if they should abide within doors and suffer the Demons to cut young Heming off from the bridge-gate, then were he lost, and if the bridge-house should fall and the bridge, then might the Demons lightly ship what force they pleased to the right bank and so closely invest them in Carcë. Of an attack on the right bank they had no fear, well knowing themselves able to sit within doors and laugh at them, since the walls were there inexpugnable. But if a battle were now brought about before the bridge-gate as they were minded, and Heming should join in the fight from the eastward, there was good hope that they should be able to crumple up the battle of the Demons, driving them in upon their centre from the west whilst Heming smote them on the other part. Whereby these should be cast into a great rout and confusion and not be able to escape away to their ships, but there in the fenlands before Carcë should be made a prey unto the Witches.

When it was the cold last hour before the dawn the generals took from the King their latest commands ere they drew forth their armies. Corinius came forth first from the King's chamber a little while before the rest. In the draughty corridor the lamps swung and smoked, making an uncertain windy light. Corinius espied by

the stair-head the Lady Sriva standing, whether watching to bid
her father adieu or but following idle curiosity. Whichever it were,
not a fico[14] gave he for that, but coming swiftly upon her whisked
her aside into an alcove where the light was barely enough to let
him see the pale shimmer of her silken gown, dark hair pinned
loosely up in deep snaky coils, and dark eyes shining. "My witty
false one, have I caught thee? Nay, fight not. Thy breath smells like
cinnamon. Kiss me, Sriva."

"I'll not!" said she, striving to escape. "Naughty man, am I
used thus?" But finding she got nought by struggling, she said in a
low voice, "Well, if thou bring back Demonland to-night, then,
let's hold more chat."

"Harken to the naughty traitress," said he, "that but last night
didst do me some uncivil discourtesies, and now speaketh me fair:
and what a devil for? if not 'cause her seemeth I'll likely not come
back after this day's fight. But I'll come back, mistress kiss-and-be-
gone; ay, by the Gods, and I'll have my payment too."

His lips fed deep on her lips, his strong and greedy hands
softly mastered her against her will, till with a little smothered cry
she embraced him, bruising her tender body against the armour he
was girt withal. Between the kisses she whispered, "Yes, yes, to-
night." Surely he damned spiteful fortune that sent him not this
encounter by an half-hour sooner.

When he was departed, Sriva remained in the shadow of the
alcove to set in order her hair and apparel, not a little disarrayed in
that hot wooing. Out of which darkness she had convenience to
observe the leave-taking of Prezmyra and her lord as they came
down that windy corridor and paused at the head of the stairs.

Prezmyra had her arm in his. "I know where the Devil keepeth
his tail, madam," said Corund. "And I know a very traitor when I
see him."

"When didst thou ever yet fare ill by following of my counsel,
my lord?" said Prezmyra. "Or did I refuse thee ever any thing thou
didst require me of? These seven years since I put off my maiden
zone for thee; and twenty kings sought me in sweet marriage, but
thee I preferred before them all, seeing the falcon shall not mate
with popinjays nor the she-eagle with swans and bustards. And will
you say nay to me in this?"

She stood round to face him. The pupils of her great eyes were
large in the doubtful lamplight, swallowing their green fires in
deep pools of mystery and darkness. The rich and gorgeous ornaments of her crown and girdle seemed but a poor casket for that
matchless beauty which was hers: her face, where every noble and

sweet quality and every thing desirable of earth or heaven had framed each feature to itself: the glory of her hair, like the red sun's glory: her whole body's poise and posture, like a stately bird's new-lighted after flight.

"Though it be very rhubarb to me," said Corund, "shall I say nay to thee this tide? Not this tide,[15] my Queen."

"Thanks, dear my lord. Disarm him and bring him in if you may. The King shall not refuse us this to pardon his folly, when thou shalt have obtained this victory for him upon our enemies."

The Lady Sriva might hear no more, harkened she never so curiously. But when they were now come to the stair foot, Corund paused a minute to try the buckles of his harness. His brow was clouded. At length he spake. "This shall be a battle mortal fierce and doubtous[16] for both parties. 'Gainst such mighty opposites as here we have, 'tis possible: No more; but kiss me, dear lass. And if: tush, 't will not be; and yet, I'd not leave it unsaid: if ill tide ill, I'd not have thee waste all thy days a-grieving. Thou knowest I am not one of your sour envious jacks, bear so poor a conceit o' them-selves they begrudge their wives should wed again lest the next husband should prove the better man."

But Prezmyra came near to him with good and merry counte-nance: "Let me stop thy mouth, my lord. These be foolish thoughts for a great king going into battle. Come back in triumph, and i' the mean season think on me that wait for thee: as a star waits, dear my lord. And never doubt the issue."

"The issue," answered he, "I'll tell thee when 'tis done. I'm no astronomer. I'll hew with my sword, love; spoil some of their guesses if I may."

"Good fortune and my love go with thee," she said.

Sriva coming forth from her hiding hastened to her mother's lodging, and there found her that had just bid adieu to her two sons, her face all blubbered with tears. In the same instant came the Duke her husband to change his sword, and the Lady Zenam-bria caught him about the neck and would have kissed him. But he shook her off, crying out that he was weary of her and her slobber-ing mouth; menacing her besides with filthy imprecations, that he would drag her with him and cast her to the Demons, who, since they had a strong loathing for such ugly tits and stale old trots, would no doubt hang her up or disembowel her and so rid him of his lasting consumption. Therewith he went forth hastily. But his wife and daughter, either weeping upon other, came down into the court, meaning to go up to the tower above the water-gate to see the army marshalled beyond the river. And on the way Sriva related all she had heard said betwixt Corund and Prezmyra.

In the court they met with Prezmyra's self, and she going with blithe countenance and light tread and humming a merry tune bade them good-morrow.

"You can bear these things more bravelier than we, madam," said Zenambria. "We be too gentle-hearted methinks and pitiful."

Prezmyra replied upon her, " 'Tis true, madam, I have not the weak sense of some of you soft-eyed whimpering ladies. And by your leave I'll keep my tears (which be great spoilers of the cheeks beside) until I need 'em."

When they were passed by, "Is it not a stony-livered and a shameless hussy, O my mother?" said Sriva. "And is it not scandalous her laughing and jestings; as I have told it thee, when she did bid him adieu, devising only how best she might coax him to save the life of yonder chambering traitorous hound?"

"With whom," said Zenambria, "she wont to do the thing I'd think shame to speak on. Truly this foreign madam with her loose and wanton ways doth scandal the whole land for us."

But Prezmyra went her way, glad that she had not by an eyelid's flicker let her lord guess what a dread possessed her mind, who had in all the bitter night seen strange and cruel visions portending loss and ruin of all she held dear.

Now, when dawn appeared, was the King's whole army drawn out in battle array before the bridge-house. Corinius held command on the left. There followed him fifteen hundred chosen troops of Witchland, with the Dukes of Trace and Estreganzia, besides these kings and princes with their outlandish levies: the king of Mynia, Count Escobrine of Tzeusha, and the Red Foliot. Corsus led the centre, and with him went King Erp of Ellien and his green-coated sling-casters, the king of Nevria, Axtacus lord of Permio, the king of Gilta, Olis of Tecapan, and other captains: seventeen hundred men in all. The right the Lord Corund had chosen for himself. Two thousand Witchland troops, the likeliest and best, hardened to war in Impland and Demonland and the southeastern borders, followed his standard, beside the heavy spearmen of Baltary and swordsmen of Buteny and Ar. Viglus his son was there, and the Count of Thramnë, Cadarus, Didarus of Largos, and the lord of Estremerine.

But when the Demons were ware of that great army standing before the bridge-gate, they put themselves in array for battle. And their ships made ready to move up the river under Carcë, if by any means they might attack the bridge by water and so cut off for the Witches their way of retreat.

It was bright low sunshine, and the splendour of the jewelled armour of the Demons and their many-coloured kirtles and the plumes that were in their helms was a wonder to behold. This was the order of their battle. On their left nearest the river was a great company of horse, and the Lord Brandoch Daha to lead them on a great golden dun with fiery eyes. His island men, Melchar and Tharmrod, with Kamerar of Stropardon and Strykmir and Stypmar, were the chief captains that rode with him to that battle. Next to these came the heavy troops from the east, and the Lord Juss himself their leader on a tall fierce big-boned chestnut. About him was his picked bodyguard of horse, with Bremery of Shaws their captain; and in his battle were these chiefs besides: Astar of Rettray and Gismor Gleam of Justdale and Peridor of Sule. Lord Spitfire led the centre, and with him Fendor of Shalgreth, and Emeron, and the men of Dalney, great spearmen; also the Duke of Azumel, sometime allied with Witchland. There went also with him the Lord Gro, that scanned still those ancient walls with a heavy heart, thinking on the great King within, and with what mastery of intellect and will he ruled those dark turbulent and bloody men who bare sway under him; thinking on Queen Prezmyra. To his sick imagining, the blackness of Carcë which no bright morning light might lighten seemed not as of old the image and emblem of the royal house of Witchland and their high magnificency and power on earth, but rather the shadow thrown before of destiny and death ready to put down that power for ever. Which whether it should so befall or no he did not greatly care, being aweary of life and life's fevers, wild longings, and exorbitant affects, whereof he thought he had now learned much: that to him, who as it seemed must still adhere to his own foes abandoning the others' service, fortune through whatever chop could bring no peace at last. On the Demon right the Lord Goldry Bluszco streamed his standard, leading to battle the south-firthers and the heavy spearmen of Mardardale and Throwater. With him was King Gaslark and his army of Goblinland, and levies from Ojedia and Eushtlan, lately revolted from their allegiance to King Gorice. The Lord Zigg, with his light horse of Rammerick and Kelialand and the northern dales, covered their flank to the eastward.[17]

Gorice the King beheld these dispositions from his tower above the water-gate. He beheld, besides, a thing the Demons might not see from below, for a little swelling of the ground that cut off their view: the marching of men far away along the Way of

Kings from the eastward: young Heming with the vassalry of Pixy-land and Maltraëny. He sent a trusty man to apprise Corund of it.

Now Lord Juss let blow up the battle call, and with the loud braying of the trumpets the hosts of the Demons swung forth to battle. And the clash of those armies when they met before Carcë was like the bursting of a thundercloud. But like a great sea-cliff patient for ages under the storm-winds' furies, that not one night's loud wind and charging breakers can wear away, nor yet a thou-sand thousand nights, the embattled strength of Witchland met their onset, mixed with them, flung them back, and stood unre-moved. Corund's iron battalions bare in this first brunt the heavi-est load, and bare it through. For the ships, with young Hesper Golthring in command most fiercely urging them, ran up the river to force the bridge, and Corund whiles he met on his front the onset of the flower of Demonland must still be shot at by these behind. Hacmon and Viglus, those young princes his sons, were charged with the warding of the bridge and walls to burn and break up their ships. And they of all hands bestirring them twice and thrice threw back the Demons when they had gotten a footing on the bridge; until in fine, both sides for a long space fighting very cruelly, it fell out very fatally against Hesper and his power, his ships all lighted in a lowe and the more part of his folk burned or drowned or slain with the sword; and himself after many and grievous wounds in his last attempt left alone on the bridge, and crawling to have got away was stabbed in with a dagger and died.

After this the ships fell back down the river, so many as might avail thereto, and those sons of Corund, their task manfully ful-filled, came forth with their folk to join in the main battle. And the smoke of the burning ships was like incense in the nostrils of the King watching these things from his tower above the water-gate.

Little pause was there betwixt this first brunt and the next, for Heming now bare down from the east, drave in Zigg's horsemen that were hampered in the heavy ground, and pressed his onset home on the Demon right. Along the whole line from Corund's post beside the river to the eastern flank where Heming joined Corinius the Witches now set on most fiercely; and now were the odds of numbers, which were at first against them, swung mightily in their favour, and under this great side-blow on his flank not all the Lord Goldry Bluszco's soldiership nor all the terror of his might in arms could uphold the Demons' battle-line. Yard by yard they fell back before the Witches, most gloriously maintaining their array unbroken, though the outland allies broke and fled. Meantime on the Demon left Juss and Brandoch Daha most stub-

364 ❖ E. R. Eddison

bornly withstood that onslaught, albeit they had to do with the first
and chosen troops of Witchland. In which struggle befell the most
bloody fighting that was yet seen that day, and the stour of battle so
asper[18] and so mortal that it was hard to see how any man should
come out from it with life, since not a man of either side would
budge an inch but die there in his steps if he might not rather slay
the foe before him. So the armies swayed for an hour like wrastlers
locked, but in the end the Lord Corund had his way and held his
ground before the bridge-gate.

Romenard of Dalney, galloping to Lord Juss where he paused
a while panting from violence of the battle brought him by Spitfire's command tidings from the right: telling him Goldry's self
could hold no longer against such odds: that the centre yet held,
but at the next onset was like to break, or the right wing else be
driven in upon their rear and all overwhelmed: "If your highness
cannot throw back Corund, all is lost."

In these short minutes' lull (if lull it were when all the time the
battle like a sounding sea rolled on with a ceaseless noise of riding
and slaying and the clang of arms), Juss chose. Demonland and the
whole world's destinies hung on his choice. He had no counsellor.
He had no time for slow deliberation. In such a moment imagination, resolution, swift decision, all high gifts of nature, are nought:
swift horses gulfed and lost in the pit which fate the enemy digged
in the way before them; except painful knowledge, stored up pa-
tiently through years of practice, shall have prepared a road sure
and clean for their flying hooves to bear them in the great hour of
destiny. So it was from the beginning with all great captains: so
with the Lord Juss in that hour when ruin swooped upon his
armies. For two minutes' space he stood silent; then sent Bremery
of Shaws galloping westward like one minded to break his neck
with his orders to Lord Brandoch Daha, and Romenard eastward
again to Spitfire. And Juss himself riding forward among his
soldiers shouted among them in a voice that was like a trumpet
thundering, that they should now make ready for the fiercest trial
of all.

"Is my cousin mad?" said Lord Brandoch Daha, when he saw
and understood the whole substance and matter of it. "Or hath he
found Corund so tame to deal with he can make shift without me
and well nigh half his strength, and yet withstand him?"

"He looseth this hold," answered Bremery, "to snatch at
safety. 'Tis desperate, but all other ways we but wait on destruction. Our right is clean driven in, the left holdeth but hardly. He
chargeth your highness break their centre if you may. They have

somewhat dangerously advanced their left, and therein is their momentary peril if we be swift enough. But remember that here, o' this side, is their greatest power before us, and if we be 'whelmed ere you can compass it——"

"No more but Yes," said Lord Brandoch Daha. "Time gallopeth: so must we."

Even so in that hour when Goldry and Zigg, giving way step by step before superior odds, were bent back well nigh with their backs to the river, and Corund on the Demons' left had after a bitter battle checked and held them and threatened now to complete in one more great blow the ruin of them all, Juss, choosing a desperate expedient to meet a danger that else must destroy him, weakened his hard-pressed left to throw Brandoch Daha and well nigh eight hundred horse into Spitfire's battle to drive a wedge betwixt Corsus and Corinius.

It was now long past noon. The tempest of battle that had quietened awhile for utter weariness roared forth anew from wing to wing as Brandoch Daha hurled his horsemen upon Corsus and the subject allies, while all along the battle-line the Demons rallied to fling back the enemy. For a breathless while, the issue hung in suspense: then the men of Gilta and Nevria broke and fled, Brandoch Daha and his cavalry swept through the gap, wheeled right and left and took Corsus and Corinius in flank and rear.

There fell in this onset Axtacus lord of Permio, the kings of Ellien and Gilta, Gorius the son of Corsus, the Count of Tzeusha, and many other noblemen and men of mark. Of the Demons many were hurt and many slain, but none of great note save Kamerar of Stropardon, whose head Corinius swapt off clean with a blow of his battle-axe, and Trentmar whom Corsus smote full in the stomach with a javelin so that he fell down from his horse and was dead at once. Now was all the left and centre of the Witches' battle thrown into great confusion, and the allies most of all fallen into disorder and fain to yield themselves and pray for mercy. The King, seeing the extent of this disaster, sent a galloper to Corund, who straightway sent to Corsus and Corinius commanding them get them at their speediest with all their folk back into Carcë while time yet served. Himself in the meantime, showing now, like the sun, his greatest countenance in his lowest estate, set on with his weary army to stem the advance of Juss, who now momently gathered fresh force against him, and to keep open for the rest of the King's forces their way by the bridge-gate into Carcë. Corinius, when he understood it, galloped thither with a band of men to aid Corund, and this did likewise Heming and Dekalajus and other captains of the Witches. But Corsus himself, counting the day lost and considering that he was an old man and had fought now long enough, gat him privily back into Carcë as quickly as he was able. And truly he was bleeding from many wounds.

By this great stand of Corund and his men was time won for a great part of the residue of the army to escape into Carcë. And ever the Witches were put aback and lost much ground, yet ever the Lord Corund by his great valiance and noble heart recomforted his folk, so that they gave back very slowly, most bloodily disputing the ground foot by foot to the bridge-gate, that they also might win in again, so many as might. Juss said, "This is the greatest deed of arms that ever I in the days of my life did see, and I have so great an admiration and wonder in my heart for Corund that almost I would give him peace. But I have sworn now to have no peace with Witchland."

Lord Gro was in that battle with the Demons. He ran Didarus through the neck with his sword, so that he fell down and was dead.

Corund, when he saw it, heaved up his axe, but changed his intention in the manage, saying, "O landskip of iniquity, shalt thou kill beside me the men of mine household? But my friendship sitteth not on a weather vane. Live, and be a traitor."

But Gro, being mightily moved with these words, and staring at great Corund wide-eyed like a man roused from a dream, answered, "Have I done amiss? 'Tis easy remedied." Therewith he turned about and slew a man of Demonland. Which Spitfire seeing, he cried out upon Gro in a great rage for a most filthy traitor, and bloodily rushing in thrust him through the buckler[19] into the brain.

In such wise and by such a sudden vengeance did the Lord Gro most miserably end his life-days. Who, being a philosopher and a man of peace, careless of particular things of earth, had followed and observed all his days steadfastly one heavenly star; yet now in the bloody battle before Carcë died in the common opinion of men a manifold perjured traitor, that had at length gotten the guerdon of his guile.

Now came the Lord Juss with a great rout of men armed on his great horse with his sword dripping with blood, and the battle sprang up into yet more noise and fury, and great man-slaying befell, and many able men of Witchland fell in that stour and the Demons had almost put them from the bridge-gate. But the Lord Corund, rallying his folk, swung back yet again the battletide, albeit he was by a great odds outnumbered. And he sought none but Juss himself in that deadly mellay; who when he saw him coming he refused him not but made against him most fiercely, and with great clanging blows they swapped together awhile, until Corund hewed Juss's shield asunder and struck him from his horse. Juss, leaping up again, thrust up at Corund with his sword and with the violence of the blow brake through the rings of his byrny about his middle and drave the sword into his breast. And Corund felled him to earth with a great down-stroke on the helm, so that he lay senseless.

Still the battle raged before the bridge-gate, and great wounds were given and taken of either side. But now the sons of Corund saw that their father had lost much of his blood and waxed feeble, and the residue of his folk seeing it too, and seeing themselves so few against so many, began to be abashed. So those sons of Corund, riding up to him on either side with a band of men, made him turn back with them and go with them in by the gate to Carcë, the which he did like a man amazed and knowing not what he doeth. And indeed it was a great marvel how so great a lord, wounded to the death, might sit on horseback.

In the great court he was gotten down from his horse. The Lady Prezmyra, when she perceived that his harness was all red with blood, and saw his wound, fell not down in a swoon as another might, but took his arm about her shoulder and so supported, with her step-sons to help her, that great frame which could no more support itself yet had till that hour borne up against the whole world's strength in arms. Leeches came that she had called for, and a litter, and they brought him to the banquet hall. But after no long while those learned men confessed his hurt was deadly, and all their cunning nought. Whereupon, much disdaining to die in bed, not in the field fighting with his enemies, the Lord Corund caused himself, completely armed and weaponed, with the stains and dust of the battle yet upon him, to be set in his chair, there to await death.

Heming, when this was done, came to tell it to the King, where from the tower above the water-gate he beheld the end of this battle. The Demons held the bridge-house. The fight was done. The King sat in his chair looking down to the battle-field. His dark mantle was about his shoulders. He leaned forward resting his chin in his hand. They of his bodyguard, nine or ten, stood huddled together some yards away as if afraid to approach him. As Heming came near, the King turned his head slowly to look at him. The low sun, swinging blood-red over Tenemos, shone full on the King's face. And as Heming looked in the face of the King fear gat hold upon him, so that he durst not speak a word to the King, but made obeisance and departed again, trembling like one who has seen a sight beyond the veil.

XXXII

THE LATTER END OF ALL THE LORDS OF WITCHLAND

Of the council of war; and how the Lord Corsus,
being rejected of the King, turned his thoughts to
other things; and of the last conjuring that was
in Carcë and the last wine-bibbing; and how yet
once again the Lady Prezmyra spake with the
lords of Demonland in Carcë.

ORICE the King held in his private chamber a council of war on the morrow of the battle before Carcë. The morning was over-cast with sullen cloud, and though all the windows were thrown wide the sluggish air hung heavy in the room, as if it too were pervaded by the cold dark humour that clogged the vitals of those lords of Witchland like a drowsy drug, or as if the stars would breathe themselves for a greater mischief. Pale and drawn were those lords' faces; and, for all they strove to put on a brave countenance before the King, clean gone was the vigour and war-like mien that clothed them but yesterday. Only Corinius kept some spring of his old valiancy and portly bearing, seated with arms akimbo over against the King, his heavy under-jaw set forward and his nostrils wide. He had slept ill or watched late, for his eyes were blood-shotten, and the breath of his nostrils was heavy with wine.

"We tarry for Corsus," said the King. "Had he not word of my bidding?"

369

Dekalajus said, "Lord, I will summon him again. These misfortunes I fear me hang heavy on his mind, and, by your majesty's leave, he is scarce his own man since yesterday."

"Do it straight," said the King. "Give me thy papers, Corinius. Thou art my general since Corund gat his death. I will see what yesterday hath cost us and what power yet remaineth to crush me these snakes by force of arms."

"These be the numbers, O King," said Corinius. "But three thousand and five hundred fighting men, and well nigh half of these over much crippled with wounds to do aught save behind closed walls. It were but to give the Demons easy victory to adventure against them, that stand before Carcë four thousand sound men in arms."

The King blew scornfully through his nostrils. "Who told thee their strength?" said he.

"It were dangerous to write them down a man fewer," answered Corinius. And Hacmon said, "My Lord the King, I would adventure my head they have more. And your majesty will not forget they be all flown with eagerness and pride after yesterday's field, whereas our men——"

"Were ye sons of Corund," said the King, breaking in quietly on his speech and looking dangerously upon him, "but twigs of your father's tree, that he being cut down ye have no manhood left nor vital sap, but straight wither in idiotish dotage? I will not have these womanish counsels spoke in Carcë; no, nor thought in Carcë."

Corinius said, "We had sure intelligence, O King, whenas they landed that their main army was six thousand fighting men; and last night myself spake with full a score of our officers, and had a true tale of some few of the Demons captured by us before they were slain with the sword. When I say to you Juss standeth before Carcë four thousand strong, I swell not the truth. His losses yesterday were but a flea-biting 'gainst ours."

The King nodded a curt assent.

Corinius proceeded, "If we might contrive indeed to raise help from without Carcë, were it but five hundred spears to distract his mind some part from usward,[1] nought but your majesty's strict command should stay me but I should assault him. It were perilous even so, but never have you known me leave a fruit unplucked at for fear of thorns. But until that time, nought but your straight command might win me to essay a sally. Since well I wot it were my death, and the ruin of you, O King, and of all Witchland."

The King listened with unmoved countenance, his shaven lip

set somewhat in a sneer, his eyes half closed like the eyes of a cat couched sphinx-like in the sun. But no sun shone in that council chamber. The leaden pall hung darker without, even as morning grew toward noon. "My Lord the King," said Heming, "send me. To overslip their guards i' the night, 'tis not a thing beyond invention. That done, I'd gather you some small head of men, enough to serve this turn, if I must rake the seven kingdoms to find 'em."

While Heming spoke, the door opened and the Duke Corsus entered the chamber. An ill sight was he, flabbier of cheek and duller of eye than was his wont. His face was bloodless, his great paunch seemed shrunken, and his shoulders yet more hunched since yesterday. His gait was uncertain, and his hand shook as he moved the chair from the board and took his seat before the King. The King looked on him awhile in silence, and under that gaze beads of sweat stood on Corsus's brow and his under-lip twitched.

"We need thy counsel, O Corsus," said the King. "Thus it is: since our ill-faced stars gave victory to the Demon rebels in yesterday's battle, Juss and his brethren front us with four thousand men, whiles I have not two thousand soldiers unhurt in Carcë. Corinius accounteth us too weak to risk a sally but and if we might contrive some diversion from without. And that (after yesterday) is not to be thought on. Hither and to Melikaphkhaz did we draw all our powers, and the subject allies not for our love but for fear sake and for lust of gain flocked to our standard. These caterpillars drop off now. Yet if we fight not, then is our strength in arms clean spent, and our enemies need but to sit before Carcë till we be starved. 'Tis a point of great difficulty and knotty to solve."

"Difficult indeed, O my Lord the King," said Corsus. His glance shifted round the board, avoiding the steady gaze bent on him from beneath the eaves of King Gorice's brow, and resting at last on the jewelled splendour of the crown of Witchland on the King's head. "O King," he said, "you demand my rede, and I shall not say nor counsel you nothing but that good and well shall come thereof, as much as yet may be in this pass we stand in. For now is our greatness turned in woe, dolour, and heaviness. And easy it is to be after-witted."

He paused, and his under-jaw wobbled and twitched. "Speak on," said the King. "Thou stutterest forth nothings by fits and girds,[2] as an ague taketh a goose. Let me know thy rede."

Corsus said, "You will not take it, I know, O King. For we of Witchland have ever been ruled by the rock rather than by the rudder. I had liever be silent. Silence was never written down."

"Thou wouldst, and thou wouldst not!" said the King.

"Whence gottest thou this look of a dish of whey with blood spit in it?³ Speak, or thou'lt anger me."

"Then blame me not, O King," said Corsus. "Thus it seemeth to me, that the hour hath struck whenas we of Witchland must needs look calamity in the eye and acknowledge we have thrown our last, and lost all. The Demons, as we have seen to our undoing, be unconquerable in war. Yet are their minds pranked with many silly phantasies of honour and courtesy which may preserve us the poor dregs yet unspilt from the cup of our fortune, if we but leave unseasonable pride and see where our advantage lieth."

"Chat, chat, chat!" said the King. "Perdition catch me if I can find a meaning in it! What dost thou bid me do?"

Corsus met the King's eye at last. He braced himself as if to meet a blow. "Throw not your cloak in the fire because your house is burning, O King. Surrender all to Juss at his discretion. And trust me the foolish softness of these Demons will leave us freedom and the wherewithal to live at ease."

The King was leaned a little forward as Corsus, somewhat dry-throated but gathering heart as he spake, blurted forth his counsel of defeat. No man among them looked on Corsus, but all on the King, and for a minute's space was no sound save the sound of breathing in that chamber. Then a puff of hot air blew a window to with a thud, and the King without moving his head rolled his awful glance forth and back over his council slowly, fixing each in his turn. And the King said, "Unto which of you is this counsel acceptable? Let him speak and instruct us."

All did sit mum like beasts. The King spake again, saying, "It is well. Were there of my council such another vermin, so sottish, so louse-hearted, as this one hath proclaimed himself, I had been persuaded Witchland was a sleepy pear, corrupted in her inward parts. And that were so, I had given order straightway for the sally; and, for his chastening and your dishonour, this Corsus should have led you. And so an end, ere the imposthume of our shame brake forth too foul before earth and heaven."

"I admire not, Lord, that you do strike at me," said Corsus. "Yet I pray you think how many Kings in Carcë have heaped with injurious indignities them that were so hardy as give them wholesome counsel afore their fall. Though your majesty were a half-god or a Fury out of the pit, you could not by further resisting deliver us out of this net wherein the Demons have gotten us caught and tied. You can keep geese no longer, O King. Will you rend me because I bid you be content to keep goslings?"

Corinius smote the table with his fist. "O monstrous vermin!"

he cried, "because thou wast scalded, must all we be afeared of cold water?"

But the King stood up in his majesty, and Corsus shrank beneath the flame of his royal anger. And the King spake and said, "The council is up, my lords. For thee, Corsus, I dismiss thee from my council. Thou art to thank my clemency that I take not thy head for this. It were for thy better safety, which well I know thou prizest dearer than mine honour, that thou show not in my path till these perilous days be overpast." And unto Corinius he said, "On thy head it lieth that the Demons storm not the hold, as haply their hot pride may incense them to attempt. Expect me not at supper. I lie in the Iron Tower to-night, and let none disturb me there at peril of his head. You of my council must attend me here four hours ere to-morrow's noon. Look to it well, Corinius, that nought shalt thou do nor in any wise adventure our forces against the Demons till thou receive my further bidding, save only to hold Carcë against any assault if need be. For this thy life shall answer. For the Demons, they were wisest praise a fair day at night. If mine enemy uproot a boulder above my dwelling, so I be mighty enow of mine hands I may, even in the nick of time that it tottereth to leap and crush mine house, o'erset it on him and pash him to a mummy."

So speaking, the King moved resolute with a great strong step toward the door. There paused he, his hand upon the silver latch, and looking tigerishly on Corsus, "Be advised," he said, "thou. Cross not my path again. Nor, while I think on't, send me not thy daughter again, as last year thou didst. Apt to the sport she is, and well enow she served my turn aforetime. But the King of Witchland suppeth not twice of the same dish, nor lacketh he fresh wenches if he need them."

Whereat all they laughed. But Corsus's face grew red as blood.

On such wise brake up the council. Corinius with the sons of Corund and of Corsus went upon the walls ordering all in obedience to the word of Gorice the King. But that old Duke Corsus betook him to his chamber in the north gallery. Nor might he abide even a small while at ease, but sate now in his carven chair, now on the windowsill, now on his broad-canopied bed, and now walked the chamber floor twisting his hands and gnawing his lip. And if he were distraught in mind, small wonder it were, set as he was betwixt hawk and buzzard, the King's wrath menacing him in Carcë and the hosts of Demonland without.

So wore the day till supper-time. And at supper was Corsus, to their much amaze, sitting in his place, and the ladies Zenambria and Sriva with him. He drank deep, and when supper was done he filled a goblet saying, "My lord the king of Demonland and ye other Witches, good it is that we, who stand as now we stand with one foot in the jaws of destruction, should bear with one another. Neither should any hide his thought from other, but say openly, even as I this morning before the face of our Lord the King, his thought and counsel. Wherefore without shame do I confess me ill-advised to-day, when I urged the King to make peace with Demonland. I wax old, and old men will oft embrace timorous counsels which, if there be wisdom and valiancy left in them, they soon renounce when the stress is overpast and they have leisure to afterthink them with a sad mind. And clear as day it is that the King was right, both in his chastening of my faint courage and in his bidding thee, O King Corinius, stand to thy watch and do nought till this night be worn. For went he not to the Iron Tower? And to what end else spendeth he the night in yonder chamber of dread than to do sorcery or his magic art, as aforetime he did, and in such wise blast these Demons to perdition even in the spring-tide of their fortunes? At no point of time hath Witchland greater need of our wishes than at this coming midnight, and I pray you, my lords, let us meet a little before in this hall that we with one heart and mind may drink fair fortune to the King's enchantery."

With such pleasant words and sympathetical insinuations, working at a season when the wine-cup had caused to unfold some gayness in their hearts that were fordone with the hard scapes and chances of disastrous war, was Corsus grown to friendship again with the lords of Witchland. So, when the guard was set and all made sure for the night, they came together in the great banquet hall, whereas more than three years ago the Prince La Fireez had feasted and after fought against them of Witchland. But now was he drowned among the shifting tides in the Straits of Melikaphkhaz. And the Lord Corund, that fought that night in such valiant wise, now in that same hall, armed from throat to foot as becometh a great soldier dead, lay in state, crowned on his brow with the amethystine crown of Impland. The spacious side-benches were untenanted and void their high seats, and the cross-bench was removed to make place for Corund's bier. The lords of Witchland sate at a small table below the dais: Corinius in the seat of honour at the end nearest the door, and over against him Corsus, and on Corinius's left Zenambria, and on his right Dekalajus son to Corsus, and then Heming; and on Corsus's left his daughter Sriva, and those two remaining of Corund's sons on his right. All were there save Prezmyra, and her had none seen since her lord's death, but she kept her chamber. Flamboys stood in the silver stands as of old, lighting the lonely spaces of the hall, and four candles shivered round the bier where Corund slept. Fair goblets stood on the board brimmed with dark sweet Thramnian wine, one for each feaster there, and cold bacon pies and botargoes and craw-fish in hippocras sauce furnished a light midnight meal.

Now scarce were they set, when the flamboys burned pale in a strange light from without doors: an evil, pallid, bale-like[4] lowe, such as Gro had beheld in days gone by when King Gorice XII. first conjured in Carcë. Corinius paused ere taking his seat. Goodly and stalwart he showed in his blue silk cloak and silvered byrny. The fair crown of Demonland, wherewith Corsus had been enforced to crown him on that great night in Owlswick, shone above his light brown curling hair. Youth and lustihood stood forth in every line of his great frame, and on his bare arms smooth and brawny, with their wristlets of gold; but somewhat ghastly was the corpse-like pallor of that light on his shaven jowl, and his thick scornful lips were blackened, like those of poisoned men, in that light of bale.

"Saw ye not this light aforetime?" he cried, "and 'twas the shadow before the sun of our omnipotence. Fate's hammer is lifted up to strike. Drink with me to our Lord the King that laboureth with destiny."

All drank deep, and Corinius said, "Pass we on the cups that each may drain his neighbour's. 'Tis an old lucky custom Corund taught me out of Impland. Swift, for the fate of Witchland is poised in the balance." Therewith he passed his cup to Zenambria, who quaffed it to the dregs. And all they, passing on their cups, drank deep again; all save Corsus alone. But Corsus's eyes were big with terror as he looked on the cup passed on to him by Corund's son.

"Drink, O Corsus," said Corinius; and seeing him still waver, "What ails the old doting disard?"[5] he cried. "He stareth on good wine with an eye as ghastly as a mad dog's beholding water."

In that instant the unearthly glare went out as a lamp in a gust of wind, and only the flamboys and the funeral candles flickered on the feasters with uncertain radiance. Corinius said again, "Drink."

But Corsus set down the cup untasted, and stayed irresolute. Corinius opened his mouth to speak, and his jaw fell, as of a man that conceiveth suddenly some dread suspicion. But ere he might speak word, a blinding flash went from earth to heaven, and the firm floor of the banquet hall rocked and shook as with an earthquake. All save Corinius fell back into their seats, clutching the table, amazed and dumb. Crash after crash, after the listening ear was well nigh split by the roar, the horror broken out of the bowels of night thundered and ravened in Carcë. Laughter, as of damned souls banqueting in Hell, rode on the tortured air. Wildfire tore the darkness asunder, half blinding them that sat about that table, and Corinius gripped the board with either hand as a last deafening crash shook the walls, and a flame rushed up the night, lighting the whole sky with a livid glare. And in that trisulk[6] flash Corinius beheld through the south-west window the Iron Tower blasted and cleft asunder, and the next instant fallen in an avalanche of red-hot ruin.

"The keep hath fallen!" he cried. And, deadly wearied on a sudden, he sank heavily into his seat. The cataclysm was passed by like a wind in the night; but now was heard a sound as of the enemy rushing to the assault. Corinius strove to rise, but his legs were over feeble. His eye lit on Corsus's untasted cup, that which was passed on to him by Viglus Corund's son, and he cried, "What devil's work is this? I have a strange numbness in my bones. By heavens, thou shalt drink that cup or die."

Viglus, his eyes protruding, his hand clutching at his breast, struggled to rise but could not.

Heming half staggered up, fumbling for his sword, then pitched forward on the table with a horrid rattle of the throat.

But Corsus leaped up trembling, his dull eyes aflame with triumphant malice. "The King hath thrown and lost," he cried, "as well I foresaw it. And now have the children of night taken him to themselves. And thou, damned Corinius, and you sons of Corund, are but dead swine before me. Ye have all drunk venom, and ye are dead. Now will I deliver up Carcë to the Demons. And it, and your bodies, with mine electuary rotting in your vitals, shall buy me peace from Demonland."

"O horrible! Then I too am poisoned," cried the Lady Zenambria, and she fell a-swooning.

" 'Tis pity," said Corsus. "Blame the passing of the cups for that. I might not speak ere the poison had chained me the limbs of these cursed devils, and made 'em harmless."

Corinius's jaw set like a bulldog's. Painfully gritting his teeth he rose from his seat, his sword naked in his hand. Corsus, that was now passing near him on his way to the door, saw too late that he had reckoned without his host. Corinius, albeit the baneful drug bound his legs as with a cere-cloth,[7] was yet too swift for Corsus, who, fleeing before him to the door, had but time to clutch the heavy curtains ere the sword of Corinius took him in the back. He fell, and lay a-writhing lumpishly, like a toad spitted on a skewer. And the floor of steatite was made slippery with his blood.

" 'Tis well. Through the guts," said Corinius. No might he had to draw forth the sword, but staggered as one drunken, and fell to earth, propped against the jambs of the lofty doorway.

Some while he lay there, harkening to the sounds of battle without; for the Iron Tower was fallen athwart the outer wall, making a breach through all lines of defence. And through that breach the Demons stormed the hold of Carcë, that never un-friendly foot had entered by force in all the centuries since it was builded by Gorice I. An ill watch it was for Corinius to lie harken-ing to that unequal fight, unable to stir a hand, and all they that should have headed the defence dead or dying before his eyes. Yet was his breath lightened and his pain some part eased when his eye rested on the gross body of Corsus twisting in the agony of death upon his sword.

In such wise passed well nigh an hour. The bodily strength of Corinius and his iron heart bare up against the power of the venom long after those others had breathed out their souls in death. But now was the battle done and the victory with them of Demonland, and the lords Juss and Goldry Bluszco and Brandoch Daha with certain of their fighting men came into the banquet hall. Smeared they were with blood and the dust of battle, for not without great blows and the death of many a stout lad had the hold been won. Goldry said as they paused at the threshold, "This is the very banquet house of death. How came these by their end?"

Corinius's brow darkened at the sight of the lords of Demon-land, and mightily he strove to raise himself, but sank back groan-ing. "I have gotten an everlasting chill o' the bones," he said. "Yon hellish traitor murthered us all by poison; else should some of you have gotten your deaths by me or ever ye won up into Carcë."

"Bring him some water," said Juss. And he with Brandoch Daha gently lifted Corinius and bare him to his chair where he should be more at ease.

Goldry said, "Here is a lady liveth." For Sriva, that sitting on her father's left hand had so escaped a poisoned draught at the passing of the cups, rose from the table where she had cowered in fearful silence, and cast herself in a flood of tears and terrified supplications about Goldry's knees. Goldry bade guard her to the camp and there bestow her in safe asylum until the morning.

Now was Corinius near his end, but he gathered strength to speak, saying, "I do joy that not by your sword were we put down, but by the unequal trumpery of Fortune, whose tool was this Corsus and the King's devilish pride, that desired to harness Heaven and Hell to his chariot. Fortune's a right strumpet, to fondle me in the neck and now yerk me one thus i' the midriff."

"Not Fortune, my Lord Corinius, but the Gods," said Goldry, "whose feet be shod with wool."

By then was water brought in, and Brandoch Daha would have given him to drink. But Corinius would have none of it, but jerked his head aside and o'erset the cup, and looking fiercely on Lord Brandoch Daha, "Vile fellow," he said, "so thou too art come to insult on Witchland's grave? Thou'dst strike me now into the centre, and thou wert not more a dancing madam than a soldier."

"How?" said Brandoch Daha. "Say a dog bite me in the ham: must I bite him again i' the same part?"

Corinius's eyelids closed, and he said weakly, "How look thy womanish gew-gaws in Krothering since I towsed[8] 'em?" And therewith the creeping poison reached his strong heart-strings, and he died.

Now was silence for a space in that banquet hall, and in the silence a step was heard, and the lords of Demonland turned toward the lofty doorway, that yawned as an arched cavern-mouth of darkness; for Corsus had torn down the arras curtains in his death-throes, and they lay heaped athwart the threshold with his dead body across them, Corinius's sword-hilts jammed against his ribs and the blade standing a foot's length forth from his breast. And while they gazed, there walked into the shifting light of the flamboys over that threshold the Lady Prezmyra, crowned and arrayed in her rich robes and ornaments of state. Her countenance was bleak as the winter moon flying high amid light clouds on a windy midnight settling towards rain, and those lords, under the spell of her sad cold beauty, stood without speech.

In a while Juss, speaking as one who needeth to command his voice, and making grave obeisance to her, said, "O Queen, we give you peace. Command our service in all things whatsoever. And first in this, which shall be our earliest task ere we sail homeward, to stablish you in your rightful realm of Pixyland. But this hour is overcharged with fate and desperate deeds to suffer counsel. Counsel is for the morning. The night calleth to rest. I pray you give us leave."

Prezmyra looked upon Juss, and there was eye-bite in her eyes, that glinted with green metallic lustre like those of a she-lion brought to battle.

"Thou dost offer me Pixyland, my Lord Juss," said she, "that

am Queen of Impland. And this night, thou thinkest, can bring me
rest. These that were dear to me have rest indeed: my lord and
lover Corund; the Prince my brother; Gro, that was my friend.
Deadly enow they found you, whether as friends or foes."

Juss said, "O Queen Prezmyra, the nest falleth with the tree.
These things hath Fate brought to pass, and we be but Fate's
whipping-tops bandied what way she will. Against thee we war not,
and I swear to thee that all our care is to make thee amends."

"O, thine oaths!" said Prezmyra. "What amends canst thou
make? Youth I have and some poor beauty. Wilt thou conjure
those three dead men alive again that ye have slain? For all thy
vaunted art, I think this were too hard a task."

All they were silent, eyeing her as she walked delicately past
the table. She looked with a distant and, to outward seeming,
uncomprehending eye on the dead feasters and their empty cups.
Empty all, save that one passed on by Viglus, whereof Corsus
would not drink; and it stood half drained. Of curious workmanship it was, of pale green glass, its stand formed of three serpents
intertwined, the one of gold, another of silver, the third of iron.
Fingering it carelessly she raised her glittering eyes once more on
the Demons, and said, "It was ever the wont of you of Demonland
to eat the egg and give away the shell in alms." And pointing at the
lords of Witchland dead at the feast, she asked, "Were these also
your victims in this day's hunting, my lords?"

"Thou dost us wrong, madam," cried Goldry. "Never hath
Demonland used suchlike arts against her enemies."

Lord Brandoch Daha looked swiftly at him, and stepped idly
forward, saying, "I know not what art hath wrought yon goblet, but
'tis strangely like to one I saw in Impland. Yet fairer is this, and of
more just proportions." But Prezmyra forestalled his outstretched hand, and quietly drew the cup towards her out of reach.
As sword crosses sword, the glance of her green eyes crossed his,
and she said, "Think not that you have a worse enemy left on earth
than me. I it was that sent Corsus and Corinius to trample Demonland in the mire. Had I but some spark of masculine virtue, some
soul at least of you should yet be loosed squealing to the shades to
attend my dear ones ere I set sail. But I have none. Kill me then,
and let me go."

Juss, whose sword was bare in his hand, smote it home in the
scabbard and stepped towards her. But the table was betwixt them,
and she drew back to the dais where Corund lay in state. There,
like some triumphant goddess, she stood above them, the cup of

venom in her hand. "Come not beyond the table, my lords," she said, "or I drain this cup to your damnation."

Brandoch Daha said, "The dice are thrown, O Juss. And the Queen hath won the hazard."

"Madam," said Juss, "I swear to you there shall no force nor restraint be put upon you, but honour only and worship shown you, and friendship if you will. That surely mightest thou take of us for thy brother's sake." Thereat she looked terribly upon him, and he said, "Only on this wild night lay not hands upon yourself. For their sake, that even now haply behold us out of the undiscovered barren lands, beyond the dismal lake, do not this."

Still facing them, the cup still aloft in her right hand, Prezmyra laid her left hand lightly on the brazen plates of Corund's byrny that cased the mighty muscles of his breast. Her hand touched his beard, and drew back suddenly; but in an instant she laid it gently again on his breast. Somewhat her orient loveliness seemed to soften for a passing minute in the altering light, and she said, "I was given to Corund young. This night I will sleep with him, or reign with him, among the mighty nations of the dead."

Juss moved as one about to speak, but she stayed him with a look, and the lines of her body hardened again and the lioness looked forth anew in her peerless eyes. "Hath your greatness," she said, "so much outgrown your wit, that you think I will abide to be your pensioner, that have been a Princess in Pixyland, a Queen of far-fronted Impland, and wife to the greatest soldier in this hold of Carcë, which till this day hath been the only scourge and terror of the world? O my lords of Demonland, good comfortable fools, speak to me no more, for your speech is folly. Go, doff your hats to the silly hind that runneth on the mountain; pray her gently dwell with you amid your stalled cattle, when you have slain her mate. Shall the blackening frost, when it hath blasted and starved all the sweet garden flowers, say to the rose, Abide with us; and shall she harken to such a wolfish suit?"

So speaking she drank the cup; and turning from those lords of Demonland as a queen turneth her from the unregarded multitude, kneeled gently down by Corund's bier, her white arms clasped about his head, her face pillowed on his breast.

When Juss spake, his voice was choked with tears. He commanded Bremery that they should take up the bodies of Corsus and Zenambria and those sons of Corund and of Corsus that lay poisoned and dead in that hall and on the morrow give them reverent burial. "And for the Lord Corinius I will that ye make a

bed of state, that he may lie in this hall to-night, and to-morrow will
we lay him in howe before Carcë, as is fitting for so renowned a
captain. But great Corund and his lady shall none depart one from
the other, but in one grave shall they rest, side by side, for their
love sake. Ere we be gone I will rear them such a monument as
beseemeth great kings and princes when they die. For royal and
lordly was Corund, and a mighty man at arms, and a fighter clean
of hand, albeit our bitter enemy. Wondrous it is with what cords of
love he bound to him this unparagoned Queen of his. Who hath
known her like among women for trueness and highness of heart?
And sure none was ever more unfortunate."

Now went they forth into the outer ward of Carcë. The night
bore still some signs of that commotion of the skies that had so
lately burst forth and passed away, and some torn palls of thunder-
cloud yet hung athwart the face of heaven. Betwixt them in the
swept places of the sky a few stars shivered, and the moon, more
than half waxen towards her full, was sinking over Tenemos. Some
faint breath of autumn was abroad, and the Demons shuddered a
little, fresh from the heavy air of the great banquet hall. The ruins
of the Iron Tower smoking to the sky, and the torn and tumbled
masses of masonry about it, showed monstrous in the gloom as
fragments of old chaos; and from them and from the riven earth
beneath steamed up pungent fumes as of brimstone burning. Ever
busily, back and forth through those sulphurous vapours, obscene
birds of the night flitted a weary round, and bats on leathern wing,
fitfully and dimly seen in the uncertain mirk, save when their passage brought them dark against the moon. And from the solitudes
of the mournful fen afar voices of lamentation floated on the night:
wild wailing cries and sobbing noises and long moans rising and
falling and quivering down to silence.

Juss laid his hand on Goldry's arm, saying, "There is nought
earthly in these laments, nor be those that thou seest circling in the
reek very bats or owls. These be his masterless familiars wailing for
their Lord. Many such served him, simple earthy divels and divels
of the air and of the water, held by him in thrall by sorcerous and
artificial practices, coming and going and doing his will."

"These availed him not," said Goldry, "nor the sword of
Witchland against our might and main, that brake it asunder in his
hand and slew his mighty men of valour."

"Yet true it is," said Lord Juss, "that none greater hath lived
on earth than King Gorice XII. When after these long wars we held
him as a stag at bay, he feared not to assay a second time, and this
time unaided and alone, what no man else hath so much as once

performed and lived. And well he knew that that which was summoned by him out of the deep must spill and blast him utterly if he should slip one whit, as slip he did in former days, but his disciple succoured him. Behold now with what loud striking of thunder, unconquered by any earthly power, he hath his parting: with this Carcë black and smoking in ruin for his monument, these lords of Witchland and hundreds besides of our soldiers and of the Witches for his funeral bake-meats, and spirits weeping in the night for his chief mourners."

So came they again to the camp. And in due time the moon set and the clouds departed and the quiet stars pursued their eternal way until night's decline; as if this night had been but as other nights: this night which had beheld the power and glory that was Witchland by such a hammer-stroke of destiny smitten in pieces.

XXXIII

QUEEN SOPHONISBA IN GALING

*Of the entertainment given by Lord Juss in
Demonland to Queen Sophonisba, fosterling of the
gods, and of that circumstance which, beyond all
the wonders fair and lovely to behold shown her
in that country, made her most to marvel:
wherein is a rare example how in a fortunate
world, out of all expectation, in the spring of the
year, cometh a new birth.*

o w the returning months brought the season of the
year when Queen Sophonisba should come according
to her promise to guest with Lord Juss in Galing. And
so it was that in the hush of a windless April dawn the
Zimiamvian caravel[1] that bare the Queen to Demonland rowed up the firth to Lookinghaven.

All the east was a bower for the golden dawn. Kartadza, sharp-
outlined as if cut in bronze, still hid the sun; and in the great
shadow of the mountain the haven and the low hills and the groves
of holm-oak and strawberry tree slumbered in a deep obscurity of
blues and purples, against which the avenues of pink almond blossom and the white marble quays were bodied forth in pale wakening beauty, imaged as in a looking-glass in that tranquillity of the
sea. Westward across the firth all the land was aglow with the

opening day. Snow lingered still on the higher summits. Cloudless, bathing in the golden light, they stood against the blue: Dina, the Forks of Nantreganon, Pike o' Shards, and all the peaks of the Thornback range and Neverdale. Morning laughed on their high ridges and kissed the woods that clung about their lower limbs: billowy woods, where rich hues of brown and purple told of every twig on all their myriad branches thick and afire with buds. White mists lay like coverlets on the water-meadows where Tivarandardale opens to the sea. On the shores of Bothrey and Scaramsey, and on the mainland near the great bluff of Thremnir's Heugh and a little south of Owlswick, clear spaces among the birchwoods showed golden yellow: daffodils abloom in the spring.

They rowed in to the northernmost berth and made fast the caravel. The sweetness of the almond trees was the sweetness of spring in the air, and spring was in the face of that Queen as she came with her attendants up the shining steps, her little martlets circling about her or perching on her shoulders: she to whom the Gods of old gave youth everlasting, and peace everlasting in Koshtra Belorn.

Lord Juss and his brethren were on the quay to meet her, and the Lord Brandoch Daha. They bowed in turn, kissing her hands and bidding her welcome to Demonland. But she said, "Not to Demonland alone, my lords, to the world again. And toward which of all earth's harbours should I steer, and toward which land if not to this land of yours, who have by your victories brought peace and joy to all the world? Surely peace slept not more softly on the Moruna in old days before the names of Gorice and Witchland were heard in that country, than she shall sleep for us on this new earth and Demonland, now that those names are drowned for ever under the whirlpools of oblivion and darkness."

Juss said, "O Queen Sophonisba, desire not that the names of great men dead should be forgot for ever. So should these wars that we last year brought to so mighty a conclusion to make us undisputed lords of the earth go down to oblivion with them that fought against us. But the fame of these things shall be on the lips and in the songs of men from one generation to another, so long as the world shall endure."

They took horse and rode up from the harbour to the upper road, and so through open pastures on to Havershaw Tongue. Lambs frisked on the dewy meadows beside the road; blackbirds flew from bush to bush; larks trilled in the sightless sky; and as they came down through the woods to Beckfoot wood-pigeons cooed in the trees, and squirrels peeped with beady eyes. The Queen spoke little. These and all shy things of the woods and field held her in thrall, charming her to a silence that was broken only now and then by a little exclamation of joy. The Lord Juss, who himself also loved these things, watched her delight.

Now they wound up the steep ascent from Beckfoot, and rode into Galing by the Lion Gate. The avenue of Irish yews was lined by soldiers of the bodyguards of Juss, Goldry, and Spitfire, and Brandoch Daha. These, in honour of their great masters and of the Queen, lifted their spears aloft, while trumpeters blew three fanfares on silver trumpets. Then to an accompaniment of lutes and theorbos and citherns[2] moving above the pulse of muffled drums, a choir of maidens sang a song of welcome, strewing the path before the lords of Demonland and the Queen with sweet white hyacinths and narcissus blooms, while the ladies Mevrian and Armelline, more lovely than any queens of earth, waited at the head of the golden staircase above the inner court to greet Queen Sophonisba come to Galing.

A hard matter it were to tell of all the pleasures prepared for Queen Sophonisba and for her delight by the lords of Demonland. The first day she spent among the parks and pleasure gardens of Galing, where Lord Juss showed her his great lime avenues, his yew-houses, his fruit gardens and sunk gardens and his private walks and bowers; his walks of creeping thyme which being trodden on sends up sweet odours to refresh the treader; his ancient water-gardens beside the Brankdale Beck, whither the water nymphs resort in summer and are seen under the moon singing and combing their hair with combs of gold.

On the second day he showed her his herb gardens, disclosing to her the secret properties of herbs, wherein he was deeply learned. There grew that Zamalenticion, which being well beaten up with fat without salt is sovran for all wounds. And Dittany, which if eaten soon puts out the arrow and healeth the wounds; and not only by its presence stayeth snakes wheresoever they be handy to it, but by reason of its smell carried by wind and they smell it they die. And Mandragora, which being taken into the middle of an house compelleth all evils out of the house, and relieveth also headaches and produceth sleep. Also he showed her Sea Holly in his garden, that is born in secret places and in wet ones, and the root of it is as the head of that monster which men name the Gorgon, and the root-twigs have both eyes and nose and colour of serpents. Of this he told her how when taking up the root, a man must see to it that no sun shine on it, and he who would

carve it must avert his head, for it is not permitted that man may
see that root unharmed.

The third day Juss showed the Queen his stables, where were
his war-horses and horses for the chase and for chariot racing
stabled in stalls with furniture of silver, and much she marvelled at
his seven white mares, sisters, so like that none might tell one from
another, given him in days gone by by the priests of Artemis in the
lands beyond the sunset. They were immortal, bearing ichor in
their veins, not blood; and the fire of it showed in their eyes like
lamps burning.

The fourth night and the fifth the Queen was at Drepaby,
guesting with Lord Goldry Bluszco and the Princess Armelline,
that were wedded in Zajë Zaculo last Yule; and the sixth and seventh nights at Owlswick, and there Spitfire made her lordly entertainment. But Lord Brandoch Daha would not have the Queen go
yet to Krothering, for he had not yet made fair again his gardens
and pleasaunces and restored his rich and goodly treasures to his
mind after their ill handling by Corinius. And it was not his will
that she should look on Krothering Castle until all was there stablished anew according to its ancient glory.

The eighth day she came again to Galing, and now Lord Juss
showed her his study, with his astrolabes of orichalc,[3] figured with
all the signs of the Zodiac and the mansions of the moon, standing
a tall man's height above the floor, and his perspectives[4] and
gloves and crystals and hollow looking-glasses; and great crystal
globes where he kept homunculi whom he had made by secret
processes of nature, both men and women, less than a span long,
as beautiful as one could wish to see in their little coats, eating and
drinking and going their ways in those mighty globes of crystal
where his art had given them being.

Every night, whether at Galing, Owlswick, or Drepaby Mire,
was feasting held in her honour, with music and dancing and
merry-making and all delight, and poetical recitations and feats of
arms and horsemanship, and masques and interludes the like
whereof hath not been seen on earth for beauty and wit and all
magnificence.

Now was the ninth day come of the Queen's guesting in
Demonland, and it was the eve of Lord Juss's birthday, when all the
great ones in the land were come together, as four years ago they
came, to do honour on the morrow unto him and unto his brethren
as was their wont aforetime. It was fine bright weather, with every
little while a shower to bring fresh sweetness to the air, colour and

refreshment to the earth, and gladness to the sunshine. Juss walked with the Queen in the morning in the woods of Moongarth Bottom, now bursting into leaf; and after their mid-day meal showed her his treasures cut in the live rock under Galing Castle, where she beheld bars of gold and silver piled like trunks of trees; unhewn crystals of ruby, chrysoprase, or hyacinth, so heavy a strong man might not lift them; stacks of ivory in the tusk, piled to the ceiling; chests and jars filled with perfumes and costly spices, ambergris, frankincense, sweet-scented sandalwood and myrrh and spikenard; cups and beakers and eared wine-jars and lamps and caskets made of pure gold, worked and chased with the forms of men and women and birds and beasts and creeping things, and ornamented with jewels beyond price, margarites and pink and yellow sapphires, smaragds and chrysoberyls and yellow diamonds.

When the Queen had had her fill of gazing on these, he carried her to his great library where statues stood of the nine Muses about Apollo, and all the walls were hidden with books: histories and songs of old days, books of philosophy, alchymy and astronomy and art magic, romances and music and lives of great men dead and great treatises of all the arts of peace and war, with pictures and illuminated characters. Great windows opened southward on the garden from the library, and climbing rose-trees and plants of honeysuckle and evergreen magnolia clustered about the windows. Great chairs and couches stood about the open hearth where a fire of cedar logs burned in winter time. Lamps of moonstones self-effulgent shaded with cloudy green tourmaline stood on silver stands on the table and by each couch and chair, to give light when the day was over; and all the air was sweet with the scent of dried rose-leaves kept in ancient bowls and vases of painted earthenware.

Queen Sophonisba said, "My lord, I love this best of all the fair things thou hast shown me in thy castle of Galing: here where all trouble seems a forgotten echo of an ill world left behind. Surely my heart is glad, O my friend, that thou and these other lords of Demonland shall now enjoy your goodly treasures and fair days in your dear native land in peace and quietness all your lives."

The Lord Juss stood at the window that looked westward across the lake to the great wall of the Scarf. Some shadow of a noble melancholy hovered about his sweet dark countenance as his gaze rested on a curtain of rain that swept across the face of the mountain wall, half veiling the high rock summits. "Yet think, madam," said he, "that we be young of years. And to strenuous minds there is an unquietude in over-quietness."

Now he conducted her through his armouries where he kept his weapons and weapons for his fighting men and all panoply of war. There he showed her swords and spears, maces and axes and daggers, orfreyed and damascened[5] and inlaid with jewels; byrnies and baldricks and shields; blades so keen, a hair blown against them in a wind should be parted in twain; charmed helms on which no ordinary sword would bite. And Juss said unto the Queen, "Madam, what thinkest thou of these swords and spears? For know well that these be the ladder's rungs that we of Demonland climbed up by to that signiory and principality which now we hold over the four corners of the world."

She answered, "O my lord, I think nobly of them. For an ill part it were while we joy in the harvest, to contemn the tools that prepared the land for it and reaped it."

While she spoke, Juss took down from its hook a great sword with a haft bound with plaited cords of gold and silver wire and cross-hilts of latoun set with studs of amethyst and a drake's head at either end of the hilt with crimson almandines for his eyes, and the pommel a ball of deep amber-coloured opal with red and green flashes.

"With this sword," said he, "I went up with Gaslark to the gates of Carcë, four years gone by this summer, being clouded in my mind by the back-wash of the sending of Gorice the King. With this sword I fought an hour back to back with Brandoch Daha, against Corund and Corinius and their ablest men: the greatest fight that ever I fought, and against the fearfullest odds. Witchland himself beheld us from Carcë walls through the watery mist and glare, and marvelled that two men that are born of woman could perform such deeds."

He untied the bands of the sword and drew it singing from its sheath. "With this sword," he said, looking lovingly along the blade, "I have overcome hundreds of mine enemies: Witches, and Ghouls, and barbarous people out of Impland and the southern seas, pirates of Esamocia and princes of the eastern main. With this sword I gat the victory in many a battle, and most glorious of all in the battle before Carcë last September. There, fighting against great Corund in the press of the fight I gave him with this sword the wound that was his death-wound."

He put up the sword again in its sheath: held it a minute as if pondering whether or no to gird it about his waist: then slowly turned to its place on the wall and hung it up again. He carried his head high like a warhorse, keeping his gaze averted from the Queen as they went out from the great armoury in Galing; yet not so skilfully but she marked a glistening in his eye that seemed a tear standing above his lower eyelash.

That night was supper set in Lord Juss's private chamber: a light regale, yet most sumptuous. They sat at a round table, nine in company: the three brethren, the Lords Brandoch Daha, Zigg, and Volle, the Ladies Armelline and Mevrian, and the Queen. Brightly flowed the wines of Krothering and Norvasp and blithely went the talk to outward seeming. But ever and again silence swung athwart the board, like a gray pall, till Zigg broke it with a jest, or Brandoch Daha or his sister Mevrian. The Queen felt the chill behind their merriment. The silent fits came oftener as the feast went forward, as if wine and good cheer had lost their native quality and turned fathers of black moods and gloomy meditations.

The Lord Goldry Bluszco, that till now had spoke little, spake now not at all, his proud dark face fixed in staid pensive lines of thought. Spitfire too was fallen silent, his face leaned upon his hand, his brow bent; and whiles he drank amain, and whiles he drummed his fingers on the table. The Lord Brandoch Daha leaned back in his ivory chair, sipping his wine. Very demure, through half-closed eyes, like a panther dozing in the noon-day, he watched his companions at the feast. Like sunbeams chased by cloud-shadows across a mountain-side in windy weather, the lights of humorous enjoyment played across his face.

The Queen said, "O my lords, you have promised me I should hear the full tale of your wars in Impland and the Impland seas, and how you came to Carcë and of the great battle that there befell, and of the latter end of all the lords of Witchland and of Gorice XII. of memory accursed. I pray you let me hear it now, that our hearts may be gladdened by the tale of great deeds the remembrance whereof shall be for all generations, and that we may rejoice anew that all the lords of Witchland are dead and gone because of whom and their tyranny earth hath groaned and laboured these many years."

Lord Juss, in whose face when it was at rest she had beheld that same melancholy which she had marked in him in the library that same day, poured forth more wine, and said, "O Queen Sophonisba, thou shalt hear it all." Therewith he told all that had befallen since they last bade her adieu in Koshtra Belorn: of the march to the sea at Muelva; of Laxus and his great fleet destroyed and sunk off Melikaphkhaz; of the battle before Carcë and its swinging fortunes; of the unhallowed light and flaring signs in heaven whereby they knew of the King's conjuring again in Carcë, of their waiting in the night, armed at all points, with charms and amulets ready against what dreadful birth might be from the King's enchantments; of the blasting of the Iron Tower, and the storming of the hold in pitch darkness; of the lords of Witchland murthered at the feast, and nought left at last of the power and pomp and terror that was Witchland save dying embers of a funeral fire and voices wailing in the wind before the dawn.

When he had done, the Queen said, as if talking in a dream, "Surely it may be said of these kings and lords of Witchland dead—

> These wretched eminent things
> Leave no more fame behind 'em than should one
> Fall in a frost, and leave his print in snow;
> As soon as the sun shines, it ever melts
> Both form and matter."

With those words spoken dropped silence again like a pall athwart that banquet table, more tristful than before and full of heaviness.

On a sudden Lord Brandoch Daha stood up, unbuckling from his shoulder his golden baldrick set with apricot-coloured sapphires and diamonds and fire-opals that imaged thunderbolts. He threw it before him on the table, with his sword, clattering among the cups. "O Queen Sophonisba," said he, "thou hast spoken a fit funeral dirge for our glory as for Witchland's. This sword Zeldornius gave me. I bare it at Krothering Side against Corinius, when I threw him out of Demonland. I bare it at Melikaphkhaz. I bare it in the last great fight in Witchland. Thou wilt say it brought me good luck and victory in battle. But it brought not to me, as to Zeldornius, this last best luck of all: that earth should gape for me when my great deeds were ended."

The Queen looked at him amazed, marvelling to see him so much moved that she had known until now so lazy mocking and so debonair.

But the other lords of Demonland stood up and flung down their jewelled swords on the table beside Lord Brandoch Daha's. And Lord Juss spake and said, "We may well cast down our swords as a last offering on Witchland's grave. For now must they rust: seamanship and all high arts of war must wither: and, now that our great enemies are dead and gone, we that were lords of all the world must turn shepherds and hunters, lest we become mere mountebanks[6] and fops, fit fellows for the chambering Beshtrians or the Red Foliot. O Queen Sophonisba, and you my brethren and my friends, that are come to keep my birthday with me to-morrow in Galing, what make ye in holiday attire? Weep ye rather, and weep again, and clothe you all in black, thinking that our mightiest feats of arms and the high southing of the bright star of our magnificence should bring us unto timeless ruin. Thinking that we, that fought but for fighting's sake, have in the end fought so well we never may fight more; unless it should be in fratricidal rage each against each. And ere that should betide, may earth close over us and our memory perish."

Mightily moved was the Queen to behold such a violent sorrow, albeit she could not comprehend the roots and reason of it. Her voice shook a little as she said, "My Lord Juss, my Lord Brandoch Daha, and you other lords of Demonland, it was little in mine expectation to find in you such a passion of sour discontent. For I came to rejoice with you. And strangely it soundeth in mine ear to hear you mourn and lament your worst enemies, at so great hazard of your lives and all you held dear, struck down by you at last. I am but a maid and young in years, albeit my memory goeth back two hundred springs, and ill it befitteth me to counsel great lords and men of war. Yet strange it seemeth if there be not peaceful enjoyment and noble deeds of peace for you all your days, who are young and noble and lords of all the world and rich in every treasure and high gifts of learning, and the fairest country in the world for your dear native land. And if your swords must not rust, ye may bear them against the uncivil races of Impland and other distant countries to bring them to subjection."

But Lord Goldry Bluszco laughed bitterly. "O Queen," he cried, "shall the correction of feeble savages content these swords, which have warred against the house of Gorice and against all his chosen captains that upheld the great power of Carcë and the glory and the fear thereof?"

And Spitfire said, "What joy shall we have of soft beds and delicate meats and all the delights that be in many-mountained Demonland, if we must be stingless drones, with no action to sharpen our appetite for ease?"

All were silent awhile. Then the Lord Juss spake saying, "O Queen Sophonisba, hast thou looked ever, on a showery day in spring, upon the rainbow flung across earth and sky, and marked how all things of earth beyond it, trees, mountain-sides, and rivers, and fields, and woods, and homes of men, are transfigured by the colours that are in the bow?"

"Yes," she said, "and oft desired to reach them."

"We," said Juss, "have flown beyond the rainbow. And there we found no fabled land of heart's desire, but wet rain and wind only and the cold mountain-side. And our hearts are a-cold because of it."

The Queen said, "How old art thou, my Lord Juss, that thou speakest as an old man might speak?"

He answered, "I shall be thirty-three years old to-morrow, and that is young by the reckoning of men. None of us be old, and my brethren and Lord Brandoch Daha younger than I. Yet as old men may we now look forth on our lives, since the goodness thereof is gone by for us." And he said, "Thou O Queen canst scarcely know our grief; for to thee the blessed Gods gave thy heart's desire: youth for ever, and peace. Would they might give us our good gift, that should be youth for ever, and war; and unwaning strength and skill in arms. Would they might but give us our great enemies alive and whole again. For better it were we should run hazard again of utter destruction, than thus live out our lives like cattle fattening for the slaughter, or like silly garden plants."

The Queen's eyes were large with wonder. "Thou couldst wish it?" she said.

Juss answered and said, "A true saying it is that 'a grave is a rotten foundation.' If thou shouldst proclaim to me at this instant the great King alive again and sitting again in Carcë, bidding us to the dread arbitrament of war, thou shouldst quickly see I told thee truth."

While Juss spake, the Queen turned her gaze from one to another round the board. In every eye, when he spake of Carcë, she saw the lightning of the joy of battle as of life returning to men held in a deadly trance. And when he had done, she saw in every eye the light go out. Like Gods they seemed, in the glory of their youth and pride, seated about that table; but sad and tragical, like Gods exiled from wide Heaven.

None spake, and the Queen cast down her eyes, sitting as if wrapped in thought. Then the Lord Juss rose to his feet, and said, "O Queen Sophonisba, forgive us that our private sorrows should make us so forgetful of our hospitality as weary our guest with a mirthless feast. But think 'tis because we know thee our dear friend we use not too much ceremony. To-morrow we will be merry with thee, whate'er betide thereafter."

So they bade good-night. But as they went out into the garden under the stars, the Queen took Juss aside privately and said to him, "My lord, since thou and my Lord Brandoch Daha came first of mortal men into Koshtra Belorn, and fulfilled the weird according to preordainment, this only hath been my desire: to further you and to enhance you and to obtain for you what you would, so far as in me lieth. Though I be but a weak maid, yet hath it seemed good to the blessed Gods to show kindness unto me. One holy prayer may work things we scarce dream of. Wilt thou that I pray to Them to-night?"

"Alas, dear Queen," said he, "shall those estranged and divided ashes unite again? Who shall turn back the floodtide of unalterable necessity?"

But she said, "Thou hast crystals and perspectives can show thee things afar off. I pray bring them, and row me in thy boat up to Moonmere Head that we may land there about midnight. And let my Lord Brandoch Daha come with us and thy brothers. But let none else know of it. For that were but to mock them with a false dawn, if it should prove at last to be according to thy wisdom, O my lord, and not according to my prayers."

So the Lord Juss did according to the word of that fair Queen, and they rowed her up the lake by moonlight. None spake, and the Queen sate apart in the bows of the boat, in earnest supplication to the blessed Gods. When they were come to the head of the lake they went ashore on a little spit of silver sand. The April night was above them, mild with moonlight. The shadows of the fells rose inky black and beyond imagination huge against the sky. The Queen kneeled awhile in silence on the cold ground, and those lords of Demonland stood together in silence watching her.

In a while she raised her eyes to heaven; and behold, between the two main peaks of the Scarf, a meteor crept slowly out of darkness and across the night-sky, leaving a trail of silver fire, and silently departed into darkness. They watched, and another came, and yet another, until the western sky above the mountain was ablaze with them. From two points of heaven they came, one betwixt the foreclaws of the Lion and one in the dark sign of Cancer. And they that came from the Lion were sparkling like the white fires of Rigel or Altair, and they that came from the Crab were haughty red, like the lustre of Antares. The lords of Demonland, leaning on their swords, watched these portents for a long while in silence. Then the travelling meteors ceased, and the steadfast stars shone lonely and serene. A soft breeze stirred among the alders and willows by the lake. The lapping waters lapping the shingly shore made a quiet tune. A nightingale in a coppice on a little hill sang so passionate sweet it seemed some spirit singing. As in a trance they stood and listened, until that singing ended, and a hush fell on water and wood and lawn. Then all the east blazed up for an instant with sheet lightnings, and thunder growled from the east beyond the sea.

The thunder took form so that music was in the heavens, filling earth and sky as with trumpets calling to battle, first high, then low, then shuddering down to silence. Juss and Brandoch Daha knew it for that great call to battle which had preluded that music in the dark night without her palace, in Koshtra Belorn, when first they stood before her portal divine. The great call went again through earth and air, sounding defiance; and in its train new voices, groping in darkness, rising to passionate lament, hovering, and dying away on the wind, till nought remained but a roll of muffled thunder, long, low, quiet, big with menace.

The Queen turned to Lord Juss. Surely her eyes were like two stars shining in the gloom. She said in a drowned voice, "Thy perspectives, my lord."

So the Lord Juss made a fire of certain spices and herbs, and smoke rose in a thick cloud full of fiery sparks, with a sweet sharp smell. And he said, "Not we, O my Lady, lest our desires cheat our senses. But look thou in my perspectives through the smoke, and say unto us what thou shalt behold in the east beyond the unharvested sea."

The Queen looked. And she said, "I behold a harbour town and a sluggish river coming down to the harbour through a mere set about with mud flats, and a great waste of fen stretching inland from the sea. Inland, by the river side, I behold a great bluff standing above the fens. And walls about the bluff, as it were a citadel. And the bluff and the walled hold perched thereon are black like old night, and like throned iniquity sitting in the place of power, darkening the desolation of that fen."

Juss said, "Are the walls thrown down? Or is not the great round tower south-westward thrown down in ruin athwart the walls?"

She said, "All is whole and sound as the walls of thine own castle, my lord."

Juss said, "Turn the crystal, O Queen, that thou mayest see within the walls if any persons be therein, and tell us their shape and seeming."

The Queen was silent for a space, gazing earnestly in the crystal. Then she said, "I see a banquet hall with walls of dark green jasper speckled with red, and a massy cornice borne up by giants three-headed carved in black serpentine; and each giant is bowed beneath the weight of a huge crab-fish. The hall is seven-sided. Two long tables there be and a cross-bench. There be iron braziers in the midst of the hall and flamboys burning in silver stands, and revellers quaffing at the long tables. Some dark young men black of brow and great of jaw, most soldier-like, brothers mayhap. Another with them, ruddy of countenance and kindlier to look on, with long brown moustachios. Another that weareth a brazen byrny and sea-green kirtle; an old man he, with sparse gray whiskers and flabby cheeks; fat and unwieldy; not a comely old man to look upon."

She ceased speaking, and Juss said, "Whom seest thou else in the banquet hall, O Queen?"

She said, "The flare of the flamboys hideth the cross-bench. I will turn the crystal again. Now I behold two diverting themselves with dice at the table before the cross-bench. One is well-looking enough, well knit, of a noble port, with curly brown hair and beard and keen eyes like a sailor. The other seemeth younger in years, younger than any of you, my lords. He is smooth shaved, of a fresh complexion and fair curling hair, and his brow is wreathed with a festal garland. A most big broad strong and seemly young man. Yet is there a somewhat maketh me ill at ease beholding him; and for all his fair countenance and royal bearing he seemeth displeasing in mine eyes.

"There is a damosel there too, watching them while they play. Showily dressed she is, and hath some beauty. Yet scarce can I commend her—" and, ill at ease on a sudden, the Queen suddenly put down the crystal.

The eye of Lord Brandoch Daha twinkled, but he kept silence. Lord Juss said, "More, I entreat thee, O Queen, ere the reek be gone and the vision fade. If this be all within the banquet hall, seest thou nought without?"

Queen Sophonisba looked again, and in a while said, "There is a terrace facing to the west under the inner wall of that fortress of old night, and walking on it in the torchlight a man crowned like a King. Very tall he is: lean of body, and long of limb. He weareth a black doublet bedizened o'er with diamonds, and his crown is in the figure of a crab-fish, and the jewels thereof out-face the sun in splendour. But scarce may I mark his apparel for looking on the face of him, which is more terrible than the face of any man that ever I saw. And the whole aspect of the man is full of darkness and power and terror and stern command, that spirits from below earth must tremble at and do his bidding."

Juss said, "Heaven forfend that this should prove but a sweet and golden dream, and we wake to-morrow to find it flown."

"There walketh with him," said the Queen, "in intimate converse, as of a servant talking to his lord, one with a long black beard curly as the sheep's wool and glossy as the raven's wing. Pale he is as the moon in daylight hours, slender, with fine-cut features and great dark eyes, and his nose hooked like a reaping-hook; gentle-looking and melancholy-looking, yet noble."

Lord Brandoch Daha said, "Seest thou none, O Queen, in the lodgings that be in the eastern gallery above the inner court of the palace?"

The Queen answered, "I see a lofty bed-chamber hung with arras. It is dark, save for two branching candlesticks of lights burning before a great mirror. I see a lady standing before the mirror, crowned with a queen's crown of purple amethysts on her deep hair that hath the colour of the tipmost tongues of a flame. A man cometh through the door behind her, parting the heavy hangings left and right. A big man he is, and looketh like a king, in his great wolf-skin mantle and his kirtle of russet velvet with ornaments of gold. His bald head set about with grizzled curls and his bushy beard flecked with gray speak him something past his prime; but the light of youth burns in his eager eyes and the vigour of youth is in his tread. She turneth to greet him. Tall she is, and young she is, and beautiful, and proud-faced, and sweet-faced, and most gallant-hearted too, and merry of heart too, if her looks belie her not."

Queen Sophonisba covered her eyes, saying, "My lords, I see no more. The crystal curdles within like foam in a whirlpool under a high force in rainy weather. Mine eyes grow sore with watching. Let us row back, for the night is far spent and I am weary."

But Juss stayed her and said, "Let me dream yet awhile. The double pillar of the world, that member thereof which we, blind instruments of inscrutable Heaven, did shatter, restored again? From this time forth to maintain, I and he, his and mine, ageless and deathless for ever, for ever our high contention whether he or we should be great masters of all the earth? If this be but phantoms, O Queen, thou'st 'ticed us to the very heart of bitterness. This we could have missed, unseen and unimagined: but not now. Yet how were it possible the Gods should relent and the years return?"

But the Queen spake, and her voice was like the falling shades of evening, pulsing with hidden splendour, as of a sense of wakening starlight alive behind the fading blue. "This King," she said, "in the wickedness of his impious pride did wear on his thumb the likeness of that worm Ouroboros, as much as to say his kingdom should never end. Yet was he, when the appointed hour did come, thundered down into the depths of Hell. And if now he be raised again and his days continued, 'tis not for his virtue but for your sake, my lords, whom the Almighty Gods do love. Therefore I pray you possess your hearts awhile with humility before the most high Gods, and speak no unprofitable words. Let us row back."

Dawn came golden-fingered, but the lords of Demonland lay along abed after their watch in the night. About the third hour before noon, the presence was filled in the high presence chamber, and the three brethren sat upon their thrones, as four years ago they sat, between the golden hippogriffs, and beside them were thrones set for Queen Sophonisba and Lord Brandoch Daha. All else of beauty and splendour in Galing Castle had the Queen beheld, but not till now this presence chamber; and much she marvelled at its matchless beauties and rarities, the hangings and the carvings on the walls, the fair pictures, the lamps of moonstone and escarbuncle self-effulgent, the monsters on the four-and-twenty pillars, carved in precious stones so great that two men might scarce circle them with their arms, and the constellations burning in that firmament of lapis lazuli below the golden canopy. And when they drank unto Lord Juss the cup of glory to be, wishing him long years and joy and greatness for ever more, the Queen took a little cithern saying, "O my lord, I will sing a sonnet to thee and to you my lords and to sea-girt Demonland." So saying, she smote the strings, and sang in that crystal voice of hers, so true and delicate that all that were in that hall were ravished by its beauty:

> Shall I compare thee to a Sommers day?
>   Thou art more lovely and more temperate:
> Rough windes do shake the darling buds of Maie,
>   And Sommers lease hath all too short a date:
> Sometime too hot the eye of heaven shines,
>   And often is his gold complexion dimn'd;
> And every faire from faire some-time declines,
>   By chance or natures changing course untrim'd;
>   But thy eternall Sommer shall not fade
>   Nor loose possession of that faire thou ow'st;
>   Nor shall Death brag thou wandr'st in his shade,
>   When in eternall lines to time thou grow'st:
> So long as men can breath, or eyes can see,
> So long lives this, and this gives life to thee.

When she had done, Lord Juss rose up very nobly and kissed her hand, saying, "O Queen Sophonisba, fosterling of the Gods, shame us not with praises that be too high for mortal men. For well thou knowest what thing alone might bring us content. And 'tis not to be thought that that which was seen at Moonmere Head last night was very truth indeed, but rather the dream of a night vision."

But Queen Sophonisba answered and said, "My Lord Juss, blaspheme not the bounty of the blessed Gods, lest They be angry and withdraw it, Who have granted unto you of Demonland from this day forth youth everlasting and unwaning strength and skill in arms, and—but hark!" she said, for a trumpet sounded at the gate, three strident blasts.

At the sound of that trumpet blown, the lords Goldry and Spitfire sprang from their seats, clapping hand to sword. Lord Juss stood like a stag at gaze. Lord Brandoch Daha sat still in his golden chair, scarce changing his pose of easeful grace. But all his frame seemed alight with action near to birth, as the active principle of light pulses and grows in the sky at sunrise. He looked at the Queen, his eyes filled with a wild surmise.[7] A serving man, obedient to Juss's nod, hastened from the chamber.

No sound was there in that high presence chamber in Galing till in a minute's space the serving man returned with startled countenance, and, bowing before Lord Juss, said, "Lord, it is an Ambassador from Witchland and his train. He craveth present audience."

ARGUMENT: WITH DATES

[Dates *Anno Carces Conditae*. The action of the story covers exactly four years; from the 22nd April 399 to 22nd April 403 A.C.C.]

375 Corinius born in Carcë.

376 Prezmyra, sister to the Prince La Fireez, second wife to Corund, and after Queen of Impland, born in Norvasp.

379 Birth of Hacmon, eldest of the sons of Corund. Mevrian, sister to Lord Brandoch Daha, born in Krothering.

380 Heming born, second of Corund's sons.

381 Dormanes born, third of Corund's sons.

382 Birth of Viglus, Corund's fourth son, in Carcë. Recedor, King of Goblinland, privily poisoned by Corsus:
Gaslark reigns in his stead in Zajë Zaculo.
Sriva, daughter to Corsus and Zenambria, born in Carcë.

383 Armelline, cousin-german to King Gaslark, after betrothed and wed to Goldry Bluszco, born in Carcë.

384 Cargo, youngest of the sons of Corund, born in Carcë.

388 Goblinland invaded by the Ghouls: the flight out of Zajë Zaculo: Tenemos burnt: the power of the Ghouls crushed by Corsus.

389 Zeldornius, Helteranius, and Jalcanaius Fostus sent by Gaslark with an armament into Impland, and there ensor-celled.

390 The Witches harry in Goblinland: their defeat by the help of Demonland on Lormeron field: the slaying of Gorice X. by Brandoch Daha: Corsus taken captive and shamed by the Demons: Gro, abandoning the Goblin cause, dwells in exile at the court of Witchland.

393 La Fireez, besieged by Fax Fay Faz at Lida Nanguna in Outer Impland, delivered by the Demons: Goldry Bluszco repulsed by Corsus before Harquem.

395 Corund weds in Norvasp with the Princess Prezmyra.

398 The Ghouls burst forth in unimagined ferocity: their harrying in Demonland and burning of Goldry's house at Drepaby.

399 Holy war of Witchland, Demonland, Goblinland, and other polite nations against the Ghouls: Laxus, with the countenance of his master Gorice XI. and by the counsel of Gro, deserts with all his fleet in the battle off Kartadza (eastern seaboard of Demonland): the Ghouls nevertheless overwhelmed by the Demons in Kartadza Sound, and their whole race exterminated: Gorice XI. demands homage of Demonland, wrastles with Goldry Bluszco, and is in that encounter slain. Gorice XII., renewing with happier fortune the artificial practices of Gorice VII. in Carcë, takes Goldry with a

sending magical: Juss and Brandoch Daha, partly straught of their wits, unadvisedly go up with Gaslark against Carcë and are there clapped up: their delivery by the agency of La Fireez, and return to their own country: Juss's dream: the council in Krothering: the first expedition to Impland. The King's revenge on Pixyland executed by Corinius, and La Fireez dispossessed and driven into exile: Corund's great march over Akra Skabranth, sudden irruption into Outer Impland, and conquest of that country: shipwreck of the Demon fleet: carnage at Salapanta: march of the Demons into Upper Impland: amorous commerce of Brandoch Daha with the Lady of Ishnain Nemartra, who lays a weird upon him: Corund besieges and captures Eshgrar Ogo: Juss and Brandoch Daha escape across the Moruna and winter by the Bhavinan.

400   News of Eshgrar Ogo brought to Carcë: Corund honoured by the King therefor with the style of king of Impland. Juss and Brandoch Daha cross the Zia Pass: fight with the mantichore: ascent of Koshtra Pivrarcha, entrance into Koshtra Belorn, and entertainment by Queen Sophonisba: Juss's vision of Goldry bound on Zora: the Queen's furtherance of their designs: the hippogriff hatched beside the Lake of Ravary: the fatal folly of Mivarsh: Juss in despite of the Queen's admonitions assays Zora Rach on foot and comes within a little of losing his life. Prezmyra Queen of Impland and Laxus king of Pixyland crowned in Carcë: the King sends an expedition to put down Demonland, setting Corsus in chief command thereof: Laxus defeats Volle by sea off Lookinghaven, and Corsus, Vizz by land at Crossby Outsikes, Vizz slain on the field: cruel and despiteful policy of Corsus: dissensions betwixt him and Gallandus: great reversal of these disasters by Spitfire, Corsus's army cut in pieces by him on the Rapes of Brima and the survivors besieged in Owlswick: discontent of the army: Corsus with his own hands murthers Gallandus in Owlswick: tidings brought by Gro to Carcë: Corsus degraded by the King, who commissions Corinius as king of Demonland to retrieve the matter: battle of Thremnir's Heugh, with the overthrow of Spitfire's power: Corinius crowned in Owlswick: arrest of Corsus and his sons and their despatch home to Witchland.

401   Reduction of eastern Demonland by Corinius, save only Galing which Bremery holds with seventy men: Corinius moves west over the Stile: his insolent demands to Mevrian: miscarriage of Gaslark's expedition to the relief of Krothering, his defeat at Aurwath: masterly retreat of Corinius from Krothering before superior numbers: his ambushing and destroying of Spitfire's army on the shores of Switchwater: fall of Krothering and surrender of Mevrian: her escape by the counsel of Gro, the help of Corund's sons, and the connivance of Laxus: her flight to Westmark and thence east again into Neverdale: Gro abandons the cause of Witchland for that of Demonland: his and Mevrian's meeting with Juss and Brandoch Daha on their return home after two years: revolt of the east and relief of Galing: masterly dispositions both by Corinius and by the Demons for a decisive encounter: battle of Krothering Side and expulsion of the Witches from Demonland.

402   Second expedition to Impland, in which Gaslark and La Fireez join the Demons, lands at Muelva on the Didornian Sea: Juss, Spitfire, Brandoch Daha, Gro, Zigg, and Astar cross the Moruna: Juss's riding of the hippogriff to Zora Rach and deliverance of Goldry: Laxus sent by the King with an overwhelming power of ships to close Melikaphkhaz Straits against the Demons on their homeward voyage: battle off Melikaphkhaz: destruction of the Witchland armada: Laxus and La Fireez slain: a single surviving ship brings the tidings to Carcë: Corund called captain general in Carcë: gathering of the Witchland armies and their subject allies: landing of the Demons in the south: parley before Carcë: the King's warning to Juss: implacable enmity between them: signs and prognosticks in the heavens: the King's desperate resolution if the fight should go against him: battle before Carcë: slaying of Gro and Corund: defeat of the King's forces: council of war in Carcë, Corinius the second time captain general: Corsus, counselling surrender, falls greatly into the King's displeasure and is by him shamed and dismissed: in despair he compasses the taking off of Corinius and the sons of Corund, and unhappily of his own son too and his duchess, by poison, but is himself slain by Corinius: blasting of the Iron Tower in the miscarriage of the King's last conjuring: the Demons enter into Carcë: their encounter there with Queen Prezmyra: her tragical end and triumph: in

all of which is completed the fall of the empire and kingdom of the house of Gorice in Carcë.

403 Queen Sophonisba in Demonland: the marvel of marvels that restored the world on Lord Juss's natal day, the thirty-third year of his life in Galing.

BIBLIOGRAPHICAL NOTES
ON THE VERSES

xxxi.	Prophecy concerning con- juring	——
xxiii.	Lines quoted by Queen Sophonisba on the fall of Witchland	Webster (beginning of 17th cen- tury); "The Duchess of Malfi," Act V. v.
	Queen Sophonisba's Son- net	Shakespeare, Sonnet xviii.

The text here printed of Wotton's poem is that of "Reliquiae Wottoni-anae," 1st ed., 1651, edited by Izaak Walton; except that I read (with the earlier texts) 1. 5 *Moone*, 1. 8 *Passions*, 1. 16 *Princess*, instead of *Sun, Voyces, Mistris* of the 1651 edition.

Shakespeare's Sonnet is from the Quarto of 1609.

The passage from Njal's Saga in the Induction is quoted from Sir George Dasent's classic translation.

E.R.E

NOTES TO THE INTRODUCTION

1. Mark Graubard discusses the ouroboros in his *Astrology and Alchemy: Two Fossil Sciences* (New York: The Philosophical Library, 1953). This ancient symbol will not be unfamiliar to students of modern philosophy, for it has been used by C. G. Jung and Erich Neumann in their discussions of development of and unity in the personality. See Jung's *Symbole der Wandlung* (Symbols of Transformation), trans. R.F.C. Hull (New Haven: Princeton UP, 1956) and Neumann's *The Origins and History of Consciousness.* The curious may see a photograph of an ancient papyrus manuscript containing a drawing of an ouroboros on page 103 of *Greek Papyri in the British Museum* (London: printed by order of the Trustees of the British Museum, 1893). A companion volume discusses the drawing: *Greek Papyri in the British Museum. Catalogue with Texts,* ed. F. G. Kenyon (London: William Clones and Sons, Ltd., 1893), see page 103.

2. The ancient alchemists conceived of gold in a metaphoric sense in addition to its literal name for the most perfect metal. Any substance with ordered proportions could be called "golden."

3. Graubard, *Astrology and Alchemy,* p. 240.

4. Robert Steele, "Alchemy," *Shakespeare's England* (Oxford: Clarendon Press, 1970) 1:462–475.

5. Eddison to K. Henderson, 5 February 1923, fol. 18 of Ms. Eng. Letters c. 231, Bodleian Library, Oxford.

6. Most readers outside the field of Scandinavian literature have never heard of the Icelandic sagas. Professor Gwyn Jones describes the sagas in his book *A History of the Vikings* (London: Oxford UP, 1973), p. 288: "The thirteenth century . . . was the classical age of saga (i.e. family saga) writing. The hundred and twenty or more sagas *(sogur)* and short stories *(thaettir)* provide us with a freely rendered and often fictional history of most of the tenth century and the first third of the eleventh, revealed through the lives of outstanding men and women and the feud-ridden traditions of notable families, but much affected by the creative imagination of storytellers, authors, and scribes, by the changes to which tradition is subject over a period of two to three hundred years, and the distortions inevitable when men of antiquarian interests and family pride portray one age partly in terms of another."

7. H. Rider Haggard to Eddison, 14 May 1922, fol. 13 of Ms. Eng. Letters c. 231, Bodleian Library, Oxford.

8. Here I am paraphrasing words and ideas expressed by J.R.R. Tolkien in his essay "On Fairy Stories" from the anthology *Essays Presented to Charles*

Williams, ed. C. S. Lewis (Grand Rapids, Michigan: Eerdmans, 1974), p. 60. These are Tolkien's words on a reader's ability to believe the fantastic in literature: "That state of mind has been called 'willing suspension of disbelief.' But this does not seem to me a good description of what happens. What really happens is that the story-maker proves a successful 'sub-creator.' He makes a Secondary World which your mind can enter. Inside it, what he relates is 'true': it accords with the laws of that world. You therefore believe it, while you are, as it were, inside. The moment disbelief arises, the spell is broken; the magic, or rather art, has failed. You are then out in the Primary World again, looking at the little abortive Secondary World from outside."

9. Tolkien to Caroline Everett, letter 199, *The Letters of J.R.R. Tolkien,* ed. Humphrey Carpenter and Christopher Tolkien (Boston: Houghton Mifflin Company, 1981), p. 258.

10. Ransome to Eddison, 10 September 1922, fol. 40 of Ms. Eng. Letters c. 231, Bodleian Library, Oxford.

11. Arthur Ransome, *The Autobiography of Arthur Ransome* (London: Jonathan Cape, 1976), p. 38.

12. Eddison to E. Brinton, 6 August 1922, SRQ 823.91 ED23, Correspondence relating to *Styrbiorn the Strong,* Local History Department, Reference Library, Central Library, Leeds.

13. SRQ 823.91 ED23, Notes relating to *Styrbiorn the Strong,* Local History Department, Reference Library, Central Library, Leeds.

14. SRQ 823.91 ED23, Correspondence relating to *Egil's Saga,* Local History Department, Reference Library, Central Library, Leeds.

15. This and all other secondary references in this section ("I will . . . deliver") are from pages xxviii–xxxii of Eddison's Introduction to his translation of *Egil's Saga* (Cambridge: Cambridge University Press, 1930).

16. Eddison, *Egil's Saga,* xix.

17. Gwyn Jones, *Eirik the Red and other Icelandic Sagas,* trans. Gwyn Jones (Oxford: Oxford University Press, 1982), p. ix.

18. Magnus Magnusson and Hermann Palson, *Njal's Saga,* trans. M. Magnusson and H. Palson (Harmondsworth, Middlesex: Penguin, 1986), p. 25.

19. Jones, *Eirik the Red,* p. xiv.

20. E. V. Gordon, *An Introduction to Old Norse* (Oxford: Clarendon Press, 1927), p. xxxii.

21. Eddison to Mrs. Ford, 24 January 1923, fol. 9 of Ms. Eng. Letters c. 231, Bodleian Library, Oxford.

22. Eddison, *Egil's Saga,* xxix.

23. Eddison to Henderson, 5 February 1923, fols. 18–21 of Ms. Eng. Letters c. 231, Bodleian Library, Oxford.

24. Priam's "wonderfully built" palace "was fashioned with smooth-stone cloister walks, and within it/were embodied fifty sleeping chambers of smoothed stone/built so as to connect with each other" (VI:242–245). *The Iliad of Homer,* trans. Richmond Lattimore (Chicago: The University of Chicago Press, 1961), p. 159.

25. See pages 177, 183, and 331 for the only references to parents.

26. H. Munro Chadwick, *The Heroic Age* (Cambridge: Cambridge University Press, 1917), p. 387.

27. Jones, *History of the Vikings,* pp. 279–287.

28. Lattimore, *Iliad;* pp. 327, 330, 331, 333.

29. *Othello,* II:iii: 257–258.

NOTES TO
The Worm Ouroboros

A note on the Notes: I have used two abbreviations throughout: "ERE" for E. R. Eddison, and *"WO"* for *The Worm Ouroboros.*

I have cited sources when necessary, but here I must credit the contributions of works consulted several times. In 1928, the Oxford University Press published at the Clarendon Press the ten-volume *Oxford English Dictionary;* in 1933 it was reissued in twelve volumes called *The New English Dictionary,* and in 1989 the revised and expanded second edition of *The Oxford English Dictionary* was published. These volumes have been my constant companions: nearly all of the archaisms and esoteric words have been glossed according to the definitions in the first and second editions. My citations of Shakespeare follow the "Through Line Numbers" method adopted by David Bevington in his third edition of the *Complete Works of Shakespeare,* first published in 1951 by Scott, Foresman and Company in Glenview, Illinois. I have taken the Homeric quotations from the sublime translations by Richmond Lattimore, whose *Iliad of Homer* was published in 1951 in Chicago by the University of Chicago Press, and whose *Odyssey of Homer* was published in 1965 in New York by Harper & Row. I have taken the Websterian quotations from *John Webster: Three Plays,* edited by D. C. Gunby and published in Harmondsworth, Middlesex, in 1972 by Penguin Books.

Where I have been able, I have tried to indicate sources having tangible influence on the text. My motives for so doing have been to reveal, more minutely than I could in the introduction, the many works of literature that delighted Eddison enough to spark his imitation of them or borrowing from them and to reveal some of the thoughts that winged through his mind during his writing of this book. Most of these indicated sources have been literary, as I am ignorant of other subjects: astronomy, for example, a science Eddison studied in some detail, I have neglected completely. Even in my efforts to illuminate the literary sources I have been negligent, for Eddison's reading delved far deeper and ranged far wider than mine has yet, and I know I have, through unobserving ignorance, passed over several allusions. Those of you having minds more richly stored with poetry than mine will see things to which I have been blind, and from you I ask for patience during your reading of my notes.

P. E. THOMAS

409

THE INDUCTION

1. The Induction: The Induction has been called the novel's "main flaw" (see note 8 to Chapter II), but ERE purposes it to set the novel's tone and atmosphere. The word has several meanings, and nearly all find some application here. First, the word is an archaism for *introduction,* and by beginning with such a word, the first of hundreds of archaisms, ERE immediately alerts us to the novel's peculiar style: it will be an eclectic mix of the modern and the archaic. The word also means the action of persuasive inducement, and in these few pages of prose ERE attempts to persuade us to go further into the story proper. ERE's method here resembles that of the Elizabethan poet Thomas Sackville. ERE's deep reading in Elizabethan literature would have brought him in the way of Sackville's famous "Induction" (1563) to the didactic composite poem *Mirrour for Magistrates* written by several poets and published in four expanding editions between 1559 and 1587. In this "Induction," which is modeled on Book VI of *The Aeneid,* personified Sorrow meets the somber narrator on a gloomy winter day and leads him from the known world into Hell. Inside the black gates, Sorrow shows the narrator a succession of grim personifications: Remorse, Dread, Revenge, Misery, Old Age, Malady, Famine, and War. Personified War carries a huge shield on which are painted great commanders of antique ages: Darius, Hannibal, Pompey, Caesar, Scilla, and Marius. Sackville describes each personification and the shield's portraits with enough detailed imagery to make Hell a place of sensuous horrors and deep gloom. This prepares readers for the *Mirrour*'s specific themes and examples, because Sackville's dark and sinister Hell, contrasting with the comforts of the sunlit world, emphasizes the poem's messages about the punishments suffered in Hell for political sins committed in the living world. In a similar way the strange nature of ERE's imaginary Mercury necessitates his Induction, but it is neither allegorical nor didactic like Sackville's. ERE must elicit belief in the imaginary world by contrasting it to earthly realities. Thus ERE gives the reader a human companion on the journey past *"les barricades mystérieuses"* to the alien world of Mercury. The success of the Induction rests in its understatement and in its unexplained plot events: these produce mystery in the text, and the mystery, in turn, produces curiosity in the reader. The oddness of the house, the naming of it "House of Peace" and "House of Postmeridian" and "House of Heart's Desire," the references to the Lotus Room with its allusion to the strangely compelling lotus fruit, which makes the eater forget his homeland (see Homer's *Odyssey,* Book IX: 82–104), the Lotus Room's relationship to Mercury, the arrival of the martlet, the winged horse and its chariot: neither ERE as the narrator nor Lessingham as the main character explains these things. The events of the Induction simply happen, and as in a mythic plot, they must be accepted, as Keats says of mysteries, "without any irritable reaching after fact & reason" (from a letter to his brothers, December 21–27, 1817). Speaking of Couperin's piece's title, *Les Barricades Mystérieuses,* Lessingham whispers to Mary: "And only you and I know what it really means." This epitomizes the entire Induction: ERE and his characters know the mysterious matter, but the reader obtains only hints that spur on his interest while lulling his acceptance of the marvels. "As in a dream," Lessingham follows the martlet, and the reader, in dreamlike curiosity, follows Lessingham to the glories of Galing Castle.

2. There was a man named Lessingham: ERE begins his novel in the manner of a saga. All the prominent Icelandic sagas begin this way: *Njal's Saga*—" There was a man named Mord . . ." (trans. Sir George Webbe Dasent [London: J. M. Dent & Sons, 1911]); *Egil's Saga*—" There was a man named Wolf . . ." (trans. E. R. Eddison [Cambridge University Press, 1930]); *The Saga of Grettir the Strong*—" There was a man named Onund . . ." (trans. G. Hight [London: J. M. Dent & Sons, 1914]); *Laxdaela Saga*—"There was a man called Ketil Flat-Nose . . ." (trans. M. Magnusson and H. Palsson [Harmondsworth, Middlesex: Penguin Books, 1969]). Beginning *WO* in saga fashion shows ERE's desire to declare his allegiance to one of his strongest influences.

3. in Wasdale . . . the Screes: To anyone who has walked or climbed in the mountain ranges of Asia, Europe, or western North America, the peaks of the English Lake District seem like dwarf mountains, and yet, on those Cumbrian fells (i.e. hills), beauty exists unlike that of any other range. ERE knew and loved Lakeland, and because of its remoteness Wasdale was one of his favorite places. This valley lies in the western part of Lakeland and contains the Wast Water, the deepest lake in the entire district (250 feet). Wasdale itself is contained within the Copeland Forest: Copeland extends over the mountains west of the Wast Water, and at its southern edge lies the quiet village of Nether Wasdale. One road, skirting the western shore of the Wast Water, connects the village of Nether Wasdale to the village of Wasdale Head at the north end of the valley. Walking north along this road, one can look east over the clear expanse of the Wast Water to the Screes, which soar precipitously from the eastern shore of the lake. The Screes, from this view, seem to transport the observer to the ruggedness of the last glacial ice age, for they seem to pour into the Wast Water incalculable tons of black, gray, brown, and white fragments of volcanic rock, and hence the name of these cliffs. The Screes vary in height and extend between two peaks: Whin Rigg (1,755 feet) and Illgill Head (1,998 feet). Lessingham's house must be in the south near the village of Nether Wasdale, but it is probably east of the Irt River, for the view from the garden looks northeastward to the lake and Gable can be seen behind the Screes. Gable, more properly called Great Gable, stands 2,949 feet high. A. Wainwright, whose seven-volume *Pictorial Guide to the Lakeland Fells* is the fell-walker's bible, describes Great Gable, "the hoary old favorite," in words far better than mine could be:

It is the undisputed overlord of the group of hills to which it belongs, and its superior height is emphasized tremendously by the deep gulf separating it from the Scafells and allowing an impressive view that reveals the whole of its half-mile altitude as an unremitting and unbroken pyramid: this is the aspect of the fell that earned the name. . . . Great Gable casts a spell. It starts as an honourable adversary and becomes a friend.

4. Njal: Mary, Lessingham's wife, reads from chapter 124 of Sir George Webbe Dasent's much admired translation of *Njal's Saga.* Titled *The Story of Burnt Njal,* it was published in two volumes by the firm of Edmonston and Douglas in Edinburgh in 1861. ERE obtained the volumes in 1900, so they had endured twenty years of loving use by the time ERE came to copy out this section for *WO,* and the "faded green cover" of Mary's book perhaps alludes directly to ERE's own. The ornate covers have two old Icelandic proverbs embossed in gold: "But a short while is hand fain of blow" and "Bare is back without brother behind it." Dasent's translation was affordably reprinted as part of the "Everyman's Library" by J. M. Dent in England and E. P. Dutton in America.

To state it perhaps too simply, the great theme of *Njal's Saga* concerns the wisdom of finding peaceful solutions to potentially violent conflicts. The sage Njal constantly works to maintain the salutary bonds of kinship and friendship while other, angrier men work to break these bonds to satisfy their anger. The saga's complicated plot tells of the failed attempts of friendship to supplant enmity, of forgiveness to becalm revenge, of humility to topple pride, and of compromise to melt stubbornness. The ominous "wolf's ride" portends the final overthrow of Njal and the triumph of violence. The man who sees the "wolf's ride," is named Hilidglum, but he has only a small place in the action of the story. The man on the gray horse with flanks "flecked with rime" (hoar frost) tells Hildiglum that Flosi's "redes" (advice or plans) are like the burning torch he carries. Flosi Thordarson, father-in-law of Hoskuld Hvitaness-Priest, plans to attack Njal's house and to kill his sons in revenge for their having killed Hoskuld. Flosi attacks Njal's house at Bergthorsknoll and burns the entrapped family with their house. It is difficult to say exactly why ERE chose to quote this particular passage in his Induction. Dasent's final words, "great tidings," could have some connection with Lessingham's journey to Mercury. The portent could also refer to the great tidings of warfare on Mercury. Knowing ERE's disliking for allegory, I hesitate to suggest any connection between the conflicting Icelanders and the conflicting Demons and Witches.

5. hawking bats: ERE means that the bats hunt insects in the same way that hawks hunt birds. Although his analogy is not correct because bats locate insects with sonar and eat them on the wing while hawks kill other birds by diving at them and ramming them at great speed, this expression is a minute example of the Elizabethan aspect of ERE's style. Shakespeare uses the verb in the same way in *Macbeth* when Ross and the old man discuss the strange portents which both preceded and followed the murder of King Duncan:

> On Tuesday last,
> A falcon, tow'ring in her pride of place,
> Was by a mousing owl hawk'd at and kill'd. (II:iv:11–13)

Mainly nocturnal hunters, owls pounce silently upon their earthbound victims. Here, an owl who normally eats mice kills a high-flying hawk by the hawk's own method.

6. *Les Barricades Mystérieuses:* François Couperin's (1668–1733) short rondeau in B flat major must be played *"vivement."*

7. Postmeridian: This term is associated with sleep and pertains to the hours after noon (P.M.).

8. martlet: Normally, these imaginary birds have no feet, and although a footless flyer appears in Chapter Twelve, Lessingham's laconic little friend seems gressible.

9. A horse it seemed: see note 6 to Chapter I.

CHAPTER I

1. two dreams walking: The martlet's words may have been inspired by some spoken by Lady Mary Seraskier in George du Maurier's *Peter Ibbetson,* a novel ERE much admired. Peter Ibbetson meets Lady Mary in a dream, and the two of them journey to the Paris of their childhood. Once there, Lady Mary warns Peter:

> And mind, also, you must take care how you touch things or
> people—you may hear, and see, and smell; but you mustn't touch,
> nor pick flowers or leaves, nor move things about. It blurs the
> dream, like breathing on a window-pane. I don't know why, but it
> does. You must remember that everything here is dead and gone by.
> With you and me it is different; we're alive and real. . . .
> (George du Maurier, *Peter Ibbetson* [London: James R.
> Osgood, McIlvaine & Co., 1896, p. 191.)

ERE has reversed the situation: in *Peter Ibbetson* the dreaming travelers are real and Paris is illusory, but in *WO* the dreaming travelers seem illusory while Mercury seems real.

2. Croesus: Ruling from 560–546 B.C., he was a powerful and wealthy king of the Lydians. He conquered Ephesus and subdued the Ionian Greeks, but he could not conquer the Ionian islands, so he made an alliance with them. (Herodotus's version of the birth of the alliance has charm: see *The History,* I:27.) When Solon, the Athenian archon and lawmaker, visited him, Croesus asked Solon who was the most blessed man on earth, and Solon said, "To me it is clear that you are very rich, and clear that you are the king of many men; but the thing that you ask me I cannot say of you yet, until I hear that you have brought your life to an end well." Croesus was not at all pleased by this answer and sent Solon away, "making no further account of him, thinking him assuredly a stupid man who would let by present goods and bid him look to the end of every matter" (Herodotus, *The History*, trans. David Grene [Chicago: The University of Chicago Press, 1987], pp. 47–48).

3. Minos: a mythical king of Crete and the son of Zeus; his wife, Pasiphae, gave birth to the Minotaur; he sacrificed seven maids and youths to the Minotaur each year; he became the judge of the dead in Hades.

4. Semiramis: many legends surround this ancient Assyrian princess who lived in the ninth century B.C. The building of Babylon and its glorious hanging gardens has been attributed to her. Some legends make her the incarnation of the goddesses Ishtar and Astarte.

5. that high presence chamber of the lords of Demonland: In 1904, when ERE was twenty-two, he obtained the John Ashton edition of *The Voiage and Travayle* of Sir John Maundeville Knight (London: Pickering & Chatto, 1887), first written in Anglo-Norman French in 1356–7. It seems probable that Maundeville's strange, imaginative book inspired ERE in his description of the Galing presence chamber. Maundeville says this of the palace of the king of Java:

> The King of this lande hath a riche palace and the best that is in the worlde, for all the greces [stairs] of his hall and chambres are all made one of gold & another of silver, & all the walls are plated with fine gold and silver, & on those plates are written stories of knightes, and batayles, and the pavimente of the hall and chambres is of golde and silver, and there is no man that woulde beleve this riches that is there except hee had sene it . . . (pp. 137–38).

Maundeville also describes the lavish palace of Prester John:

> . . . there is his principall palaice that is so riche that marvayle is to tell . . . and the principal gates of this palaice are of precious stones that men call Saraine & the borders of the barres are of Ivory, & windowes of the hall and chambers are of Crystall, and tables that they eat of, some Emerandes, some are of Mayk [amethysts], some of golde and precious stones, and the pillers that beare the tables are of such stones also, and the greces on the which the Emperour goeth to his sege [seat] where he sitteth at meat, one is of Mastik [onyx], another of Cristal, another of green Jasphy [jasper], another of Diasper [amethyst], another of Serdin [sardonyx], another of Cornelin [red chalcedony], another of Seuton [?], & that he setteth his fote upon, is of Crisolites, and all these greces are bordered with fine gold, and well set with great perles and other precious stones . . . (pp. 205–6).

6. hippogriff: Unlike Ovid's Pegasus this word, in Italian *ippogrifo*, was first used by the sixteenth-century Italian poet Ariosto to label a combination of the horse and the griffin:

[The] horse was not a fiction, but instead
The offspring of a griffin and a mare.
Its plumage, forefeet, muzzle, wings and head
Like those of its paternal parent were.
The rest was from its dam inherited.
It's called a hippogriff. Such beasts, though rare
In the Rhiphaean mountains, far beyond
The icy waters of the north, are found.
(Orlando Furioso, trans. Barbara Reynolds [Harmondsworth,
Middlesex: Penguin Books, 1975], Canto IV: stanza 18)

Ariosto also declares, facetiously, that the hippogriff is a natural beast to distinguish it from the winged horse in the *Orlando Innamorato* of Boiardo, the poem and poet that partly inspired Ariosto. The winged horse that takes Lessingham to Mercury resembles Ariosto's beast, and it is fitting that Lessingham's conveyance is the symbol of Demonland.

7. conger: a saltwater eel common to the coasts of Britain; it attains lengths of six to ten feet and is used for food.

8. harpy: ERE studied Virgil at Oxford, and he may have had these lines from *The Aeneid* in mind when he wrote of the screaming monster:

No monster
is more malevolent than these, no scourge
of gods or pestilence more savage ever
rose from the Stygian waves. These birds may wear
the face of virgins, but their bellies drip with
a disgusting discharge, and their hands
are talons, and their features pale and famished.
(trans. A. Mandelbaum [Berkeley: The University
of California Press, 1971], Book III: lines 281–87)

Aeneas, narrating his travels at Dido's feast, then speaks of the harpies attacking with "terrifying scream" (A. Mandelbaum) and "with hideous cry and clattering wings" (Dryden).

9. fire-drake: The dragon killed by Beowulf was called "fyr-draca" (line 5,371), and the word was used by Elizabethans to mean a fire-breathing dragon.

10. cockatrice: See note 17 to Chapter IV.

11. cyclops: giants having one round eye in the center of their foreheads. Many used to dwell on Sicily, but all are now extinct.

12. chimaera: a fire-breathing monster with a lion's head, a goat's body, and a snake's tail.

13. leviathan: In ancient Hebrew poetry this name referred to a giant aquatic animal either real or imaginary. To the Elizabethans it referred either to a whale or to an imaginary sea monster.

14. crystolite: (chrysolite?) A yellowish variety of the precious beryl.

15. beryl: a transparent stone of pale green, sometimes with the addition of light blue, yellow, or white colors.

16. amethyst: a compound stone of manganese and quartz which is a transparent purple or bluish violet color.

17. To give light to the presence chamber were seven escarbuncles: (carbuncle) The word refers to any of several large red precious stones; the most common is the ruby. Between the fourteen and the seventeenth centuries the name was applied to a mythical gem stone that glowed with light. References to the glowing stone can be found in writers as notable as William Caxton and Sir Walter Raleigh, but ERE found the legendary stone in Sir John Maundeville's *Voiage and Travayle*. While describing Prester John's palace at Suse, Maundeville says that "about the principall toure of the palaice are two pomels of gold all round, and eche one of those hath two carbuncles great & large, that shine ryght clere in the night . . ." (Chapter XCVIII). In Chapter LXXII Maundeville describes the palace of the Ok-lar-Khan, the emperor of the Tartars: "And he hath in his chambre a pillar of golde in the which lighteth all his chambre by night. . . ."

18. lapis lazuli: a sulphurous silicate stone of bright blue color.

19. cloth of tissue: an expensive fabric often interwoven with gold and silver thread. Elizabethans and Jacobeans valued it highly. ERE may have learned of it from John Webster. In II: 1 of *The White Devil* the Duke of Florence upbraids Brachiano with suspicions of Brachiano's adulterous affair with Vittoria Corombona, and he believes that Brachiano pays Vittoria to be his mistress:

> Her husband is lord of a poor fortune—
> Yet she wears cloth of tissue.

20. tiffany: a thin, transparent silk or a gauze muslin.

21. carcanets: necklaces inset with jewels.

22. white-armed Helen: Helen of Troy had such great beauty that she earned the envy of Aphrodite. "Terrible is the likeness of her face to immortal goddesses," says one of Priam's counselors (*Iliad*, trans. Lattimore, III: 158).

23. Arcadian Atalanta: ERE admired Swinburne enough to purchase a nineteen-volume set of his complete works. In Swinburne's *Atalanta in Calydon*, Meleager the Prince of Calydon loves and reveres the Arcadian maiden:

> For thy name's sake and awe toward thy chaste head,
> O holiest Atalanta, no man dares
> Praise thee, though fairer than whom all men praise,
> And godlike for thy grace of hallowed hair
> And holy habit of thine eyes . . .

24. Phryne: A lovely Greek woman of the fourth century B.C. She modeled for Praxiteles when he created the "Cnidian Aphrodite," the first life-size and free-standing female nude in classical Greek art.

25. Queen for ever among the dead that be departed: Persephone, the daughter of Zeus and Demeter, was carried off by Hades to the underworld; she ate food there and so committed herself to staying with Hades for six months of every year.

26. sylph: a spirit inhabiting the air.

27. Will-o'-the-Wisp: literally, a naturally occurring fire in a marsh or peat bog; because it wanders with a compelling and mysterious light, the term is used figuratively for anything which is alluring but misleading.

28. sendaline: (sendal) a thin, rich silken material; also, fine linen.

29. Recedor . . . murthered: This occured in 382; see the "Argument."

30. in the battle with the Ghouls: According to the "Argument," this war began in 399. In a letter (16 March 1942) to an American friend named J. M. Howard, ERE compared the war with Germany to the war against the Ghouls. He made a distinction between "the contentions of life-giving action" like the joyous wars "of Galing against Carcë which, by their ending, brought such woeful and empty handed bereavement upon Juss and his friends" and the sorrowful, hateful, wretchedly destructive war against Hitler's ideology:

> . . . this is war against the Ghouls: a war of destruction: a heavy, unescapable, ugly job, having as its end and sanction the extirpation of things which, until by our own strength and manhood we extirpate them, stand between mankind and the life which—if we are to remain men—is alone worth having. (Fol. 124 of Ms. Eng. Lett., c. 231, Bodleian)

CHAPTER II

1. withal: in addition.

2. combe: a valley or a hillside cut by a glacier.

3. withies: (withy) the flexible branch of a willow.

4. the wrastling ground: ERE models this episode on the Icelandic institution of judicial combat called the "holmgang." Until the year 1006, both defendants and plaintiffs had the right to call for a holmgang as a method for settling legal disputes. For an example of a holmgang, see chapter 65 of *Egil's Saga.*

5. byrnies: (singular: byrny) a shirt or coat of mail.

6. greaves: armor for the lower leg, covering the shin.

7. neat: a bovine animal; an ox or a bull.

8. but wait for these things' unfolding: These are Lessingham's last words. Orville Prescott believes that ERE's use of Lessingham is awkward:

> "Since this is a romantic epic about an imaginary world Eddison felt it necessary to set his stage and explain things before launching into his story proper. This he did awkwardly, by sending an English gentleman in a magic dream to the planet Mercury to observe events there. It is a distracting and clumsy notion; but since Eddison forgot

all about his earthborn observer after the first twenty pages no pro-
spective reader should allow himself to be troubled by his fleeting
presence" (from the Introduction to the 1967 Ballantine Books edition of this novel).

Lin Carter, quoting the above passage, says that Prescott "laid his finger
on the book's main flaw" (*Tolkien: a Look Behind the Lord of the Rings* [New
York: Ballantine, 1969] 143). It is true that Lessingham's participation in
the novel ends abruptly, but the lacking explanation for this sudden ending is not necessarily a flaw. Perhaps Lessingham's silence through the
rest of the novel is the expression of his declaration "to dance to none of
their tunes, but wait for these things' unfolding." Or, perhaps ERE intends for Lessingham's resolution to signal his full use of a sagalike
narrator who does not interpret action or judge characters. On the other
hand, perhaps the explanation is there. The martlet carefully explains
Lessingham's status on Mercury: "Thou and I will journey up and down
for a season. . . . But here thou canst not handle aught, neither make the
folk ware of thee. . . . For thou and I walk here impalpable and invisible,
as it were two dreams walking" (p. 6). ERE clearly states that Lessingham
is really outside this world (as the reader is) though he is watching it, and
having established his presence as a constant observer, ERE may have felt
it unnecessary to say any more about him.

9. Lord Gro: In *The Book of Drawings* (see section 2 of the Introduction)
Gro emerges a complicated figure. He acts much more heroically in the
drawings than he does in *WO*. One drawing shows "Lord Gro cutting the
javelin of the son of Corund in two": a pretty piece of swordsmanship that
only men like Gunnar and Kolskegg of *Njal's Saga* are capable of. Another
drawing is captioned "The Demons seeking to hold back and disarm Lord
Gro until the son of Corsus has escaped." In this drawing Gro stands as a
hero larger and stronger than the Demons, and no fewer than three
Demons are having difficulty restraining him. Gro's greatest moment in
The Book of Drawings occurs when he leads a charge against an army of
Witches: "Gorice was certainly conquering, but suddenly Lord Gro, with
fifty men, came to the rescue. He charged down upon the Witches, & when
their leader came to cut him down, he drew his revolver, & shot him
dead." In *WO*, Gro does nothing so conventionally heroic, though he does
fight in the final battle before Carcë. What is more, in *The Book of Drawings*,
Gro is unwaveringly on the side of the Demons: he does not have the
turncoat desires, born of his hero-worshiping heart, which beset him in
WO. Nevertheless, Gro is pictured in situations which make one think that
he has some of the characteristics of the cunning Machiavel he is in *WO*.
Two drawings show Gro shooting another lord in the back. Another is
captioned "Lord Gro stabbing Lord Gandari as he drinks." Surely not
moments of courage equal to his tremendous charge upon Gorice. Another is captioned "Lord Gro shooting his old accomplice." I do not know
why Gro shoots this man, but the picture shows Lord Gro turning upon
someone who was once his ally. Since some drawings of Gro show widely

differing traits, I believe that, even at this early stage, Gro was already becoming the most complicated character in ERE's imagination.

10. his long black beard was tightly curled: ERE has in mind the bearded figures in the bronze, stone, and relief sculptures of ancient Akkad, Assyria, and Babylon. ERE believed strongly in the beauty of the beard, and in 1930 he declared his views in an imaginative unpublished essay called "A Night Piece on Hair":

> In England today the fashion of shaving is so nearly universal that you may go about for months and years without seeing a natural beard. Between the native beauty of a great beard that never was touched by razor (here I stroked my hand down the soft Assyrian blackness of my own) and the harsh stiff trimmed beards, and these as a rule, too, old men's beards, of today, there is as much difference as between the stately elm and its poor limb-lopped brothers in Kensington Gardens. So that the beard has become, from the chief ornament of manhood, the badge of a doddering age grown too idle to use the razor; and that "bloom of youth," the soft young growth of the beard on a young man's cheek that the Greeks so much delighted in, is, in this country, as extinct as the osprey or the bustard.

ERE, within his narrative persona, cannot help but identify himself with the great bearded sculptures of the Assyrians. ERE wore a moustache through most of his adult life. During a trip to Iceland in 1926, he grew a beard, and on his return, his wife, Winifred, and his daughter, Jean, pleaded with him to shave it. To their relief he razored the beard, but, not wanting to relinquish completely his ornament of manhood, he retained the moustache for the rest of his days. (Ms. Eng. Misc., c. 456, Bodleian)

11. widdershins: in a direction contrary to the normal: i.e., backwards.

12. madder: a climbing plant whose roots yield red pigments for dye.

13. Corinius: This Witchlander possesses some, but certainly not all, of the traits of his namesake in Geoffrey of Monmouth's *Historia Regum Britanniae.* Geoffrey's fictional hero, Brutus, while leading his people to Albion, meets the Trojan exile Corineus, "a sober-minded man, wise in counsel, yet of great courage and audacity," in Mauretania. Corineus and his people join Brutus, and they all sail to the Aquitaine, where Corineus, already famed as a fighter against giants, impresses Brutus by leading the warriors in the conquest of the Aquitainians: "Corineus brandished his battle-axe among the retreating battalions. . . . At a single blow he struck off one man's head, while from another he cut away the legs." (trans. Lewis Thorpe [Harmondsworth, Middlesex: Penguin Books, 1966] p. 68). ERE probably read Geoffrey in his youth. Though ERE's hero has the same courage as Geoffrey's, ERE's young carouser is surely not sober minded.

14. flittermouse: a bat.

15. angelica: the root of this aromatic herb was used medicinally against disease and poison.

16. mickle: much.

17. he heaved the King over his head: *Egil's Saga* is the source for Goldry's act of violence. In the episode imitated by ERE, Skallagrim (Grim), the father of Egil, swells with the frenzy of rage during a ball game resembling rugby, and his strength swells proportionately:

> Grim became then so strong that he grabbed Thord and drave him down so hard that he was all to-broken, and straightway gat his bane. (trans. E. R. Eddison [Cambridge: Cambridge University Press, 1930] 76)

See the subsequent note, which describes the nature of Skalagrim's and Goldry's temporary battle-fury.

18. Goldry's wrath departed from him and left him strengthless: Goldry's sudden swelling to anger, his temporary insanity ("wood with anger"), his gnashing teeth and foaming mouth, his swift and extraordinary violence, and the sudden dissipation of both his anger and his strength are some of the characteristics of a "berserk." This Old Icelandic term refers to a warrior whose mind and body become impassioned with "battle-fury" or *"furor athleticus,"* as Tacitus described it among the German tribes. Controversy still exists over the word's full meaning: some scholars believe that it describes warriors who enter battle wearing only a bearskin shirt; others believe it describes warriors who enter battle without a byrny or mail-coat. ERE, aware of this controversy and perhaps unwilling to take a side, made Goldry and Gorice XI fight naked! *Egil's Saga* gives an authoritative description of the "berserk-gang" or berserk fit:

> So is it said of those men that were shape-strong or of them on whom was the berserk-gang, that for so long as that held, they were so strong that there was no holding against them, but forthwith when that was passed over, then were they unmightier than of wont. And it was so with Kveldulf that, as soon as the berserk rage was gone from him, then knew he his weariness after those onslaughts he had made, and then was he altogether without might, so that he laid him down in his bed. (trans. E. R. Eddison [Cambridge: Cambridge University Press, 1930] 53)

For a man to be "shape strong" means he has the ability to change his shape, usually to the shape of a wolf or a bear, and thus, Kveldulf, who was "exceeding shape-strong" (p. 1) has a name that means "evening wolf." The shape-strong or werewolf tradition is often attached to the berserk tradition in Old Norse literature. The folklore of most cultures contains a tradition of lycanthropy.

CHAPTER III

1. arvale: this word usually refers to a funeral feast; here it seems to refer to a drink or toast at a funeral feast.

2. firkin: a small cask with a capacity of eight or nine gallons.

3. theorbo: a lute with two fretted necks and two sets of tuning pegs; the upper neck contains the treble strings, and the lower neck, the base strings.

4. hautboy: a wooden double-reed instrument with a highly pitched range of two and a half octaves; it became the modern oboe.

5. Aeolian mode: a scale on which some Gregorian chants were based; a late addition to the church modes, it was used in the sixteenth century.

6. trublit: troubled.

7. feblit: made feeble.

8. *Timor Mortis conturbat me:* Dread fear of death worries me.

9. plesance: a garden; here used to mean the material world.

10. bruckle: fragile, brittle, frail.

11. slee: sly.

12. sary: sorry.

13. dansand mirry: grows happy; comes into happiness.

14. like to die: seeming likely to perish.

15. wicker: a willow branch; possibly, a candle.

16. wannis: "wan is"; wan = faded, sickly.

17. Estatis: kingdoms, governments.

18. baith: both.

19. mellie: here, a chivalric battle; usually, a tournament or mock-battle.

20. sowkand: suckling.

21. campion: champion.

22. stour: battle.

23. closit in the tour: protected in the castle.

24. piscence: strength (puissance).

25. straik: stroke.

26. bodkin: a short, pointed dagger.

27. Pavane: a stately dance in slow 2/2 time.

28. Allemande: a name given to various German dances.

29. Fandango: a fast Spanish dance in 3/4 time.

30. Bacchanals: the wild, drunken dances of the priestesses of Bacchus.

31. Galliard: a swift dance in triple meter.

32. Gigue: a dance in 6/8 time.

33. Coranto: a lively French dance in triple meter.

34. Estridges: ostriches.

35. Bustards: large European flightless birds capable of running with great speed. Bustards are now rare in Europe; the great bustard was once common in England, but it is extinct now.

36. sackbut: trombone.

37. lode-star: a guiding star used in navigation, especially Polaris.

38. infirm of purpose: Cf. Lady Macbeth's reproachful words to her husband when he fears to return the daggers to Duncan's chamber: "Infirm of purpose! / Give me the daggers. The sleeping and the dead / Are but as pictures" (*Macbeth*, II:ii:50–52).

39. egromancy: (negromancy, necromancy) popularly, "black magic" referring to conjuring; originally, the art of foretelling future events through communication with the dead.

40. and there was written: The rare word *chirt* (to squeeze out) and the spelling of *brenne* (for *burn*) would place this bit of prose in the early sixteenth century. However, by 1500, most writers spelled *hous* with a final *e,* so that word must be placed somewhat earlier. The spelling of *shippe* can be found in Caxton. So, considering these words together, this writing can be placed, roughly, at the end of the fifteenth century. It contrasts to the characters' speech, which echoes, and sometimes quotes, the English writers of the late sixteenth and early seventeenth centuries. By making the verbal abilities of his characters span at least three centuries, Eddison maintains an alchemic eclecticism in his prose style. (See also note 13 to Chapter VIII.)

CHAPTER IV

1. corbel: a projection of stone imbedded in a wall and jutting out to support the weight of a structure above it; the corbel table at Carcë supports the tower and the parapet.

2. machicolation: an opening between two corbel supports; through it molten lead or boiling water can be poured.

3. fen: a marsh; low land covered wholly or partially with shallow water.

4. gat his bane: obtained his destruction.

5. sithence: seeing that, or, since that time.

6. donjon keep: the innermost and strongest part of a castle.

7. retort: a glass vessel with a long, thin, downward-bending neck; used to distill liquids.

8. astrolabe: an obsolete instrument formerly used for calculating altitudes; it took various forms, but it commonly had metal hoops corresponding to the planetary orbits.

9. alembic: a gourd-shaped vessel used for distilling.

10. bain-marie: a flat vessel containing steaming water; smaller vessels are placed within it, and the water heats their contents.

11. wist: guessed, knew.

12. cormorant: a black bird about three feet in length; they inhabit the seashores of the northern hemisphere and are commonly thought to be insatiably voracious.

13. puissaunce: power, strength.

14. grammarie: (gramarye) occult learning, magic, conjuring.

15. pismire: an ant.

16. phantasmagoria: an exhibition of optical illusions.

17. a more material horror: This is the cockatrice or basilisk, a small but deadly monster hatched from a hen's egg by an incubating serpent. As with the Gorgon (see subsequent note), a glance from its eye can kill. ERE's builds his description upon Elizabethan folklore. Even gentle Juliet speaks of "the death-darting eye of cockatrice" *(Romeo and Juliet,* III: ii: 47).

18. gorgon: Phorcus, a sea deity, fathered the three gorgons, whose heads were covered with snakes and whose eyes turned men to stone. Medusa, whom Perseus killed, was his most famous offspring.

19. aspick: a plant from which a volatile, aromatic oil is procured.

20. ensorcelled: enchanted, bewitched.

21. unhallowed processes . . . nearing maturity: The listed terms are alchemic processes. Fixation is the process of reducing a volatile spirit to permanent bodily form; in modern chemistry, of combining a gas with a solid. Conjunction is the process of uniting components of matter. Deflagration is the sudden combustion of a substance for the purpose of producing a change in its composition. Putrefaction is the decaying or decomposing of a substance by chemical action. Rubefication is the process of heating a base metal to redness.

22. phial: a small glass bottle.

23. decoction: the process of boiling a substance in water to extract its soluble parts.

24. kestrel: a small hawk.

25. costly essences: Shell of gold is gold for painting or writing and is stored in a mussel shell. Saffron of gold is a saffron-colored chemical preparation. Amianth is alum. Mandragora is a poisonous plant used as a narcotic. (See note 58 to Chapter VII.) Sal armoniack is ammonium chloride. Monkshood and black hellebore are poisonous plants. The thornapple is a plant used as a narcotic and is so called for its round fruit and thorny stems. Aphroselmia, asem, strypteria of Melos, and vinum ardens are such esoteric substances that public knowledge of them has been forbidden since the sixteenth century.

26. aurum potabile: in alchemy, the much-sought-after elixir of perfection that would prolong life and give perfect health.

27. instruments innumerable of rare design: These are vessels used in alchemy. An aludel is a pear-shaped vessel of glass or earthenware open at both ends. A sand-bath is a vessel of heated sand used to heat other vessels. A matrass is a round glass vessel with a long neck used in distilling. An athanor is a furnace with constant, self-fueling heat.

CHAPTER V

1. kirtle: a tunic or coat sometimes reaching to the knees; usually worn over a shirt and under a cloak.

2. Tyrian purple: Tyre, the land from which the great Carthaginian Queen

Dido escaped, was renowned for its purple dye. It is a fact little known that ancient Mediterranean peoples traded with the Mercurians.

3. black-a-moor: a black-skinned person.

4. alectorian: a dim water-colored stone supposedly located in the throat of a rooster.

5. preparing my body to melancholy, and madness itself: Brandoch Daha here experiences the emotional progression of a berserk, but the fit does not come upon him. (See note 18 to Chapter II.)

6. flower-de-luces: flowers of the wind.

CHAPTER VI

1. brailed up: sails tied with small ropes called brails and then furled.

2. cupshotten: drunk.

3. wood: insane, out of one's mind.

4. mellay: a close, hand-to-hand battle.

5. stoat: an ermine or weasel.

6. mine eyes dazzle: ERE so loved John Webster's two Italian tragedies that his imagination enfolded them and held them to his heart. Many of Webster's lines floated about in ERE's imagination, and here he shows how readily his thoughts took verbal shape within Elizabethan expressions because he uses one of Webster's most famous lines in a relatively mundane remark:

> Cover her face. Mine eyes dazzle: she died young.

Ferdinand speaks these words while looking upon the body of his twin sister the Duchess. He ordered her murder. (*The Duchess of Malfi:* IV: ii: 263).

7. kemperie-men: fighting men; a "kemp" or "kemper" was a name for a big fighter or wrestler in the medieval German languages and *kemping* is also a verb for fighting.

8. birched: flogged with a birch rod.

9. scotched: crippled, rendered inoperative, held motionless.

CHAPTER VII

1. howe: a valley, basin, depression in the earth.

2. spleenwort: a name for several kinds of fern.

3. assafoetida: a resinous gum with a strong garliclike flavor; obtained from plants in central Asia.

4. arbor vitae: a popular name for several evergreen shrubs.

5. aconite: a genus of poisonous plants commonly called monkshood or wolfsbane.

6. quince: a hard, acid, yellowish, pear-shaped fruit used to flavor other fruit dishes.

7. tinselled: cloth intertwined with threads of silver and gold.

8. gate: way, path, direction, or a habitual practice.

9. purl: thread or cord of twisted silver.

10. sennet: a trumpet fanfare used to announce the entrance of an important person; in Elizabethan drama, to announce the entrance of players.

11. alarum: a call to arms or a call of arousal and attention.

12. hippocras: wine flavored with spices.

13. gyves: shackles, fetters.

14. dight: prepare, cover.

15. saved his life six winters back in Impland the More: See the "Argument: with dates" for the year 393.

16. caryatide: a female figure used as a pillar to support a lintel or an entablature.

17. a barbaric music: music from one of the outer provinces of Witchland's empire.

18. Pasque flower: a species of anemone with bell-shaped purple flowers; they are common April blooms on English chalk downs.

19. oleander hawk-moth: These lovely moths have wing shapes resembling modern jet fighter planes and wing colors mixing many shades of green with swirling bands of white, yellow, pink, and a touch of lavender. The caterpillar lives on the oleander, a poisonous evergreen shrub with red and white flowers. The moth can be seen in warm Mediterranean Europe, but it is more common in Africa.

20. pickled grigs: pickled eel meat.

21. whilk: a nickname for a species of wild duck.

22. pilchard: a small sea fish, smaller than the herring.

23. hogs' haslets: hearts and livers of hogs.

24. carbonado: fish, meat, or fowl scored across and grilled over coals.

25. chitterling: the smaller intestines of pigs; sometimes filled with mincemeat and served as sausages.

26. thistle-down: the light, flimsy, featherlike substance which surrounds the seeds of the thistle and which allows them to spread their species by carrying the seeds on the wind.

27. jerkin: a close-fitting jacket or short coat.

28. bryony: a vinous plant of southern England. The three varieties are known as red, white, and black bryony.

29. nightshade: a plant with white flowers and black, poisonous berries.

30. fumado: a small smoked sea fish.

31. chine: the backbone.

32. potations: a potion, an unhealthy drink.

33. Hyperborean: pertaining to the extreme north of the earth.

34. madge-howlet: a barn owl.

35. brawn: arm or leg muscles of animals, especially of the wild boar.

36. sowst: immersed, drenched, or pickled.

37. noynt: anoint.

38. mockado: a woolen material of lesser quality than silk or velvet; made primarily in the low countries and much used in the sixteenth and seventeenth centuries.

39. hortolan: a small species of the bunting bird; found in Europe, northern Africa, and western Asia; valued for its flavor.

40. botargoes: salted fish spawn, Italian caviale.

41. enterprises of such pitch and moment have ended thus, in a kind of nothing: ERE makes fine use of two quotations from some of Shakespeare's and Webster's verses about ambition. He first quotes Hamlet's concluding thoughts in his most famous speech:

> Thus conscience does make cowards of us all,
> And thus the native hue of resolution
> Is sicklied o'er with the pale cast of thought,
> And enterprises of great pitch and moment
> With this regard their currents turn awry
> And lose the name of action.
> *(Hamlet,* III: i: 84–89)

For Hamlet conscience, thought, and "the dread of something after death" (III: i: 79) "puzzles the will" (III: i: 81) and sickens resolution so that ambitious plans "lose the name of action." The deftness of ERE's use of the quotation lies in the contrast between Gaslark's behavior and that which Hamlet describes: Gaslark's ambitions lost the name of action not because he was too circumspect but because he did not plan well enough. Juss calls Gaslark's plan to attack Carcë "a wild fancy" and says that Spitfire and Brandoch Daha are "mad as March hares" and that they "seem to catch wisdom by imitating her voice" when they agree with Gaslark's plans (pp. 63–64). When plans lose the name of action they become, as King Gorice says, "a kind of nothing." With this phrase ERE, through Gorice, quotes John Webster's honorless, bitter, and self-despising Bosola, who, having been mortally wounded himself, grimly smiles in the satisfaction of knowing that his blow will dispatch the icy and ruthless Cardinal, a man guilty of several black sins:

> I do glory
> That thou, which stood'st like a huge pyramid
> Begun upon a large and ample base,
> Shalt end in a little point, a kind of nothing.
> *(The Duchess of Malfi,* V: v: 76–79)

Although Gaslark has nothing in common with Webster's Cardinal, his wound, like the Cardinal's, ends his ambitious plans for great action.

42. smoored: smothered.

43. concerning the toad and the spider: In the Elizabethan years the study of neither amphibians nor arachnids was advanced enough to pierce the popular folklore surrounding spiders and toads. Edward Topsell, in his *Historie of Serpents* (1608), classifies both toads and spiders as venomous serpents, for he defines the word to include "all venomous beasts, whether creeping without legges, as adders and snakes, or with legges, as crocodiles and lizards, or more neerly compacted bodies, as toads, spiders, and bees." Robert Greene believed in 1592 that spiders suck their poison out of flowers. Shakespeare shares in this belief for his Richard II asks his "gentle earth" to "feed not thy sovereign's foe," but rather to "let thy spiders, that suck up thy venom,/And heavy-gaited toads lie in their way" (*Richard II,* III: ii: 12–15). Though the toad "ugly and venomous,/ Wears yet a precious jewel in his head" (*As You Like It,* II: i: 13–14), it was a toad, whose "sweltered venom" was produced by its sleeping under a cold stone for thirty-one days, that the weird sisters placed in the cauldron (*Macbeth,* IV: i: 6–9). By maintaining these ideas in Witchland, ERE was merely adding another Elizabethan attitude to the culture of his Mercury. With Baconian pragmatism and experimentation, Sir Thomas Browne debunked this Elizabethan attitude, and his prose is ERE's source for Prezmyra's practical experiment:

> The antipathy between a toad and a spider, and that they poisonously destroy each other, is very famous, and solemn stories have been written of their combats, wherein most commonly the victory is given unto the spider. . . . But what we have observed herein, we cannot in reason conceal; who having in a glass included a toad with several spiders, we behold the spiders, without resistance to sit upon his head and pass over all his body; which at last upon advantage he swallowed down, and that in few hours, unto the number of seven.
>
> (*Pseudodoxia Epidemica;* Third Book, Chapter 27, section 6)

ERE obtained three volumes of Sir Thomas Browne's works in 1916, and he admired them all his life. He often acknowledged his debt to Browne.

44. pistick nuts: pistachios.

45. thy theoric crumbleth apace: your theory is quickly falling apart.

46. horn-mad: stark mad, mad with rage, furious.

47. haskardly: vulgar, low, base.

48. scud of wind: a sudden, strong gust of wind.

49. marchpane: a cake made of almond paste and sugar.

50. prattling popinjay: ERE was probably thinking of Hotspur's astounding opening lines in *1 Henry IV* in which he tells the king that he did not deliver up his prisoners because he was "so pestered with a popinjay":

> Came there a certain lord, neat and trimly dressed,
> Fresh as a bridegroom; and his chin new reap'd
> Showed like a stubble-land at harvest home.
> He was perfumed like a milliner
>   . . . and still he smiled and talked.
> . . . With many holiday and lady terms
> He questioned me. . . .
>
> (I: iii: 33–47)

Corinius assents to Heming's remark "that La Fireez is the showiest of men in all that belongeth to gear and costly array" (p. 80), and yet the narrator tells us that, when mocked for his own attire, Corinius "somewhat reddened . . . about the cheeks and shaven jowl, for surely was none in that hall more richly apparelled than he" (p. 81). *Popinjay* was an Elizabethan word for *parrot* and a derogatory slang label, with a homosexual connotation, for a dainty and effeminate man with a showy wardrobe.

51. I will make Beshtrian cutworks in his guts: ERE has lifted this threat from John Webster's *The White Devil*. In his anger over his banishment, Count Lodovico threatens the Duke of Florence and the Duke of Brachiano: "I'll make Italian cut-works in their guts/if ever I return" (I:i: 51–2). "Italian cut-work" was a type of embroidery done with cut or stamped cloth, and it was popular in Italy during the sixteenth and seventeenth centuries. ERE judiciously relocated this popular pastime on Mercury.

52. capon: a castrated rooster.

53. flamboys: torches made of several thick wicks dipped in wax.

54. cark: load, burden, labor, toil.

55. Day ne'er broke up till now: Brandoch Daha quotes John Webster's fascinating, impetuous, exuberant, ruthless, and amoral Flamineo from *The White Devil.* See V:i: 2.

56. fitchew: a polecat.

57. fleer: to make faces and laugh mockingly.

58. thou didst dig up two mandrakes shall bring sorrow and death: The mandrake bears poisonous fruit which have been used as narcotics or as enemas, and since ancient times it has been valued as an aphrodisiac. Prezmyra speaks of the mandrake root, to which, because it is shaped like a forked radish and resembles the lower half of a human form, Elizabethans attached many superstitions. F. L. Lucas discusses these superstitions in detail:

> "It is in fact "a forked radish" resembling a man, just as Justice Shallow resembled "a forked radish". From this weird likeness doubtless arose the strange idea that the plant grew under gibbets from the droppings of the dead; the male mandrake from men and the female from women. And hence also the even stranger idea that, human-like, they "give a shriek upon eradication"; "arising perhaps," Sir Thomas Browne continues, "from a small and stridulous noise, which, being firmly rooted, it maketh upon divusion of parts". And since it was death to whoever pulled up this magic plant, a dog was always employed for this purpose, and expired instantly; while in order to prevent the madness caused by hearing the shriek, the gatherer sealed up his own ears."
>
> (F. L. Lucas, *The Complete Works of John Webster,* 4 vols.
> [London: Chatto & Windus, 1928] 1: 227–228)

Prezmyra uses "sorrow" to mean the madness resulting from uprooting the mandrake plant.

CHAPTER VIII

1. In the stainless spaces . . . from the waves: In this paragraph one can hear echoes of Coleridge's *The Rime of the Ancient Mariner*, perhaps the work of Coleridge that ERE most admired:

> The fair breeze blew, the white foam flew
> The furrow followed free
> We were the first that ever burst
> Into that silent sea.   (1834 text: 103–106)
> The stars were dim, and thick the night,
> The steersman's face by his lamp gleam'd white;
> From the sails the dew did drip—
> Till clomb above the eastern bar
> The horned Moon, with one bright star
> Within the nether tip.
> (1843 text: 206–211)

2. house-carles: in Old Norse a *huskarl* was a manservant; in Old English the term described members of a king's bodyguard.

3. a mosaic of tiny stones: Jet is black marble. Serpentine is a dark green mineral. Dark hyacinth is a precious dark blue stone. Bloodstone is jasper or any of several precious stones with red spots or streaks.

4. alaunt: (alan) a wolfhound.

5. almerie hasped: (ambry) a secure closet or cupboard like a modern safe; Juss's almerie is "hasped" or "fastened, girded and buckled" with gold.

6. So rode they . . . feasting on the sun: ERE's knowledge of wildflowers came first hand. The ox-eye daisy is the common white and yellow daisy found in fields between June and August. The bluebell can be any of several wild herbs with large leaves and small, bell-shaped lavender flowers. The yellow goatsbeard is a smooth-stemmed flower blooming throughout the summer; it has green grasslike blades beneath its many-petaled flower, and black flecks the central yellow petals. The sea campion is probably the white campion or evening lychnis, a many-branched plant with white flowers and an inflated calyx. The deep blue gentians are the rare fringed gentians, which flower in autumn; the fringed petals of their trumpet-shaped flowers curl outward. The agrimony is a plant with compound leaves and wandlike clusters of small yellow flowers. The wild marjoram is a common plant in limestone or chalky districts; its herb is highly valued in cooking. Hedge bindweed is a twining vine having pinkish funnel-shaped flowers with white stripes; it resembles the morning glory. As a boy ERE rambled about the tree-covered hills of Adel, the village of his birth and now a suburb of Leeds. As a young man he walked the Yorkshire Dales and the fells of Lakeland. Later he visited Iceland, Canada, and Switzerland. In a letter to me dated 15 May 1983, ERE's daughter, Jean G. R. Latham, spoke of his love of nature: "He was so fond of life

& the arts & I learnt so much from him, as well as a great joy in animals, birds, flowers, & mountain holidays."

7. onyx: a variety of quartz reflecting many colors from its inner crystal planes; related to the agate.

8. hyaline: a name for the sea when it is glassy smooth and calm.

9. corsage: a bodice; the torso of a woman's dress.

10. caravanserai: a temporary dwelling or meeting place.

11. balustrades: rows of columns surmounted with a railing to form an ornamental wall at the edge of a balcony or terrace.

12. withers: the highest part of the back; between the shoulder blades.

13. Over the gate was written in letters of gold: This odd inscription combines the archaic *ye* with words of Scottish dialect *(an', a', awa', frae)* and a word from dialects of Wiltshire or West Somerset *(skeered)*. This inscription is another example of ERE's alchemic eclecticism. All of his characters communicate in English, and yet he sets broad boundaries for their idiom: their ways of speaking and writing may, at any time, echo geographically diverse dialects, and they may span the centuries from the fifteenth to the twentieth.

14. crabbedly: crossly, ill-temperedly, sourly.

15. mediamnis: an island in a river.

16. lynge, mores: heather, moors.

17. usid: used, active.

18. supervivid: the past participle of the verb *supervive,* which means "to survive" and which was used only rarely by fifteenth- and sixteenth-century writers.

19. frambousier: a raspberry bush.

20. What be these mantichores . . . ?: In this section on the mantichores ERE shows part of his composing method: a habitual consulting of *The Oxford English Dictionary* to ensure the proper use of archaisms. Here he quotes the dictionary's citations from John Skelton, G. Wilkins, and James Howell. Skelton (from *Phyllyp Sparowe):* "The mantycors of the montaynes Myght fede them on thy braynes." Wilkins (from *The Miseries of Inforst Marige*—this gorgeous title makes me wonder about the context of the following quotation!): "Mantichoras, monstrous beastes, enemies to mankinde, that have double rowes of teeth in their mouthes." Howell (from *Lustra Ludovici):* "The Beast Marticora which is of a red colour, and hath the head of a man lancing out sharpe prickles from behind."

CHAPTER IX

1. verjuice: the acid juice of unripe grapes; used in cooking and as a medicine.

2. muckhills: a manure heap; or compost.

3. spy-fortalice: a small hold used as an outpost for observing the land.

4. pennoned spear: a spear having a banner that will extend with the wind when the spear is raised aloft.

5. lodestone: a magnet.

6. casque: helmet.

7. eld: old age.

8. or: before.

9. Erebus: In Hesiod's *Theogony* Erebus is the primeval darkness born of Chaos. He and his sister, Night, are the parents of Ether and Day. Usually, Erebus is a name for the Underworld.

10. ensorcelled: entranced, held in a magic spell.

11. enow: the plural form of *enough.*

12. catarrh or rheum: a running nose produced by a cold.

13. wottest: know.

14. ling and bent: heather and stiff, grasslike reeds.

15. the dark ferryman who tarrieth for no man: Zeldornius refers to the impatient and insolent Charon, the boatman of Styx, whose task is to carry the souls of the buried dead to the Fields of Mourning. Virgil describes him in Book VI of *The Aeneid* when the Sibyl conducts Aeneas through the Underworld as he goes to meet the shade of his father Anchises:

> Grim Charon is the squalid ferryman,
> is guardian of these streams, these rivers; his
> white hairs lie thick, disheveled on his chin;
> his eyes are fires that stare, a filthy mantle
> hangs down his shoulder by a knot. Alone,
> he poles the boat and tends the sails and carries
> the dead in his dark ship, old as he is . . .
>   (trans. A. Mandelbaum [Los Angeles:
>   University of California Press, 1971], Book VI: 394–400)

CHAPTER X

1. fixed with nails of diamond: In John Webster's *White Devil* Flamineo, the secretary to Brachiano and his panderer in his affair with Vittoria, assures Vittoria of her tryst with Brachiano: "Shalt meet him, 'tis fixed, with nails of diamonds to inevitable necessity" (I: ii: 158–159).

2. strath: a wide valley traversed by a river and bounded by hills.

3. cymophanes: a synonym for *chrysoberyl;* a yellowish green gem.

4. breath of myrrh and nard and ambergris: These are perfumes. Myrrh is a gum-resin produced by the myrrh-shrub; it is associated with the Middle Eastern countries. Nard is an aromatic ointment extracted from the nard plant by boiling. Ambergris is an odorous secretion from the intestines of a sperm whale.

5. . . . from the chamber: This episode at Eshgrar Ogo his been partly inspired by and partly lifted from *The Voiage and Travayle of Sir John Maundeville Knight* (1357):

> And from thence men go through lyttle Armony [Armenia] & in that countrey is an olde castell that is on a rock, that men call the castell of Spirys, & there men finde an hawke sitting upon a perch right well made & a faire lady of Fayre that keepeth it, & he that will wake this same hawke seven days and seven nightes, and some say that it is not but three days and three nightes, alone without any company and without slepe, this faire ladie shall come unto him at the vii dayes or iii dayes ende & shall graunte unto him the first thing that he will aske of worldly things, and that hath often ben proved. And so uppon a time it befell that a man which that tyme was Kinge of Armonye that was a righte doughty man waked uppon a tyme, and at the seven dayes ende the lady came to him and bade him aske what he would for he had wel done his devoure [work, duty, = Fr., *devoir*], and the king aunswered and sayde that he was a great lorde and in good peace, and he was riche, so that he would aske nothing but all onely the body of the fayre lady, or to haue his will of hir. Then this fayre lady aunswered and sayde unto him, that he was a foole, for he wist not what he asked, for he might not have hir, for he shoulde not haue asked hir but worldly thinges & she was not worldly. And the king sayde he woulde nought else, and she said sith he would aske nought else, she should graunt him three thinges and all that came after hym, and sayde unto him, Sir kinge you shall haue warre without peace unto the ix degree, and you shall be in subjection of your enemies, and you shall have greate nede of good and cattell, and sithen that tyme all the Kynges of Armonye have been in wartre and nedefull and under trybute of the Sarasyns. (ed. John Ashton [London, Pickering & Chatto, 1887] pp. 110–112)

Eddison reduces the seven-night vigil with the hawk to one night, but the entire adventure with the lady lasts seven nights while Juss and Spitfire sleep. In allowing Brandoch Daha to make love to the woman, Eddison grants the wish which Maundeville denies to the poor Armenian king.

6. the weird: In modern times this word has been used universally as an adjective to describe something strangely odd or abnormal. This modern adjectival usage descends mainly from "the weird sisters" in *Macbeth,* for these women look weird: they have beards, and, as Banquo says, they are "so withered and so wild in their attire/That look not like th' inhabitants o' th' earth,/and yet are on't" (I: iii: 44–46). However, *weird* is originally an Old English noun spelled "wyrd" and meaning, in several poems, fate, destiny, experience, or the course of events. Two quotations from "The Wanderer" (a lyric poem composed in the seventh century; to describe it simply but inadequately, this lovely poem is a poignant elegy relating the wintertime meditations of a lonely and desolate man without a lord and a place in society) will illustrate the usage: *"Wyrd bith ful araed"* (line 5)— Destiny is completely fixed; *"Ne maeg werig mod wyrde withstandon"* (line 15) —A discouraged mind cannot withstand destiny. Shakespeare uses the word grammatically as an adjective but semantically as a noun: when Macbeth and Banquo refer to the three witches as the weird sisters, they are speaking of the witches as the ministers of destiny or fate. ERE, through Brandoch Daha, uses the word to name the destiny which the Lady of Ishnain Nemartra has placed upon the Demon lord.

CHAPTER XI

1. let dight supper: commanded supper to be prepared and set.
2. The devel damn me black as buttermilk: Here Corund, in a light moment with Gro, speaks facetious irony by twisting some lines which Macbeth, the fifth-act Macbeth of "valiant fury," speaks to a tremulous messenger who comes to warn him of the approaching English army: "The devil damn thee black, thou cream-fac'd loon!/Where got'st thou that goose look?" (V: iii: 11–12). The epithet *cream-fac'd loon* probably suggested *buttermilk* to ERE, and buttermilk's color, of course, is far from black.
3. cold dark humours in the body: Medieval and Renaissance European medicine categorized the moods of temperament and disposition according to four humors or complexions. In the sanguine humor, blood predominates and produces a red-faced person who is cheerful, hopeful, courageous, and amorous. In the phlegmatic humour, phlegm predominates and produces either a reserved, cool, and self-possessed person, or a lazy, sluggish, and dull person. In the choleric humor, yellow bile predominates and produces a bilious, irascible, passionate, aggressive, wrathful person. In the melancholic humor, black bile predominates and produces a gloomy, sad, depressed person. Surgeons tried to temper uncontrolled humors through blood letting, diet, and drugs.
4. skipjack: a pert, insolent, shallow man; a conceited fop; a pretty boy.
5. sand-leverick: the sand lark or laverock, which lives on sandy shores.
6. cocksure: absolutely safe and secure from danger.
7. it skills not what: it does not matter what you offer him.
8. cogs and stops: frauds and obstacles.
9. grith: security; safe-conduct, protection.
10. firkin: a small cask capable of holding eight or nine gallons.
11. a great yerk beneath the ribs: Here ERE uses a line from *Othello* in which Iago attempts to show his loyalty to Othello by telling his desire to murder Brabantio: "Nine or ten times/I had thought t' have yerk'd him here under the ribs" *(Othello,* I: ii: 4–5).
12. van: the foremost part of an army.
13. obscene beasts . . . feasted on their bodies by the light of the moon: This image, common to heroic poetry, has particular horror for heroes and their families because an important part of a hero's final glory and reputation rests in his being properly buried or burned, and if his body remains on the field to be pecked by scavenging animals, this final

glory is denied him. The opening lines of the *Iliad* find this horror directly. The hideous consequence of the wrath of inexorable Achilleus is that

> it put pains thousandfold upon the Achaians,
> hurled in their multitudes to the house of Hades strong souls
> of heroes, but gave their bodies to be the delicate feasting
> of dogs, of all birds
>
> *(Iliad,* I: 2–5).

14. libel it me out: write it out for me.

15. dastard: a cowardly person who attempts to avoid danger.

16. fazart: an obscure Scottish name for a coward.

17. and fight alone, against a sworder: In Act III scene xiii of *Antony and Cleopatra,* the mercurial Antony decides to challenge Octavius Caesar to a single combat "sword against sword, Ourselves alone" (III: xiii: 27–28). Upon hearing this, Antony's friend and officer Enobarbus, already bitterly disappointed in Antony due to his latest failure in the naval battle against Octavius, scoffs in an aside:

> Yes, like enough, high-battled Caesar will
> Unstate his happiness, and be stag'd to th' show
> Against a sworder!

Enobarbus concludes the aside by doubting Antony's command ability: "Caesar, thou hast subdued his judgment too" (III: xiii: 29–37).

18. springes: traps.

19. gallimaufry: mincemeat; also a ragout dish made from minced meat.

CHAPTER XII

1. Queen Sophonisba: The name comes from a tragedy written in 1606 by John Marston. ERE most likely came to the name and the play through John Webster, who admired Marston's work.

2. Tartarian: from Tartarus, the region in the Underworld of Roman mythology in which the guilty spirits or shades of mortals were punished.

3. in the infernal glens of Pyriphlegethon or Acheron: Pyriphlegethon is more commonly known as Phlegethon, which is one of the rivers of the Underworld of Roman mythology and which means, literally, "blazing"; prefixing *pyri* to the name simply adds the Latin word for *hearth.* Acheron is the river of sorrow in the Roman Underworld but is also used as a name for the Underworld. Christopher Marlowe's damned Faustus, amid rich scholastic rhetoric, swears by both rivers: "Now by the kingdoms of infernal rule,/Of Styx, or Acheron, and the fiery lake/of ever-burning Phlegethon, I swear/That I do long to see the monuments/And situation of bright splendent Rome" (*The Tragedy of Doctor Faustus,* III: ii: 47–51). Perhaps ERE had these verses in mind when he wrote this chapter, for he greatly admired Marlowe. ERE obtained the Mermaid Series edition of Marlowe's plays in 1904 and kept them until his death.

4. hight the Gates of Zimiamvia: The verb *hight* means "is called." This is the first reference to the place which, ten years later and during the writing of *Mistress of Mistresses,* became the name for the "private heaven" of ERE's characters Edward Lessingham and Mary Scarnside Lessingham. These characters, because they occur in *WO*'s "Induction," provide a link between the two novels, which were published fourteen years apart. The geographic position of Zimiamvia on Mercury, here so clear, becomes cloudy in the later books, where Mercury is never mentioned.

5. leech: a physician; one who practices the healing art.

CHAPTER XIII

1. Furies steaming up from the pit: Born from the drops of blood streaming from the genitals of wounded Uranus, the three Furies became winged creatures having snakes coiling in their hair. They are associated with hatred, rage, and revenge. To stir the native Italian tribes to war against the immigrant Trojans of Aeneas, Juno summons the Fury Allecto:

> And from the home of the appalling Furies
> and hellish darkness she calls up the dread
> Allecto, in whose heart are gruesome wars
> and violence and fraud and injuries
> (*The Aeneid,* trans. A. Mandelbaum [Berkeley: The
> University of California Press, 1971], Book VII: 429–32)

2. nickers of the sea: Probably a nicker *(nicor)* is a shark or a killer whale, but some have thought it a walrus or even a hippopotamus. To the Anglo-Saxons these were sea goblins or monsters, and Beowulf fights some of them and suffers great pain (see *Beowulf,* lines 422–23). Personally, I like the idea of a bunch of hippos giving Beowulf a run for his money.

3. viands: articles of food.

4. the gate of horn: In Greek legends true dreams come through the gate of horn, and false ones through the gate of ivory.

5. dispart in sunder: to fly apart and open up; to crack in pieces.

CHAPTER XIV

1. couchant: lying down.

2. him we wot of: the man of whom we are thinking.

3. aught of dross: anything of worthlessness.

4. purpose cool: Cf. Macbeth's lines before his slaughterous attack on

Macduff's castle in Fife: "No boasting like a fool;/This deed I'll do before the purpose cool" (IV: i: 153–154).

5. here is that secret glome or bottom of our days: The "glome" is the lowest point. In 1916 ERE obtained the *Pseudodoxia Epidemica, Religio Medici*, and *Hydriotaphia* of Sir Thomas Browne (1605–1682). Here ERE quotes Browne's view of God's providence from § 43 of *Religio Medici:* "There is therefore a secret glome or bottome of our days: 'twas his wisdom to determine them; but his perpetual and waking providence that fulfills and accomplisheth them. . . ."

6. the flies hemerae take life with the sun and die with the dew: ERE quotes Robert Greene's *The Honorable Historie of Frier Bacon and Frier Bongay* (1594).

7. sovran: (sovereign); in a supreme degree.

8. in middle earth: this is the name for the lands inhabited by men. The modern term comes from the Old English word *middangeard*, which means "earth" or "world." Since I quoted from "The Wanderer" earlier (see note 6 to Chapter X) let it serve again: ". . . *thes middangeard/ealra dogra gehwam dreoseth ond fealle*" (62–63)—"This middle earth each and every day perishes and falls in ruin." J.R.R. Tolkien has made the term a household word, but he did not divorce the term from its terrestrial associations:

> "Middle-earth," by the way, is not a name of a never-never land without relation to the world we live in (like the Mercury of Eddison). It is just a use of Middle English *middel-erde* (or *erthe*), altered from Old English *Middangeard:* the name for the inhabited lands of Men "between the seas." And though I have not attempted to relate the shape of the mountains and land-masses to what geologists may say or surmise about the nearer past, imaginatively this "history" is supposed to take place in a period of the actual Old World of this planet.
> *(The Letters of J.R.R. Tolkien,* ed. Humphrey Carpenter and Christopher Tolkien [Boston: Houghton Mifflin, 1981], p. 220)

Maintaining the earthly connection was essential for Tolkien, because he wanted his legends to have a portal to English history through the Anglo-Saxon name Aelfwine ("elf friend"), which Tolkien gave to a mariner who sails west and learns the history of the Elves in the lonely isle of Tol Eressea.

CHAPTER XV

1. chrysolite: a green gem stone; a silicate of magnesium and iron.

2. put the wite on Witchland: to put the blame on King Gorice XII.

3. grammercy: literally, "grant mercy" and short for "may God grant you mercy"; i.e., "thank you."

4. fey: doomed, fated.

5. gangrel-woman: a wandering beggar-woman.

6. out of all ho: beyond normal limits or the boundary of moderation.
7. gleeking and galling: tricking and harassing. "Gleeke" was a card game familiar to Jacobeans and Elizabethans. John Webster refers to it in *The Devil's Law Case*, II: i: 57.
8. roisterer: a swaggering bully; a noisy young drunkard.
9. shittle-cock: (shuttle-cock) a small piece of cork fitted with a circle of feathers; the precursor to the "birdie" in modern badminton.
10. battledore: a wooden raquet or bat used to hit a shuttle-cock.
11. dock: the cork end of the shuttle-cock.
12. chub-faced meacock: a cowardly man with a face like a carp.
13. for the nonce: for the occasion; for the time being. This is one of Chaucer's favorite stock phrases.

CHAPTER XVI

1. marmolite: a laminated marble with a pale green lustrous color.
2. brocade: costly fabric woven with raised or textured patterns.
3. chalice: the blossom.
4. bona roba: a "good dress"; an Italian euphemism for a mistress.

CHAPTER XVII

1. minish: diminish.
2. towereth: a hunting falcon soars in circles at a great height before dropping upon its prey at high speed; this high circling is called "towering."
3. mounty: in falconry, the action of rising in pursuit of a quarry.
4. tiffany: thin silk or gauze muslin.
5. Is it not passing brave . . . over all the earth?: Here Prezmyra paraphrases Christopher Marlowe's Tamburlaine:

> Is it not brave to be a king, Techelles!
> Usumcasane and Theridamas,
> Is it not passing brave to be a king,
> And ride in triumph through Persepolis?
> *(Tamburlaine the Great, Part One,* II: v: 51–54)

6. goshawk: a large, short-winged hawk.
7. the gallop galliard: lively, brisk, high-spirited galloping.
8. curvets and caprioles: In horsemanship a curvet is a leap in which the horse raises its forelegs and then springs up with its hind legs before the forelegs reach the ground. A capriole is a leap followed by a lateral spin on the hind legs.
9. austringer: a keeper of goshawks.

10. merlin: a very small but very bold European falcon.

11. my haggard eagle: an eagle caught after growing to adulthood in the wild. Once birds of prey have lived through their first molting in the wild, they are more fierce and more difficult to train for hunting.

12. jesses . . . varvels . . . hood: In falconry the jesses are the tethers attached to a falcon's legs and to the perch. The varvels are metal rings connected to the jesses and to longer leashes. The hood is a small leather sack fitted over the head of a falcon and used to keep it docile.

13. frump: a sneer; a mocking expression or gesture.

14. sathanas: an archaic spelling of Satan.

15. appanage: a province for the maintenance of a prince.

16. doit: a very small piece or part of anything.

17. hazard: gambling with dice; the three subsequent sentences continue a dicing metaphor.

18. langret: false die.

19. dwale: the deadly nightshade plant.

20. bill: a halberd or concave battle-axe with a spike and a long shaft.

CHAPTER XVIII

1. serpentine: marble.

2. quicklime a-slaking: When limestone is burned to the point of decomposing, it releases carbonic acid while calcium oxide or quicklime remains behind and must be slaked or washed out with water. Quicklime has a pale yellowish color.

3. scarab fly: a name for any beetle that, supposedly, reproduces in and feeds on dung.

4. I have scotched it: It is fitting that after a most Macbeth-like murder, Corsus uses one of Macbeth's expressions. Crowned yet full of anxious fears, Macbeth tells his wife that more crimes must be committed before they can be safe: "We have scotched the snake, not killed it" (III: ii: 15—Bevington uses the Folio printing, "scorched").

5. ere all be shent: before all is lost.

6. strike us into the hazard: An obsolete tennis term, the hazards were three winning places on the court; if the ball were struck into one of them, a point would be scored.

7. bloodstone: green quartz spotted or streaked with red.

8. bryony: a vinelike climbing plant.

9. Corsus hath proved haggard: Although Gro muttered, in the preceding chapter, that the haggard eagle's plucking out the eyes of the hunting hound was "ominous," he did not urge any interpretation upon the King, and Gorice, seemingly, dismissed the incident from his mind. Here the King perhaps speaks without conscious reference to the disobedient bird, and yet the King's metaphor confirms the incident as an evil omen: the haggard eagle represents Corsus; the hound, Gallandus; the boar,

Demonland; and the plucking of the eyes, the murder of Gallandus by Corsus. The King's words also echo one of Othello's lines spoken when Iago's "medicine" has first begun to work upon him: "If I do prove her haggard . . ." (III: iii: 266).

CHAPTER XIX

1. balas: originally a proper name for the district near Sarmarcand where rubies are found.

2. shear up the war-arrow: In tenth century Norway, symbolic arrows of iron and wood were circulated through the countryside when a lord needed to gather an army hastily. See *Egil's Saga,* Chapter 3.

3. Spitfire, beware of Thremnir's Heugh: (A "heugh" is a steep and rugged cliff overhanging the sea.) This little scene is yet another of ERE's eclectic combinations. The old man seems to be Odin, for his appearance (aside from his having two eyes) resembles that of Odin in the *Volsunga Saga.* In that story Odin appears five times, and always he is "an old man, long bearded," "unknown of aspect to all men," and he wears "a slouched hat upon his head," and he is "one eyed," and he vanishes suddenly (see *The Story of the Volsungs and Niblungs,* trans. William Morris and Eirikr Magnusson). Yet the old man's meeting with Spitfire bears a closer resemblance to Shakespeare's dramatization of the soothsayer's approaching Julius Caesar and saying the words "Beware the ides of March" (*Julius Caesar,* I:ii:18).

4. Wood angry . . . carle: insanely angry . . . common man.

5. the larboard tack: sailing toward the left hand or port side.

6. I shall give thee a choke-pear: Here ERE borrows a line from John Webster's *The White Devil.* Cardinal Monticelso, chiding Vittoria for her sarcasm spoken during her trial for adultery, says "Go to, go to./After your goodly and vain-glorious banquet,/I'll give you a choke-pear" (III:ii:231–33). A "choke-pear" is any unripe, tough, and bitter pear.

7. throstle-cock: the male song-thrush.

8. watchet-coloured cloak: a light blue cloak.

9. corrie: a more or less circular hollow on a mountainside, surrounded with steep slopes or precipices.

10. scree-shoot: a hillside down which broken rock fragments fall.

11. bane-sore: mortal wound.

12. black horehound and millefoil: The first is a labiate herb with leaves covered in a white cottony pubescence (a hairlike fluffiness); the second is the common yarrow, a roadside herb with a tough grayish stem, finely divided bipinnate leaves, and close clusters of dull white flower heads.

13. umbles: normally, the edible inward parts of a deer.

CHAPTER XX

1. **adamant:** diamond.
2. **taffety:** a thin, lustrous silk.
3. **weet:** know; present tense of *wot.*
4. **cameline:** a genus of plants with four flowers growing in the form of a cross.
5. **I do you to wit:** I want you to know.
6. **smoking from the battle:** The smoke is steam from hot human blood spilled on a cold morning. The battle that opens *Macbeth,* certainly fought under the clouds in the chilly Scottish air, is one in which Macbeth wins golden opinions for his heroics "with his brandish'd steel,/Which smok'd with bloody execution" (I:ii:19–20).
7. **choler:** anger, wrath stemming from a queasy stomach (see note 3 to Chapter XI).
8. **plaudits:** clapping of hands; emphatic expressions of approval.
9. **thrawart ways:** improper or perverse methods.
10. **leal:** loyal.

CHAPTER XXI

1. **divine Huntress:** in Greece, the goddess Artemis; in Rome, Diana.

CHAPTER XXII

1. **bowled a hoop:** the old and warlike Ravnor shows unexpected frivolity by making a reference to having played croquet.
2. **"I would know their names":** see note 12 to Chapter XXVII.
3. **a glaive crimson-hafted:** a spear with a crimson-colored shaft.
4. **toward:** in progress, being done, going on.
5. **misprision:** a wrong action; a failure of duty.
6. **jasper:** a quartz rock with many colors.
7. **to the top of our bent:** extending to our fullest inclinations.
8. **howster:** to oust, to root out.
9. **dado:** a continuous wall-like pedestal supporting pillars.
10. **in all their delicate beauty:** ERE may have had Shelley's *Prometheus Unbound* in mind when he wrote this sentence:

> Prometheus saw, and waked the legioned hopes
> Which sleep within folded Elysian flowers,
> Nepenthe, Moly, Amaranth, fadeless blooms . . .
>
> (II:iv:59–61)

The amaranth is an imaginary flower whose blossom never withers. The nepenthe is a plant famous for the drug obtained from its leaves rather than its flower, but ERE, like Shelley, praises its blooms; the nepenthe drug brings forgetfulness and sorrow. Hermes gave moly, an herb with white flowers, to Odysseus to protect him from Circe. Elysian asphodel received its name from Homer, who, in *The Odyssey* (XI:539), stated that the asphodel covers the meadows of Elysium.

11. nie: near.

12. fallow doe: a female deer without a fawn. This deer is pregnant.

13. leman: lover.

14. hauberk: a mail coat.

15. in the arms of the Queen of Love: Demodokos the clear voiced sings of "the love of Ares and sweet-garlanded Aphrodite," and of their being ensnared in the bed by Hephaistos, and of the other gods' raucous laughter at the spectacle of Ares and Aphrodite *(Odyssey,* VIII:266–366).

CHAPTER XXIII

1. invested it: He camped closely around it so that none of Mevrian's party could leave or enter undetected.

2. comfit-box: a comfit is a sweetmeat made of fruit and preserved in sugar; the box holds the preserve.

3. astonied: stunned, insensible, paralyzed by a blow.

4. peisant: having great weight, heavy, ponderous.

CHAPTER XXIV

1. let dight a banquet: commanded a banquet to be prepared and set.

2. fordone: exhausted, overcome, tired out.

3. smacketh: has suggestions of.

4. sendal . . . sarcenett: Both are fine, soft silken materials.

5. My lord, unman not thyself by such a bestial transformation: Cf. Lady Macbeth's chiding of her husband during his fitful, bellowing hysterics upon seeing the ghost of Banquo at the feast: "What, quite unmann'd in folly?" *(Macbeth,* III:iv:74)

6. with harness on our backs: The phrase means "wearing armor." Cf. Macbeth's valiant fury when he hears that Birnam forest has been seen moving toward Dunsinane hill: "Ring the alarum-bell! Blow, wind! Come, wrack!/At least we'll die with harness on our back" *(Macbeth,* V:vii:51–52).

7. a Roland for thine Oliver: In the twelfth-century French oral epic, *Le Chanson de Roland (The Song of Roland),* the greatest of the French *chansons des gestes* (songs of deeds), Oliver and Roland were fast friends and the two greatest knights among Charlemagne's chivalry. In the cause of Frankish heroism and Frankish Christianity, the poet fictionizes and gives epic scope to a small but bloody incident that occurred in the Pyrenees near Roncesvalles on 15 August 778: Gascon peasants ambushed, killed, and looted some French knights in the rear guard of Charlemagne's army as the men were marching north to France after fighting the Saracens in Spain. In the poem Roland and Oliver and ten other great knights die while fighting off nearly four hundred thousand Saracens.

8. go his gate: go his own way.

9. Atropos: She was the oldest of the three Fates, the deities who determine human destiny (sometimes their decrees bind the gods too) in Greek mythology.

CHAPTER XXV

1. strath: a wide valley traversed by a river and bounded on either side by hills or forests.

2. gossip: a friend, a familiar companion; as a noun this has usually been a sexist term, but Gro's horse is not a mare.

3. lakelet: a small lake.

4. conies: rabbits, not chili dogs.

5. moorcock: a male red grouse.

6. coolth: coolness.

7. beck: a brook or stream.

8. capripeds: goat-footed creatures.

9. Oreads: nymphs of the mountains.

10. eft: a small lizard or salamander.

11. Parnassus: a mountain in Greece; sacred to Apollo.

12. never yet did kite bring forth a good flying hawk: A kite is a bird of prey with long wings and a forked tail. Mevrian seems to equate Gro with the kite that will not kill the good hunting falcon, herself.

13. garth: a small piece of enclosed ground used as a yard.

CHAPTER XXVI

1. why then . . . to the hammer: Cf. Webster's Bosola. Having grown to hate the wretched deeds he has done in the base service as spy for the Cardinal and his wolfish brother Ferdinand, Bosola turns against his masters: "O, my fate moves swift./I have this Cardinal in the forge already;/ Now I'll bring him to th' hammer" (*The Duchess of Malfi*, V:iv:77–79).

2. dive-dapper: a small duck with bright plumage.

3. the farmer at Holt: This man and his daughter and son constitute ERE's only acknowledgment of the husbandry class in the novel and the only departure from aristocratic characters. Because the man is a farmer but also an old warrior, and because his son fights for his lord Brandoch Daha, the family resemble an Icelandic household of the saga time.

4. meadow-pipit: a bird resembling the lark.

5. morion-cap: a sixteenth century helmet having no visor.

6. But a little while is hand fain of blow: see note 4 to the Induction.

7. shiel-house: a small wooden cottage or a temporary summer house for shepherds.

8. millefoil: (milfoil) the common yarrow, a plant with clusters of small white flowers.

9. partisan: a long-handled spear with lateral blades in addition to a point; sometimes called a halberd or gisarme; used in the sixteenth and seventeenth centuries.

10. haply: by chance.

11. shielings: see note 7.

12. masque: an elaborate costume party.

13. . . . who went not to it with his whole heart and mind: When writing this paragraph, the first portion of Henry V's St. Crispin's Day speech must have echoed in ERE's mind, since for four hundred years it has been the greatest single piece of English military patriotism:

> Rather proclaim it, Westmorland, through my host,
> That he which hath no stomach to this fight,
> Let him depart; his passport shall be made
> And crowns for convoy put into his purse.
> We would not die in that man's company
> That fears his fellowship to die with us.
>
> *(King Henry V,* IV:iii:34–39)

14. speered: questioned.

15. syth: satisfaction.

16. spate: a sudden flood of a river; caused by melting snow.

17. from crown to belly: Only the greatest heroes, like Roland, are capable of such stuff. Here Count Roland kills the Saracen prince Grandoyne:

> The Count assails him with such ferocious valour
> That to the nasal the whole helmet is shattered,
> Cloven the nose and the teeth and the palate,
> The jaz'rain [scale armor] hauberk and the breastbone and backbone,
> Both silver bows from off the golden saddle;
> Horseman and horse clean asunder he slashes,
> Lifeless he leaves them and the pieces past patching. (Laisse 124)
>
> *(The Song of Roland,* trans. Dorothy Sayers [Harmondsworth,
> Middlesex: Penguin Books, 1957], p. 115)

18. come sailing home again: Here ERE's Arnod echoes the famous Scottish ballad of "Sir Patrick Spens":

> O lang, lang may their ladies sit
> Wi' their fans into their hand,

> Or ere they see Sir Patrick Spens
> Come sailing to the land.
>
> O lang, lang may the ladies stand
> Wi' their gold kems in their hair,
> Waiting for their ain dear lords,
> For they'll see them na mair.

Captain Spens and his men wreck in a storm and go down with their ship "half o'er" to Aberdeen.

19. jimp: slender, slim, delicate, graceful.

20. one boy would catch 'tother: This section, in its detailed, comparative description, approaches a Homeric simile, but it also echoes some verses in *Macbeth*, in which the bloody and wounded captain tells King Duncan of the battle against Macdonald and his supporters:

> Doubtful it stood,
> As two spent swimmers, that do cling together
> And choke their art. (I:ii:9–11.)

21. twined: to put asunder, to part.

22. grith: guaranteed security; protection.

CHAPTER XXVII

1. betimes: at an early hour.

2. busked and boun: both verbs mean "prepared" or "set in order."

3. Huntress . . . Queen: Artemis . . . Aphrodite.

4. not strest: not compelled, not obligated.

5. she gave her heart: La Fireez turns the words of some lines Othello speaks to Desdemona. While holding and contemplating his wife's hand, Othello says "The hearts of old gave hands; / But our new heraldry is hands, not hearts" (III: iv: 46–47). Othello means that in ages past people touched hands to signify the giving of their hearts, but now in these corrupt days people merely touch hands without giving their hearts. La Fireez places his sister among the sincere and faithful ones who give hearts with hands.

6. teen: vexation, sorrow, irritation (usually an adjective or verb).

7. chrysoprase: a golden-green semiprecious stone of the beryl family.

8. coppices: small woods or thickets.

9. conceit: a concept or idea placed within an apt form.

10. certes: for certain.

11. his gorget and baldrick: The first is a piece of armor that surrounds and protects the throat; the second is a belt of leather that holds a sword and is worn over the shoulder.

12. So she showed him all as they rode by: In Book III of the *Iliad* Paris and Menelaos prepare to fight a single combat over Helen. Before the

combat old King Priam asks Helen to sit with him in one of the palace
towers so that she may point out and tell him of the Greek heroes who
move about on the field below. Helen and King Priam speak together in
lines 161–242 and Helen identifies and describes Agamemnon, Odysseus,
and Aias, before she concludes her list by saying, "I see them/all now, all
the rest of the glancing-eyed Achaians,/all whom I would know well by
sight, whose names I could tell you" (III:233–245). Although no symbolic
correspondence exists, Gro occupies the place of Priam, and Mevrian of
Helen, in this scene. ERE imitates this scene twice, for on page 258
Mevrian has Priam's place and Ravnor has Helen's place. See also note 17
to Chapter XXXI for a discussion of epic catalogs.

13. surcoat: a coat made of rich material and worn over armor.
14. lustihood: robustness, vigor, strength of body.
15. cog: to trick, trap, or cheat.
16. snell and frore: adverbs; the first means "sharp, quick, and swift"; the
second means "with intense cold."
17. blasted wolds: open country, moorland.

CHAPTER XXVIII

1. to witch: to bewitch or entrance.
2. gowany: covered with daisies (gowan flowers).
3. the dark-tressed Earthshaker: Poseidon.
4. him: Hades.
5. Father of All: Zeus.
6. ateem: teeming, seething.
7. strakes: streaks, wisps.
8. eldritch: hideous, weird, ghostly.
9. graithed: adorned, clothed, furbished.
10. grisful: terrible.
11. guerdon: reward, recompense.

CHAPTER XXIX

1. leveable: believable.

CHAPTER XXX

1. arras: rich tapestry fabric; also a name for a tapestry.
2. smaragds: emeralds.
3. layes: poems, songs.

4. Philomell: a poetic name for the nightingale.

5. galbanum: fragrant gum resin from Persian trees.

6. fray-bugs: ghosts, specters, bogies.

CHAPTER XXXI

1. these forced besides with some that should be ours: Having heard of the approach of the conjoined English and Scottish armies led by Prince Malcolm and MacDuff, having lost the alliance of many of his thanes and their armies to Malcolm, and knowing that his small force will have to rely upon the strength of Dunsinane castle to resist the invaders, Macbeth bitterly snarls in alliteration suggesting the clash of sword upon shield: "Were they not forc'd with those that should be ours/We might have met them dareful, beard to beard,/And beat them backward home" *(Macbeth,* V:v:5–7).

2. gaberlunzie: a strolling beggar.

3. perdue: in military terms a very advanced and dangerous position.

4. acquit: vow, swear, promise.

5. I'd liever: I would rather.

6. tassel-gentle: tercel hawk.

7. demasked and embossed: adorned and richly covered.

8. crab-fish: This sentence originates in the *Arcadia* of Sir Philip Sidney. Webster admired it enough to imitate it too. See *The Complete Works of John Webster,* ed. F. L. Lucas (London: Chatto & Windus, 1928) 2:137.

9. Thou dost thee and thou me: Juss refers to the formal (you, you) and informal (thou, thee) second person pronouns which are moribund in modern English. Modern Romance languages maintain this distinction between formal and familiar diction.

10. electuaries: medicinal pastes consisting of a powder mixed with honey or some other sweet base. Sometimes they are used as a reference to aphrodisiacs: "These politic enclosures for paltry mutton, makes more rebellion in the flesh than all the provocative electuaries doctors have uttered since last jubilee" (John Webster, *The White Devil,* I:ii:96–98).

11. succubi and incubi: spirits that engage in sexual intercourse with mortals; the succubus is feminine and the incubus is masculine.

12. conned: studied, examined.

13. urchin-show: the appearance of goblins or elves.

14. fico: fig.

15. tide: occasion.

16. doubtous: full of terror; fearful, dreadful, terrible.

17. Now, when dawn appeared . . . to the eastward: By listing the commanders and the troops of the Witches and Demons, ERE imitates the conventions of the heroic epic which originated in the *Iliad.* In Book II of the *Iliad* Homer catalogs the ships and armies of the Achaians (the Danaans, Argives, Myrmidons, and others) in lines 494–759, and those of the Trojans and their allies in lines 816–877. Following Homer's practice, Virgil listed the Italian armies opposing Aeneas's Trojans in lines 854–1,072 of Book VII of the *Aeneid*. The imitators of Virgil—Tasso and Milton and T. E. Lawrence—included catalogs in their epics: *Gerusalemme Liberata*, Canto I: stanzas 37–64; *Paradise Lost*, Book I: 392–521; and *Seven Pillars of Wisdom*, Book II, Chapter 25. Through continued usage the catalog of armies has been recognized as one of the conventional ingredients that define the classical or Aristotelian epic (an epic that has "unity of action" by telling a single story from beginning to end, as opposed to a romance epic, which has several intertwined and episodic plots). The classical form requires only one catalog, but ERE has written two others in addition to this one: he lists the companies of the Witchland army for the invasion of Demonland in Chapter XVII, and he lists the companies of the allied fleet of Demonland for the journey to Impland in Chapter XXVII.

18. asper: harsh, rugged, savage, warlike, cruel.
19. buckler: the strap of a helmet that fastens beneath the chin.

CHAPTER XXXII

1. usward: toward us.
2. girds: rapid, rushing starts
3. Speak on . . . Thou stutterest . . . as an ague taketh a goose . . . Whence gottest thou this look of a dish of whey with blood spit in it?: In these phrases and clauses the King echoes the furious fifth-act Macbeth when he upbraids the frightened servant who tells him of Malcolm and the approaching English army:

> MACB: The devil damn thee black, thou cream-fac'd loon!
> Where got'st thou that goose look?
> SERV: There is ten thousand—
> MACB: Geese, villain?
> SERV: Soldiers, sir.
> MACB: Go prick thy face, and over-red thy fear,
> Thou lily-liver'd boy. What soldiers, patch?
> Death of thy soul! Those linen cheeks of thine
> Are counselors to fear. What soldiers, whey-face?
>   (V:iii:11–17)

ERE also plays on these verses on (p. 132) when Corund says "The devil damn me black as buttermilk."
4. bale-like: malignant, tormenting, mischievous, hurting.
5. disard: (dizzard) a jester or fool.
6. trisulk: a thunderbolt.
7. cere-cloth: a waxed winding sheet used to wrap a dead body.
8. towsed: handled roughly, used like a dog.

CHAPTER XXXIII

1. caravel: a small, light ship.
2. theorbos and citherns: the first is a double-necked lute; the second is an instrument resembling a guitar but having wire strings, which are plucked and not strummed.
3. orichalc: a yellow ore, or a copper alloy; sometimes a term for brass.
4. perspective: an Elizabethan term for telescope.
5. orfreyed and damascened: the first names the process of gold embroidery; the second names a process of ornamentation with designs incised in a surface and filled with silver.
6. mountebank: one who resorts to degrading means to obtain fame.
7. with a wild surmise: Here ERE echoes the famous early sonnet by John Keats, "On First Looking into Chapman's Homer":

> Much have I travelled in the realms of gold,
> And many goodly states and kingdoms seen;
> Round many western islands have I been
> Which bards in fealty to Apollo hold.
> Oft of one wide expanse had I been told
> That deep-browed Homer ruled as his demesne;
> Yet did I never breathe its pure serene
> Till I heard Chapman speak out loud and bold:
> Then felt I like some watcher of the skies
> When a new planet swims into his ken;
> Or like stout Cortez when with eagle eyes
> He stared at the Pacific—and all his men
> Looked at each other with a wild surmise—
> Silent, upon a peak in Darien.

The allusion is apt, for the trumpet blast restores life, meaning, adventure, and much loved danger to the Demons. When they guess at the meaning of the trumpet, they stand silent, like Cortez (Keats confused Cortez with Balboa) and his men on the peak, and they see their world reforming.